Robert Jordan was born in 1948 in Charleston, South Carolina, and died in 2007. He taught himself to read when he was four with the incidental aid of a twelve-years-older brother, and was tackling Mark Twain and Jules Verne by five. He is a graduate of the Citadel, the Military College of South Carolina, with a degree in physics, and served two tours in Vietnam with the U.S. Army. Among his decorations are the Distinguished Flying Cross with bronze oak leaf cluster, the Bronze Star with "V" and bronze oak leaf cluster, and two Vietnamese Gallantry Crosses with Palm. He has written historical novels, and dance and theatre criticism, but it is the many volumes of his epic Wheel of Time series that have made him one of the bestselling and best loved fantasy writers of modern times.

Find out more about Robert Jordan and other Orbit authors by registering for the free monthly newsletter at www.orbitbooks.net

GW00659941

By Robert Jordan

The Wheel of Time®
The Eye of the World
The Great Hunt
The Dragon Reborn
The Shadow Rising
The Fires of Heaven
Lord of Chaos
A Crown of Swords
The Path of Daggers
Winter's Heart
Crossroads of Twilight
Knife of Dreams
The Gathering Storm (by Robert Jordan and
Brandon Sanderson)
Towers of Midnight (by Robert Jordan and
Brandon Sanderson)

New Spring

The World of Robert Jordan's The Wheel of Time®
(with Teresa Patterson)

*

The Conan Chronicles 1
The Conan Chronicles 2

THE CONAN CHRONICLES 2

Conan the Magnificent
Conan the Triumphant
Conan the Destroyer

Robert Jordan

www.orbitbooks.net

ORBIT

This omnibus edition first published in Great Britain by Legend Books 1997
Reprinted by Orbit 1999, 2000, 2004, 2006, 2009, 2010, 2011

This omnibus edition copyright © Conan Properties Inc. 1997

Conan the Magnificent
First published by Legend Books in 1997
Copyright © Conan Properties Inc. 1984

Conan the Triumphant
First published by Legend Books in 1997
Copyright © Conan Properties Inc. 1983, 1984

Conan the Destroyer
First published by Legend Books in 1997
Copyright © Conan Properties Inc. 1984

The moral right of the author has been asserted.

*All characters and events in this publication, other than those
clearly in the public domain, are fictitious, and any resemblance
to real persons, living or dead, is purely coincidental.*

All rights reserved.
No part of this publication may be reproduced, stored in a
retrieval system, or transmitted, in any form or by any means, without
the prior permission in writing of the publisher, nor be otherwise circulated
in any form of binding or cover other than that in which it is published
and without a similar condition including this condition being
imposed on the subsequent purchaser.

A CIP catalogue record for this book
is available from the British Library.

ISBN 978-1-85723-749-8

Typeset by Hewer Text Ltd, Edinburgh
Printed in Great Britain by Clays Ltd, St Ives plc

Papers used by Orbit are from well-managed forests
and other responsible sources.

MIX
Paper from
responsible sources
FSC
www.fsc.org
FSC® C104740

Orbit
An imprint of
Little, Brown Book Group
100 Victoria Embankment
London EC4Y 0DY

An Hachette UK Company
www.hachette.co.uk

www.orbitbooks.net

Contents

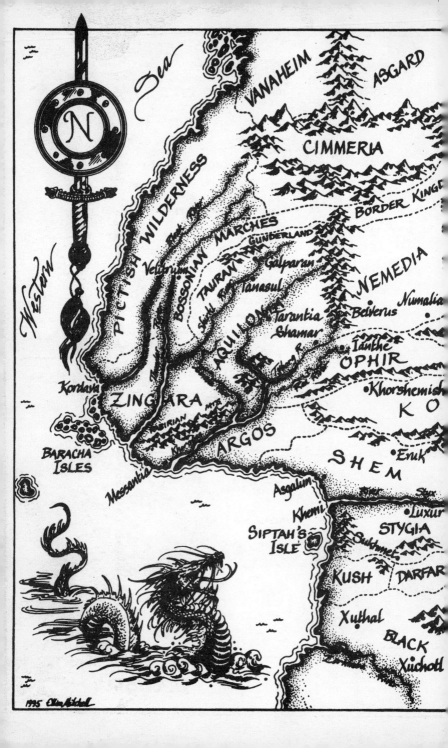

TUNDRAS
Haloga
HYPERBOREA
DESERTS
OM
BRYTHUNIA
MTS.
STEPPES
KEZANKIAN
HYRKANIA
CORINTHIA
ZAMORA
TURAN
Sultanapur
KARPASH MTS.
Shadizar
Arenjun
VILAYET SEA
KHITAI
Isle of Iron Statues
KHAURAN
T H
Akit
Aghrapur
KHORAJA
DESERTS
Samara
Shangara
Xapur
Zamboula
Khawarism
Kuthchernes
Pteion
Alkmeenon
Kassali
KESHAN
Keshla
PUNT
VENDHYA
KINGDOMS
ZEMBABWEI
IRANISTAN

Conan
the
Magnificent

prologue

I cy air hung deathly still among the crags of the Kezankian mountains, deep in the heart of that arm of those mountains which
stretched south and west along the border between Zamora and
Brythunia. No bird sang, and the cloudless azure sky was empty, for even
the ever-present vultures could find no current on which to soar.

In that eerie quiesence a thousand fierce, turbanned Kezankian hillmen
crowded steep brown slopes that formed a natural amphitheater. They
waited and merged with the silence of the mountains. No sheathed tulwar
clattered against stone. No booted foot shifted with the impatience that
was plain on lean, bearded faces. They hardly seemed to breathe. Black
eyes stared down unblinkingly at a space two hundred paces across,
floored with great granite blocks and encircled by a waist-high wall as
wide as a man was tall. Granite columns, thick and crudely hewn, lined
the top of the wall like teeth in a sun-dried skull. In the center of that
circle three men, pale-skinned Brythunians, were bound to tall stakes of
black iron, arms stretched above their heads, leather cords digging cruelly
into their wrists. But they were not the object of the watcher's attention.
That was on the tall, scarlet-robed man with a forked beard who stood
atop a tunnel of massive stone blocks that pierced the low wall and led
back into the mountain behind him.

Basrakan Imalla, dark face thin and stern beneath a turban of red, green
and gold, threw back his head and cried, "All glory be to the true gods!"

A sigh of exaltation passed through the watchers, and their response
rumbled against the mountainsides. "All glory be to the true gods!"

Had Basrakan's nature been different, he might have smiled in
satisfaction. Hillmen did not gather in large numbers, for every clan
warred against every other clan, and the tribes were riddled by blood
feuds. But he had gathered these and more. Nearly ten times their number
camped amid the jagged mountains around the amphitheater, and scores
of others joined them every day. With the power the true gods had given

him, with the sign of their favor they had granted him, he had done what no other could. And he would do more! The ancient gods of the Kezankians had chosen him out.

"Men of the cities," he made the word sound obscene, "worship false gods! They know nothing of the true gods, the spirits of earth, of air, of water. And of fire!"

A wordless roar broke from a thousand throats, approbation for Basrakan and hatred for the men of the cities melting together till even the men who shouted could not tell where one ended and the other began.

Basrakan's black eyes burned with fervor. Hundreds of Imallas wandered the mountains, carrying the word of the ancient gods from clan to clan, kept safe from feud and battle by the word they carried. But it had been given to him to bring about the old gods' triumph.

"The people of the cities are an iniquity in the sight of the true gods!" His voice rang like a deep bell, and he could feel his words resonate in the minds of his listeners. "Kings and lords who murder true believers in the names of the foul demons they call gods! Fat merchants who pile up more gold in their vaults than any clan of the mountains possesses! Princesses who flaunt their half-naked bodies and offer themselves to men like trulls! Trulls who drench themselves in perfumes and bedeck themselves in gold like princesses! Men with less pride than animals, begging in the streets! The filth of their lives stains the world, but we will wash it away in their blood!"

The scream that answered him, shaking the gray granite beneath his feet, barely touched his thoughts. Deep into the warren of caverns beneath this very mountain he had gone, through stygian passages lit only by the torch he carried, seeking to be closer to the spirits of the earth when he offered them prayers. There the true gods led him to the subterranean pool where eyeless, albescent fish swam around the clutch of huge eggs, as hard as the finest armor, left there countless centuries past.

For years he had feared the true gods would turn their faces from him for his study of the thaumaturgical arts, but only those studies had enabled him to transport the slick black spheres back to his hut. Without the knowledge from those studies he could never have succeeded in hatching one of the nine, could never have bound the creature that came from it to him, even as imperfectly as he had. If only he had the Eyes of Fire . . . no, *when* he had them all bonds, so tenuous now, would become as iron.

"We will kill the unbelievers and the defilers!" Basrakan intoned as the tumult faded. "We will tear down their cities and sow the ground whereon they stood with salt! Their women, who are vessels of lust, shall be scourged of their vileness! No trace of their blood shall remain! Not even a memory!" The hook-nosed Imalla threw his arms wide. "The sign of the true gods is with us!"

In a loud, clear voice he began to chant, each word echoing sharply from the mountains. The thousand watching warriors held their collective breath. He knew there were those listening who sought only gold looted from the cities rather than the purification of the world. Now they would learn to believe.

The last syllable of the incantation rang in the air like struck crystal. Basrakan ran his eyes over the Brythunian captives, survivors of a party of hunters who had entered the mountains from the west. One was no more than sixteen, his gray eyes twisted with fear, but the Imalla did not see the Brythunians as human. They were not of the tribes. They were outsiders. They were the sacrifice.

Basrakan felt the coming, a slow vibration of the stone beneath his feet, before he heard the rough scraping of claws longer than a man's hand.

"The sign of the true gods is with us!" he shouted again, and the creature's great head emerged from the tunnel.

A thousand throats answered the Imalla as the rest of the thick, tubular body came into view, more than fifteen paces in length and supported on four wide-set, massive legs. "The sign of the true gods is with us!" Awe and fear warred in that thunderous roar.

Blackened plates lined its short muzzle, overlapped by thick, irregular teeth designed for ripping flesh. The rest of that monstrous head and body were covered by scales of green and gold and scarlet, glittering in the pale sun, harder than the finest armor the hand of man could produce. On its back those scales had of late been displaced by two long, leathery boils. Drake, the ancient tomes called it, and if those volumes were correct about the hard, dull bulges, the sign of the true gods' favor would soon be complete.

The creature turned its head to stare with paralyzing intensity directly at Basrakan. The Imalla remained outwardly calm, but a core of ice formed in his stomach, and that coldness spread, freezing his breath and the words in his throat. That golden-eyed gaze always seemed to him filled with hatred. It could not be hatred of him, of course. He was blessed by the true gods. Yet the malevolence was there. Perhaps it was the contempt of a creature of the true gods for mere mortal men. In any case, the wards he had set between the crudely hewn granite columns would keep the drake within the circle, and the tunnel exited only there. Or did it? Though he had often descended into the caverns beneath the mountain—at least, in the days before he found the black drake eggs—he had not explored the tenth part of them. There could be a score of exits from that tangle of passages he had never found.

Those awesome eyes turned away, and Basrakan found himself drawing a deep breath. He was pleased to note there was no shudder in it. The favor of the old gods was truly with him.

With a speed that seemed too great for its bulk, the glittering creature moved to within ten paces of the bound men. Suddenly the great, scaled head went back, and from its gaping maw came a shrill ululation that froze men's marrow and turned their bones to water. Awed silence fell among the watchers, but one of the prisoners screamed, a high, thin sound with the reek of madness in it. The boy fought his cords silently; blood began to trickle down his arms.

The fiery-eyed Imalla brought his hands forward, palms up, as if offering the drake to the assemblage. "From the depths of the earth it comes!" he cried. "The spirits of earth are with us!"

Mouth still open, the drake's head lowered until those chill golden eyes regarded the captives. From those gaping jaws a gout of rubescent flame swept across the captives.

"Fire is its breath!" Basrakan shouted. "The spirits of fire are with us!"

Two of the prisoners were sagging torches, tunic and hair aflame. The youth, wracked with the pain of his burns, shrieked, "Mitra help me! Eldran, I—"

The iridescent creature took two quick paces forward, and a shorter burst of fire silenced the boy. Darting forward, the drake ripped a burning body in half. The crunching of bones sounded loudly, and gobbets of charred flesh dropped to the stone.

"The true gods are with us!" Basrakan declaimed. "On a day soon, the sign of the gods' favor will fly! The spirits of air are with us!" The old tomes had to be right, he thought. Those leathery bulges would burst, and wings would grow. They would! "On that day we will ride forth, invincible in the favor of the old gods, and purge the world with fire and steel! All praise be to the true gods!"

"*All praise be to the true gods!*" his followers answered.

"All glory to the true gods!"

"*All glory to the true gods!*"

"Death to the unbelievers!"

The roar was deafening. "*DEATH TO THE UNBELIEVERS!*"

The thousand would stay to watch the feeding, for they were chosen by lot from the ever-growing number encamped in the surrounding mountains, and many had never seen it before. Basrakan had more important matters to tend to. The drake would return to its caverns of its own accord when the bodies were consumed. The Imalla started up a path, well worn now in the brown stone by many journeys, that led from the amphitheater around the mountainside.

A man almost as tall as Basrakan and even leaner, his face burning with ascetic fanaticism above a plaited beard, met him and bowed deeply. "The blessings of the true gods be on you, Basrakan Imalla," the newcomer said. His turban of scarlet, green and gold marked him as Basrakan's acolyte, though his robe was of plain black. "The man Akkadan has come. I have had him taken to your dwelling."

No glimmer of Basrakan's excitement touched his stern face. The Eyes of Fire! He inclined his head slightly. "The blessings of the true gods be on you, Jbeil Imalla. I will see him now."

Jbeil bowed again; Basrakan went on, seemingly unhurried, but without even the inclination of his head this time.

The path led around the slope of the mountain to the village of stone houses, a score in number, that had grown up where once stood the hut in which Basrakan had lived. His followers had spoken of building a fortress for him, but he had no need of such. In time, though, he had allowed the construction of a dwelling for himself, of two stories and larger than all the rest of the village placed together. It was not a matter of pride, he often reminded himself, for he denied all pride save that of the old gods. The structure was for *their* glory.

Turbanned and bearded men in stained leather vests and voluminous trousers, the original color of which was a mystery lost in age and dirt, bowed as he passed, as did women covered from head to foot in black cloth, with only a slit for their eyes. He ignored them, as he did the two guards before his door, for he was openly hurrying now.

Within, another acolyte in multi-hued turban bent himself and gestured with a bony hand. "The blessings of the true gods be on you, Basrakan Imalla. The man Akkadan—"

"Yes, Ruhallah." Basrakan wasted not even moments on honorifics. "Leave me!" Without waiting to be obeyed, the tall Imalla swept through the door Ruhallah had indicated, into a room sparsely furnished with black-lacquered tables and stools. A hanging on one wall was a woven map of the nations from the Vilayet Sea west to Nemedia and Ophir.

Basrakan's face darkened at the sight of the man who waited there. Turban and forked beard proclaimed him hillman, but his fingers bore jeweled rings, his cloak was of purple silk and there was a plumpness about him that bespoke feasting and wine.

"You have spent too much time among the men of the cities, Akkadan," Basrakan said grimly. "No doubt you have partaken of their vices! Consorted with their women!"

The plump man's face paled beneath its swarthiness, and he quickly hid his beringed hands behind him as he bowed. "No, Basrakan Imalla, I have not. I swear!" His words tumbled over each other in his haste. Sweat gleamed on his forehead. "I am a true—"

"Enough!" Basrakan spat. "You had best have what I sent you for, Akkadan. I commanded you not to return without the information."

"I have it, Basrakan Imalla. I have found them. And I have made plans of the palace and maps—"

Basrakan's shout cut him short. "Truly I am favored above all other men by the true gods!"

Turning his back on Akkadan, he strode to the wall hanging, clenched fists raised in triumph toward the nations represented there. Soon the Eyes of Fire would be his, and the drake would be bound to him as if part of his flesh and will. And with the sign of the true gods' favor flying before his followers, no army of mortal men would long stand against them.

"All glory to the true gods," Basrakan whispered fiercely. "Death to all unbelievers!"

1

Night caressed Shadizar, that city known as "the Wicked," and veiled the happenings which justified that name a thousand times over. The darkness that brought respite to other cities drew out the worst in Shadizar of the Alabaster Towers, Shadizar of the Golden Domes, city of venality and debauchery.

In a score of marble chambers silk-clad nobles coerced wives not theirs to their beds, and many-chinned merchants licked fat lips over the abductions of competitors' nubile daughters. Perfumed wives, fanned by slaves wielding snowy ostrich plumes, plotted the cuckolding of husbands, sometimes their own, while hot-eyed young women of wealth or noble birth or both schemed at circumventing the guards placed on their supposed chastity. Nine women and thirty-one men, one a beggar and one a lord, died by murder. The gold of ten wealthy men was taken from iron vaults by thieves, and fifty others increased their wealth at the expense of the poor. In three brothels perversions never before contemplated by humankind were created. Doxies beyond numbering plied their ancient trade from the shadows, and twisted, ragged beggars preyed on the trulls' wine-soaked patrons. No man walked the streets unarmed, but even in the best quarters of the city arms were often not enough to save one's silver from cutpurses and footpads. Night in Shadizar was in full cry.

Wisps of cloud, stirred by a warm breeze, dappled the moon sitting high in the sky. Vagrant shadows fled over the rooftops, yet they were enough for the massively muscled young man, swordbelt slung across his broad chest so that the worn hilt of his broadsword projected above his right shoulder, who raced with them from chimney to chimney. With a skill born in the savage wastes of his native Cimmerian mountains he blended with the drifting shades, and was invisible to the eyes of the city-born.

The roof the muscular youth traveled came to an end, and he peered down into the blackness hiding the paving stones of the street, four stories below. His eyes were frozen sapphires, and his face, a square-cut lion's mane of black held back from it by a leather cord, showed several ordinary lifetimes' experience despite its youth. He eyed the next building, an alabaster cube with a freize of scrollwork running all the way around it an arm's length below the roof. From deep in his throat came a soft growl. A good six paces wide, the street was, although it was the narrowest of the four that surrounded the nearly palatial structure. What he had not noticed when he chose this approach—eying the distances from the ground—was that the far roof was sloped. Steeply! Erlik take Baratses, he thought. And his gold!

This was no theft of his own choosing, but rather was at the behest of the merchant Baratses, a purveyor of spices from the most distant realms of the world. Ten pieces of gold the spice dealer had offered for the most prized possession of Samarides, a wealthy importer of gems: a goblet carved from a single huge emerald. Ten pieces of gold was the hundredth part of the goblet's worth, one tenth of what the fences in the Desert would pay, but a run of bad luck with the dice had put the Cimmerian in urgent need of coin. He had agreed to theft and price, and taken two gold pieces in advance, before he even knew what was to be stolen. Still, a bargain sworn to must be kept. At least, he thought grimly, there was no guard atop the other building, as there were on so many other merchants' roofs.

"Crom!" he muttered with a last look at Samarides' roof, and moved back from the edge, well back into the shadows among the chimneys. Breathing deeply to charge his lungs, he crouched. His eyes strained toward the distant rooftop. Suddenly, like a hunting leopard, he sprang forward; in two strides he was sprinting at full speed. His lead foot touched the edge of the roof, and he leaped, hurling himself into the air with arms outstretched, fingers curled to grab.

With a crash he landed at full length on the sloping roof. And immediately began to slide. Desperately he spread his arms and legs to slow himself; his eyes searched for a projection to grasp, for the smallest nub that might stop his fall. Inexorably he moved toward the drop to the pavement.

No wonder there was no watchman on the roof, he thought, furious at himself for not questioning that lack earlier. The rooftiles were glazed to a surface like oiled porcelain. In the space of a breath his feet were over the edge, then his legs. Abruptly his left hand slid into a gap where a tile was missing. Tiles shattered as his weight smashed his vainly gripping hand through them; fragments showered past him into the gloom beneath. Wood slapped his palm; convulsively he clutched. With a jerk that wrenched at the heavy muscles of his shoulder he was brought up short to swing over the shadowed four-story drop.

For the first time since his leap he made a sound, a long, slow exhalation between his teeth. "Ten gold pieces," he said in a flat voice, "are not enough."

Suddenly the wooden roof-frame he was grasping gave with a sharp snap, and he was falling again. Twisting as he dropped, he stretched, caught the finger-joint-wide ledge at the bottom of the frieze by his fingertips, and slammed flat against the alabaster wall.

"Not nearly enough," he panted when he had regained his breath. "I've half a mind to take the accursed thing to Zeno after this." But even as he said it he knew he would not go to the Nemedian fence. He had given his word.

At the moment, he realized, his problem lay not in how to dispose of the emerald goblet, but in how to leave his present position with a whole skin. The only openings piercing the alabaster wall at this height were ventilation holes the size of his fist, for the top floor and the attic were given over to storage and quarters for servants and slaves. Such needed no windows, to the mind of Samarides, and if they had them would only lean out and spoil the appearance of his fine house. No other ledges or friezes broke the smoothness of the walls, nor were there balconies overlooking the street. The roof he had first leaped from might as well have been in Sultanapur, the roof above as well have been beyond the clouds. That, the dangling youth reluctantly concluded, left only the windows of the third floor, their arched tops a good armspan lower than his feet.

It was not his way to dally when his course was decided. Slowly, hanging by his fingertips, he worked his way along the narrow ledge. The first two arched windows to pass beneath his feet glowed with light. He could not risk meeting people. The third, however, was dark.

Taking a deep breath, he let go his hold and dropped, his body brushing lightly against the wall. If he touched the wall too much, it would push him out and away to fall helplessly. As he felt his legs come in front of the window, he moved his feet inward, toward the window sill. Stone smashed against his soles, his palms slapped hard against the sides of the window, and he hung precariously, leaning outward. The thickness of the wall, the depth of the window, denied even a fingernail's hold. Only the outward pressure of his hands kept him form hurtling to the street.

Muscles knotted with the strain, he drew himself forward until he could step within Samarides' dwelling. As his foot touched the carpet-strewn floor, his hand went to the worn leather of his sword hilt. The room was dark, yet his night-accustomed eyes could make out the dim shapes of cushioned chairs. Tapestries, their colors reduced to shadings of gray, hung on the walls, and a dimly patterned carpet covered the marble floor. With a sigh he relaxed, a trifle, at least. This was no sleeping chamber, with someone to awaken and scream an alarm. It was about time something went right on this night of continuous near-disaster.

There were still problems, though. He was unsure whether the worst of these was how to get out of the dwelling—or how to get to his goal. Samarides' house was arranged around a central garden, where the gem merchant spent a great deal of his time among the fountains. The only door of the room in which he displayed his treasures opened onto the ground-floor colonnade around that garden.

It would have been easy to climb down from the roof to the garden, and Baratses had told him exactly the location of the door to the treasure room. Now he must make his way through the corridors, and risk coming on servants or guards.

Opening the door a crack, he peered into the hall, lit by gilded brass oil lamps hung on chains from bronze wall sconces. Tables inlaid with mother-of-pearl stood at intervals along walls mosaicked in intricate patterns with thousands of tiny, multihued tiles. No one trod the polished marble floor. Silently he slipped into the corridor.

For a heartbeat he stood, picturing the plan of the house in his mind. The treasure room was in *that* direction. Ears straining for the slightest hint of another's footstep, he hurried through the halls with a tread as light as a cat. Back stairs led downward, then others took him down again. Their location and the fact that their dark red tiles were dull and worn marked them as servant's stairs. Twice the scuff of sandals from a crossing corridor gave warning, and he pressed his back to a wall, barely breathing, while unseeing servants in pale blue tunics scurried by, too intent on their labors to so much as glance down the branching way.

Then he was into the central garden, the high, shadowed walls of the house making it a small canyon. Splash and burble echoed softly from half-a-score fountains, scattered among fig trees and flowering plants and alabaster statuary. The treasure room lay directly opposite him across the garden.

He took a step, and froze. A dim shape hurried toward him down one of the garden paths. Silently he moved further to the side, away from the light spilling from the doorway. The approaching figure slowed. Had he been seen, he wondered. Whoever was coming moved very slowly, now, seeming almost to creep, and made no sound at all. Abruptly the figure left the slated walk and moved toward him again. His jaw tightened; no other muscle of him moved, not so much as an eyelid blinking. Closer. Ten paces. Five. Two.

Suddenly the strangely still-dim figure froze, gasped. The big youth sprang. One hand cut off sound by covering the mouth that uttered it. His other arm pinned the figure's arms. Teeth dug into his calloused palm, and his captive flung about wildly, kicks thudding against his legs.

"Erlik take you!" he hissed. "You fight like a woman! Stop that, and I'll not hurt—"

It penetrated his mind that the body he held was rounded, if firm. He side-stepped to the edge of the light from the doorway, and found himself studying large, brown eyes that were suddenly frowning above his hand. It *was* a woman, and a pretty one, with satiny, olive skin and her hair braided tightly about her small head. The biting stopped, and he loosed his grip on her jaw. He opened his mouth to say he would not harm her if she gave no outcry, but she cut him off.

"I am a sorceress," she whispered hoarsely, "and I know you, Conan, far-traveler from Samaria, or Cymria, or some such place. You think you are a thief. Release me!"

The hairs on the back of his neck stirred. How could she know? He seemed to have a talent for running afoul of sorcerers, a talent he would just as soon lose. His grip was loosening when he became aware of the amused gleam in her big eyes, and the way her small, white teeth were biting a full lower lip. For the first time he took in her garb, snug, dull black from neck to toes. Even her feet were covered in ebon cloth, with the big toe separated like the thumb on a mitten.

Holding her out from him by her upper arms, he was unable to suppress a smile. Slender, she was, and short, but the close fit of her odd garments left no doubts as to her womanhood. She kicked at him, and he caught it on his thigh.

"Sorceress?" he growled softly. "Then why do I think you'll change your story should I take a switch to your rump?"

"Why do I think that at the first blow I'll howl loudly enough to bring half the city?" she whispered back. "But truly I don't wish to. My name is Lyana, and I've heard of you, Conan. I've seen you in the streets. And admired you. I just wanted to sound mysterious, so I could compete with your other women." She shifted in his grasp, and her round breasts, large on her diminutive slimness, seemed even more prominent. Her tongue wet her lips, and she smiled invitingly. "Could you please put me down? You're so strong, and you're hurting me."

He hesitated, then lowered her feet to the ground. "What is this garb you wear, Lyana?"

"Forget that," she breathed, swaying closer. "Kiss me."

Despite himself his hands came up to clasp her face. Before his fingers touched her cheeks, she dropped to her knees and threw herself into a forward tumble past him. Stunned, he still managed to whirl after her.

One tiny foot flashing from the middle of her roll caught him under the ribs, bringing a grunt, slowing him enough for her to come to her feet facing the wall . . . and she seemed to go up it like a spider.

With an oath Conan leaped forward. Something struck his arm, and he grabbed a soft, black-dye rope, hanging from above.

"Mitra blast me for a fool!" he grated. "A thief!"

Soft laughter floated down from close enough over his head to make him peer sharply upwards. "You are a fool." The girl's soft tones brimmed with mirth. "And I am indeed a thief, which you'll never be. Perhaps, with those shoulders, you could be a carter. Or a cart horse."

Snarling, Conan took hold of the rope to climb. A flicker caught the corner of his eye, and he felt more than heard something strike the ground by his foot. Instinctively, he jumped back, losing his grip on the rope. His grab to regain it brushed only the free end as it was drawn up.

"It would have struck you," the girl's low voice came again, "had I intended it so. Were I you, I'd leave here. Now. Fare you well, Conan."

"Lyana?" he whispered roughly. "Lyana?" Mocking silence answered him.

Muttering under his breath, he searched the ground around his feet, and tugged a flat, black throwing knife from the dirt. He tucked it behind his swordbelt, then stiffened as if stabbed.

The girl was a thief, and she had come from the direction of the treasure room. Cursing under his breath he ran, heedless of the rare shrubs and plants he passed.

An arched door led into the chamber where Samarides kept his most valuable possessions, and that door stood open. Conan paused a moment to study the heavy iron lock. That the girl had opened it he had no doubt, but if she had been within, then any traps must have been disabled, or else be easily avoided.

The Cimmerian hesitated a moment longer, then started across the chamber, floored in diamond-shaped tiles of alternating red and white. The emerald goblet, he had been told, stood at the far end of the room on a pedestal carved of serpentine. At his second step a diamond tile sank beneath his foot. Thinking of crossbows mounted on the wall—he had encountered such before—he threw himself flat on the floor. And felt another tile sink beneath his hand. From the wall came a rattling clink and clatter he had been a thief long enough to recognize. The sinking tiles had each released a weight which was pulling a chain from a wheel. And that in turn would activate . . . what?

As he leaped to his feet a bell began to toll, then another. Cursing, he ran the length of the room. Twice more tiles sank beneath him, and by the time he reached the dull green mottled pedestal, four bells clanged the alarm. The pedestal was bare.

"Erlik take the wench!" he snarled.

Spinning, he dashed from the chamber. And ran head-on into two spear-carrying guards. As the three fell to the floor it flashed into Conan's head that it was just as well he had not dallied to choose something to make up for the loss of the goblet. His fist smashed into the face of one guard, nose and teeth cracking in a spray of red. The man jerked and sagged, unconscious. The other scrambled to his feet, spear ready to thrust. Had he delayed, Conan thought, they could likely have held him in the chamber long enough for others to arrive. His sword flickered from its sheath, caught the spear just behind the head, and the second guard found himself holding a long stick. With a shout the man threw the pole at Conan and fled.

Conan ran, too. In the opposite direction. At the first doorway of the house he ducked inside, bursting into the midst of servants nervously chattering about the still ringing bells. For an instant they stared at him, eyes going wider and wider, then he waved his sword in the air and roared at the top of his lungs. Shrieking men and women scattered like a covey of Kothian quail.

Confusion, the Cimmerian thought. If he spread enough confusion he might get out of there yet. Through the house he sped, and every servant he met was sent flying by fierce roars and waving blade, till cries of "Help!" and "Murder!" and even "Fire!" rang down every corridor. More than once the young Cimmerian had to duck down a side hall as guards clattered by, chasing after screams and yelling themselves, until he began to wonder how many men Samarides had. Cacophony run riot filled the house.

At last he reached the entry hall, surrounded on three sides by a balcony with balustrades of smoke-stone, beneath a vaulted ceiling worked in alabaster arabesques. Twin broad stairs of black marble curved down from that second-floor balcony to a floor mosaicked in a map of the world, as Zamorans knew it, with each country marked by representations of the gems imported from it.

All of this Conan ignored, his eyes locked on the tall, iron-studded doors leading to the street. A bar, heavy enough to need three men for the lifting, held them shut, and the bar was in turn fastened in place by iron chains and massive locks.

"Crom!" he growled. "Shut up like a fortress!"

Once, twice, thrice his broadsword clashed against a lock, with him wincing at the damage the blows were doing to his edge. The lock broke open, and he quickly pulled the chain through the iron loops holding it against the bar. As he turned to the next chain, a quarrel as thick as two of his fingers slammed into the bar where he had been standing. He changed his turn into a dive to the floor, eyes searching for the next shot.

Instantly he saw his lone opponent. Atop one flight of stairs stood a man of immense girth, whose skin yet hung in folds as if he had once been twice so big. Lank, thinning hair surrounded his puffy face, and he wore a shapeless sleeping garment of dark blue silk. Samarides. One of the gem merchant's feet was in the stirrup of a heavy crossbow, and he laboriously worked the handles of a windlass to crank back the bowstring, a rope of drool running from one corner of his narrow mouth.

Quickly judging how long it would be before Samarides could place another quarrel in the crossbow, Conan bounded to his feet. A single furious blow that struck sparks sent the second lock clattering to the floor. Sheathing his sword, the Cimmerian tugged the chain free and set his hands to the massive bar.

"Guards!" Samarides screamed. "To me! Guards!"

Muscles corded and knotted in calves and thighs, back, shoulders and arms, as Conan strained against the huge wooden bar. By the thickness of a fingernail it lifted. Sweat popped out on his forehead. The thickness of a finger. The width of a hand. And then the massive bar was clear of the support irons.

Three slow, staggering steps backwards Conan took, until he could turn and heave the bar aside. Mosaic tiles shattered as it landed with a crash that shook the floor.

"Guards!" Samarides shrieked, and pounding feet answered him.

Conan dashed to the thick, iron-studded doors and heaved one open to crash against a wall. As he darted through, another quarrel slashed past his head to gouge a furrow in the marble of Samarides' portico. Tumult rose behind him as guards rushed into the entry hall, shouting to Samarides for instructions, and Samarides screamed incoherently back at them. Conan did not look back. He ran. Mind filled with anger at a young woman thief with a too-witty tongue, he ran until the night of Shadizar swallowed him.

11

That quarter of Shadizar called the Desert was a warren of crooked steets reeking of offal and despair. The debaucheries that took place behind closed doors in the rest of the city were performed openly in the Desert, and made to pay a profit. Its denizens, more often in rags than not, lived as if death could come with the next breath, as it quite often did. Men and women were scavengers, predators or prey, and some who thought themselves in one class discovered, frequently too late, that they were in another.

The tavern of Abuletes was one of the Desert's best, as such was accounted there. Few footpads and fewer cutpurses were numbered among its patrons. Graverobbers were unwelcome, though more for the smells that hung about them than for how they earned their coin. For the rest, all who had the price of a drink were welcome.

When Conan slapped open the tavern door, the effluvia of the street fought momentarily with the smell of half-burned meat and sour wine in the big common room where two musicians playing zithers for a naked dancing girl competed unsuccessfully with the babble of the tavern's custom. A mustachioed Nemedian coiner at the bar fondled a giggling doxy in a tall, red-dyed wig and strips of green silk that did little to cover her generously rounded breasts and buttocks. A plump Ophirean procurer, jeweled rings glittering on his fingers, held court at a corner table; among those laughing at his jokes—so long as his gold held out, at least—were three kidnappers, swarthy, narrow-faced Iranistanis, hoping he would throw a little business their way. A pair of doxies, dark-eyed twins, hawked their wares among the tables, their girdles of coins clinking as their hips swayed in unison.

Before the Cimmerian had taken a full step, a voluptuous, olive-skinned woman threw her arms around his neck. Gilded brass breastplates barely contained her heavy breasts, and a narrow girdle of gilded chain, set low on her well-rounded hips, supported a length of diaphanous blue silk, no more than a handspan in width, that hung to her braceleted ankles before and behind.

"Ah, Conan," she murmured throatily, "what a pity you did not return earlier."

"Have some wine with me, Semiramis," he replied, eying her swelling chest, "and tell me why I should have come back sooner. Then we can go upstairs—" He cut off with a frown as she shook her head.

"I ply my trade this night, Cimmerian." At his frown, she sighed. "Even I must have a little silver to live."

"I have silver," he growled.

"And I cannot take coin from you. I will not."

He muttered an oath under his breath. "You always say that. Why not? I don't understand."

"Because you're not a woman." She laughed softly and traced a finger along his jaw. "A thing for which I am continually grateful."

Conan's face tightened. First Lyana had made a fool of him this night, and now Semiramis attempted the same. "Women never say their minds straight out. Very well. If you've no use for me tonight, then I'm done with you as well." He left her standing with her fists on her hips and her mouth twisted in exasperation.

At the bar he dug into his purse and tossed coppers onto the cracked wooden surface. As he had known it would, the sound of coins penetrated the wall of noise in the room and drew Abuletes, wiping his fat fingers on the filthy apron he wore over a faded yellow tunic. The tavernkeeper made the coins disappear with a deft motion.

"I want wine for that," Conan said. Abuletes nodded. "And some information."

"'Tis enough for the wine," the tavernkeeper replied drily. He set a wooden tankard, from which rose the sour smell of cheap wine, before the big youth. "Information costs more."

Conan rubbed his thumb over a gouge in the edge of the bar, made by a sword stroke, drawing the fat man's piggish eyes to the mark. "There were six of them, as I recall," he said absently. "One with his knife pricking your ribs, and ready to probe your guts if you opened your mouth without his leave. What was it they intended? Taking you into the kitchen, wasn't it? Didn't one of them speak of putting your feet in the cookfire till you told where your gold is cached?"

"I have no gold," Abuletes muttered unconvincingly. He could spot a clipped coin at ten paces, and was reliably rumored to have the first copper he had ever stolen buried somewhere in the tavern.

"Of course not," Conan agreed smoothly. "Still, it was Hannuman's own luck for you I saw what was happening, when none else did. 'Twould have been ... uncomfortable for you, with your feet in the coals and naught to tell them."

"Aye, you saw." The fat man's tone was as sour as his wine. "And laid about you with that accursed sword, splintering half my tables. Do you know what they cost to replace? The doxies were hysterical for all the blood you splattered around, and half my night's custom disappeared for fear you'd cut them down as well."

Conan laughed and drank deeply from the tankard, saying no more. Never a night passed without blood shed on the sawdust-strewn floor, and it was no rare sight to see a corpse being dragged out back for disposal in an alley.

Abuletes' face twisted, and his chin sank until his chins doubled in number. "This makes it clear between us. Right?"

The Cimerian nodded, but cautioned, "If you tell me what I want to hear. I look for a woman." Abuletes snorted and gestured to the doxies scattered through the common room. Conan went on patiently. "She's a thief, about so tall," he marked with one big hand at the height of his chest, "and well rounded for her size. Tonight she wore black leggings and a short tunic, both as tight as her skin. And she carried this." He laid the thowing knife on the bar. "She calls herself Lyana."

Abuletes prodded the black blade with a grimy-knuckled finger. "I know of no woman thief, called Lyana or aught else. There was a man, though, who used knives like this. Jamal, he was named."

"A woman, Abuletes."

The fat tapster shrugged. "He had a daughter. What was her name? Let me see." He rubbed at a suety cheek. "Jamal was shortened a head by the City Guard, it must be ten years back. His brothers took the girl in. Gayan and Hafid. They were thieves, too. Haven't heard of them in years, though. Too old for the life now, I suppose. Age gets us all, in the end. Tamira. That was her name. Tamira."

The muscular youth stared expressionless at Abuletes until the fat tavernkeeper fell silent. "I ask about a girl called Lyana, and you spin me a tale of this Tamira. And her entire Mitra-accursed family. Would you care to tell me about her mother? Her grandfather? I've a mind to put your feet in the fire myself."

Abuletes eyed Conan warily. The man with the strange blue eyes was known in the Desert for his sudden temper, and for his unpredictability. The tavernkeeper spread his hands. "How hard is it to give a name not your own? And didn't I say? Jamal and his brothers wore the black garments you spoke of. Claimed it made them all but invisible in the dark. Had all sorts of tricks, they did. Ropes of raw silk dyed black, and I don't know what all. No, Tamira's your female thief, all right, whatever she calls herself now."

Black ropes, Conan thought, and suppressed a smile. Despite his youth he had had enough years as a thief to learn discretion. "Perhaps," was all he said.

"Perhaps," the tapster grumbled. "You mark me on it. She's the one. This makes us even, Cimmerian."

Conan finished his wine in three long gulps and set the empty tankard down with a click. "If she *is* the woman I seek. The question now is where to find her and make certain."

Abuletes threw up his pudgy hands. "Do you think I keep track of every woman in the Desert? I can't even keep track of the trulls in my own tavern!"

Conan turned his back on the tavernkeeper's grinding teeth. Tamira and Lyana, he was sure, were one and the same woman. Luck must be with him, for he had expected days of asking to find a trace of her. Denizens of the Desert left as few tracks as the animals of that district's namesake. Surely discovering so much so quickly was an omen. No doubt he would leave the tavern in the morning and find her walking past in the street. Then they would see who would make a fool of whom.

At that moment his eye fell on Semiramis, seated at a table with three Kothian smugglers. One, with his mustache curled like horns and big gilded hoops in his ears, kneaded her bare thigh as he spoke to her urgently. Nodding in sudden decision, Conan strode to the table where the four sat.

The Kothians looked up, and Semiramis frowned. "Conan," she began, reaching toward him cautioningly.

The big Cimmerian grasped her wrist, bent and, before anyone could move, hoisted her over his shoulder. Stools crashed over as the Kothians leaped to their feet, hands going to sword hilts.

"You northland oaf!" Semiramis howled, wriggling furiously. Her fist pounded futilely at his back. "Unhand me, you misbegotten spawn of a camel! Mitra blast your eyes, Conan!"

Her tirade went on, getting more inventive, and Conan paused to listen admiringly. The Kothians hesitated with swords half drawn, disconcerted at being ignored. After a moment Conan turned his attention to them, putting a pleasant smile on his face. That seemed to unsettle the three even more.

"My sister," he said mildly. "She and I must speak of family matters."

"Erlik flay your hide and stake your carcass in the sun!" the struggling woman yelled. "Derketo shrivel your stones!"

Calmly Conan met each man's gaze in turn, and each man shivered, for his smile did not extend to those glacial blue orbs. The Kothians measured the breadth of his shoulders, calculated how encumbered he would be by the woman, and tossed the dice in the privacy of their minds.

"I wouldn't interfere between brother and sister," the one with hoops in his ears muttered, his eyes sliding away. Suddenly all three were engrossed in setting their stools upright.

Semiramis' shouts redoubled in fury as Conan started for the rickety stairs that led to the second floor. He smacked a rounded buttock with his open palm. "Your sweet poetry leads me to believe you love me," he said, "but your dulcet tones would deafen an ox. Be quiet."

Her body quivered. It took him a moment to realize she was laughing. "Will you at least let me walk, you untutored beast?" she asked.

"No," he replied with a grin.

"Barbarian!" she murmured, and snuggled her cheek against his back.

Laughing, he took the stairs two at a time. Luck was indeed with him.

III

The Katara Bazaar was a kaleidoscope of colors and a cacophony of voices, a large, flagstone-paved square near the Desert where sleek lordlings, perfumed pomanders at their nostrils, rubbed shoulders with unwashed apprentices who apologized with mocking grins when they jostled the well-born. Silk-clad ladies, trailed by attentive slaves to carry their purchases, browsed unmindful of the ragged urchins scurrying about their feet. Some vendors displayed their goods on flimsy tables sheltered by faded lengths of cloth on poles. Others had no more than a blanket spread beneath the hot sun. Hawkers of plums and ribbons, oranges and pins, cried their wares shrilly as they strolled through the throng. Rainbow bolts of cloth, carved ivories from Vendhya, brass bowls from Shadizar's own metalworkers, lustrous pearls from the Western Sea and paste "gems" guaranteed to be genuine, all changed hands in the space of a heartbeat. Some were stolen, some smuggled. A rare few had even had the King's tax paid on them.

On the morning after his attempt at Samarides' goblet—the thought made him wince—Conan made his way around the perimeter of the bazaar, searching without seeming to among the beggars. Mendicants were not allowed within the confines of the great square, but they lined its edges, their thin, supplicating cries entreating passerby for a coin. There was a space between each ragged man and the next, and unlike beggars elsewhere in Shadizar these cooperated to the extent of maintaining that distance. Too many too close together would reduce each man's take.

Exchanging a copper with a fruitmonger for two oranges, the big Cimmerian squatted near a beggar in filthy rags, a man with one leg twisted grotesquely at the knee. A grimy strip of cloth covered his eyes, and a wooden bowl with a single copper in the bottom sat on the flagstones before him.

"Pity the blind," the beggar whined loudly. "A coin for the blind, gentle people. Pity the blind."

Conan tossed one orange into the bowl and began stripping the peel from the other. "Ever think of going back to being a thief, Peor?" he said quietly.

The "blind" man turned his head sightly to make sure no one else was close by and said, "Never, Cimmerian." His cheerful voice was pitched to reach Conan's ear and no further. He made the orange disappear beneath his tunic of patches. "For later. No, I pay my tithe to the City Guard, and I sleep easy at night knowing my head will never go up on a pike over the West Gate. You should consider becoming a beggar. 'Tis a solid trade. Not like thieving. Mitra-accursed mountain slime!"

Conan paused with a segment of orange half-lifted to his mouth. "What?"

Barely moving his head, Peor motioned to a knot of six Kezankian hillmen, turbanned and bearded, their dark eyes wide with ill-concealed amazement at the city around them. They wandered through the bazaar in a daze, fingering goods but never buying. From the scowls that followed them, the peddlers were glad to see their backs, sale or no. "That's the third lot of those filthy jackals I've seen today, and a good two turns of the glass till the sun is high. They should be running for the rocks they crawled out from under, what with the news that's about this morning."

The beggar got little chance between sunrise and sunset to say anything beyond his pleading cry, and the occasional fawning thanks. It could not hurt to let him talk, Conan thought, and said, "What news?"

Peor snorted. "If it was about a new method of winning at dice, Cimmerian, you'd have known of it yesterday. Do you think of anything but women and gambling?"

"The news, Peor?"

"They say someone is uniting the Kezankian tribes. They say the hillmen are sharpening their tulwars. They say it could mean war. If 'tis so, the Desert will feel the first blow, as always."

Conan tossed the last of the orange aside and wiped his hands on his thighs. "The Kezankians are far distant, Peor." His grin revealed strong white teeth. "Or do you think the tribesmen will leave their mountains to sack the Desert? It is not the place I would chose, were I they, but you are older than I and no doubt know better."

"Laugh, Cimmerian," Peor said bitterly. "But when war is announced the mob will hunt for hillman throats to slit, and when they cannot find enough to sate their bloodlust, they'll turn their attentions to the Desert. And the army will be there—'to preserve order.' Which means to put to the sword any poor sod from the Desert who thinks of actually resisting the mob. It has happened before, and will again."

A shadow fell across them, cast by a woman whose soft robes of emerald silk clung to the curves of breasts and belly and thighs like a caress. A belt woven of golden cords was about her waist. Ropes of pearls encircled her wrists and neck, and two more, as large as a man's thumbnail, were at her ears. Behind her a tall Shemite, the iron collar of a slave on his neck and a bored expression on his face, stood laden with packages from the Bazaar. She dropped a silver coin in Peor's bowl, but her sultry gaze was all for Conan.

The muscular youth enjoyed the looks women gave him, as a normal matter, but this one examined him as if he were a horse in the auction barns. And to make matters worse a scowl grew on the Shemite's face as though he recognized a rival. Conan's face grew hot with anger. He opened his mouth, but she spoke first.

"My husband would never approve the purchase," she smiled, and walked away with undulating hips. The Shemite hurried after her, casting a self-satisfied glance over his shoulder at Conan as he went.

Peor's bony fingers fished the coin from the bowl. With a cackle that showed he had regained at least some of his humor, he tucked it into his pouch. "And she'd pay a hundred times so much for a single night with you, Cimmerian. Two hundred. A more pleasant way to earn your coin than scrambling over rooftops, eh?"

"Would you like that leg broken in truth?" Conan growled.

The beggar's cackles grew until they took him into a fit of coughing. When he could breathe normally again, he wiped the back of his hand across his thin-lipped mouth. "No doubt I would earn even more in my bowl. My knee hurts of a night for leaving it so all day, but that fall was the best thing that ever happened to me."

Conan shivered at the thought, but pressed on while the other held his good mood. "I did not come today just to give you an orange, Peor. I look for a woman called Lyana, or perhaps Tamira."

Peor nodded as the Cimmerian described the girl and gave a carefully edited account of their meeting, then said, "Tamira. I've heard that name, and seen the girl. She looks as you say."

"Where can I find her?" Conan asked eagerly, but the beggar shook his head.

"I said I've seen her, and more than once, but as to where she might be . . ." He shrugged.

Conan put a hand to the leather purse at his belt. "Peor, I could manage a pair of silver pieces for the man who tells me how to find her."

"I wish I knew," Peor said ruefully, then went on quickly. "But I'll pass the word among the Brotherhood of the Bowl. If a beggar sees her, you'll hear of it. After all, friendship counts for something, does it not?"

The Cimmerian cleared his throat to hide a grin. Friendship, indeed! The message would come to him through Peor, and the beggar who sent it would be lucky to get as much as one of the silver pieces. "That it does," he agreed.

"But, Conan? I don't hold with killing women. You don't intend to hurt her, do you?"

"Only her pride," Conan said, getting to his feet. With the beggars' eyes as his, he would have her before the day was out. "Only her pride."

Two days later Conan threaded his way through the thronging crowds with a sour expression on his face. Not only the beggars of Shadizar had become his eyes. More than one doxy had smiled at the ruggedly handsome young Cimmerian, shivered in her depths at the blue of his eyes, and promised to watch for the woman he sought, though never without a pout of sultry jealousy. The street urchins, unimpressed by broad shoulders or azure eyes, had been more difficult. Some men called them the Dust, those homeless, ragged children, countless in number and helpless before the winds of fate, but the streets of Shadizar were a hard school, and the urchins gave trust grudgingly and demanded a reward in silver. But from all those eyes he had learned only where Tamira had been, and never a word of where she was.

Conan's eyes searched among the passersby, seeking to pierce the veils of those women who wore them. At least, the veils of those who were slender and no taller than his chest. What he would do when he found her was not yet clear in his mind beyond the matter of seeking restitution for his youthful pride, but find her he would if he had to stare into the face of every woman in Shadizar.

So intent was he on his thoughts that the drum that cleared others from the street, even driving sedan chairs to the edge of the pavement, did not register on his mind until it suddenly came to him that he stood alone in the middle of the street. Turning to see where the steady thumb came from, he found a procession bearing down on him.

At its head were two spearmen as tall as he, ebon-eyed men with capes of leopard skin, the clawed paws hanging across their broad, bare chests. Behind came the drummer, his instrument slung by his side to give free swing to the mallets with which he beat a cadence. A score of men in spiked helms and short, sleeveless mail followed the drummer. Half bore spears and half bows, with quivers on their backs, and all wore wide, white trousers and high, red boots.

Conan's eyes went no further down the cortege than the horsemen who came next, or rather the woman who led them, mounted on a prancing black gelding a hand taller than any her followers rode. Tall she was, and well rounded, a delight both callimastian and callipygean. Her garb of tight tunic and tighter breeches, both of tawny silk, with a scarlet cloak thrown well back across her horse's rump, did naught to hide her curves. Light brown hair, sun-streaked with gold, curled about her shoulders and surrounded a prideful face set with clear gray eyes.

She was a woman worth looking at, Conan thought. And besides, he knew of her, as did every thief in Shadizar. The Lady Jondra was known for many things, her arrogance, her hunting, her racing of horses, but among thieves she was known as the possessor of a necklace and tiara that had set more than one man's mouth watering. Each was set with a flawless ruby, larger than the last joint of a big man's thumb, surrounded by sapphires and black opals. In the Desert men taunted each other with the stealing of them, for of all those who had tried, the only one not taken by the spears of her guards had died with Jondra's own arrows in his eyes. It was said she had been more furious that the thief entered her chambers while she was bathing than at his bungled attempt at theft.

Conan prepared to step from the procession's path, when the spearmen, not five paces from him now, dropped their spears to the ready. They did not slow their pace, but came on as if the threat should send him scurrying for cover.

The big Cimmerian's face tightened. Did they think him a dog, then, to beat from their way? A young man's pride, dented as much as he could stand in recent days, hardened. He straightened, and his hand went to the worn, leather-wrapped hilt of his broad-sword. Dead silence fell among the crowd lining the sides of the street.

The spearmen's eyes widened at the sight of the young giant standing his ground. The streets always cleared before their mistress, the drum usually sufficing, and never more than the gleam of a spearpoint in the sunlight required at most. It came to each in the same instant that this was no apprentice to be chivvied aside. As one man they stopped and dropped into a crouch with spears presented.

The drummer, marching obliviously, continued his pounding until he was between the two spearmen. There his mallets froze, one raised and one against the drumhead, and his eyes darted for a way out. The three men made a barricade across the street that perforce brought the rest of Lady Jondra's cortege to a halt, first the mailed hunters, then the horsemen, and so back down the line, till all stood stopped.

The ludicrousness of it struck Conan, and he felt mirth rising despite himself. How did he get himself into these predicaments, he wondered.

"You there!" a husky woman's voice called. "You, big fellow with the sword!" Conan looked up to find the Lady Jondra staring at him over the heads of her spearmen and archers. "If you can stop Zurat and Tamal in their tracks, perhaps you can face a lion as well. I always need men, and there are few who deserve the name in Shadizar. I will take you into my service." A tall, hawk-faced man riding next to her opened his mouth angrily, but she cut him off with a gesture. "What say you? You have the shoulders for a spearman."

The laughter broke through, and Conan let it roar, though he was careful not to take his eyes from the spearmen or his hand from his sword. Jondra's face slowly froze in amazement. "I am already in service," he managed, "to myself. But, my lady, I wish you good day and will no longer block your passage." He made a sweeping bow—not deep enough to lose sight of the spear points—and strode to the side of the street.

For an instant there was stunned silence, then the Lady Jondra was shouting. "Zurat! Tamal! March on! Junio! The beat!"

The spearmen straightened, and the drummer stiffly took up his cadence again. In moments the procession was moving. Jondra rode past stiffly, her eyes drifting to the big Cimmerian as if she did not realize what she did. The hawk-faced man rode beside her, arguing volubly, but she seemed not to hear.

A knot of barefooted street urchins, all color long faded from their tattered tunics, suddenly appeared near Conan. Their leader was a girl, though at an age when her scrawniness could pass for either sex. Half a head taller than her followers, she swaggered to the muscular youth's side and studied the array of hunters. The lion dogs passed, heavy, snarling brutes with spiked collars, pulling hard on the leashes held by their handlers.

"Dog like that could take your leg off," the girl said. "Big man, you get a spear in your belly, and who's going to pay us?"

"You get paid when you've found her, Laeta," Conan replied. The trophies of the hunt were borne by, skins of leopards and lions, great scimitar antelope horns, the skull of a huge wild ox with horns as thick and long as a man's arm, all held aloft for the view of the onlookers.

She cast a scornful glance at him. "Did I not say as much? We found the wench, and I want those two pieces of silver."

Conan grunted. "When I am sure it's her."

This was not the first report of Tamira he had had. One had been a woman more than twice his age, another a potter's apprentice with only one eye. The last of Jondra's procession passed, pack animals and high-wheeled ox-carts, and the throng that had stood aside flowed together behind like water behind a boat.

"Take me to her," Conan said.

Laeta grumbled, but trotted away down the street, her coterie of hard-eyed urchins surrounding her like a bodyguard. Under every ragged tunic, the Cimmerian knew, was a knife, or more than one. The children of the street preferred to run, but when cornered they were as dangerous as a pack of rats.

To Conan's surprise they moved no closer to the Desert, but rather father away, into a district peopled by craftsmen. The din of brass-smiths' hammers beat at them, then the stench of the dyers' vats. Smoke from kiln fires rose on all sides. Finally the girl stopped and pointed to a stone building where a sign hanging from chains showed the image of a lion, half-heartedly daubed not too long past with fresh carmine.

"In there?" Conan asked suspiciously. Taverns attracted likes, and a thief would not likely be welcome amid potters and dyers.

"In there," Laeta agreed. She chewed her lip, then sighed. "We will wait out here, big man. For the silver."

Conan nodded impatiently and pushed open the tavern door.

Inside, the Red Lion was arranged differently from the usual tavern. At some time in the past a fire had gutted the building. The ground floor, which had collapsed into the cellar, had never been replaced. Instead, a balcony had been built running around the inside of the building at street level, and the common room was now in what had been the cellar. Even when the sun was high on the hottest day, the common room of the Red Lion remained cool.

From a place by the balcony rail just in front of the door, Conan ran his gaze over the interior of the tavern, searching for a slender female form. A few men stood on the balcony, some lounging against the railing with tankard in hand, most bargaining quietly with doxies for time in the rooms abovestairs. A steady stream of serving girls trotted up and down stairs at the rear of the common room with trays of food and drink, for the kitchen was still on the ground level. Tables scattered across the stone floor below held potters whose arms were flecked with dried clay and leather-aproned metal workers and apprentices with tunics stained by rainbow splashes.

The ever-present trulls, their wisps of silk covering no more here than they did in the Desert, strolled the floor, but as he had expected Conan could see no other women among the tables. Satisfied that Laeta was mistaken or lying, he started to turn for the door. From the corner of his eye he saw a burly potter, with a round-breasted doxy running her fingers through his hair, look away from her bounty to glance curiously at a spot below where the big Cimmerian stood. Another man, his leather apron lying across the table before him and a squealing jade on his knees, paused in his pawing of her to do the same. And yet another man.

Conan leaned to look over the railing, and there Tamira sat beneath him, demurely clothed in pale blue robes, face scrubbed to virginal freshness . . . and a wooden mug upended at her mouth. With a sigh she set the mug on the table upside-down, a signal to the serving girls that she wanted it refilled.

Smiling, Conan slipped the flat throwing knife from his belt. A flicker of his hand, and the black blade quivered in the upturned bottom of her mug. Tamira started, then was still except for the fingers of her left hand drumming on the tabletop. The Cimmerian's smile faded. With a muttered oath he stalked to the stairs and down.

When he reached the table the throwing knife had disappeared. He ignored the wide-eyed looks of men at nearby tables and sat across from her.

"You cost me eight pieces of gold," were his first words.

The corners of Tamira's mouth twitched upward. "So little? I received forty from the Lady Zayella."

Conan's hand gripped the edge of the table till the wood creaked in protest. Forty! "Zarath the Kothian would give a hundred," he muttered, then went on quickly before she could ask why he was then only to receive eight. "I want a word with you, wench."

"And I with you," she said. "I didn't come to a place like this, and let you find me, just to—"

"Let me find you!" he roared. A man at a nearby table hurriedly got up and moved away.

"Of course, I did." Her face and voice were calm, but her fingers began to tap on the table again. "How could I fail to know that every beggar in Shadizar, and a fair number of the trulls, were asking after my whereabouts?"

"Did you think I would forget you?" he asked sarcastically.

She went on as if he had not spoken. "Well, I will not have it. You'll get in my—my uncles' attention. They'll not take kindly to a stranger seeking after me. I led you here, well away from the Desert, in the hopes they'll not hear of our meeting. You'll find yourself with a blade in your throat, Cimmerian. And for some reason I don't quite understand, I would not like that."

Conan looked at her silently, until under his gaze her large, dark eyes began blinking nervously. Her finger-drumming quickened. "So you do know my country of birth."

"You fool, I am trying to save your life."

"Your uncles look after you?" he said abruptly. "Watch over you? Protect you?"

"You will find out how carefully if you do not leave me alone. And what's that smug grin for?"

"It's just that now I know I'll be your first man." His tone was complacent, but his every muscle tensed.

Tamira's mouth worked in silent incredulity, and scarlet suffused her cheeks. Suddenly a shriek burst from her lips, and the throwing knife was in her hand. Conan threw himself from his bench as her arm whipped forward. Beyond him an appentice yelped and stared disbelieving at the tip of his nose, from which a steady drip of red fell to put new blotches on his dye-stained tunic.

Warily Conan got to his feet. Tamira shook her small fists at him in incoherent fury. At least, he thought, she did not have another of those knives. It would be out, otherwise. "But you must ask me," he said as if there had been no interruption. "That will make up for the eight gold pieces you stole from me, when you ask me."

"Erlik take you!" she gasped. "Mitra blast your soul! To think I worried . . . to think I . . . You're nothing but an oaf after all! I hope my uncles do catch you! I hope the City Guard puts your head on a pike! I hope—I hope—oh!" From head to toe she shook with rage.

"I eagerly await our first kiss," Conan said, and dodged her mug, aimed at his head.

Calmly turning his back on her wordless shouts, he strolled up the stairs and out of the tavern. As soon as the door closed behind him, his casual manner disappeared. Urgently he looked for Laeta, and smiled when she appeared with her palm out.

Before she could ask he tossed her two silver coins. "There's more," he said. "I want to know everywhere she goes, and everyone she sees. A silver piece every tenday for you, and the same for your followers." Baratses' gold was disappearing fast, he thought, but with luck it should last just long enough.

Laeta, with her mouth open to bargain, could only nod wordlessly.

Conan smiled in satisfaction. He had Tamira now. After his performance she thought he was a buffoon intent on seduction to salve his pride. He doubted if she even remembered her slip of the tongue. Almost she had said he would get in her way. She planned a theft, and wanted no encumbrance. But this time *he* would get there first, and *she* would find the empty pedestal.

IV

Much of the Zamoran nobility, the Lady Jondra thought as she strolled through her palace garden, deplored that the last of the Perashanids was a woman. Carefully drawing back the vermilion silk sleeve of her robe, she dabbled her fingers in the sparkling waters of a fountain rimmed with gray-veined marble. From the corner of her eye she watched the man who stood next to her. His handsome, dark-eyed face radiated self-assurance. A heavy gold chain, each link worked with the seal of his family, hung across the crisp pleats of his citrine tunic. Lord Amaranides did not deplore her femininity at all. It meant that all the wealth of the Perashanids went with her hand. If he could manage to secure that hand.

"Let us walk on, Ama," she said, and smiled at his attempt to hide a grimace for the pet name she had given him. He would think the smile was for him, she knew. It was not in him to imagine otherwise.

"The garden is lovely," he said. "But not so lovely as you."

Instead of taking his proffered arm she moved ahead down the slate-tiled walk, forcing him to hurry to catch up to her.

Eventually she would have to wed. The thought brought a sigh of regret, but duty would do what legions of suitors had been unable to. She could not allow the Perashanid line to end with her. Another sigh passed her full lips.

"Why so melancholy, my sweetling?" Amaranides murmured in her ear. "Let me but taste your honey kiss, and I will sweep your moodiness away."

Deftly she avoided his lips, but made no further discouraging move. Unlike most nobly born Zamoran women, she allowed few men so much as a kiss, and none more. But even if she could not bring herself to stop her occasional tweaking of his well-stuffed pomposity, Amaranides must not be put off entirely.

At least he was tall enough, she thought. She never allowed herself to contemplate the reason why she was taller than most Zamoran men, but she had long since decided that her husband must be taller than she. Amaranides was a head taller, but his build was slender. With an idle corner of her mind she sketched the man she wanted. Of noble lineage, certainly. An excellent horseman, archer and hunter, of course. Physically? Taller than Amaranides by nearly a head. Much broader of shoulders, with a deep, powerful chest. Handsome, but more ruggedly so than her companion. His eyes . . .

Abruptly she gasped as she recognized the man she had drawn in her mind. She had dressed him as a Zamoran nobleman, but it was the sky-eyed street-ruffian who had disrupted her return from the hunt. Her face flooded with scarlet. Blue eyes! A barbarian! Like smoky gray fires her own eyes blazed. That she could consider allowing such a one to touch her, even without realizing it! Mitra! It was worse done without realizing it!

". . . And on my last hunt," Amaranides was saying, "I killed a truly magnificent leopard. Finer than any you've taken, I fancy. It will be a pleasure for me to teach you the finer points of hunting, my little sweetmeat. I . . ."

Jondra ground her teeth as he rattled blithely on. Still, he *was* a hunter, not to mention nobly born. If he was a fool—and of that there was little doubt in her mind—then he would be all the more easily managed.

"I know why you've come, Ama," she said.

". . . Claws as big as . . ." The nobleman's voice trailed off, and he blinked uncertainly. "You know?"

She could not keep impatience from her voice. "You want me for your wife. Is that not it? Come." Briskly she set out through the garden toward the fletcher's mound.

Amaranides hesitated, then ran after her. "You don't know how happy you've made me, sweetling. Sweetling? Jondra? Where are you . . . ah!"

Jondra fended off the arms he tried to throw around her with a recurved bow she had taken from a gilded rack standing on a grassy sward. Calmly she slipped a leather bracer onto her left arm for protection from the bowstring. Another bow, a second bracer, and two quivers, clustered fletchings rising above their black-lacquered sides, hung on the rack.

"You must . . . equal me," she said, gesturing toward a small round target of thickly woven straw hanging at the top of a wide wooden frame, which was three times the height of a man, a hundred paces distant. She had intended to say "best," but at the last could not bring herself to it. In truth, she did not believe *any* man could best her, either with a bow or on horseback. "I can marry no man who is not my equal as an archer."

Amaranides eyed the target, then took the second bow with a smug smile. "Why so high? No matter. I wager I'll beat you at it." He laughed then, a shocking bray at odds with his handsome features. "I've won many a purse with a bow, but you will be my finest prize."

Jondra's mouth tightened. Shaking back the hanging sleeves of her robes, she nocked an arrow and called, "Mineus!"

A balding man, in the short white tunic of a servant, came from the bushes near the frame and tugged at a rope attached near the target. Immediately the target, no bigger than a man's head, began to slide down a diagonal, and as it slid it swung from side to side on a long wooden arm. Clearly it would take a zig-zag path, at increasing speed, all the way to the ground.

Jondra did not raise her bow until the target had traversed half the first diagonal. Then, in one motion, she raised, drew and released. With a solid thwack her shaft struck, not slowing the target's descent. Before that arrow had gone home her second was loosed, and a third followed on its heels. As the straw target struck the ground, she lowered her bow with an arrow nocked but unreleased. It was her seventh. Six feathered shafts decorated the target. "The robes hamper me somewhat," she said ruefully. "With your tunic, you may well get more than my six. Let me clothe myself in hunting garb—are you ill, Ama?"

Amaranides' bow hung from a limp hand. He stared, pale of face, at the target. As he turned to her, high color replaced the pallor of his cheeks. His mouth twisted around his words. "I have heard that you delight in besting men, but I had not thought you would claim yourself ready to wed just to lure me to . . . this!" He spat the last word, hurling the bow at the riddled target. "What Brythunian witch-work did you use to magic your arrows?"

Her hands shook with rage as she raised her bow and drew the nocked arrow back to her cheek, but she forced them to be steady. "Remove yourself!" she said grimly.

Mouth falling open, the dark-faced nobleman stared at the arrow pointed at his face. Abruptly he spun about and ran, dodging from side to side, shoulders hunched, as if simultaneously attempting to avoid her arrow and steel himself against its strike.

She followed every skip and leap, keeping the arrow centered on him until he had disappeared among the shrubs. Then she released the breath in her tight lungs and the tension on her bowstring together. Thoughts she had disciplined from her mind came flooding back.

Lord Karentides, her father, had been a general of the Zamoran Army, as well as the last scion of an ancient house. Campaigning on the Brythunian border he chose a woman from among the prisoners, Camardica, tall and gray-eyed, who claimed to be a priestess. In the normal course of events there would have been nothing strange in this, for

Zamoran soldiers often enjoyed themselves with captive Brythunian women, and the Brythunian slaves in Zamora were beyond counting. But Karentides married his captive. Married her and accepted the ostracism that became his.

Jondra remembered his body—his and . . . that woman's—lying in state after the fever that slew so many in the city, sparing neither noble nor beggar. She had been raised, educated, protected as what she was, heiress to vast wealth, to blood of ancient nobility. The marks were on her, though—the height and the accursed eyes of gray—and she had heard the whispers. Half-breed. Savage. Brythunian. She had heard them until her skill with a bow, her ready temper and her disregard of consequences silenced even whispers in her hearing. She was the Lady Jondra of the House Perashanid, daughter of General Lord Karentides, last of a lineage to rival that of King Tiridates himself, and ware to anyone who mentioned aught else.

"He would not have hit it once, my lady," a quiet voice said at her elbow.

Jondra glanced at the balding servant, at the concern on his wrinkled face. "It is not your place to speak so, Mineus," she said, but there was no rebuke in her voice.

Mineus' expression folded into deference. "As you say, my lady. If my lady pleases, the girl sent by the Lady Roxana is here. I put her in the second waiting room, but I can send her away if that is still your wish."

"If I am not to wed," she said, replacing her bow carefully on the rack, "I shall have need of her after all."

The second waiting room was floored with a mosaic of arabesques in green and gold, in the middle of which stood a short, slender girl in a short tunic of dark blue, the color Lady Roxana put on her serving maids. Her dark hair was worked in a simple plait that fell to the small of her back. She kept her eyes on the tiles beneath her small feet as Jondra entered the room.

An ebony table inlaid with ivory held two wax tablets fastened face-to-face with silken cords. Jondra examined the seals on the cords carefully. Few outside the nobility or the merchant classes could write, but servants had been known to try altering their recommendations. There were no signs of tampering here. She cut the cords and read.

"Why do you wish to leave the Lady Roxana's service?" she asked abruptly. "Lyana? That's your name?"

"Yes, my lady," the girl answered without raising her head. "I want to become a lady's maid, my lady. I worked in the Lady Roxana's kitchens, but her handmaidens trained me. The Lady Roxana had no place for another handmaiden, but she said that you sought one."

Jondra frowned. Did the chit not even have enough spirit to meet her eyes? She abhorred a lack of spirit, whether in dogs or horses or servants. "I need a girl to tend my needs on the hunt. The last two found the rigors too great. Do you think your desire to be a lady's maid will survive heat and flies and sand?"

"Oh, yes, my lady."

Slowly Jondra walked around the girl studying her from every angle. She certainly *looked* sturdy enough to withstand a hunting camp. With fingertips she raised the girl's chin. "Lovely," she said, and thought she saw a spark in those large, dark eyes. Perhaps there was some spirit here after all. "I'll not have my hunts disrupted by spearmen panting after a pretty face, girl. See you cast no eyes at my hunters." Jondra smiled. There had definitely been a flash of anger that time.

"I am a maiden, my lady," the girl said with the faintest trace of tightness in her voice.

"Of course," Jondra said noncommittally. Few serving girls were, though all seemed to think the condition made them more acceptable to their mistresses. "I'm surprised the Lady Roxana allowed you to leave her, considering the praises she heaps on your head." She tapped the wax tablet with a fingernail. "In time I will discover if you deserve them. In any case, know that I will allow no hint of disobedience, lying, stealing or laziness. I do not beat my servants as often as some, but trangression in these areas will earn you stripes." She watched the sparks in the girl's eyes replaced with eagerness as the meaning of her words broke through.

"My lady, I swear that I will serve you as such a great lady deserves to be served."

Jondra nodded. "Mineus, show her to the servants' quarters. And summon Arvaneus."

"It shall be done, my lady."

She dismissed the matter from her mind then, the sounds of Mineus leading the girl from the room seeming to fade to insignificance. Replacing the tablets on the ebony table, she crossed the room to a tall, narrow cabinet of profusely carved rosewood. The doors opened to reveal shelves piled with scrolls of parchment, each bound with a ribbon. Hastily she pawed through the pale cylinders.

The incident with Amaranides had crystallized a decision. That the whispers about her parentage were still being bruited about was reason enough to end her consideration of marriage. Instead . . .

Amaranides had said she liked to best men. Could she help it that men, with their foolish pride, could not accept the fact that she was better than they, whether with bow or horse or on the hunt? Well, now she would best them properly. She would do what none of them had either the skill or the courage to do.

She untied the ribbon about a scroll and searched down the parchment until she found what she sought.

The beast, my lady, is said to be scaled like a serpent, but to move on legs. Winnowing out obvious exaggerations caused by fear, I can reliably report that it has slain and eaten both men and cattle. Its habitat, my lady, seems, however, to be the Kezankian Mountains near the border between Zamora and Brythunia. With the current unrest of the hill tribes, I cannot suggest . . .

The parchment crumpled in her hands. She would bring this strange beast's hide back as her trophy. Let one of Amaranides' ilk suggest he could do as much. Let him just dare.

Tamira scurried down palace corridors in Mineus' wake, barely hearing when the balding old man told her of her duties, or when he spoke to other servants. Until the very last moment she had not been certain her plan would work, even after so much planning and labor.

Forty gold pieces she had obtained from Zayella, and all had gone in preparation for this. Most went to Roxana's chamberlain, who provided the use of the Lady's private seal. There would be no checking, though, to trip her up, for the Lady Roxana had departed the city a day past. Tamira allowed herself a smile. In a day or two she would have Jondra's fabulous necklace and tiara.

"Give attention, girl," Mineus said impatiently. "You must know this to help prepare for the Lady Jondra's hunt."

Tamira blinked. "Hunt? But she just returned from a hunt."

"You saw me speak to Arvaneus, the chief huntsman. No doubt you will depart as soon as supplies are gathered."

Panic flashed through her. It had been none of her intention to actually go on one of Jondra's forays. There was no point to her sweating in a tent while the jewels remained in Shadizar. Of course, they would be there when she returned. But so might the Lady Roxana. "I—I have to see . . . about my belongings," she stammered. "I left clothing at the Lady Roxana's palace. And my favorite pin. I must fetch—"

Mineus cut her short. "When you've had instructions as to your duties in preparing for the hunt. Not only must you see that my lady's clothing and jewels are packed, but you must see to her perfumes, the soaps and oils for her bathing, and—"

"She—my lady takes her jewels hunting?"

"Yes, girl. Now pay attention. My lady's rouges and powders—"

"You mean a few bracelets and brooches," Tamira insisted.

The old man rubbed his bald spot and sighed. "I mean nothing of the sort, girl. Of an evening my lady often adorns herself to dine in her finest. Now, since you seem distracted for some reason, I will see you through your tasks."

For the rest of the morning and into the afternoon Tamira was prodded and pushed from one labor to the next, always under Mineus' watchful eye. She folded Jondra's garments of silks and laces—three times she folded them before reaching Mineus' satisfaction—and packed them in wicker panniers. Rare perfumes from Vendhya and powders from far Khitai, rouges from Sultanapur, costly oils and unguents from the corners of the world, all she wrapped in soft cloths and packed, with the balding old man hovering close to remind her that every vial and jar must be handled as gently as a swaddling child. Then, staggering under the weighty panniers, she and another serving-woman carried them down to the stableyard, where the pack-animals would be loaded on the morrow.

On each trip through Jondra's chambers, the chests for transporting the noblewoman's jewelry, thick-sided boxes of iron, made her mouth water. They sat so tantalizingly against a tapestry-hung wall. But they were empty iron now, for they would not be filled until the last instant. Still, the gems would be going with her. She could not help smiling.

Aching from the unaccustomed labor, Tamira found that Mineus had led her to a side door of the palace. "Fetch your belongings, girl," he said, "and return quickly. There will be more work."

Before she could speak she had been thrust outside, and the door closed in her face. For a long moment she stared wonderingly at the red-painted wood. She had forgotten her panic-induced invention of possessions. Her original plan called for remaining inside Jondra's palace until the necklace and tiara were in her hands. In that way Conan would never discover what she was up to. The huge barbarian seemed intent on . . .

It dawned on her that she *was* outside the palace, and she spun around to study the narrow street. A turbaned Kezankian hillman squatted disconsolately against a wall across the street, and a few ragged urchins played tag on the rough paving stones. She heaved a sigh of relief. There was neither a beggar nor a doxy in sight. Her uncles could provide a bundle to satisfy Mineus. Keeping a careful watch for Conan's many eyes, she hurried down the street.

Unseen by her, three of the urchins broke of their play and trailed after her.

The hillman watched her go with lustful eyes, then reluctantly returned to his surveillance of the palace.

V

At a corner table in Abuletes' common room, Conan glowered into a leathern jack half-filled with cheap Kothian wine. Semiramis, in a girdle of coins and two strips of thin scarlet silk, was seated in the lap of a Turanian coiner across the crowded room, but for once that was not the reason for the Cimmerian's dour face. What remained of Baratses' two gold pieces had been lessened at dice the previous night. With all of his mind on Tamira, he had given no thought to how to get more. And worst, he had had no word from Laeta. It was only a day since he had set the urchin to watch Tamira, but he was certain—as certain as if he had been told by the dark-eyed thief herself—that she moved already on the theft she planned. The theft he had vowed to beat her to. And he had no word!

Grimacing, he raised his wine and gulped the remainder of it down. When he lowered the jack a tall, bony man stood across the table from him. A fine black Khauranian cloak, edged with cloth of gold, was pulled tightly around him as if to hide his identity.

"What do you want, Baratses?" Conan grumbled. "I keep the two gold pieces for the attempt, and you should be thankful to have it made so cheaply."

"Do you have a room in this . . . establishment?" The spice merchant's black eyes darted about the raucous tavern as if he expected to be attacked at any moment. "I would talk with you in privacy."

Conan shook his head in disbelief. The fool had obviously dressed himself in what he considered plain fashion, but just as obviously he was no denizen of the Desert. His passage had certainly been noted, and footpads no doubt awaited nine deep in the street for his departure, but here, where he was safe from such, he feared robbery.

"Come," Conan said, and led the way up the rickety wooden stairs at the back of the common room.

His own room was a simple box of rough wooden planks, with a narrow window shuttered in a vain attempt to keep out the stench of the alley behind the tavern. A wide, low bed, a table with one short leg, and a lone stool were all the furnishings. The Cimmerian's few possessions—aside from the ancient broadsword he always wore—hung on pegs in one wall.

Baratses glanced around the room disdainfully, and Conan bristled. "I cannot afford a palace. Yet. Now, why are you here? Something more to be stolen? You'll give a fair price this time, or find someone else."

"You've not yet fulfilled your last commission, Cimmerian." Though the door was closed, the merchant kept his cloak clutched about him. "I have the rest of your gold here, but where is my goblet? I know Samarides no longer possesses it."

"Nor do I," Conan replied ruefully. "Another was there before me." He hesitated, but could not rid himself of the belief that the man deserved at least some information for his two gold pieces. "I have heard the Lady Zayella has the goblet now."

"So she offered you more than I," Baratses murmured. "I had heard you had some odd concept of honor, but I see I was wrong."

The Cimmerian's eyes grew icy. "Do not call me liar, merchant. Another took the goblet."

"The room is close," Baratses said. "I am hot." He twitched the cloak from his shoulders, swirling it before him.

Instinct flared a warning in Conan. As the cloak moved aside his big hand slapped down to grasp Baratses' wrist, stopping a black-bladed Karpashian dagger a handspan from his middle. "Fool!" he said.

Blood and teeth sprayed from the merchant's face beneath Conan's fist. The dagger dropped from nerveless fingers and struck the floor no more than an instant before Baratses himself.

The big Cimmerian frowned at the man lying unconscious before him. A sheath on Baratses' forearm had held the black blade. Conan bent to remove that, and tossed it and the dagger atop the cloak. "An attempt on my life," he muttered finally, "surely earns me the gold you brought."

Unfastening the merchant's purse from his belt, Conan emptied it onto his palm. There was no gold, only silver and copper. He counted it and grimaced. Three coppers more than a single gold piece. It seemed his death had been intended whether he had the goblet or not. Pouring the coins back into the purse, he added it to the dagger and sheath.

On the floor Baratses stirred and moaned.

Knotting his fist in the bony man's tunic, Conan lifted him erect and shook him till his eyes fluttered open. Baratses let out a gurgling groan as his tongue explored splintered teeth.

"I do not have the goblet," the Cimmerian said grimly. Easily he hoisted the merchant's feet clear of the floor. "I have never had the goblet." He took a step and smashed Baratses against the shutter, which burst open. The bloody-faced man dangled above the alley at arm's length from the window. "And if I ever see you again, I'll break the rest of your teeth." Conan opened his hand.

Baratses' wail cut off as he landed with a squelch in equal parts of mud, offal and the emptyings of chamber pots. A scrawny dog, disturbed at its rootings, began to bark at him furiously. Scrambling shakily to his feet, Baratses stared wildly about him, then broke into a slipping, sliding run. "Murder!" he screamed. "Murder!"

Conan sighed as he watched the merchant disappear down the alley. His cries would bring no aid in the Desert, but once he was beyond those cramped streets the City Guard would come quickly enough. And listen attentively to a respectable merchant's tale. Perhaps it would have been better had he slit the man's throat, yet murder had never been his way. He would have to leave the city for a time, until the furor died down. The fist that had broken Baratses' teeth pounded the window frame. And by the time he returned Tamira would have accomplished her theft. He might never even know what it was, much less in time to get there first.

Hastily he made his preparations. The contents of Baratses' purse were added to his own. The dagger in its sheath he fastened to his left forearm, then settled the black cloak about his broad shoulders. It fit a trifle snugly, but was ten times better than what he had.

He frowned at a lump over his chest, and felt inside the cloak. A small pouch of cloth was sewn there. From it he drew a small silver box, its lid set with blue gems. Inferior sapphires, his experienced eye told him. He flipped it open; his lip curled contemptuously at the sickly verduous powder within. Pollen from the green lotus of Vendhya. It seemed Baratses liked his dreams to come when he desired them. The small quantity in his hand would bring ten gold pieces. Upending the silver box, he tapped it against the heel of his hand to make sure all of the pollen fell to the floor. He did not deal in such things.

Quickly he ran an eye over the rest of his possessions. There was nothing there worth the bother of bundling. Near two years of thievery, and this was all he had to show for it. A fool like Baratses could throw away on stolen dreams as much as he could earn in a night of risking his life. Pushing open the door, he slapped the worn leather hilt of his broadsword with a mirthless laugh. "This is all I need anyway," he told himself.

At the bar Abuletes came slowly in response to the big Cimmerian's beckoning gesture. "I need a horse," Conan said when the fat innkeeper was finally before him. "A good horse. Not one ready for the boneyard."

Abuletes' black eyes, deepest in wells of suet, went from the cloak on

Conan's shoulders to the stairs. "You need to leave Shadizar quickly, Cimmerian?"

"There's no body to be found," Conan reassured him. "Just a disagreement with a man who can get the ear of the City Guard."

"Too bad," Abuletes grunted. "'Tis cheaper to dispose of a body than to purchase a horse. But I know a man—" Suddenly he glared past Conan's shoulder. "You! Out! I'll have none of you filthy little thieves in my place!"

Conan glanced over his shoulder. Laeta stood just inside the door, glaring fiercely back at the tavern-keeper. "She has come to see me," the Cimmerian said.

"She?" Abuletes said incredulously, but he was speaking to Conan's back.

"You have news of Tamira?" Conan asked when he reached the girl. It was like his luck of late, he thought, that the news would come when he could not use it.

Laeta nodded, but did not speak. Conan dug two silver pieces from his purse, but when she stretched out a hand for them he lifted them out of her reach and looked at her questioningly.

"All right, big man," she sighed. "But I had better get my coin. Yestermorn your wench went to the palace of the Lady Jondra."

"Jondra!" So she was after the necklace and tiara. And he had to leave the city. Grinding his teeth, he tossed the coins to Laeta. "Why didn't you tell me then?"

She tucked the silver under her torn tunic. "Because she left again. And," she added reluctantly, "we lost her trail in the Katara Bazaar. But this morning I set Urias to watch Jondra's palace, and he saw her again. This time she left dressed like a serving girl and riding a supply cart in Jondra's hunting party. The lot of them departed the city by the Lion Gate. A good six turns of the glass ago, it was. Urias took his time telling me, and I'm docking him his share of this silver for it."

Conan studied the girl, wondering if she had spun this tale. It seemed too fantastic. Unless . . . unless Tamira had discovered Jondra was taking the fabled necklace and tiara with her. But on a hunt? No matter. He had to leave Shadizar anyway. As well ride north and see for himself what Tamira was up to.

He started to turn away, then stopped, looking at Laeta's dirt-smudged face and big, wary eyes, truly seeing her for the first time. "Wait here," he told her. She eyed him quizzically, but stood there as he walked away.

He found Semiramis leaning against the wall at the back of the common room, one foot laid across her knee so she could rub it. Quickly he separated out half the coin in his purse and pressed it into her hand.

"Conan," she protested, "you know I'll not take money from—"

"It's for her," he said, jerking his head toward Laeta, who was watching him suspiciously. Semiramis arched a questioning eyebrow. "In another year she'll not be able to pass as a boy any longer," he explained. "Already she's putting dirt on her face to hide how pretty she is. I thought, maybe, that you . . ." He shrugged awkwardly, unsure of what he did mean.

Semiramis raised herself on tiptoes and brushed her lips against his cheek.

"That's no kiss," he laughed. "If you want to say goodbye—"

She laid her fingers against his lips. "You are a better man than you try to pretend, Cimmerian." With that she slipped by him.

Wondering if women were made by the same gods as men, he watched her approach Laeta. The two spoke quietly, looked at him, then moved toward an empty table together. As they sat, he suddenly recalled his own needs. He strode back to the bar and caught the tavernkeeper's arm as the fat man passed.

"About this horse, Abuletes . . ."

VI

Dark hung silently over Shadizar, at least in the quarter where lay the Perashanid palace. A hatchet-faced man in a filthy turban and stained leather jerkin, his beard divided into three braids, moved from the shadows, freezing when the barking of a dog rent the night. Then quiet came again.

"Farouz," the bearded man called softly. "Jhal. Tirjas."

The three men named appeared from the dark, each followed by half a score other turbaned Kezankian hillmen.

"The true gods guide our blades, Djinar," one man murmured as he passed hatchet-face.

Booted feet thudding on the paving stones, each small column hurried toward its appointed goal. Farouz would take his men over the garden's west wall, Jhal over the north. Tirjas was to watch the front of the palace and assure that no one left . . . alive.

"Come," Djinar commanded, and ten grim hillmen hurried after him to the east wall of the palace garden.

At the base of the wall two of his men bent to present cupped hands for his booted feet. Boosted thus, Djinar caught the top of the wall and scrambled over to drop inside. Moonlight put a silver glow on the trees and flowers of the garden. He wondered briefly at the labor involved. So much sweat, and for plants. Truly the men of the cities were mad.

Soft thuds announced the arrival of his companions. Swords were drawn with the susurration of steel on leather, and from one man came a fierce mutter. "Death to the unbelievers!"

Djinar hissed for silence, unwilling to speak lest his feelings at being within a city became plain in his voice. So many people gathered in one place. So many buildings. So many walls, closing him in. He motioned the hillmen to follow.

Silently the stony-eyed column slipped through the garden. No doors barred their entrance to the palace. It was going well, Djinar thought. The others would be entering the palace at other places. No alarm had been given. The blessings of the old gods must be on them, as Basrakan Imalla had said.

Abruptly a man in the white tunic of a servant appeared before him, mouth opening to shout. Djinar's tulwar moved before he could think, the tip of the curved blade slicing open the other man's throat.

As the corpse twitched in a pool of crimson, spreading across the marble floor, Djinar found his nervousness gone. "Spread out," he commanded. "None must live to give an alarm. Go!"

Growling deep in their throats, his men scattered with ready blades. Djinar ran as well, seeking the chamber that had been described to him by a sweating Akkadan beneath the iron gaze of Basrakan Imalla. Three more servants, roused by pounding boots, fell beneath his bloody steel. All were unarmed, one was a woman, but all were unbelievers, and he gave them no chance to cry out.

Then he was at his goal, and it was as the plump man had said. Large square tiles of red, black and gold covered the floor in geometric patterns. The walls were red and black brick to the height of a man's waist. Furnishings he did not notice. That lamps were lit so that he could see them was all that was important.

Still gripping his sanguine sword, Djinar hurried to the nearest corner and pushed against a black brick four down from the top row and four out from the corner. He gave a satisfied grunt when it sank beneath his pressure. Quickly he moved to the other three corners in turn; three more black bricks sank into the wall.

A clatter of boots in the corridor brought him to his feet, tulwar raised. Farouz and other hillmen burst into the room.

"We must hurry," Farouz snarled. "A bald-headed old man broke Karim's skull with a vase and escaped into the garden. We'll never find him before he raises an alarm."

Djinar bit back an oath. Hurriedly he positioned four men on their knees, forming the corners of a square beside widely separated golden tiles. "Press all together," he ordered. "Together, mind you. Now!"

With sharp clicks the four tiles were depressed as one. A grinding noise rose from beneath their feet. Slowly, two thick sections of the floor swung up to reveal stairs leading down.

Djinar darted down those stairs, and found himself in a small chamber carved from the stone beneath the palace. Dim light filtered from above, revealing casket-laden shelves lining the walls. In haste he opened a casket, then another. Emeralds and sapphires on golden chains. Opals and pearls mounted in silver brooches. Carved ivories and amber. But not what he sought. Careless of the treasures he handled, the hillman spilled the contents of caskets on the floor. Gems and precious metals poured to the marble. His feet kicked wealth enough for a king, but he gave it not a second glance. With a curse he threw aside the last empty casket and ran back up the stairs.

More hillmen had come, crowding the room. Now some pushed past him to the chamber below. Squabbling, they stuffed their tunics with gems and gold.

"The Eyes of Fire are not here," Djinar announced. The men below, panting with greed, paid no mind, but those in the chamber with him grew long faces.

"Perhaps the woman took them with her," suggested a man with a scar where his left ear had been.

Farouz spat loudly. "It was you, Djinar, who said wait. The strumpet goes to hunt, you said. She will take her guards, and we shall have an easier time of it."

Djinar's thin lips curled back from his teeth. "And you, Farouz," he snarled. "Did you cry for us to press on? Did you spend no time in the places where women barter their flesh for coin?" He clamped his teeth on his rage. The feeling of walls trapping him returned. What was to be done? To return to Basrakan Imalla empty-handed after being commanded to bring the Eyes of Fire . . . He shuddered at the thought. If the Zamoran jade had the Eyes of Fire, then she must be found. "Does none of these vermin still live?"

Mutters of negation filled the room, but Farouz said, "Jhal keeps a wench alive till his pleasure is spent. Do you now abandon the Imalla's quest to join him?"

Djinar's dagger was suddenly in his hand. He tested the edge on a well-calloused thumb. "I go to ask questions," he said, and strode from the room.

Behind him the hubbub of argument over the looting rose higher.

VII

Conan let his reins fall on the neck of his horse, moving at a slow walk, and took a long pull on his water-skin. His expression did not change at the stale taste of the tepid fluid. He had drunk worse at times when the sun did not beat down so strongly from a cloudless sky as it did now, though it had risen not three handspans above the horizon. His cloak was rolled and bound behind his saddle pad, and a piece of his tunic was held on his head like a kaffiyeh by a leather cord. Rolling hills, with here and there an outcrop of rock or a huge, half-buried boulder, stretched as far as the eye could discern, with never a tree, nor any growth save sparse patches of rough grass.

Twice since leaving Shadizar he had crossed the tracks of very large bodies of men, and once he had seen Zamoran infantry in the distance, marching north. He kept himself from their sight. It did not seem likely that Baratses had influence enough to set the army on his trail, but a man in Conan's profession quickly learned to avoid chance encounters with large numbers of soldiers. Life was more peaceful, less complicated without soldiers. Of the Lady Jondra's hunting party he had seen no sign.

Plugging the spout of the skin, he slung it from his shoulder and returned to a study of the tracks he followed now. A single horse, lightly laden. Perhaps a woman rider.

He booted the roan into a trot, its quickest pace. He intended to have a word with Abuletes when he returned to Shadizar, a quiet converse about messages sent to horse traders. The tavernkeeper's friend had denied having another animal beside this gelding on its last legs, and bargained as if he knew the big youth had reason to leave Shadizar quickly. Conan dug in his heels again, but the animal would move no faster.

Snarls, growing louder as he rode, drifted to him over the next rise. Topping the swell of ground, he took in the scene below in one glance. Half a score of wolves quarreled over the carcass of a horse. Some eyed him warily without ceasing their feast. Twenty paces away the Lady

CONAN THE MAGNIFICENT 55

Jondra crouched precariously atop a boulder, her bow clutched in one hand. Five more of the massive gray beasts waited below, their eyes intent on her.

Suddenly one of them took a quick step forward and leaped for the girl on the rock. Desperately she drew her feet up and swung the bow like a club. The wolf twisted in mid-air; powerful jaws closed on the bow, ripping it from her grasp. The force of it pulled her forward, slipping down the side of the boulder. She gave a half-scream, grabbed frantically at the stone, and hung there, closer now to the creatures below. She pulled her legs up, but the next leaper would reach them easily.

"Crom," Conan muttered. There was no time for planning, or even for conscious decisions. His heels thudded into the roan's ribs, goading it into a sliding charge down the hillside. "Crom!" he bellowed, and his broadsword whispered from its worn shagreen scabbard.

The wolfpack gained its feet as one, gray forms crouching to await him. Jondra stared at him in wild disbelief. The roan, eyes wide and whinnying in terror, suddenly broke into a gallop. Two of the wolves darted for the horse's head, and two more dashed in behind to snap at its hamstrings. A forehoof shattered a broad gray-furred head. Conan's blade whistled down to split the skull of a second wolf. The roan kicked back with both hind legs, splintering the ribs of a third, but the fourth sank gleaming fangs deep into one of those legs. Screaming, the horse stumbled and fell.

Conan stepped from his saddle pad as the animal went down, just in time to meet leaping gray death with a slashing blade. Half cut in two the great wolf dropped. Behind him Conan heard the roan scramble to its feet, whinnying frantically, and the solid thuds of hooves striking home. There was no opportunity to so much as glance at his mount, though, or even to look at Jondra, for the rest of the pack swarmed around him.

Desperately the big Cimmerian cut and hacked at deadly shapes that darted and slashed like gray demons. Blood splashed cinereous fur, and not all of it was theirs, for their teeth were like razors, and he could not keep them all from him. With cold certainty he knew he could not afford to go down, even for an instant. Let him once get off his feet, and he was meat for the eating. Somehow he managed to get the Karpashian dagger into his left hand, and laid about him with two blades. All thought left him save battle; he fought with as pure a fury as the wolves themselves, asking no quarter and giving none. To fight was all he knew. To fight, and let the losers go to the ravens.

As suddenly as the combat had begun it was ended. One instant steel battled slashing fangs, the next massive gray forms were loping away over the hills, one limping on three legs. Conan looked around him, half wondering that he still lived. Nine wolves lay as heaps of blood-soaked fur. The roan was down again, and this time it would not rise again. A gaping wound in its throat dripped blood into a dark pool that was already soaking into the rocky soil.

A scrabbling sound drew Conan's eyes. Jondra slid from the boulder and took her bow from the ground. Snug tunic and riding breeches of russet silk delineated every curve of her full-breasted form. Lips pursed, she examined the gouges in the bow's glued layers of bone and wood. Her hands shook.

"Why did you not put arrows into a few?" Conan demanded. "You might have saved yourself before I came."

"My quiver . . ." Her voice trailed off at the sight of her half-eaten horse, but she visibly steeled herself and went to the carcass. From under the bloody mass she tugged a quiver. A crack ran down one side of the black lacquerwork. Checking the arrows, she discarded three that were broken, then slung the quiver on her back. "I had no chance to reach this," she said, adjusting the cords that held the lacquered box on her back. "The first wolf hamstrung my gelding before I even saw it. It was Hannuman's own luck I made it to that rock."

"This is no country for a woman to ride alone," Conan grumbled as he retrieved the rolled cloak and wiped his bloody blade on his saddle pad. He knew he should take a different course with this woman. He had, after all, ridden halfway across Zamora for the express purpose of getting close enough to steal her gems. But there he stood with his horse dead, a dozen gashes that, if not serious still burned and bled, and no mind to walk easily with anyone.

"Guard your tongue!" Jondra snapped. "I've ridden—" Suddenly she seemed to see him fully for the first time. Taking a step back, she raised the bow before her as if it were a shield. "You!" Her voice was a breathless whisper. "What do you do here?"

"What I do is walk, since my horse is slain in the saving of your life. For which, I mind me, I've heard no word of thanks, nor an offer to bind my wounds in your camp."

Mouth dropping open, Jondra stared at him, astonishment warring with anger on her face. Drawing a deep breath, she shook herself as if waking from a dream. "You saved my life . . ." she began, then trailed off. "I do not even know your name."

"I am called Conan. Conan of Cimmeria."

Jondra made a small bow, and her smile trembled only a little. "Conan of Cimmeria, I offer you my heartfelt thanks for my life. As well, I offer the use of my camp for as long as you choose to stay." She looked at the wolf carcasses and shuddered. "I have taken many trophies," she said unsteadily, "but I never thought to be one. The skins are yours, of course."

The Cimmerian shook his head, though it pained him to abandon useful pelts. And valuable ones, too, could they be gotten back to Shadizar. He hefted his waterskin, showing a long rent made by slashing jaws. A last few drops of water dripped to the ground.

"Without water, we can waste no time with skinning in this heat." He shaded his eyes with a broad palm and measured how far the sun had yet to rise to reach its zenith. "It will get hotter before it cools. How far is it to your camp?"

"On horses we could be there by the time the sun is high, or shortly after. On foot . . ." She shrugged, making her heavy breasts move under the tight silk of her tunic. "I walk little, and so am no judge."

Conan made an effort to keep his mind on the matter at hand. "Then we must start now. You will have to keep up, for if we stop in this heat we shall likely never move again. Now, which way?"

Jondra hesitated, clearly as unused to taking commands as to walking. Haughty gray eyes dueled with cool sapphire blue; it was gray that fell. Without another word, but with an irritated expression painted on her features, the tall noblewoman fitted a shaft to her bow and began walking, headed south of the rising sun.

Conan stared after her before following, and not for the pleasant rolling motion of her rump. The fool woman had not wanted him behind her. Did she fear he would take her by force? And why had she seemed shaken by fear when she recognized him? Slowly, however, his questions were submerged in the pleasure of watching her make her way over the rolling hills. The silk riding breeches fit her buttocks like skin, and the view as she toiled upslope ahead of him was enough to make any man forget himself.

The sun climbed on, a ball of luteous fire baking the air dry. Shimmers rose from the rocky ground, and boot soles burned as if they rested on coals. Every breath sucked moisture from the lungs, dried the throat. Across the sky marched the sun, to its zenith and beyond, roasting the flesh, baking the brain.

The sun, Conan realized as he labored uphill in Jondra's wake, had replaced the woman as the center of his thoughts. He tried to calculate the time he had left to find water, the time before the strength of his thews began to fail. The effort of wetting his cracking lips was wasted, for the dampness did not last beyond the doing. He saw no use in offering up prayers. Crom, the Lord of the Mound, the god of his harsh native land, listened to no prayers, accepted no votive offerings. Crom gave a man but two gifts, life and will, and never another. Will would carry him till dark, he decided. Then, having survived a day, he would set about surviving the night, and then the next day, and the next night.

Of the girl he was not so sure. Already she had begun to stagger, tripping over stones she would easily have stepped over when they left the horses. Abruptly a rock smaller than her fist turned under her boot, and she fell heavily. To hands and knees she rose, but no further. Her head hung weakly, and her sides heaved with the effort of drawing a decent breath from the bone-dry air.

Scrambling up beside her, Conan pulled her to her feet. She hung limply from his hands. "Is this the right direction, girl? Is it?"

"How—dare—you," she managed through cracked lips.

Fiercely he shook her; her head lolled on her neck. "The direction, girl! Tell me!"

Unsteadily she looked around them. "Yes," she said finally. "I—think."

With a sigh, Conan lifted her over his shoulder.

"Not—dignified," she panted. "Put—me—down."

"There's no one to see," he told her. And perhaps never would be, he told himself. A well-honed instinct for direction would keep him moving on the path Jondra had set as long as he was able to move; an instinct for survival and an indomitable will would keep him moving long after the limits of ordinary human endurance had been breeched. He would find her camp. If she actually followed the true path. If he had not waited too late to question her. If . . .

Putting his doubts and Jondra's weak struggles alike from his mind, Conan set out slightly to the south of the line the sun had followed in rising. Constantly his eyes searched for signs of water, but in vain. It was too much to hope for palm fronds waving above a spring. Now, however, he could not find even the plants that would show him where to dig for a seep hole. No trace of green met his eyes save the short, wiry grass that could grow where a lizard would die of thirst. The sun blazed its way westward.

Conan's gaze swept toward the horizon. No smoke marked a campsite, no track disturbed the stony flanks of the hills before him. A steady, ground-eating pace he kept, tirelessly at first, then, as shadows lengthened before him, with an iron determination that denied the possibility of surrender. With water the coming night would have been a haven. Without it, there would be no stopping, for if they stopped they might well never take another step.

Darkness swooped, with no twilight. The stretching shadows seemed to merge and permeate the air in moments. The searing heat dissipated quickly. Stars blinked into being, like flecks of crystal on black velvet, and with them came a chill that struck to the bone as fiercely as had the sun. Jondra stirred on his shoulder and murmured faintly. Conan could not make out what she said, nor waste the energy to wonder what it had been.

He began to stumble, and he knew it was not only the dark. His throat was as dry as the rocks that turned under his feet, and the cold gave little relief to the sun-cracked skin of his face. All he could see were the unwinking stars. Locking his eyes on the horizon, a thin line where sable merged into ebon, he trudged on. Abruptly he realized that three of those stars did seem to shimmer. And they lay below the horizon. Fires.

Forcing his feet to move faster, Conan half-ran toward the camp, for such it must be, whether Jondra's or another. Whoever's camp it was, they must go in, for they had to have water. With his free hand he loosened his sword in its scabbard. They needed water, and he meant to have it.

The "stars" clearly became fires built high, surrounded by two-wheeled carts and round tents, with picket lines of animals beyond. Conan stumbled into the firelight; men in short mail tunics and baggy white trousers leaped to their feet. Hands reached for spears and tulwars.

The Cimmerian let Jondra fall and put a hand to his sword hilt. "Water," he croaked. The one word was all he could manage.

"What have you done?" a tall hawk-faced man demanded. Conan worked for the moisture to ask what the man meant, but the other did not wait. "Kill him!" he snarled.

Conan's broadsword slid smoothly free, and it was not the only steel bared to gleam in the light of the fires. Some men raised their spears to throw.

"No!" The faint command came in a thirst-hoarsened voice. "No, I say!"

Conan risked a glance from the corner of his eye. One of the mail-shirted men held a water-skin solicitously to Jondra's lips, and her shoulders were supported by Tamira, in the short, white tunic of a servant.

Not lowering his sword—for few of the others had lowered theirs—Conan began to laugh, a dry, rasping sound of relief. It hurt his throat, but he did not care.

"But, my lady," the hawk-faced man protested. Conan remembered him, now, at Jondra's shoulder that day in Shadizar.

"Be silent, Arvaneus," Jondra barked. She took two more thirsty gulps from the waterskin, then pushed it aside and held out an imperious hand, demanding to be helped to her feet. The man with the waterskin hastened to comply. She stood unsteadily, but pushed him aside when he tried to support her. "This man saved me from wolves, Arvaneus, and carried me when I could not walk. While you huddled by the fires, he saved my life. Give him water. Tend his hurts, and see to his comfort."

Hesitantly, eying Conan's bare blade, the man with the waterskin handed it to the big Cimmerian.

Arvaneus spread his hands in supplication. "We searched, my lady. When you did not return, we searched until dark, then built the fires high that you might see them and be guided to the camp. At first light we would have—"

"At first light I would have been dead!" Jondra snapped. "I will retire to my tent now, Arvaneus, and give thanks to Mitra that my survival was not left to you. Attend me, Lyana." Her rigid-backed departure was spoiled slightly by a stumble, and she muttered a curse as she ducked into her scarlet-walled pavillion.

Conan cast an eye about the encampment—the tulwars and spears were no longer in evidence—and sheathed his own blade. As he was raising the waterskin, he met Arvaneus' gaze. The huntsman's black eyes were filled with a hatred rooted in his marrow. And he was not the only one staring at the Cimmerian. Tamira's glare was one of frustration.

"Lyana!" Jondra called from her tent. "Attend me, girl, or . . ." The threat was implicit in her tone.

For the barest moment Tamira hesitated, giving Conan a well-honed look, then she darted for the tent.

Arvaneus' face was still a mask of malignity, but Conan neither knew the reason nor cared. All that mattered was that he would now surely reach the necklace and tiara before the young woman thief. That and nothing more. With a rasping chuckle he tilted up the waterskin and drank deeply.

VIII

The tall, gray-eyed young man kicked his horse into a trot as the lay of the country told him he neared his village. The last wisps of morning fog lingered among the towering forest oaks, as it often did in this part of Brythunia, not far from the Kezankian Mountains. Then the village itself came in view. A few low, thatch-roofed houses of stone, those of the village's wealthiest men, were dotted among the wattle structures that clustered around two dirt streets that lay at right angles to each other.

People crowded the street as he rode into the village. "Eldran!" they shouted, and dogs ran beside his horse, adding their barking to the uproar. "You have come! Boudanecea said you would!" The men were dressed as he, their tunics embroidered at the neck, with cross-gaitered fur leggings that rose to the knee. The women's dresses were longer versions of the tunics, but in a profusion of scarlets and yellows and blues where the men's were brown and gray, and embroidered at hem and at the ends of the sleeves as well.

"Of course I've come," he said as he dismounted. "Why should I not?" They gathered about him, each trying to get close. He noticed that every man wore a sword, though few did in the normal course of days, and many leaned on spears and carried their round shields of linden wood rimmed with iron. "What has happened here? What has the priestess to do with this?" A tumult answered him, voices tumbling over each other like brook water over stones.

". . . Burned the farmsteads . . ."

". . . Men dead, women dead, animals dead . . ."

". . . Some eaten . . ."

". . . Devil beast . . ."

". . . Went to hunt it . . ."

". . . Ellandune . . ."

". . . All dead save Godtan . . ."

61

"Hold!" Eldran cried. "I cannot hear you all. Who spoke of Ellandune? Is my brother well?"

Silence fell, save for the shuffling of feet. No one would meet his eyes. A murmur spread from the rear of the crowd, and they parted for the passage of a tall woman with a face serene and ageless. Her hair, the black streaked with gray, hung to her ankles and was bound loosely back with a white linen band. Her dress was of pristine linen as well, and the embroideries were of the leaves and berries of the mistletoe. A small golden sickle hung at her belt. She could walk anywhere in Brythunia and the poorest man in the land would not touch that sickle, nor the most violent raise a finger against her.

Eldran's clear gray eyes were troubled as they met hers of dark brown. "Will you tell me, Boudanecea? What has happened to Ellandune?"

"Come with me, Eldran." The priestess took his arm in a strong grasp. "Walk with me, and I will tell you what I can."

He let her lead him away, and none of the rest followed other than with sympathetic eyes that made fear rise in him. In silence they walked slowly down the dusty street. He kept a rein on his impatience, for he knew of old she would not be rushed.

Before the gray stone house where she lived, Boudanecea drew him to a halt. "Go in, Eldran. See Godtan. Speak with him. Then I will tell you."

Eldran hesitated, then pushed open the door of pale polished wood. A short, slight woman met him inside, dressed like Boudanecea, but with her dark, shiny hair braided in tight spirals about her head as a sign that she was still an acolyte.

"Godtan," was all he could say. What of Ellandune, he wanted to shout, but he had begun to fear the answer.

The acolyte silently drew aside a red woolen door-hanging and motioned him to enter the room. A stomach-wrenching melding of smells drifted out. Medicinal herbs and poultices. Burned meat. Rotting meat. He swallowed and ducked through. She let the hanging fall behind him.

It was a simple room, with a well-swept floor of smooth wooden planks and a single window, its curtains pulled back to admit light. A table with a glazed pottery basin and pitcher stood beside the bed on which lay the naked shape of a man. Or what had once been a man. The right side of his face was burned away, a fringe of gray hair bordering what remained. From the shoulder to the knee his right side was a mass of charred flesh, crimson showing through cracks in the black. There were no fingers on the twisted stick that had once been his right arm. Eldran remembered that right arm well, for it had taught him the sword.

"Godtan." The name caught in his throat. "Godtan, it is I, Eldran."

The horribly burned man's remaining eye flickered weakly open, swiveled toward him. Eldran groaned at the madness in it.

"We followed," Godtan said, his voice a gurgling croak. "Into—the mountains. Kill it. We were—going to—. We didn't—know. The colors—of it. Beautiful. Beautiful—like death. Scales—turned—our arrows—like straws. Spears wouldn't—. Its breath—is fire!"

That mad eye bulged frantically, and Eldran said, "Rest, Godtan. Rest, and I'll—"

"No!" The word came from that twisted mouth with insistence. "No rest! We—fled it. Had to. Hillmen—found us. Took Aelric. Took—Ellandune. Thought—I was—dead. Fooled them." Godtan gave a rasping bark; Eldran realized with a shiver that it was meant to be laughter. "One—of us—had to—bring word—what happened. I—had to." His one eye swiveled to Eldran's face, and for a moment the madness was replaced by bewilderment and pain. "Forgive—me. I—did not—mean—to leave him. Forgive—Eldran."

"I forgive you," Eldran said softly. "And I thank you for returning with word of what happened. You are still the best man of us all."

A grateful smile curved the half of Godtan's mouth that was left, and his eye drifted shut as if the effort of keeping it open were too great.

Grinding his teeth, Eldran stalked from the building, slapping the door open so that it banged against the wallstones. His eyes were the gray of forged iron, hard and cold from the quenching, and when he confronted Boudanecea his fists were clenched till the nails dug into his palms in an effort to control his anger.

"Will you tell me now?" he grated.

"The beast of fire," she began, but he cut her off.

"A tale for children! Tell me what happened!"

She shook a fist under his nose, and her fury blazed back at him as strongly as his own. "How think you Godtan took his burns? Think, man! A tale for children, you call it. Ha! For all the breadth of your shoulders I've alway had trouble thinking of you as a man grown, for I helped your mother birth you, and wrapped your first swaddling cloths about you with these hands. Now you bring my doubts home again. I know you have the fierce heart of a man. Have you the brain as well?"

Despite his chill rage Eldran was taken aback. He had known Boundanecea since his childhood, and never had he seen her lose her temper. "But, Godtan . . . I thought . . . he's mad."

"Aye, he's mad, and as well he is. All the way from the Kezankians he came, like that, seeking to tell us the fate of his companions, seeking the help of his people. Seeking my help. But none of my spells or potions can help him. The greenrot had set in too deeply by the time I saw him. Only a necromancer could help him now." She touched the golden sickle at her belt to ward off the evil of the thought, and he made the sign of the sickle.

"So the . . . the devil beast came," Eldran said.

Her long hair swayed as she nodded. "While you were in the west. First one farmstead was burned, all of the building, and only gnawed fragments of people or cattle left. Men made up stories to settle their minds, of a fire that killed the family and the animals, of wolves getting at the remains when the fire burned down. But then a second farmstead was destroyed, and a third, and a fourth, and . . ." She took a long breath. "Twenty-three, in all, and all at night. Seven on the last night alone. After that the hotheads took matters into their own hands. Aelfric. Godtan. Your brother. A score of others. They talked like you when I spoke of the beast of fire after the first farmstead. A tale for children. Then they found spoor, tracks. But they still would not believe me when I said no weapon forged by the hands of ordinary men could harm the creature. They made their plans in secret, and sneaked from the village before dawn to avoid my eye."

"If no weapon forged by man . . ." Eldran's hands worked futilely. "Boudanecea, I will not let it rest. The hillmen must pay for my brother, and the beast must be slain. Wiccana aid me, it must! Not only for revenge, but to stop it coming again."

"Aye." The priestess breathed the word. "Wait here." In what would have been hurry for one without her stately dignity, she disappeared into her house. When she returned she was followed by a plump acolyte with merry brown eyes. The acolyte carried a flat, red-lacquered chest atop which were neatly folded white cloths and a pitcher of white-glazed pottery. "From this moment," Boudanecea told him, "you must do exactly as you are told, and no more. For your life, Eldran, and your sanity, heed. Now, come."

They formed a procession then, the priestess leading and the acolyte following behind Eldran. The women marched with a measured tread, and he found himself falling into it as if an invisible drum beat the steps.

The hair of the back of his neck stirred as he realized where they were taking him. The Sacred Grove of Wiccana, eldest of the sacred groves of Brythunia, where the boles of the youngest oaks were as thick and as tall as the largest elsewhere in the forest. Only the priestesses and acolytes went to the sacred groves now, though once, countless centuries in the past, men had made that journey. As sacrifices to the goddess. The thought did not comfort Eldran.

Limbs as thick as a man's body wove a canopy above their heads, and the decaying leaves of the past season rustled beneath their feet. Abruptly a clearing appeared before them, where a broad, low grassy mound lay bare to the sky. A rough slab of granite, as long and as wide as the height of a man, lay partially buried in the side of the mound before them.

"Attempt to move the stone," Boudanecea commanded.

Eldran stared at her. He was head and shoulders taller than most men of the village, well muscled and with broad shoulders, but he knew the weight was beyond him. Then, remembering her first instructions, he obeyed. Squatting beside the great stone, he tried to dig down with his hands to find the lower edge. The first handfuls moved easily, but abruptly the dirt took on the consistency of rock. It looked no different than before, yet his nails could not scratch it. Giving up on that, he threw his weight against the side of the slab, attempting to lever it over. Every sinew of him strained, and sweat ran in rivulets down his face and body, but the granite seemed a fixed part of the mound. It did not stir.

"Enough," Boudanecea said. "Come and kneel here." She indicated a spot before the slab.

The acolyte had laid open the top of the chest, revealing stoppered vials and bowls of a glaze that seemed the exact green of mistletoe. Boudanecea firmly turned Eldran's back to the plump woman and made him kneel. From the white pitcher she poured clear water over his hands, and wiped them with soft white cloths. Other cloths were dampened and used to wipe sweat from his face.

As she cleansed his face and hands the graying priestess spoke. "No man or woman can move that stone, nor enter that mound save with Wiccana's aid. *With* her aid . . ."

The acolyte appeared at her side, holding a small green bowl. With her golden sickle Boudacenea cut a lock of Eldran's hair. He shivered as she dropped it into the bowl. Taking each of his hands in turn, she pricked the balls of his thumbs with the point of the sickle and squeezed a few drops of his blood on top of the hair. The acolyte and bowl hurried from his view again.

Boudanecea's eyes held his. He could hear the plump woman clinking vials, murmuring incantations, but he could not look away from the priestess' face. Then the acolyte was back, and Boudanecea took from her the bowl and a long sprig of mistletoe, which she dipped into the bowl.

Head back, the priestess began to chant. The words she spoke were no words Eldran had ever heard before, but the power of them chilled him to the bone. The air about him became icy and still. A thrill of terror went through him as he held out his hands, palms up, without instruction. It was as if he suddenly had known that he must do it. Mistletoe slapped his hands, and terror was replaced by a feeling of wholeness and wellbeing greater than any he had ever known before. Boudanecea chanted on, her paean rising in tone. The dampened sprig of mistletoe struck one cheek, then the other. Abruptly his body seemed to have no weight; he felt as if he might drift on the lightest breeze.

Boudanecea's voice stilled. Eldran wavered, then staggered to his feet. The peculiar sense of lightness remained with him.

"Go to the stone." Boudanecea's voice hung like chimes in the crystallized air. "Move the stone aside."

Silently Eldran moved to the slab. It had not changed that he could see, and rather than feeling stronger, he seemed to have no strength at all. Still the compulsion of her words was on him. Bending beside the stone, he fitted his hands to it, heaved . . . and his mouth fell open as the stone rose like a feather, pivoted on its further edge, and fell soundlessly. He stared at the stone, at his hands, at the sloping passage revealed in the side of the mound, at Boudanecea.

"Go down," she told him. Tension froze her face, and insistence made her words ring more loudly. "Go down, and bring back what you find."

Taking a deep breath, Eldran stumbled down the slanting, dirt-floored passage. No dust rose beneath his feet. Broad, long slabs of stone had been carefully laid for walls and roof to the passage, their crude work showing their age. Quickly the passage widened into a round chamber, some ten paces across, walled and roofed in the same gray stone as the way down. There were no lamps, but a soft light permeated the room. Nor were there the cobwebs and dust he had expected. A smell of freshly grown green things hung in the air, a smell of spring.

There could be no doubt as to what he was to bring up, for the chamber was bare save for a simple pedestal of pale stone, atop which rested a sword of ancient design. Its broad blade gleamed brightly, as if it had just come, newly made and freshly oiled, from the smith's hand. The bronze hilt was wrapped with leather that could have have been tanned that season. Its quillons ended in claws that seemed designed to hold something, but they were empty now.

A sense of urgency came on him as he stared at the sword. Seizing it, he half-ran back to the sunlight above.

As he took his first step onto the ground of the clearing he heaved a sigh of relief. And suddenly he felt as he had before coming there. All the strange sensations were gone. Almost against his will he looked over his shoulder. The great stone rested where it had originally lain, with no sign that it had ever been disturbed. Even the place where he had dug beside it was no longer there.

A shudder ran down his bones. Only the weight of the sword in his hand—an ordinary-seeming, if ancient, blade—remained to convince him something had actually happened. He clung hard to sanity, and did not wonder about what that something had been.

"Flame Slayer," Boudanecea said softly. Her hand stretched toward the sword, but did not touch it. "Symbol of our people, sword of our people's heroes. It was forged by great wizards nearly three thousand years ago, as a weapon against the beasts of fire, for the evil of Acheron had launched a plague of them, creations of their vile sorceries, upon the world. Once those claws held two great rubies, the Eyes of Fire, and the sword could control the beasts as well as slay them. For it *can* slay the beast."

"Why didn't you tell me of it?" Eldran demanded. "Why did you bring me here unknowing, like a sheep to . . ." His voice trailed off, for he did not like the thoughts that image brought back.

"It is part of the *geas* laid on the sword," the priestess replied, "and on we who keep it. Without the aid of a priestess, no one can reach the sword. But no priestess may speak of the sword to any who does not hold it. Great care must be taken in choosing to bring a man to the blade, for as well as its uses against the beasts of fire it can be a locus of great power to one who knows the ways of such things."

He hefted the sword curiously. "Power? Of what kind?"

"Do you seek power, Eldran?" she asked gravely. "Or do you seek to slay the beast?"

"The beast," he growled, and she nodded approval.

"Good. I chose you when first I knew what the beast was. You are acknowledged the finest man in Brythunia with sword or horse or bow. It is said that you move through the forest, and the trees are unaware of your passage, that you can track the wind itself. Such a man will be needed to hunt down the beast of fire. And this you must remember. Do not allow the sword to leave your possession, even while you sleep, or you will never regain its hilt. Instead the sword will, Wiccana alone knows how, return to its place beneath the stone. Many times it has been lost, but always, when it is needed and the stone is lifted aside, the sword is there. That will not help you should you lose it, though, for the sword may be given to any man but once in his life."

"I will not lose it," Eldran said grimly. "It will do its work, and I will return it here myself. But now I must take it from here." He began to move toward the trees, out of the sacred grove; his first nervousness was returning, as if this was not a place for men to remain long. "There is no time to waste, so I must choose the rest of my party quickly."

"Rest?" Boudanecea exclaimed, halting him at the edge of the trees. "I intended you to go alone, one swift hunter to slay the—"

"No. There must be blood price for Aelric and Ellandune, and for any others who fell to the hillmen. You know it must be so."

"I know," she sighed. "Your mother was like my own sister. I had hoped to hold her grandson one day, hoped for it many a day before this. Now I fear I never shall."

"I will come back," he said, and laughed suddenly, shocking himself. "You will get to see me wed yet, Boudanecea."

She raised the mistletoe in benediction, and he bowed his head to accept it. But even as he did he was listing in his mind the men he would take into the mountains with him.

IX

easing himself in his high-pommeled Zamoran saddle, Conan studied the country toward which the hunting party traveled. The flat, rolling hills through which they rode had changed little in the three days since his rescue of Jondra, except that the short grass was more abundant here and a brown tangle of thornbushes occasionally covered a stony slope. Ahead, though, the hills rose quickly higher, piling up on one another till they melded into the jagged, towering peaks of the Kezankians.

These were an arm of that range that stretched south and west along the border between Zamora and Brythunia. Conan knew of no game in them that would attract a hunter like Jondra save for the great spiral-horned sheep that lived amid the sheer cliffs in the heart of the range. In the heart of the mountain tribes, as well. He could not believe she meant to venture there.

The hunting party was a vile-tempered snake twisting its way among the low hills, avoiding the crests. Spearmen muttered oaths as their sandaled feet slipped on stony slopes, exchanging insults with mounted archers. Pack animals brayed and muleteers cursed. Ox drivers shouted and cracked their long whips as the oxen strained to pull the high-wheeled supply carts. The string of spare horses, raising an even taller plume of dust than all the rest of the party, was the only part of the column not adding to the tumult. Jondra rode before it all with Arvaneus and half a score other mounted hunters, oblivious of the noise behind them. It was no way to enter the country of the hill tribes. Conan was only thankful the dogs had been left behind in Shadizar.

Tamira, perched precariously atop lashed bundles of tenting on a lurching cart, waved to him, and Conan moved his horse up beside the cart. "You surprise me," he said. "You have avoided me these three days past."

"The Lady Jondra finds many labors for me," she replied. Eying the carter, walking beside his oxen, she edged more to the rear of the high-wheeled vehicle. "Why did you follow me?" she whispered fiercely.

Conan smiled lazily. "Followed you? Perhaps I seek the country air. Invigorating rides are good for the lungs, I'm told."

"Invigorating—" She spluttered indignantly. "Tell me the truth, Cimmerian! If you think to cut me out—"

"Already I have told you my plans for you," he broke in.

"You . . . you are serious?" she said, a rising note of incredulity in her voice. As if fearing he might seize her on the instant, she wiggled to the far side of the cart and peered at him over the top of the rolled tenting. "The Lady Jondra requires that her handmaidens be chaste, Cimmerian. You may think that saving her life will gain you license, but she is a noble, and will forget her gratitude in a moment if you transgress her rules."

"Then I will have to be careful, won't I?" Conan said, letting his horse fall behind. She peered after him anxiously as the cart trundled on. Conan wore a satisfied smile.

He was sure she did not believe that he had no interest in Jondra's jewels—she was no fool, or she could not have thieved as long as she had in Shadizar— but she would at least think his mind was divided between the gems and her. Most women, he had found, would believe that a man lusted after them on the slightest provocation. And if Tamira believed that, she would be nervously looking over her shoulder when she should be getting her hands on the gems.

A blackened hillside caught the big Cimmerian's eye, off from the line of march, and he turned his horse aside from curiosity. Nothing was left of the thornbushes that had once covered the slope save charred stumps and ashes. It did not have the look of lightning strike, he thought, for the bolt would have struck the hilltop, not its side.

Abruptly his mount stopped, nostrils flaring, and gave a low, fearful whicker. Conan tried to urge the animal closer, but it refused, even taking a step back. He frowned, unable to see anything ominous. What would frighten a horse he had been told was trained for the hunting of lions?

Dismounting, he dropped his reins, then watched to be sure the animal would stand. Its flanks shivered, but training held it. Satisfied, Conan approached the burn. And loosened his sword, just in case.

At first his booted feet stirred only ashes over blackened soil and rock. Then his toe struck something different. He picked up a broken wild ox horn with a fragment of skull attached. The horn was charred, as were the shreds of flesh adhering to the bone, but the piece of skull itself was not. Slowly he searched through the entire burn. There were no other bones to be found, not even such cracked bits as hyenas would leave after scavenging a lion's kill. He extended his search to the area around the char.

With a clatter of hooves Arvaneus galloped up, working his reins to make his horse dance as he stared down at Conan. "If you fall behind, barbar," the hawk-faced man said contemptuously, "you may not be so lucky as to find others to take you in."

Conan's hands tightened on the horn. The gems, he reminded himself firmly. "I found this in the ashes, and—"

"An old ox horn," the huntsman snorted, "and a lightning strike. No doubt it signifies some portent to one such as you, but we have no time for wasting."

Taking a deep breath, Conan went on. "There are tracks—"

"I have trackers, barbar. I have no need of you. Better you do fall behind. Leave us, barbar, while you can." Wheeling his mount in a spray of rocks and dirt, Arvaneus galloped after the fast-disappearing column.

There was a sharp crack, and Conan discovered that the ox horn had broken in his grip. "Zandru's Nine Hells!" he muttered.

Tossing the shattered remnants of horn aside, he knelt to examine the track he had found. It was only part of an animal's print, for the stony soil did not take tracks well. At least, he thought it was an animal's print. Two toes ending in long claws, and scuffings that might have indicated the rest of the foot. He laid a forefinger beside one of the claw marks. The claw had been easily twice as large as his finger.

He had never heard of a beast that made tracks as large as these. At least, he thought, Jondra did not hunt this. Nor did he think he would warn her of it. What he knew of her suggested she would leap at the chance to hunt an unknown creature, especially if it was dangerous. Still, he would keep his own eyes open. Swinging into the saddle, he galloped after the hunting party.

Sooner than Conan expected, he caught up with them. The column was halted. Men held the horses' heads to keep them silent, and the carters held the oxen's nose-rings so they would not low. Tamira paused in beating dust from her short white tunic to grimace at Conan as he walked his horse past the cart of tenting. From somewhere ahead came a faint, steady pounding of drums.

At the front of the line Jondra and a handful of her hunters lay on their bellies near the crest of a hill. Leaving his horse at the foot of the slope, Conan made his way up to them, dropping flat before his head overtopped the hill. The drumbeat was louder here.

"Go, barbar," Arvaneus snarled. "You are not needed here."

"Be silent, Arvaneus," Jondra said softly, but there was iron in her tone.

Conan ignored them both. A third of a league distant another column marched, this one following a knife-edge line, caring not whether it topped hills or no. A column of the Zamoran Army. Ten score horsemen in spiked helms rode in four files behind a leopard-head standard. Behind came twenty drummers, mallets rising and falling in unison, and behind them ... The Cimmerian made a rough estimate of the numbers of sloped spears, rank on rank on rank. Five thousand Zamoran infantry made a drum of the ground with their measured tread.

Conan turned his head to gaze at Jondra. Color came into her cheeks beneath his eyes. "Why do you avoid the army?" he asked.

"We will camp," Jondra said. "Find a site, Arvaneus." She began moving backwards down the slope, and the huntsman slithered after her.

Conan watched them go with a frown, then turned back to peer after the soldiers until they had marched out of sight beyond the hills to the north.

The camp was set up when Conan finally left the hill, conical tents dotting a broad, flat space between two hills. Jondra's large tent of bright scarlet stood in the center of the area. The oxen had been hobbled, and the horses tied along a picket line beyond the carts. No fires were lit, he noted, and the cooks were handing out dried meat and fruit.

"You, barbar," Arvaneus said around a strip of jerky. "I see you waited until the work was done before coming in."

"Why does Jondra avoid the army?" Conan demanded.

The hawk-faced man spit out a wad of half-chewed meat. "The *Lady* Jondra," he snapped. "Show a proper respect toward her, barbar, or I'll . . ." His hand clutched the hilt of his tulwar.

A slow smile appeared on Conan's face, a smile that did not extend to suddenly steely eyes. There were dead men who could have told Arvaneus about that smile. "What, huntsman? Try what is in your mind, if you think you are man enough." In an instant the black-eyed man's curved blade was bare, and, though Conan's hand had not been near his sword hilt, his broadsword was out in the same breath.

Arvaneus blinked, taken aback at the big Cimmerian's quickness. "Do you know who I am, barbar?" There was a shakiness to his voice, and his face tightened at it. "Huntsman, you call me, but I am the son of Lord Andanezeus, and if she who bore me had not been a concubine I would be a lord of Zamora. Noble blood flows in my veins, barbar, blood fit for the Lady Jondra herself, while yours is—"

"Arvaneus!" Jondra's voice cracked like a whip over the camp. Pale faced, the noblewoman came to within a pace of the two men. Her close-fitting leather jerkin was laced tightly up the front, and red leather boots rose to her knees. Arvaneus watched her with a tortured expression on his face. Her troubled gray eyes touched Conan's face, then jerked away. "You overstep yourself, Arvaneus," she said unsteadily. "Put up your sword." Her eyes flickered to Conan. "Both of you."

Arvaneus' face was a mosaic of emotion, rage and shame, desire and frustration. With a wordless shout he slammed his blade back into its scabbard as if into the tall Cimmerian's ribs.

Conan waited until the other's sword was covered before sheathing his own, then said grimly, "I still want to know why you hide from your own army."

Jondra looked at him, hesitating, but Arvaneus spoke up quickly, urgently. "My lady, this man should not be among us. He is no hunter, no archer or spearman. He does not serve you as . . . as I do."

With a deep chuckle, Conan shook his black-maned head. "It is true I am my own man, but I am as good a hunter as you, Zamoran. And as for the spear, will you match me at it? For coin?" He knew he must best the man at something, or else contend with him as long as he remained with the hunters. And he carefully had not mentioned the bow, of which he knew little beyond the holding of it.

"Done!" the huntsman cried. "Done! Bring the butts! Quickly! I will show this barbarian oaf the way of the spear!"

Jondra opened her mouth as if to speak, then closed it again as the camp erupted in a bustle of men, some scurrying to clear a space for the throwing, others rushing to the carts to wrestle with a heavy practice butt. The thick bundle woven of straw was a weighty burden to carry on a hunting expedition, but it did not break arrows or spear points, as did casting and shooting at trees or at targets on a hillside.

A shaven-headed man with a long nose leaped on an upturned keg. "I'll cover all wagers! I give one to twenty on Arvaneus, twenty to one on the barbarian. Don't crowd." A few men wandered over to him, but most seemed to take the outcome as foregone.

Conan noticed Tamira among those about the keg. When she left she strolled by him. "Throw your best," she said, "and I'll win a silver piece . . ." She waited until his chest began to expand with pride, then finished with a laugh, ". . . Since I wagered on the other."

"It will be a pleasure to help you lose your coppers," he told her dryly.

"Stop flirting, Lyana," Jondra called sharply. "There's work for you to be doing."

Tamira made a face the tall woman could not see, bringing a smile to Conan's face despite himself, then scurried away.

"Will you throw, barbar?" Arvaneus asked tauntingly. The tall huntsman held a spear in his hand and was stripped to the waist, revealing hard ropes of muscle. "Or would you rather stay with the serving girl?"

"The girl is certainly more pleasing to look on than your face," Conan replied.

Arvaneus' face darkened at the ripple of laughter that greeted the Cimmerian's words. With the blade of his spear the Zamoran scratched a line on the ground. "No part of your foot may pass this line, or you lose no matter how well you throw. Though I doubt I must worry about that."

Doffing his tunic, Conan took a spear handed to him by another of the hunters and moved to the line. He eyed the butt, thirty paces away. "It does not look a great distance."

"But see the target, barbar." The swarthy huntsman smiled, pointing. A lanky spearman was just finishing attaching a circle of black cloth, no bigger than a man's palm, to the straw.

Conan made his eyes go wide. "Aaah," he breathed, and the hawk-faced man's smile deepened.

"To be fair," Arvaneus announced loudly, "I will give you odds. One hundred to one." A murmur rose among the watchers, and all in the camp were there. "You did mention coin, barbar. Unless you wish to acknowledge me the better man now."

"They seem fair odds," Conan said, "considering the reputation you have with yourself." The murmur of astonishment at the odds offered became a roar of laughter. He considered the weight of his purse. "I have five silver pieces at those odds." The laughter cut off in stunned silence. Few there thought the hawk-faced man might lose, but the sheer magnitude of his unlikely loss astounded them.

Arvaneus seemed unmoved. "Done," was all he said. He moved back from the line, took two quick steps forward, and hurled. His spear streaked to the center of the black cloth, pinning it more firmly to the butt. Half a score of the hunters raised a cheer, and some began trying to collect their bets now. "Done," he said again, and laughed mockingly.

Conan hefted his spear as he stood at the line. The haft was as thick as his two thumbs, tipped with an iron blade as long as his forearm. Suddenly he leaned back, then whipped forward, arm and body moving as one. With a thud that shoved the butt back his spear buried its head not a finger's width from the other already there. "Mayhap if it were further back," he mused. Arvaneus ground his teeth.

There was silence in the camp till the man on the keg broke it. "Even odds! I'll give even odds on Arvaneus or—what's his name? Conan?—or on Conan! Even odds!"

"Shut your teeth, Telades!" Arvaneus shouted, but men crowded around the shaven-headed man. Angrily the huntsman gestured toward the butt. "Back! Move it back!" Two men rushed out to drag it a further ten paces, then returned quickly with the spears.

Glaring at Conan, Arvaneus took his place back from the line again, ran forward and threw. Again his spear struck through the cloth. Conan stepped back a single pace, and again his throw was one single continuous motion. His spear brushed against Arvaneus's, striking through the black cloth even more closely than the first time. Scattered shouts of delighted surprise rose among the hunters. The Cimmerian was surprised to see a smile on Jondra's face, and even more surprised to see another on Tamira's.

Arvaneu's face writhed with fury. "Further!" he shouted when the spears were returned once more. "Further! Still further!"

An expectant hush settled as the butt was pulled to sixty paces distant. It was a fair throw for the mark, Conan conceded to himself. Perhaps more than a fair throw.

Muttering under his breath, the huntsman set himself, then launched his spear with a grunt. It smacked home solidly in the butt.

"A miss!" Telades called. "It touched the cloth, but a miss! One to five on Conan!"

Arm cocked, Conan hurtled toward the line. For the third time his shaft streaked a dark line to the cloth. A tumultuous cry went up, and men pounded their spears on the ground in approbation.

Telades leaped from his keg and capered laughing through the crowd to clasp Conan's hand. "You've cost me coin this day, northerner, but 'twas worth every copper to see it done."

Eyes bulging in his head, Arvaneus gave a strangled cry. "No!" Suddenly he was running toward the butt, pushing men from his path. He began wrestling the heavy mass of straw further away. "Hit this, barbar dog!" he shouted, fighting his weighty burden still. "Erlik take you and your accursed cheating tricks! Hit this!"

"Why, 'tis a hundred paces," Telades exclaimed, shaking his head. "No man could—" He cut off with a gasp as Conan took a spear from the hand of a nearby hunter. Like antelope scattering before a lion, men ran to get from between the Cimmerian and the distant target.

Arvaneus' voice drifted back to them, filled with hysterical laughter. "Hit this, barbar! Try!"

Weighing the spear in his hand, Conan suddenly moved. Powerful legs drove him forward, his arm went back, and the spear arched high into the air. The hawk-faced huntsman stared open-mouthed at the spear arcing toward him, then screamed and hurled himself aside. Dust lifted from the butt as the spear slashed into the straw beside the two already there.

Telades ran forward, peering in disbelief, then whirled to throw his arms high. "By all the gods, he hit cloth! You who call yourselves spearmen, acknowledge your master! At a hundred paces he hit the cloth!"

A throng of hunters crowded around Conan, shouting their approval of his feat, striving to clasp his hand.

Abruptly the shouts faded as Jondra strode up. The hunters parted before her, waiting expectantly for what she would say. For a moment, though, she stood, strangely diffident, before speaking.

"You asked me a question, Cimmerian," she said at last, looking over his shoulder rather than at him. "I do not give reasons for what I do, but you *did* save my life, and your cast was magnificent, so I will tell you alone. But in private. Come." Back rigid and looking neither to left nor right, she turned and walked to her scarlet tent.

Conan followed more slowly. When he ducked through the tent flap, the well-curved noblewoman stood with her back to the entrance, toying with the laces of her leather jerkin. Fine Iranistani carpets, dotted with silken pillows, made a floor, and golden lamps stood on low, brass tables.

"Why, then?" he said.

She started, but did not turn around. "If the army is out in such force," she said distractedly, "they must expect trouble of some sort. They would surely try to turn back a hunting party, and I do not want the trouble of convincing some general that I will not be ordered about by the army."

"And you keep this secret?" Conan said, frowning. "Do you think your hunters have not reasoned some of this out themselves?"

"Is Lyana as you said?" she asked. "Pleasing to look on? More pleasing than I?"

"She is lovely." Conan smiled at the stiffening of her back, and added judiciously, "But not so lovely as you." He was young, but he knew enough of women to take care in speaking of one woman's beauty to another.

"I will pay Arvaneus's wager," Jondra said abruptly. "He does not have five hundred pieces of silver."

The tall Cimmerian blinked, taken aback by her sudden shift. "I will not take it from you. The wager was with him."

Her head bowed, and she muttered, seemingly unaware that she spoke aloud. "Why is he always the same in my mind? Why must he be a barbarian?" Suddenly she turned, and Conan gasped. She had worked the laces from her jerkin, and the supple leather gaped open to bare heavy, round breasts and erect, pink nipples. "Did you think I brought you to my tent merely to answer your questions?" she cried. "I've allowed no man to touch me, but you will not even stretch out a hand. Will you make me be as shameless as—"

The young noblewoman's words cut off as Conan pulled her to him. His big hands slid beneath her jerkin, fingers spreading on the smooth skin of her back, to press her full breasts against him. "I stretch out both hands," he said, working the leather from her shoulders to fall to the carpets.

Clutching at him, she laid her head against his broad chest. "My hunters will know . . . they will guess what I . . . what you . . ." She shivered and held to him harder.

Gently he tipped her head back and peered into her eyes, as gray as the clouds of a mountain morning. "If you fear what they think," he said, "then why?"

The tip of her small pink tongue wet her lips. "I could never have made that spear cast," she murmured, and pulled him down to the silken cushions.

X

Conan tossed aside the fur coverlet and got to his feet with an appreciative look at Jondra's nude form. She sighed in her sleep, and threw her arms over her head, tightening the domes of her breasts in such a way as to make him consider not dressing after all. Chuckling, he reached for his tunic instead. The locked iron chests containing her gems got not a wit of his attention.

Three days since the spear casting, he reflected, and for all her fears of what her hunters might think, it would take a man both blind and deaf to be still unaware of what occurred between Jondra and him. She had not let him leave her tent that first night, not even to eat, and the past two had been the same. Each morning, seemingly oblivious of the hunters' smiles and Arvaneus' glares, she insisted that Conan "guide" her while she hunted, a hunt that lasted only until she found a spot well away from the line of march where there was shade and a level surface large enough for two. The chaste, noble Lady Jondra had found that she liked lying with a man, and she was making up for lost opportunities.

Not that her absorption in the flesh was total. That first day she had been unsatisfied on their return with how far the column had traveled. Up and down the line she galloped, scoring men with her tongue till they were as shaken as if she had used her quirt. Arvaneus she took aside, and what she said to him no one heard, but when he galloped back his lips were a tight, pale line, and his black eyes smouldered. There had not been another day when the progress of the column failed to satisfy her.

Settling his black Khauranian cloak around his shoulders, Conan stepped out into the cool morning. He was pleased to see that the cookfires had at last been made with dried ox dung, as he had suggested. No smoke rose to draw eyes to them, and that was more important than ever, now. A day to the north of where they camped, at most two days amid the now steep-sloped hills, lay the towering ranges of the Kezankian, dark and jagged against the horizon.

The camp itself squatted atop a hill amidst trees twisted and stunted by arid, rocky soil. Every man wore his mail shirt and spiked helm at all times, now, and none went so far as the privy trenches without spear or bow.

A sweating Tamira, dodging from fire to fire under the watchful eye of the fat cook, gave Conan a grimace as she twisted a meat-laden spit half a turn. Arvaneus, sitting cross-legged near the fires, sullenly buried his face in a mug of wine when he saw the Cimmerian.

Conan ignored them both. His ears strained for the sound he thought he had heard. There. He grabbed Tamira's arm. "Go wake J . . . your mistress," he told her. Hands on hips, Tamira stared at him wryly. "Go," he growled. "There are horsemen coming from the south." A look of startlement passed over her face, then she darted for the big scarlet tent.

"What offal do you spout now?" Arvaneus demanded. "I see nothing."

Telades came running across the camp to the hawk-faced man's side. "Mardak claims he hears horses to the south, Arvaneus."

With an oath the huntsman tossed his mug to the ground and scrambled to his feet. A worried frown creased his face. "Hillmen?" he asked Telades, and the shaven-headed man shrugged.

"Not likely from the south," Conan said. "Still, it couldn't hurt to let the rest of the camp know. Quietly."

"When I need your advice," Arvaneus snarled, but he did not finish it. Instead he turned to Telades. "Go among the men. Tell them to be ready." His face twitched, and he added a muttered, "Quietly."

Unasked, the Cimmerian added his efforts to those of Telades, moving from man to man, murmuring a word of warning. Mardak, a grizzled, squint-eyed man with long, thin mustaches also was passing the word. The hunters took it calmly. Here and there a man fingered the hilt of his tulwar or pulled a lacquered quiver of arrows closer, but all went on with what they were doing, though with eyes continually flickering to the south.

By the time Conan returned to the center of the camp, ten horsemen had topped the crest of the next hill and were walking their horses toward the camp.

Arvaneus grunted. "We could slay all of them before they knew we were here. What are they, anyway? Not hillmen."

"Brythunians," Telades replied. "Is there really cause to kill them, Arvaneus?"

"Barbarian scum," the hawk-faced hunter sneered. "They don't even see us."

"They see us," Conan said, "or they'd never have crossed that crest. And what makes you think we see all of them?"

The two Zamorans exchanged surprised looks, but Conan concentrated on the oncoming men. All wore fur leggings and fur-edged capes, with broadswords at their waists and round shields hung behind their saddles. Nine of them carried spears. One, who led them, carried a long, recurved bow.

The Brythunian horsemen picked their way up the hill and drew rein short of the camp. The man with the bow raised it above his head. "I am called Eldran," he said. "Are we welcome here?"

A sour look on his face, Arvaneus stood silent.

Conan raised his right hand above his head. "I am called Conan," he said. "I welcome you, so long as you mean harm to none here. Dismount and share our fires."

Eldran climbed from his horse with a smile. He was almost as tall as Conan, though not so heavily muscled. "We cannot remain long. We seek information, then we must move on."

"I seek information as well," Jondra said as she strode between the men. Her hair, light brown sun-streaked with blonde, was tousled, and her tight riding breeches and tunic of emerald silk had an air of having been hastily donned. "Tell me . . ." Her words died as her eyes met those of Eldran, as gray as her own. Her head was tilted back to look up at him, and her mouth remained open. Finally she said unsteadily, "From . . . from what country are you?"

"They're Brythunians," Arvaneus spoke up. "Savages."

"Be silent!" Jondra's enraged scream caught the men by surprise. Conan and Eldran stared at her wonderingly. Arvaneus' face paled. "I did not speak to you," she went on in a voice that shook. "You will be silent till spoken to! Do you understand me, huntsman?" Not waiting for his answer, she turned back to Eldran. The color in her cheeks was high, her voice thin but cool. "You are hunters, then? It is doubly dangerous for you to hunt here. The Zamoran army is in the field, and there are always the hillmen."

"The Zamoran Army does not seem to find us," the Brythunian answered. His still-mounted men laughed. "As for the hillmen . . ." There was an easiness to his voice, but grim light flashed in his eyes. "I have given my name, woman, but have not heard yours."

She drew herself up to her greatest height, still no taller than his shoulder. "It is the Lady Jondra of the House Perashanid of Shadizar, to whom you speak, Brythunian."

"An honorable lineage, Zamoran."

His tone was neutral, but Jondra flinched as if he had sneered. Strangely, it seemed to steady her in some fashion. Her voice firmed. "If you are a hunter, perhaps you have seen the beast I hunt, or its sign. I am told its body is that of a huge serpent, covered with scales in many colors. Its track—"

"The beast of fire," one of the mounted Brythunians murmured, and others made a curving sign in the air before them as if it were a charm.

Eldran's face was tight. "We seek the beast as well, Jondra. Our people know it of old. Perhaps we can join forces."

"I need no more hunters," Jondra said quickly.

"The creature is more difficult to slay than you can imagine," the tall Brythunian said urgently. His hand gripped tightly at the hilt of his sword, a weapon of ancient pattern with quillons ending in claws like an eagle's. "Its breath is fire. Without us you can but die in the seeking of it."

"So say you," she said mockingly, "with your children's tales. I say I will slay the beast, and without your aid. I also say that I had better not find you attempting to poach my kill. This trophy is mine, Brythunian. Do you understand me?"

"Your eyes are like the mists of dawn," he said, smiling.

Jondra quivered. "If I see you again, I'll put arrows in both of *your* eyes. I'll—"

Suddenly she grabbed a bow from one of her archers. Brythunian spears were lowered, and their horses pranced nervously. Hunters reached for their tulwars. In one smooth motion Jondra drew and released, into the air. Far above the camp a raven gave a shrill cry and began to flutter erratically, dropping toward a far hill.

"See that," Jondra exclaimed, "and fear my shafts."

Before the words were out of her mouth the distant raven jerked downward, turning over as it plummeted to reveal a second arrow transfixing its feathered corpse.

"You are a fine shot," Eldran said as he lowered his bow. Smoothly he swung into his saddle. "I would stay to shoot with you, but I have hunting to do." Without a backward glance he wheeled his horse and rode down the hill, his men following as if unaware that their backs were bare to the camp's archers.

That thought occurred quickly to Arvaneus. "Archers," he began, when Jondra whirled on him, glaring. She said no word, nor needed to. The huntsman backed away from her, eyes down, muttering, "Your forgiveness, my lady."

Next she turned her attentions to Conan. "You," she breathed. "He spoke to me like that, and you did nothing. Nothing!"

The big Cimmerian eyed her impassively. "Perhaps he is right. I found signs of a beast that may kill with fire. And if he is right about that, perhaps he is right about the difficulty of killing it. Perhaps you should return to Shadizar."

"Perhaps, perhaps, perhaps!" She spat each word. "Why was I not told of these signs? Arvaneus, what do you know of this?"

The huntsman darted a malice-filled gaze at Conan. "A fire begun by lightning," he said sullenly, "and a few old bones. This one is frightened by his own shadow. Or by the shadow of the mountains."

"That is not true, is it?" Jondra's eyes were doubtful on Conan's face. "You do not make invention for fear of dying at the hillmen's hands, do you?"

"I do not fear death," Conan said flatly. "The dark will come when it comes. But none save a fool seeks it out needlessly."

The noblewoman tossed her head haughtily. "So," she said, and again, "So." Without another look at Conan, she stalked away, calling loudly, "Lyana! Prepare my morning bath, girl!"

Arvaneus grinned at Conan malevolently, but the Cimmerian youth did not see him. Matters had become complex far beyond his simple plans on leaving Shadizar, Conan thought. What was he to do now? There was one way he knew to concentrate his mind for the solution of a problem. Producing a small whetstone from his pouch, he drew his sword and settled cross-legged to touch up the edge on the ancient blade and think.

Basrakan Imalla glared at the raven lying dead on his chamber floor and tugged at the forks of his beard in frustration. The watch-ravens were not easily come by. Nestlings must be secured, and only one pair in twenty survived the incantations that linked them so that one of the two saw and experienced what the other did. Time to secure the birds, time to work the spells. He had no time for replacing the accursed bird. Likely the other had fallen to a hawk. And he had so few of them.

With a grunt he kicked the dead bird, smashing it into the bare stone wall. "Filthy creature," he snarled.

Tugging his crimson robes straight, he turned to the six tall perches that stood in the center of the floor. On five of the perches ravens sat, tilting their heads to watch him with eyes like shiny black beads. Their wings, clipped so they could not fly, dropped listlessly. There were few furnishings in the room other than those perches. A table inlaid with mother-of-pearl bore a brass lamp and a scattering of implements for the dark arts. A shelf along one wall held the volumes of necromantic lore that he had gathered in a lifetime. No one entered that room, or the others reserved to his great work, save him, and none save his acolytes knew what occurred there.

Lighting a splinter of wood at the lamp, Basrakan began to trace an intricate figure in the air before the first bird. The tiny eyes followed the flame, which was mirrored in their black surfaces. As he traced, Basrakan chanted words from a tome copied on vellum made of human skin rather than sheepskin, words that floated in the air till the walls seemed to shimmer. With each word the tracing grew more solid, till an unholy symbol in fire hung between himself and the raven.

The raven's beak opened with painful slowness, and creaking words, barely recognizable, emerged. "Hills. Sky. Trees. Clouds. Many many clouds."

The sorcerer clapped his hands; the fiery image vanished, and the words ceased to come. It was often thus with the creatures. By the spells that held them they would speak of men before all else, but if there were no men they would mutter about whatever they happened to see, go on forever if he did not silence them.

The same ritual before the next bird gained him the same reply, with only the terrain changed, as did the next and the next. By the time he reached the last raven he was hurrying. An important matter awaited his attention in the next room, and he was certain by now what the creature would report. Chanting, he traced the symbol in fire, preparing even as it came into being to clap his hands.

"Soldiers," the raven croaked. "Many many. Many many."

Barakan's breath caught in his throat. Never more than now had he regretted the inability of the ravens to transmit numbers. "Where?" he demanded.

"South. South of mountains."

Thoughtfully the stern-faced Imalla stroked his beard. If they came from the south, they must be Zamorans. But how to deal with them? The bird that had actually seen the soldiers could be made to return and guide his warriors back to them. The men would see it as a further sign of the favor of the old gods, for birds were creatures of the spirits of the air. And it would the first victory, the first of many against the unbelievers.

"Return!" Basrakan commanded.

"Return," the raven croaked agreement, and he broke the link.

How many soldiers, he wondered as he strode from the chamber, and how many warriors of the true gods to send against them?

As he passed through the next chamber, he paused to ponder the girl who cowered against a wall paneled in polished oak, as rare and costly in these mountains as pearls. Her dark eyes streamed tears, and her full mouth quivered uncontrollably. Her skin was smooth and supple, and his view of it was not hampered by garments.

Basrakan grimaced in disgust and wiped his hands on the front of his scarlet robes. Only eighteen, and already she was a vessel of lust, attempting to ensnare the minds of men. As did all women. None were truly pure. None were worthy of the ancient gods.

Shaking himself from his dark reverie, the holy man hurried on. He had no fear for the girl's wandering. The *geas* he had put on her would not allow her to leave that chamber until he gave her permission, until he found her worthy.

In the corridor he found Jbeil Imalla just entering his abode. The lean man bowed, his black robes rustling stiffly. "The blessings of the true gods be on you, Basrakan Imalla. I come with ill tidings."

"Ill tidings?" Basrakan said, ignoring the greeting. "Speak, man!"

"Many warriors have joined our number, but most of them have never seen the sign of the true gods' favor." Jbeil's dark eyes burned with the fervor of the true believer above his plaited beard, and his mouth twisted with contempt for those less full of faith than himself. "Many are the voices crying out to witness a sacrifice. Even some who have seen now whisper that the creature sent by the ancient gods has abandoned us, since it has not been seen in so many days. A few, among the newcomers, say that there *is* no sign, that it is all a lie. These last speak now in private places, among themselves, but they will not forever, and I fear the hearts of the doubters may be easily swayed."

Basrakan's teeth ground in frustration. He had had the same fears of abandonment himself, and scourged himself at night, alone, for his lack of belief. He had tried to summon the beast to fire, tried and failed. But it was still there, he told himself. Still beneath the mountain, waiting to come forth once more. Waiting for—his breath caught in his throat—a sign of their faith.

"How many warriors are gathered?" he demanded.

"More than forty thousand, Imalla, and more come every day. It is a great strain to feed so many, though they are, of course, the faithful."

Basrakan pulled himself to his full height. Renewed belief shone on his dark narrow face. "Let the warriors know that their lack of faith is not secret." He intoned the words, letting them flow from him, convinced they were inspired by the true gods. "Let them know that an act of faith is demanded of them if they would have the sight they crave. A bird will come, a raven, a sign from the spirits of the air. Half of those gathered are to follow it, and it will guide them to unbelievers, soldiers of Zamora. These they must slay, letting none escape. Not one. If this is done as it is commanded, the sight of the true gods' favor will be granted to them."

"A bird," Jbeil breathed. "A sign from the spirits of the air. Truly are the ancient gods mighty, and truly is Basraken Imalla mighty in their sight."

Basrakan waved away the compliment with a negligent hand. "I am but a man," he said. "Now, go! See that it is done as I have commanded."

The black-robed man bowed himself from the sorcerer's presence, and Basrakan began to rub at his temples as soon as he was gone. So many pressures on him. They made his head hurt. But there was the girl. Showing her the evil within her, saving her from it, would ease the pain. He would chastise the lust from her. His face shining with the ascetic look of one who suffered for his duty, Basrakan retraced his steps.

XI

Djinar lay on his belly in the night and studied the hunter's camp, lying still and quiet on the next hill. His dark robes blended with the shadows of his own stony hilltop. Only smouldering beds of ashes remained of the cook fires, leaving the camp in darkness, its tents and carts but dim mounds, save for the soft glow of lamps within a large tent of scarlet. The moon rode high over the jagged peaks to the north, but dense dark clouds let its pale light through only an occasional brief rent. A perfect night for attack. He tugged at the triple braids of his beard. Perhaps the ancient gods *were* with them.

It had certainly seemed so during the days when the trail of the hunting party led north like an arrow aimed at the encampment of Basraken Imalla. Could it be that the Eyes of Fire were drawn in some fashion to the Imalla, that the true gods stirred themselves among men, even through the Zamoran slut? A chill like the trickle of an icy mountain stream ran down Djinar's spine, and the hairs on the back of his neck rose. It seemed to him that the ancient gods walked the earth within sight of his eyes. Rocks grated behind him; Djinar gasped, and almost fouled himself.

Farouz dropped down beside him on the stony ground.

"Sentries?" Djinar asked finally. He was pleased at the steadiness of his voice.

The other man snorted in contempt. "Ten of them, but all more asleep than awake. They will die easily."

"So many? The soldiers set guards in such numbers, but not hunters."

"I tell you, Djinar, they all but snore. Their eyes are closed."

"A score of eyes," Djinar sighed. "All it takes is one pair to be alert. If the camp is awakened, and we must ride uphill at them . . ."

"Bah! We should have attacked when first we found them, while they were yet on the march. Or do you still fear the Brythunian dogs? They are gone long since."

Djinar did not answer. Only because Sharmal had gone off alone to answer a call of nature had the Brythunians been seen, ghosting along the trail of the hunters from Shadizar. There was no great love lost between Brythunian and Zamoran, it was true, but either would turn aside from slaying the other to wet his blade with the blood of a hillman. Farouz would have placed them between their two enemies—at least two score of the Brythunians; half again so many Zamorans—without a thought save how many he could kill.

"If your . . . caution brings us to failure," Farouz muttered, "do not think to shield yourself from Basrakan Imalla's wrath by casting blame on others. The truth will be known."

Farouz, Djinar decided, would not survive to return to the Imalla's encampment of the faithful. The old gods themselves would see the justice of it.

Again boots scrabbled on the rocks behind him, but this time Djinar merely looked over his shoulder. Sharmal, a slender young man with his wispy beard worked into many thin braids, squatted near the two men. "The Brythunian unbelievers ride yet to the east," the young man said.

"They did not stop at dark?" Djinar demanded, frowning. He did not like behavior out of the ordinary, and men did not travel by night without pressing reason, not in sight of the Kezankians.

"When I turned back at sundown," Sharmal answered, "they still rode east. I . . . I did not wish to miss the fighting."

"If there is to be any," Farouz sneered.

Djinar's teeth ground loudly. "Mount your horses," he commanded. "Surround the camp and advance slowly. Strike no blow until I call, unless the alarm be given. Well, Farouz? You speak eager words. Can your arm match them?"

With a snarl Farouz leaped to his feet and dashed down the hill to where their shaggy, mountain-bred horses waited.

Djinar followed with a grim smile and climbed into the high-pommeled saddle. Carefully he walked his mount around the side of the hill, toward the camp atop the next stony rise. The rattle of unshod hooves on rock did not disturb him, not now. He guided his horse upslope. To the core of him he was convinced the Zamorans would not rouse. The ancient gods were with him. He and the others were one with the dark. He could make out a sentry, leaning on his spear, unseeing, unaware of one more shadow that drifted closer. Djinar loosed his tulwar from its scabbard. The true gods might walk the camp before him, but there was another presence as well. Death. He could smell it. Death for many men. Death for Farouz.

Smiling, Djinar dug in his heels; his mount sprang forward. The sentry had time to widen his eyes in shock; then the curved blade with the strength of Djinar's arm and the weight of the charging horse behind it took the man's head from his shoulders. Djinar's cry rent the darkness. "By the will of the true gods, slay them! No quarter!" Screaming hillmen slashed out of the night with thirsty steel.

Conan's eyes slitted open, where he lay wrapped in his cloak and the night beneath the sky. After her behavior he had chosen not to go to Jondra's tent, despite the lamps that remained invitingly lit even now. It had not been thoughts of the silken body that had wakened him, though, but a sound out of place. He could hear the breathing of the sentry nearest him, a breathing too deeply regular for a man alert. The fools would not hear his advice, he thought. They listened, but would not hear. There were other things they did not hear, as well. The sentry's half-snore was overlaid by another sound; stones slid and clicked on the hillside. On *all* sides of the hill.

"Crom!" he muttered. In a continuous motion he threw aside his black cloak, rose to his feet and drew steel. His mouth opened to shout the alarm, and in that instant there was need no longer.

On the heels of the hollow "thunk" of a blade striking flesh came, "By the will of the true gods, slay them! No quarter!"

Chaos clawed its way out of the dark, hillmen appearing on every side screaming for the blood of unbelievers, hunters scrambling from their tents crying prayers to their gods for another dawn.

The big Cimmerian ran toward the sentry he had listened to. Shocked to wakefulness the hunter tried to lower his long-pointed spear, but a slashing stroke across the face from a tulwar spun him shrieking to the ground.

"Crom!" Conan roared.

The hillman jerked at his reins, spun his shaggy mount above the downed sentry toward the huge man who loomed out of the night. "The true gods will it!" he yelled. Waving his bloody blade above his turban, he booted his shaggy mount into a charge.

For the space of a heartbeat Conan halted, planted his feet as if preparing to take the charge. Suddenly he sprang forward, ducking under the whistling crescent of steel, his own blade lancing into the hillman's middle. The shock of the blow rocked the Cimmerian to his heels as the hillman seemed to leap backwards over his horse's rump to crash to earth.

Placing his foot on the chest of the corpse, Conan pulled his sword free. Warned by a primitive sense, by a pricking between his shoulderblades, he whirled to find another mounted foe, and a tulwar streaking for his head. But his steel was rising as he turned, its razor edge slicing through the descending wrist. Tulwar and hand flew, and the keening hillman galloped into the night with the fountaining stump of his wrist held high, as if he could thus keep the blood from pouring out of him.

Already two high-wheeled carts were towering bonfires, and flames swiftly ate five of the round tents. Over all hung the din of battle, the clang of steel on steel, the screams of the wounded, the moans of the dying. Another cart burst afire. The burnings cast back the night from struggling pairs of men who danced with sanguine blades among the bodies that littered the hilltop. Of those who lay still, more wore the mail shirts and spiked helms of Zamorans than wore turbans.

All this Conan took in in an instant, but one sight among all the others drew his eyes. Jondra, drawn from her sleeping furs and naked save for a quiven slung over her shoulder, stood before her crimson-walled tent, nocking arrows and firing as calmly as if she shot her bow at straw targets. And where her shafts went hillmen died.

Another had become aware of her, the Cimmerian saw. A hillman at the far end of the camp suddenly gave an ululating cry and kicked his mount into a gallop for the bare-skinned archer.

"Jondra!" Conan shouted, but even as he did he knew she could not hear above the tumult. Nor would all his speed take him to her side in time.

Tossing his sword to his left hand, he flung himself in two bounds back to the sentry who lay with his face a ruined mask staring at the sable sky. Ruthlessly he put a foot on the man's outstretched arm, ripped free the heavy hunting spear from the death-grip that held it. With desperate quickness he straightened, turned and threw, freezing as the spear left his hand. No will or thought was left for motion, for all rode with that thick shaft. The hillman's mount was but two strides from Jondra, his blade heartbeats from her back, but still she neither heard nor turned. And the hillman convulsed as a forearm-long blade transfixed his chest. His horse galloped on, and he slowly toppled backwards, falling like a sack before the woman he meant to slay. Jondra started as the body hit the ground almost at her feet, but for a moment continued to fumble at her empty quiver in search of another arrow. Abruptly she tossed aside her bow and snatched the tulwar from the dead man's hand.

Conan found he could breathe again. He took a step toward her . . . and something sliced a line of fire across his back. The big youth threw himself into a forward roll and came to his feet searching for his attacker. There were men behind him, both hillmen and hunters, but all save Arvaneus and Telades were killing or being killed, and even as he looked they engaged turbanned foes. He had no time to seek out particular enemies, Conan thought. There were enough for all. The dark blood-rage rose in him, cold enough to burn.

When he turned back Jondra was gone, but thoughts of her were buried deep now in the battle-black of his mind. Some men are said to be born for battle; Conan had been born on the field of battle. The scent drawn in with his first breath had been the coppery smell of fresh-spilled blood. The first sound to greet his ears had been the clash of steel. The first sight his eye beheld had been ravens circling in the sky, waiting till living men departed and they ruled what remained.

With the battle fury that had been his birthright he strode through the flames and screams of the encampment, and death rode on his steel. He sought the turbanned men, the bearded men, and those he found went before Erlik's Black Throne with eyes of azure fire their last memory of the world of men. His ancient broadsword flashed banefully in the light of burning tents, flashed till its encrimsoned length could flash no more, but seemed rather to eat light as it ate life. Men faced him, men fell before him, and at last men fled him.

The time came when he stood alone, and no turbans could his questing eye find but those on dead men. There were standing men, he realized as the haze of battle-rage thinned and cleared his eyes, Zamoran hunters gathered in a loose circle about him, staring in wonder tinged with fear. He turned to face each man in turn, and each fell back a step at his gaze. Even Arvaneus could not hold his ground, though his face flushed with anger when he realized what he had done.

"The hillmen?" Conan demanded hoarsely. He stripped the rough woolen cloak from a hillman's corpse and wiped his blade clean.

"Gone," Telades said in a high voice. He paused to clear his throat. "Some few fled, I think, but most . . ." His gesture took in the entire hilltop, strewn with bodies and burned-out tents, illumined by flaming carts. "It was your work that saved us, Cimmerian."

"Hannuman's Stones!" Arvaneus roared. "Are you all women? It was your own arms saved you, swords in your own hands! If the barbar slew one or two, it was his skin he sought to save."

"Do not speak the fool," Telades retorted. "You of all men should not speak against him. Conan fought like a demon while the rest of us struggled to realize that we were awake, that it was not a nightmare we faced." A murmur of agreement came from the circle of men.

Face twisted darkly, Arvaneus opened his mouth, but Conan cut him off. "If some of them escaped, they may return with others. We should be gone from this place, and quickly."

"There stands your hero," Arvaneus sneered. "Ready to run. Few hillman bands are larger than the number which attacked us, and most of them now wait for the worms. Who else will come against us? I, for one, think we slew all of the mountain dogs."

"Some did flee," Telades protested, but Arvaneus spoke on over him.

"I saw none escaping. If I had, they wouldn't have lived to escape. If we run like rabbits, then like rabbits we run from shadows."

"Your insults begin to disturb me, huntsman," Conan said, hefting his sword. "In the past I have forborne killing you for one reason or another. Now, it is time for you to still your tongue, or I will still it for you."

Arvaneus stared stiffly back at him, his tulwar twitching in his hand, but he did not speak. The other hunters moved back to give room.

Into the silence Jondra stepped, a robe of brocaded sky-blue silk covering her to the ankles and held tightly at her neck with both hands. She studied the two men confronting each other before speaking. "Conan, why do you think the hillmen will return?"

She was attempting to ignore the tension, the Cimmerian knew, and so disarm it, but he thought the answer to her question was more important than killing Arvaneus. "It is true that bands of hillmen are usually small, but in Shadizar it is said the Kezankian tribes are gathering. The soldiers we saw marching north bear this out, for it is also said the army is being sent to deal with them. To go risks nothing; to stay risks that the few who fled may bring back a thousand more."

"A thousand!" the hawk-faced man snorted. "My lady, it is well known how the hill tribes war constantly with one another. A thousand hillmen in one place would kill each other in the space of a day. And if, by some miracle, so many were gathered together, their attention would surely be on the soldiers. In any case, I cannot believe in this bazaar rumor of a gathering of the tribes. It goes against all that I know of the hillmen."

Jondra nodded thoughtfully, then asked, "And our injured? How many are they, and how badly hurt?"

"Many nicks and cuts, my lady," Arvaneus told her, "but only fourteen hurt badly enough to be accounted as wounded, and but two of those seriously." He hesitated. "Eleven are dead, my lady."

"Eleven," she sighed, and her eyes closed.

"'Twould have been more, my lady, save for Conan," Telades said, and Arvaneus rounded on him.

"Cease your chatter of the barbar, man!"

"Enough!" Jondra barked. Her voice stilled the hunters on the instant. "I will reach a decision on what is to be done tomorrow. For now the wounded must be tended, and the fires put out. Arvaneus, you will see to it." She paused to take a deep breath, looking at no one. "Conan, come to my tent. Please?" The last word was forced, and as she said it she turned away quickly, her robe flaring to give a glimpse of bare thighs, and hurried from the circle of men.

Conan's visits to Jondra's tent and sleeping furs had been an open secret, but an unacknowledged one. Studiously the men all avoided looking at Conan, or at each other, for that matter. Arvaneus seemed stunned. Tamira alone met his eyes, and she glared daggers.

With a shake of his head for the vagaries of women, the big Cimmerian sheathed his sword and followed Jondra.

She was waiting for him in her scarlet tent. As he ducked through the tent-flap, she slipped the silk robe from her shoulders, and he found his arms full of sleek bare skin. Full breasts bored into his ribs as she clutched at him, burying her head against his broad chest.

"I . . . I should not have spoken as I did earlier," she murmured. "I do not doubt what you saw, and I do not want you to stay away from my bed."

"It is well you believe me," he said, smoothing her hair, "for I saw as I said. But now is no time to speak of that." She sighed and snuggled closer, if that was possible. "It is time to speak of turning back. Your hunters have taken grievous hurt from the hillmen, and you are yet a day from the mountains. Do you enter the mountains with carts and oxen, you'll not escape further attention from the tribes. Your men will be slain, and you will find yourself the slave of an unwashed tribesman whose wives will beat you constantly for your beauty. At least, they will until the harsh life and the labor leaches your youth as it does theirs."

Word by word she had stiffened in his arms. Now she pushed herself from him, staring up at him incredulously. "It has been long years," she said in breathless fury, "since I apologized to any man, and never have I b . . . asked one to my bed before you. Whatever I expected for doing so, it was not to be lectured."

"It must be spoken of." He found it hard to ignore the heavy, round breasts that confronted him, the tiny waist that flared into generous hips and long legs, but he forced himself to speak as if she were draped in layers of thick wool. "The hillmen are roused. Ants might escape their notice, but not men. And should you find this beast you hunt, remember that it is a hunter as well, and one that kills with fire. How many men will you see roasted alive to put a trophy on your wall?"

"A folk tale," she scoffed. "If hillmen cannot frighten me off, do you think I will run before a myth?"

"Eldran," he began with a patience he no longer felt, but her screech cut him off.

"No! I will not hear of that . . . that Brythunian!" Panting, she struggled to gain control of herself. At last she drew herself up imperiously. "I did not summon you here for argument. You will come to my bed and speak only of what we do, or you will leave me."

Conan's anger coiled to within a hair's breadth of erupting, but he managed to keep his reply to a mocking, "As my lady wishes." And he turned his back on her nudity.

Her furious cries followed him into the fading night, echoing across the camp. "Conan! Come back here, Mitra blast you! You cannot leave me like this! I command you to return, Erlik curse you forever!"

No man looked up from his labor, but it was clear from the intensity with which they minded their work that none was deaf. Those prodding burning bundles from the carts with spears abruptly redoubled their efforts to save what had not already caught fire. The newly set sentries suddenly peered at the failing shadows as if each hid a hillman.

Tamira was passing among the wounded lying in a row on blankets in the middle of the camp, holding a waterskin to each man's mouth. She looked up with a bright smile as he passed. "So you'll sleep alone again tonight, Cimmerian," she said sweetly. "A pity." Conan did not look at her, but a scowl darkened his face.

One of the carts had been abandoned to burn, and flaming bundles lay scattered about the others. The fat cook capered among the men, waving a pewter tray over his head and complaining loudly at their use of his implements for shoveling dirt onto the fires. Conan took the tray from the rotund man's hands and bent beside Telades to dig at the rocky soil.

The shaven-headed hunter eyed him sideways for a time, then said carefully, "There are few men would walk out on her without reason."

Instead of answering the unasked question, Conan snarled, "I've half a mind to tie her to her horse so you can lead her back to Shadizar."

"You've half a mind if you think that you could," Telades said, throwing a potful of dirt and small stones on a fiery bale, "or that we would. The Lady Jondra decides where to go, and we follow."

"Into the Kezankians?" Conan said incredulously. "With the tribes stirring? The army didn't come north for the weather."

"I've served the House Perashanid," the other man said slowly, "since I was a boy, and my father before me, and his before him. The Lady Jondra *is* the house, now, for she is the last. I cannot desert her. But you could, I suppose. In fact, perhaps you should."

"And why would I do that?" Conan asked drily.

Telades answered as though the question had been serious. "Not all spears are thrown by the enemies you expect, northlander. If you do stay, watch your back."

Conan paused in the act of stooping for more dirt. So the spear that grazed his back had not been cast by a hillman's hand. Arvaneus, no doubt. Or perhaps some other, long in the Perashanid's service, who did not like the last daughter of the house bedding a landless warrior. That was all he needed. An enemy behind him—at least one—and the hillmen surrounding. Tomorrow, he decided, he would make one last try at convincing Jondra to turn back. And Tamira, as well. There were gems aplenty in Shadizar for her to steal. And if they would not, he would leave them and go back alone. Furiously he scooped dirt onto the tray and hurled it at the flames. He would! Erlik take him if he did not.

In the gray dawn Djinar stared at the pitiful following that remained to him. Five men with shocked eyes and no horses.

"It was the giant," Sharmal muttered. His turban was gone, and his face was streaked with dirt, and dried blood from a scalp wound. His eye focused on something none of the rest could see. "The giant slew who he would. None could face him." No one tried to quiet him, for the mad were touched by the old gods, and under their protection.

"Does any man think we can yet take the Eyes of Fire from the Zamoran woman?" Djinar asked tiredly. Blank stares answered him.

"He cut off Farouz's hand," Sharmal said. "The blood spurted from Farouz's arm as he rode into the night to die."

Djinar ignored the youth. "And does any man doubt the price we will pay for failing Basrakan Imalla's command?" Again the four who retained their senses kept silent, but again the answer was in their dark eyes, colored now by a tinge of horror.

Sharmal began to weep. "The giant was a spirit of the earth. We have displeased the true gods, and they sent him to punish us."

"It is decided, then." Djinar shook his head. He would leave much behind, including his favorite saddle and two young wives, but such could be more easily replaced than blood from a man's veins. "In the south the tribes have not yet heeded Basrakan's call. They care only for raiding the caravans to Sultanapur and Aghrapur. We will go there. Better the risk no one will take us in than the certainty of Basrakan's anger."

He did not see Sharmal move, but suddenly the young man's fist thudded against his chest. He looked down, perplexed that his breath seemed short. The blow had not been that hard. Then he saw the hilt of a dagger in the fist. When he raised his eyes again, the other four were gone, unwilling to meddle in the affairs of a madman.

"You have been attainted, Djinar," Sharmal said in a tone suitable for instructing a child. "Better this than that you should flee the will of the true gods. Surely you see that. We must return to Basrakan Imalla, who is a holy man, and tell him of the giant."

He had been right, Djinar thought. Death had been in that camp. He could smell it still. He opened his mouth to laugh, and blood poured out.

XII

Amid the lengthening shadows of mid-afternoon, some semblance of normality had returned to the hunter's camp. The fires were out, and those carts that could not be salvaged had been pushed to the bottom of the hill, along with supplies too badly burned for use. Most of the wounded were on their feet, if not ready for another battle, and the rest soon would be. The dead—including now the two most seriously wounded—had been buried in a row on the hillside, with cairns of stones laid atop their graves to keep the wolves from them. Zamoran dead, at least, had been treated so. Vultures and ravens squawked and contended beyond the next hill, where the corpses of hillmen had been dragged.

Sentries were set now not only about the hilltop camp itself, but on the hills surrounding. Those distant watchers, mounted so they could bring an alarm in time to be useful, had been Conan's idea. When he put the notion forward Jondra ignored it, and Arvaneus scorned it, but the sentries were placed, if without acknowledgement to the Cimmerian.

It was not for pique, however, that Conan stalked through the camp with a face like a thunderhead. He cared nothing who got credit for the sentries, so long as they were placed. But all day Jondra had avoided him. She had hurried about checking the wounded, checking the meals the cook prepared, meddling in a score of tasks she would normally have dismissed once she ordered them done. All in the camp save Conan she had kept at the run. And every particle of it, he knew, was to keep from talk with him.

Tamira trotted by in her short white tunic, intently balancing a flagon of wine and a goblet on a tray, and Conan caught her arm. "I can't stop now," she said distractedly. "She wants this right away, and the way she's been today I have no wish to be slow." Suddenly the slender thief chuckled. "Perhaps it would have been better for us all if you *hadn't* slept alone last night."

"Never mind that," Conan growled. "It's time for leaving, Tamira. Tomorrow will see us in the mountains."

"Is that what you said to Jondra to anger her so?" Her face tightened. "Did you ask her to go back with you, too?"

"Fool girl, will you listen? A hunting trophy is no reason to risk death at the hands of hillmen, nor are those gems."

"What of Jondra?" she said suspiciously. "She won't turn back."

"If I can't talk her into it, I will go without her. Will you come?"

Tamira bit her full under-lip and studied his face from beneath her lashes. Finally, she nodded. "I will. It must be in the night, though, while she sleeps. She'll not let me leave her service, if she knows of it. What would she do without a handmaiden to shout at? But what of your own interest in the rubies, Cimmerian?"

"I no longer have any interest," he replied.

"No longer have," Tamira began, then broke off with a disbelieving shake of her head. "Oh, you must think I am a fine fool to believe that, Cimmerian. Or else you're one. Mitra, but I do keep forgetting that men will act like men."

"And what does that mean?" Conan demanded.

"That she's had you to her bed, and now you will not steal from her. And you call yourself a thief!"

"My reasons are no concerns of yours," he told her with more patience than he felt. "No more than the rubies should be. You leave with me tonight, remember?"

"I remember," she said slowly. As her large brown eyes looked up at him, he thought for a moment that she wanted to say something more.

"Lyana!" Jondra's voice cracked in the air like a whip. "Where is my wine?"

"Where is my wine?" Tamira muttered mockingly, but she broke into a run, dodging around Telades, who labored under one end of a weighty brass-bound chest.

"Mayhap you shouldn't have angered her, Cimmerian," the shaven-headed hunter panted. "Mayhap you could apologize." The man at the other end of the chest nodded weary agreement.

"Crom!" Conan growled. "Is everyone in the camp worrying about whether I . . ." His words trailed off as one of the sentries galloped his horse up the hill. Unknowingly, easing his broadsword in its scabbard, he strode to where the man was dismounting before Jondra. The hunters left off their tasks to gather around.

"Soldiers, my lady," the sentry said, breathing heavily. "Cavalry. Two, perhaps three hundred of them, coming hard."

Jondra pounded a fist on a rounded thigh. Her salmon silk tunic and riding breeches were dusty and sweat-stained from her day's labors. "Erlik take all soldiers," she said tightly, then took a deep breath that made her heavy breasts stir beneath the taut silk of her tunic. "Very well. If they come, I'll receive their commander. Arvaneus! See that any man who's bandaged is out of sight. If the soldiers arrive before I return, be courteous, but tell them nothing. Nothing, understand me! Lyana! Attend me, girl!" Before she finished speaking she was pushing through the assembled hunters, not waiting for them to move from her path.

The hawk-faced huntsman began shouting commands, and hunters and carters scattered in all directions, hastening to prepare the camp for visitors. Moving the wounded inside tents was the least of it, for most of them could walk without assistance, but Jondra's industriousness had left bales and bundles, piles of cooking gear and stacks of spears scattered among the remaining tents till the camp seemed struck by a whirlwind.

Ignoring the bustle behind him, Conan settled into a flat-footed crouch at the edge of the camp, his eyes intent on the direction from which the sentry had come. More than once his hand strayed unconsciously to the worn hilt of his ancient broadsword. He did not doubt that the sentry had seen Zamoran soldiers and not hillmen, but he had as little regard for one as for the other. Relations between the army and a thief were seldom easy.

A ringing clatter of shod hooves on loose stone heralded the soldiers' approach well before the mounted column came into sight. In ranks of four, with well-aligned lance-points glittering in the afternoon sun, they wended their way along the small valleys between the hills. A banner led them, such as Zamoran generals were wont to have, of green silk fringed with gold, its surface embroidered in ornate gold script recounting victories. Conan snorted contemptuously at the sight of the honor standard. At that distance he could not read the script, but he could count the number of battles listed. Considering the number of true battles fought by Zamoran arms in the twenty years past, that banner gave honor to many a border skirmish and brawl with brigands.

At the foot of the hill the column drew up, two files wheeling to face the camp, the other two turning their mounts the other way. The standard bearer and the general, marked by the plume of scarlet horsehair on his golden helmet and the gilding of his mail, picked their way up the hill through the few stunted trees and scattered clumps of waist-high scrub.

At Arvaneus' impatient signal two of the hunters ran forward, one to hold the general's bridle, the other his stirrup, as he dismounted. He was a tall man of darkly handsome face, his upper lip adorned by thin mustaches. His arrogant eye ran over the camp, pausing at Conan for a raised brow of surprise and a sniff of dismissal before going on. The

Cimmerian wondered idly if the man had ever actually had to use the jewel-hilted sword at his side.

"Well," the general said suddenly, "where is your mistress?"

Arvaneus darted forward, his face set for effusive apologies, but Jondra's voice brought him to a skidding halt. "Here I am, Zathanides. And what does Zamora's most illustrious general do so far from the palaces of Shadizar?"

She came before the general with a feline stride, and her garb brought gasps even from her hunters. Shimmering scarlet silk, belted with thickly woven gold and pearls, moulded every curve of breasts and belly and thighs, rounded and firm enough to make a eunuch's mouth water.

It was not the raiment that drew Conan's attention, however. On her head rested a diadem of sapphires and black opals, with one great ruby larger than the last joint of a big man's thumb lying above her brows. Between her generous breasts nestled that ruby's twin, depending from a necklace likewise encrusted with brilliant azure sapphires and opals of deepest ebon. The Cimmerian's gaze sought out Tamira. The young woman thief was demurely presenting to Zathanides a tray bearing a golden goblet and a crystal flagon of wine, with damp, folded cloths beside. She seemed unaware of the gems she had meant to steal.

"You are as lovely as ever, Jondra," the general said as he wiped his hands and tossed the cloths back onto the tray. "But that loveliness might have ended gracing some hillman's hut if I hadn't found this fellow Eldran."

Jondra stiffened visibly. "Eldran?"

"Yes. A Brythunian. Hunter, he said." He took the goblet Tamira filled for him, gracing her with a momentary smile that touched only his lips. "I wouldn't have believed his tale of a Zamoran noblewoman in this Mitra-forsaken place if it had not been for his description. A woman as tall as most men, ravingly beautiful of face and figure, a fair shot with a bow. And your gray eyes, of course. I knew then it could be none but you." He tilted back his head to drink.

"He dared describe me so? A fair shot?" She hissed the words, but it had been "ravingly beautiful" that made her face color, and the mention of her eyes that had clenched her fists. "I hope you have this Eldran well chained. And his followers. I . . . I have reason to believe they are brigands."

Conan grinned openly. She was not a woman to take kindly to being bested.

"I fear not," Zathanides said, tossing the empty goblet back to Tamira. "He seemed what he called himself, and he was alone, so I sent him on his way. In any case, you should be thankful to him for saving your life,

Jondra. The hillmen are giving trouble, and this is no place for one of your little jaunts. I'll send a few men with you to see that you get back to Shadizar safely."

"I am no child to be commanded," Jondra said hotly.

The general's heavy-lidded eyes caressed her form, and his reply came slowly. "You are certainly no child, Jondra. No, indeed. But go you must."

Jondra's eyes flickered to Conan. Abruptly her posture softened, and her voice became languorous. "No, I am not a child, Zathanides. Perhaps we can discuss my future plans. In the privacy of my tent?"

Startlement passed over Zathanides' face to be replaced by pleasure. "Certainly," he said with an unctuous smile. "Let us . . . discuss your future."

Arvaneus' swarthy face was a blend of despair and rage as he watched the pair disappear into the scarlet tent. Conan merely scooped up a handful of rocks and began tossing them down the hill one by one. Telades squatted next to him.

"More trouble, Cimmerian," the shaven-headed man said, "and I begin to wonder if you are worth it."

"What have I to do with anything?" Conan asked coldly.

"She does this because of you, you fool northlander."

"She makes her choice." He would not admit even to himself that this flirting with Zathanides sat ill with him. "She's not the first woman to choose a man for wealth and titles."

"But she is no ordinary woman. I have served her since she was a child, and I tell you that you were the first man to come to her bed."

"I know," Conan said through gritted teeth. He was unused to women casting him aside; he liked neither the fact of it nor the discussing of it.

A woman's scream came from the tent, and the Cimmerian threw another stone. The tightness of his jaw eased, and a slight smile touched his lips. Arvaneus took a single step toward the scarlet pavilion, then froze in indecision. From where she knelt by the tent flap, Tamira cast an agonized glance at Conan. All the rest of the camp seemed stunned to immobility. Another shriek rent the air.

Telades leaped to his feet, but Conan caught the hunter's arm. "I will see if she requires aid," he said calmly, tossing aside his handful of stones. Despite his tone the Cimmerian's first steps were quick, and by the time he reached the tent he was running.

As he ducked through the tent-flap, the story was plain. Jondra struggled among the cushions, her scarlet robe rucked up above her rounded hips, long legs kicking in the air, while Zathanides lay half atop her, fumbling with his breeches and raining kisses on her face. Her small fists pounded futilely at his back and sides.

With a snarl Conan grasped the man by the neck of his gilded mail shirt and the seat of his breeches, lifting him straight into the air. Zathanides gave a shout, then began cursing and struggling, clawing at his sword, but the huge Cimmerian easily carried him to the entrance and threw him from the tent to land like a sack.

Conan took a bare instant to assure himself that Jondra was unharmed. Her jewelry was discarded on the cushions, and her robe was torn to expose one smooth shoulder, but she seemed more angry than hurt as she scrambled to her feet, pushing her silk down over her sleek nudity. Then he followed Zathanides outside. The general had risen to one knee, his mouth twisted with rage, and his sword came out as Conan appeared. The Cimmerian's foot lashed out. The jeweled sword went flying; Zathanides yelped and clutched his wrist. The shout of outraged pain faded as Conan's blade point touched the general's throat.

"Stop!" Jondra cried. "Conan, put up your sword!"

Conan lowered his steel slowly, though he did not sheath it. It had been she who was assaulted, and by his thinking Zathanides' life was hers to dispose of as she saw fit, or even to spare. But he would not disarm himself until the man was dead or gone.

"I'll have your head, barbarian," Zathanides snarled as he got painfully to his feet. "You'll discover the penalty for attacking a Lord of Zamora."

"Then you will discover the penalty for . . . for manhandling a Lady of Zamora," Jondra said coldly. "Tread warily, Zathanides, for your head and Conan's will share the same fate, and the choice is yours."

Zathanides' dark eyes bulged, and spittle dripped from the corner of his mouth. "Make what charges you will, you half-breed Brythunian trull. Do you think there is anyone in Zamora who has not heard the stories of you? That you bed a man before you take him in service as a hunter? Who will believe that one such as I would touch such a slut, such a piece of—"

He cut off and took a step back as Conan's sword lifted again, but Jondra grabbed the Cimmerian's massive arm, though both her hands could not come near encircling it. "Hold, Conan," she said unsteadily. "Make your choice, Zathanides."

The dark-faced general scrubbed at the spittle on his chin with the back of his hand, then nodded jerkily. " 'Tis you who has made a choice, Jondra. Keep your savage lover. Enter the mountains if you will, and find a hillman." Stamping to where his jewel-hilted blade lay, he snatched it from the ground and slammed it home in the sheath at his side. "For all I care, you can go straight to Zandru's Ninth Hell!"

Satisfaction glimmered beneath Conan's anger as he watched the general's stiff-backed march to his horse. Zathanides might wish to abandon Jondra to her fate, but too many of his own soldiers knew that he had found her. The attempted rape might well be covered up—especially if other nobles felt about Jondra as the general did—but failing in his attempt to turn a woman back from the mountains would place his manhood in an unfavorable light indeed. At least, that was the way the Cimmerian believed a man of Zathanides' ilk would look at the matter. Conan felt he could safely wager that the next day would see the appearance of a force under orders to escort the hunting party to Shadizar, without regard for what Jondra had to say.

As Zathanides and his standard bearer galloped down the hill, Arvaneus approached the crimson-walled tent, his manner at once arrogant and hesitant "My lady," he said hoarsely, "if you command it, I will take men and see that Lord Zathanides does not survive the night."

"If I command it," Jondra replied in an icy tone, "you will sneak in the night and murder Zathanides. Conan did not await my command. He faced Zathanides openly, without fear of consequences."

"My lady, I . . . I would die for you. I live only for you."

Jondra turned her back on the impassioned huntsman. Her eyes fastened on Conan's broad chest as if afraid to meet his gaze. "You begin to make a habit of saving me," she said softly. "I see no reason for us to continue to sleep apart." Arvaneus' teeth ground audibly.

Conan said nothing. If his thoughts concerning Zathanides were correct, then he should be gone from the camp before the night ended, for the general's instructions would certainly include the death of one large northlander. Too, there was his plan of departing with Tamira. Leaving from Jondra's bed would necessitate explanations he did not want to make.

The tall noblewoman drew a shuddering breath. "I am no tavern wench to be toyed with. I will have an answer now."

"I did not leave your bed for wanting to," he said carefully, and cursed his lack of diplomatic skill when her chin went up and her eyes flared. "Let us not argue," he added quickly. "It will be days before the wounded have their strength back. They should be days of rest and enjoyment." Days spent in her return to Shadizar, he thought, but his satisfaction vanished at her scornful laugh.

"Can you be so foolish? Zathanides will brood on his manhood and the pride he lost here, then convince himself that he can escape any charges I might bring. Tomorrow will see more soldiers, Conan, no doubt with orders to take me back in chains if I'll go no other way. But they will need to seek me in the mountains." Abruptly her face stilled, and her voice hardened. "You are *not* so foolish as that. You know as well as I the soldiers will return. You would have waited and seen me carried back to Shadizar like a bundle. Well, go, if you fear the mountains. Go! I care not!"

As abruptly as she had turned her back on Arvaneus, she turned to face the huntsman again. "I intend to press on at first light," she told the hawk-faced man, "and to move quickly. All baggage must be discarded except what can be carried on pack animals. The wounded and all men who cannot be mounted will turn back with the ox-carts. Perhaps their trail will confuse Zathanides for a time . . ."

As her list of instructions went on, Arvaneus shot a look over her shoulder at Conan, smug satisfaction mingled with a promise of violence. There would be more trouble from that quarter. Or rather, the Cimmerian reminded himself, there would be if he continued with the hunters, which he had no intention of doing. And since such was his plan, it was time for him to be making preparations for his leave-taking.

Slowly Conan moved away from the noblewoman's flow of commands. With studied casualness he drifted beyond the cookfires. The fat cook, frowning over a delicate dish for Jondra's table, never looked up as the Cimmerian rooted among the supplies. When Conan walked on, he carried two fat leather pouches of dried meat in the crook of his arm. Taking one quick look to make certain he was unobserved, he cached the meat beneath a thornbush on the edge of the encampment. Soon he had added four waterbags, and blankets of blue-striped wool. He was inured to sleeping with naught but his cloak for protection from the cold, or even without it, but he could not think a city woman like Tamira was so hardy.

The horses had to wait until the point of leaving—they certainly could not be saddled now without drawing unwanted attention—but he walked to the picket line anyway. It was easier to choose out a good mount when there was light to see. The big black he had been riding would do for him; Tamira needed a horse with good endurance as well, though. He had intended to move down the line of animals without stopping, so as to give no hint of his interest, but as he came to a long-legged bay mare—just the sort he would choose for Tamira—his feet halted of their own accord. On the ground at the mare's head rested a high-pommeled saddle, a bulging waterbag, and a tightly tied leather sack.

"In the night, Tamira?" he said softly. "Or while I sit waiting for darkness to come?" The picture of the rubies lying on the cushions of Jondra's tent was suddenly bright in his mind.

With a calm he did not feel, Conan strode through the camp, his eyes seeking Tamira. Once more the encampment was an anthill, hunters scurrying at Jondra's commands. For an instant the noblewoman paused, gazing at Conan as if she wished to speak, or waited for him to speak, but when he did not slow she turned angrily back to supervising the preparations for the next morning. Nowhere did Conan see Tamira. But that, he thought grimly, might mean he was not too late.

Conan knew how he would have entered the scarlet tent, had he chosen to steal the rubies with the camp aroused. A glance told him no one was watching, and he quickly slipped behind Jondra's pavilion. Down the back of the tent a long slit had been made. Parting it a fingerwidth, he peered in. Tamira knelt within, rooting among the cushions. With a muffled laugh she drew out the sparkling length of the necklace. The tiara was gripped in her other hand.

Soundlessly Conan slipped through the slit. The first announcement of his presence Tamira received was his hand closing over her mouth. His free arm encircled her, pinning her arms and lifting her before she had time to do more than gasp into his palm. She had dropped the gems, he saw, but that was the end of his moment of peace. Tamira exploded into a wriggling, kicking, biting bundle. And footsteps were approaching the front of the tent.

With a muttered oath the Cimmerian ducked back through the slit with his struggling burden. Behind the tent was no place to stop, however, not if someone was going to enter the tent, not with Tamira as likely as not to scream that *he* had been thieving. Cursing under his breath, he scrambled down the stony slope until he found a clump of scrub brush that hid them from the camp. There he tried to set her down, but she kicked him fiercely on the ankle, rocks slid beneath his foot, and he found himself on the ground with Tamira beneath him, her eyes starting from her head from the force of the fall.

"You great oaf!" she wheezed after a moment, "Do you try to break my ribs?"

"I did not kick myself," he growled. "I thought we agreed to leave in the night. What were you doing in Jondra's tent?"

"Nothing was said about the rubies," she retorted "I haven't changed my plans for them, even if you have. Perhaps," she finished angrily, "you find what Jondra gives you more valuable than rubies, but as I am not a man I have a different view of the matter."

"Leave Jondra out of this," he snapped. "And do not try to change the subject. You have a horse waiting this very instant."

Tamira shifted uneasily beneath him, and her eyes slid away from his. "I wanted to be ready," she muttered. "For the night."

"Do you think I'm a fool," he said, "that I take you for a fool? The saddle cannot escape discovery till nightfall. But if someone planned to steal the rubies and leave the camp within the turn of a glass . . . You could not have been planning such a thing, could you?"

"They would not have held you to blame." Her tone was sullenly excusatory. "Jondra would not blame you if she found you with the rubies in your pouch. And if she did, it would be less than you deserve."

"Jondra," he breathed. "Always Jondra. What is it to you whose bed I share? You and I are not lovers."

Tamira's large brown eyes grew even wider. Scarlet suffused her cheeks, and her mouth worked for a long moment before sound finally came out. "We most certainly are not!" she gasped. "How dare you suggest such a thing? Let me up! Get off me, you great ox! Let me up, I say!" Her small fists punctuated her words, pounding at his shoulders, but suddenly her fingers had tangled in his hair, and she was pressing her lips to his.

Conan blinked once in surprise, then returned her kiss with as much fervor as she was putting into it.

"Don't think this will convince me to stay," he said when they broke apart for air. "I'm not such a fool."

"If you stop," she moaned, "then you *are* a fool."

With one last silent reminder that he would *not* be a fool, Conan gave up talk and thought alike for pleasures at once simpler and more complex.

XIII

He was not a fool, Conan told himself once more as he guided his horse along a trail halfway up a nameless peak on the fringe of the Kezankians. If he kept saying it, he thought he might convince himself in time. Before and behind him stretched the hunting party, all mounted and many leading pack animals, wending their way deeper into the hillman domains. The sun stood barely above the horizon. They had left the camp in the hills before the first glimmer of dawn. The ox-carts with the wounded would be on their way back to Shadizar.

Lost in his own thoughts, Conan was surprised to find that Jondra had reined aside to await him. He had not spoken to her since she turned her back on him, but he noted that at least she was smiling now.

She drew her horse in beside his. The trail was wide enough for the animals to walk abreast. "The day is fine, is it not?" she said brightly.

Conan merely looked at her.

"I hoped you would come to me in the night. No, I promised myself I would not say that." Shyly she peered at him through lowered lashes. "I knew you could not leave me. That is . . . I thought . . . you *did* stay because of me, did you not?"

"I did," he said glumly, but she appeared not to notice his tone.

"I knew it," she said, her smile even more radiant than before. "Tonight we will put the past behind us once and for all." With that she galloped up the line of mounted men to resume her place at their head.

Conan growled deep in his throat.

"What did she want?" Tamira demanded, guiding her mount up beside his. It was the same bay mare she had chosen out for her flight. She glared jealously after the noblewoman.

"Nothing of consequence," Conan replied.

The young woman thief grunted contemptuously. "'Tis likely she thinks you are still here because of the over-generous charms she displays so freely. But you came because of me. Didn't you?"

"I came for you," Conan told her. "But unless you want to see how strongly Jondra wields a switch, you had best not let her see us talking too often."

"Let her but try."

"Then you intend to explain to her that you are not Lyana the handmaiden, but Tamira the thief?"

"If she faced me in a fair fight," the slender woman began with a toss of her head, then broke off in a laugh. "But it is not talk I want from you. She can have that. Till tonight, Conan."

The big Cimmerian sighed heavily as she let her horse fall behind his. It was no easy task he had ahead of him, and all because he could not allow a woman who had shared his bed—much less two of them—to enter the Kezankians while he rode back to Shadizar. He supposed those men who called themselves civilized and him barbarian could have managed it easily. It was beyond him, though, and his pride was enough to make him believe he could bring both safely out of the mountains. Of course, he knew, soon or late each woman would find out about the other. At that point, he was sure, he would rather face all the hillmen of the Kezankians than those two females.

The thought of hillmen brought him back to his surroundings. If he did not keep watch, they might not even make it fully into the mountains, much less out. His eyes scanned the steep brown mountain slopes around him, dotted with trees bizarrely sculpted by wind and harsh clime. He searched the jagged peaks ahead. No signs of life did he discern, but the breeze brought a sound to him, faint yet disturbing. It came from behind.

He reined his horse around to look back, and felt the hair stir on the back of his neck. Far below and far distant among the foothills a battle raged. He could make out little save dust rising as smoke from the hills and the small forms of men swarming like ants, yet for an instant he saw what he could swear was a Zamoran honor standard atop a hill. Then it was ridden down, and the men who rode over it wore turbans. Most of the other shapes he could make out were turbanned as well.

"What is the matter?" Jondra shouted, galloping down the trail. She had to force her way through a knot of hunters gathered behind Conan. "Why are you halted?"

" 'Tis a battle, my lady," Telades said, shading his eyes with one hand to peer down at the hills. "I cannot say who fights."

"Hillmen," Conan said. "From the look of it hillmen are killing some part of the Zamoran Army."

"Nonsense!" Arvaneus snapped. "The army would sweep any hillman rabble aside. Besides, the tribes never gather in such numbers, and . . . and . . . " The force of his words weakened as he spoke, and he finished lamely with, "It is impossible to make out details at this distance. That could be anyone fighting. Perhaps it is not a battle at all."

"Perhaps it is a folk dance," Conan said dryly.

Jondra touched his arm. "Is there aught we can do to aid them?"

"Not even if we had wings," the big Cimmerian replied.

Relief was writ plain on the faces of the hunters at his reply, but it was relief tinged with fear. It was all very well to talk of entering the Kezankians and risking the wrath of the hill tribes. To actually see that wrath, even at a distance, was something else, and most especially when it seemed to be dealt out by more hillmen than a man might expect to see in a lifetime of roaming the mountains.

Jondra looked from face to face, then put on a smile. "If so many hillmen are down there, then we shall have the mountains to ourselves." Her words had little effect on the hunters' expressions. A raven appeared, flying around the side of the mountain. "There," Jondra said, drawing her bow from its lacquered case behind her saddle. "Should there be a hillman or two left in the mountains, we'll deal with them as easily as this." Her bowstring slapped against her forearm leather; the raven's wings folded, and the bird dropped like a stone. Conan thought he heard her mutter something about "Brythunian" as she recased her bow. "Now let us ride," she commanded, and galloped back up the trail.

Slowly the column of hunters formed again behind the noblewoman. As Tamira passed Conan, she gave him an anxious, wide-eyed look. Perhaps he *was* a fool, he thought, but he could be no other than what he was. With a reassuring smile for the young woman thief, he joined the file of horsemen picking its way up the mountain.

Eldran ran a judicious eye over the two score men following him through a field of boulders deeper into the mountains, and said, "We stop for a rest."

"About time," said a round-cheeked man with gray streaking the long hair that was held back from his face by a leather cord. "We've ridden since before first light, and I'm not so young as I once was."

"If you tell me about your old bones one more time, Haral," Eldran laughed, and the others joined in, though their laughter was strained. Haral's age and plumpness were belied by the scars on his face, and the wolf whose fur trimmed his cloak had been slain with his bare hands. "A short stop only," Eldran went on. "These mountains feel ill, and I would be done with what we came for and out of them quickly."

That cooled their mirth, as he had intended it should. The laugh had been good for easing the disquiet, and perhaps more than disquiet, that had fallen over them all since they entered the mountains, but they must be ever mindful of what they were about and where they were if they were to leave with their lives.

As the others sat or lay or even walked a bit to stretch their legs, Eldran reclined with his reins wrapped loosely about one hand. He had had his own difficulties in keeping his mind cleanly on his purpose in the Kezankians. Even through the unease that hung about him like a miasma, a tall Zamoran beauty with arrogance enough for a score of kings had a way of intruding on his thoughts when he was not careful. But was she truly Zamoran, he wondered. Her manner, acting as if she ruled whatever ground she stood on, said yes. But those eyes. Like the mists of morning clinging to the oaks of the forest. No Zamoran ever had such eyes, as gray as his own.

Angrily he reminded himself of his purpose, to avenge his brother and those who went with him into the Kezankians, never to return. And to avenge as well those who had died attempting to defend their farmholds against the beast of fire. To make certain that more deaths did not come from the beast. If he and every man with him died, it would be small price for success. They had all agreed to that before ever they left Brythunia.

A raven circled high above him. Like the bird he and Jondra had shot, he thought. Angrily he leaped to his feet. Could nothing put the woman from his mind? Well, he would not be reminded of her longer by that accursed bird. He pulled his bow from its wolf-hide case behind his saddle.

"Eldran!" From a space clear of boulders higher on the mountain, a bony man with a pointed nose waved to him frantically. "Come quickly, Eldran!"

"What is it, Fyrdan?" Eldran called back, but he was scrambling up the slope as he spoke. Fyrdan was not one to become excited over nothing. Others of the band followed.

"There," the bony man said, flinging out an arm to point as Eldran joined him.

Eldran cupped his hands beside his eyes to improve his seeing, but there was little to make out save boiling dust and the tiny figures of struggling men on the hills far below. "Hillmen," he said finally.

"And Zamorans," Fyrdan added. "I saw the banner their general carried go down."

Slowly Eldran's hands dropped to his sides. "Forgive me, Jondra," he said softly.

"Perhaps the soldiers had not fetched her yet," Haral said. "Perhaps these are the other soldiers we saw."

Eldran shook his head. "The others were further west. And I watched their camp until their general left to find her."

"A Zamoran wench," Fyrdan said scornfully. "There are plenty of good Brythunian women eager for a tumble with . . ." His words trailed off under Eldran's glare.

"We will speak no more of the woman," the gray-eyed man said. "We will talk of other things, things that must be said. We have tracked the beast here to its home ground, and its spoor is on the mountains themselves. The very rocks are baneful, and the air reeks of maleficence. Let no man say he has not felt it as I have."

"Next you will be claiming second sight," Haral grumbled, then added with a chuckle, "Unless you've changed greatly since last we swam together, you cannot qualify to become a priestess." No one echoed his jollity; grave eyes watched Eldran, who went on in grim tones.

"I have no need of second sight to scent death. Who follows me from here must resign himself that his bones will go unanointed. I will not think ill of any man who turns back, but let him do it now."

"Do you turn back?" Haral asked gently. Eldran shook his head. "Then," the plump man said, "I will not either. I am old enough to choose the place of my dying, an it comes to that."

"My brother rode with yours, Eldran," Fyrdan said. "My blood burns as hot for vengeance as yours." One by one the others made it known that they, too, would go on, and Eldran nodded.

"Very well," he said simply. "What will come, will come. Let us ride."

The raven was gone, he saw as he made his way back down to the trail. Birds of ill omen, they were, yet he could not find gladness in him for its absence. It had reminded him of Jondra, and whether she lived or no he could not think he would ever see her again. But then, he thought bleakly, there would be ravens beyond counting deeper in the Kezankians, and bones aplenty for them to pick.

XIV

Basrakan Imalla stalked the floor of his oaken-paneled chamber with head bowed as if his multi-hued turban were too heavy. His blood-red robes swirled with the agitation of his pacing. So many worries weighing on his shoulders, he thought. The path of holiness was not an easy one. There was the matter of another dead raven in the next chamber. Men, it had said before dying. But how many, and where? And to have two of the birds slain in only a few days. Did someone know of the ravens' function? Someone inimical to him? Another had reported men as well. Not soldiers; the birds could distinguish them. But the inability to count meant there could be ten or a hundred. It might even be the same party seen by the dead raven. He would have to increase his patrols and find these interlopers, however many groups of them there were.

At least the bird that accompanied the men he had sent against the soldiers had reported victory. No, not merely victory. Annihilation. But even with that came burdens. The warriors he had sent forth camped now, so said the raven. Squabbling among themselves over the looting of the dead, no doubt. But they would return. They had to. He had given them a victory, a sign from the old gods.

Unbidden the true source of his worries rushed back to mock him, though he tried as he had so often in days past to force it from him. A sign from the old gods. The sign of the ancient gods' favor. Seven times, now, he had tried to summon the drake, each attempt carefully hidden from the eyes even of his own acolytes, and seven times he had failed. Unrest grew in the camps for the lack of the showing. And those he had sent after the Eyes of Fire had not returned. Could the old gods have withdrawn their grace from him?

Wrapping his arms around him, he rocked back and forth on his heels. "Am I worthy, O gods of my forefathers?" he moaned. "Am I truly worthy?"

"Our question exactly, Imalla," a voice growled.

Basrakan spun, and blinked to find three hillmen confronting him. He struggled to recover his equilibrium. As he drew himself up, two of the bearded men shrank back. "You dare disturb me?" he rasped. "How did you pass my guards?"

The man who had stood his ground, his mustaches curled like the horns of a bull, spoke. "Even among your guards there are doubts, Imalla."

"You are called Walid," Basrakan said, and a flicker of fear appeared in the other's black eyes.

There were no sorceries involved, though. This Walid had been reported to him as one of the troublemakers, the questioners. It had taken him a moment to remember the man's description. He had not thought the troublemaking had gone so far as this, however. But he had prepared for every eventuality.

With false calmness he tucked his hands into the long sleeves of his crimson robe. "What doubts do *you* have, Walid?"

The man's thick mustache twitched at the repetition of his name, and he half turned his head as if looking for support from his companions. They remained well behind him, meeting neither his eyes nor Basrakan's. Walid drew a deep breath. "We came here, many of us, because we heard the old gods favored you. Those who came before us speak of a fabulous beast, a sign of that favor, but I have seen no such creature. What I *have* seen is thousands of hillmen sent to battle Zamoran soldiers, who have ever before slaughtered us when we fought them in numbers. And I have seen none of those warriors return."

"That is all?" Basrakan asked.

His suddenly mild tone seemed to startle Walid. "Is it not enough?" the mustached man demanded.

"More than enough," Basrakan replied. Within his sleeves his hands clasped small pouches he had prepared only a day past, when the unrest among the gathered tribes first truly began to worry him. Now he praised his foresight. "Much more than enough, Walid."

Basrakan's hands came out of his sleeves, and in a continuous motion he scattered the powder from one pouch across Walid. As the powder struck, the Imalla's right hand made arcane gestures, and he chanted in a tongue dead a thousand years.

Walid stared down at his chest in horror for a moment as the chilling incantation went on, then, with a shout of rage and fear, he grabbed for his tulwar. Even as his hand touched the hilt, though, fire spurted from his every pore. Flame surrounded him as clothes and hair turned to ash. His roar of anger became a shrill shriek of agony, then the hiss of boiling grease. A plume of oily black smoke rose from the collapsing sack that had been a man.

The other two men had stood, eyes bulging with terror, but now one burst for the door, and the other fell to his knees crying, "Forgiveness, Imalla! Forgiveness!"

In two quick strides Basrakan was on them, throwing the powder over the fleeing man and the kneeling one alike. His long-fingered hands gestured, and the chant rose once more. The running man made it to the door before fire engulfed him. The other fell on his face, wriggling toward Basrakan, then he, too, was a living pyre. Their screams lasted only moments, blending into a shrill whistle as flame consumed their bones.

At last even the black smoke guttered out. Only small heaps of dark, oily ash were left on the floor, and sooty smudges on the ceiling. The fierce-eyed Imalla viewed the residues of his accusers with satisfaction, but it faded quickly to grim anger. These men would have brothers, cousins, and nephews, scores of male relatives who, while they might fear to confront Basrakan openly, would most certainly now be a source of further dissension. Some might even go beyond words. The tribesmen lived and died by the blood feud, and nothing could turn them from it save death.

"So be it," he pronounced intently.

Dark face as cold and calm as if he had a lifetime for the task, Basrakan gathered a sampling from each pile of ash, scraping them into folded scraps of parchment with a bone knife four times blessed in rites before the ancient gods of the Kezankians. Ash from each dead man went into a thick-walled mortar of plain, unworked gold. The sorcerer's movements quickened as he added further ingredients, for speed now was essential. Powdered virgin's eye and ground firefly. Salamanders' hearts and the dried blood of infants. Potions and powders, the ingredients of which he dared not even think of. With the thigh bone of a woman strangled by her own daughter he ground the mixture, twelve times widdershins, intoning the hidden names of the ancient gods, names that chilled the marrow and made vapors of frost hang in the air. Twelve times the other way. Then it was done, this first step, leaving the golden vessel filled almost to the brim with black powder that seemed to swirl like smoke in its depths.

Gingerly, for the blending was deadly to the touch now, Basrakan carried the mortar to a cleared space on the pale stone floor. There, dipping a brush tipped with virgins' eyelashes into the moist mixture, he carefully scribed a precise pattern on the smooth stone. It was a cross, its arms of equal length exactly aligned to north and south, east and west. Tipping each arm was a circle, within which he drew the four ideograms of the ancient gods, the secret signs of earth, air, water, and fire. Next a triangle, its apex at the meeting of the arms of the cross, enclosed the symbol for the spirits of fire, and that same character was placed on each point of the triangle.

Basrakan paused, staring at what he had wrought, and his breath came fast. He would not admit to fear despite a tightening in his bowels, but this was more dangerous than anything he had yet attempted. An error in any phase, one completed or one to come, and the rite would rebound on him. Yet he knew there was no turning back.

Deftly he tipped the last of the powder into a silver censer on the end of a silver chain. Ordinary flint and steel provided the spark and set it smouldering. Aligning his feet carefully on the broad base of the triangle, he swung the censer in an intricate pattern. Wisps of smoke wafted upward from the silver ball, and Basrakan's incantation rose with the odoriferous vapors. With each swing of the censer one crystalline word rang in the air, words that even the fiery-eyed Imalla could not hear, for they were not meant for human ears, and the human mind could not comprehend them.

Around him the very air seemed to glisten darkly. Smoke from the censer thickened and fell to the stone floor, aligning itself unnaturally with the pattern drawn there. Basrakan's chant came faster, and more loudly. The words pealed hollowly, like funereal tolling from the depths of a cavern. Within the ropes of smoke now covering the configuration came a glow, ever fiercer and hotter, till it seemed as if all the fires of the earth's bowels were bound in those roiling thongs of black. Sweat rolled down Basrakan's thin cheeks from the heat. The glow became blinding, and his words rose higher and higher, the walls shivering under their impact.

Suddenly Basrakan ceased his cry. Silence came, and in that instant, glow and smoke and drawn pattern all vanished. Even the smoke from the censer failed.

Done, Basrakan thought. Weariness filled him. Even his bones felt weak. But what had had to be done, had been done.

A tremor shook him as his eye fell on the remains of his accusers. On each pile of ash, from which all that could be burned had been burned, danced pale flames. Even as he watched they licked into extinction. He drew a deep breath. This was no cause for fear, but rather for exaltation.

Jbeil burst into the chamber, panting, with one hand pressed hard to his side. "The bless . . . the bless . . . the blessings . . ."

"An Imalla must be dignified," Basrakan snapped. Returning confidence, returning faith, washed away the dregs of his fear. "An Imalla does not run."

"But the camps, Imalla," Jbeil managed past gulps of air. "Fire. Men are burning. Burning, Imalla! Warriors, old men, boys. Even babes unweaned,

Imalla! They simply burst into flame, and not water or dirt can extinguish them. Hundreds upon hundreds of them!"

"Not so many, I think," Basrakan replied coolly. "A hundred, perhaps, or even two, but not so many as you say."

"But, Imalla, there is panic."

"I will speak to the people, Jbeil, and calm them. Those who died were of tainted blood. Did the means of their dying tell you nothing?"

"The fire, Imalla?" Jbeil said uncertainly. "They offended the spirits of fire?"

Basrakan smiled as if at a pupil who had learned his lesson well. "More than offended, Jbeil. Much more. And all males of their blood shared their atonement." A thought struck him, a memory of words that seemed to have been spoken days in the past. "My guards, Jbeil. Did you see them as you came in?"

"Yes, Imalla. As I came to you. The two who were at your door accompanied Ruhallah Imalla on some errand." His eyes took on a sly cast. "They ran, Imalla. Ruhallah knows little of dignity. Only the urgency of my message brought me to such haste."

"Ruhallah had his own urgency," Basrakan said so softly he might have been speaking to himself. He fixed the other man with an eye like a dagger. "Ruhallah is to blame for the fiery deaths this day. He and those false guards who flee with him. Ruhallah led those men of the blood that perished this day into false beliefs and tainted ways." It could be so, he thought. It must be so. Assuredly, it *was* so. "Ruhallah and the guards who flee with him must be brought back to face payment for what they have done." Few things amused Basrakan, but the next thought to visit him brought a smile to his thin lips. "They are to be given to the women of the men who died by fire this day. Let those who lost kith and kin exact their vengeance."

"As you command, Imalla, so will it be." Jbeil froze in a half-bow, and his eyes went wide. "Aaiee! Imalla, it had been driven from my mind by the burnings and . . ." Basrakan glared at him, and he swallowed and went on. "Sharmal has returned, Imalla. One of those you sent after the Eyes of Fire, Imalla," he added when the tall holy man raised a questioning eyebrow.

"They have returned?" Basrakan said, excitement rising in his voice. "The Eyes of Fire are mine! All praise to the old gods!" Abruptly he was coldly calm, only an intensity of tone remaining of the emotion that had filled his speech. "Bring the gems to me. Immediately, fool! Nothing should have kept you from that. Nothing! And bring the men, as well. They will not find their rewards small."

"Imalla," Jbeil said hesitantly, "Sharmal is alone, and empty handed.

He babbles that the rest are dead, and other things, as well. But there is little of sense in any of it. He . . . he is mad, Imalla."

Basrakan ground his teeth, and tugged at his forked beard as if he wanted to pull it out by the roots. "Empty handed," he breathed at last, hoarse and icy. He could not be cheated of his desires now. He *would* not be. "What occurred, Jbeil? Where are the Eyes of Fire? I will know these things. Put this Sharmal to the question. Strip him of his skin. Sear him to the bone. I will have answers!"

"But, Imalla," Jbeil whispered, "the man is mad. The protection of the old gods is on him."

"Do as I command!" Basrakan roared, and his acolyte flinched.

"As . . . as you command, Imalla, so will it be." Jbeil bowed deeply, and moved backwards toward the door.

So much had happened, Basrakan thought, in such a short time. There was something he was forgetting. Something . . . "Jbeil!" The other man jerked to a halt. "There are strangers in the mountains, Jbeil. They are to be found, and any survivors brought to me for offering to the true gods. Let it be done!" He gestured, and Jbeil nearly ran from the room.

XV

"We will make camp now," Jondra announced while the sun still rose. Arvaneus' voice rose, echoing her command, and obediently her hunters dismounted and began seeing to the pack animals and their own mounts.

Conan caught her eye questioningly, and she favored him with a smile. "When hunting a rare animal," she said, "care must be taken not to bypass its feeding grounds. We will spend days in each camp, searching."

"Let us hope this animal is not also searching," Conan replied. The noblewoman frowned, but before she could speak Arvaneus came to stand at her stirrup.

"Do you wish the trackers out now, my lady?" he asked.

Jondra nodded, and a shiver of excitement produced effects to draw male eyes. "It would be wonderful to get a shot at my quarry on the first day. Yes, Arvaneus. Put out your best trackers."

She looked expectantly at Conan, but he pretended not to notice. His tracking skill was the equal of any of the hunters', but he had no interest in finding the creature Jondra sought. He wanted only to see the two women returned to the safety of Shadizar, and he could offer them no protection if he was out tracking.

Jondra's face fell when Conan did not speak, but the dark-eyed huntsman smiled maliciously. "It takes a great special skill to be a tracker," he said to no one in particular. "My lady." He made an elegant bow to Jondra, then backed away, calling as he straightened. "Trackers out! Telades! Zurat! Abu!" His list ran on, and soon he and nine others were trotting out of the camp in ten different directions. They went afoot, for the slight spoor that a tracker must read as a scribe read words on parchment could be missed entirely from the back of a horse.

With the trackers gone, the beauteous noblewoman began ordering the placement of the camp, and Conan found a place to settle with a honing stone, a bit of rag and a vial of olive oil. A sword must be tended to, especially if it would soon find use, and Conan was sure his blade would not be idle long. The mountains seemed to overhang them with a sense of foreboding, and something permeated the very stones that made him uneasy. The honing stone slid along his blade with quiet sussuration. Morning grew into afternoon.

The camp, Conan decided after a time, was placed as well as it could be under the circumstances. The stunted trees that were scattered so sparsely through the Kezankians were in this spot gathered into what might pass for a grove, though an exceedingly thin one. At least they added some modicum to the hiding of the camp.

Jondra's scarlet tent, which she had never considered leaving behind, stood between two massive granite boulders and was screened from behind by the brown rock of a sheer cliff. No other tents had been brought—for which small favor the Cimmerian was grateful—and the hunters' blankets were scattered in twos and threes in a score of well-hidden depressions. The horses were picketed in a long, narrow hollow that could be missed even by a man looking for it. To one unfamiliar with the land the encampment would be all but invisible. The trouble, he thought sourly, was that the hillmen were more than familiar with their mountains. There would be trouble.

As though his thought of trouble had been a signal, a sound sliced through the cool mountain air, and Conan's hand stopped in the act of oiling his sword blade. Through the jagged peaks echoed a shrill, ululating cry, piercing to the bone and the heart. He had never heard the like of that sound, not from the throat of any man or any creature.

The big Cimmerian was not alone in being disturbed by the hunting call—for such he was sure it was. Hunters sat up in their blankets, exchanging worried glances. Some rose to walk a few paces, eyes searching the steep, encircling slopes. Jondra came to the flap of her tent, head tilted questioningly, listening. She wore leather now, jerkin and breeches, as always fitting her curves like a second skin, but plain brown, suitable for the hunt. When the sound was not repeated she retreated inside once more.

"What in Mitra's thrice-blessed name was that?" Tamira said, dropping into a crouch near Conan. She adjusted her short white robe to provide a modicum of decency, and wrapped slim arms about her knees. "Can it be the creature Jondra hunts?"

"I would not be surprised if it was," Conan said. He returned to the oiling of his blade. "Little good those rubies will do you if you end in the belly of that beast."

"You try to talk me into fleeing," she retorted, "leaving you with a clear path to the gems."

"I have told you," he began, but she cut him off.

"A clear path to Jondra's sleeping furs, then."

Conan sighed and slid his broadsword into his sheath. "You were in my arms this night past, and she not for two days. And I said that I came into these thrice-accursed mountains for you. Do you now call me liar?"

Her eyes slid away from his, to the rugged spires of granite surrounding them. "Do you think the trackers will find it? This beast, I mean? Perhaps, if they do not, we will leave these mountains. I would as well steal the rubies while returning to Shadizar."

"I would as soon they found naught but sore feet," Conan said. He remembered the half-charred fragment of skull and horn. "This beast will not be so easy to slay as Jondra believes, I fear. And you will not steal the rubies."

"So you *do* mean to take them yourself."

"I do not."

"Then you intend to save them for your paramour. For Jondra."

"Hannuman's Stones, woman! Will you give over?"

Tamira eyed him sharply. "I do not know whether I want you to be lying or not."

"What do you mean by that?" he asked in puzzlement.

"I intend to steal the rubies, you understand, no matter what you say or do." Her voice tightened. "But if you did not come for the rubies, then you came for me. Or for Jondra. I am uncertain whether I wouldn't rather have the sure knowledge that all you wanted was the gems."

Conan leaned back against the boulder behind him and laughed until he wheezed. "So you don't believe me?" he asked finally.

"I've known enough men to doubt anything any of you says."

"You have?" he exclaimed in feigned surprise. "I would have sworn I was the very first man you'd known."

Color flooded her cheeks, and she leaped to her feet. "Just you wait until—"

Whatever her threat was to be, Conan did not hear its finish, for Telades hurried into the camp, half out of breath and using his spear as a walking staff. Men hastened to surround him, and the Cimmerian was first among them.

A hail of words came from the hunters.

"Did you find tracks?"

"We heard a great cry."

"What did you see?"

"It must have been the thing we hunt."

"Did you see the beast?"

Telades tugged off his spiked helm and shook his shaved head. "I heard the cry, but I saw neither animal nor tracks."

"Give your report to me," Jondra snapped. The hunters parted to let her through. Her eagerness was betrayed by the bow in her hand. "Or am I to wait until you've told everyone else?"

"No, my lady," Telades replied abashedly. "I ask forgiveness. What I saw was the army, my lady. Soldiers."

Again a torrent of questions broke over the man.

"Are you sure?"

"From the lot we saw fighting?"

"How could they get into the mountains ahead of us?"

Jondra's cool gray eyes swept across the assembled hunters, and the torrent died as though she had cracked a whip.

"Where are those soldiers, Telades?" Conan asked. Jondra looked at him sharply, but closed her mouth and said nothing.

"Not two leagues to the north and east of us," Telades replied. "Their general is Lord Tenerses. I got close enough to see him, though they did not see me."

"Tenerses," Conan mused. "I have heard of him."

"They say he hunts glory," the shaven-headed hunter said, "but it seems he thinks well enough to know when danger is about. His camp is so well hidden, in a canyon with but one entrance, that I found it only by merest chance. And I could not see how many men he has with him."

"Not one fewer than Zathanides," Conan said, "if what I have heard of him is true. He is a man with a sense of his own importance, this Tenerses."

Jondra broke in in flat tones. "If you two are quite finished discussing the army, I would like to hear the results I sent this man for in the first place. Did you find tracks, Telades, or did you not?"

"Uh, no, my lady. No tracks."

"There are still nine others," the noblewoman said half to herself. "As for these soldiers," she went on in a more normal tone, "they have naught to do with us, and we naught to do with them. I see no reason why they should be a subject of further discussion, nor why they should even become aware of our existence. Am I understood?"

Her gaze was commanding as it met each man's eyes in turn, and each man mumbled assent and grew intent in his study of the ground beneath his feet, until she came to Conan. Eyes of chilling azure looked back at her in unblinking calmness, and it was smoky gray orbs that dropped to break the mesmerizing contact.

When she looked at him again, it was through long eyelashes. "I must talk with you, Conan," she murmured. "In my tent. I . . . would have your advice on the hunt."

Over Jondra's shoulder Conan saw Tamira watching him intently, hands on hips. "Perhaps later," he said. When the noblewoman blinked and stared, he added quickly, "The mountains are dangerous. We cannot spare even one watcher." Before she could say more—and he could see from the sparks in her eyes that she intended to say *much* more—he retreated across the camp to his place by the boulder.

As he settled once more with his back to the stone, he noticed that both women were looking at him. And both were glaring. The old saying was certainly proving true, he thought. He who has two women oft finds himself in possession of none. And not one thing could he think to do about it. With a sigh he set back to tending his steel. Some men claimed their blades had the personalities of women, but he had never known a sword to suffer jealousy.

The other trackers began returning at decreasing intervals. Jondra allowed these no time to become involved in extraneous—to her—matters with the other hunters. She met each man as he entered the camp, and her sharp gaze kept the rest back until she finished her questioning and gave the tracker leave to go.

One by one the trackers returned, and one by one they reported . . . nothing of interest to Jondra. One, who had searched near Telades, had found the cheekpiece of a soldier's helmet. Another had seen a great mountain ram with curling horns as long as a man's arm. Jondra angrily turned her back on him before he finished telling of it. Several saw hillmen, and in numbers enough to make a prudent man wary, but none had found the spoor of the beast, or anything that might remotely be taken as a sign of its presence or passage. The gray-eyed noblewoman heard each man out, and strode away from each impatiently tapping her bow against her thigh.

The last to return was Arvaneus, trotting into the camp to lean on his spear with an arrogant smile.

"Well?" Jondra demanded as she stalked up to him. "I suppose you have seen nothing either?"

The hawkfaced huntsman seemed taken aback at her tone, but he recovered quickly and swept a bow before her. "My lady, what you seek, I give to you." He shot a challenging look at Conan as he straightened. "*I*, Arvaneus, son of Lord Andanezeus, give it to you."

"You have found it?" Excitement brightened her face. "Where, Arvaneus?"

"A bare league to the east, my lady. I found the marks of great claws as long as a man's hand, and followed them for some distance. The tracks were made this day, and there cannot be another creature in these mountains to leave such spoor as human eyes have never before seen."

The entire camp stared in amazement as Jondra leaped spinning into the air, then danced three steps of a jig. "It must be. It must. I will give you gold to make you wealthy for this, Arvaneus. Find this beast for me, and I will give you an estate."

"I want no gold." Arvaneus said huskily, his black eyes suddenly hot. "Nor estates."

Jondra froze, staring at him, then turned unsteadily away. "Prepare horses," she commanded. "I would see these tracks."

The huntsman looked worriedly at the sky. The sun, giving little warmth in these mountains, lay halfway to the western horizon from its zenith. "It is late to begin a hunt. In the morning, at first light—"

"Do you question my commands?" she snapped. "I am no fool to start a hunt for a dangerous beast with night approaching, but I will see those tracks. Now! Twenty men. The rest will remain in camp and prepare for the hunt tomorrow."

"As you command, my lady," Arvaneus muttered. He glared malevolently at Conan as Jondra turned to the big Cimmerian and spoke in a soft voice.

"Will you ride with me, Conan? I . . . I would feel much safer." The awkwardness of her words and the coloring of her cheeks gave her the lie. With obvious difficulty, she added, "Please?"

Wordlessly Conan rose and walked to the picket line. Arvaneus barked orders, and others joined the Cimmerian. As Conan was fastening his saddle girth, he became aware of Tamira, making a great show of idly petting the nose of a roan next to his tall black.

"Will you ride with me, Conan?" she mimicked softly. "I will feel *so* much safer." She twisted up her face as if to spit.

Conan let out a long breath. "I'd not like to see either of you dead, or a hillman's slave. You will be safer here than will she out there, so I go with her."

He stepped up into the high-pommeled Zamoran saddle. Tamira trotted alongside as he rode from the hollow where the horses were picketed. "You will be out there," she told him, "and so will she. You could return to find me gone, Conan. And the rubies. What is to keep me here?"

"Why, you'll be waiting for me," he laughed, booting his mount to a trot. A hurled rock bounced off his shoulder, but he did not look back.

XVI

The party of Zamoran hunters made their way in single file along the gullies and clefts that lined the mountains like wrinkles of ancient age on the face of the earth. Arvaneus led, since he knew the way, and Jondra rode close behind him. Conan, in turn, kept close to the tall noblewoman. There would be little time to spare when protection was needed. The mountains seemed to press in on them malignly, even when their way opened enough for a score of men or more to ride abreast.

The big Cimmerian's eyes searched the jagged crags and steep slopes around them constantly, and with instincts long buried in civilized men he probed for his enemies. No sign of hillmen did he see, no hint of them came to his senses, but menace still oozed from the stones. Outwardly he seemed at ease, but he was dry tinder waiting for a spark.

Abruptly Arvaneus drew rein where the walls of rock were steep and close. "There, my lady," the huntsman said, pointing to the ground. "Here is the first track I found."

Jondra scrambled from her saddle to kneel by a small patch of clay. The deep marks of two massive claws and part of a third were impressed there. "It is larger than I thought," she murmured, running two slender fingers into one impression.

"We have seen the tracks," Conan said. The oppressive air seemed thicker to him. "Let us return to the camp."

Arvaneus' lip curled in a sneer. "Are you afraid, barbar? My lady, there are more tracks further on. Some are complete."

"I must see that," Jondra exclaimed. Swinging into her saddle she galloped ahead, and Arvaneus spurred after her.

Conan exchanged a look with Telades—by the shaven-headed hunter's sour face he liked this as little as the Cimmerian—then they and the rest of the column of horsemen followed.

As it had often before, the narrow passage opened out. This time it led into a small canyon, perhaps a hundred paces wide, with five narrow draws cutting its steep brown walls. Conan eyed those openings suspiciously. Any enemy hidden in those would be on them before they had time to react. The hillmen's favorite tactic was the ambush.

On the floor of the canyon the spoor of the beast was plentiful. Tracks leading both in and out showed that the beast had explored the narrow cuts. Unease permeated the column; hunters shifted their spears nervously, or reached back to touch the cased bows behind their saddles, and horses danced and shied. Jondra uncased her bow as she dismounted at the track Arvaneus pointed out, and nocked an arrow before kneeling to examine it. The hawk-faced huntsman frowned at the ground around him, attempting with only partial success to control his mount's quick sidesteps.

Conan found himself wondering about that frown. Arvaneus had seen this canyon and the tracks that filled it only a short time before. What was there for him to frown about? The big Cimmerian's breath caught in his throat. Unless there were *more* tracks than he had seen before. If that was true they must leave immediately.

Conan opened his mouth, and a shrill ululation split the air, chilling the blood, making the horses buck and scream. Jondra's mount tore the reins from her hands and bolted, nostrils flaring and eyes rolling wildly, leaving the noblewoman standing like a statue of ice. With difficulty the Cimmerian pulled his big black around. "Crom," he breathed into the din filling the stone walls.

Into the canyon came a monstrous creature, huge, on massive legs. Multi-hued scales glittered in the sinking sun, broken only by dark, leathery-appearing bulges on its back. Adamantine claws gouged the stone beneath them. The broad head was thrown back, the widespread maw revealing jagged teeth like splinters of stone, and that piercing cry struck men to their souls.

The hunters were men who had faced death many times, and if it had never before confronted them in such form, still death was no stranger to them. As that malevolent howl ended they forced themselves into movement, fighting horses half-mad with terror to spread and surround the gargantuan form. The man nearest the beast leveled his spear like a lance and charged. With a clang as of steel against stone the spear struck, and the rider was shivered from his saddle. The great head lowered, and flame roared from that gaping mouth. Man and horse shrieked as one, a shrillness that never seemed to end, as they were roasted alive.

A gasp rose from the other hunters, but they were already launching their attack, men charging in from from either flank. Even had they wished to turn aside, the beast gave them no chance. More swiftly than any leopard it moved, claws sweeping bloody rags that had once been men to the ground, jaws crushing men and horses alike. Spears splintered like straws against the iridescent scales, and the cries of the dying drowned out all save thought, and fear became the only thought in the hunter's minds.

Through that howling maelstrom of certain death Conan galloped, swinging low out of his saddle to snatch an unbroken spear from the bloody ground. Those great golden eyes, he thought. The eyes had to be vulnerable, or the long, dark protuberances on its back. He forced his mount to turn—it struggled to run on, away from the horror—and the sight that met his eyes sent a quiver through him as not even the beast's hunting cry had.

Jondra stood not ten paces from the creature's head. Even as he saw her, an arrow left her bow. Squarely on one malevolent golden eye the shaft struck. And ricocheted away. The beast lunged, claws streaking toward her. Frantically she leaped back, but the tip of one claw snagged in the laces of her red leather jerking, and she was jerked into the air to dangle before the creature's eyes. Ignoring the carnage around it, the shouting, screaming men, the beast seemed to study her.

A thrill of horror coursed through Conan. There was a light of intelligence in those auric globes. But if the brain behind them could reason, it was a form of reasoning too inhuman for the mind of man to know it. It did not see the beautiful woman as other than prey. The spike-toothed mouth opened, and Jondra was drawn closer.

Conan's spear came up. "Crom!" he bellowed, and his heels thudded his fear-ridden mount into a charge. His spearpoint held steady on one leathery bulge. He clamped his knees tightly on the animal against the shock he had seen throw others to the ground, but even so the force of the blow rocked through him, staggering his horse to its knees.

With sinuous grace and blinding speed the glittering beast twisted, smashing Conan with the leg from which Jondra dangled. Breath rushed from the big Cimmerian as he was lifted and hurled through the air. Stony ground rushed up to slam what little air remained from his chest. Desperately he fought to breathe, forced numbed muscles to move, rolled to hands and knees, staggered to his feet. Jondra lay on her back near him, writhing, bare breasts heaving as she struggled for air.

The beast turned its attention to the Cimmerian, Jondra's jerkin still tangled in its claws. What remained of his horse lay quivering beneath the creature; gobbets of flesh fell from its fanged jaws.

In what he knew was a futile gesture Conan drew his ancient broadsword. Steel made no mark on those infrangible scales. He could not move quickly enough to escape the creature's attack unburdened, much less carrying Jondra, and he could not leave her behind. Yet he would not die without fighting.

"Ho, Conan!" Swaying in his saddle, Telades rode toward the beast from behind. The mail over his chest was rent, and blood drenched him, but he gripped his spear firmly. "Get her away, northlander!" Pounding his boots into his horse's flanks, he forced it forward.

Iridescent scales flashed as the creature spun.

"No!" Conan shouted.

Flame engulfed the shaven-headed hunter, and the beast leaped to tear at smouldering flesh.

The Cimmerian would not waste Telades' sacrifice. Sheathing his blade, he scooped Jondra from the ground and darted into a narrow cleft, pursued by the sounds of crunching bone.

As the terrible grinding faded behind him, Jondra stirred in his arms. "I did not mean for them to die," she whispered. Her eyes were horror-laden pools.

"You wanted to hunt the beast," he said, not slowing his steady stride. Under other circumstances he would have searched for survivors. Now he thought only of getting Jondra far from that charnel scene, back to the relative safety of the camp.

Jondra pressed herself more firmly against his broad chest as if sheltering from storm winds in the safety of a huge boulder. "Telades gave his life for me," she murmured, shivering. "Truly, I did not wish it to be. Oh, Conan, what can I do?"

Conan stopped dead, and she huddled in his arms as though hiding from his icy blue gaze. "Leave these mountains," he said harshly. "Go back to Shadizar. Forget this beast, and always remember the men who died for your foolishness and pride."

Anger and arrogance flared across her face. Her fist rose, then abruptly fell limp. Tears leaked down her cheeks. "I will," she wept. "Before all the gods, I swear it."

"It will not repay Telades' sacrifice," he said, "but it will at least mean that you value what he did."

Gently she touched Conan's cheek. "Never have I wanted a man to guide me, but you almost make me . . ." Small white teeth bit her full underlip, and she dropped her eyes. "Will you come back to Shadizar with me?" she said softly, shifting in his grasp again so that her full, round breasts were exposed to his gaze.

"Perhaps," he replied gruffly, and began walking once more, with his full concentration on the twists of the cleft and the stony ground beneath his feet. Only a fool would refuse a woman like the one he held. And only a fool would disregard the advice he had given. But Telades had become a friend, and the man had died for him as well as for her.

A part of the Cimmerian's code demanded that Telades' death, offered in place of his own, should be repaid, just as another part of that code demanded that he see Jondra and Tamira to safety. At the moment the second seemed much more easily accomplished than the first! How, he thought, could he slay a beast that steel could not harm? If he took no notice of the charms Jondra displayed in his arms, it was no wonder.

XVII

amira was the first person Conan saw when he strode into the camp with his arms full of half-naked noblewoman and the sun a bloody ball balanced on jagged peaks. The slender young thief regarded him with fists on hips and a jaundiced eye for the way Jondra clung to him. Then Jondra looked around dazedly, revealing her tear-stained face. Tamira's jaw dropped, and she dashed into the red-walled tent to return with a cloak.

As Conan stood Jondra upright, the smaller woman enfolded her in soft blue wool. When he released his hold on her, the noblewoman sank to her knees. Tamira knelt beside her, drawing Jondra's head to her shoulder and glaring up at the big Cimmerian.

"What happened?" she demanded hotly.

"We found the beast she hunts. Hunted. Have any of the others returned?"

Dark eyes widening with sudden fear, Tamira shook her head. "None. They . . . they could not all be dead?"

"Of course not," Conan said. He would be very surprised ever to see another of them alive, but there was no point in terrifying the wench more than she already was. Better to find work to occupy her mind. "See to her," he told Tamira. "She never stopped crying for a hundred paces together all the way back here."

"And no wonder," Tamira replied hotly, "with no better care than you've taken of her." She bundled the unresisting noblewoman off to her tent, leaving Conan standing open-mouthed.

He would never understand women, he decided. Never. Then he became aware of the remaining hunters gathered around him, looking at him worriedly. Looking to him for commands, he realized with some surprise. Firmly he put all thoughts of women from his mind.

"At dawn," he told them, "we leave for Shadizar. But first we must survive until then. No man sleeps tonight, unless he wants to risk

128

waking with his throat cut. And no fires. Break open the supply packs."

With as much haste as Conan could manage, the hunters prepared themselves. All of the arrows were shared out, three quivers per man, and each man had an extra spear, as well as a waterbag and a pouch of dried meat. A coward or two might flee, with the means at hand, but he would not condemn the others to death if flight was required.

An assault from hillmen might come at any time, from any quarter save the cliff that backed Jondra's tent. Even if the first thrust were beaten off, they could not afford to be there when daylight came, pinned like bugs beneath a butcher bird's claws. They would attempt to retreat after an attack, or during, if it could not be driven back. And if they were on the point of being overwhelmed, every man would have to see to his own survival as best he could.

Worst of all would be an attack by the beast. As he moved through the darkening twilight from man to man, Conan left each with same final words. "Do not try to fight the beast. If it comes, run, and hope your gods feel kindly toward you."

Not far from Jondra's tent Conan settled into a flat-footed squat. Did the worst come, the others had only themselves to think of. He would need to be close to the women if he was to get them away.

A crunch of stone underfoot announced Tamira's approach, and he shifted his pair of spears to make a space for her.

"She's asleep," the slender woman sighed as she dropped to the ground beside him. "She wore herself out with tears. And who's to question it, after what she saw?"

"It happened by her command," Conan said quietly, "and for her pride. That Brythunian told her of the beast, and I told her what I had discovered of it."

"You are a hard man, Cimmerian. As hard as these mountains."

"I am a man," he told her simply.

For a time Tamira was silent. Finally she said, "Jondra says you are returning to Shadizar with her."

Conan gave a sour grunt. "It seems she talked a lot for a woman on the point of exhaustion."

"She plans to have apartments constructed for you in her palace."

"Ridiculous."

"She intends to dress you all in silk, with wristlets and armbands of gold to show off your muscles."

"What?" He thought he heard a giggle beside him in the deepening dark, and glared at her. "Enjoy your jokes, girl," he growled. "I, myself, do not find them funny."

"You were *her* first man, too, Conan. You cannot know what that means to a woman, but I do. She cares for you. Or perhaps it is for the image of you that she cares. She asked me if there were other men like you. She even compared you with Eldran, that Brythunian. She pretended not to remember his name, but she did."

Something in her voice struck him. "Mitra blind me if you don't pity her." His tone was incredulous.

"She knows less of men than I," the slender thief replied defensively. "It is a hard thing to be a woman in a world with men."

"It would be harder in a world without them," he said drily, and she fisted him in the ribs.

"I don't find *your* jokes," she began, but his hand closed over her mouth. Intently he listened for the sound he was sure he had heard before. There. The scrape of a hoof—an *unshod* hoof—on stone.

"Go to the tent," he whispered, giving her a push in the right direction. "Rouse her, and be ready to flee. Hurry!"

At that instant a cry broke the night. "By the will of the true gods!" And hordes of hillmen swarmed through the camp on shaggy mountain horses, curved tulwar blades gleaming in the pale moonlight as they rose and fell.

Conan hefted a spear and threw at the nearest target. A turbaned rider, transfixed, screamed and toppled from his galloping horse. Another hillman, calling loudly on his gods, closed with raised steel. There was no chance for the Cimmerian to throw his second spear. He dropped flat and swung it like a club at the legs of the charging animal. With a sharp crack the haft of the spear struck; horse and rider somersaulted. Before the hillman could rise, Conan put a forearm's length of spear through his chest.

All about the Cimmerian steel clanged against steel. Men shouted battle cries, shouted death rattles. In that deadly, bloody tempest an ingrained barbarian sense gave Conan warning. Pulling the spear free, he whirled in time to block a slashing tulwar. Deftly he rotated his spear point against the curved blade, thrust over it into his bearded attacker's throat. Dying, the hillman clutched the weapon that killed him with both hands. His horse ran out from under him, and as he fell he wrenched the spear from Conan's grip.

"Conan!" Tamira's shriek cut through the din to the Cimmerian's ears. "Conan!"

Desperately the Cimmerian's eyes sought for the slender woman . . . and found her, lifted to a hillman's saddle by a fist in her hair. Grinning broadly through his beard, the tribesman tauntingly lowered his blade toward her throat. With one hand she frantically attempted to fend off the razor edge, while the other clutched at his robes.

Conan's broadsword came into his hand. Two bounds took him to Tamira's side; the hillman's head went back, and his mouth fell open as the Cimmerian's steel slid smoothly between his ribs. Lifeless fingers loosened in Tamira's hair, and Conan caught her as she fell. Trembling arms snaked round his neck; she sobbed limply against his chest.

With a corpse on its back the horse galloped on, and in the space of a breath Conan had taken in the situation in the camp. The fight went badly. Had gone badly, for there was little of it left. Few of the turbaned warriors remained in the camp, and they were occupied with mutilating the dead. Murderous cries from the dark told of hillmen spreading in pursuit of hunters. Jondra's tent was in flames.

A chill went through the big Cimmerian. As he watched, the last of the tent collapsed, sending a shower of sparks into the night. If Jondra was in that, there was no hope for her. He hoped that she had gotten out, but he could not help her now. He had a woman to care for, and no time to spare for another.

Bending to catch Tamira behind the knees, he heaved her onto his shoulder like a sack. A half-formed protest came through her weeping, but the flow of tears did not slow. None of the tribesmen slashing at corpses noticed the muscular youth or his well-curved burden as he faded into the night.

Like a spirit Conan moved from shadow to shadow. Darkness alone, however, was no shield, he knew. From the clouded velvet sky a nacreous moon shed little light, but enough to make movement plain to a discerning eye, and Tamira's short, white robe made matters no better. The night-clad rocks were filled with the clatter of galloping hooves on stone, the shouts of hunting hillmen. They hunted, and, given time, they would find.

The Cimmerian kept moving, always away from the noise of the hillmen, and his eyes searched for a hiding place. A line of deeper blackness within the dark caught his gaze. He made his way to it and found a horizontal fracture in the face of a cliff. It was wide enough to hold Tamira, deep enough for her to remain hidden from all but someone sticking an arm into it.

Lowering the girl from his shoulder, he thrust her into the crack. "Stay quiet," he told her in low tones, "and do not move. I'll be back as quickly as I can. Listen to me, woman!"

"He . . . he was going to kill me," she sobbed. "He was l-laughing." She clutched at him, but he gently removed her hands from his shoulders.

"'Tis over, now. You are safe, Tamira."

"Don't leave me."

"I must find Jondra. Remain here till I return, and I will get the three of us out of these mountains." He had thought his voice full of confidence—certainly more confidence than he felt, at the moment—but she drew back from him into the crack in the cliff.

"Go then," she said sullenly. He could not see her, but her tears seemed to dry up suddenly. "Well? Go, if you want to."

He hesitated, but Jondra was still to be found, and whether alive or dead he did not know. Tamira would be safe here until he could return. "I will come back quickly," he said, and slipped away into the night.

Tamira peered from the crevice, but though her night vision was like that of a cat, she could see nothing. Conan had disappeared. She settled back sulkily.

She had nearly been killed, had been taunted with her own death, and he went after *her* when it should have been clear even to a blind man that she needed the comfort of his arms. But then, were not all men blind? It was not fair that he could affect her so much, while he cared so little. Once she had been able to think calmly and logically about any man. Once—it seemed a hundred years ago—before she allowed the young Cimmerian giant to . . . Even alone in the dark she blushed at the thought.

She would not think of him any more, she decided. Drawing herself to the front of the crack, she tried once more to pierce the darkness. It was futile, like attempting to peer through a raven's wing. A chill wind whined through the mountains, and she pulled her knees up, huddling, painfully aware of how little warmth was to be had from her short tunic.

Where *had* he gone? To look for Jondra, he claimed, but how did he intend to find her in the night? Was the noblewoman even alive? The tent had been aflame, Tamira remembered. Nothing could have survived in that. Except . . . the iron chests containing Jondra's jewels.

Tamira's eyes gleamed with delight, and she bit her lip to suppress a giggle. "Let him search for Jondra," she whispered. "He'll return to find me gone. Gone from the mountains, and the rubies with me."

With the suppleness of a cat she rolled from the crevice, came to her feet in the night. The cold breeze ruffled her white tunic about her thighs. For an instant she considered the problem of that garment's paleness.

"Well, I cannot go naked," she said finally, then clamped her teeth shut. She could not afford to make a sound, now.

Silently she glided into the dark, moving with all the stealthy skill she possessed. No matter what was said in Shadizar, in the taverns of the Desert, concerning Conan, she *was* the best thief in the city.

A sound halted her, a grating as of boots on rock, and she wished she had her daggers. Whoever it was, she thought contemptuously, he was clumsy. Noiselessly she moved away from he-who-stepped-on-rocks . . . and was buried beneath a rush of smelly robes and unwashed flesh.

She kicked at the cursing men who swarmed over her, struck at them until her wrists were caught in a grip like a vise. Hands fumbled at her body. She saw a bearded face, merciless and hard, and a curved dagger raised high. A scream choked in her throat. So many men to kill one woman. It was unfair, she thought dully. Her tunic was grasped at the neck and ripped open to the waist.

"See!" a voice said hoarsely. "It is as I said. A woman, and young."

The hard face did not change. "A lowland woman! A vessel of lust and corruption!"

"Even so," a third man said, "remember the Imalla's commands. And remember Walid's fate before you think to disobey." The hard-faced man blinked at that, and frowned.

"Take me to the Imalla," Tamira gasped. She knew that Imallas were holy men among the hill tribes. Surely a holy man would protect her.

The hard face split in an evil grin. "Let it be as the wench wishes. Mayhap she will come to regret not choosing my blade." And he began to laugh.

XVIII

I n the canescent pre-dawn light Conan flattened himself on a narrow granite ledge as a file of hillmen rode by on a narrow path below, between steep walls. Their numbers had thinned as the night waned, but there were still too many of the bearded men to suit him. As the last of the horsemen disappeared up the twisting track, the big Cimmerian scrambled from fingerhold to fingerhold, down from the ledge, and set off at a trot in the opposite direction, toward the campsite that had become a bloody shambles so short a time before, toward Tamira's hiding place.

Two hundred paces down the trail he passed the remains of one of the Zamoran hunters. He could not tell which. The headless body, covered with blackened blood and bright green flies, lay with limbs twisted at unnatural angles. Conan gave the corpse not a glance as he went by. He had found too many others during the night, some worse than this, and at each one he had only been grateful it was not Jondra. Now worry for Tamira filled his mind. He was sure she was safe—even in daylight that crack would not be easily noticed—but she had been alone for the entire night, a night filled with hillmen and the memories of murder.

Along the slope of a mountain he trotted, eyes ever watchful. Dropping to his belly, he crawled to the top of a rough stone outcropping. Below him lay the camp, blackened ground and ash where Jondra's tent had stood against the cliff. Half a score bodies, many in more than one piece, were scattered among the stunted trees—Zamoran bodies only, for the hillmen had carried their own dead away. There was no sound but the somber droning of flies.

Conan took a deep breath and went over the ridgetop, half sliding down the other side on loose rocks and shale. The dead he let lie, for he had no time to waste on burials or funeral rites. Instead he concentrated on what might be of use to the living. A spear, whole and overlooked by the hillmen. A waterbag unslashed and bulging damply. A pouch of dried meat.

The tribesmen had been thorough in their looting, however, and there was little to find. Broken spear-points, the cook's pots, even the rope used for picketing horses had been taken, and the ashes of Jondra's tent had been sifted for anything not consumed by the flames. He did find his black Khauranian cloak, tucked where he had left it beneath the edge of a boulder. He added it to the pitiful pile.

"So you are a thief, a looter!"

At the hoarse words Conan grabbed up the spear and whirled. Arvaneus shuffled toward him, black eyes glittering, knuckles white on his spear haft. The huntsman's head was bare; dust covered him, and his baggy white breeches were torn.

"It is good to see another of Jondra's party alive," Conan said. "All thought you were slain by the beast."

The huntsman's eyes slid off to the side, skipped from body to body. "The beast," he whispered. "Mortal men could not face it. Any fool could see that. That cry . . ." He shivered. "They should have fled," he went on plaintively. "That was the only thing to do. To try to fight it, to stay even a moment . . ." His gaze fell on the pile Conan had made, and he tilted his head to look sidelong at the big Cimmerian. "So you are a thief, stealing from the Lady Jondra."

Hair stirred on the back of Conan's neck. Madness was not something he had encountered frequently, especially in one he had known when sane. "These supplies may save Jondra's life," he said, "when I find her. She is lost, Arvaneus. I must find her quickly if she is to get out of these mountains alive."

"So pretty," Arvaneus said softly, "with her long legs, and those round breasts meant to pillow a man's head. So pretty, my Lady Jondra."

"I am going now," Conan said, stretching out one hand to pick up his cloak. He was careful not to take his eyes from Arvaneus, for the other man still gripped his spear as if ready to use it.

"I watched her," the swarthy huntsman went on. The mad light in his eyes deepened. "Watched her run from the camp. Watched her hide from the hillmen. She did not see me. No. But I will go to her, and she will be grateful. She will know me for the man I am, not just as her chief huntsman."

Conan froze when he realized what Arvaneus was saying. The Cimmerian let out a long breath, and chose his words carefully. "Let us go to Jondra together. We can take her back to Shadizar, Arvaneus. She will be very grateful to you."

"You lie!" The huntsman's face twisted as if he was on the point of tears; his hands flexed on his spear haft. "You want her for yourself! You are not good enough to lick her sandals!"

"Arvaneus, I—"

Conan cut his words short as the huntsman thrust at him. Whipping his cloak up, the Cimmerian entangled the other man's spearpoint, but Arvaneus ripped his weapon free, and Conan was forced to leap back as gleaming steel lanced toward him once more. Warily, the two men circled, weapons at the ready.

"Arvaneus," Conan said, "there is no need for this." He did not want to kill the man. He needed to know where Jondra was.

"There is need for you to die," the hawk-faced man panted. Their spearpoints clattered as he felt for weakness and Conan deflected his probes.

"We have enemies enough around us," Conan told him. "We should not do their killing for them."

"Die!" Arvaneus screamed, rushing forward, spear outthrust.

Conan parried the thrust, but the huntsman did not draw back. He came on, straight onto the Cimmerian's spearpoint. Arvaneus' weapon dropped to the ground, but he took yet another step forward, clawed hands reached for Conan, impaling himself further. Surprise flooded his face; jerkily he looked down at the thick wooden shaft standing out from his chest.

The big Cimmerian caught Arvaneus as he collapsed, eased him to the stony ground. "Where is she?" Conan demanded. "Erlik blast you, where is Jondra?"

Laughter wracked the huntsman. "Die, barbar," he rasped. "Die." Blood welled up in his mouth, and he sagged, eyes glazing.

With a muttered curse Conan got to his feet. At least she was alive, he thought. If it was not all a fantasy constructed by a mad mind. Gathering up his supplies, he set out for Tamira's hiding place.

From the shaded shelter of huge stone slabs, split from the cliff behind her by an earthquake centuries gone, Jondra stared longingly at the tiny pool of water far below and licked her lips. Had she known it was there while dark still covered the Kezankians, she would not have thought twice before assuaging her thirst. But now . . . She peered to the east, to a sun still half-hidden by the jagged peaks. It was full enough light to expose her clearly to the eyes of any watchers.

And expose, the voluptuous noblewoman thought wryly, was exactly the right word. Save for the dust of flight on her legs, she was quite naked.

"Not the proper dress for a noble Zamoran woman while hunting," she whispered to herself. But then, Zamoran nobles were seldom roused from their slumber by murderous hillmen or tents burning around them. Nor did they take part in the hunt as the prey.

She turned once more to study the pool, and licked lips that were dry again in moments. To reach it she would have to traverse a steep, rocky slope with not so much as a blade of grass for cover. At the bottom of the slope was a drop; she could not be sure how far from this angle, but it did not look enough to cause difficulty. The pool itself beckoned her enticingly. A patch of water she could doubtless wade in three strides without sinking to her knees, with three stunted trees on its edge, and at that moment it seemed more inviting than her palace gardens.

"I will not remain here until my tongue swells," she announced to the air. As if the sound of her own voice had spurred her to action, she crawled from the shelter of the stone slabs and started down the slope.

At first she moved carefully, picking her way over the loose stone. With every step, however, she became more aware of her nudity, of the way her breasts swayed with every movement, of how her skin flashed palely in the sunlight. First night and then the stone slabs had provided some illusion of being less naked. She had often lain naked in her garden, luxuriating in the warmth of the sun, but here sunlight stripped the illusion as bare as she. Here she could not know who watched her. Reason told her if there was a watcher, she had greater problems than nudity, but reason prevailed nothing against her feelings. Curling one arm over her breasts helped little, and she found herself crouching more and more, hurrying faster, taking less care of where she put her feet.

Abruptly the stones beneath her turned, and she was on her back, sliding amid a cloud of dust. Desperately she clawed for a hold, but each stone she grasped merely set others sliding. Just as she was ready to moan that matters could not get worse, she found herself falling. Only for long enough to be aware of the fall did she drop, then a jolt pulled her up short. The slide of rocks and dirt she had begun did not cease, however. A torrent of rubble showered down on her. Covering her face with her arms, spiting to clear dust from her mouth, she reflected that she would be a mass of bruises from shoulders to ankles after this day.

The rain of dirt and stones slowed and halted, and Jondra examined her position with a sinking feeling. The first shock was that she hung upside down, against the face of the drop she had been sure would present no difficulty. A twisted tree stump no thicker than her wrist held her ankle firmly in the V it formed with the face of the drop. Beneath her a pile of rubble from her fall reached just high enough for her to touch the stones with her fingertips.

Deliberately she closed her eyes and took three deep breaths to calm herself. There had to be a way out. She always found a way to get what she wanted, and she did *not* want to die hanging like a side of mutton. She would, she decided, just have to get hold of the stump and lift her ankle free.

At her first attempt to bend double a jolt of pain shot from her ankle, and she fell back gasping. The ankle was not broken, she decided. She would not accept that it was. Steeling herself against the pain, she tried again. Her fingers brushed the stump. Once more, she thought.

A rustle drew her eyes toward the pool, and terror chilled her blood. A bearded hillman stood there in filthy yellow tunic and stained, baggy trousers. He licked his lips slowly, and his staring black eyes burned with lust. He started toward her, already loosening his garments. Suddenly there was a noise like a sharp slap, and the hillman stopped, sank to his knees. Jondra blinked, then saw the arrow standing out from his neck.

Frantically she searched for the shaft's source. A movement on a mountain caught her eye, a moment's view of something that could have been a bow. Three hundred paces, the archer in her measured calmly, while the rest of her nearly wept for relief. Whichever of her hunters it was, she thought, she would gift him with as much gold as he could carry.

But she was not about to let anyone, least of all a man in her service, find her in such a helpless position. Redoubling her efforts, she split several splinters of wood from the stump and chipped her fingernails, but got no closer to freeing herself.

Suddenly she gasped in renewed horror at the sight of the man who appeared walking slowly toward her. This was no hillman, this tall form with fur leggings and clean-shaven face and gray eyes. She knew that face and the name that went with it, though she would have given much to deny it. Eldran. Vainly she tried to protect her modesty with her hands.

"You!" she spat. "Go away, and leave me alone!"

He continued his slow advance toward her, one hand resting lightly on the hilt of his broadsword, his fur-lined cloak slung back from his shoulders. No bow or quiver was in evidence. His eyes were fixed on her, and his face was grim.

"Stop staring at me!" Jondra demanded. "Go away, I tell you. I neither need nor want your help."

She flinched as three hillmen burst silently from the rocks behind the Brythunian, rushing at him with raised tulwars. Her mouth opened to scream . . . and Eldran whirled, the broadsword with its clawed quillons seeming to flow into his hand. In movements almost too fast for her to follow the four danced of death. Blood wetted steel. A bearded head rolled in the dust. And then all three hillmen were down, and Eldran was calmly wiping his blade on the cloak of one.

Sheathing the steel, he stepped closer to her. "Perhaps you do not want my help," he said quietly, "but you do need it."

Jondra realized her mouth was still open and snapped it shut. Then she decided silence would not do, but before she could speak the big Brythunian had stepped onto the pile of rubble, taken hold of her calves and lifted her clear of the stump that had held her. One arm went behind her knees, and she was swung up into his arms. He cradled her there as easily as did Conan, she thought. He was as tall as the Cimmerian, too, though not so broad across the shoulders. For the first time since the attack she felt safe. Color abruptly flooded her face as the nature of her thoughts became clear to her.

"Put me down," she told him. "I said, put me down!"

Silent, he carried her to the pool and lowered her gently by its edge. "You are down," he said. She winced as he felt her ankle. "A bad bruise, but it should heal in a few days."

There was dried blood on his forehead, she saw. "How came you by that? Have you met other hillmen?"

"I must get my bow," he said curtly, and stalked away.

As well if he did not return, she thought angrily, but the thought brought a twinge of anxiety. Suppose he did *not* return. Suppose he decided to abandon her, naked and alone in this wilderness. When he reappeared she gave a small sigh of relief, and then was angry with herself for that.

He set his bow and a hide quiver of arrows down, then turned to her with a bleak face. "We met other hillmen, yes. Two score men followed me into these accursed mountains, and I failed to keep them safe until we accomplished our purpose. Hillmen, hundreds of them, found our camp. I do not know if any of my companions still live." He sighed heavily. "I surmise the same fate befell you. I wish I could promise to see you to safety, but there is a task I have yet to accomplish, and it must take precedence even over you. I will do what I can for you, though. I must regret that I cannot take days to sit here and just look at you."

It came to her that he *was* looking at her, looking as if he intended to commit what he saw to memory. It also came to her that she was naked. Quickly she scrambled to her knees, crouching with her arms over her breasts. "A civilized man would turn his back," she snapped.

"Then the men you call civilized do not appreciate beauty in a woman."

"Give me your cloak," she commanded. "I am no tavern wench to be stared at. Give it to me, I say!"

Eldran shook his head. "Alone in the heart of the Kezankians, naked as a slave girl on the auction block, and still you demand and give orders. Take garments from the hillmen, if you wish, but do so quickly, for we must leave this place. There are others of their sort about. If you do not wish me to watch, I will not." Taking up his bow again, he nocked an arrow, and his eyes scanned the mountain slopes. "Hurry, girl."

Face flushed with anger and some other emotion she did not quite understand, Jondra refused even to look at the corpses. "Their garments are filthy and bloodstained," she said, biting off each word. "You must provide me decent garb. Such as your cloak!"

"Wiccana has cursed me," the Brythunian said as if she had not spoken, "that she made your eyes touch my soul. There are many women in my native land, but I must come to here, and see you. I look into your eyes, and I feel your eyes touch me, and there are no other women. It is you I want to bear my children. A petulant, pampered woman whose very blood is arrogance. Why should I so want a woman such as you? Yet my heart soars at the sight of you."

Jondra's mouth worked in soundless fury. Petulant! Bear his children! And he went on, saying unbearable things, things she did not want to hear. Her hand found a fist-sized rock by the water, and, with no more thought than white-hot rage, she hurled it. She gave a shocked gasp when Eldran crumpled bonelessly A thin line of blood trickled down his temple.

"Eldran?" she whispered.

Frantically she crawled to his unmoving form, held a hand before his mouth. He still breathed. Relief filled her, stronger than she would have believed possible. She hesitated over touching the bloody gash where the stone had struck, then instead gently smoothed back his curling brown hair.

Suddenly her hand jerked back as if burned. What was she doing? She had to be gone before he regained consciousness. At best he would start his ranting again, about her bearing his children and the like. At worst . . . She remembered the ease with which he had carried her—and firmly pushed away the memory of feeling protected while he did so. He was strong. Strong enough to force his will with her. She must go quickly.

The first of her needs was water, and she dropped down beside the pool to drink until she felt she would burst at one more swallow. The cool water invigorated her. Limping, she walked back to Eldran. He must be the source of what she needed. Truly she could not bring herself to touch the hillmen's garments, but things of his were another matter.

His bow she snatched up with an excited murmur, and raised it to test the pull. In astonishment she stared from the bow to the man on the ground. She had never met the man who could pull a stronger bow than she, but this bow she could not draw a handspan. Reluctantly she laid it on the ground beside him.

The sword she did not touch, for she had no skill with the weapon. Instead she slipped the tall Brythunian's dagger from his belt. Once she made slits in his fur-lined cape for her head and arms, it made a passable tunic, when belted with one of the rawhide thongs that had tied his fur leggings. The leggings themselves she cut to wrap around her feet, then tied with pieces of the other thong.

And then she was ready to go. For long moments she knelt by Eldran's side, hesitating. Some men never awoke from head injuries. What if he needed care?

"Jondra?" he murmured. Though his eyes remained closed, his hands reached out as if searching for her. She started back from it as from a snake. He must care for himself, she decided.

At the start she kept her pace slow, for the mountainous terrain was rough at best. Her ankle would give no trouble if she did not overtax it, she thought. But after a time her thoughts drifted to Eldran, too. He had been near to waking when she left. He would be dazed, at first, but not too dazed to know she was gone, nor to remember what she had done. He was a hunter. Her hunters could track. There was no reason to suppose the Brythunian could not. And Eldran had two good legs on which to walk.

Almost without realizing it she began to press for speed. The ache in her ankle grew, but she ignored it. Eldran would be following her. She had to keep ahead of him. Her breath came in gulps. Her mouth was dry as if she had never drunk, and her throat as well. She was a hunter, too, she told herself. She knew how to watch for prey; she could also watch for a pursuer. Constantly she studied her backtrail, till she spent nearly as much time looking over her shoulder as looking ahead.

Rounding a thick, stone spire, she had taken three staggering, limping strides before she saw the halfscore hillmen, sitting their horses and staring at her in amazement.

"A gift from the old gods!" one of them shouted, and booted his horse forward.

Jondra was too tired to struggle as he tangled a hand in her hair and pulled her belly-down across his mount before his saddle pad. Weeping in exhausted despair, she sagged unresisting as the hillman flipped up the tail of Eldran's cloak and fondled her bare buttocks.

"He will save me," she sobbed softly into the shaggy fur beneath her face. "He will save me." And a part of her mind wondered why the countenance she conjured was that of the Brythunian.

XIX

Conan's teeth ground as he stared into the crevice where he had hidden Tamira. Staring, he knew, would do no good. She was not likely to appear from the mere force of his looking.

Forgetting the crack in the stone, he examined the ground and frowned. There was little that was enlightening. The ground was too stony to take footprints, but he had learned to track in the mountains of Cimmeria, and the ground in one set of mountains was not too unlike that in another. Here a rock was scraped. There another had its dark bottom turned up to the light. The story he found was perplexing. Tamira had left. That, and nothing more. He could find no sign that hillmen or anyone else had come to take her. She had simply gone. Nor had she waited long after his own departure to do so, for he could see remnants of the night's dew on some of the overturned stones.

"Fool wench," he growled. "Now I have two of you to find." And when he found the thief, he vowed, he would wear out a switch.

Carrying his spear at the trail, Conan set out at a lope, easily following the scattered sign. As he did he felt like cursing. It was clear where she had headed. The camp. The rubies. Perhaps she finally had them, for he remembered the iron chests had not been in the ashes of Jondra's tent.

Suddenly he stopped, frowning at the rocky ground. There had been a struggle here, among several people. He picked up a torn scrap of white cloth. It was a piece of a servant's tunic, like the one Tamira had been wearing. He crumpled it in his fist.

"Fool wench," he said again, but softly.

Warily, now, he went on, eyes searching as much for hillmen as for signs of passage. After a time he became aware that he was following three tracks. Two were of men on horseback, one the set he followed, one much fresher. Newest of all were the tracks of several men afoot. Hillmen did not travel far without their shaggy horses, and there were not enough of them to be soldiers. He could think of no other group at large in the mountains, for if any of the Zamoran hunters remained alive they were certainly seeking the lowlands as fast as they could.

Suspicions roused, he looked even more carefully for likely ambush sites. The Kezankians had a wealth of such places, which did not make his task easier. Sharp bends around precipitous slopes and narrow passages between sheer walls were common. Yet it was a small valley bordered by gentle slopes that first halted him.

From the end of a deep ravine that opened into the valley, he studied it. Motionless, he stood close against the rock wall. It was motion which drew the eye more than anything else. Stunted trees dotted the slopes, but in numbers too small to provide cover. From the valley floor to the peaks there were few boulders or depressions to hide attackers, and those lay halfway to the summit on both sides. Hillmen liked to be close for their ambushes, to allow their prey little time to react. Everything his eyes could see told him the valley was safe, but instinct prickled in the back of his skull. Instinct, which had saved him more than once, won out.

Swiftly he retreated down the ravine. At a place where the wall had collapsed in a fan of rock, nearly blocking the way, he climbed up and out. Patient as a hunting cat he moved from boulder to boulder, twisted tree to twisted tree, following every fold and dip in the land.

Finally he found himself on the slope above the valley. Below him, crouched behind a jagged boulder with bow in hand, was a man. Conan grunted softly in surprise. Though he lacked fur leggings, the embroidered tunic marked the ambusher as a Brythunian. In fact, Conan knew him for the leader of those who had come to Jondra's camp in the hills. Frowning, he eased silently down the incline. Just above the watcher he stopped, settled his cloak about his shoulders and sat with his spear leaning against his shoulder.

"Whom do you wait for, Eldran of Brythunia?" he asked conversationally.

The Brythunian did not start. Instead he looked calmly over shoulder. "You, Conan of Cimmeria," he said. "Though I will admit I did not know it was you who followed us."

"Not you," Conan said. "Hillmen. And you can tell the rest of your men to come out. Unless you think they really have need to watch my back."

Grinning, Eldran sat up. "So we both know what we are about." He waved his arm, and one by one seven men in fur-leggings and embroidered tunics appeared on the slope, trotting to join them. "Do you, too, seek to rescue Jondra, then, Cimmerian?"

Conan drew a long breath. "So she is in the hands of the hillmen. Yes, I seek her, though it was another woman, also a captive, I first set out to find. But you speak as if you also wish to rescue Jondra. This puzzles me, considering the warmth of your last meeting with her."

"We have met since, she and I," Eldran said ruefully, "and there was even less warmth on her part. Some time after, I found where she had fallen captive to hillmen." He fingered his rough gray woolen cloak, dirty and torn; it was a hillman's cloak, Conan saw, stained and dirty. "There are matters I must discuss sharply with that woman."

One of the other Brythunians, a bony man with a pointed nose, spat. "I still say forget the woman. We came to slay the beast of fire, and we must do it if we all die. We have no time for foreign women."

Eldran did not reply, though his face tightened. Another of them murmured, "Peace, Frydan," and the bony man subsided, albeit with an ill grace.

"So you hunt the beast as Jondra did," Conan said. "She learned better after twenty of her hunters died, torn apart or burned alive. Only she, myself and one other survived that enounter, and we barely. I would see the thing dead, too, Brythunian, but there are easier ways to kill yourself."

"The Zamoran wench finds the beast," Frydan muttered disgustedly, "while we find only tracks. Mayhap we do need her."

Again Eldran ignored him. "Jondra hunted for a trophy," he said. "We hunt to avenge dead kin, and to prevent more deaths. Your steel could not prevail against the beast of fire, Conan, nor any mortal-wrought metal. But this," he laid a hand on the hilt of his broadsword, "was forged by mages for that very purpose."

The big Cimmerian eyed the weapon with sudden interest. Objects of sorcery were not beyond his experience. Betimes he could feel the aura of their power in his hands. If this weapon was indeed as Eldran said, then his debt to Telades could yet be repaid. "I would heft the weapon that could slay that creature," he said, but the gray-eyed Brythunian shook his head.

"Once it leaves my possession, Cimmerian, it will journey, Wiccana alone knows how, back to the place where it was given me, and I shall never regain it in this life. Such is the way of its ensorcelment."

"I understand," Conan said. Perhaps it was as the Brythunian said, and perhaps not, but did Eldran fall, he vowed, he would see that wherever the blade journeyed, it came first to his hand. One way or another, if he lived, the debt to Telades would be paid. "But before the beast, the women. Agreed?"

"Agreed," Eldran replied. "As our trails have converged, perhaps we will find both women together. Haral continued after the hillmen who have Jondra, and he will mark the way so we may follow quickly."

Conan got to his feet. "Then let us tarry no longer if we would save them before they are harmed." Yet as they filed down the slope his heart was grim. Women captives did not receive kind treatment from hillmen. Let them only have courage, he thought. Let them only survive till he could find them.

For the twentieth time Tamira examined her bonds, and for the twentieth time knew the futility of such study. Leather cuffs about her wrists and ankles were attached to stout chains fastened in the ceiling and floor of the windowless, stone-walled chamber, holding her rigidly spread-eagled in mid-air. The slender thief's sweat-slick nudity glistened in the light from bronze lamps. The air was chill; the sweat came from fear, fear more of something half-sensed in the room than of her captivity.

Jondra hung suspended as she was, facing her, and Tamira exchanged glances with the noblewoman. The taller woman's body also gleamed, every curve of breast and hip and thigh highlighted. Tamira hoped she also shared the other woman's calmness of face, though it was slightly spoiled by Jondra's constant wetting of her lips.

"I am the Lady Jondra of the House Perashanid of Zamora," Jondra said, her voice quaking. "A generous ransom will be paid for my safe return, and that of my serving woman. But we must be clothed and well-treated. Did you hear me? I will give our weight in gold!"

The crimson-robed man who labored at their feet, drawing a strange pattern on the floor with powders poured from small clay bowls, did not glance up. He gave no sign at all that he had heard, as he had given no sign since they were brought to him. He murmured constantly as he drew, words that Tamira could barely hear, and could not understand at all.

Tamira tried not to listen, but the steady drone bored into her ears. She clenched her teeth to keep them from chattering. Basrakan Imalla, the men who had thrown her at his feet had called him. She would have wept for her belief that a holy man would protect her, but she feared that if she began she might never stop.

"I am the Lady Jondra of the House . . ." Jondra licked her lips nervously. Her head tossed as she attempted to jerk at her bonds; a quiver ran down the length of her, but no more. "I will give you twice our weight in gold." Her voice was fringed with panic, and the tone of panic grew with every word. "Three times! Four! Any amount you wish! Anything! But whatever you intend, do not do it! Do not! Oh, Mitra protect me, do not!"

The beautiful noble sobbed and struggled wildly, and her fear sparked Tamira's own to flame. The thief knew now what she sensed in the chamber, what she had not allowed herself to even think of. Sorcery. The very walls reeked of sorcery. And something else, now that she let herself feel it. A malevolent hatred of women. Sobs wracked her, and tears streamed from beneath eyelids squeezed shut as if she could hide behind them.

"You are vessels of iniquity!" The harsh voice cut through Tamira's weeping. Unwillingly she looked. Basrakan stood stroking his forked beard, and his black eyes glittered despite at them. "All women of the cities are unclean vessels of lust. The old gods themselves will prove it on your bodies. Then I will chastise you of your vileness, that you may go to the ancient gods of these mountains in purity."

Shuddering, Tamira tore her eyes from him, and found herself looking down at the design he had drawn, an elongated diamond with concave sides. A short, black candle on one of the points flickered beneath her, another beneath Jondra. The configuration of lines within the diamond pulled at her gaze, drew it hypnotically. Her thoughts fragmented, became a maze, and unrecognizable images came into her mind, images that brought terror. Shrieking in the depths of her mind she tried to flee, to find a refuge, but all was chaos and horror.

Suddenly the maze itself shattered. Gasping, she found that she could look away from the diamond. The stern-faced Imalla had seated himself cross-legged at one end of the unholy pattern. He struck a small gong of burnished brass that stood by his side, and she realized it had been that sound which had released her from the maze. Again the gong sounded, and he began a new chant. Once more the gong chimed. And again. Again.

She told herself that she would not listen, but her bones seemed to vibrate with his words, with the reverberations of the brass. The air within the chamber grew chill; it thickened and stirred. Its caress on her body was palpable, like the feathery stroking of soft hands that touched her everywhere at once. And the heat, rising.

In disbelief she stared down at the candle beneath her. The flame stood firm, untroubled by the breezes she felt stirring, yet it could not possibly be the source of the waves of heat that seemed to rise from it. But the heat came, from somewhere, licking through her limbs, making her belly roll and heave, changing. She tried to shake her head, tried to deny the desire that curled and coiled within her. Dimly she heard a groan of negation from Jondra. Vaguely she saw the noblewoman, head thrown back, hips jerking uncontrollably, and she knew that she writhed as well.

Her lips parted; a moan was wrenched from her. "Conan!" With the tattered shreds of reason left to her, she recognized an answering cry from Jondra. "Eldran!" It would not stop. Her blood boiled.

With a crash the doors of the chamber flew open. Tamira gasped as if plunged into icy water; all sensation of desire fled from her in an instant. Weeping replaced it, tears for the uncleanness that seemed to cover her.

Basrakan leaped to his feet. "Do you desire death, Jbeil?" he snarled. "Do you desire to join Sharmal?"

The gaunt man in the door bowed deeply. "Forgiveness, Basrakan Imalla," he said hastily, "but it is the Eyes of the Fire."

Basrakan pulled him erect by fistfuls of black robe. "Speak, fool! What of the Eyes?"

"Sharmal claims that a woman brings the Eyes into the mountains. And he describes her." Jbeil flung a hand, pointing to Jondra.

Through her tears Tamira met the noblewoman's eyes, and got a confused stare and a shake of the head in return.

Basrakan's blood-red robes swirled as he spun. Tamira would have flinched from his gaze if she could. Before it had been malign. Now she could read in them skin being flayed, flesh stripped from bone. Her skin. Her flesh.

"Two camps of outsiders were destroyed this night past." The Imalla's voice was quiet, like the first brush of a knife against a throat. "This woman came from one of them, Jbeil. Find every scrap that was taken from that camp. Find the Eyes of Fire. Find them, Jbeil."

Jbeil ran from the chamber as if his own throat had felt that blade's caress.

Basrakan's eyes, like ebon stones, were locked on Jondra, but Tamira could not break her own gaze from them. As she stared helplessly, she found herself praying to every god she knew that whatever Basrakan sought was brought to him. Quickly.

XX

From the scant shelter of a sparse clump of twisted trees above the hillman village, Conan frowned at a two-story stone structure in its center. Armed men swarmed in hundreds about the score of crude stone huts, but it was the slate-roofed building that held his eyes. Around him lay the Brythunians, and they, too, watched.

"I have never heard of a dwelling like that among hillmen," Eldran said quietly. "For the Kezankians, it is a palace."

"I have never heard of so many hillmen in one place," Frydan said nervously. His eyes were not on the village, but on the surrounding mountains. Half a score camps were visible from where they lay, one close enough for the breeze to bring the sour smell of cooking and the shouts of men searching through the low tents. They had seen more clusters of the low, earth-colored tents in reaching their present vantage. "How many are there, Haral?"

"A score of thousands, perhaps." The plump Brythunian's voice was a study in casualness. "Perhaps more. Enough to go around, in any case." Frydan stared at him, then closed his eyes wearily.

Through a gap between mountains Conan caught sight of crude stone columns. "What is that?" he asked, pointing.

Haral shook his head. "I have done little looking about, Cimmerian. I saw the woman, Jondra, taken into that building below, and since I have watched, and waited for Eldran."

"Rescuing her will not be easy," Conan sighed. "Are you sure you did not see another woman captive?" Once more Haral shook his head, and the Cimmerian resumed his study of what lay below.

"It would take an army to go down there," Frydan protested. "Eldran, we did not come to die attempting to rescue a Zamoran wench. We seek the beast of fire, or do you forget? Let us be about it." Some of the other Brythunians murmured agreement.

148

"I will have her out of there," Eldran replied quietly, "or die in the trying."

An awkward silence hung over them for a moment, then Haral abruptly said, "There is an army in these mountains."

Frydan's mouth twisted sarcastically. "The Zamorans? I am sure they would come to help us if we only asked."

"Perhaps they would," Conan said with a smile, "if they were asked properly." The others looked at him doubtfully, obviously wondering if he made a joke, so he went on. "Their general is one Tenerses, I understand, a lover of glory and easy victories. He has been sent into the mountains to put down a gathering of the hill tribes. Well, here it is."

Even Haral was skeptical. "Unless this Tenerses is a fool, Cimmerian, he'll not attack here. Why, he'd be outnumbered four to one at the very least."

"That is true," Conan agreed. "But if he thought there were but a thousand or so hillmen, and they on the point of leaving before he could gain his victory . . ." He grinned at the others, and slowly, as the idea caught hold, they grinned back. All save Frydan.

"The tribesmen would all rush to meet his attack," Eldran said, "giving us as good as a clear path to Jondra's prison. Perhaps your woman—Tamira?—is there as well. Both sets of tracks came to this village."

Conan's smile faded. He had stopped counting hillman camps when he reached twenty, but Tamira could be in any one of ten thousand dingy tents. He could do nothing save rescue Jondra and hope to find the slender thief after. It was a faint hope at the moment, but he had no more. "Who will go to lure Tenerses?" he said grimly.

"Fyrdan has a silver tongue," Eldran said, "when he wishes to use it so."

"We should be about our charge. It is what we came for," the bony man said stiffly.

Eldran put a hand on his shoulder. "I cannot leave this woman," he said quietly.

Frydan lay still for a moment, then sighed and sat up. "If I can steal one of the sheep these hill scum call a horse, I will reach the Zamorans in half a turn of the glass. A moment to snare this general with my tale and get his block-footed soldiers marching." He squinted at the sun, approaching its zenith. "The earliest I could get them here is mid-afternoon, Eldran. With luck."

"Wiccana will give you her luck, and guide your words," Eldran said.

Conan turned from the leavetaking among the Brythunians to resume his study of the stone building. "I will get you out," he vowed under his breath. "Both of you."

* * *

Pain had long since come and gone in Tamira's shoulders, wracked by her suspension. Even the numbness that replaced pain had faded into the background, leaving only fear. She did not have to look at Jondra to know the noblewoman's eyes were directed, as were hers, at Basrakan, the man who held their fate on the tip of his tongue. She could as soon have grown wings as taken her eyes from his dark presence.

The Imalla sat, now, on a low stool. Idly he stroked his forked beard and watched the two bound women with eyes as black as bottomless pits. For the first turn of the glass he had stalked the room, muttering dire threats and imprecations at those who moved slowly to obey him, to obey the will of the true gods, muttering about the Eyes of Fire. Twice so long he had sat quietly, and Tamira wished he would pace again, rant, anything but look at her. His eyes no longer glittered; they seemed devoid of life or even the barest shreds of humanity. In their depths she read tortures that did not even have names. That which called itself Tamira cowered in the furthest recesses of her mind in a vain attempt to escape that diabolic ebon gaze, but she could not look away.

At the doors came a scratching. It was like the slash of a knife in the dead silence. Tamira shuddered; Jondra whimpered and began to sob softly.

Basrakan's scarlet robes rippled as he rose fluidly. His voice was filled with preternatural calmness. "Bring the Eyes to me."

One door opened a crack, and Jbeil entered diffidently. "I have not your knowledge, Basrakan Imalla," the gaunt man said as if he dared not breathe, "but these fit the description my poor ears heard." The gems he extended in his hands gleamed in the lamp light.

Tamira's eyes widened. The black-robed man held Jondra's necklace and tiara.

Basrakan put out a hand; the jewelry was laid in his palm. From beneath his blood-red robes he produced a dagger. Almost delicately he picked at the settings around the two great rubies. Gold, sapphires and black opals he threw aside like trash. Slowly his hands rose before his face, each cupping one sanguine gem.

"They are mine at last," he said as if to himself. "All power is mine." His head swiveled—no other muscle moved—to regard the two naked women suspended in chains. "Before this sun sets the doubters will have their proof. Confine these women, Jbeil. This day they will be given to the old gods."

Tamira shivered, and for an instant she teetered on the brink of unconsciousness. Given to the old gods. Sacrificed—it could mean no other. She wanted to cry out, to plead, but her tongue clove to the roof of her mouth. Wildly she stared at the swarthy, turbaned men who appeared to take her from her bonds. Her limbs would not work; she could not stand unaided. As she was carried from the room, her eyes sought desperately for Basrakan, the man who had the power of life and death here, the man who could, who must change his edict. The stern-faced Imalla stood before a table on which rested the rubies, his long fingers busy among vials and flasks.

The door closed, shutting off Tamira's view, and a wordless wail of despair rose in her throat. She tried to find moisture in her mouth so that she might beg the cold-eyed men who bore her unheeding of her nudity. To them she might as well not be a woman. Sacrificial meat, she shrieked in her mind.

Inexorably, she was carried on, down winding stone steps into musty corridors. A thick iron-bound door opened, and she was thrown to land heavily on hard-packed earth. With a hollow boom the door slammed.

Escape, she thought. She was a thief, a skilled thief, used to getting into places designed to keep her out. Surely she could get out of one meant to keep her in. Awkwardly, for the stiffness of her arms and legs, she pushed up to her knees and surveyed her prison. The dirt floor, rough stone walls, the obdurate door. There was nothing else. Dim light filtered down from two narrow slits near the ceiling, twice the height of a tall man above her head. Her momentary burst of hope faded away.

A whimper reminded her that she was not alone. Jondra lay huddled on the dirt, her head in her arms. "He will never find me," the noblewoman wept bitterly.

"He will find us," Tamira said stoutly, "and save us." To her shock she realized that, though all her other hopes were gone, one still remained. She had never asked favor or aid from any man, but she knew with unshakeable certainty that Conan would find her. She clung to an image of him breaking down the heavy, iron-bound door and bearing her away, clutched at it the way a drowning man would clutch a raft.

Jondra did not stop her slow, inconsolable sobbing. "He does not know where I am. I hit him with a rock, and . . . I do not want to die."

Tamira crawled to the taller woman and shook her by a shoulder. "If you give up, then you are dead already. Do you think I did not know terror to my soul in that chamber above?" She made a disgusted sound deep in her throat. "I've seen virgin girls on the slave block with more courage than you. All of that vaunted pride was camouflage for a sniveling worm ready to crawl on her belly."

Jondra glared up at her with some spark of her old spirit, but there was still a plaintive note in her voice. "I do not want to die."

"Nor do I," Tamira replied, and abruptly the two women were clinging to each other, trembling with their fear yet drawing strength each from the other. "You must say it," Tamira whispered fiercely. "Say it, and believe it. *He will save us.*"

"He will save us," Jondra said hoarsely.

"*He will save us.*"

"He will save us."

Basrakan intoned the last word, and his eyes opened wide with awe at the rush of strength through his veins. He felt as if a single bound would take him the length of the room. He drew a deep breath and thought he could detect each separate odor in the room, sharp and distinct. So this was what it was to be bonded with the drake.

On the table the glow faded from the rubies, from the lines of power drawn there in virgins' blood and powdered bone and substances too dreadful for mortal men to speak their names. But the glow that permeated Basrakan's very marrow did not fade. Triumph painted his face.

"We are one," he announced to the chamber, to the dangling chains where the women had hung. "Our fates are one. It *will* obey my summons now."

Tamira started as the door opened, crashing back against the stone wall. She felt Jondra tense as Basrakan appeared in the opening.

"It is time," the Imalla said.

"He will save us," Tamira whispered, and Jondra echoed, "He will save us."

"They are stirring," Eldran said.

Conan nodded, but did not take his eyes from the two-story stone structure below. From all the camps hillmen were moving, thick lines of them filing toward the stone columns that peeked through the gap between mountains. In the village five score turbaned men stood before the stone building. A red-robed man with a forked beard and multi-hued turban stepped out, and a muffled roar rose from the waiting hillmen, the words of it lost with the distance.

The Cimmerian stiffened as Jondra appeared, naked, arms bound behind her, a guard to either side with drawn tulwar. And behind her came Tamira, tied and bare as well.

"They are together," Eldran said excitedly. "And unharmed, so far as I can see. Alive, at least, praise Wiccana."

"So far," Conan said.

The skin between the Cimmerian's shoulderblades prickled. There was much about the scene below that did not please him, much beside the way the women were being treated. Where were they being taken, and why? Why?

The hundred hillmen formed a rough, hollow circle about the red-robed man and the two women. The procession joined the streams flowing toward the distant columns.

"This feels ill," Conan said. Unconsciously he eased his ancient broadsword in its worn shagreen sheath. "I do not think we can wait longer."

"Just a little longer," Haral pleaded. "Fyrdan will bring the soldiers soon. He will not fail."

"Not soon enough, it seems," Conan said. He got to his feet and dusted his hands together. "I think I will take a stroll among the hillmen."

With a grin, Eldran straightened. "I feel the need of stretching my legs as well, Cimmerian."

"You young fools!" Haral spluttered. "You'll get your heads split. You'll . . . you'll . . ." With a growl he stood up beside them. "We'll need turbans, if we're to pass for hillmen long enough to keep our heads." The others were on their feet now, too.

"There is a camp just down the mountain," Conan said, "and none in it save women and children, that I can see."

"Then let us be about our walk," Eldran said.

"These old bones aren't up to this any more," Haral complained.

The small file of men started down the mountain.

". . . For the time of our glory has come," Basrakan cried to the throngs of turbaned men jammed shoulder to shoulder on the mountainsides about the amphitheater. Their answering roar washed over him. "The time of the old gods' triumph is upon us!" he called. "The sign of the true gods is with us!"

He spread his arms, and the flow of power through his bones made him think he might fly. Loudly he began to chant, the words echoing from the slopes. Never had so many seen the rite, he thought as the invocation rang out. After this day there would be no doubters.

His dark eyes flickered to the two naked women dangling from their wrists against the iron posts in the center of the circle of crude stone pillars. It was fitting, he thought, that those who brought him the Eyes of Fire should be the sacrifice now, when the new power that was in him was made manifest to his people. They struggled in the bonds, and one of them cried a name, but he did not hear. The glory of the old gods filled him.

The last syllable hung in the air, and vibration in the stone beneath his feet told Basrakan of the coming. He drew breath to announce the arrival of the sign of the true gods' favor.

From the masses on the slopes shouts and cries drifted, becoming louder. Basrakan's face became like granite. He would have those who dared disturb this moment flayed alive over a slow fire. He would . . . There were men within the circle! Abruptly the words penetrated his mind.

"Soldiers!" was the cry. "We are attacked!"

Walking hunched to disguise his height, with his cloak drawn tightly around him, Conan pushed through the pack of hillmen quickly, giving no man more than an instant to see his face. Grumbles and curses followed him. A roughly wound turban topped his black mane, and his face was smeared with soot and grease from a cooking pot, but he was grateful that men saw what they thought they should see, no matter what their eyes told them. The wide circle of crude stone columns was only a few paces away. Conan kept his head down, but his eyes were locked on the two women. A few moments more, he thought.

A murmur ran through the crowd, growing louder. Far down the mountain someone shouted, and other voices took up the cry. It had been more than the big Cimmerian expected to go undetected so long. Best to move before the alarm became general. Grasping his sword hilt firmly, Conan tore off the turban and leaped for the circle of columns.

As he passed between two of the roughly hewn pillars he realized what words were being shouted. "Soldiers! We are attacked! Soldiers!" Over and over from a thousand throats. Fyrdan, he thought, laughing. They might live through this yet.

Then he was running across the uneven granite blocks, blade bared. The red-robed man, forked beard shaking with fury, shouted at him from atop a tunnel built of stone that seemed to reach back into the mountain, but Conan did not hear. Straight to the blackened iron posts he ran. Tears sprang into Tamira's eyes when she saw him.

"I knew you would come," she laughed and cried at the same time. "I knew you would come."

Swiftly Conan sawed apart the leather cords on her wrists. As she dropped, he caught her with an arm around her slim waist, and she tried to twine her arms about his neck.

"Not now, woman," he growled. In a trice he had her slender nudity bundled in his cloak. From the corner of his eye he saw that Eldran had treated Jondra the same. "Now to get out," he said.

Haral and the other Brythunians were within the columned circle, all facing outwards with swords in hand. From outside, bearded faces stared at them, some with disbelief, some with anger. And some, Conan saw in amazement, some with fear. Tulwar hilts were fingered, but none moved to cross the low granite wall atop which the columns stood.

From afar came the sounds of Zamoran drums beating furiously. The clash of steel drifted faintly in the air, and the shouts of fighting men.

"Mayhap we can just stay here till the soldiers come," Haral said unsteadily.

A ripple ran through the hillmen pressed against the circle's perimeter.

"Stay back!" the red-robed man cried. "The unbelievers will be dealt with by—"

Screaming at the top of their lungs, a score of turbaned warriors leaped into the circle with steel flashing against the Brythunians. By ones and twos, others joined them. Conan wished he knew what held the rest back, but there was suddenly no time for thought.

The Cimmerian blocked a tulwar slash aimed at his head, booted another attacker full in the belly. The second man fell beneath the feet of a third. The Cimmerian's steel pivoted around his first opponent's curved blade to drive through a leather-vested chest. He wanted to spare a glance for Tamira, but more hillmen were pressing on him. A mighty swing of his ancient broadsword sent a turbaned head rolling on the granite blocks, then continued on to rip out a bearded throat in a spray of blood.

Battle rage rose in him, the fiery blood that drowned reason. Hillmen rushed against him, and fell before a whirlwind of murderous steel. His eyes burned like azure flames, and all who looked into them knew they saw their own death. In some small corner of his mind sanity remained, enough to see Eldran, facing three hillmen and pushed almost to the low stone wall, fighting with broadsword in one hand and tulwar in the other. Haral and another Brythunian stood back to back, and a barricade of corpses slowed others who tried to reach them.

Abruptly the hillman who faced Conan backed away, dark eyes going wide with horror as he stared past the Cimmerian's shoulder. The tribesmen outside the circle were silent, pressing back from the stone columns. Conan risked a backward glance, and clamped his teeth on an oath.

Slowly the iridescent form of the beast of fire moved from the stone tunnel, its great golden eyes coldly surveying the arena filled with men who slowed and ceased their struggles as they became aware of it. One of the leathery bulges on its back had split; the edge of what appeared to be a wing, like that of a great bat, protruded. And almost beneath its feet crouched Tamira and Jondra.

"Behold!" the red-robed mage cried, flinging wide his arms. "The sign of the true gods is with us!"

For an instant there was silence save for the dimly heard sounds of distant battle. Then Eldran shouted. "Cimmerian!" The Brythunian's arm drew back; the ancient broadsword with its strange, clawed quillons arced spinning through the air.

Conan shifted his own sword to his left hand, and his right went up to catch the hilt of the thrown blade.

As if his movement, or perhaps the sword, had drawn its eyes, the brightly scaled beast stepped toward the Cimmerian. Memory of their last encounter was strong in Conan, and as the spike-toothed maw opened he threw himself into a rolling tumble. Flame roared. The hillman he had faced screamed as beard, hair and filthy robes blazed.

Conan knew well the quickness of the beast. He came to his feet only to dive in a different direction, one that took him closer. Fire scorched the stone where he had stood. The glittering creature moved with the speed of a leopard, Conan like a hunting lion. With a mutter of hope that Eldran spoke truly about the weapon, the big Cimmerian struck. A shock, as of sparks traveling along his bones, went through him. And the blade sliced through one golden eye, opening a gaping wound down the side of the huge scaled head, a wound that dripped black ichor.

Atop the stone tunnel the red-robed man screamed shrilly and threw his hands to his face. The beast reared back its head and echoed the scream, the two sounds merging, ringing through the mountains.

Conan felt his marrow freezing as the cry lanced into him, turning his muscles to water. Anger flared in him. He would not wait so to die. Fury lent him strength. "Crom!" he roared. Rushing forward, he plunged the ensorceled weapon into the creature's chest.

With a jerk, the beast's movement tore the hilt from his hand. Onto its hind legs it rose, towering above them all. If its cry had been one of pain before, now it was a shriek of agony, a scream that made the very stones of the mountains shiver.

The red-robed man was down on his knees, one hand to his face, the other clutching his chest. His black eyes on the scaled form were pools of horror. "No!" he howled. "No!"

Slowly the monstrous shape toppled. The stones of the tunnel cracked at its fall. A damp, leathery wing emerged from the broken bulge on its back, quivered once and was still. From beneath the beast extended a corner of scarlet robe, rivulets of crimson blood and black ichor falling from it.

From the hillmen on the slopes a keening went up, an eery wail of despair. Suddenly the thousands of them broke into fear-ridden flight. Even now they tried to avoid the circle of columns, but their numbers were too great, their panic too strong. Those close to the low stone wall were forced over it, screaming denial, by the press of human flesh. The circle became a maelstrom, hundreds trampling each other in their eagerness to flee.

Like a rock Conan breasted the flood, his eyes searching desperately for Tamira and Jondra. The men streaming around him had no thought left but escape, no desire but to claw through the pack, grinding underfoot anyone who slowed them. No man raised a hand against the Cimmerian except to try to pull him from their path. None touched a weapon, or even seemed to see him with their terrified eyes. They would not stop to harm the women deliberately, but if either woman went down beneath those trampling feet . . .

Eldran's height made him stand out as he waded through the shorter hillmen with Jondra in his arms. The Brythunian scrambled over the low stone wall and disappeared in the wash of dirty turbans.

Then Conan caught sight of the gold-edged black cloak, well beyond the circle, being borne around the mountain by the tide of flight. "Fool woman," he growled.

The clash of steel was closer, driving fear deeper into the hearts of men still trying to flee. There was no room to draw or swing a sword, but here and there daggers were out now, and hillman spilled hillman's blood to carve a way through to safety. With hammering fists and swordhilt, Conan hewed his own path through the mob, ruthless in his need to reach Tamira. Screaming men went down before his blows, and those who fell beneath the feet of that frenzied horde did not rise again.

The hillman village came into sight. Around the two-story stone building swarmed a hell of panting, desperate men dragging screaming black-swathed women with squalling babes in their arms and children clutching their long skirts. Here knots of men could break off from the seething mass to seek their camps. Other paused in flight to grab what they could from the stone huts. Bright steel flashed and reddened, and possessions changed hands thrice in the space of a breath.

Conan's sword and the breadth of his shoulders kept a space clear about him, but he barely even saw the men who slunk away from him like curs. He could no longer find Tamira among the now spreading streams of hillmen.

Abruptly the slender woman thief dashed from the stone structure that towered over the others in the village. She gasped and snugged the gold-edged black cloak tightly about her as Conan grabbed her arm.

"What in Mitra's name are you doing?" the Cimmerian demanded fiercely.

"My clothes," she began, and shrieked when he raised his sword.

Deftly Conan brought his blade over her head to run through a black-robed man who ran from the building with a dagger in his hand and murder in his eye. The hillman's multi-hued turban rolled from his head as he fell.

"I was just," Tamira began again, holding the cloak even more tightly, but she cut off with a squeal as Conan swung her over his shoulder.

"Fool, fool woman," he muttered, and with a wary eye for other hillmen with more than flight on their minds, he headed for the mountain heights.

Behind him, clangor rose as the Zamoran Army topped the rise overlooking the village.

Epilogue

L eaning back against a boulder, Conan allowed himself a real smile for the first time in days. They were at the edge of the mountains, and in their journey they had seen no hillman who was not fleeing. Certainly there had been none interested in attacking outsiders.

". . . And when Tenerses realized how many hillmen he faced," Fyrdan was saying, "he began shouting for me and his torturer all in one breath."

"There was little fun where we were, either," Haral told him. "These old bones cannot take this adventuring any more."

Jondra and Tamira, still swathed in their borrowed cloaks, huddled close to a small fire with their heads together. They showed more interest in their own talk than that of the men.

"It was hard enough with the Zamorans," the bony man laughed. "I thought I would have my hide stripped off on the instant. Then that . . . that sound came." He shivered and pulled his cloak closer about him. "It turned men's bowels to water. The hillmen stood for only a moment after that, then broke."

"That was Conan," Eldran said from where he examined the two shaggy horses they had found wandering, saddled but riderless, in the mountains. There had been others that they could not catch. "He slew the beast of fire, and it . . . screamed."

"And the Zamoran gained his victory," Haral said, "and his glory. It will be years before the hill tribes so much as think of uniting again. He will be acclaimed a hero in Shadizar, while the Cimmerian gets nothing."

"Let Tenerses have his glory," Conan said. "We have our lives, and the beast is dead. What more can we ask?"

Eldran turned suddenly from the horses. "One more thing," he said sharply. "A matter of debt. Jondra!"

Jondra stiffened and looked over her shoulder at the tall Brythunian. Tamira rose swiftly, carefully holding the black cloak closed, and moved to Conan's side.

"I know of no debt I owe you." The gray-eyed noblewoman's voice was tight. "But I would speak with you about garments. How long am I to be forced to wear no more than this cloak? Surely you can find me *something* more."

"Garments are a part of your debt," Eldran told her. He ticked off items on his fingers. "One cloak lined with badger fur. One pair of wolf fur leggings. And a good Nemedian dagger. I will not speak of a crack on the head. Since I see no chance of having them returned, I will have payment."

Jondra sniffed. "I will have their weight in gold sent to you from Shadizar."

"Shadizar?" Eldran laughed. "I am a Brythunian. What do I care of gold in Shadizar?" Abruptly he leaped, bearing the tall noblewoman to the ground. From his belt he produced long leather thongs like those used to tie leggings. "If you cannot pay me," he said into her disbelieving face, "then I will have you in payment."

Conan rose to his feet, one hand going to his sword hilt, but Tamira laid both of her small hands atop his. "Do nothing," she said softly.

The big Cimmerian frowned down at her. "Do you hate her so?"

Tamira shook her head, smiling. "You would have to be a woman to understand. Her choice is to return to being a wealthy outcast, scorned for her blood, or to be the captive of a man who loves her. And whom she loves, though she cannot bring herself to admit it. It is a choice any woman could make in an instant."

Conan admitted to himself that Jondra did not seem to be struggling as hard as she might, though she almost made up for it with her tirade. "You Brythunian oaf! Erlik blast your soul! Unhand me! I'll have your head for this! Derketo shrivel your manhood! I will see you flayed alive! Ouch! My ransom will be more wealth than you've ever seen if I am unharmed, Mitra curse you!"

Eldran straightened from her with a grin. She was a neat bundle in the cloak, now, snugly tied from shoulders to ankles with the leather thongs. "I would not take all the wealth of Zamora for you," he said. "Besides, a slave in Brythunia can have no interest in gold in Shadizar." He turned his back on her indignant gasp. "You understand, Cimmerian?"

Conan exchanged a glance with Tamira; she nodded. "I have had it explained to me," he answered. "But now it is time to take my leave."

"Wiccana watch over you, Cimmerian," Eldran said. Frydan and Haral echoed the farewell.

Conan swung into the saddle of one of the two horses. "Tamira?" he said, reaching down both hands. As he lifted her up behind him, her cloak became disarrayed, exposing soft curves and satin skin, and she had to press herself to his back to preserve her modesty.

"Be more careful," she complained.

The big Cimmerian only smiled, and spoke to the others. "Fare you well, and take a pull at the hellhorn for me if you get there before me."

As their shaggy mount carried them away from the small camp, Tamira said, "Truly you do not have to worry for her, Conan. I'll wager by the end of the year she has not only managed to make him free her, but that they are wed as well."

Conan only grunted, and watched for the first appearance of the lowlands through the gap ahead.

"It is a pity we must go back to Shadizar empty-handed, is it not?"

Still Conan did not reply.

"No doubt some hillman has the rubies, now," Tamira sighed heavily. "You must understand, I do not hold it against you. I would like to see you once we return to Shadizar. Perhaps we could meet at the Red Lion."

"Perhaps we could." Delving into the pouch at his belt Conan drew out the two great rubies from Jondra's regalia. They seemed to glow with a crimson light on his calloused palm. "Perhaps I might spend some of what I receive for these on you." Tamira gasped; he felt her rumaging within the cloak, and smiled. "Did you think I would not know of the pouch sewn inside my own cloak?" he asked. "I may not have been raised as a thief, but I have some skill with my fingers."

A small fist pounded at his shoulder. "You said you would not steal from her," the slender thief yelped.

"And so I did not," he answered smoothly. "I stole them from you."

"But you would not steal from her because you slept with her, and you ... I ... we ..."

"But did *you* not say that should not trouble a thief?" he chuckled.

"Do not go to sleep," Tamira said direly. "Do not even close your eyes. Do you hear me, Cimmerian? You had better heed my words. Do you think I'll allow ..."

Conan tucked the rubies back into his pouch, then thoughtfully moved the pouch around on his belt where it would be harder for her to reach. He might not receive the triumphal parade that Tenerses would get, but his would not be a bad return to Shadizar. Laughing, he booted his horse into a gallop.

Conan

The

Triumphant

prologue

The great granite mound called Tor Al'Kiir crouched like a malevolent toad in the night, wearing a crown of toppled walls and ruined columns, memories of failed attempts by a score of Ophirean dynasties to build there. Men had long since forgotten the origin of the mountain's name, but they knew it for a place of ill luck and evil, and laughed at the former kings who had not had their sense. Yet their laughter was tinged with unease for there was that about the mountain that made it a place to avoid even in thought.

The roiling black clouds of the storm that lashed Ianthe, that sprawling golden-domed and alabaster-spired city to the south, seemed to center about the mountain, but no muffled murmur of the thunder that rattled roof-tiles in the capital, no flash of light from lightnings streaking the dark like dragons' tongues, penetrated to the depths of Tor Al'Kiir's heart.

The Lady Synelle knew of the storm, though she could not hear it. It was proper for the night. Let the heavens split, she thought, and mountains be torn asunder in honor of *his* return to the world of men.

Her tall form was barely covered by a black silk tabard, tightly belted with golden links, that left the outer curves of breasts and hips bare. None of those who knew her as a princess of Ophir would have recognized her now, dark eyes glittering, beautiful face seemingly carved from marble, spun-platinum hair twisted about her head in severe coils and bearing a coronet of golden chain. There were four horns on the brow of that coronet, symbol that she was High Priestess of the god she had chosen to serve. But the bracelets of plain black iron that encircled her wrists were a symbol as well, and one she hated, for the god Al'Kiir accepted only those into his service who admitted themselves to be his slaves. Ebon silk that hung to her ankles, the hem weighted by golden beads, stirred against her long, slender legs as, barefoot, she led a strange procession deeper into the mountain through rough-hewn passages, lit by dark iron cressets suggesting the form of a horrible, four-horned head.

A score of black-mailed warriors were strange enough, their faces covered by slitted helmets bearing four horns, two outthrust to the sides and two curling down before the helmet, making them seem more demons than men. The quillons of their broadswords were formed of four horns as well, and each wore on his chest, picked out in scarlet, the outline of the monstrous horned head only hinted by the fiery iron baskets suspended by chains from the roof of the tunnel.

Stranger still was the woman they escorted, clothed in Ophirean bridal dress, diaphanous layers of pale cerulean silk made opaque by their number, caught at the waist with a cord of gold. Her long hair, black as a raven's wing, curling about her shoulders, was filled with the tiny white blossoms of the tarla, symbol of purity, and her feet were bare as a sign of humility. She stumbled, and rough hands grasped her arms to hold her erect.

"Synelle!" the black-haired woman called woozily. A hint of her natural haughtiness came through her drug-induced haze. "Where are we, Synelle? How did I come here?"

The cortege moved on. Synelle gave no outward sign that she had heard. Inwardly her only reaction was relief that the drug was wearing off. It had been necessary in order to remove the woman from her palace in Ianthe, and it had made her easier to prepare and bring this far, but her mind must be clear for the ceremony ahead.

Power, Synelle thought. A woman could have no real power in Ophir, yet power was what she craved. Power was what she would have. Men thought that she was content to order the estates she had inherited, that she would eventually marry and give stewardship of those lands— ownership in all but name—to her husband. In their fools' blindness they did not stop to think that royal blood coursed in her veins. Did ancient laws not forbid a woman taking the crown, she would stand next in succession to the childless King now on the throne in Ianthe. Valdric sat his throne, consumed with chivying his retinue of sorcerers and physicians to find a cure for the wasting sickness that killed him by inches, too busy to name an heir or to see that, for this failure to do so, the noble lords of Ophir struggled and fought to gain the seat his death would vacate.

A dark, contented smile touched Synelle's full red lips. Let those proud men strut in their armor and tear at one another like starving wolfhounds in a pit. They would wake from their dreams of glory to find that the Countess of Asmark had become Queen Synelle of Ophir, and she would teach them to heel like whipped curs.

Abruptly the passage widened into a great, domed cavern, the very memory of which had passed from the minds of men. Burning tapers on unadorned walls hacked from the living stone lit the smooth stone floor, which bore only two tall, slender wooden posts topped with the omnipresent four-horned head. Ornament had been far from the minds of those who had burrowed into a nameless mountain in a now forgotten age. They had meant it as prison for the adamantine figure, colored like old blood, that stood dominating the grotto, as it would have dominated the greatest place ever conceived. A statue it seemed, yet was not.

The massive body was as that of a man, though half again as tall as any human male, save for the six claw-tipped fingers on each broad hand. In its malevolent, horned head were three lidless eyes, smouldering blackly with a glow that ate light, and its mouth was a broad, lipless gash filled with rows of needle-sharp teeth. The figure's thick arms were encircled by bracers and armlets bearing its own horned likeness. About its waist was a wide belt and loinguard of intricately worked gold, a coiled black whip glistening metallically on one side, a monstrous dagger with horned quillons depending on the other.

Synelle felt the breath catch in her throat as it had the first time she had seen her god, as it did each time she saw him. "Prepare the bride of Al' Kiir," she commanded.

A choking scream broke from the bridal-clothed woman's throat as she was hurried forward by the guards who held her. Quickly, with cords that dug cruelly into her soft flesh, they bound her between the twin posts on widely straddled knees, arms stretched above her head. Her blue eyes bulged, unable to tear themselves away from the great form that overtowered her; her mouth hung silently open as she knelt, as if terror had driven even the thought of screaming from her.

Synelle spoke. "Taramenon."

The bound woman started at the name. "Him, also?" she cried. "What is happening, Synelle? Tell me! Please!" Synelle gave no answer.

One of the armored men came forward at the summons, carrying a small, brass-bound chest and knelt stiffly before the woman who was at once a princess of Ophir and a priestess of dark Al'Kiir.

Muttering incantations of protection, Synelle opened the chest and drew out her implements and potions, one by one.

As a child had Synelle first heard of Al'Kiir, a god forgotten by all but a handful, from an old nurse-maid who had been dismissed when it was learned what sort of evil tales she told. Little had the crone told her before she went, but even then the child had been enraptured by the power said to be given to the priestesses of Al'Kiir, to those women who would pledge their bodies and their souls to the god of lust and pain and death, who would perform the heinous rites he demanded. Even then power had been her dream.

Synelle turned from the chest with a small, crystal-stoppered vial, and approached the bound woman. Deftly she withdrew the clear stopper and, with its damp end, traced the sign of the horns on the other woman's forehead.

"Something to help you attain the proper mood for a bride, Telima." Her voice was soft and mocking.

"I don't understand, Synelle," Telima said. A breathy quality had come into her voice; she tossed her head with a gasp, and her hair was a midnight cloud about her face. "What is happening?" she whimpered.

Synelle returned the vial to its resting place in the chest. Using powdered blood and bone, she traced the sign of the horns once more, this time in broad strokes on the floor, with the woman at the posts at the horns' meeting. A jade flask contained virgin's blood; with a brush of virgin's hair she anointed Al'Kiir's broad mouth and mighty thighs. Now there was naught left save to begin.

Yet Synelle hesitated. This part of the rite she hated, as she hated the iron bracelets. There were none to witness save her guards, who would die for her, and Telima, who would soon, in one way or another, be of no import to this world, but she herself would know. Still it must be done. It must.

Reluctantly she knelt facing the great figure, paused to take a deep breath, then fell on her face, arms outspread.

"O, mighty Al'Kiir," she intoned, "lord of blood and death, thy slave abases herself before thee. Her body is thine. Her soul is thine. Accept her submission and use her as thou wilt."

Trembling, her hands moved forward to grasp the massive ankles; slowly she pulled herself across the floor until she could kiss each clawed foot.

"O, mighty Al'Kiir," she breathed, "lord of pain and lust, thy slave brings thee a bride in offering. Her body is thine. Her soul is thine. Accept her submission and use her as thou wilt."

In ages past, before the first hut was built on the site of Acheron, now eons gone in dust, Al'Kiir had been worshipped in the land that would become Ophir. The proudest and most beautiful of women the god demanded as offerings, and they were brought to him in steady streams. Rites were performed that stained the souls of those who performed them and haunted the minds of those who witnessed them.

At last a band of mages vowed to free the world of the monstrous god, and had the blessings of Mitra and Azura and gods long forgotten placed on their foreheads. Alone of that company had the sorcerer Avanrakash survived, yet with a staff of power had he sealed Al'Kiir away from the world of men. That which stood in the cavern beneath Tor Al'Kiir was no statue of the god, but his very body, entombed for long ages.

Two of the guards had removed their helmets and produced flutes. High, haunting music filled the cavern. Two more stationed themselves behind the woman kneeling between the posts. The rest unfastened their scabbarded broad-swords from their belts and began to pound the stone floor in rhythm to the flutes.

With boneless sinuosity Synelle rose and began to dance, her feet striking the floor in time with the pounding of the scabbards. In a precise pattern she moved, cat-like, each step coming in an ancient order, and as she danced she chanted in a tongue lost to time. She spun, and weighted black silk stood straight out from her body, baring her from waist to ankles. Sensuously she dipped and swayed from the looming shape of the god to the kneeling woman.

Sweat beaded Telima's countenance, and her eyes were glazed. She seemed to have lost awareness of her surroundings and she writhed uncontrollably in her bonds. Lust bloomed on her face, and horror at the realization of it.

Like pale birds Synelle's hands fluttered to Telima, brushed damp dark hair from her face, trailed across her shoulders, ripped away one single layer of her bridal garb.

Telima screamed as the men behind her struck with broad leather straps, again and again, criss-crossing from shoulders to buttocks, yet her jerking motions came as much from the potion as from the lashing. Pain had been added to lust, as required by the god.

Still Synelle danced and chanted. Another layer of diaphanous silk was torn from Telima, and as her shrieks mounted the chant wove into them, so that the cries of pain became part of the incantation.

The figure of Al'Kiir began to vibrate.

Where neither time, nor place, nor space existed, there was a stirring, a half awakening from long slumber. Tendrils of pleasurable feeling caressed, feeble threads of worship that called. But to where? Once appetites had been fed to satiation. Women had been offered in multitudes. Their essences had been kept alive for countless centuries, kept clothed in flesh forever young to be toys for the boundless lusts of a god. Memories, half dreams, flickered. In the midst of eternal nothingness was suddenly a vast floor. A thousand women born ten thousand years before danced nude. But they were merely shells, without interest. Even a god could not keep frail human essence alive forever. Petulance, and dancers and floor alike were gone. From whence did these feelings come, so frequently of late after seemingly endless ages of absence, bringing with them irritating remembrance of what was lost? There was no direction. A shield was formed and blessed peace descended. Slumber returned.

*   *   *

Synelle slumped to the stone floor, panting from her exertions. There was no sound in the cavern except for the sobs of the midnight-haired beauty kneeling in welted nudity.

Painfully the priestess struggled to her feet. Failure again. So many failures. She staggered as she made her way to the chest, but her hand was steady as she removed a dagger that was a normal-sized version of the blade at the god's belt.

"The bowl, Taramenon," Synelle said. The rite had failed, yet it must continue to its conclusion.

Telima moaned as Synelle tangled a hand in her black hair and drew her head back. "Please," the kneeling woman wept.

Her sobs were cut off by the blade slashing across her throat. The armored man who had borne the chest thrust a bronze bowl forward to catch the sanguinary flow.

Synelle watched with disinterest as final terror blazed in Telima's eyes and faded to the glaze of death. The priestess's thoughts were on the future. Another failure, as there had been so many in the past, but she would continue if a thousand women must die in that chamber. She would bring Al'Kiir back to the world of men. Without another glance at the dead woman, she turned to the completion of the ceremony.

1

T he long pack train approaching the high crenellated granite walls of Ianthe did not appear to be moving through a country officially at peace. Twoscore horsemen in spiked helms, dust turning their dark blue wool cloaks gray, rode in columns to either side of the long line of sumpter mules. Their eyes constantly searched even here in the very shadow of the capital. Half carried their short horse-bows at the ready. Sweaty-palmed muledrivers hurried their animals along, panting with eagerness to be done now that their goal was in sight.

Only the leader of the guards, his shoulders broad almost to the point of busting his metal jazeraint hauberk, seemed unconcerned. His icy blue eyes showed no hint of the worry that made the others' eyes dart, yet he was as aware of his surroundings as they. Perhaps more so. Three times since leaving the gem and gold mines on the Nemedian border, the train had been attacked. Twice his barbarian senses had detected the ambush before it had time to develop, the third time his fiercely wielded broadsword smashed the attack even as it began. In the rugged mountains of his native Cimmeria, men who fell easily into ambush did not long survive. He had known battle there, and had a place at the warriors' fires, at an age when most boys were still learning at their father's knees.

Before the northeast gate of Ianthe, the Gate of Gold, the train halted. "Open the gates!" the leader shouted. Drawing off his helm, he revealed a square-cut black mane and a face that showed more experience than his youth would warrant. "Do we look like bandits? Mitra rot you, open the gates!"

A head in a steel casque, a broken-nosed face with a short beard, appeared atop the wall. "Is that you, Conan?" He turned aside to call down, "Swing back the gate!"

Slowly the right side of the iron-bound gate creaked inward. Conan galloped through, pulling his big Aquilonian black from the road just inside to let the rest of the train pass. A dozen mail-clad soldiers threw their shoulders behind the gate as soon as the last pack-laden mule ran by. The huge wooden slab closed with a hollow boom, and a great bar, thicker than a man's body, crashed down to fasten it.

The soldier who had called down from the wall appeared with his casque beneath his arm. "I should have recognized those accursed eastern helmets, Cimmerian," he laughed. "Your Free-Company makes a name for itself."

"Why are the gates shut, Junius?" Conan demanded. "'Tis at least three hours till dark."

"Orders, Cimmerian. With the gates closed, perhaps we can keep the troubles out of the city." Junius looked around, then dropped his voice. "It would be better if Valdric died quickly. Then Count Tiberio could put an end to all this fighting."

"I thought General Iskandrian was keeping the army clear," Conan replied coolly. "Or have you just chosen your own side?"

The broken-nosed soldier drew back, licking his thin lips nervously. "Just talking," he muttered. Abruptly he straightened, and his voice took on a blustering tone. "You had better move on, Cimmerian. There's no loitering about the gates allowed now. Especially by mercenary companies." He fumbled his casque back onto his head as if to give himself more authority, or perhaps simply more protection from the Cimmerian's piercing gaze.

With a disgusted grunt Conan touched boot to his stallion's ribs and galloped after his company. Thus far Iskandrian—the White Eagle of Ophir, he was called; some said he was the greatest general of the age—had managed to keep Ophir from open civil war by holding the army loyal to Valdric, though the King seemed not to know it, or even to know that his country was on the verge of destruction. But if the old general's grip on the army was falling . . .

Conan scowled and pressed on. The twisted maze of maneuverings for the throne was not to his liking, yet he was forced to keep an understanding of it for his own safety, and that of his company.

To the casual observer, the streets of Ianthe would have showed no sign that nobles' private armies were fighting an undeclared and unacknowledged war in the countryside. Scurrying crowds filled narrow side streets and broad thoroughfares alike, merchants in their voluminous robes and peddlers in rags, silk-clad ladies shopping with retinues of basket-carrying servants in tow, strutting lordlings in satins and brocades with scented pomanders held to their nostrils against the smell of the sewers, leather-aproned apprentices tarrying on their errands to bandy words with young girls hawking baskets of oranges and pomegranates, pears and plums. Ragged beggars, flies buzzing about blinded eyes or crudely bandaged stumps, squatted on every corner—more since the troubles had driven so many from their villages and farms. Doxies strutted in gilded bangles and sheer silks or less, often taking a stance before columned palaces or even on the broad marble steps of temples.

Yet there was that about the throng that belied the normalcy of the scene. A flush of cheek where there should have been only calm. A quickness of breath where there was no haste. A darting of eye where there was no visible reason for suspicion. The knowledge of what occurred beyond the walls lay heavily on Ianthe even as the city denied its happening, and the fear that it might move within the walls was in every heart.

When Conan caught up to the pack train, it was slowly wending its way through the crowds. He reined in beside his lieutenant, a grizzled Nemedian who had had the choice of deserting from the City Guard of Belverus or of being executed for performing his duty too well, to the fatal detriment of a lord of that city.

"Keep a close watch, Machaon," the Cimmerian said. "Even here we might be mobbed if this crowd knew what we carried."

Machaon spat. The nasal of his helm failed to hide the livid scar that cut across his broad nose. A blue tattoo of a six-pointed Kothian star adorned his left cheek. "I'd give a silver myself to know how Baron Timeon comes to be taking this delivery. I never knew our fat patron had any connections with the mines."

"He doesn't. A little of the gold and perhaps a few gems will stay with Timeon; the rest goes elsewhere."

The dark-eyed veteran gave him a questioning look, but Conan said no more. It had taken him no little effort to discover that Timeon was but a tool of Count Antimides. But Antimides was supposedly one of the few lords of Ophir *not* maneuvering to ascend the throne at the death of the King. As such he should have no need of secret supporters, and that meant he played a deeper game than any knew. Too, Antimides also had no connection with the mines, and thus as little right to pack-saddles loaded with gold bars and chests of emeralds and rubies. A second reason for a wise man to keep his tongue behind his teeth till he knew more of the way things were, yet it rankled the pride of the young Cimmerian.

Fortune as much as anything else had given him his Free-Company in Nemedia, but in a year of campaigning since crossing the border into Ophir they had built a reputation. The horse archers of Conan the Cimmerian were known for their fierceness and the skill of him who led them, respected even by those who had cause to hate them. Long and hard had been Conan's climb from a boyhood as a thief to become a captain of mercenaries at an age when most men might only dream of such a thing.

It had been, he thought, a climb to freedom, for never had he liked obeying another's commands; yet here he played the game of a man he had never even met, and it set most ill with him. Most ill, indeed.

As they came in sight of Timeon's palace, a pretentiously ornamented and columned square of white marble with broad stairs, crowded between a temple of Mitra and a potter's works, Conan suddenly slid from his saddle and tossed his reins and helmet to a surprised Machaon.

"Once this is all safely in the cellars," he told his lieutenant, "let those who rode with us have until dawn tomorrow for carousing. They've earned it."

"The baron may take it badly, Conan, you leaving before the gold is safely under lock and key."

Conan shook his head. "And I see him now, I may say things best left unsaid."

"He'll likely be so occupied with his latest leman that he'll not have time for two words with you."

One of the company close behind them laughed, a startling sound to come from his sephulcral face. He looked like a man ravaged nearly to death by disease. "Timeon goes through almost as many women as you, Machaon," he said. "But then, he has wealth to attract them. I still don't see how you do it."

"If you spent less time gaming, Narus," Machaon replied, "and more hunting, perhaps you'd know my secrets. Or mayhap it's because I don't have your spindly shanks."

A dozen of the company roared with laughter. Narus' successes with women came with those who wanted to fatten him up and nurse him back to health; there seemed to be a surprising number of them.

"Machaon has enough women for five men," laughed Taurianus, a lanky, dark-haired Ophirean, "Narus dices enough for ten, and Conan does enough of both for twenty." He was one of those who had joined the company since its arrival in Ophir. But nine of the original score remained. Death had done for some of the rest; others had simply tired of a steady diet of blood and danger.

Conan waited for the laughter to subside. "If Timeon's got a new mistress, and it's about time for him to if he's running true to form, he'll not notice if I'm there or no. Take them on in, Machaon." Without waiting for a reply the Cimmerian plunged into the crowd.

Other than staying away from Timeon until he was in better temper, Conan was unsure of what he sought. A woman, perhaps. Eight days the journey to the mines and back had taken, without so much as a crone to gaze on. Women were forbidden at the mines; men condemned to a life digging rock were difficult enough to control without the sight of soft flesh to incite them, and after a year or two in the pits the flesh would not have to be that soft.

A woman, then, but there was no urgency. For a time he would simply wander and drink in the bustle of the city, so different even with its taint from the open terror that permeated the countryside.

Ophir was an ancient kingdom; it had coexisted with the mage-ridden empire of Acheron, gone to dust these three millennia and more, and had been one of the few lands to resist conquest by that dark empire's hordes. Ianthe, its capital, might have been neatly planned and divided into districts at some time in its long history, but over the centuries the great city of spired towers and golden-domed palaces had grown and shifted, winding streets pushing through haphazardly, buildings going up wherever there was space. Marble temples, fronted by countless rows of fluted columns and silent save for the chants of priests and worshippers, sat between brick-walled brothels and smoking foundries filled with the clanging of hammers, mansions and alabaster between rough taverns and silversmiths' shops. There was a system of sewers, though more often than not the refuse thrown there simply lay, adding to the effluvia that filled the streets. And stench there was, for some were too lazy even to dispose of their offal in the sewers, emptying chamber pots and kitchen scraps into the nearest alley. But for all its smells and cramped streets, for all its fears, the city was alive.

A trull wearing a single strip of silk threaded through her belt of coins smiled invitingly at the big youth, running her hands through her dark curls to lift well-rounded breasts, wetting her lips for the breadth of his shoulders. Conan answered her inviting smile with one that sent a visible shiver through her. Marking her as likely for later, though, he moved on, the doxy's regretful gaze following him. He tossed a coin to a fruit-girl and took a handful of plums, munching as he went, tossing the seeds into a sewer drain when he saw one.

In the shop of a swordsmith he examined keen blades with an expert eye, though he had never found steel to match that of his own ancient broadsword, ever present at his side in its worn shagreen scabbard. But the thought of a woman rose up in him, the memory of the whore's thighs. Perhaps there was some small urgency to finding a woman after all.

From a silversmith he purchased a gilded brass necklace set with amber. It would go well on the neck of that curly-head wench, or if not her, about the neck of another. Jewelry, flowers and perfume, he had learned, went further with any woman, be she the most common jade of the streets or a daughter of the noblest house, than a sack of gold, though the trull would want her coins as well, of course. The perfume he obtained from a one-eyed peddler with a tray hung on a strap about his scrawny neck, a vial of something that smelled of roses. Now he was ready.

He cast about for a place to throw the last of his plum pits, and his eye fell on a barrel before the shop of a brass smith, filled with scraps of brass and bronze obviously ready for melting down. Lying atop the metallic debris was a bronze figure as long as his forearm and green with the verdigris of age. The head of it was a four-horned monstrosity, broad and flat, with three eyes above a broad, fang-filled gash of a mouth.

Chuckling, Conan straightened the statuette in the barrel. Ugly it was, without doubt. It was also naked and grotesquely male. A perfect gift for Machaon.

"The noble sir is a connoisseur, I see. That is one of my best pieces."

Conan eyed the smiling, dumpy little man who had appeared in the doorway of the shop, with his plump hands folded over a yellow tunic where it was strained by his belly. "One of your best pieces, is it?" Amusement was plain in the Cimmerian's voice. "On the scrap heap?"

"A mistake on the part of my apprentice, noble sir. A worthless lad." The dumpy fellow's voice dripped regretful anger at the worthlessness of his apprentice. "I'll leather him well for it. A mere two gold pieces, and it is—"

Conan cut him off with a raised hand. "Any more lies, and I may not buy it at all. If you know something of it, then speak."

"I tell you, noble sir, it is easily worth—" Conan turned away, and the shopkeeper yelped. "Wait! Please! I will speak only the truth, as Mitra hears my words!"

Conan stopped and looked back, feigning doubt. This fellow, he thought, would not last a day among the peddlers of Turan.

There was sweat on the shopkeeper's face, though the day was cool. "Please, noble sir. Come into my shop, and we will talk. Please."

Still pretending reluctance, Conan allowed himself to be ushered inside, plucking the figure from the barrel as he passed. Within, the narrow shop was crowded with tables displaying examples of the smith's work. Shelves on the walls held bowls, vases, ewers and goblets in a welter of shapes and sizes. The big Cimmerian set the statuette on a table that creaked under its weight.

"Now," he said, "name me a price. And I'll hear no more mention of gold for something you were going to melt."

Avarice struggled on the smith's plump face with fear of losing a purchaser. "Ten silvers," he said finally, screwing his face into a parody of his former welcoming expression.

Deliberately Conan removed a single silver coin from his pouch and set it on the table. Crossing his massive arms across his chest, he waited.

The plump man's mouth worked, and his head moved in small jerks of negation, but at last he sighed and nodded. "Tis yours," he muttered bitterly. "For one silver. It's as much as it is worth to melt down, and without the labor. But the thing is ill luck. A peasant fleeing the troubles brought it to me. Dug it up on his scrap of land. Ancient bronzes always sell well, but none would have this. Ill favored, they called it. And naught but bad luck since it's been in my shop. One of my daughters is with child, but unmarried; the other has taken up with a panderer who sells her not three doors from here. My wife left me for a carter. A common carter, mind you. I tell you, that thing is . . ." His words wound down as he realized he might be talking himself out of a sale. Hurriedly he snatched the silver and made it disappear under his tunic. "Yours for a silver, noble sir, and a bargain greater than you can imagine."

"If you say so," Conan said drily. "But get me something to carry it through the streets in." He eyed the figure and chuckled despite himself, imagining the look on Machaon's face when he presented it to him. "The most hardened trull in the city would blush to look on it."

As the smith scurried into the back of his shop, two heavy-set men in the castoff finery of nobles swaggered in. One, in a soiled red brocade tunic, had had his ears and nose slit, the penalties for first and second offences of theft. For the next he would go to the mines. The other, bald and with a straggly black beard, wore a frayed wool cloak that had once been worked with embroidery of silver or gold, long since picked out. Their eyes went immediately to the bronze figure on the table. Conan kept his gaze on them; their swords, at least, looked well tended, and the hilts showed the wear of much use.

"Can I help you?" the shopkeeper asked, reappearing with a coarsely woven sack in his hand. There was no "noble sir" for this sort.

"That," slit-ear said gruffly, pointing to the statuette. "A gold piece for it."

The smith coughed and spluttered, glaring reproachfully at Conan.

"It's mine," the Cimmerian said calmly, "and I've no mind to sell."

"Two gold pieces," slit-ear said. Conan shook his head.

"Five," the bald man offered.

Slit-ear rounded on his companion. "Give away your profit, an you will, but not mine! I'll make this ox an offer," he snarled and spun, his sword whispering from its sheath.

Conan made no move toward his own blade. Grasping the bronze figure by its feet, he swung it sideways. The splintering of bone blended with slit-ear's scream as his shoulder was crushed. The bald man had his sword out now, but Conan merely stepped aside from his lunge and brought the weighty statuette down like a mace, splattering blood and brains. The dead man's momentum carried him on into the tables, overturning those he did not smash, sending brass vases and bowls clattering across the floor. Conan whirled back to find the first man thrusting with a dagger held left-handed. The blade skittered off his hauberk, and the two men crashed together. For the space of a breath they were chest to chest, Conan staring into desperate black eyes. This time he disdained to use a weapon. His huge fist traveled more than half the length of his forearm, and slit-ear staggered back, his face a bloody mask, to pull shelves down atop him as he crumpled to the floor. Conan did not know if he was alive or dead, nor did he care.

The smith stood in the middle of the floor, hopping from one foot to the other. "My shop!" he wailed. "My shop is wrecked! You steal for a silver what they would have given five gold pieces for, then you destroy my place of business!"

"They have purses," Conan growled. "Take the cost of your repairs from—" He broke off with a curse as the scent of roses wafted to his nose. Delving into his pouch, he came out with a fragment of vial. Perfume was soaking into his hauberk. And his cloak. "Erlik take the pair of them," he muttered. He hefted the bronze figure that he still held in one hand. "What about this thing is worth five gold pieces? Or worth dying for?" The shopkeeper, gingerly feeling for the ruffians' purses, did not answer.

Cursing under his breath Conan wiped the blood from the figure and thrust it into the sack the smith had let drop.

With a shout of delight the smith held up a handful of silver, then drew back as if he feared Conan might take it. He started, then stared at the two men littering his floor as if realizing where they were for the first time. "But what will I do with them?" he cried.

"Apprentice them," Conan told him. "I'll wager they won't put anything valuable in the scrap barrel."

Leaving the dumpy man kneeling on the floor with his mouth hanging open, Conan stalked into the street. It was time and more to find himself a woman.

In his haste he did not notice the heavily veiled woman whose green eyes widened in surprise at his appearance. She watched him blend into the crowd then, gathering her cloak about her, followed slowly.

11

The *Bull and Bear* was almost empty when Conan entered, and the half-dread silence suited his mood well. The curly-haired trull had been leaving with a customer when he got back to her corner, and he had not seen another to compare with her between there and this tavern.

An odor of stale wine and sweat hung in the air of the common room; it was not a tavern for gentlefolk. Half a dozen men, carters and apprentices in rough woolen tunics, sat singly at the tables scattered about the stone floor, each engrossed in his own drinking. A single doxy stood with her back to a corner, not plying her trade but seeming rather to ignore the men in the room. Auburn hair fell in soft waves to her shoulders. Wrapped in layers of green silk, she was more modestly covered than most noble ladies of Ophir, and she wore none of the gaudy ornaments such women usually adorned themselves with, but the elaborate kohl of her eyelids named her professional, as did her presence in that place. Still, there was a youthful freshness to her face that gave him cause to think she had not long been at it.

Conan was so intent on the girl that he failed at first to see the graying man, the full beard of a scholar spreading over his chest, who muttered to himself over a battered pewter pitcher at a table to one side of the door. When he did, he sighed, wondering if the wench would be worth putting up with the old man.

At that moment the bearded man caught sight of Conan, and a drunken, snaggle-toothed grin split his wizened face. His tunic was patched in a rainbow of colors, and stained with wine and food. "Conan," he cried, gesturing so hard for the big youth to come closer that he nearly fell from his stool. "Come. Sit. Drink."

"You look to have had enough, Boros," Conan said drily, "and I'll buy you no more."

"No need to buy," Boros laughed. He fumbled for the pitcher. "No need. See? Water. But with just a little . . ." His voice trailed off into mumbles, while his free hand made passes above the pitcher.

"Crom!" Conan shouted, leaping back from the table. Some in the room looked up, but seeing neither blood nor chance for advantage all went back to their drinking. "Not again while you're drunk, you old fool!" the Cimmerian continued hastily. "Narus still isn't rid of those warts you gave him trying to cure his boil."

Boros cackled and thrust the pitcher toward him. "Taste. 'S wine. Naught to fear here."

Cautiously Conan took the proffered pitcher and sniffed at the mouth of it. His nose wrinkled, and he handed the vessel back. "You drink first, since it's your making."

"Fearful, are you?" Boros laughed. "And big as you are. Had I your muscles . . ." He buried his nose in the pitcher, threw back his head, and almost in the same motion hurled the vessel from him, gagging, spluttering and spitting. "Mitra's mercies," he gasped shakily, scrubbing the back of a bony hand across his mouth. "Never tasted anything like that in my life. Must have put a gill or more down my gullet. What in Azura's name is it?"

Conan suppressed a grin. "Milk. Sour milk, by the smell."

Boros shuddered and retched, but nothing came up. "You switched the pitcher," he said when he could speak. "Your hands are swift, but not so swift as my eye. You owe me wine, Cimmerian."

Conan dropped onto a stool across the table from Boros, setting the sack containing the bronze on the floor at his side. He had little liking for wizards, but properly speaking Boros was not such a one. The old man had been an apprentice in the black arts, but a liking for drink that became an all-consuming passion had led him to the gutter rather than down crooked paths of dark knowledge. When sober he was of some use in curing minor ills, or providing a love philtre; drunk, he was sometimes a danger even to himself. He was a good drinking companion, though, so long as he was kept from magic.

"Here!" the tavernkeeper bellowed, wiping his hands on a filthy once-white apron as he hurried toward them. With his spindly limbs and pot belly, he looked like a fat spider. "What's all this mess on the floor? I'll have you know this tavern is respectable, and—"

"Wine," Conan cut him off, tossing coppers to clatter on the floor at his feet. "And have a wench bring it." He gestured to the strangely aloof doxy. "That one in the corner will do."

"She don't work for me," the tavernkeeper grunted, bending to collect the pitcher and the coins. Then he got down on hands and knees to fetch one copper from under the table and grinned at it in satisfaction. "But you'll have a girl, never fear."

He disappeared into the rear of the building, and in short moments a plump girl scurried out, one strip of blue silk barely containing her bouncing breasts and another fastened about her hips, to set a pitcher of wine and a pair of dented tankards before the two men. Wriggling, she moved closer to Conan, a seductive light in her dark eyes. He was barely aware of her; his eyes had gone back to the auburn-haired jade.

"Fool!" the serving wench snapped. "As well take a block of ice in your arms as that one." And with a roll of her lips she flounced away.

Conan stared after her in amazement. "What is Zandru's Nine Hells got into her?" he growled.

"Who understands women?" Boros muttered absently. Hastily he filled a tankard and gulped half of it. "Besides," he went on in bleary tones once he had taken a deep breath, "now Tiberio's dead, we'll have too much else to be worrying about . . ." The rest of his words were drowned in another mouthful of wine.

"Tiberio dead?" Conan said incredulously. "I spoke of him not too hours gone and heard no mention of this. Black Erlik's Throne, stop drinking and talk. What of Tiberio?"

Boros set his tankard down with obvious reluctance. "The word is just now spreading. Last night it was. Slit his wrists in his bath. Or so they say."

Conan grunted. "Who will believe that, and him with the best blood claim to succeed Valdric?"

"Folk believe what they want to believe, Cimmerian. Or what they're afraid not to believe."

It had had to come, Conan thought. There had been kidnappings in plenty, wives, sons, daughters. Sometimes demands were made, that an alliance be broken or a secret betrayed; sometimes there was only silence, and fear to paralyze a noble in his castle. Now began the assassinations. He was glad that a third of his Free-Company was always on guard at Timeon's palace. Losing a patron in that fashion would be ill for a company's reputation.

"'Tis all of a piece," Boros went on unsteadily. "Someone attempts to resurrect Al'Kiir. I've seen lights atop that accursed mountain, heard whispers of black knowledge sought. And this time there'll be no Avanrakash to seal him up again. We need Moranthes the Great reborn. It would take him to bring order now."

"What are you chattering at? No matter. Who's next in line after Tiberio? Valentius, isn't it?"

"Valentius," Boris chuckled derisively. "He'll never be allowed to take the throne. He's too young."

"He's a man grown," Conan said angrily. He knew little of Valentius and cared less, but the count was a full six years older than he.

Boros smiled. "There's a difference between you two, Cimmerian. You've put two hard life-times' experience into your years. Valentius has led a courtier's life, all perfumes and courtesies and soft words."

"You're rambling," Conan barked. How had the other man read his thoughts? A fast rise had not lessened his touchiness about his comparative youth, nor his anger at those who thought him too young for the position he held. But he had better to do with his time than sit with a drunken failed mage. There was that auburn-haired wench, for instance. "The rest of the wine is yours," he said. Snatching up the sack with the bronze in it, he stalked away from the table, leaving Boros chortling into his wine.

The girl had not moved from the corner or changed her stance in all the time Conan had been watching her. Her heart-shaped face did not change expression as he approached, but her downcast eyes, blue as a northland sky at dawn, widened like those of a frightened deer, and she quivered as if prepared for flight.

"Share some wine with me," Conan said, motioning to a table nearby.

The girl stared at him directly, her big eyes going even wider, if such were possible, and shook her head.

He blinked in surprise. That innocent face might belie it, but if she wanted directness . . . "If you don't want wine, how does two silvers take you?"

The girl's mouth dropped open. "I don't . . . that is, I . . . I mean . . ." Even stammering, her voice was a soprano like silver bells.

"Three silvers, then. A fourth if you prove worth it." She still stared. Why was he wasting time with her, he wondered, when there were other wenches about? She reminded him of Karela, that was it. This girl's hair was not so red, nor her cheekbones so high, but she recalled to him the woman bandit who had shared his bed—and managed to disrupt his life—every time their paths had crossed. Karela was a woman fit for any man, fit for a King. But what use raking up old memories? "Girl," he said gruffly, "if you don't want my silver, say so, and I'll take my custom elsewhere."

"Stay," she gasped. It was an obvious effort for her to get the word out.

"Innkeeper," Conan bellowed, "a room!" The wench's face went scarlet beneath the rouge on her cheeks.

The spidery tapster appeared on the instant, a long hand extended for coin. "Four coppers," he growled, and waited until Conan had dropped them into his palm before adding, "Top of the stairs, to the right."

Conan caught the furiously blushing girl by the arm and drew her up the creaking wooden stairs after him.

The room was what he had expected, a small box with dust on the floor and cobwebs in the corners. A sagging bed with a husk-filled mattress and none-too-clean blankets, a three-legged stool, and a rickety table were all the furnishings. But then, what he was there for went as well in a barn as in a palace, and often better.

Dropping the sack on the floor with a thump, he kicked the door shut and put his hands on the girl's shoulders. As he drew her to him he peeled her silken robes from her shoulders to her waist. Her breasts were full, but upstanding, and pink-nippled. She yelped once before his mouth descended on hers, then went stiff in his arms. He could as well have been kissing a statue.

He drew back, but held her still in the circle of his arms. "What sort of doxy are you?" he demanded. "A man would think you'd never kissed a man before."

"I haven't," she snapped, then began to stammer. "That is, I have. I've kissed many men. More than you can count. I am very . . . experienced." She bared her teeth in what Conan suspected was meant to be an inviting smile; it was more a fearful rictus.

He snorted derisively and pushed her out to arms' length. Her hands twitched toward her disarrayed garments, then were still. Heavy breathing made her breasts rise and fall in interesting fashion, and her face slowly colored again. "You don't talk like a farm wench," he said finally. "What are you? Some merchant's runaway daughter without sense enough to go home?"

Her face became a frozen mask of arrogant pride. "You, barbarian, will have the honor of taking a noblewoman of Ophir to . . . to your bed." Even the stumble did not crack her haughty demeanor.

Taken together with her manner of dress—or undress, rather—it was too much for the Cimmerian. He threw back his head and bellowed his laughter at the fly-specked ceiling.

"You laugh at me?" she gasped. "You dare?"

"Cover yourself," he snapped back at her, his mirth fading. Anger sprouted from stifled desires; she was a tasty bit, and he had been looking forward to the enjoyment of her. But a virgin girl running away from a noble father was the last thing he needed, or wanted any part of. Nor could he walk away from her if she needed help, either. That thought came reluctantly. Softhearted, he grumbled to himself. That was his trouble. To the girl he growled, "Do it, before I take my belt to your backside."

For a moment she glared at him, sky-blue eyes warring with icy sapphire. Ice won, and she hastily fumbled her green robes back into place, muttering under her breath.

"Your name," he demanded. "And no lies, or I'll pack you to the

Marline Cloisters myself. Besides the hungry and the sick, they take in wayward girls and unruly children, and you look to be both."

"You have no right. I've changed my mind. I do not want your silver." She gestured imperiously. "Stand away from that door."

Conan gazed back at her calmly, not moving. "You are but a few words away from a stern-faced woman with a switch to teach you manners and proper behavior. Your name?"

Her eyes darted angrily to the door. "I am the Lady Julia," she said stiffly. "I will not shame my house by naming it in this place, not if you torture me with red-hot irons. Not if you use pincers, and the knout, and . . . and . . ."

"Why are you here, Julia, masquerading as a trull, instead of doing needlework at your mother's knee?"

"What right have you to demand . . . ? Erlik take you! My mother is long dead, and my father these three months. His estates were pledged for loans and were seized in payment. I had no relations to take me in, nor friends who had use for a girl with no more than the clothes on her back. And you will call me Lady Julia. I am still a noblewoman of Ophir."

"You're a silly wench," he retorted. "And why this? Why not become a serving girl? Or a beggar, even?"

Julia sniffed haughtily. "I would not sink so low. My blood—"

"So you become a trull?" He noted she had the grace to blush. But then, she did that often.

"I thought," she began hesitantly, then stopped. When she resumed her voice had dropped to a murmur. "It seemed not so different from my father's lemans, and they appeared to be ladies." Her eyes searched his face, and she went on urgently. "But I've done nothing. I am still . . . I mean . . . Oh, why am I telling any of this to you?"

Conan leaned against the door, the crudely cut boards creaking at his weight. If he were a civilized man, he would abandon her to the path she was following. He would have his will of her and leave her weeping with her coins—or cheat her of them, for that was the civilized way. Anything else would be more bother than she was worth. The gods alone knew what faction she might be attached to by blood, for all they had not helped her so far, or what faction he might offend by aiding her.

His mouth twisted in a grimace, and Julia flinched, thinking it was for her. He was thinking too much of factions of late, spending too much time delving the labyrinthine twists of Ophirean politics. This he would leave to the gods. And the wench.

"I am called Conan," he said abruptly "and I captain a Free-Company. We have our own cook, for our patron's kitchens prepare fussed-over viands not fit for a man's stomach. This cook, Fabio, needs a girl to fetch and serve. The work is yours, an you want it."

"A pot girl!" she exclaimed. "Me!"

"Be silent, wench!" he roared, and she rocked back on her heels. He waited to be certain she would obey, then nodded in satisfaction when she settled with her hands clasped at her throat. And her mouth shut. "Do you decide it is not too far beneath you, present yourself at Baron Timeon's palace before sunfall. If not, then know well what your future will be."

She let out one startled squeak as he took the step necessary to crush her to his chest. He tangled his free hand in her long hair, and his mouth took its pleasure with hers. For a time her bare feet drummed against his shins, then slowly her kicking stopped. When he let her heels thud to the floor once more, she stood trembling and silent, tremulous azure eyes locked on his face.

"And I was gentle compared to some," he said. Scooping up the sack containing the bronze, he left her standing there.

III

Boros was gone from the common room when Conan returned below, for which the Cimmerian was just as glad.

The spidery innkeeper rushed forward, though, rubbing his hands avariciously. "Not long with the girl, noble sir. I could have told you she'd not please. My Selina, now . . ."

Conan snarled, and the fellow retreated hastily. Crom! What a day, he thought. Go out searching for a wench and end up trying to rescue a fool girl from her own folly. He had thought he had outgrown such idiocy long ago.

Outside the street was narrow and crooked, little more than an alley dotted with muddy potholes where the cracked paving stones had been pried up and carried away, yet even here were there beggars. Conan tossed a fistful of coppers into the nearest out-thrust bowl and hurried on before the score of others could flock about him. A stench of rotted turnip and offal hung in the air, held by stone buildings that seemed to lean out over the way.

He had not gone far when it dawned on him that the mendicants, rather than chasing after him crying for more, had disappeared. Such men had the instincts of feral animals. His hand went to his sword even as three men stepped into the cramped confines of the street before him. The leader had a rag tied over where his right eye had been. The other two wore beards, one no more than a straggly collection of hairs. All three had swords in hand. A foot grated on paving stone behind the Cimmerian.

He did not wait for them to take another step. Hurling the bag containing the bronze at the one-eyed man, he drew his ancient broadsword and dropped to a crouch in one continuous motion. A blade whistled over his head as he pivoted, then his own steel was biting deep into the side of the man behind. Blood spurting, the man screamed, and his legs buckled.

Conan threw himself into a dive past the collapsing man, tucking his shoulder under, and rolled to his feet with his sword at the ready just in time to spit one-eye as he rushed forward with blade upraised. For an instant Conan stared into a lone brown eye filling with despair and filming with death, then one of the others was crowding close, attempting to catch the big Cimmerian while his sword was hung up in the body. Conan snatched the poignard from one-eye's belt and slammed it into his other attacker's throat. The man staggered back with a gurgling shriek, blood pumping through the fingers clutching his neck to soak his filthy beard in crimson.

All had occurred so quickly that the man impaled on Conan's blade was just now beginning to fall. The Cimmerian jerked his blade free as one-eye dropped. The first attacker gave a last quiver and lay still in a widening sanguinary pool.

The man with the straggly beard had not even had time to join the fight. Now he stood with sword half-raised, dark eyes rolling from one corpse to another and thin nose twitching. He looked like a rat that had just discovered it was fighting a lion. "Not worth it," he muttered. "No matter the gold, it's not worth dying." Warily he edged backwards until he came abreast of a crossing alley; with a last frightened glance he darted into it. In moments even the pounding of his feet had faded.

Conan made no effort to follow. He had no interest in footpads, of which the city had an overabundance. These had made their try and paid the price. He bent to wipe his sword, and froze as a thought came to him. The last man had mentioned gold. Only nobles carried gold on their persons, and he was far from looking that sort. Gold might be paid for a killing, though the life of a mercenary, even a captain, was not usually considered worth more than silver. Few indeed were the deaths that would bring gold. Except . . . assassination. With a shout that rang from the stone walls Conan snatched up the sack-wrapped statuette and was running in the same motion, encarmined blade still gripped in his fist. With him out of the way it might be easier to get through his company to Timeon. And that sort of killing had already begun. His massive legs pumped harder, and he burst out of the alley onto a main street.

A flower-girl, screeching at the giant apparition wielding bloody steel, leaped out of his way; a fruit peddler failed to move fast enough and caromed off Conan's chest, oranges exploding from his basket in all directions. The peddler's imprecations, half for the huge Cimmerian and half for the apprentices scurrying to steal his scattered fruit, followed Conan down the crowded street, but he did not slow his headlong charge. Bearers, scrambling to move from his path, overturned their sedan chairs, spilling cursing nobles into the street. Merchants in voluminous robes and serving girls shopping for their masters' kitchens scattered screaming and shouting before him.

Then Timeon's palace was in sight. As Conan pounded up the broad alabaster stairs, the two guards he had set on the columned portico rushed forward, arrows nocked, eyes searching the street for what pursued him.

"The door!" he roared at them. "Erlik blast your hides! Open the door!"

Hurriedly they leaped to swing open one of the massive bronze doors, worked with Timeon's family crest, and Conan rushed through without slowing.

He was met in the broad entry hall by Machaon and half a score of the company, their boots clattering on polished marble tiles. Varying degrees of undress and more than one mug clutched in a fist showed they had been rousted from their rest by his shouts, but all had weapons in hand.

"What happens?" Machaon demanded. "We heard your shouts, and—"

Conan cut him off. "Where is Timeon? Have you seen him since arriving?"

"He's upstairs with his new leman," Machaon replied. "What—"

Spinning, Conan raced up the nearest stairs, a curving sweep of alabaster that stood without visible support. Pausing only an instant Machaon and the others followed at a dead run. At the door to Timeon's bedchamber, tall and carved with improbable beasts, Conan did not pause. He slammed open the door with a shoulder and rushed in.

Baron Timeon leaped from his tall-posted bed with a startled cry, his round belly bouncing, and snatched up a long robe of red brocade. On the bed a slender, naked girl clutched the coverlet to her small yet shapely breasts. Ducking her head, she peered shyly at Conan through a veil of long, silky black hair that hung to her waist.

"What is the meaning of this?" Timeon demanded, furiously belting the robe about his girth. After the current fashion of the nobility, he wore a small, triangular beard on the point of his chin. On his moon face, with his found, protuberant eyes, it made him look like a fat goat. An angry goat, now. "I demand an answer immediately! Bursting into my chambers with sword drawn." He peered suddenly at the blade in Conan's hand. "Blood!" he gasped, staggering. He flung his arms around one of the thick intricately carved posts of his bed as if to hold himself erect, or perhaps to hide himself behind. "Are we attacked? You must hold them off till I escape. That is, I'll ride for aid. Hold them, and there'll be gold for all of you."

"There's no attack, Lord Timeon," Conan said hastily "At least, not here. But I was attacked in the city."

Timeon glanced at the girl. He seemed to realize he had been far from heroic before her. Straightening abruptly, he tugged at his robe as if adjusting it, smoothed his thinning hair. "Your squabbles with the refuse of Ianthe have no interest for me. And my pretty Tivia is too delicate a blossom to be frightened with your tales of alley brawls, and your gory blade. Leave, and I will try to forget your ill manners."

"Lord Timeon," Conan said with forced patience, "does someone mean you harm, well might they try to put me out of the way first. Count Tiberio is dead this last night at an assassin's hand. I will put guards at your door and in the garden beneath your windows."

The plump noble's water blue eyes darted to the girl again. "You will do no such thing. Tiberio took his own life, so I heard. And as for assassins—" he strode to the table where his sword lay, slung the scabbard into a corner and struck a pose with the weapon in hand—"should any manage to get past your vigilance, I will deal with them myself. Now leave me. I have . . . " he leered at the slender girl who still attempted unsuccessfully to cover herself, "matters to attend to."

Reluctantly Conan bowed himself from the room. The instant the door was shut behind him, he growled, "That tainted sack of suet. An old woman with a switch could beat him through every corridor of this palace."

"What are we to do?" Machaon asked. "If he refuses guards . . ."

"We guard him anyway," Conan snorted. "He can take all the chances he wants to with us to protect him, and he will so long as there's a woman to impress, but we cannot afford to let him die. Put two men in the garden, where he can't see them from his windows. And one at either end of this hall, around the corners where they can hide if Timeon comes out, but where they can keep an eye on his door."

"I'll see to it." The scarred warrior paused. "What's that you're carrying?"

Conan realized he still had the bronze, wrapped in its sack, beneath his arm. He had forgotten it in the mad rush to get to Timeon. Now he wondered. If the men who had attacked him had not been trying to open a way to the baron—and it now seemed they had not—perhaps they had been after the statuette. After all, two others had been willing to kill, and die, for it. And they had thought it worth gold. It seemed best to find out the why of it before giving Machaon a gift that might bring men seeking his life.

"Just a thing I bought in the city," he said. "Post those guards immediately. I don't want to take chances, in case I was right the first time."

"First time?" Machaon echoed, but Conan was already striding away.

The room Conan had been given was spacious, but what Timeon thought suitable for a mercenary captain. The tapestries on the walls were

of the second quality only, the lamps were polished pewter and brass
rather than silver or gold, and the floor was plain red tiles. Two arched
windows looked out on the garden, four floors below, but there was no
balcony. Still, the mattress on the big bed was goose down, and the tables
and chairs, if plain varnished wood, were sturdy enough for him to be
comfortable with, unlike the frail, gilded pieces in the rooms for noble
guests.

He tossed the rough sacking aside and set the bronze on a table. A
malevolent piece, it seemed almost alive. Alive and ready to rend and
tear. The man who had made it was a master. And steeped in abomination,
Conan was sure, for otherwise he could not have infused so much evil
into his creation.

Drawing his dagger, he tapped the hilt against the figure. It was not
hollow; there could be no gems hidden within. Nor did it have the feel or
heft of bronze layered over gold, though who would have gone to *that*
much trouble, or why, he could not imagine.

A knock came at the door while he was still frowning at the horned
shape, attempting to divine its secret. He hesitated, then covered it with
the sack before going to the door. It was Narus.

"There's a wench asking for you," the hollow-cheeked man said.
"Dressed like a doxy, but her face scrubbed like a temple virgin, and
pretty enough to be either. Says her name is Julia."

"I know her," Conan said, smiling.

Narus' mournful expression did not change, but then it seldom did. "A
gold to a silver there's trouble in this one, Cimmerian. Came to the front
and demanded entrance, as arrogant as a princess of the realm. When I
sent her around back, she tried to tell me her lineage. Claims she's noble
born. The times are ill for dallying with such."

"Take her to Fabio," Conan laughed. "She's his new pot girl. Tell him
to put her peeling turnips for the stew."

"A pleasure," Narus said, with a brief flicker of a smile, "after the way
her tongue scourged me."

At least one thing had gone well with the day, Conan thought as he
turned from the door. Then his eye fell on the sacking covered bronze on
the table, and his moment of jollity faded. But there were other matters
yet to be plumbed, and the feeling at the back of his neck told him there
would be deadly danger in doing so.

IV

The sly-faced man who called himself Galbro wandered nervously around the dusty room where he had been told to wait. Two great stuffed eagles on perches were the only decoration, the amber beads that had replaced their eyes seeming to glare more fiercely than ever any living eagle's eyes had. The lone furnishing was the long table supporting the leather bag in which he had brought what he had to sell. He did not like these meetings; despite all the silver and gold they put in his purse, he did not like the woman who gave him the coin. Her name was unknown to him, and he did not want to know it, now anything else about her. Knowledge of her would be dangerous.

Yet he knew it was not the woman alone who made him pace this time. That man. A northlander, Urian said he was. From whencever he came, he had slain five of Galbro's best and walked away without so much as a scratch. That had never happened before, or at least not since he came to Ophir. It was an ill omen. For the first time in long years he wished that he was back in Zingara, back in the thieves' warren of alleys that ran along the docks of Kordava. And that was foolish, for if he was not shortened a head by the guard, his throat would be slit by the denizens of those same alleys before he saw a single nightfall. There were penalties attached to playing both sides in a game, especially when both sides discovered that you cheated.

A light footstep brough him alert. *She* stepped into the room, and a shiver passed through him. No part of her but her eyes, dark and devoid of softness, was visible. A silver cloak that brushed the floor was gathered close about her. A dark, opaque veil covered the lower half of her face, and her hair was hidden by a white silk headcloth, held by a ruby pin, the stone as large as the last joint of his thumb.

The ruby invoked no shreds of greed within him. Nothing about her brought any feeling to him except fear. He hated that, fearing a woman,

191

but at least her coin was plentiful. His taste for that was all the greed he dared allow himself with her.

With a start he realized she was waiting for him to speak. Wetting his lips—why did they dry so in her presence?—he opened his bag, spread his offerings on the table. "As you can see, my lady, I have much this time. Very valuable."

One pale, slender hand extended from the cloak to finger what he had brought, object by object. The brass plaque, worked with the head of the demon that so fascinated her, was thrust contemptuously aside. He schooled his face not to wince. Leandros had labored hard on that, but of late she accepted few of the Corinthian's forgeries. Three fragments of manuscript, tattered and torn, she studied carefully, then lay to one side. Her fingers paused over a clay head, so worn with age he had not been certain it was meant to be the creature she wanted. She put it with the parchments.

"Two gold pieces," she said quietly when she was done. "One for the head, one for the codexes. They but duplicate what I already have."

A gold for the head was good—he had expected two for each of the manuscripts. "But, my lady," he whined, "I can but bring you what I find. I cannot read such script, or know if you already possess it. You know not what difficulties I face, what expenses, in your service. Five of my men slain. Coin to be paid for thefts. Men to be—"

"Five men dead?" Her voice was a whipcrack across his back, though she had not raised it.

He squirmed beneath her gaze; sweat rolled down his face. This cold woman had little tolerance for failure, he knew, and less for men who drew attention to themselves, as by leaving corpses strewn in the streets. He had Baraca as example for that. The Kothian had been found hanging by his feet with his skin neatly removed, yet still alive. For a few agonized hours of screaming.

"What have you been into, Galbro," she continued, her low words stabbing like daggers, "to lose five men?"

"Naught, my lady. A private matter. I should not have mentioned it, my lady. Forgive me, please."

"Fool! Your lies are transparent. Know that the god I serve, and whom you serve through me, gives me the power of pain." She spoke words that his brain did not want to comprehend; her hand traced a figure in the air between them.

Blinding light flashed behind his eyes, and agony filled him, every muscle in his body writhing and knotting. Helpless, he fell, quivering in every limb, bending into a backbreaking arch till only his head and drumming heels touched the floor. He tried to shriek, but shrieks could not pass the frozen cords of his throat, nor even breath. Blackness veiled his eyes, and he found a core within him that cried out for death, for anything to escape the all-consuming pain.

Abruptly the torment melted away, and he collapsed in a sobbing heap.

"Not even death can save you," she whispered, "for death is one of the realms of my master. Behold!" Again she spoke words that seared his mind.

He peered up at her pleadingly, tried to beg, but the words stuck in his throat. The eagles moved. He knew they were dead; he had touched them. But they moved, wings unfolding. One uttered a piercing scream. The other swooped from its perch to the table, great talons gripping the wood as it tilted its head to regard him as it might a rabbit. Tears rolled uncontrollably down his thin cheeks.

"They would tear you to pieces at my command," the veiled woman told him. "Now speak. Tell me all."

Galbro began to babble. Words spilled from his mouth like water from a fountain. The bronze figure, described in minute detail. How he learned of it, and the attempts to secure it. Yet even in his terror he held back the true description of the giant northlander. Some tiny portion of him wanted to be part of killing this man who had endangered him; a larger part wanted whatever the veiled woman might pay for the piece. Did she know how to obtain it without him she might decide his usefulness was at an end. He knew she had others like him who served her, and Baraca reminded him of the deadliness of her wrath. When his torrent of speech ended, he lay waiting in dread.

"I dislike those who keep things from me," she said at last, and he shivered at the thought of her dislike. "Secure this bronze, Galbro. Obey me implicitly, and I will forgive your lies. Fail . . ."

She did not have to voice the threat. His whirling mind provided a score of them, each worse than the last. "I will obey, my lady," he sobbed, scrubbing his face in the dust of the floor. "I will obey. I will obey."

Not until her footsteps had faded from the room could he bring himself to stop the litany. Raising his head he stared wildly about the room, filled with joyous relief that he was alone and still alive. The eagles caught his eye, and he moaned. They were still again, but one leaned forward with wings half raised as if ready to swoop at him from its perch. The other still clung to the table, head swiveled to pierce him with its amber gaze.

He wanted to flee, yet he knew with a sinking feeling that he could not run far enough or fast enough to escape her. That accursed northlander was responsible for this. If not for him everything could have gone on as before. Rage built in him, comforting rage that overlaid his terror. He would make the northlander pay for everything that had happened to him. That big man would pay.

Synelle waited until she was in her palanquin—unadorned for anonymity—with the pale gray curtains safely drawn before lowering her veil. The bearers carried her from the courtyard of the small house where she had met Galbro without a word needed from her. Tongueless, so they could not speak of where they had borne her, they knew the need to serve her perfectly as well as did the sly-faced thief.

It was well she always went to these meetings prepared. A cloth on which Galbro had wiped his sweat, obtained by another of her minions, a few feathers plucked from the eagles, these had given her the means to quell the thief. She could rest at her ease knowing the man's soul was seared with the need for absolute obedience. And yet for once the gentle swaying of the platform did not lull her as she lolled on silken cushions.

Something about the sly little man's description of the bronze produced an irritating tickle in the back of her mind. She had encountered many representations of Al'Kiir's head, many medallions and amulets embossed with his head or the symbol of the horns, but never before a complete figure. It sounded so detailed, perhaps an exact duplicate of the actual body of the god. Her face went blank with astonishment. In one of the manuscript fragments she had gathered there was . . . something. She was sure of it.

She parted the forward curtains a slit. "Faster!" she commanded. "Erlik blast your souls, faster!"

The bearers increased their pace to a run, forcing their way through the crowds, careless of the curses that followed them. Synelle would do more than curse if they failed to obey. Within, she pounded a small fist against her thigh in frustration at the time it took to cross the city.

As soon as the palanquin entered the courtyard of her mansion, before the bearers could lower it to the slate tiles, Synelle leaped out. Even in her haste hate flickered through her at the sight of the house. As large as any palace in the city, it still was not a palace. The white-stuccoed walls and red-tiled roof were suitable for the dwelling of a merchant. Or a woman. By ancient law no woman, not even a princess, could maintain a palace within the walls of Ianthe. But she would change that. By the gods, if what she thought were true she would change it within the month. Why wait for Valdric to die? Not even the army could stand against her. Iskandrian, the White Eagle of Ophir, would kneel at her feet along with the great lords of Ophir.

Dropping her cloak for a serving maid to tend to, she raised her robes to her hips and ran, heedless of servants who stared at bare, flashing limbs.

To the top floor of the mansion she ran, to a windowless room where only one other but herself was allowed, and that one with her mind ensorceled to forget what lay within, to die did anyone attempt to force the awful knowledge from her.

Golden sconces on the walls held pale, perfumed candles, yet all their light could not thrust back an air of darkness, the feel of a shrine to evil. Shrine it was, in a way, though there was no idol, no place for votive offerings. Three long tables, polished till they gleamed, were all the furnishings the room contained. On one were flasks of liquids that bubbled in their sealed containers or glowed with eery lights, vials of powders noxious and obscene, the tools of her painfully learned craft. The second was covered with amulets and talismans; some held awesome powers she could detect but not yet wield. Al'Kiir would give them to her.

It was to the third table she hurried, for there were the fragments of scroll, the tattered pages of parchment and vellum that she had slowly and carefully gathered over the years. There was the dark knowledge of sorceries the world had attempted to forget, sorceries that would give her power. Hastily she pawed through them, for once careless of flakes that dropped from ancient pages. She found what she sought, and easily read in a language dead a thousand years. She was perhaps the last person in the world capable of reading that extinct tongue, for the scholar who had taught her she had had strangled with his own beard, his wife and children smothered in their beds to be doubly sure. Death guarded secrets far better than gold.

An eager gleam lit her dark eyes, and she read again the passage she had found.

> Lo, call to the great god, entreating him, and set before the image,
> the succedaneum, the bridge between worlds, as a beacon to glorify
> the way of the god to thee.

She had thought this spoke of the priestess as bridge and beacon, placing herself before the image of Al'Kiir, but that which lay beneath the mountain was not an image. It was material body of the god. It must be the image that was to be placed before the priestess during the rites. The image. The bronze figure. It had to be. A thrill of triumph coursed through her as she swept from the room.

In the corridor a serving girl busily lighting silver lamps hung from the walls awkwardly made obeisence clutching her coal-pot and tongs.

Synelle had not realized how close the fall of darkness came. Twilight was almost on the city; precious time wasted away as she stood there. "Find Lord Taramenon," she commanded, "and bid him come to my dressing chamber immediately. Run, girl!" The serving girl ran, for the Lady Synelle's displeasures brought punishments best not thought of.

There was no need to ask if the handsome young lord was in her mansion. Taramenon wished to be king, a foolish desire for one with neither the proper blood lines nor money, and one he believed he had hidden from her. It was true he was the finest sword in Ophir—she had made a point of binding the best bladesmen of the land to her service—but that counted little in the quest for a throne. He followed Synelle in her own seeking because he believed in his arrogance that she would find it impossible to rule without a husband by her side, because he thought in his pride that he would be that husband. Thus he would gain his crown. She had done nothing to dissuade him from the belief. Not yet.

Four tirewomen, lithe matched blondes in robes that seemed to be but vapors of silk, paused only to bend knee before hurrying forward, moving as gracefully as dancers, as Synelle entered her dressing chamber. Her agents had gone to great efforts to find the four, sisters of noble Corinthian blood with but a year separating each from the next; Synelle herself had seen to the breaking and training of them. They followed her submissively and silently as she strolled about the room, removing her garments without once impeding her progress in any way. In nakedness more resplendant than any satins or silks, long-limbed, full-breasted and sleek, Synelle allowed them to minister to her. One held an ivory-framed mirror while another used delicate fur brushes to freshen the kohl on Synelle's eyelids and the rouge on her lips. The others wiped her softly with cool, damp clothes, and annointed her with rare perfume of Vendhya, priced at one gold coin the drop.

The heavy tread of a man's boots sounded in the antechamber, and the tirewomen scurried to fetch a lounging robe of scarlet velvet. Synelle refused to hold out her arms for them to slip it on until the steps were at the very door.

Taramenon gasped at the tantalizing flash of silken curves, quickly sheathed, that greeted his entrance. He was tall, broad of shoulders and deep of chest, with an aquiline nose and deep brown eyes that had melted the hearts of many women. Synelle was glad that he did not follow the fashion in beards, being rather clean shaven. She was also pleased to note the quickening of his breath as he gazed at her.

"Leave me," she commanded, belting tight the red satin sash of her robe. The girls filed obediently from the room.

"Synelle," Taramenon said thickly as soon as they were gone, and stepped forward as if to take her in his arms.

She stopped him with an upraised hand. There was no time for such frivolity, no matter how amusing it might usually be to make him writhe with a desire she had no intention of slaking. Her studies told her there were powers to be gained from allowing a man to take her, and dedicating that taking to Al'Kiir, but she knew Taramenon's plans for her. And she had seen too many proud, independent women give themselves to a man only to discover they had given pride and independence as well. Not for her listening breathlessly for a lover's footstep, smiling at his laughter, weeping at his frowns, running to tend to his wants like the meanest slave. She would not risk such an outcome. She would never give herself to any man.

"Send your two best swordsmen after yourself to find and follow Galbro," she said, "without allowing him to become aware of it. He seeks a bronze, an image of Al'Kiir the length of a big man's forearm, but it is too important to trust to him. When he has located it for them, they are to secure it and bring it to me at once. Do you understand, Taramenon? Are you listening?"

"I listen," he said hoarsely, a touch of anger in his voice. "When you summoned me to your dressing chamber, at this hour, I thought something other than an accursed figure was on your mind."

A seductive smile caressed her full lips, and she moved closer to him, until her breasts were pressed against him. "There will be time for that when the throne is secure," she said softly. Her slender fingers brushed his mouth. "All the time in the world." His arms began to come up around her, but she stepped smoothly out of his embrace. "First the throne, Taramenon, and this bronze you call accursed is vital to attaining that. Send the men tonight. Now."

She watched a multitude of emotions cross his face, and wondered yet again at how transparent were the minds of men. No doubt he thought his features unreadable, yet she knew he was adding this incident to a host of others, cataloguing the ways he would make her pay for them once she was his.

"It will be done, Synelle," he growled at last.

When he was gone her smile turned to one of ambition triumphant. Power would be hers. The smile became full-throated laughter. It would be hers, and hers alone.

V

The night streets of Ianthe were dark and empty, yet near the palace of Baron Timeon a shadow moved. A cloaked and hooded figure pressed itself to the thickly-ornamented marble walls, and cool green eyes, slightly tilted above high cheekbones, surveyed the guards marching their rounds among the thick, fluted columns of alabaster. All very well, those guards, but would he who lay sleeping within remember his own thief's tricks?

The cloak was discarded, revealing a woman in tight-fitting tunic and snug breeches of buttery leather, with soft red boots on her feet. Moonlight shimmered on titian hair tied back from her face with a cord. Quickly she undid her sword belt and refastened it with her Turanian scimitar hanging down her back, then checked the leather sack hanging at her side. Strong, slender fingers tested the niveous marble carvings of the wall, and then she was climbing like a monkey.

Below the edge of the flat roof she paused. Boots grated on slate tiles. He remembered. Yet for all the reputation this Free-Company was building in the country, they were yet soldiers. Those on the roof walked regular paths, as sentries in a camp. The measured tread came closer, closer. And then it was receding.

As agile as a panther, she was onto the roof, running on silent feet, losing herself in the shadows of two score chimneys. At the drop of the central garden around which the entire palace was arranged, she fell to her belly and peered down. There were the windows of his sleeping chamber. They were dark. So he did sleep. She would have expected him to be carousing with yet another in a long line of all too willing wenches. It was one of the things she remembered most about him, his eye for women and theirs for him.

Knowledge had been easily come by. Not even bribes had been necessary. All that had been required was for her to pretend to be a serving woman—though that had been no small a task in itself, given her lush beauty; serving maids with curves like hers soon found themselves promoted to the master's bed—and chat to the women of Baron Timeon's palace in the markets. They had been eager to tell about the great house in which they served, about their fat master and his constantly changing parade of women, about the hard-eyed warriors who had hired themselves to him. Especially about the warriors they had been willing to talk, giggling and teasing each other about returning from the stable with hay covering the back of a robe and stolen moments in secluded corners of the garden.

She would have wagered there were guards in that garden as well as on the roof, but those did not worry her. From the leather sack she produced a rope woven of black-dyed silk, to the end of which was fastened a padded grapnel. The metal prongs hooked on the scrollwork along the roof-edge; the rope fell invisibly into the darkness below. It was just long enough to reach the window she sought.

A short climb downward, and she was inside the room. It was as black as Zandru's Seventh Hell. A dagger found its way into her hand . . . and she stopped dead. What if there were some error in her information? She did not want to kill the wrong man. She had to be sure.

Mentally cursing her own foolishness, she felt in the darkness for a table, for a lamp . . . and yes, a coal-box and tongs. She puffed softly on the coal till it glowed, held it to the wick. Light bloomed, and she gasped at the apparition on the table beside the brass lamp. Horned malevolence glared at her. It was but a bronze figure, yet she sensed evil in the thing, and primeval instinct deep within her told her that evil was directed at women. Could the man she sought have changed so much as to keep such monstrosity in his chamber? The man she sought!

Heart pounding, she spun, dagger raised. He still slept, a young giant sprawled in his slumber, Conan of Cimmeria. Soft-footed she crept closer to his bed, her eyes drinking him in, the planes of his face, the breadth of his shoulders, the massive arms that had . . .

Stop, she commanded herself. How many wrongs had this man committed against her? She had lived on the plains of Zamora and Turan with the freedom of the hawk till Conan had come, and brought with him the destruction of her band of brigands. For his stupid male honor and the matter of a silly oath she had made him swear in a moment of anger, he had allowed her to be sold into slavery, into a zenana in Sultanapur. Every time the switch had kissed her buttocks, every time she had been forced to dance naked for the pleasure of the fat merchant who had been her master and his friends, all these could be laid at Conan's feet.

When at last she had escaped and fled to Nemedia, become the queen of the smugglers of that country, he had appeared again. And before he was done she must needs pack her hard-acquired wealth on sumpter animals and flee again.

She had escaped him, then, but she could not escape his memory, the memory of his building fires in her, fires that she came to crave like the smoker of the yellow lotus craved his pipe. That memory had hounded her, driven her into riotous living and excesses that shocked even the jaded court of Aquilonia. Only when all her gold was gone had she known freedom again. Once more she had taken up the life she loved, living by her wits and her sword. She had sought a new country, Ophir, and raised a new band of rogues.

How many months gone had the first rumors come to her of a huge northerner whose Free-Company was a terror to all who opposed him? How long had she tried to convince herself that it was not the same man who always brought ruin to her? Once more she found herself within the same borders as he, but this time she would not flee. She would be free of him at last. With a sob she raised the dagger high and brought it down.

A strange sound penetrated Conan's dreams—a woman's sob, he thought drowsily—and brought him awake. He had just time to see a shape beside his bed, see the descending dagger, and then he was rolling aside.

The dagger slashed into the mattress where his chest had been, and the force of the missed stab brought his attacker down on top of him. Instantly he seized the shape—the back of his brain noted a curious softness—and hurled it across the room. In the same motion he leaped from the bed, seized the worn leather-wrapped hilt of his broadsword and slung the scabbard aside. It was then that he saw his assailant clearly for the first time.

"Karela!" he exclaimed.

The auburn-haired beauty rising warily from the floor near the wall snarled at him. "Yes, Derketo blast your eyes! And would she had made you sleep just one moment more."

His gaze went to the dagger thrust into his mattress, and his eyebrows raised. But all he said was, "I thought you went to Aquilonia to live the life of a lady."

"I am no lady," she breathed. "I am a woman! And woman enough to put an end to you once and for all!" Her hand went to her shoulder, and suddenly she was rushing at him, brandishing three feet of curved razor-sharp steel.

Anger blazed in Conan's icy blue eyes, and he swung his sword to meet hers with a crash. Shock appeared on Karela's face, her mouth dropping open with incredulity as her blade was nearly wrenched from her grasp. She took a step back, and from that moment was ever defending from his flashing edge. He did not force her back, but every pace backwards she took, he followed. And she could not but move backwards, away from the force of those blows, panting, desperate to attack yet with no slightest opportunity. If he made certain that his sword struck only hers, he also made certain that every blow had his full strength behind it, rocking her to her heels. The cool smile on his face, calm even as he battled her, struck to her heart. It mocked her, wounding more deeply than ever steel could.

"Derketo take you, you over-muscled barbar," she rasped.

With a sharp ring her scimitar was hurled from her. For a breath she froze, then dove for the fallen blade.

Conan tossed his broadsword aside and seized the back of her tunic as she leaped. Fabric already strained by more than generous callimastian curves split down the front; her momentum carried her partly out of her tunic, stripping her half-way to the waist. In an instant Conan had twisted his fistful of cloth, trapping her arms at her sides. He found he had caught a spitting, kicking wildcat. But, he noted, a wildcat who still had the finest, roundest set of breasts he had seen in many a day.

"Coward!" she shouted. "Spawn of a diseased goat! Fight me blade to blade, and I'll spit you like the capon you are!"

Easily he pulled her over to the bed, seated himself, and jerked her across his knees. Easily he controlled her frenzied thrashings.

"Oh, no!" she gasped. "Not that! Cimmerian, I'll cut your heart out! I'll slice your manhood for—"

Her diatribe was cut off with a howl as his big hand landed forcefully on her taut-breeched buttocks.

A fist thumped against the heavy wooden door, and Machaon's voice sounded from the corridor. "What's happening in there, Conan? Are you all right?"

"All is well," Conan replied. "I'm tending to an unruly wench."

That provoked furious struggles from Karela, futile against his iron grasp. "Release me, Cimmerian," she growled, "or I'll see you hanging by your heels over a slow fire. Unhand me, Derketo shrivel your manhood!"

Conan answered her with a smack that brought another howled curse. "You tried to kill me, wench," he said slowly, punctuating each word with his calloused palm. "You've been untrustworthy from the first day I laid eyes on you. In Shadizar you'd have let me be slain without a word of warning." Karela's shrieked imprecation became incoherent; she kicked frantically at the air, but he did not pause. "In the Kezankian Mountains you betrayed me to a sorcerer. I saved your life there, but in Nemedia you bribed my jailors with gold to torture me. Why? Why a knife for my heart while I lay sleeping? Have I ever harmed you? Is your soul filled with treachery, woman?"

A half-formed plea among her cries penetrated his rage, killing his anger and staying his hand. Karela pleading? Whatever she had done or tried to do, that was not right. As he could not kill her, neither could he bring himself to break her pride completely. He pushed her off his lap to fall with a thump to her knees.

Her tear-streaked face twisted with sobs, Karela's slender hands stole back gingerly to her buttocks. Then, as if suddenly remembering Conan's presence, she tore them away again; moist green eyes glared daggers at him. "May Derketo blast your eyes, Cimmerian," she said jerkily, "and Erlik take your soul for a plaything. No man has ever treated me as you do and lived."

"And no one," he said quietly, "man or woman, has ever dealt with me as treacherously as you have without incurring my enmity. And yet I cannot find it in me to hate you. But this! Murder was never your way, Karela. Was it for gold? You've always loved gold above all else."

"It was for me!" she spat at him, pounding a small fist on her thigh. Her eyes squeezed shut, and her voice dropped to a whisper. "Your presence turns my muscles to wine. Your eyes on me sap my will. How can I not want you dead?"

Conan shook his head in wonderment. Never had he pretended to understand women, least of all this fierce female falcon. Once more he was convinced that whatever gods had created men had not been the gods who created women.

As she knelt there in disarray, naked to the waist, Conan felt other stirrings than amazement. She was a woman of marvelous curves to brighten the eye, a wonderful blend of softness and firmness to delight the touch. Always she had been able to rouse his desire, though she often attempted to use that to bend him to her will. Abruptly he decided that learning why and how she had come to Ophir could wait. Gently he drew her between his knees.

Her clear green eyes, still tremulous, fluttered open. "What are you doing?" she demanded unsteadily.

He lifted the tattered tunic from her and threw it aside.

Small white teeth bit into her full underlip, and she shook her head. "No," she said breathlessly. "I will not. No. Please."

Easily he lifted her to the bed, disposed of her soft boots, peeled the tight breeches from her long legs.

"I hate you, Conan." But there was a curious note of pleading in her voice for such a statement. "I came to kill you. Do you not realize that?"

He plucked her dagger from his mattress and held it in two fingers before her gaze. "Take it, if you truly wish me dead."

For the space of three breaths his eyes held hers. Convulsively she turned her face aside. Conan smiled and, casually tossing the dagger to the floor, set about producing cries from her that had naught to do with pain.

VI

Sunlight steaming through the windows woke Conan. He opened
his eyes and found himself staring at Karela's dagger, once more
driven to the hilt into his mattress. The blade held a fragment of
parchment. Karela was gone.

"Blast the woman," he muttered, ripping the parchment free. It was
covered with a bold, sprawling hand.

> Another debt added to those you already owe me. The next time
> you will die, Cimmerian. I will not run from another country
> because of you. By the Teats of Derketo I swear, I will not.

Frowning, he crumpled the parchment in his fist. It was like the woman,
leaving before he woke, with threats but without answers to any of his
questions. He had thought she was done with threats altogether; she had
enjoyed the night as well as he, of that she had left no doubt.

Hurriedly he dressed and headed into the bowels of the palace. He was
still settling his swordbelt about his waist when he entered the long room
where his company took their meals, near the kitchen Timeon had given
over to them. The simple hearty provender Fabio prepared offended his
own cooks, so the lord said. Some score and a half of the mercenary
warriors, unarmored but weapons as always belted on, were scattered
among crude trestle-tables that had been rooted out of storage in the
stables. Machaon and Narus sat by themselves, their attention to the
leather jacks of ale in their fists and the wooden bowls of stew before them
not so great that they did not note his entrance.

"Ho, Cimmerian," Machaon called out loudly. "How was that, ah,
unruly wench last night?" A sprinkling of rough laughter made it clear he
had shared his story with the rest.

Could not the accursed fool keep his tongue behind his teeth, Conan
thought. Aloud he said, "Double the guards on the roof, Machaon. And

see they keep eyes and ears open. A parade of temple virgins would be undetected up there as it is."

Narus laughed dolefully into his ale as Conan straddled a bench across from them. "The wench was *too* unruly, was she? 'Tis the way of all women, to be least accomodating when you want them most."

"Do you have to beat all of them?" Taurianus called, a jealous edge to his bantering tone. "I thought her shrieks would bring the roof down."

"Food!" Conan bellowed. "Must I die of hunger?"

"There's a morsel in that kitchen," Machaon chuckled, "I could consume whole." He nudged Narus as Julia hurried from the kitchen, balancing with some difficulty a bowl of stew, a loaf of bread and a mug of ale.

She was much changed from the last time Conan had seen her. Her long auburn hair was tied with a green ribbon, and pulled back from a face bare of rouge or kohl but streaked with sweat from the heat of the kitchen fires. Her long robe of soft white wool, soot smudged and damp with soapy water, was meant to be modest, he assumed, but it clung to her curves in a way that drew the eye of every man in the room.

"You must speak to that man," she said as she set Conan's meal before him. He stared at her questioningly, and she flung out an arm dramatically toward the kitchen. "That man. Fabio. He threatened me . . . with a switch. Tell him who I am."

Conan scooped up a horn spoon full of stew. In one form or another it served the men of the company for both meals of the day, morning and night. "You work in the kitchens," he said. "That is Fabio's domain. Did a queen somehow come to scrub his pots he'd switch her an she did it badly. You'd best learn to do as he tells you."

Julia sputtered in indignation, the more so when Machaon laughed.

"You've too many airs, wench," the grizzled veteran chortled. "Besides, you're well padded for it." And he applied a full-fingered pinch to punctuate his claim.

Squealing, the auburn-haired girl leaped. To seize Conan's bowl and upend it over Machaon's head. Narus convulsed with laughter so hard that he began coughing.

"Fool girl," Conan growled. "I was eating that. Fetch me another, and quick about it."

"Fetch your own," she snapped back. "Or starve, if you wish to eat with the likes of him." Spinning on her heel, she stalked into the kitchen, her back rigid.

A stunned Machaon sat raking thick gobbets of stew from his face with his fingers. "I've a mind to take a switch to that conceited jade myself," he muttered.

"Go easy with her," Conan said. "She'll learn in time, whether she will or no. She is used to a gentler way of life than that which faces her now."

"I'd like to gentle her," Machaon replied. "But I'll keep my hands from her as she's yours, Cimmerian."

Conan shook his head. "She's not mine. Nor yours either, till she says she is. There are bawds aplenty in the town, is that your need."

The two men stared at him perplexedly, but they nodded, and he was satisfied. They might think he was in truth laying claim to the girl— though doubtless wondering why he wished to make a secret of it—but they would not demand more of her than she was willing to give. And they would speak it among the company, giving her protection with the others as well. He was not sure why he did not, save for Karela. It was difficult for him to think too much of other women when that fiery wench was about.

In any case, she was likely to give him ten times the trouble Julia did, and without trying half so hard. Karela was a woman who kept her word. If he did not find a way to stop her she would put steel between his ribs yet. Worse, she had a mind for vengeance like a Stygian. It would be like her to destroy the Free-Company, if she could, before killing him.

"Have either of you heard rumors of a woman bandit?" he asked in a carefully casual tone.

"I'll have to bathe to get clean of this," Machaon growled, picking a lump of meat from his hair. He popped it into his mouth. "I've heard no such tales. Women are meant for other things than brigands."

"Nor I," Narus said. "Women are not suited to the violent trades. Except perhaps that red-haired jade we encountered in Nemedia. She claimed to be a bandit, though I'd never heard of her. The buxom trull was offended I did not know her fame. Remember?"

"She's no trull," Conan said, "and she'll carve your liver does she hear you name her so." Immediately the words were gone he wished he had held his tongue.

"She's here!" Machaon exclaimed. "What was her name?"

"Karela," Narus said. "A temper like a thornbush, that one has."

Machaon laughed suddenly. "She was the wench last night." He shrugged at Conan's glare. "Well, there's no woman in the palace who'd need her bottom warmed to crawl into your blankets. It must have been her. I'd not bed her without my sword and armor, and mayhap a man to watch my back."

"It was her," the Cimmerian said, and added grudgingly, "She tried to put a dagger in me."

"That sounds like the woman I remember," Narus chortled. "From the yells, I'd say you taught her better manners."

" 'Twould be sport," Machaon crowed, "to stuff her and our Julia into a sack together."

Tears ran down Narus' face from his laughter. "I would pay coin to see that fight."

"Erlik take the pair of you," Conan snarled. "There's more danger in that woman than sport. She thinks she has a grievance against me, and she will cause trouble for the company if she can."

"What can a woman do?" Narus said. "Nothing."

"I would not like to wager my life on that," Conan told him. "Not when the woman is Karela. I want you to ask questions in the taverns and the brothels. 'Tis possible she's changed her name, but she cannot change the way she looks. A red-haired woman bandit with a body like one of Derketo's handmaidens will be known to someone. Tell the others to keep their eyes open as well."

"Why can you not manage her grievance as you did last night?" Machaon asked. "A smack on the bottom and to bed. Oh, very well—" he raised his hands in surrender as Conan opened his mouth for more angry words—"I will ask questions in the brothels. At least it gives me an excuse to spend more time at the House of the Doves."

"Forget not the House of the Honeyed Virgins," Narus added.

Conan scowled wordlessly. The fools did not know Karela as he did. He hoped for the sake of the company that they had time to learn before it was too late. Abruptly he became aware of the horn spoon of stew he still held, and put it in his mouth. "Fabio's cooking horse again," he said when he'd swallowed.

Narus froze with his own spoon half lifted. "Horse?" he gasped. Machaon stared at his bowl as if he expected it to leap from the table at him.

"Horse," Conan said, tossing his spoon to the rough planks. Narus gagged. Not until he was out of the room did the Cimmerian permit a smile to grow on his face. The meat tasted like beef to him, but those two deserved the worrying they were going to do over what Fabio was feeding them.

"Conan!" Julia ran out of the door he had just exited, bouncing off his chest as he turned. Her hands clutched her robe at the waist, twisting nervously. "Conan, you didn't . . . that is, last night . . . I mean . . ." She stopped and took a deep breath. "Conan, you must speak to Fabio. He struck me. Look." Half-turning she lifted her robe to expose the alabastrine rounds of her buttocks.

Conan was barely able to make out a pink stripe across the undercurve. He raised his gaze to her face. Her eyes were closed; the tip of her tongue continually wetted her full lips.

"I'll speak to him," he said gravely. He eyes shot open, and a smile blossomed on her face. "I'll tell him he must strike harder than that to make any impression on a stubborn pot-girl."

"Conan!" she wailed. Hastily she covered herself, smoothing the pale wool over her hips. Her eyes became as hard as sapphires. "You had a woman in your . . . your chamber last night. I . . . I was passing in the corridor, and I heard."

He smiled, and watched a blush spread over her cheeks. So she had had her ear pressed to his door, had she? "And what concern is that of yours?" he asked. "You are here to scrub pots and stir the stew, to fetch and carry for Fabio. Not to be wandering parts of the palace where you have no business."

"But you kissed me," she protested. "And the way you kissed me! You cannot make me feel like that, then calmly walk away. I'm a woman, curse you! I'm eighteen! I will not be dismissed like a plaything."

For the second time in the space of hours, he mused, a woman was protesting her womanhood to him. But what a contrast between them. Karela was bold and defiant even as she melted with passion; Julia frightened despite her bluff front. Karela knew well the ways of men and women; Julia was ravaged by a kiss. Karela knew who she was and what she wanted; Julia . . .

"Do you want to come to my bed?" he said softly, taking her chin in his hand and tilting her face up. Scarlet suffused her face and neck, but she did not try to wrench free. "Say yes, and I'll carry you there this moment."

"The others," she whispered. "They'll know."

"Forget them. 'Tis you must chose."

"I cannot, Conan." She sobbed when he released her, and leaned toward him as if seeking his touch. "I want to say yes, but I fear to. Can you not just . . . take me? Men do such things, I know. Why must you put this burden I do not want on me?"

Barely four years separated them, yet at that moment he felt it could as well be four hundred. "Because you are not a slave, Julia. You say you are a woman, but when you are truly a woman you will be able to say yes or no, and know it is what you mean to say. But till then . . . well, I take only women to my bed, not frightened girls."

"Erlik curse you," she said bitterly. Instantly she was contrite, one hand raised to touch his cheek. "No, I didn't mean that. You confuse me so. When you kissed me you made me want to be a woman. Kiss me again, and make me remember. Kiss me, and give me the courage I need."

Conan reached for her, and at that instant a bellow of pain and rage echoed down the halls. He spun, grabbing instead for the leather-wrapped hilt of his sword. The cry came again, from above he was certain.

"Timeon," he muttered. His blade came into his hand, and he was running, shouting as he ran. "Rouse yourselves, you poxed rouges! 'Tis the baron screaming like a woman in birth! To arms, curse you!"

Servants and slaves ran hysterically, shrieking and waving their arms at his shouts. Men of the company knocked them aside without compunction as they poured out of the corners where they had been taking their ease. Helmets were tugged on and swords waved as a growing knot of warriors followed the big Cimmerian up marble stairs.

In the corridor outside Timeon's chamber the two guards Conan had caused to be set there stood staring dumbfounded at the ornately carved door. Conan slammed into that door at a dead run, smashing it open.

Timeon lay in the middle of a multi-hued Iranistani carpet, his body wracked by convulsions, heels drumming, plump hands clawing at his throat. His head was thrown back, and every time he managed to fight a breath he loosed it again in a scream. Tivia, his leman, stood with her back to a wall, clutching a cloak about her tightly, her eyes, large and dark, fixed on the helplessly jerking man in an expression of horror. An overturned goblet lay near Timeon, and a puddle of wine soaking into the rug.

"Zandru's Hells!" Conan growled. His eye lit on Machaon, forcing his way through the men crowding the hall. "A physician, Machaon. Quickly! Timeon's poisoned!"

"Boros is in the kitchens," the tattooed man called back. Conan hesitated, and the other saw it. "Curse it, Cimmerian, it'll take half the day to get another."

Timeon's struggles were growing weaker; his screams had become moans of agony. Conan nodded. "Fetch him, then."

Machaon disappeared, and Conan turned back to the man on the floor. How had the fool gotten himself poisoned? The answer might mean life or death to him and the rest of the company. And he had to have the answer before the matter was turned over to the King's torturers. Valdric might ignore the great part of what was happening in his country, but he would not ignore the murder of a noble in the very shadow of his throne.

"Narus!" Conan shouted. The hollow-faced man stuck his head into the room. "Secure the palace. No one leaves, nor any message, till I say. Hurry, man!"

As Narus left Machaon hurried Boros into the room. The former mage's apprentice looked sober at least, Conan was glad to see.

"He's poisoned," the Cimmerian said.

Boros looked at him as he might at a child. "I can see that."

Fumbling in his pouch the gray-bearded man knelt beside Timeon. Quickly he produced a smooth white stone the size of a man's fist and a small knife. With difficulty he straightened one of the baron's arms, pushed up the sleeve of his robe, and made a deep cut. As blood welled up he pressed the white stone to the cut. When he took his hand away the stone remained, tendrils of black appearing in it.

"Bezoar-stone," Boros announced to the room. "Sovereign for poison. A physician's tool, strictly speaking, but I find it useful. Yes."

He tugged at his full beard and bent to study the stone. It was full black, now, and as they watched it became blacker, as a burned cinder, as a raven's wing, and blacker still. Suddenly the stone shattered. In the same moment a last breath rattled in Timeon's throat, and the fat baron was still.

"He's dead," Conan breathed. "I thought you said that accursed stone was sovereign for poison!"

"Look at it!" Boros wailed. "My stone is ruined. 'Twould take poison enough to kill ten men to do that. I could not have saved him with a sack full of bezoar-stones."

"It is murder, then," Narus breathed. A murmur of disquiet ripplied through the men in the corridor.

Conan's hand tightened on his sword. Most of the three-score who followed him now he had recruited in Ophir, a polyglot crew from half a dozen lands, and their allegiance to him was not as strong as that of the original few. They had faced battle with him often—such was the way of the life they led, and accepted by them—but unless he found the murderer quickly fear of being put to the question would do what no enemy had ever been able to. Send them scattering to the four winds.

"Do you want me to find who put the poison in the wine?" Boros asked.

For a moment Conan could only gape. "You can do that?" he demanded finally. "Erlik blast you, are you sober enough? An you make some drunkard's mistake, I'll shave your corpse."

"I'm as sober as a priest of Mitra," Boros replied. "More so than most. You, girl. The wine came from that?" He pointed to a crystal flagon, half-filled with ruby wine, on a table near the bed. Tivia's mouth opened, but no words came out. Boros shook his head. "No matter. I see no other, so the wine must have come from there." Climbing to his feet with a grunt, he delved into his pouch once more.

"Is he truly sober?" Conan said quietly to Machaon.

The grizzled man tugged nervously at the three thin gold rings dangling from the lobe of his right ear. "I think so. Fabio likes his company, but doesn't let him drink. Usually."

The Cimmerian sighed. Avoiding the hot irons meant trusting a man who might give them all leprosy by mistake.

With a stick of charcoal Boros scribed figures on the tabletop around the flagon of wine. Slowly he began to chant, so softly that the words were inaudible to the others in the room. With his left hand he sprinkled powder from a twist of parchment over the flagon; his right traced obscure patterns in the air. A red glow grew in the crystal container.

"There," Boros said, dropping his hands. "A simple thing, really." He stared at the flagon and frowned. "Cimmerian, the poisoner is close by. The glow tells."

"Crom," Conan muttered. The men who had been in the doorway crowded back into the hall.

"The closer the wine is the one who poisoned it," Boros said, "the more strongly it will glow."

"Get on with it," Conan commanded.

Picking up the flask, Boros moved closer to Machaon. The glow remained unchanged. As he moved past the door, briefly thrusting the flask toward the men outside, it dimmed. Abruptly the bearded man pressed the wine-filled vessel against Narus' chest. The hollow-cheeked man started back; the glow did not brighten.

"A pity," Boros murmured. "You look the part. And that leaves only . . ."

All eyes in the room went to Tivia, still standing with her back pressed against the wall. Under their gaze she started, then shook her head vigorously, but still said nothing. Boros padded toward her, holding the flagon of glowing wine before him. With each step the light from the wine became brighter until, as he stopped not a pace from the girl, the crystal he held seemed to contain red fire.

She avoided looking at the luminous vessel. "No," she cried. "'Tis a trick of some sort. He who placed the poison in the wine put a spell on it."

"Sorcerer as well as poisoner?" Boros asked mildly.

With an oath Conan strode across the room. "The truth, girl! Who paid you?" She shook her head in denial. "I've no stomach for torturing woman," he continued, "but mayhap Boros has some spell to force the truth from you."

"Well, let me see," the old man mused. "Why, yes, I believe I have just the thing. Aging. The longer you take to tell the truth, the older you'll become. But it works rapidly, child. I should speak quickly, were I you, or you may well leave this room a toothless crone. Pity."

Tivia's eyes swiveled desperately from the grim-faced Cimmerian to the kindly-appearing man, calmly stroking his beard, who had voiced the awful threat. "I do not know his name," she said, sagging against the wall. "He wore a mask. I was given fifty pieces of gold and the powder, with fifty more to come when Timeon was dead. I can tell you no more."

Sobbing, she slid to the floor. "Whatever you do to me, I can tell you no more."

"What do we do with her now?" Machaon asked. "Give her over to the judges?"

"They'll have her beheaded for slaying a noble," Narus said. "A shame, that. She's too pretty to die like that, and it should hardly count a crime to kill a fool like Timeon."

"Giving her to the judges won't help us," Conan said. He wished he could carry on this conversation with Machaon and Narus in privacy, but the door was open and most of the company had jammed themselves into the corridor. Shut them out now and there might not be a dozen left when the door was opened again. He took a deep breath and went on. "We've lost our patron to an assassin. Ordinarily that would be the death knell for a Free-Company." Uneasy mutters rose in the hall, and he lifted his voice to a roar. "Ordinarily, I said. But Timeon was a supporter of Count Antimides to succeed Valdric. Perhaps we can take service with Antimides, if I deliver the murderer to his hands." At least it was a chance, he thought. Antimides might well find them employment simply to keep secret his own ambitions.

"Antimides?" Machaon said doubtfully. "Cimmerian, 'tis said he's one of the few nobles who does *not* seek the throne at Valdric's death." There were murmured agreements from the hall.

"Timeon spoke too freely in his cups," Conan said. "Of how Antimides was so clever he had fooled everyone. Of how he himself would be one of the most powerful lords of Ophir once Antimides took the throne."

"Well enough," Machaon said, "but will Antimides take us in service? If he pretends to be aloof from the struggle to succeed Valdric, how will he have need for a Free-Company?"

"He'll take us," Conan said with more confidence than he felt. "Or find us service. I'll take oath on it." Besides, he thought, it was the only course they had open.

"That aging spell," Narus said suddenly. "It seems a strange sort of spell, even for folk as strange as sorcerers are reputed to be. Why would you learn a thing like that?"

"Cheese," Boros replied with a chuckle. "I had a taste for well-aged cheese when I was young, and I created the spell for that. My master flogged me for wasting time. In truth, I doubt it would work on a human."

"You tricked me," Tivia gasped. "Whoreson dog!" she shrieked, launching herself at the bearded man with fingernails clawed. Conan caught her by the arms, but she still struggled to get to the old man, who stared at her in amazement. "I'll pluck your eyes, you old fraud! You dung beetle's offspring! I'll take your manhood off in slices! Your mother was a drunken trull, and your father a poxed goat!"

"Get me a cord to tie her wrists," Conan said, then added, "And a gag." Her tirade was becoming obscene to the point where Machaon was listening with interest. The Cimmerian glared at Narus, who looked abashed as he hurried to fetch what Conan required. It was all he needed, to have to carry a shrieking girl through the streets. Narus returned with strips of cloth, and, muttering to himself, Conan bound his writhing prisoner.

VII

C onan drew few stares as he made his way through Ianthe, even with a wiggling, cloak-wrapped woman over his massive shoulder. Or because of the woman. In the streets of the capital, eaten by fear and riddled with suspicion, no one wanted to interfere in something that might even possibly involve them in the troubles beyond the walls of the city. They could see a kidnapping take place or murder done and walk by looking the other way. Who the young giant might be, or why he carried a woman like a sack of grain, no one wanted to know. It could be dangerous to know. It could be dangerous even to appear curious. Therefore none looked too closely at the big Cimmerian or his burden.

He had already been to Antimides' palace. With more than a little difficulty—for the well-fed chamberlain, as proud in his manner as any noble of the land, had seen no reason to give any information whatsoever to a stranger, and a barbarian at that—he learned that the count was a guest of the King. King Valdric liked Antimides' conversation, claiming it was better tonic than any of his physicians or sorcerers could compound. Lord Antimides would be remaining at the royal palace for several days. It was remarkable how free the chamberlain had become with his tongue once a big hand had lifted him until his velvet shoes dangled clear of the floor.

The royal palace of Ophir was a fortress rather than the marble and alabaster edifices erected in the city by nobles. It was not by chance that the King dwelt behind massive granite walls while his lords spent their days in the capital in manors more suited to pleasure than defense. More than once the throne of Ophir had only been held secure by a King taking refuge behind those walls, betimes even refuge from his own nobles. They, having no strong points within Ianthe, had always been forced to abandon the city to the King. And as control of Ianthe was the key to keeping the crown, it was said that whoever held the royal palace held Ophir.

The guards at the towering barbican gate before the royal palace stirred themselves at Conan's approach. A paunch-bellied sergeant, the small triangular beard that was in favor among the nobles waggling on his chins, stepped forward and raised a hand for the Cimmerian to halt.

"What's this, then? Do you mercenaries now think to give us your leftover women?" He chuckled over his shoulder to the pikemen behind him, enjoying his own wit. "Off with you. The royal palace is no place for your drunken carousing. And if you must bind your women, keep them from sight of the army or we will be forced to take cognizance of it."

"She's a gift for Count Antimides," Conan replied, and managed a conspiratorial wink. "A tasty pastry from my patron. Perhaps he wishes to curry favor with a great lord." Tivia redoubled her squirming; unintelligible noises came from behind the twist of rag gagging her.

"She seems not to like the idea," the sergeant chortled.

Conan grinned back at him. "I wager Lord Antimides will know what to do with her, whether she likes it or not."

"That he will. Wait you here." Belly shaking with mirth, the soldier disappeared through the gate. In a few moments he was back with a slender man, his black hair streaked with gray, in a tabard of gold and green, Antimides' colors.

The slender man turned a supercilious gaze on the big Cimmerian. "I am Ludovic," he said sharply, "Count Antimides' steward. You've come to see the count? Who are you?" He appeared to ignore Conan's burden.

"I am Conan of Cimmeria, Captain of the Free-Company in service to Baron Timeon."

Ludovic stroked his beard thoughtfully with a single finger, his eyes traveling to the wriggling girl over Conan's shoulder, then nodded. "Follow me," he commanded. "Perhaps the count will grant you a brief time."

Conan's mouth tightened. All this obsequiousness and play-acting was enough to turn his stomach. But he followed the slender man under the portcullis and into the royal palace.

If a fortress from the outside, the seat of the Kings of Ophir was still a palace within. Gleaming white marble walls, floors covered with a profusion of many-hued mosaicks, fluted alabaster columns. Golden lamps depending on silver chains from high vaulted ceilings, painted with scenes from Ophir's glorious history. Gardens, surrounded by shaded colonnades and filled with rare blossoms from the far corners of the world. Courtyards, tiled with greenstone, where ladies of the court in diaphanous gowns that concealed little of their curves dabbled pale fingers in the babbling waters of ornate fountains.

Their passage left a wake of giggles and murmurs, and stares at the towering Cimmerian and the burden across his broad shoulder. No fear was there here in noticing the unusual, and commenting on it. High-born, hot-eyed women speculated loudly on the pleasures to be found in being carried so—without the cords, of course.

The slender man scowled and increased his pace, muttering under his breath. Conan followed and wished the steward would go faster still.

Finally Ludovic stopped before a wide door carved with the ancient arms of Ophir. "Wait," he said. "I will see if the count will give you audience."

Conan opened his mouth, but before he could speak, the slender man disappeared through the door, carefully closing it behind him. Audience, he thought disgustedly. Antimides already acted as if he wore the crown.

The door swung open, and Ludovic beckoned him. "Hurry, man. Count Antimides can spare you but a few moments."

Muttering to himself Conan bore his burden within. Immediately he saw the room, his eyebrows lifted in surprise. Perhaps to the casual observer the room would not seem odd, but to one who knew Antimides' ambitions it was clearly a small throne room. An arras depicting a famous battle scene, Moranthes the Great defeating the last army of Acheron in the passes of the Karpash Mountains, hung across one wall. On a dais before the great tapestry was a massive chair with a high back, its dark wood carved with a profusion of leopards and eagles, the ancient symbols of Ophirean Kings.

If the chair seemed not grand enough by itself for a throne, the man seated there made it so. Deep-seated, piercing black eyes flanked a strong, prominent nose. His mouth was hard above a firm chin with its precisely trimmed fashionable beard. Long fingers bearing swordsman's callouses played with a ruby chain hanging across the chest of a robe of cloth-of-gold, slashed to show emerald silk beneath.

"My lord count," Ludovic said, bowing to the man on the dais, "this is the man calling himself Conan of Cimmeria."

" 'Tis my name," Conan said. He lowered Tivia to the thick-carpeted floor, layered in costly multi-colored rugs from Vendhya and Iranistan. She crouched there silently, fright seeming at last to have stilled her rage.

"Count Antimides," Ludovic pronounced grandly, "wishes to know why you have come to him."

"The girl is Tivia," Conan replied, "late mistress of Baron Timeon. Until she did poison him this morn."

Antimides raised a finger, and Ludovic spoke again. "But why have you brought her to him? She should be given to the King's justices."

Conan wondered why the count did not speak for himself. But the ways of nobles were as strange as those of sorcerers. And there were more troublesome matters to concern him. Time for his gamble had come. "As Baron Timeon supported Count Antimides in his quest to succeed Valdric, it seemed proper to bring her before the count. My Free-Company is now without a patron. Perhaps the count can find—"

"My quest!" Antimides burst out, his face choleric with rage. "How dare you accuse me of . . ." He broke off, grinding his teeth. Ludovic stared at him in obvious surprise. Tivia, her mouth working futilely at her gag, seemed transfixed by his gaze. "You, jade," he breathed. "So you poisoned your master, and were caught at it by this barbar mercenary. Pray that justice is mercifully swift for you. Take her away, Ludovic."

Desperately and futilely Tivia attempted to force words past the cloth gagging her. She flung herself against her bonds as the steward seized her, but the slender man bore her behind the arras with little effort. A door opened and closed behind the hanging, and her cries were cut off.

The Cimmerian reminded himself that Tivia was a self-confessed murderer, and for gold. Still, it pained him to have a hand in a woman's death. In his belief women were not meant to die violently; such was for men. He forced himself to stop thinking of her, and put his attention on the hawk-eyed man on the dais. "Count Antimides, there is still the matter of my Free-Company. Our reputation is well known, and—"

"Your reputation!" Antimides snarled. "Your patron assassinated, and you speak of your reputation. Worse, you come to me with vile accusations. I should have your tongue torn out!"

"Pray, Antimides, what accusations are these to put you in such a rage?"

Both men started at the question; so intent had they been on each other that neither had noticed the entrance of another. Now that Conan saw her, though, he drank her in appreciatively. Long of leg and full of breast, an exotic beauty blending the extraordinary combination of hair like fine, spun silver and large, dark eyes that spoke of deep wells of untapped passion, she moved with sinuous grace, her shimmering scarlet robe, barely opaque and slit up one thigh to a rounded hip, clinging to the curves of breast and thigh.

"Why do you come here, Synelle?" Antimides demanded. "I will not be bothered by your sharp tongue today."

"I have not seen this chamber since you came to the royal palace, Antimides," she said with a dangerous smile. "Seeing it, a suspicious mind might think you sought the crown after all, no matter your public pronouncements of disdain for those who strive beyond the city walls." Antimides' face darkened, and his knuckles grew white on the arms of the chair; Synelle's smile deepened. "But as to why I came. It is said in the palace that a giant northlander came to you bearing a woman wrapped like a package from a fishmonger. Surely I could not miss seeing that? But where is this gift? She is a gift, is she not?"

"This does not concern you, Synelle," Antimides grated. "Go back to your woman's concerns. Have you not needlework waiting?"

Synelle merely arched her eyebrows and moved closer to Conan. "And this is the barbarian? He is certainly as large as was reported. I have a liking for big men." Shivering ostentatiously, she fingered the small, overlapping steel plates on his hauberk. "Are you a mercenary, my handsome northlander?"

He smiled down at her, preening under her sultry look despite himself. "I am captain of a Free-Company, my lady. My name is Conan."

"Conan." Her lips caressed the name. "And why do you come to Antimides, Conan?"

"Enough, Synelle," Antimides barked. "That lies between me and this barbar." He had shot a hard look at the big Cimmerian, a warning to silence.

Conan bristled, and glared back. "I came seeking employment for my company, my lady, but the count has nothing for us." Did the fool think he had no sense? Speaking of Timeon, and the baron's connection to Antimides, would gain him naught and perhaps cost much.

"Nothing?" Pity dripped from Synelle's voice. "But why do you not enter my service?" She raised her eyes boldly to his, and he thought he read a promise in them. "Would you not like to . . . serve me?"

Antimides snorted derisively. "You outdo yourself, Synelle. Are you not satisfied with Taramenon? Do you need an entire company of rogues to satisfy you? Or do you think to contend for the throne yourself?" He roared with laughter at his own wit, but jealous anger colored his glare at Conan.

Synelle's face hardened, and Conan thought she bit back words. At last she spoke in icy tones. "My house is as ancient as yours, Antimides. And did the succession depend on blood alone, I would stand first after Valdric." She drew a deep, shuddering breath, and her smile returned. "I *will* take your company in service, Conan. At twice the gold Antimides would give."

"Done," Conan said. It was not the sort of service he had sought, but the men of his company would at least be pleased with the gold.

The stern-faced count seemed bewildered over what had happened. "Can you be serious, Synelle?" he asked incredulously. "What use have you for such men? You throw your gold away like a foolish girl, on a whim."

"Are not my holdings subject to bandit attacks as others are, now that the army keeps to the cities? Besides," she added with a smouldering look at the Cimmerian, "I like his shoulders." Her voice hardened. "Or do you try to deny me even the right to take men-at-arms in service?"

"Women who need men-at-arms," Antimides replied hotly, "should make alliance with a man who can provide them."

"Why, so I have," she said, her mercurial mood becoming all gaiety. "Come with me, Conan. We have done here."

Conan followed as she moved from the chamber, leaving a fuming Antimides on his wooden throne.

In the corridor she turned suddenly, her mouth open to speak. Conan, caught by surprise, almost walked into her. For a moment she stood, words forgotten and dark eyes wide, staring up at him. "Never have I seen such a man," she whispered then, as if to herself. "Could you be the one to . . ." Her words trailed off, but she still stood gazing at him as if in a trance.

A woman-wise smile appeared on Conan's face. He had not been sure if her flirting in the other room had been for his benefit or Antimides', but of this he had no doubt. Lifting her into his arms, he kissed her. She returned his kiss with fiery lips, cupping his face with both hands, straining her body to him.

Abruptly she pulled back, horror filling her eyes; her hand cracked against his face. "Loose me!" she cried. "You forget yourself!"

Confused, he set her feet back on the floor. She took two quick steps back from him, one trembling hand to her lips.

"Your pardon, my lady," he said slowly. Did the woman play a game with him?

"I will not have it," she breathed unsteadily. "I will not." Slowly her composure returned, and when she went on her voice was as cold as it had ever been for Antimides. "I will forget what just happened, and I advise you to do the same. I have a house on the Street of Crowns where you may quarter your company. There are stables behind for your horses. Ask for it, and you will be directed. Go there, and await my instructions. And forget, barbarian, as you value your life."

Did women ever know their own minds, Conan wondered as he watched her stiff back recede down the corridor. How then did they expect men to know them? His consternation could not last long, however. Once more he had managed to save his company. For a time, at least, and that was all a man could ask. All that was left was to convince them there was no disgrace in taking service with a woman. Thinking on that he set about finding his way out of the palace.

VIII

The massive walls and great outer towers of the royal palace had stood for centuries unchanged, but the interior had altered with every dynasty till it was a warren of corridors and gardens. Soon Conan felt he had visited all of them without making his way to the barbican gate.

Servants rushing through the halls on their duties would not even pause at question from the young barbarian in well-used armor. They were nearly as arrogant as the nobles who lounged in the fountained courts, and inquiries made to richly-clad folk got him little from the haughty men except gibes that brought him close to drawing his sword a time or two. The sleek, languorous women gave inviting smiles and even offers as open as those of any trull on the streets. Such might have appealed had he not been in haste to return to the Free-Company, but even they had only amusement for his ignorance of the palace, tinkling laughter and directions that, followed, sent him in circles.

Conan stepped into yet another courtyard, and found he was staring at King Valdric himself, trailing his retinue as he crossed the greenstone tiles. The King looked worse than Narus, the young Cimmerian thought. Valdric's gold-embroidered state robes hung loosely on a shrunken body that had once weighed half again as much as it did now, and he used the tall, gem-encrusted scepter of Ophir as a walking staff. His golden crown, thickly set with emeralds and rubies from the mines on the Nemedian border, sat low on his brow; and his eyes, sunken deep in a hollow-cheeked face, held a feverish light.

The retinue consisted mainly of men with the full beards of scholars, leavened with a sprinkling of nobles in colorful silks and soldiers of rank in gilded armor, crested helms beneath their arms. The bearded men held forth continuously, competing loudly for Valdric's ear as the procession made its slow way across the courtyard.

"The stars will be favorable this night for an invocation to Mitra," one cried.

"You must be bled, your majesty," another shouted. "I have a new shipment of leeches from the marshes of Argos."

"This new spell will surely cast the last of the demons from you," a third contributed.

"'Tis time for your cupping, my King."

"This potion . . ."

"The balance of fluxes and humors . . ."

Conan made an awkward bow, though none of them seemed to notice him. Kings, he knew, were particular about such things.

When he straightened, King and retinue had gone; but one, a white-haired soldier, had stayed behind and was looking at him. Conan knew him immediately, though he had never met the man. Iskandrian, the White Eagle of Ophir, the general who kept the army aloof from the struggle to succeed Valdric. Despite his age and white hairs, the general's leathery face was as hard as the walls of the palace, his bushy-browed gray eyes clear and sharp. The calloused hand that rested on his sword hilt was strong and steady.

"You're the one who brought the girl to Antimides," the white-haired general said abruptly. "What is your name?"

"Conan of Cimmeria."

"Mercenary," Iskandrian said drily. His attitude toward mercenaries was well known. To his mind no foreign warrior should tread the soil of Ophir, not even if he *was* in service to an Ophirean. "I've heard of you. That fat fool Timeon's man, are you not?"

"I am no one's man but my own," Conan said hotly. "My company did follow Baron Timeon, but we have lately taken the Lady Synelle's colors." At least, they would once he drummed the fact into their heads.

Iskandrian whistled between his teeth. "Then, mercenary, you have gotten yourself a problem along with your lady patron. You've a set of shoulders like an ox, and I suppose women account you handsome. 'Twill light a fire in Taramenon's head to have a man like you near Synelle."

"Taramenon?" Conan remembered Antimides mentioning that name as well. The count had implied this Taramenon had some interest in Synelle, or she in him.

"He is the finest swordsman in Ophir," Iskandrian said. "Best sharpen your blade and pray to your gods for luck."

"A man makes his own luck," Conan said, "and my sword is always sharp."

"A good belief for a mercenary," Iskandrian laughed. "Or a soldier." A frown quickly replaced his mirth. "Why are you in this part of the palace, barbarian? You are far from the path from Antimides' chambers to the gate."

Conan hesitated, then shrugged ruefully. "I am lost," he admitted, and the general laughed again.

"That does not sound like what I've heard of you. But I'll get you a guide." With a wave of his hand he summoned a servant, who bowed low before Iskandrian and ignored Conan. "Take this man to the barbican gate," the general commanded.

"My thanks," the Cimmerian told him. "Yours are the first words I have heard in some time that were neither mocking nor lies."

Iskandrian eyed him sharply. "Make no mistake, Conan of Cimmeria. You have a reputation for daring and tactical sense, and were you Ophirean, I'd make you one of my officers. But you are a mercenary, and an outlander. Do I have my way, the day will come when you'll leave Ophir with all the haste you can muster or have your ashes scattered here." With that he stalked away.

By the time Conan got back to Timeon's palace, he was uncertain if he had ever had so many opposed to him before. Iskandrian seemed to like him personally, and would see him dead given the chance. Antimides hated him to the bone, and without doubt would like to put him on his funeral fires whether he went to them alive or dead. Synelle he was unsure of; what she said she wanted and what her body said she wanted were opposites, and a man could be shaved at the shoulders for involving himself with such a one as that. Karela claimed that she desired him dead, for all she had not taken the opportunity granted her, and she had a knack of making her desires come true that would make a statue sweat in the circumstances. Then there was the thrice-accursed horned figure. *Had* the second group of attackers been after it, as those first two had been? If they were, he could wager good coin on future attempts, though he still had no clue as to why.

Of course, he could rid himself of the threat of attack by ridding himself of the bronze, but that smacked too much of fright to suit him. Let him but discover why it was worth killing and dying for, and he would willingly shed himself of it, but it was not his way to run from trouble. The Cimmerian almost laughed when he realized that the murder of Timeon was the only trouble to come his way of late that had been resolved.

The guards on the white-columned portico looked at him expectantly, and he put on a smile for their benefit. "All is well," he told them. "We have a patron, and gold to tempt the wenches."

He left them slapping each other's back in relieved laughter, but once he was inside his own smile disappeared. Did they know half of what faced them, they would likely throw down their bows on the spot and desert.

"Machaon!" he called, the name echoing in the high-ceilinged entry hall.

Narus, on the balcony above, shouted down. "He's in the garden. How went matters with Antimides?"

"Assemble the men here," Conan told him, hurrying on.

The tattooed veteran was in the garden as Narus had said, on a bench with a girl, his arms wrapped around her and hers around him. Trust Machaon, the Cimmerian thought with a chuckle, even when waiting to see if they must flee the country. It was about time he found something for merriment in the day.

"Leave her be," he said jovially. "There'll be time for wenches lat—" He broke off as the girl leaped to her feet. It was Julia, cheeks scarlet and breasts heaving.

Clutching her skirts with both hands she looked helplessly at him, turned suddenly tear-filled eyes on Machaon, then ran wailing past the Cimmerian into the palace.

Machaon flung up his hands as Conan rounded on him angrily. "Hear me out before you speak, Cimmerian. She came about me, teasing, and taunted me about kissing her. And she did not try to run when I did it, either."

Conan scowled. He had saved her from a life as a trull, given her honest employment, for this? "She's no camp-follower, Machaon. If you want her, then court her. Don't grab her like a doxy in a tavern."

"Mitra's mercies, man! Court her? You speak as if she were your sister. Zandru's Hells, I've never taken a woman against her will in my life."

The young Cimmerian opened his mouth for an angry retort, and found that none came. If Julia wanted to be a woman fully-fledged, who was he to say her nay? And Machaon was certainly experienced enough to make her enjoy her learning.

"I'm trying to protect someone who apparently doesn't want it any more, Machaon," he said slowly. His reason for seeking out the grizzled man returned to him. "Events have turned as I said they would. We have our patron." Machaon barked a laugh and shook a fist over his head in triumph. "Narus is bringing some of the men to the entry hall. You fetch the rest, and I'll tell the company."

The wide, tapestry-hung hall filled rapidly, threescore men—less the guards posted, for there was no reason to be foolish—crowding it from wall to wall. All looking expectantly to him, Conan thought as he watched them from a perch on the curving marble stair. Boros was among them, he saw, but after the gray-bearded man had ferreted out Tivia for him, he was willing to let him remain. So long as he remained sober and stayed away from magic, at least.

"The company has a new patron," he announced, and the hall exploded in cheers. He waited for the tumult to subside, then added, "Our payment is twice what we were getting." After all, he thought while they renewed their shouts of glee, Synelle had offered to double Antimides' best offer; why would she not do the same for Timeon's? "Listen to me," he called to them. "Quiet, and listen to me. We'll be quartering in a house on the Street of Crowns. We leave here within the hour."

"But whom do we serve?" Taurianus shouted. Others took up the cry.

Conan drew a deep breath. "The Lady Synelle." Flat silence greeted his words.

At last Taurianus muttered disgustedly, "You'd have us serve a woman?"

"Aye, a woman," the Cimmerian answered. "Will her gold buy less when you clink it on the table in a tavern? And how many of you have worried as to how we'd fare if, when someone does succeed Valdric, it turned out we followed the wrong side? We'll be out of that. A woman cannot succeed to the throne. There'll be naught to do but guard her holdings from bandits and spend her gold."

"Twice as much gold?" Taurianus said.

"Twice as much." He had them, now. He could see it in their faces. "Get your belongings together quickly. And no looting! Timeon has heirs somewhere. I want none of you rogues hauled before the justices for theft."

Laughing again, the company began to disperse, and Conan dropped to a seat on the stair. At times it seemed as much of a battle to hold the company together as to fight any of the foes they had been called on to face.

"You handled that as well as any king," Boros said, creakily climbing the stairs.

"Of kings I know little," Conan told him. "All I know are steel and battle."

The gray-bearded man chuckled drily. "How do you think kings get to be kings, my young friend?"

"I neither know nor care," the Cimmerian replied. "All I want is to keep my company together. That and no more."

Sweat glistened on the body of the naked woman stretched taut on the rack, reflecting the flames of charcoal-filled iron cressets of the damp-streaked stone walls of the royal palace dungeon. Nearby, the handles of irons thrust from a brazier of glowing coals, ready in case they were called for. From the way she babbled her tale, punctuating it periodically with screams as the shaven-headed torturer encouraged her with a scourge, they would not be needed.

She had taken money to poison Timeon, but she did not know the man who paid her. He was masked. She became frightened when the first dose of poison showed no effect on the baron, and had placed all she had been given in his wine at once. Before all the gods, she did not know who had paid her.

Antimides listened quietly as the torturer did his work. It amazed him how the struggle for even a chance at life could continue when the person involved had to know there was no hope of it. Time and again, with men and women alike, had he seen it. As soon as he had spoken and seen the expression on Tivia's face, he was aware that she recognized his voice, that she knew him for the man behind the black silk mask. Yet even with the rack and the whip she denied, praying that he would spare her if he thought his secret was safe.

It was odd, too, how dangers suddenly multiplied just when he was in sight of his goal. Had the girl administered the poison in daily doses as directed the finest physician would have said Timeon died of natural causes, and he would have been free of a fool who drank too much and talked too freely when drunk. Then there was the barbarian with the outlandish name, bringing her to him, drawing attention to him when he least wanted it. No doubt that could be laid to Timeon's tongue. But what were the chances the man would fail to tell Synelle what he knew or suspected?

He, Antimides, had been the first to learn of Valdric's illness, the first to prepare to take the throne at his death, and all, he was certain, without being suspected by anyone. While the others fought in the countryside, he remained in Ianthe. When Valdric finally died, they who thought to take the throne, those few who managed to survive his assassins, would find that he held the royal palace. And he who held the royal palace held the throne of Ophir. Now all of his careful plans were endangered, his secrecy threatened.

Something would have to be done about Synelle. He had always had plans for that sharp-tongued jade. Prating about her bloodlines. Of what use were bloodlines in a wench, except with regard to the children she could produce? He had planned to take great pleasure in breaking her to heel, and in using those bloodlines she boasted of to make heirs with an even stronger claim to the throne than himself. But now she had to be done away with, and quickly. And the barbarian as well.

He perked an ear toward Tivia. She was repeating herself. "Enough,

Raga," he said, and the shaven-headed man desisted. Antimides pressed a gold coin into the fellow's thick-thingered hand. Raga was bought long since, but it never hurt to ensure loyalties. "She's yours," Antimides told the man. Raga beamed a gap-toothed smile. "When you are done, dispose of her in the usual fashion."

As the count let himself out of the dungeon Tivia's shrieks were rising afresh. Lost in his planning for Synelle and the barbarian, Antimides did not hear.

IX

T he house on the Street of Crowns was a large square, two stories high, around a dusty central court, with the bottom floor of the two sides being given over to stables. A wooden-roofed balcony, reached by stairs weakened from long neglect, ran around the courtyard on the second level. Dirty red roof tiles gleamed dully in the late afternoon sun; flaking plaster on the stone walls combined with shadows to give the structure a leprous appearance. An arched gate, its hinges squealing with rust, led from the street to the courtyard, where a dusty fountain was filled with withered brown leaves.

"Complete with rats and fleas, no doubt," Narus said dolefully as he dismounted.

Taurianus sat his horse and glared about him. "For this we left a palace?" A flurry of doves burst from an upper window. "See! We're expected to sleep in a roost!"

"You've all grown too used to the soft life in a palace," Conan growled before the mutters could spread. "Stop complaining like a herd of old women, and remember the times you've slept in the mud."

"'Twas better than this, that mud," Taurianus muttered, but he climbed down from his saddle.

Grumbling men began carrying blanket rolls and bundles of personal belongings in search of places to settle themselves. Others led their horses into the stables; curses quickly floated out as to the number of rats and cobwebs. Rotund Fabio hurried in search of the kitchens, trailed by a half-running Julia, her arms full of soot-blackened pots and bundles of herbs, strings of garlic and peppers dangling from her shoulders. Boros stood at the gate staring about him in amazement, though he certainly slept in little better as a matter of course. Synelle, Conan thought, had much to learn about what was properly provided a Free-Company.

They had attracted entirely too much attention for Conan's taste during their search for the house. Three-score armored men on horseback, laden with sacks and cloak-wrapped bundles till they looked like a procession of country peddlers, could not help but draw eyes even in a city that assiduously attempted to avoid seeing anything that might be dangerous. The Cimmerian would just as soon they could all have become invisible till the matter of Timeon's death was forgotten. And he was none too eager to look into any of those bundles, many of which clinked and seemed heavier than they had a right to be. For all his injunction against looting he was sure they were filled with silver goblets and trinkets of gold. More of those following him than not, the Ophireans most certainly, were light-fingered at the best of times.

Giving his horse over to one of the men, the big Cimmerian went in search of a room for himself, his blanket roll over one shoulder and the sack containing the bronze under his arm. Save for weapons and armor, horse and change of clothes, they were all the possessions he had.

Soon he found a large, corner room on the second floor, with four windows to give it light. A wad of straw in one corner showed that a rat had been nesting there. Two benches and a table stood in the middle of the floor, covered with heavy dust. A bed, sagging but certainly large enough even for his height, was jammed against a wall. The mattress crackled with the sound of dried husks when he poked it, and he sighed, remembering the goose-down mattress in Timeon's palace. Think of the mud, he reminded himself sternly.

Machaon's voice drifted up from the courtyard. "Conan, where are you? There's news!"

Tossing his burdens on the bed, Conan hurried out onto the balcony. "What word? Has Synelle summoned us?"

"Not yet, Cimmerian. The assassins were busy last night. Valentius fled his palace after three of his own guards turned their blades on him. 'Tis said others of his men cut them down, but the lordling now seems affrightened of his own shadow. He has taken refuge with Count Antimides."

Conan's eyebrows went up. Antimides. The young fool had unknowingly put himself in the hands of one of his rivals. Another lord removed from the race, this one by his own hand, in a manner of speaking. Who stood next in the bloodright after Valentius? But what occurred among the contending factions, he thought, no longer concerned him or his company.

"We're done with that, Machaon," he laughed, "Let them all kill each other."

The grizzled veteran joined his laughter. "An that happens, mayhap we can make you King. I will settle for count, myself."

Conan opened his mouth to reply, and suddenly realized a sound that should not be there had been impinging on his brain. Creaking boards from the room he had just left. No rat made boards creak. His blade whispered from its sheath, and he dove through the door, followed by Machaon's surprised shout.

Four startled men in cast-off finery, one just climbing in the window, stared in shock at the appearance of the young giant. Their surprise lasted but an instant; as he took his first full step into the room, swords appeared in their fists and they rushed to attack.

Conan beat aside the thrust of the first to reach him, and in the same movement planted a foot in the middle of his opponent's dirty gray silk tunic. Breath left the man in an explosive gasp, and he fell in a heap at the feet of a thick-mustached man behind him. The mustached man stumbled, and the tip of Conan's blade slashed his throat in a fountain of blood. As the dying man fell atop the first attacker, a man with a jagged scar down his left cheek leaped over him, sword hacking wildly. Conan dropped to a crouch—whistling steel ruffled the hair atop his head—and his own blade sliced across scar-face's stomach. With a shriek the man dropped in a heap, both hands clutching at thick ropes of entrails spilling from his body. A sword thrust from the floor slid under the metal scales of Conan's hauberk, slicing his side, but the Cimmerian's return blow struck through gray-tunic's skull at the eyes.

"Erlik curse you!" the last man screamed. Sly-faced and bony, he had been the last into the room, and had not joined in the wild melee. "Eight of my men you've slain! Erlik curse all your seed!" Shrieking, he dashed at Conan with frenzied slashes.

The Cimmerian wanted to take this man alive, in condition to answer questions, but the furious attack was too dangerous to withstand for long. A half-mad light of fear and rage gleamed in the man's sweaty face, and he screamed with every blow he made. Three times their blades crossed, then blood was spurting from the stump of sly-face's neck as his head rolled on the floor.

With a clatter of boots mercenaries crowded into the room, led by Machaon, all with swords in hand. "Mitra, Cimmerian," the tattooed man said, scanning the scene of carnage. "Couldn't you have saved just one for us?"

"I didn't think of it," Conan replied drily.

Julia forced her way through the men. When she saw the bodies her hands went to her face, and she screamed. Then her eyes lit on Conan, and her composure returned as quickly as it had gone. "You're wounded!" she said. "Sit on the bed, and I will tend it."

For the first time Conan became aware of a razor's edge of fire along his ribs, and the blood wetting the side of his hauberk. " 'Tis but a scratch," he told her. "Get these out of here," he added to Machaon, gesturing to the corpses.

Machaon told off men to cart the dead away.

Julia, however, was not finished. "Scratch or not," she said firmly, "if it is not tended you may grow ill. Fetch me hot water and clean clothes," she flung over her shoulder, as she attempted to press Conan toward the bed. "Clean, mind you!" To everyone's surprise two of the mercenaries rushed off at her command.

Amused, Conan let her have her way. Muttering to herself she fussed over getting his metal-scaled leather tunic off. Gently she palped the flesh about the long, shallow gash, a thoughtful frown on her face. She seemed unconcerned about his blood on her fingers.

"It seems you are ahead once more," Machaon said ruefully, before leaving them alone.

"What did he mean by that?" she asked absently. "Don't talk. Let the wound lie still. There are no ribs broken, and I will not have to sew it, but after it is bandaged you must take care not to exert yourself. Perhaps if you lie—" She broke off with a gasp. "Mitra protect us, what is that evil thing?"

Conan followed her suddenly frightened gaze to the bronze figure, lying on the bed and now out of the sack. "Just something I bought as a gift for Machaon," he said, picking it up. She backed away from him. "What ails you, girl? The thing is but dead metal."

"She is right to be affrighted," Boros said from the door. His eyes were fixed on the bronze as on a living demon. "It is evil beyond knowing. I can feel the waves of it from here."

"And I," Julia said shakily. "It means me harm. I can feel it."

Boros nodded sagely. "Aye, a woman would be sensitive to such. The rites of Al'Kiir were heinous. Scores of men fighting to the death while the priestesses chanted, with the heart of the survivor to be ripped from his living body. Rites of torture, with the victim kept alive and screaming on the altar for days. But the most evil of all, and the most powerful, was the giving of women as sacrifices. Or as worse than sacrifices."

"What could be worse than being sacrificed?" Julia asked faintly.

"Being given to the living god whose image that is," Boros answered, "to be his plaything for all eternity. Such may well have been the fate of the women given to Al'Kiir."

Julia swayed, and Conan snapped, "Enough, old man! You frighten her. I remember now that you mentioned this Al'Kiir once before, when you were drunk. Are you drunk now? Have you dredged all this from wine fumes in your head?"

"I am deathly sober," the gray-bearded man replied, "and I wish I were pickled in wine like a corpse. For that is not only an image of Al'Kiir, Cimmerian. It is a necessary, a vital part of the worship of that horrible god. I thought all such had been destroyed centuries ago. Someone attempts to bring Al'Kiir again to this world, and did they have that unholy image they might well succeed. I, for one, would not care to be alive if they do."

Conan stared at the bronze gripped in his big hand. Two men had died attempting to take it from him in the shop. Three more perished in the second attack, and that that had been for the same thing he no longer doubted. Before he himself died, sly-face had accused Conan of slaying about eight of his men. The numbers were right. Those who wanted to bring back this god knew the Cimmerian had the image they needed. In a way he was relieved. He had had stray thoughts that some of these attacks, including the one just done, were Karela's work.

The men fetching the hot water and bandages entered the room; Conan thrust the image under his blanket roll and signed the others to silence until they were gone.

When the three were alone again, Julia spoke. "I'll tend your wound, but not if you again remove that evil thing from its hiding. Even there I can sense it."

"I'll leave it where it is," the young Cimmerian said, and she knelt beside him and busied herself with bathing and bandaging his wound. "Go on with your telling, Boros," he continued. "How is it this god cannot find his own way to the world of men? That seems like no god to fear greatly, for all his horns."

"You make jokes," Boros grumbled, "but there is no humor in this. To tell you of Al'Kiir I must speak of the distant past. You know that Ophir is the most ancient of all the kingdoms now existing in the world, yet few men know ought of its misty beginnings. I know a little. Before even Ophir was, this land was the center of the worship of Al'Kiir. The strongest and handsomest of men and the proudest and most beautiful of women were brought from afar for the rites of which I have spoken. But, as you might imagine, there were those who opposed the worship of Al'Kiir, and foremost of these were the men who called themselves the Circle of the Right-Hand Path."

"Can you not be shorter about it?" Conan said. "There's no need to dress the tale like a storyteller in the marketplace."

Boros snorted. "Do you wish brevity, or the facts? Listen. The Circle of the Right-Hand Path was led by a man named Avanrakash, perhaps the most powerful practitioner of white magic who has ever lived."

"I did not know there was such a thing as white magic," Conan said.

"Never have I seen a sorcerer who did not reek of blackness and evil as a dunghill reeks of filth."

This time the old man ignored him. "These men made contact with the very gods, 'tis said, and concluded a pact. No god would stand against Al'Kiir openly, for they feared that in a war between gods all that is might be destroyed, even themselves. Some—Set, supposedly, was one—declared themselves apart from what was to happen. Others, though, granted those of the Right-Hand Path an increase in powers, enough so that they in concert could match a single god. You can understand that they would not give so much to a single man, for that would make him a demigod at the least, nor enough to all of them that they could not be vanquished easily by as few as two of the gods in concert."

Despite himself Conan found himself listening intently. Julia, her mouth hanging open in wonderment, held the ties of the Cimmerian's bandages forgotten as she followed Boros' words.

"In the battle that followed, the face of the land itself was changed, mountains raised, rivers altered in their courses, ancient seas made desert. All of those who marched against Al'Kiir, saving only Avanrakash, perished, and he was wounded to the death. Yet in his dying he managed with a staff of power to sever Al'Kiir from the body the god wore in the world of men, to seal the god from that world.

"Then came rebellion among the people against the temples of Al'Kiir, and the first King of Ophir was crowned. Whole cities were razed so that not even their memory remains. All that kept so much as the name of Al'Kiir in the minds of men was destroyed.

"The earthly body of the god? Men tried to destroy that as well, but the hottest fires made no mark, and the finest swords shattered against it. Finally it was entombed beneath a mountain, and the entrances sealed up, so that with time men should forget its very existence.

"They both succeeded and failed, they who would have destroyed the god's name and memory, for the name Tor Al'Kiir was given to the mountain, but for centuries gone only a scattered few have known the source of that name, though all men know it for a place of ill luck, a place to be avoided.

"I believed I was the last to have the knowledge I possess, that it would go to my funeral fires with me. But I have seen lights in the night atop Tor Al'Kiir. I have heard whispers of knowledge sought. Someone attempts to bring Al'Kiir back to this world again. I was sure they would find only failure, for the lack of that image or its like, but do they get their hands on it, blood and lust and slavery will be the portion of all men."

Conan let out a long breath when the old man at last fell silent. "The answer is simple. I'll take the accursed thing to the nearest metalworker's shop and have it melted down."

"No!" Boros cried. A violent shudder wracked him, and he combed his long beard with his fingers in agitation. "Without the proper spells that would loose such power as would burn this city from the face of the earth, and perhaps half the country as well. Before you ask, I do not know the necessary spells, and those who do would be more likely to attempt use of the image than its destruction."

"That staff," Julia said suddenly. "The one Avanrakash used. Could it destroy the image?"

"A very perceptive question, child," the old man murmured. "The answer is, I do not know. It might very well have that power, though."

"Much good that does," Conan muttered. "The staff is no doubt rotted to dust long ago."

Boros shook his head. "Not at all. 'Tis a staff of power, after all, that Staff of Avanrakash. Those men of ancient times revered its power, and made it the scepter of Ophir, which it still is, though covered in gold and gems. It is said 'twas the presence of that scepter, carried as a standard before the armies of Ophir, that allowed Moranthes the Great to win his victories against Acheron. If you could acquire the scepter, Conan . . ."

"I will not," Conan said flatly, "attempt to steal King Valdric's scepter on the off chance that it might have some power. Zandru's Nine Hells, the man uses the thing as a walking staff! It's with him constantly."

"You must understand, Cimmerian," Boros began, but Conan cut him off.

"No! I will put the thrice-accursed beneath the floor boards yonder until I can find a place to bury it where it will never be found. Crack not your teeth concerning any of this until I can do so, Boros. And stay away from the wine till then as well."

Boros put on a cloak of injured dignity. "I have been keeping this particular secret for nearly fifty years, Cimmerian. You've no need to instruct me."

Conan grunted, and let Julia lift his arm to finish her bandaging. It was yet another rotten turnip to add to the stew before him. How to destroy a thing that could not be destroyed, or as well as could not, given the lack of trustworthy sorcerer, and such were as rare as virgin whores. Still, he was worried more about Karela than any of the rest. What, he wondered, was that flame-haired wench plotting?

X

K arela reined in her bay mare at the edge of the tall trees, thick with the shadows of the setting sun, and studied the small peak-roofed hut in the forest clearing. A single horse was tethered outside, a tall black warmount colorfully caprisoned for a noble, though its scarlet and black bardings bore the sign of no house. A lone man was supposed to meet her there, but she would wait to make sure.

The snap of a fallen twig announced the arrival of a man in coarse woolen tunic and breeches of nondescript brown that blended well with the shadows. The sound was deliberate, she knew, that she, being warned, would not strike with the Turanian scimitar she wore on her belt at his sudden appearance; Agorio could move in the woods as silently as the fall of a feather, did he choose. Both the man's ears had been cropped for theft, and his narrow face bore a scar that pulled his right eye into a permanent expression of surprise. "He came alone, my lady, as you instructed," he said.

Karela nodded. They were not so good as her hounds of the Zamoran plains, the men who followed her now. Most had been poachers, and petty thieves if the opportunity presented itself, when she found them, and they had little liking for the discipline she forced on them, but given time, she would make them as good and as feared as any band of brigands that ever rode.

She rode slowly into the clearing, sitting her saddle as proudly as any queen. She disdained to show more caution than she had already. As she dismounted she drew her curved sword, and pushed open the crude plank door of the hut with the blade.

Within was a single room with the rough furnishings to be expected in such a place, dimly lit by a fire on the hearth. Dust covered everything, and old, dried cobwebs hung from the bare, shadowed rafters. A man with a plain scarlet surcoat over his armor stood in the center of the dirt floor, his thumbs hooked casually in the wide, low-slung belt that supported his scabbarded longsword. He was almost as tall as Conan, she noted, with shoulders nearly as broad. A handsome man, with an eye for women from the smile that came to his lips when she entered.

She kicked the door shut with her heel and waited for him to speak. She did not sheath her blade.

"You are not what I expected, girl," he said finally. His dark eyes caressed the curves beneath her snug-fitting jerkin and breeches. "You are quite beautiful."

"And you've made your first mistake." There was danger in her voice, though the man did not seem to realize it. "No man calls me girl. I'll have the answers to some questions before we go further. Your message came to me through ways I thought known only to a trusted few. How did you come to know of them? Who are you, and why would you send me fifty golds, not knowing if I'd come or not?" For that was the amount that had accompanied the message.

"Yet you did come," he said, radiating cool confidence. From beneath his surcoat he produced two bulging leather purses and tossed them to the table. They clinked as they landed. "And here are a hundred more pieces of gold, if you will undertake a commission for me, with as many to follow at its completion."

Her tone hardened. "My questions."

"Regrettably I cannot answer," he said smoothly. "You need have no fear of being seized, my inquisitive beauty. I came alone, as I said I would. There are no men in the trees about us."

"Except my own," she said, and was pleased to see surprise flicker across his face.

He recovered his aplomb quickly. "But that is to be expected. When I heard of a bandit band led by a . . . a woman, I knew they must be very good indeed to long survive. You see, you're becoming famous. Put up your blade. Eastern, is it not? Are you from the east, my pretty brigand? You have not the coloring of the eastern beauties I have known, though you are as lovely as all of them together."

His smile deepened, a smile she was sure sent he expected to send tingles through every woman favored with it. And likely had his expectations met, she admitted. She also knew that only her danger at his manner—girl, indeed! My pretty brigand. Ha!—armored her against it. She held hard to that anger, prodded at it. She did, however, sheathe her sword.

"I'll not tell you my history," she growled, "when I get not even your name in return. At least you can tell me what I am to do for these two hundred gold pieces."

His smoldering-eyed study of her did not end, but at least it abated. "Baron Inaros is withdrawing from his keep to his palace in Ianthe. He is not involved in the current struggles. Rather, he is afraid of them. 'Tis the reason for his move, seeking the safety of the capital. His guards will be few in number, not enough to trouble a bold band of brigands. For the two hundred you will bring me his library, which he brings with him in two carts. And of course you may keep anything else you take from his party."

"A library!" Karela burst out. "Why would you pay two hundred pieces of gold, two hundred and fifty, in truth, for a collection of dusty scrolls?"

"Let us simply say I am a collector of rarities, and that there are works in Inaros' possession I am willing to pay that price for."

Karela almost laughed. This man as a collector of rare parchments was one thing she would not believe. But there was no profit in calling him liar. "Very well," she said, "but I will have two hundred gold pieces upon delivery of these, ah, rarities." It was her turn to smile. "Are you willing to pay *that* price?"

He nodded slowly, once more eyeing her up and down. "I could almost consider it cheap, though you'd best not try to press me too far, or I may take my commission to another who, if not so pretty, is also not so greedy. Now let us seal the bargain."

"What," she began, but before she could finish he took a quick step and seized her. Roughly he crushed her against him; she could not free an arm enough to draw her sword.

"I have a special way of sealing pacts with women," he chuckled. "Struggle if you wish, but you will enjoy it before 'tis done." Suddenly he froze at the sharp prick of her dagger point against his neck.

"I should slit your throat," she hissed, "like the pig you are. Back away from me. Slowly."

Obediently he stepped backwards, his face a frozen mask of rage. As soon as he was clear of her dagger stroke, his hand went to his sword.

She flipped the dagger, catching it by the point. "Will you wager your life that I cannot put this in your eye?" His hand fell back to his side.

Desperately Karela fought her own desire to kill him. He deserved it clearly, to her thinking, but how could she keep it secret that she had slain a man come to hire her? Such things never remained buried long. All who heard the tale would think she had done it for the coins on the table, and there would be no more offers of gold.

"You codless spawn of a diseased camel!" she spat in frustration. "But recently I saw a figure that reminds me of you. An ugly thing to curdle any woman's blood, as you are. All horns and fangs, with twice as much manhood as any man, and like to think with that manhood, as you do, were it alive. If you have any manhood."

He had gone very still as she spoke, anger draining from his face, and there was barely contained excitement in his voice as he spoke. "This figure? How many horns did it have? How many eyes? Was it shaped otherwise like a man?"

Karela stared at him in amazement. Was this some attempt to draw her off guard, it was most surely a strange one. "What interest can you have in it?"

"More than you can possibly know. Speak, woman!"

"It was like a man," she said slowly, "except that it had too many fingers and toes, and claws on all of them. There were four horns, and three eyes. And a reek of evil as strong as yours."

His smile returned, but not for her this time. To her surprise it was a smile of triumph. "Forget Inaros," he said. "Bring me that figure, and I will give you *five* hundred pieces of gold."

"Think you I'd still take your gold," she said incredulously, "after this?"

"I think you'd take five hundred pieces of it if it came from Erlik himself. Think, woman. Five hundred!"

Karela hesitated. It was a tempting amount. And to think she could earn it at the Cimmerian's expense made it more so. But to deal with this one. "Done," she was surprised to hear herself say. "How shall we meet again, when I have the thing?"

He tugged off his brilliant red surcoat, revealing gilded armor beneath. "Have a man wearing this over his tunic stand before the main gate of the royal palace when the sun is at its zenith, and on that day at dusk I will come to this hut with the gold."

"Done," Karela said again. "I will leave you, now, and I advise you to wait the time it takes to count one thousand—an you can count—before following, else you will discover whether that pretty armor will avail you against crossbow bolts." With that she backed from the hut, and scrambled into her saddle.

As she rode into the forest she found that she almost felt like singing. Five hundred pieces of gold and another stroke against the Cimmerian, if a small one. But there would be greater, the first already under way. This time it would be Conan who was forced to flee, not her. He would flee, or he would die.

Synelle paced the floor of her sleeping chamber like a caged panther, hating her agitation yet unable to quell it. Silver lamps lit the room against the night at the windows, lending a sheen to the gossamer hangings about her bed. Her pale hair hung damp with sweat, though the night was cool. Normally she guarded her exotic beauty jealously, never allowing a curl to be out of place or the slightest smudging of rouge even when she was alone, but now turmoil filled her to the exclusion of all else.

For the hundreth time she stopped before a mirror and examined her full, sensuous lips. They looked no different than they always had, but they felt swollen. With a snarl of rage she resumed her pacing, her long robe of canescent silk clinging to every curve of her body. She was aware of every particle of the sleek gray material sliding on the smoothness of her skin.

Ever since that . . . that barbarian had kissed her she had been like this. She could not stop thinking about him. Tall, with shoulders like a bull and eyes like a winter lake. A crude, unmannered lout. Wild and untamed, like a lion, with arms that could crush a woman in his embrace. She felt like bubbling honey inside. She could not sleep; already this night she had tossed for hours in torment, filled to the brim with feelings she had never before experienced.

Why had she even taken the Free-Company in service? Only to spite Antimides, as had always given her pleasure in the past. There was no reason to keep it, except that Antimides would certainly think he had won in some fashion if she dismissed them. And there was the barbarian.

Desperately she tried to force her mind away from Conan. "I will not give myself to him!" she cried. "Not to any man! Never!"

There were other things to think about. There had to be. The women. Yes. Of the bronze image of Al'Kiir, she was certain now. The men Taramenon had sent after Galbro would bring it to her. But she needed a woman for the rite, and not any woman would do. This woman must be beautiful above all others about her, proud to the point of fierceness. Proud women there were, but plain or old or disqualified on a score of other points. Beautiful women abounded, and some had pride, but where was the fierceness? Without exception they would tremble at a man's anger, give way to his will eventually, for all they might resist a time.

Why did they have to be so? Yet she could understand a little now. What woman could resist a man like the barbarian. Him again! She pounded a small fist on her sleek thigh in frustration. Why did he continually invade her thoughts?

Suddenly her face firmed with determination. She strode to a marble-topped table against the tapestried wall, touched her fingers to a twist of parchment there. Within were three long, black, silky hairs, left on her robe when the barbarian . . . Her hand trembled. She could not think of that now; her mind must be clear. It must be.

Why did it have to be him? Why not Taramenon? Because he had never affected her as Conan did? Because she had toyed with him so long that only the pleasure of toying remained?

"It will be Conan," she whispered. "But it will be as I wish." Her hand closed on the parchment, and she swept from the room.

Slaves, scrubbing floors in the hours when their mistress was not usually about, scrambled from her path, pressing their faces to the marble tiles in obeisance. She took no more notice of them than she did of the furnishings.

Straight to her secret chamber she went, closing the door behind her and hurriedly lighting lamps. Triumph sped her movements, the certainty of triumph soon to be realized.

At the table covered with beakers and flasks she carefully separated one hair from the packet. One would be enough, and that would leave two in case further magicks must be worked on the huge barbarian.

On a smooth silver plate she painted the sign of the horns, the sign of Al'Kiir, in virgin's blood, using a brush made from the hair of an unborn child and handled with a bone from its mother's finger. Next two candles were affixed to the plate, one on either side, and lit. Black, they were, made from the rendered tallow of murdered men, stolen from their graves in blessed ground.

Haste was of the essence, now, but care, too, lest disaster come in place of what she sought. Gripping her tongue between her teeth, she painted the final symbols about the edge of the plate. Desire. Lust. Need. Wanting. Passion. Longing.

Quickly she threw aside the brush, raised her hands above her head, then lowered them before her, palms up, in a gesture of pleading. In the arcane tongue she had learned so painfully, Synelle chanted, soft spoken words that rebounded from the pale walls like shouts, invoking powers linked to Al'Kiir yet not of him, powers of this world, not of the void where he was imprisoned. In the beginning she had attempted to use those powers to make contact with Al'Kiir. The result had been a fire that gutted a tower of her castle, lying halfway to the Aquilonian border, a burning with flames that no water could extinguish, flames that died only when there was not even a cinder left to burn. For long after that she had feared to try again, not least for the stares directed at her and the whispers of sorcery at the castle of Asmark. To cover herself she had brought charges of witchcraft against a woman of the castle, a crone of a scullery maid who looked the part of a witch, and had her burned at the stake. Synelle had learned care from that early mistake.

Slowly the candles guttered out in pools of their own black tallow, and

Synelle lowered her hands, breathing easily for the first time in hours.
The painted symbols on the plate, the hair, all were ash. A cruel smile
touched her lips. No more was there need to fear her desires. The
barbarian was hers, now, to do with as she would. Hers.

XI

Conan's skin crawled as he walked across the dusty courtyard of the house where his company was quartered. The hairs on his body seemed to move by themselves. Bright sunlight streamed from the golden globe climbing into the mourning sky; chill air seemed to surround him. It had been so ever since he woke, this strangeness, and he had no understanding of why.

Fear the big Cimmerian dismissed as a cause. He knew his fears well, and had them well in hand. No fear could ever affect him so, who had, in his fear years, faced all manner of things that quelled the hearts of other men. As for the image, and even Al'Kiir, he had confronted demons and sorcerers before, as well as every sort of monster from huge flesh-eating worms to giant spiders dripping corrosive poison from manibles that could pierce the finest armor to a dragon of adamantine scales and fiery breath. Each he had conquered, and if he was wary of such, he did not fear them.

"Cimmerian," Narus called, "come get yourself a cloak."

"Later," Conan shouted back to the hollow-faced, who was rooting with others of the company in the great pile of bales and bundles that had been delivered by carts that morning.

Synelle had finally seen to the needs of the Free-Company she had taken in service. Bundles of long woolen cloaks of scarlet, the color of her house, had been tumbled into the courtyard, along with masses of fresh bedding and good wool blankets. There had been knee-high Aquilonian boots of good black leather, small mirrors of polished metal from Zingara, keen-bladed Corinthian razors, and a score of other things, from a dozen countries, that a soldier might need. Including a sack of gold coin for their first pay. The mercenaries had turned the morning into a holiday with it all. Fabio had kept Julia running all morning, staggering under sacks of turnips and peas, struggling with quarters of beef and whole lamb carcasses, rolling casks of wine and ale to the kitchens.

Fabio found Conan by the dry fountain. The fat, round cook was mopping his face with a rag. "Conan, that lazy wench you saddled me with has run off and hidden somewhere. And look, she hasn't swept a quarter of the courtyard yet. Claims she's a lady. Erlik take her if she is! She has a mouth like a fishwife. Flung a broom at my head in my own kitchen, and swore at me as vilely as I've ever heard from any man in the company."

Conan shook his head irritably. He was in no mood to listen to the man's complaints, not when he felt as if ants were skittering over his body. "If you want the courtyard swept," he snapped, "see to it yourself."

Fabio stared after him, open-mouthed, as he stalked away.

Conan scrubbed his fingers through his hair. What was the matter with him? *Could* that accursed bronze, the evil of it that Julia claimed to sense, have affected him from beneath the floor while he slept?

"Cimmerian," Boros said, popping out of the house, "I've been seeking you everywhere."

"Why?" Conan growled, then attempted to get a hold of himself. "What do you want?" he asked in a slightly more reasonable tone.

"Why, that image, of course." The old man looked around, then lowered his voice. "Have you given any thought to destroying it? The more I think on it, the more it seems the Staff of Avanrakash is the only answer."

"I am not stealing the Erlik-accursed scepter," Conan grated. When he saw Machaon approaching, the Cimmerian felt ready to burst.

The grizzled mercenary eyed the bigger man's grim face quizzically, but said only, "We're being watched. This house, that is."

Conan gripped his swordbelt tightly with both hands. This was business of the company, perhaps important business, and he had worked too long and too hard for that to allow even his own temper to damage it.

"Karela's men?" he asked in what was almost his normal voice. It took a great effort to maintain it.

"Not unless she's begun taking fopling youths into her band," Machaon replied. "There are two of them, garbed and jeweled for a lady's garden, with pomanders stuck to their nostrils, wandering up and down the street outside. They show an especial interest in this house."

Young nobles, Conan thought. They could be Antimides' men, if the count was concerned as to how much Conan was talking of what he knew. Or they could be seeking the image, though nobles hardly meshed with the sort who had tried for it thus far. They might even be this Taramenon, Synelle's jealous suitor, and a friend, come to see for themselves what manner of man the silvery-haired beauty had taken in service. Too many possibilities to reason out, certainly not in his present state of mind.

"If we seize them when next they pass," he began, and the two listening to him recoiled.

"You must be mad," Boros gasped. "'Tis the image, Cimmerian. it affects you ill. It must be destroyed quickly."

"I know not what this old magpie is chattering about," Machaon said, "but seizing nobles . . . in broad daylight from a street in the middle of Ianthe . . . Cimmerian, it would take more luck than ten Brythunian sages to get out of the city with our heads still on our shoulders."

Conan squeezed his eyes shut. His brain whirled and spun, skittering through fogs that veiled reason. This was deadly dangerous; he *must* be able to think clearly, or he could lead them all to disaster.

"My Lord Conan?" a diffident voice said.

Conan opened his eyes to find a barefoot man in the short white tunic of a slave, edged in scarlet, had joined them. "I'm no lord," he said gruffly.

"Yes, my lor . . . uh, noble sir. I am bid tell you the Lady Synelle wishes your presence at her house immediately."

Images of the sleek, full-breasted noblewoman flickered into Conan's mind, clearing aside all else. His unease was washed away by a warm flow of desire. Sternly he reminded himself that she no doubt wanted to consult with him about the company's duties, but the reminder could as well have been whispered into a great storm of the Vilayet Sea. When first he kissed her, she had responded. Whatever her words said, her body had told the truth of her feelings. It *must* have.

"Lead on," Conan commanded, then strode through the gate and into the street without waiting. The slave had to scurry after him.

Conan gave little heed to the man half-running beside him to keep up as he moved swiftly through throng-filled streets. With every stride his visions of Synelle grew stronger, more compelling, and his breath came faster. Each line of her became clear in his mind, the swell of round breasts above a tiny waist his big hands could almost span, the curve of sleek things and sensuously swaying hips. She filled his mind, clouded his eyes so that he saw none of the teeming crowds nor remembered anything of his journey.

Once within Synelle's great house the man in the short tunic rushed ahead to guide Conan up stairs and through corridors, but the Cimmerian was certain he could have found the way by himself. His palms sweated for the smooth satin of her skin.

The slave bowed him into Synelle's private chamber. The pale-skinned beauty stood with one small hand at her alabaster throat, dark eyes seeming to fill a face surrounded by silken waves of spun-platinum hair. Diaphanous silk covered her ivory lushness, but concealed nothing.

"Leave us, Scipio," she said unsteadily.

Conan was unaware of the slave leaving, closing the door behind him. His breath was thick in his throat; his nails dug into calloused palms. Never had he taken a woman who did not want him, yet he knew he was at the brink. One gesture from her, one word that he might take as invitation; it would be enough. Battle raged within the giant Cimmerian, ravening lust warring with his will. And for the first time in his life he felt his will begin to bend.

"I called you here, barbarian," she began, then swallowed and began again. "I summoned you to me . . ."

Her words faded away as he covered the floor between them. His hands took her shoulders gently; how great the struggle not to rip that transparently mocking garment from her. As he gazed down at her upturned face, he read fear there, and longing. Her melting eyes were bottomless pools into which he could fall forever; his were azure flames.

"Do not fear me," he said hoarsely. "I will never harm you."

She pressed her cheek to his chest, crushing her full breasts against him. Unseen by him a small smile curved her lips, softening, though not supplanting, the fear in her eyes. "You are mine," she whispered.

"When first I kissed you," Conan panted, "you wanted me. As I want you. I knew I had not imagined it."

"Come," she said, taking his hand as she backed from him. "My bed lies beyond that archway. I will have wine brought, and fruits packed in snow from the mountains."

"No," he growled. "I can wait no longer." His hand closed on sheer silk; the robe shredded from her ripe nakedness. Careless of her protests of servants who might enter, he pulled her to the floor. Soon she protested no more.

XII

The sun was rising toward its height once more as Conan left Synelle's house, and he wondered wearily at the passing of unnoticed hours. But she had so occupied him with herself that there had been no room for time. Had she not been gone from her bed at his waking, he might not be leaving yet. For all of a day and a night together, and little sleeping in it, a knot of desire still burned in his belly, flaring whenever he thought of her. Only the need to see to his Free-Company, and her absence, had stirred him to dress and go.

Bemused he strode through the crowded streets as if they were empty of all but him, seeing only the woman who still held his mind in thrall with her body. Merchants in voluminous hooded robes and tarts in little save gilded bangles scurried from his way lest they be trampled; satin-clad nobles and long-bearded scholars abandoned dignity to leap aside when they incredulously saw he would not alter his path. He heard the curses that followed him, but the stream of abuse from scores of throats did not register. It was so much meaningless babble that had naught to do with him.

Suddenly a man who had not stepped aside bounced off Conan's chest, and the Cimmerian found himself staring into an indignant face as the memory of Synelle's silken thighs dimmed, but did not fade. The man was young, no older than he himself, but his tunic of blue brocade slashed with yellow, the golden chain across his chest, his small, fashionable beard, the pomander clutched in his hand, all named him nobly born.

"You there, thief," the youthful lord sneered. "I have you now."

"Get out of my way, fool," Conan growled. "I've no time or desire to play lordlings' games." The man wore a sword strapped around his waist, the Cimmerian noted, unusual with the garb he wore.

Conan tried to step around the brocaded youth, but another young noble, with thin mustachios in addition to his beard, stepped in front of him with a swagger. Jeweled rings bedecked all his fingers, and he, too, wore a sword. "This outlander," he said loudly, "has robbed my friend."

Conan wondered for whose benefit he was speaking so; no one in the teeming street paid the three any mind. In fact, a large space had opened about them as passersby studiously avoided their vicinity. Whatever sport these two sought, he wanted none of it. He wished only to see that all was well with his company and return as quickly as possible to Synelle. Synelle of the alabaster skin as soft as satin.

"Leave be," he said, doubling a massive fist, "or I'll set your ears to ringing. I've stolen nothing."

"He attacks," the mustachioed lordling cried, and his sword swept from its sheath as his fellow flung his rose-scented pomander at Conan's face.

Even with his brain fogged by a woman's memory the big Cimmerian had survived far too many battles to be taken so easily by surprise. The blade that was meant to take his head from his shoulders passed through empty air as he leaped aside. Anger washed his mind clean of all but battle rage. The sport these fops sought was his death, a killing for which, with the times as they were and the fact that he was an outlander, they would not be brought to book. But they had chosen no easy meat. Even as Conan's own steel was coming into his fist, he booted the first young noble who had accosted him squarely in the crotch; the youth shrieked like a girl and crumpled, clutching himself.

Whirling, Conan beat aside the thrust the mustachioed lordling had meant for his back. "Crom!" he bellowed. "Crom and steel!" And he waded ferociously into the combat, his sword a flashing engine of destruction.

Step by step his opponent was forced back, splashes of blood appearing on his tunic as his desperate defenses failed to turn aside the Cimmerian's blade quickly enough. Disbelief grew on his face, as if he could not understand that he faced a man better with the sword than he. Recklessly he attempted to go over to attack. Only once more did Conan's steel strike, but this time it split the lordling's skull to his black mustachios.

As the body fell the grate of the boot on pavement gave Conan warning, and he turned to block the first noble's slash. Chest to straining chest they stood, blades locked.

"I am better than ever Demetrios was," his youthful attacker sneered. "In this hour you will meet your gods, barbar."

With a heave of his mighty shoulders Conan sent the other staggering back. "Run to your mother's breast, youngling," he told him, "and live to do your boasting to women. If you know their use."

With a cry of fury the man rushed at Conan, a blur of steel before him. Eight times their blades met, striking sparks with the force of the blows, filling the street with a ringing as of a blacksmith's hammer and anvil. Then the Cimmerian's broadsword was slicing through ribs and flesh to the heart beneath.

Once more, for a moment, Conan stared into those dark eyes. "You were better," he said, "but not by enough."

The young lord opened his mouth, but blood spilled out instead of words, and death dulled his eyes.

Hastily Conan freed his blade and cleaned it on the tunic of blue brocade. The space about them still was clear, and as if an invisible wall separated him and the two dead from those hurrying by, no one so much as glanced toward them. Given the mood of the city, it was more likely than not that no one of them would admit to what he had seen, short of being put to the question by the King's torturers, but there was no point in standing there until a score of Iskandrian's warriors appeared. Sheathing his sword, Conan melded into the crowd. Within a few paces they had closed around him, cloaking him in their number.

No more did thoughts of Synelle clog his mind. With the death of the second of his attackers he had remembered Machaon telling him of two young nobles watching the house where the Free-Company was quartered. That two different lordlings should attack him on the very next day was beyond his belief. The one had called loudly that Conan had robbed the other, as if inviting witnesses. Hardly the act of one intending murder, but perhaps slaying him had been but part of their plan.

Had they succeeded, who in Ianthe would have taken the part of a dead barbarian over that of two from noble houses? The people rushing by had done their best to ignore what happened, but if collared by a noble and pressed, which of them would not remember that Conan had been accused of theft and had then attacked the two, proving his guilt? With a King's Justice and a column of Ophirean infantry, Demetrios and his friend could have descended on the Free-Company, demanded the object they claimed had been stolen—and which they could no doubt describe as well as Conan—and have the house torn apart to find it. The bronze would have been in the hands of those who sought to use it. Boros might try to speak of evil gods and rites beneath Tor Al'Kiir, or Julia, but no ear would pay heed to the pratings of a drunken former apprentice mage, nor the babblings of a pot-girl.

Conan quickened his pace, brimming with an urgent need to assure himself that the image still lay beneath the floorboards of his sleeping chamber. He had become convinced of one thing. He would not have another night of rest in Ophir until that malevolent figure was beyond the reach of men.

*   *   *

The black candles guttered out, and Synelle lowered her hands with a satisfied sigh. The spell binding the barbarian had been altered. He was still held, but with more subtle desires than before.

With a weary groan she sagged to a low stool, wincing with the movement, and brushed spun silver hair back from her face. She pulled her cloak—that unadorned covering of scarlet wool had been all she had taken time to snatch in her flight, and it *had* been flight—about her nakedness. Her breasts were swollen and tender, her thighs and bottom bruised by Conan's fierce desires.

"How could I have known what would be unleashed in him?" she whispered. "Who could have thought a man could be so . . ." She shivered uncontrollably.

In the barbarian's arms she had felt gripped by a force of nature as irresistible as an avalanche. Fires he had built in her, feeding them till they raged out of control. And when the leaping flames had consumed all before them, when he had quenched and slaked what he had aroused, he stoked still new fires. She had tried to bring that endless cycle to a halt, more than once she had tried—memories flooded her, memories of incoherent cries when words could not be formed and reason clung by the slenderest of threads to but a single corner of her passion-drugged mind—but her sorcery had not only wakened lust in him, it had magnified that lust, made it insatiable, overwhelming. His powerful hands had handled her like a doll. His hands, so strong, so knowing and sure of her.

"No," she muttered angrily.

She would not think of his hands. That way led to weakness. She would remember instead the humiliation of crawling weakly from her own bed when the barbarian fell at last to slumber, slinking like a thief for fear of waking him, of waking the desire that would bloom in him when his eyes touched her. On the floor of her secret chamber she had slept, curled on the hard marble with only the cloak for covering and lacking even the mat the meanest of her slaves would have, too exhausted to think or dream. Remember that, she told herself, and not the pleasures that sent tendrils of heat through her belly even in remembrance.

A ragged cry broke from her throat, and she staggered to her feet to pace the room. Her eye fell on the silver plate, black tallow hardening at its edges, the ash of blood and hair lying on its surface. The spell *was* altered. Not again would she have to face a night where she was a mote caught in the stormwind of the giant barbarian's desires. Her breathing slowed, grew more normal. He was still hers, he would still bring her to rapture, but his lusts would be more controllable. Controllable by her, that is.

"Why did I fear it so long?" she laughed softly. Taken altogether, this thing of men was quite wonderful. "They must simply be controlled, and then their vaunted strength and power can avail them nothing."

That was the lesson women had not learned, that she had only just come to. If women would not be controlled by men, then they must rather control men. She had always coveted power. How strange and beautiful that power should be the key to safety in this as well!

A knock at the door shattered her musings. Who would dare disturb her there? The rapping came again, more insistent this time. Gathering her cloak across her breasts with one hand, she flung open the door, tongue ready to flay whoever had violated her sanctorum.

A surprised, "You!" slipped out instead.

"Yes, me," Taramenon said. His face was tight with barely controlled anger. "I came to speak to you last night, but you were . . . occupied."

Laying a hand gently on his chest, she pushed him back—how easily he moved, even in his rage—and closed the door firmly behind her. No man, not even he, would ever enter that chamber.

"It is well you are here," she said as if he had had no accusation in his words. "There are matters of which we must speak. A woman must be found—"

"You were with him," the tall nobleman grated. "You gave that barbarian swine what was promised to me."

Synelle drew herself to her full height, and flung cold fury at him like a dagger. "Whatever I gave was *mine* to give. Whatever I did was *mine* to do, and none with right to gainsay me."

"I will slay him," Taramenon moaned in anguish, "like a dog in the dirt."

"You will slay whom I tell you to slay, when I tell you to slay them." Synelle softened her voice; shock had driven anger from Taramenon's face. There were still uses for the man, and she had long since learned means of controlling him that had naught to do with sorcery. "The barber will be useful for a time. Later you may kill him if you wish."

The last had been a sudden thought. Conan was a wonderful lover, but why limit herself to one? Men did not limit themselves to one woman. Yet the young giant would always hold a place in her affections for the vistas of pleasure he opened to her; when she was Queen of Ophir she would have a magnificent tomb erected for him.

"I found the brigand you wanted," Taramenon muttered sullenly. "A woman."

Synelle's eyebrows arched. "A *woman* bandit? A hardened trull, no doubt, with greasy hair and gimlet eye."

"She is," he replied, "the most beautiful woman I have ever seen."

Synelle flinched, and her jaw tightened. Why had the fool forced his presence on her before her tire-maids could see to her toilet? "So long as she brings me the scrolls from Inaros' library, I care not what she looks like." He chuckled, and she stared at him. Suddenly he was more relaxed, as if he thought he was in command. "If you think to make sport of me," she began dangerously.

"I did not send her after Inaros' scrolls," Taramenon said.

Words froze in her throat. When she found speech again she hissed at him. "And pray tell me why not?"

"Because I sent her after the image of Al'Kiir that you speak. She knows where it is. She described it to me. It will be I who provide you with what you so desperately need. Did you think you could hide your impatience, your eagerness beyond that you've ever shown for all the parchments and artifacts you have gathered placed together? I bring it to you, Synelle, not that barbar animal, and I expect at least the reward that he got."

Her pale, dark-eyed beauty became icy still. She let her cloak gap open to the floor; Taramenon gasped, and sweat beaded his forehead. "You will come to my bed," she began softly, but abruptly her words became lashes of a whip tipped with steel, "when I summon you there. You will come, yes, perhaps sooner than you dream, certainly sooner than you deserve, but at *my* command." Slowly and calmly she covered herself once more. "Now when will the image be delivered to your hand?"

"The signal that she has it," he mumbled sulkily, "will be a man in my red surcoat standing before the main gate of the royal palace at noon. That night at dusk I will meet her at a hut in the forest."

Synelle nodded thoughtfully. "You say this woman is beautiful? A beautiful woman who does what men do, who leads men rather than belonging to them. She must have great pride. I shall be at that meeting with you, Taramenon." From the corner of her eye she saw a slave creeping down the corridor toward them, and rounded on him, furious at the interruption. "Yes?" she snapped.

Falling to his knees, the man pressed his face to the marble tiles. "A message, my gracious lady, from the noble Aelfric." Without lifting his head he held up a folded parchment.

Synelle frowned and snatched the message. Aelfric was Seneschal of Asmark, her ancestral castle, a man who served her well, but who liked as well the fact that she seldom visited or troubled him. It was not his way to invite her attention. Hastily she broke the lump of wax sealed with Aelfric's ring.

To My Most Gracious Lady Synelle,

    With pain I send these tidings. In the day past have vile brigands most cowardly struck at my Lady's manor-farms, burning fields, touching barns, driving oxen and cattle into the forests. Even as your humble servant writes these dire words, the night sky glows red with new fires. I beseech my Lady to send aid, else there will be no crops left, and starvation will be the lot of her people.

I remain obediently,
your faithful servitor,
Aelfric

Angrily she crumpled the letter in her fist. Bandits attacking *her* holdings? When she held the throne she would see every brigand in the country impaled on the walls of Ianthe. For now Aelfric would have to fend for himself.

But wait, she thought. With the power of Al'Kiir she could seize the throne, overawe both lords and peasants, yet would it not be even better had she some incident to point to that showed she was more than other women? Did she take Conan's warriors into the countryside and quell these bandits herself . . .

She prodded the slave with her foot. "I am leaving for the country. Tell the others to prepare. Go."

"Yes, my lady," the slave said, backing away on his knees. "At once, my lady." Rising, he bowed deeply and darted down the hall.

"And you, Taramenon," she went on. "Set a man to watch for this woman's signal and bring me word, then ride you for Castle Asmark. Await me there, and this night your waiting will be ended." She almost laughed at the lascivious anticipation that painted his visage. "Go," she said, in the same tone she had used with the slave, and Taramenon ran as quickly as the other had.

It was all a matter of maintaining proper control she told herself. Then she went in search of writing materials, to send a summons to the barbarian.

XIII

onan straightened from checking his saddle girth and glared about him at the assemblage pausing for yet another rest at Synelle's command. Three and twenty high-wheeled carts, each drawn by two span of yoked oxen, were piled high with what the Countess of Asmark considered necessary for removing to her castle in the country, rolled feather mattresses and colorful embroidered silk cushions, casks of the rarest wines from Aquilonia and Corinthia and even Khauran, packages of delicate viands that might not be readily available away from the capital, chests upon chests of satins and velvets and laces.

Synelle herself traveled in a gilded litter, borne by eight muscular slaves and curtained with fine silken net to admit the breeze yet keep the sun from her alabastrine skin. Her four blonde tirewomen crouched in the shade of a cart, fanning themselves against the midday heat. Their lithe sleekness drew many eyes among the thirty mercenaries surrounding the carts, but the women were attuned only to listening for the next command from the litter. Nearly three score other servants and slaves hunkered out of the sun or tended to errands, drivers for the oxen, maids, seamstresses, even two cooks who were at that moment arguing vociferously over the proper method of preparing humming-birds' tongues.

"Watch the trees, Erlik take you!" Conan shouted. Abashedly the mercenaries tore their eyes from the blondes to scan the forest that ran along two sides of the broad, grassy meadow where they had halted.

The Cimmerian had opposed halting; he had opposed each stop they had made thus far. Slowed by the oxcarts, they would not arrive at Synelle's castle until the following afternoon did they make the best speed the lumbering animals were capable of. Even one night in the forests with this strange cortege was more than he might wish for, much less risking a second such camp. A pavilion would have to be erected for Synelle to sleep in, another in which she would bathe, and yet a third for her tire-women's mats. There would be a fire to warm Synelle, fires for the cooks, fires to keep the maids from becoming affrighted of the night, and all no doubt large enough to announce their presence and location to anyone with eyes.

Machaon led his horse over to Conan. "I've word of Karela, Cimmerian," he said. "I crossed paths last night at the *Blue Bull* with a weedy scoundrel, a panderer who lost his women, and thus his income, to another, and whose tongue was free after his third pitcher of ale. I meant to speak of it earlier, but what with our patron's summons arriving hard on your heels this morn I forgot."

"What did you hear?" Conan asked eagerly.

"She uses her own name again, for one thing. She has not been long in Ophir, but already some twenty rogues follow her, and she is making reputation enough that Iskandrian has put twenty pieces of gold on her head."

"Such a small price must anger her," Conan laughed. "I fear not it will remain so low for long. But what of getting a message to her, or finding her? What did he say of that?"

"After a time the fellow seemed to realize he was babbling, and shut his teeth." At the Cimmerian's look of disappointment Machaon smiled. "But he let fall enough for me to question others. North of Ianthe, an hour's ride on a good horse, part of an ancient keep still stands, overgrown by the Sarelian Forest. There Karela camps her band on most nights. I am sure of it."

Conan grinned broadly. "I'll make her admit she has no grievance against me if I have to paddle her rump until she does."

"A treatment I could recommend for others," the tattooed man said with a significant look at the litter.

Conan followed his look and sighed. "We have been halted long enough," was all he said.

As the young Cimmerian walked toward the net-curtained palanquin he tried to make some slight sense of these last two days, not for the first time that morning. The previous day and night seemed like a dream, but a fever-born dream of madness, with lust burning all else from his mind. Had what he remembered—Synelle's sweat-slicked thighs and wanton moans flashed, in his mind—actually happened? It all seemed distant and dim.

When he answered her summons this morn, he had felt no such all-consuming desire. He wanted her, wanted her more than he had ever wanted any woman, more than he had wanted all the many women of his life together, but there had been a sense of restraint within him, strictures unnatural to his nature holding him in check. He did not lose control of himself with women—were his memories of the day before true?—but neither did he face them feeling bound with stout ropes.

And he had deferred to her! When, as haughty and regal as any queen, she commanded him as to how to order his men on the march, his urge had been to snort and tell her brusquely that such matters were his province. Instead he had found himself almost pleading with her, painfully convincing her that she should leave the command of his company to him. He had met kings and potentates and not acted so. How did this woman affect him in this manner? This time, he vowed, it would be different.

He stopped before Synelle's curtained litter and bowed. "If it pleases my lady, we should be moving on." Inwardly he snarled at himself. He was no man to break vows, and this had gone as swiftly as if it had never been made. What was the matter with him? Yet he could change nothing. "It is dangerous, my lady, to stay still so long with bandits and worse about."

A delicate hand parted the mesh curtain, and Synelle looked out at him calmly, a small smile curling her full lips. Her traveling garb of cool linen clung to her, revealing the curves and shadows of her. Conan's mouth went dry, and his palms dampened, at the sight.

"It would not be so dangerous," she said, "had you obeyed me and brought your entire company."

Conan gritted his teeth. Half of him wanted to tell this fool woman that she should leave the trade of arms to those who knew it; the other half wanted to stammer an apology. "We must be moving, my lady," he said finally. It had been an effort to say only that, and he feared he did not want to know what else he might have said.

"Very well. You may see to it," she said, letting the curtain fall.

Conan bowed again before turning away.

His stomach roiled as he strode back to his horse. Perhaps he *was* going mad. "To horse!" he roared, swinging into his saddle. "Mount and prepare to move! Oxdrivers to your animals!" Chattering men and giggling women darted along the row of carts. "Keep those maids off the carts!" he shouted. "We need what speed we can manage, and no extra weight for the animals! Move you!"

Harness creaked as massive beasts took up the strain; mercenaries scrambled to their mounts in a rattle of armor.

Conan raised his arm to signal the advance, and at that instant a mass of horsemen in chain-mail charged from the trees. Shrieks rose from terrified women, and the oxen, sensing the humans' fear, bellowed mournfully. This was what the Cimmerian had feared since leaving Ianthe, but for that reason he was ready for it.

"Bows!" he commanded, and short, curved horse-bows came into thirty hands beside his own.

Those powerful bows, unknown in the west except for Conan's Free-Company, could not be drawn as ordinary bows were. Nocking an arrow with a three-fingered grip on the bowstring, the huge Cimmerian placed those fingers against his cheek and thrust the bow out from him.

There were close to a hundred of them, he estimated as he drew, wearing the sign of no house and carrying no banners or pennons, yet armored too well for bandits. He loosed, and thirty more shafts flew after his. They were still too distant to pick individual targets, but the mass of them made target enough. Saddles emptied, but the onrushing men-at-arms, their wordless battle cries rising, came on. By the time Conan let his third arrow fly—the feathered shaft lanced through the eye-slit of the foremost horseman's white-plumed helmet; the man threw his hands to his face and rolled backwards over the rump of his still racing horse—the enemy had closed too much for bows to be of further use.

"Out swords!" he called, thrusting his bow back into its lacquered wooden scabbard behind his saddle. As he drew sword and thrust his left arm through the leather straps of his round shield with its spiked boss, he realized his helm still hung from his pommel. Battle rage was on him; let them see who killed them, he thought. "Crom!" he shouted. "Crom and steel!"

At the pressure of his knees, the big Aquilonian black burst forward into a gallop. Conan caught sight of Synelle, standing by her litter with her mouth open in a scream he could not hear for the blood pounding in his ears, then his mount was smashing into another horse, riding the lighter animal down, trampling its armored rider beneath steel-shod hooves.

The huge Cimmerian caught a blade on his shield, and his answering stroke severed the arm wielding it at the shoulder. Immediately he reversed to a backslash that cut deep into the neck of another foe.

Dimly he was aware of others of his men about him in the frenzied melee, but such were of necessity a series of individual combats; only when the vagaries of battle drew two comrades together did men of one side or the other stand together against their enemy.

A chain-mailed man rode close with broadsword raised high to chop, and Conan drove the spike on his shield into the man's chest, ripping him from the saddle with one jerk of a massive arm. War-trained, his big black lashed out with flashing fore-hooves at foremen's horses as he hacked deeper into the press with his murderous steel.

From beyond the swirling frenzy of slashing, shouting, dying men came a cry. "Conan! For the Cimmerian!"

About time, a cool corner of Conan's brain thought, and Narus, with twenty more mercenaries following, charged into the rear of the enemy. There was no time for more thought, for he was trading furious sword-strokes with a man whose chain-mail was splashed with blood not his own. He saw one of his men go down, head half-severed. The killer came galloping past, waving his gory blade and screaming a warcry. Conan kicked a foot free of its stirrup and booted the shouting man from his horse. The Cimmerian's blade freed itself from his opponent's and thrust under the other's chin, shattering the steel links of his mail coif and bringing a scarlet gout from his ruined throat. The man Conan had kicked from his saddle scrambled to his feet as his fellow fell, but the young giant's broadsword struck once, battering down his upraised steel, twice, and his headless corpse dropped across his comrade's body.

"Crom and steel!"

"Conan! Conan!"

"For the Cimmerian!"

It was too much for the mailed attackers, embattled before and behind, a huge northland beserker in their midst and no knowing in the fog of battle how many it was they faced. First a single man fled the combat, then another. Panic rippled through them, and cohesion was gone. By twos and threes they fought to get away. As they scattered some of the mercenaries set out in pursuit, echoing the halloing cry of hunters riding down deer.

"Back, you fools!" Conan bellowed. "Back, Black Erlik rot you!"

Reluctantly the mercenaries gave over the chase, and in moments the last of the mailed men still able to flee had melted into the forest. The men of the company who had pursued trotted back, waving gory swords and rasing shouts of victory.

"A most excellent plan, Cimmerian," Narus laughed as he galloped up, "having us trail behind as a surprise for unwelcome guests." His jazeraint hauberk was splattered with blood, no drop of which was his. The gaunt-faced man, disease-riddled though he appeared, was equal to Machaon with a blade, and none but Conan was their master. "Ten to one in gold they never knew how many hit them."

"A difficult wager to settle," Conan said, but half his mind on the other. "Machaon," he called, "what's the butcher's price?"

"I'm taking a count, Cimmerian." Quickly the tattooed veteran finished and rode to join them. "Two dead," he retorted, "and a dozen who'll need the carts to get back to Ianthe."

Conan nodded grimly. Well over a score of the enemy lay on the hoof-churned ground, meadow grass and soil now seeming plowed, and only a few moved weakly. As many more were scattered back to the trees, sprouting feathered shafts. In the grim world of the mercenary it was little better than an even trade, for enemies were always there and easily found, but new companions were hard to come by.

"See if one of them lives enough to answer questions," the Cimmerian commanded. "I would know who sent them against us, and why."

Hurriedly Machaon and Narus dismounted. Moving among the bodies, stopping occasionally to heave one over, they returned supporting between them a bloodstreaked man with a wicked gash down the side of his face and neck.

"Mercy," he gasped faintly. "I cry mercy."

"Then name he who sent you," Conan demanded. "Were you to kill us all, or one in particular?"

The Cimmerian had no intention of slaying a wounded and helpless man, but the prisoner clearly feared the worst. Almost eagerly he said, "Count Antimides. He bid us slay you and seize the Lady Synelle. Her we were to bring to him naked and in chains."

"Antimides!" Synelle hissed. The men shifted uneasily to see her picking her way across the bloody ground; such sights as lay about them, men hacked and torn by the savagery of battle, were not for women's eyes. Synelle did not seem to notice. "He dares so much against me?" she continued. "I will have his eyes and his manhood! I will—"

"My lady," Conan said, "those who attacked us may rejoin and seek you again." And he also, he added to himself, though that did not concern him as much as the other. "You must return to Ianthe, and quickly. You must ride one of the horses."

"Back to the city?" Synelle nodded vigorously. "Yes. And when I get there Antimides will learn the price of an attack on my person!" Her eyes were bright with eagerness for that teaching.

Conan began seeing to preparations, ordering men who hurried to obey. The warriors, at least, knew their vulnerability should the enemy return, perhaps with reinforcements. "Machaon, tell off ten men to ride with the carts. Unload everything except the Lady Synelle's jewelry and clothes to lighten the oxen's loads. Leave the litter here, so they can see she's no longer with the carts. Crom, of course we bring in our dead! Spread the wounded among the carts so they're not crowded, and have the maids tend them. Yes, their wounded as well."

"No!" Synelle snapped. "Leave Antimides' men! Fetch me naked and chained, will they? Let them die!"

Conan's hands tightened on his reins until his knuckles were white. His temples throbbed like drums. "Load their wounded, too," he said, and drew a shuddering breath. Almost he had not been able to get the words out.

Synelle looked at him strangely. "A strong will," she said musingly. "And yet there could be pleasure in—" Abruptly she stopped, as if she thought she had said too much, but the Cimmerian could understand nothing of it.

"My lady," he said, "you must ride astride. We have no side-saddle."

She held out a hand to him. "Your dagger, barbarian."

When she took it from him it felt as though sparks jumped from her hand to his. Deftly she slit the front of her robe. Narus led forward a horse, and she mounted with flashing limbs, exposed to the tops of her pale thighs, nor did she do anything to cover them once in the saddle. Conan could feel her eyes on him as solidly as a touch, but of which sort he could not tell. He tore his gaze from her long legs, and heard a laugh softly, the sound burning in his brain.

"We ride!" he commanded hoarsely, and galloped toward Ianthe, the rest streaming behind.

XIV

Karela kept the hood of her dark blue woolen cloak pulled well forward; there were those about her in the crowd-filled streets of Ianthe who would put aside their habit of ignoring what occurred around them for a chance at Iskandrian's reward.

She snorted at the thought. Twenty pieces of gold! A thousand times so much had been placed on her head by the Kings of Zamora and Turan. The merchants of those countries had offered more, and would have considered it cheap to rid their caravans of her depredations at the price. High Councils had had debated methods of dealing with her, armies had pursued her, and no man took passage from one city to another without offering prayers that she would spare his purse, all with equal futility. Now, she found herself reduced to an amount of coin that spoke of petty irritation. The humiliation of it was so great that barely could she keep her mind on her purpose for entering the city.

The house where Conan's company of rogues was gathered lay just ahead. That morning she had watched him ride out with half his company. A short time later another large contingent of his men had departed by another gate and trailed after the first. Wily Cimmerian! She had long since gotten over the foolishness of failing to respect his abilities. He would be taken in no ordinary trap. But then she was no ordinary woman.

Unbidden, her thoughts went back to that woman of the nobility he had been escorting. Did she know him, he had already visited the wench's bed. He had always had an eye for willing wenches, and few were those who were not willing did he once smile at them. The red-haired woman wished she could get her hands on this Synelle. Lady, indeed. She would not soil her hands with the like of those who called themselves ladies. Karela would show her what a real woman looked like, then send her back to Conan as a present, stuffed naked into a sack. When someone had offered her gold to burn the jade's farms, she had not stopped to ask why or query who the man with the deep-set, commanding eyes was behind his mask of black silk. It had been a chance to strike at Conan, and his precious Synelle, and she leaped at it. She would prick him and prick him until he was forced to flee, and if he would not . . .

Angrily she pulled her mind back to the matter at hand. She no longer cared what women he took, she told herself. Such interest in the man had brought her naught but grief. With the men he had taken to protect his new trull, he could not have left many behind. She looked through the arched gateway as she passed. Yes. There were only a handful to be seen, playing at dice against the side of the fountain in the courtyard. He who had made the cast cursed, and the others laughed as they scooped up his losings.

Karela raised a hand to her face as if brushing away a fly, and two men pushing a handcart toward her, its flat bed piled high with wooden boxes held in place by ropes, suddenly turned it into the alley beside the house. Karela followed them. The men glanced at her questioningly; she nodded, and they turned to watch the street.

One, a dark-faced Zamoran with drooping mustaches, whom she had taken on out of memory of better days, said softly, "No one looks."

In the space of two breaths Karela scrambled up the carefully arranged boxes and into a window on the second floor. It was Conan's room. Her sources of information had discovered that for her easily enough.

Her lip curled contemptuously as she looked around the bare chamber. So this was what he had come to since forsaking a palace in Nemedia. She had never heard the straight of his departing that land when he had been offered honors and wealth by the King, but it brought a measure of continuing satisfaction that he had not profited from the adventures which ended in her flight. It did her good to think of him brought low. Yet the blankets were folded neatly on the bed. There were no cobwebs on the ceiling, no dust in the corners, and the floor had been freshly swept. A woman, she thought, and not likely it was his fine Synelle. The Cimmerian gathered a zenana about him like an easterner.

Sternly she reminded herself of her lack of interest in Conan's women. She had come for that obscene bronze figure, and nothing more. But where to begin searching? There did not look to be many places for hiding. Beneath the bed, perhaps.

Before she could take a step, the door opened and a girl wearing plain white robes walked in. There was something oddly familiar about her face and hair, though Karela could swear she had never seen the girl before.

"Keep your silence, wench," Karela commanded. "Close the door and answer my questions quickly, and you'll come to no harm."

"Wench!" the girl said, her eyes flashing indignantly. "What are you doing here . . . wench? I think I'll let you see if you like Fabio's switch. Then you can answer questions for me."

"I told you," Karela began, but the girl was already turning back to the door. With a curse the woman bandit jumped across the room and grappled with her, managing to kick the door shut as she did.

She expected the girl to surrender, or try to scream for help at most, but with a sqawl of rage the other woman buried her hands in Karela's red hair. The two women fell to the floor in a kicking, nail-clawing heap.

Derketo, Karela thought, she did not want to kill the jade, but she had defended herself too long with a sword to remember well this woman-fighting. She almost screamed as the other sank teeth into her shoulder; handfuls of her hair were at the point of being ripped from her head. Desperately she slammed a knee into the girl's belly. Breath left the other woman in a gasp, and Karela wriggled forward to kneel on her arms. Her dagger slipped into her hand, and she held it before the girl's face.

"Now be silent, Derketo take you!" she panted. The girl glared up at her defiantly, but held her tongue.

Abruptly Karela realized what was familiar about the girl. The eyes were different, but the color of her hair, the shape of her face. Conan had found himself an imitation of herself. She could not think whether to laugh, or cry, or slit the wench's throat. Or wait for the Cimmerian and slit his. No interest, she told herself again. No interest at all.

"What is your name?" she grated. That would never do. She made an effort to sound more friendly, if that was possible while brandishing a dagger in the wench's face. "What's your name, girl? I like to know who I'm talking to."

The woman beneath her hesitated, then said, "Julia. And that is all you will get from me."

Karela dressed her face with a smile. "Julia, Conan has a bronze figure that I must have, a filthy thing with horns. An you've seen it, you'll not have forgotten. No woman could. Tell me where it is, and I'll leave you unharmed when I go."

"I'll tell you nothing!" Julia spat. But her eyes had flickered to a corner of the room.

There was nothing there at all that Karela could see. Still . . . "Very well, Julia, I must search without your help then. But I'll have to bind you. Now hear my warning well. Do you try to fight or flee, either one, this," she gestured with her blade, "will find a home in your heart. Do you understand?"

Julia's face was still filled with fury, but she nodded, albeit with obvious reluctance.

Carefully Karela cut away Julia's robe. The girl flinched, but otherwise did not change her hatefilled expression. As Karela was slicing strips from the robe with her dagger she could not help noticing her naked prisoner's body. The Cimmerian always had had a liking for full-breasted women, she thought sourly. But hers were better. That was, if she had still been interested in him in that way, which she was not.

"Roll over," she commanded, nudging Julia with her foot. When the girl obeyed, Karela swiftly tied her hands and feet. The wench groaned through clenched teeth as she pulled the bindings together in the small of the naked woman's back, but the threat of the dagger was enough to keep the protest muted. Not comfortable, Karela thought savagely, but then the girl had not truly answered her question. A wadding of cloth fastened with another strip of cloth did her a gag, but before Karela left she lifted Julia's face by a handful of hair. "Conan likes round bottoms," she said with a biting smile. "You have a bottom like a boy."

Julia jerked wildly at her bonds and made angry sounds behind her gag, but Karela was already studying the corner the girl's eyes had indicated. There *was* nothing there. Neither crack in the plaster nor new work gave sign that anything had been hidden behind the wall, and no opening in the fly-specked ceiling . . . A board sagged beneath her foot, and she smiled.

Swiftly she knelt and levered up the floorboard with her dagger. The malevolent bronze lay beneath, nestled in decades of dirt and rat droppings. Fitting, she thought. She reached for the horned figure, but her fingers stopped, quivering, a handsbreadth away. She could not bring herself to touch it. The evil she had felt before still radiated from it, twisting her stomach. Contact with it would surely have her retching. Hastily she fetched a blanket from the bed, folded it around the bronze, and gathered it up like a sack, holding the weighty burden well away from her. Even so she could sense the abomination of the thing, but so long as she did not have to look at it she could stand carrying it.

At the window she paused. "Thank Conan for me," she told the struggling girl. "Tell him I thank him for five hundred pieces of gold."

With that she dropped through the window and scampered down the boxes. In the alley she hid the blanket-wrapped figure inside a box on the cart. And the relief it was to get rid of it, she thought, even after so brief a contact.

"We'll meet in one turn of the glass," she told the mustached Zamoran, "at the Carellan Stables."

As she slipped back into the crowded street, the hood of her cloak once more shielding her face, she glanced regretfully at the sun. Too late today to post a man before the royal palace. On the morrow, though, the signal would be sent, and by nightfall she would have her five hundred pieces of gold. She wished fervently that she could see the Cimmerian's face when he learned how much he had lost.

XV

Silvery hair and slit robe alike flowing behind her, Synelle raced through the wide corridors of her great house, heedless of the horrified cries of servants and slaves at her dusty dishevelment, unhearing of their pleas after her welfare and concern for her precipitate return. Conan had left ten of his archers, now standing watch at the entrances, to protect her, then rode off before she could stop him. To deal with Count Antimides, one of those left behind had told her. But she would not wait for him to deal with the Mitra-accursed wretch. Antimides had struck at her—at her!—and his destruction, utter and complete, was her right and hers alone. The means of it must be exquisite, so that when the truth of it could at last be proclaimed to the world the expunging of that excrescence would be told and retold for centuries. His desire for the crown and and chains he had meant to emprison her in, that was it.

From a wall she snatched a mirror of silvered glass. With that under her arm, she swept into her secret chamber. From amidst the scintillant flasks and seething beakers of vile substances she took a vial of Antimides' blood. He had been a useful, if unknowing, tool until now, adding to the confusion and weakening those she would eventually have to cow, but always had she been aware that he might become dangerous to her. That blood had been obtained from an ensorceled serving girl, one who often shared Antimides' bed and passed on to Synelle, for the bewitchment that held her, all she learned of the great lord's plans, and kept against just such a day as this. Necromantic spells that could hold a corpse incorruptible for a thousand years kept it liquid.

With great care she sketched the crown of Ophir on the mirror in the count's blood. Below that she drew a sanguine chain.

"See yourself with the crown you seek upon your head, Antimides," she whispered. "But only for a time. A brief, painful time." Laughing cruelly, she bent back to her dark work.

* * *

"We attract attention," Machaon announced to no one in particular.

The file of nineteen armored horsemen in spiked helms with round shields slung on the arms, led by Conan, made its way slowly through the streets of Ianthe, and the crowds who parted before them did indeed stare. Deadly intensity hung about them like a cloud, stunning even those who would have looked away, numbing their reticence to see.

"There will be trouble for this," Narus said dolefully. He rode next in line behind Machaon. "Even can we slay Antimides—and the gods alone know how many guards he has—Iskandrian will not look the other way for our killing of a noble within the very walls of the capital. We shall have to flee Ophir, if we can."

"And if we do not slay him," Conan said grimly, "then still we must flee. Or would you ever be sitting with your back to a wall for protection, ever looking across your shoulder for his next attack?"

And more attacks there would be, the Cimmerian was sure. Whatever Antimides' reason for wanting to seize Synelle, he could only be seeking Conan's death to still his tongue. The attacks would continue until Conan was dead, or Antimides was.

"I didn't say we should not kill him," Narus sighed. "I simply said we must flee afterwards."

"If we must flee in any case," Taurianus demanded, "why should we then take this risk? Let the lord live, and let us be gone from Ianthe with all our blood in us." The lanky man looked more glum even than Narus, and the dark hair that straggled from under his helm was damp with anxious sweat.

"You'll never make a captain, Ophirean," the gaunt-faced mercenary replied. "A Free-Company lives by its name, and dies by it, as well. Can we be attacked with impunity, then the company is as dead as if we have all had our weazands slit, and we are no better than vagabonds and beggars."

Taurianus muttered under his breath, but spoke no more complaints aloud.

"There is Antimides' palace," Machaon said abuptly. He frowned suspiciously at the sprawling, golden-domed edifice of marble and alabaster. "I see no guards. I do not like this, Cimmerian."

Antimides' palace was second in size within Ianthe only to the royal palace itself, a massive structure of columns and terraces and spired towers, with broad, deep steps leading up from the street. There were no guards in sight on those steps, and one of the great bronze doors stood ajar.

A trap perhaps, Conan thought. Had Antimides learned of his failure already? Was he inside with his guards gathered close about him for protection? Such would be a foolish move, sure to have been protested by any competent captain. Yet a lord with Antimides' arrogance might well have bludgeoned his guard commander into complacent compliance long since.

He turned in his saddle, studying the men behind. The seven besides Machaon and Narus who had crossed the border from Nemedia with him were there. They had followed him far, and loyally.

Long and hard had he labored to build this company, and to keep it, yet fairness made him say, "What numbers we face inside I do not know. Does any man wish to leave, now is the time."

"Speak not foolishness," Machaon said. Taurianus opened his mouth, then closed it again without speaking.

Conan nodded. "Four men to hold the horses," he ordered as he dismounted.

With steady, purposeful tread they climbed the white marble steps, drawing swords as they did. Conan stepped through the open door, its broad bronze face scribed hugely with the arms of Antimides' house, and found himself in a long, dome-ceilinged hall, with grand, alabaster stairs sweeping up to a columned balcony that encircled the hall.

A buxom serving girl in plain green robes that left her pretty legs bare to the tops of her thighs dashed out of a door to one side of the hall, a large, weighty bag over her shoulders. A scream bubbled out of her when she saw the armed and armored men invading the palace. Dropping the bag, she sped wailing back the way she had come.

Narus thoughtfully eyed the array of golden goblets and silver plate that had spilled out of the bag. "A guess as to what happens here?"

"Antimides fleeing our righteous wrath?" Machaon hazarded hopefully.

"We cannot afford let him escape us," Conan said. He did not believe the count would flee, but there was strangeness here that worried him. "Spread out. Find him."

They scattered in all directions, but warily, swords at the ready. Too many battles had they faced, too many traps had been sprung around them, for complacency. The continued survival of a mercenary lay in his readiness to give battle on an instant. Any instant.

A lord's chambers would be above, the Cimmerian thought. He took the curving stairs upward.

Room by room he searched, finding no one, living or dead. Everywhere there were signs of hasty flight, and of a desire to carry away everything of value. Marks where tapestries had been pulled from the walls and carpets taken up. Tables overturned, whatever they had borne gone. Golden lamps wrenched halfway from brackets that had resisted being pried from the walls. Oddly, every mirror he saw was starred with long cracks.

Then he pushed open a door with his sword, and looked into a room that seemed untouched. Furniture stood upright, golden bowls and silver vases in place, and tapestries depicting heroic scenes of Ophir's past hung from the walls. The one mirror in the room was cracked, however, as the others were. An intricately carved chair was set before it, the high back to the door, but the voluminous, gold-embroidered green silk sleeve of a man's robe hung over one gilded wooden arm.

With the strides of a great hunting cat the giant Cimmerian crossed the room, presented his sword to the throat of the man seated there. "Now, Antimides—" Conan's words died abruptly, and the hairs on the back of his neck stirred.

Count Antimides sat with eyes bulging from an empurpled face and blackened tongue protruding between teeth clenched and bared in a rictus of agony. The links of a golden chain were buried in the swollen flesh of his neck, and his own hands clutched the ends of that chain, seeming even in the iron grip of death to strain at drawing it tighter.

"Crom!" Conan muttered. He would not believe that fear of his vengeance had been enough to make Antimides sit before a mirror and watch as he strangled himself. The Cimmerian had met sorcery often enough before to know the smell of it.

"Conan! Where are you?"

"In here!" he replied to the shout from the hall.

Machaon and Narus entered with a slender, frightened youth in filthy rags that had been fine satin robes not long past. His wrists bore the bloody marks of manacles; the pallor of his skin and the thinness of his face spoke of long days in darkness and missed meals.

"Look what we found chained below," the tattooed man said.

Not so much of a youth, Conan saw at second glance; there was that in the man's manner—a petulant thrust of a too-full lower lip; a sulkiness of eye and stance—that gave an air of boyishness.

"Well, who is he?" the Cimmerian asked. "You speak as if I should know him."

The youthful appearing man lifted his chin with almost feminine hauteur. "I am Valentius," he said in a high voice that strained for steadiness, "count now, but King to be. I give you my thanks for this rescue." His dark eyes flickered uncertainly to Narus and Machaon. "If rescue it indeed is."

Narus shrugged. "We told him why we are here," he said to Conan, "but he does not believe. Or not fully."

"There are two guards below with their gullets slit," Machaon said, "but we've seen no one living. There is madness in this place, Cimmerian. Has Antimides truly fled?"

For an answer Conan jerked his head toward the high-backed chair. The other three hesitated, then moved quickly to look.

Shockingly, Valentius giggled. "However did you make him do this? No matter. 'Tis fitting for his betrayal of my trust." His fine-featured face darkened quickly. "I came to him for aid and shelter, and he laughed at me. At me! Then he clapped me in irons and left me to rot and fight rats for my daily bowl of swill. So pious, he was. So unctuous. He would not have my blood on his hands, he said, and laughed. He would leave that to the rats."

"I've seen death on many fields, Conan," Machaon said, "but this is an ugly way to slay a man, for all he deserved killing." His knuckles were white on his sword hilt as he gazed on the corpse. Narus formed his fingers into a sign to ward off evil.

"I did not kill him," Conan told them. "Look at his hands on the chain. Antimides slew himself."

Valentius laughed again, shrilly. "However 'twas done, it was done well." Moods shifting like quicksilver, his face screwed up viciously, and he spat in the corpse's bloated face. "I but regret I could not see the doing."

Conan exchanged glances with his two friends. This was the man with the best blood claim to succeed Valdric on the throne of Ophir. The young Cimmerian shook his head in disgust. The urge to be rid of the youth quickly was strong, but did he simply leave him the fool would have his throat cut in short order. Perhaps that would be the better for Ophir, but such was not his decision to make.

To Valentius he said, "We will take you to the royal palace. Valdric will give you protection."

The slender young man stared at him, wild-eyed and trembling. "No! No, you cannot! Valdric will kill me. I am next in line for the throne. He will kill me!"

"You speak foolishness," Conan growled. "Valdric has no care for aught but saving his own life. 'Tis likely in a day he'll not even remember you are in the palace."

"You do not understand," Valentius whined, wringing his hands. "Valdric will look at me, knowing that he is dying, knowing that I will be King after. He will think of the long years I have before me, and he will hate me. He will have me slain!" He looked desperately from one face to the next, and finished with a sullenly muttered, " 'Tis what I would do, and so will he."

Machaon spat on the costly Turanian carpet. "What of blood kin?" he asked gruffly "What of friends, or allies?"

The cringing man shook his head. "How can I know who among them to trust? My own guards turned on me, men who have served my house faithfully for years." Suddenly his voice quickened, and his dark eyes took on a sly light. "You protect me! When I am King, I will give you wealth, titles. You shall have Antimides' palace, and be count in his stead. You and your men shall be the King's personal bodyguard. Riches beyond imagining I shall grant you, and power. Choose a woman, noble or common, and she will be yours. Two, do you wish them, or three! Name the honor you desire! Give it name, and I shall grant it!"

Conan grimaced. It was true that there could be no better service for a Free-Company than what Valentius offered, but he would sooner serve a viper. "What of Iskandrian?" he said. "The general takes no part in these struggles, follows no faction."

Valentius nodded reluctantly. "If you will not serve me," he said sulkily.

"Then let us leave this place," Conan said, "and quickly. It would be ill to be found standing over Antimides' corpse." As the others hurried from the room, though, he paused for one last look at the dead man. Whatever sorcery Antimides had enmeshed himself in, the Cimmerian was glad it did not touch him. With a shiver he followed the others.

XVI

D usk was falling as Conan returned to the house where his company was quartered, and the gray thickening of the air, the coming blackness, fitted his mood well. Iskandrian had taken Valentius under his protection at the army's barracks readily enough, but the old general had listened to their story with a suspicious eye on the Cimmerian. Only for Valentius' agreement that Antimides appeared to have strangled himself had the mercenaries left those long, stone buildings unchained, and the petulant glare the young lord gave Conan as he said the words was as clear as a statement that he would have spoken differently could he but he sure he would not himself be implicated.

And then there had been Synelle. Conan had found her in a strange mixture of fury and satisfaction. She already knew of Antimides' death, though he was not aware the word had spread so quickly; that accounted for her contentment. But she had upbraided him savagely for riding away without her permission, and for taking the time to bring Valentius to Iskandrian's care.

The last seemed to infuriate her more than the first. He was in her service, not that of the fopling Valentius, and he would do well to remember it. To his own amazement he had listened meekly, and worst of all had had to fight with himself to stop from begging her forgiveness. He had never begged anything from man or woman, god or demon, and it made his stomach turn to think how close he had come.

He slammed open the door of his room, and stopped dead. In the dimness. Julia, naked and bound hand and foot, frowned up at him with her mouth working frantically at a gag.

"Machaon!" he shouted. "Narus!" Hastily he untied her gag. Her bonds had been tightly tied, and she had pulled them tighter with her struggles. He had to wield his dagger carefully to cut only the strips of cloth and not her flesh. "Who did this?" he demanded as he labored to free her.

With a groan she expelled a damp wad of cloth from her mouth, and worked her jaw before speaking. "Do not let him see me like this," she pleaded. "Hurry! Hurry!"

Machaon, Narus and Boros tumbled through the door, all shouting questions at once, and Julia screamed. As Conan severed the last binding, she jerked free of him and scrambled to the bed, snatching a blanket to cover herself.

"Go away, Machaon!" she cried, cowering back. Rubiate color suffused her cheeks. "I will not have you see me so. Go away!"

"'Tis gone," Boros said drunkenly, pointing to the corner where Conan had hidden the bronze figure.

For the first time the Cimmerian realized the board was lifted aside, and the space beneath it empty. A chill as of death oozed through him. It seemed meet that this day should end so, with disaster peering at him like the vacant eye-sockets of a skull.

"Mayhap," Boros muttered, "do we ride hard, we can be across the border before it's used. I've always wished to see Vendhya, or perhaps, Khitai. Does anyone know a land more distant?"

"Be quiet, you old fool," Conan growled. "Julia, who took the bronze? Crom, woman, stop worrying about that accursed blanket and answer me!"

Not ceasing her efforts to make the blanket cover all of her bountiful curves, and less precariously, Julia glared at him and sniffed. "'Twas a trull in men's breeches and wearing a sword." She glanced at Machaon out of the corner of her eye. "She said I have a boy's bottom. My bottom is as round as hers, only not so big."

Conan ground his teeth. "Her eyes," he asked impatiently. "They were green? Her hair red? Did she say anything else?"

"Karela?" Machanon said. "I thought she meant to kill you, not steal from you. But why is Boros so frighted by this thing she took? You've not got us meddling with sorcerers again, Cimmerian?"

"You know her," Julia said accusingly. "I thought so from what she said about my . . ." She cleared her throat and began again. "All I remember of what she said is that she swore by Derketo and thanked you for five hundred pieces of gold. Have you truly given her so much? I remember my father's lemans, and I'd not think this Karela was worth a silver."

Conan pounded a huge fist on his thigh. "I must find her, Machaon, without delay. She has stolen a bronze figure that came to me by happenstance, a thing of evil power that will wreak destruction un-dreamed of, does she sell it to those I fear she will. Give me precise directions to find that ruined keep."

Julia moaned. "That is what she meant about gold? She takes the hellish thing to those Boros spoke of? Mitra protect us all, and the land!"

"I understand not a word of all this," Machaon said, "but one thing I do know. An you enter the Sarelain Forest in the night, you'll break your neck. That tangle is bad enough to travel in daylight. Twould take a man born there to find his way in the dark."

"I can find her," Boros said, swaying, "so long as she has the bronze. Its evil is in truth a beacon." He pushed his sleeves up bony arms. "A simple matter of—"

"An you attempt magic in your condition," Conan cut him off, "I'll put your head on a spike over the River Gate with my own hands." The gray-bearded man looked hurt, but subsided, muttering under his breath. Conan turned to Machaon. "There is no time to waste. Daylight may be too late."

Machaon nodded reluctantly, but Narus said, "Then take a score of us with you. Her band—"

"—would hear so many coming and melt away," the Cimmerian finished for him. "I go alone. Machaon?"

Slowly the tattooed veteran spoke.

Machaon was right, Conan thought as an unseen branch whipped across his face for what seemed the hundredth time. A man could easily break his neck in that blackness. He forced his horse on through the heavy thicket of vines and undergrowth, hoping he moved in the right direction. As a boy he had learned to guide himself by the stars, but the sky was seldom visible, for the forest was ancient, filled with huge oaks whose thick interwoven branches formed a canopy with few openings above his head.

"You've come far enough," a voice called from the dark, "unless you want a quarrel in your ribs!"

Conan put a hand to his sword.

"None of that!" another man said, then chuckled. "Me and Tenio grew up in this forest, big man, poaching the King's deer by night. He sees better than I do, and you might as well be standing under a full moon for all of me."

"I seek Karela," Conan began, but got no further.

"Enough talk," the first voice said. "Take him!"

Suddenly rough hands were pulling the big Cimmerian from his horse, into the midst of a knot of men. He could not even see well enough to count how many, but he seized an arm and broke it, producing a scream. There was no room to draw his sword, nor light to see where to strike; he snatched his dagger instead and laid about him, bringing yells and curses when he slashed flesh. In the end their numbers were too great, and he was pressed to the dirt by the weight of them, his wrists bound behind him and a cord tied between his ankles for a hobble.

"Anybody hurt bad?" panted the man who had chuckled earlier.

"My arm," someone moaned, and another voice said, "Bugger your arm! He near as cut my ear off!"

Cursing the dark—not all had cat's eyes—they pulled Conan to his feet and pulled him through the trees, dragging him, when the hobble caught roots and tripped him, until he managed to get his feet under him again.

Abruptly a blanket was pulled aside before him, and he was thrust into a stone-walled room lit by rush torches in rusted iron sconces on the walls. A huge hearth with a roaring fire of logs as big as a man's leg, a great iron pot suspended on pivoting arm above it, filled one wall. Blankets at the windows—narrow arrow-slits, in fact—kept the light from spilling into the surrounding forest. A dozen men, as motley a collection of ruffians as Conan had ever seen, sprawled on benches at crude trestle tables, swilling wine from rough clay mugs and wolfing down stew from wooden bowls.

Karela got to her feet as Conan's captors crowded in after him, complaining loudly about their wounds and bruises. Her dark leather jerkin, worn over tight breeches of pale gray silk tucked into red boots, was laced snugly, yet gaped enough at the top to reveal the creamy upper slopes of her full, heavy breasts. A belt worn low on her well-rounded hips supported her scimitar.

"So," she said, "you're more fool than I thought you, Cimmerian. You'll force me to kill you yet."

"The bronze, Karela," he said urgently. "You must not sell it. They're trying—"

"Silence him!" she snapped.

"—to raise Al'Kiir," he managed to get out, then a club smashed against the back of his head, and darkness claimed him.

XVII

The fool, Karela thought as she stared at Conan's huge prostrate form. Was his masculine arrogance so great that he could believe all he must needs do to retrieve the figure was ride up and take it? She knew him for a priceful man, and knew as well that the pride was justified. By himself, with naught but his broadsword, he was more than a match for . . .

Abruptly she cursed to herself. The Cimmerian was no longer the same man who had emprisoned a part of her and carried it away with him. She had been thinking of him as he was when she first knew him, a thief and a loner with naught but his wits and the strength of his sword arm. Now he commanded men, and men who, she reluctantly admitted, were a more dangerous pack than the hounds she led.

"Was he alone?" she demanded. "An you've led his Free-Company here, I'll have your hides for boots!"

"Didn't see nobody else," Tenio muttered. "That means there weren't nobody else." A small, ferrety man with a narrow face and sharp nose, he spat a tooth into his palm and glared at it. "I say kill him." Some of those nursing broken ribs and knife gashes growled assent.

Marusas, her Zamoran, produced a dagger in his long, calloused fingers. "Let us wake him, instead. He looks strong. He would scream a long time before he died."

Instantly all of the men were shouting, arguing for one course or the other.

"Kill him now! He's too dangerous!"

"He's just a man. Flay him, and he'll scream like any other."

"You didn't fight him out there! You don't know!"

"He cut me to the bone with ten of us on him, and broke Agorio's arm!"

"Silence, you dogs!" Karela roared, and the bickering ceased as they turned to stare at her. "I say who dies, and I say he doesn't. Not yet, at least! Do any of you mangy curs care to dispute me? To your kennels!"

She put a hand to her scimitar hilt, and a dangerous light glowed in her green eyes. One by one they dropped their eyes from hers, muttered, and shuffled back to their drinking or to tend their wounds. Jamaran, a huge, shaven-headed Kushite with shoulders broader than Conan's and the thick fingers of a wrestler, was the last to remain glowering at her, his dark face twisted with anger. A split of his cheek showed where Conan's fist had landed in the struggle.

"Well, Jamaran?" she said. She knew he wanted to replace her, and take her to his bed as well, though he did not know she was aware of his desires. He had thoughts about the proper place for women; sooner or later she would have to show him the error of his ways or slay him. "Are you ready to dispute my rule?"

Surprise glimmered on his face, and was quickly supplanted by a sneering smile. "Not yet," he growled. "I will tell you when, my red-haired pretty." His black eyes ran over her body like a caress, then with incredible lightness on his feet for a man of his size he stalked to the nearest table and snatched up a mug, tossing back his head to drink deeply.

Karela quivered in shocked outrage as she glared at his broad back. Never before had he been so open. She would have to kill him, she thought, after this. But it could not be done now. The temper of her band was too delicately balanced. As much as she hated admitting it, a wrong move now could wreck all she had labored for. With a snarl she released her sword.

It was not like the days in Zamora, she thought grimly. Then none of her band dared to challenge her word, or to think of her as a woman. It was all Conan's fault. He had changed her in some way she did not understand, some way she did not want to be changed. He had woven a thread of weakness into her fabric, and other men could sense it.

As if her thoughts of him had been a call the Cimmerian groaned and stirred.

"Gag him," she ordered. "Move, Derketo curse you! I'll not be bothered by his babblings!"

Conan shook himself as Tenio and Jamaran knelt beside him. "Karela," he said desperately, "listen to me. These men are dangerous. They mean to bring an evil—"

Tenio tried to shove a rag into his mouth, and screamed as the Cimmerian sank teeth into his hand. Jamaran smashed a fist into Conan's jaw; the ferret-faced man jerked his hand free, sprinkling drops of blood as he shook it. Before Conan could speak again Jamaran had thrust the wadding home and bound it. As he got to his feet the shaven-headed man kicked Conan in the ribs and pulled back his booted foot for another.

Tenio drew his dagger with his undamaged hand, a murderous gleam in his eyes.

"Stop that," Karela commanded. "Did you hear me? Leave him!"

Slowly, reluctantly, the two drew away from the Cimmerian.

She could feel those sapphire eyes on her. He shook his head furiously, fighting the gag, making angry noises behind it. Shivering, she turned her back to stare into the fire.

Karela knew she could not afford to let herself listen to the young giant. He had always been able to talk her into anything. Did he put his hands on her, her will melted. This time, she told herself, this time it would be different.

The night went slowly for her, and she was aware that it was because of Conan's eyes on her back. The rest of the bandits took themselves off to sleep, most simply pulling blankets about them on the stone floor, but sleep would not come near Karela. Like a leopard in a cage she paced, and the goad that made her pace was an unblinking icy blue gaze. She would have had him blind-folded, except that she would not admit even to herself that simply his eyes on her could affect her so greatly.

Finally the titian-haired beauty settled before the great hearth and studied the leaping flames as if they were the most important thing in the world. Yet even then she could not escape the Cimmerian, imagining him writhing in the fire, imagining him suffering all the tortures of the damned, all the tortures he so richly deserved. She could not understand why that seemed to make her feel even worse, or why from time to time she had to surreptitiously wipe tears from her cheeks.

At first light she sent Tenio riding for Ianthe with the scarlet surcoat. The rest of the day she spent in ignoring Conan. Food and drink she denied him.

"Let him eat and drink when I have gone," she commanded.

The men scattered about the room, most devoting their energies to dice or cards, gave her muttered assent and strange looks. She did not care. Not for the briefest moment would she allow the Cimmerian to be ungagged in her presence. Not until she had the five hundred pieces of gold in her hands to taunt him with. Not until she managed to settle herself, and that seemed strangely difficult to do.

Then the sun was making its downward journey. Time for Karela to leave for the hut. The bronze she had left, still wrapped in the blanket from Conan's bed, outside beneath a tree. There was no one about to steal it, and she would not have it under the same roof with her could she avoid it.

As she was tying the blanket-swathed bundle behind her saddle—and muttering to herself for the sickness it made her feel in the pit of her stomach—Jamaran came out of the lone tower that remained of the ancient keep.

"That thing is valuable," he said challengingly. "Five hundred gold pieces, you say."

Karela did not answer him. This morning was no better time to kill him than last night had been.

"I should go with you," the huge man went on when she remained silent. "To make certain you return safely with the gold. This noble you go to may prove treacherous. Or perhaps something else might delay you, a woman alone with so much gold."

Karela's face tightened. Did the fool think she planned to run off with the coin? Or did he think to take the gold and her both? "No!" she snapped as she swung into the saddle. "You are needed here to help guard the prisoner."

"There are a score to watch him. So much gold—"

"Fool!" She made the word a sneering whiplash. "You must learn to think if you would lead men. That one inside, bound as he is, is more dangerous than any man you've ever seen. I but hope there are enough of you to keep him till I return."

Before Jamaran could speak the furious words she could read plainly on his face, Karela put spurs to her fleet eastern bay, and darted down a narrow path that was little more than a deer track. Many such crossed and criss-crossed in the thick forest, and she was soon gone beyond following.

In truth, she did not think all of her followers were necessary to keep Conan imprisoned. What she had told the big Kushite was true. The Cimmerian giant was dangerous enough to make even her wary, and she prided herself on walking carefully about no man. She had seen him struggle when defeat was inevitable, slay when his own death was certain, win when only doom lay ahead. Bound hand and foot, however, and guarded by twenty men, she did not doubt Conan would be waiting as she had left him when she returned.

Nor did she think Jamaran could take the gold—or what else he wanted from her—without her steel drinking his life in the attempt. But her pride would not allow the nameless noble to see the open disrespect the shaven-headed man now showed her. Besides, this noble would certainly have other commissions—he had already offered one, though changing it to acquiring the bronze—but he would not likely offer them if he thought she could not keep discipline in her own band.

When Karela reached the clearing where the rude hut stood, the sun was a bloody ball half-obscured by the treetops, and long shadows stretched toward the east. The scarlet-and-black caprisoned warhorse stood alone as before. Slowly she made a circuit of the clearing, within the shaded shelter of the trees. It was a desultory search, she was well aware, but she was also aware of the bronze tied behind her. More than once had she found herself riding forward on her saddle to avoid the brush against her buttocks of the rough wool that contained it. She knew a desperate urgency to be rid of the figure.

With a snorted laugh for her own sensitivity, Karela galloped into the clearing and dismounted. She carried the blanket gripped like a sack, and kicked open the rough door of planks. "Well, Lord Nameless, do you have my . . ." Her words trailed away in surprise.

The tall nobleman stood as he had at the first meeting, but this time he was not alone. A woman with a scarlet cloak pulled around her, the hood pulled well forward, stood beside him, cool dark eyes studying Karela over a veil of opaque silk.

Karela stared back boldly, tossing the blanket to the dirt floor at their feet. "Here is your accursed image. Now where is my gold?"

The veiled woman knelt, hastily pulling aside the folds of coarse wool. A reverent sigh came from her as the horned figure was revealed. With delicate hands she lifted it to the crude table. Karela wondered how she could bear to touch it.

"It is Al'Kiir," the veiled woman breathed. "It is what I sought, Taramenon."

Karela blinked. *Lord Taramenon?* If half what she had heard of his swordplay were true, he would be no easy opponent. She let her hand drift to the hilt of her scimitar. "There are five hundred pieces of gold to be handed over before it is yours."

The other woman's eyes swiveled to her.

"Is she what you seek also?" Taramenon asked.

The veiled woman nodded thoughtfully. "She seems so. How are you called, wench?"

"I am Karela, wench!" the red-haired bandit snapped, emphasizing the last word. "Now let me tell your fates, if you have not brought the coin agreed on. You, my fine lordling, I will sell into Koth, where your pretty face may please a mistress." Taramenon's face darkened, but the veiled woman laughed. Karela turned her attention to her. "And you I will sell into Argos, where you may dance naked in a tavern in Messantia, and please the patrons one by one for the price of a mug of ale."

"I am a princess of Ophir," the veiled woman said coldly, "who can have you impaled on the walls of the royal palace. Do you dare speak so to one before whom you should tremble?"

Karela sneered. "I not only dare speak so, by Derketo's Teats, if my gold is not forthcoming I'll strip you on the spot to see if an Argossean tavern will have you. Most Ophirean noblewomen are bony wenches who could not please a man did they try with all their might." Steel whispered across leather as her blade left its scabbard. "I'll have my gold now!"

"She will indeed do," the scarlet-cloaked woman said. "Take her."

Karela spun toward Taramenon, had an instant to see him watching with a bemused smile on his face, making no move toward her or his sword, then two men in the leather armor of light cavalry dropped from the dark rafters atop her. In a struggling heap she was borne to the packed-earth floor.

"Derketo blast you!" she howled, writhing futilely in their grip. "I'll spit you like capons! Codless jackals!"

Taramenon plucked her sword from her hand and tossed it into a corner. "You'll not be needing that any longer, girl."

Despite her frenzied striving, the cavalrymen dragged Karela to her feet. Fool! she berated herself. Taken like a virgin in a kidnapper's nets! Why had she not wondered why there was no horse for the woman?

"I suppose it's too much to hope for that she's a maiden," the woman said.

Taramenon laughed. "Much too much, I should say."

"Treacherous trull!" Karela snarled. "Catamite fopling! I'll peel your hides in strips! Release me, or my men will stake you out for the vultures! Are you fool enough to think I came alone?"

"Perhaps you did not," Taramenon said calmly, "though I saw no one the last time you claimed to have men about this hut. In any case, my shout will bring fifty men-at-arms. Shall we see what your miserable brigands can do against them?"

"Enough, Taramenon," the veiled woman said. "Do not bandy words with the baggage. There was talk of stripping." She eyed Karela's tight breeches and snug-laced leather jerkin, and a note of malicious amusement entered her voice. "I would see that she is not . . . too bony for my purpose."

Taramenon laughed, and the three men set to with a will. Karela fought furiously, and when they were done there was blood on her nails and teeth, but she stood naked, heavy round breasts heaving with her effort. Lecherous male eyes probed her beauty, slid along the curves of lush thighs and narrow waist. Dark feminine eyes regarded her more coldly, and with a touch of jealousy lighting them. Pridefully the green-eyed woman stood as erect as the twisting of her arms behind her back would allow. She would not cringe like a shrinking girl on her wedding night for these of any others.

The tall nobleman touched his cheek, now decorated by four parallel sanguinary streaks, and examined the blood on his fingertips. Suddenly his hand flashed out; the force of his slap was such that Karela and the two men holding her all staggered.

"Do not damage her!" the veiled woman said sharply. "Your beauty is not ruined, Taramenon. Now bind her for transport."

"A taste of the strap will do her no damage, Synelle," the darkly handsome lord growled, "and I would teach her her proper place."

The name so shocked Karela that she missed the veiled woman's retort. Conan's patroness! Could the woman have learned of her own connection with the Cimmerian and be thinking to dispose of a rival? Well, she had the Cimmerian to bargain for her release, and if Derketo favored her she would have this treacherous noblewoman to hang by her heels beside him.

Karela opened her mouth to make her offer—Conan's freedom in return for her own—and a wadded rag pushed the words back into her throat. Like a starving panther she stuggled, but three men were too much for her. With ease that seemed to mock her they corded her into a neat package, wrists strapped to ankles, knees beneath her chin, thin straps laced around and around her, digging deep into her flesh. When one of the cavalrymen produced a large leather sack the memory of her plans for Synelle, including her method of returning her to Conan, flooded her face with scarlet.

"At least she can still blush," Synelle laughed as Karela was stuffed into the sack. "From her language, I thought she was lost to all decency. Carry her to the horses. We must hurry. Events proceed more quickly than I would like, and we must meet them."

"I must return to the palace to pay my respects," Taramenon said. "I will join you as quickly as I can."

"Do so quickly," Synelle said smoothly, "or I may put Conan in your place."

As Karela's dark prison was heaved swaying into the air, she felt tears running down her cheeks. Derketo curse the Cimmerian! Once again he had brought her humilation. She hoped Jamaran would slit his throat. Slowly.

XVIII

Conan lay on the dirt-strewn stone floor as he had for a day and a night now, bound and biding his time with the patience of a jungle predator, all of his mind and energies given over to waiting and watching. Karela's injunction to give him food and water had been ignored, and he was dimly aware of hunger and thirst, but they affected him little. He had gone longer without either, and he knew he would have both once the men who guarded him were dealt with. Soon or late a mistake would be made, and he would take advantage. Soon or late, it would come.

Brass lamps had been lit against the deepening night, but with Karela gone no one had rehung blankets to cover the tall, narrow arrow slits. Rough clay jars of wine had been passed more freely with the red-haired woman's departure, and the four brigands who had not already staggered to one of the upper rooms of the tower for drunken sleep were engrossed in drinking more and gaming with dice. The fire on the long hearth burned low; the last of the thick logs that had been stacked against the wall had long since gone into the flames, and no more had been brought from outside. None of them had thought to tend the iron kettle suspended over the flames, and the smell of burning stew blended with the unwashed stench of bandits.

Abruptly Tenio hurled dice and leather dicecup aside. "She should have returned by now," he muttered. "What keeps her?"

"Perhaps she keeps herself," Jamaran growled. His black eyes went to Conan, and he bared large, yellow teeth in a snarl. "Leaving us with this one she seems so affrighted of."

Marusas paused in the act of scooping up the dice. "You think she has run away with the gold? It sounds a tidy sum, but her share of our raids has been as much in the last month alone."

"Erlik take you, play!" snapped a man with a slitted leather patch tied over where his nose had been cut off. His pale eyes had a permanent look of suspicious anger, as if he knew and hated what men thought when they saw his disfigurement. "I'm twenty silvers down with coin on the table. Play, curse you!" The three ignored him.

Jamaran slammed a fist the size of a small ham on the table top. "And that's another thing. Why should a woman receive ten times the share that the rest of us do? Let her try our work alone and see what sport the men she tries to rob will have with her. Without us, she'd be no more than a cutpurse, bargaining when she was caught to escape having her cheek branded for a grant of the favors she is so stingy with now."

"Without her," Tenio rebutted, "what are we? How much did we get on our own? Now you moan about only fifty golds in a month, but you didn't never get ten before her."

"She's a woman!" the huge Kushite said. "A woman's place is in a man's bed, or cooking for him, not giving orders."

Marusas laughed and tugged at his drooping black mustaches. "I would like riding her myself. Much fun in breaking that one to bridle, eh?"

"'Tis more than the pair of you could do together," Tenio sneered. "I don't like taking orders from a woman no better than you, but she puts gold in my purse, more than *I've* seen before. And I know I'd have to keep her tied hand and foot or risk waking with my own dagger in my throat. Or worse."

"No cods at all on you," Jamaran snorted. He nudged the Zamoran with a huge elbow. "I always knew there was more woman than man in him. Likely spends all his hours in Ianthe at the House of the Yearling Lambs." The two of them roared with laughter, and patch-nose joined in as if despite himself.

All the blood left Tenio's face, and his narrow-bladed dagger flickered into his hand. "I don't take that from nobody," he snarled.

"From me you take what I give," Jamaran said, all mirth gone from his voice, "or I'll use that blade of yours to make *sure* you've no cods."

"Curse the lot of you for chattering old women!" patch-nose shouted. "Am I suddenly not good enough to dice with?"

Conan made a sound behind his gag; had his throat not been parched it would have been a chuckle. A while longer and they would kill each other, leaving him only his bonds to worry about.

Flinging his mug across the room in a spray of wine, Jamaran heaved himself from his bench and strode on legs as big around as a normal man's waist to stand over the Cimmerian. Conan's icy azure gaze calmly met the dark glower directed at him.

"Big man," Jamaran said contemptuously, and his foot thudding into Conan's ribs lifted the Cimmerian from the stone floor. "You seem not so big to me." Again his foot drove Conan back. "Why does Karela want you kept safe? Is she afraid of you? Or maybe she loves you, huh? Perhaps I'll let you watch while I enjoy her, if she comes back." Each sentence he punctuated with a massive booted foot, until Conan lay struggling for breath on the very edge of the hearth. The Cimmerian glared at Jamaran as the shaven-headed man squatted beside him, doubling a heavy fist. "Ten men have I beaten to their death with this. You will be number eleven. I do not think Karela will return—she's been gone too long already—but I'll wait a bit longer. I want her to see it. Watching a man killed that way does something to a woman." Laughing, the huge Kushite straightened. With a last kick he turned back to the table. "Where's my mug?" he roared. "I want wine!"

Cursing behind his gag Conan jerked himself out of the coals he had landed in, but his mind was not on his burns. So intent had he been on awaiting his chance for escape that their talk of Karela's lateness had barely impinged on his thoughts. He knew her well enough to be sure she had not fled with the gold. Boros' words came back to him. The most beautiful and proudest women of the land were sacrificed to Al'Kiir. Few were the women more beautiful than Karela, and to her pride he could well attest. The fool wench had not only taken those who wanted to raise the god the means to do so, she had delivered herself as a sacrifice. He was sure of it. Now he must rescue her from her own folly. But how? How even to free himself?

He shifted to ease his weight on a burn on his arm, and suddenly his lips curled in a smile around his gag. Careless of searing flame he thrust his bound wrists into the fire. Gritting his teeth on his gag against fiery agony, he strained mighty arms against the ropes, massive muscles knotting and writhing. Sweat beaded his face.

The reek of burning hemp came to him; he wondered how the others could fail to be aware of it, but none of the four so much as looked in his direction. They were immersed in their mugs of wine, and patch-nose kept up his arguing for a chance to win back his loses. Abruptly, the ropes parted, and Conan pulled his half-cooked wrists from the flames, careful to keep them yet behind his back. His gaze sought his ancient broadsword, leaning against the wall behind the drinking men. There would be no chance to grasp it before he came to grips with the men between him and his steel.

With a crash patch-nose kicked over his bench. Conan froze. Snarling the man snatched up his mug and began to stalk back and forth across the room, muttering angrily about men who won and then would not gamble, and shooting dark glances at the other three, still intent on their drink. His eyes did not stray to the Cimmerian, lying rigid on the hearth-stone.

Slowly, so as to draw no attention, Conan slid his booted feet back until he could feel the heat of flames licking about them. To the smell of burning rope was added that of scorching leather, but the latter was no more noticed than the first. Then those cords were burned through as well. There was no time to waste on the gag. Rolling to his feet the big Cimmerian snatched a long, black fire-iron from the hearth.

Patch-nose was the first to see Conan free of his bonds, but the man had only time to goggle before wine sprayed out of his mouth and his skull was crushed by the fire-iron. Shouting, the others scrambled to their feet. Tenio produced his dagger, but Conan drove the fire-iron point-first through the ferret-faced man's chest and caught the blade as it dropped from the transfixed man's nerveless fingers. Marusas' sword leaped into his hand, then the Zamoran was staggering back, trying to scream around the dagger that had blossomed in fountains of scarlet in his throat.

Roaring, Jamaran leaped to grapple with the Cimmerian, throwing bear-like arms about his waist, heaving him into the air. Conan felt the man's huge fists locked in the small of his back, felt his spine begin to creak. Conan smashed his linked hands down on the nape of the huge man's bull neck, once, twice, thrice, to no effect. Jamaran's grip tightened inexorably. In moments, the Cimmerian knew, his back would snap. Desperately he slammed his palms against the other's ears.

With a scream Jamaran let him drop. Even as his heels hit the stone floor, Conan's bladed hand struck the huge Kushite's throat. Jamaran gagged, yet lashed out with a massive fist in the same instant. Conan blocked the blow, winding his arm around the shaven-headed man's to pull him close, With hammer-like blows the Cimmerian pounded the big man's body, feeling ribs splinter beneath his fist.

In the night a trumpet sounded the Ophirean army call for the attack. "Company one, ready torches!" a voice called. "Company two, attack! Take no prisoners!" Feet pounded on the floors above; frantic yells rose.

In his desperate struggle Conan had no time to worry about the new danger. Jamaran smashed his head against the Cimmerian's; Conan staggered, clinging to consciousness. The huge Kushite tried to enfold Conan once more in his crushing embrace, but Conan rammed a knee into his crotch, lifting the man to his toes with bulging eyes. Like thunderbolts the heels of Conan's hands struck Jamaran's chin. The shaven head went back with a loud crack as the Kushite's neck broke, and he fell in a boneless heap.

Conan ripped the gag from his mouth and threw it atop the body of the man who had threatened to beat him to death. A torch was thrust through one of the arrow slits, then another. Putting a hand on the table top Conan vaulted across it to grab his sword hilt, baring the blade by slinging the worn shagreen scabbard away. When soldiers spoke of taking no prisoners they generally slew whatever moved, without questioning whether it was enemy or captive. Conan did not mean to die easily.

A man darted in at the door, sword ready; Conan swung his steel . . . and stopped a handbreadth away from splitting Machaon's skull. Narus rushed in behind the grizzled veteran, and two more of the company.

"You!" Conan exclaimed. "You are the Ophirean army?"

Narus shrugged and held up a battered brass trumpet. "An odd talent of mine, but useful from time to time." He looked around at the bodies on the stone floor. "Once more you leave nothing for the rest of us."

"There are more above," Conan said, but Narus shook his head.

"They leaped from breaks in the walls, thinking we were who we claimed, and fled into the night."

"We've still bloody work to do," Conan told him. "Karela has been taken prisoner, and I mean to rescue her." Atop Tor Al'Kiir, he thought. Boros said he had seen lights there, and he had no other clue. "We must move quickly, if you will come with me."

"Mitra, Conan," Machaon growled, "will you let me say a word? There's no time for wenches, not even her. We came after you because Zandru's Hells have come to sup in Ophir."

"Al'Kiir." Conan's heart sank. "They've raised the god already."

"I know naught of gods," Machaon muttered, "but Valdric lies dead of the sickness that consumed him, and Iskandrian has seized the royal palace."

Conan started in surprise. "Iskandrian!"

"The old general has declared for Valentius," Narus explained. "And that young coxcomb has taken the name Maranthes II, as if a name could make him a great king. I hear he didn't wait for funeral rites or even a priest, but took the crown from Valdric's corpse before it was cold and put it on his own head."

"Will you stop your nattering, Narus!" Machaon barked. "Most of the nobles think as you did, Cimmerian. They gather their forces, but Iskandrian moves to put them down before they can. He marched with most of the Ianthe garrison an hour after he put Valentius on the throne. If that isn't enough, Taurianus is talking loudly that the company should join the nobles. He's telling everyone if Iskandrian wins it means the end of Free-Companies in Ophir." His tattooed face grew grim. "I'll tell you, Conan, he's right on that. Iskandrian will give short shrift to mercenaries."

"We'll worry about Iskandrian later," Conan said. "Karela comes first, and matters even more important than her. How many of the company did you bring, Machaon?"

"Seven, including Narus and myself, all of whom crossed the Nemedian border with us. Two I left to guard Julia. The mood of the others is bad, Cimmerian. You must return now if you mean to hold them together. Karela can take care of herself for a time if any woman can."

"We found your black picketed with this lot's mounts," Narus added.

"Crom!" Conan muttered. The numbers were not enough if they faced what he feared atop Tor Al'Kiir. "We ride for Ianthe, to gather the company and ride out again. No, not to join the nobles. To Tor Al'Kiir. There'll be time for questions later. To horse, Erlik blast your hides. To horse, and pray to whatever gods you can think of that we are in time."

XIX

Iron-shod hooves struck sparks from paving stones as Conan galloped through the dark and empty streets of Ianthe, seven men trailing behind with their cloaks standing out in the wind of their charge. Atop the malevolent granite hump of Tor Al'Kiir torches flickered, distant points of light in the moonless sky mocking his efforts at haste. He cursed to himself, regretting even the time it had taken to bribe the gate-watch for entry.

He wanted to shout at the sleepers who felt a momentary safety behind their walls of brick and stone. Mourning cloths draped from shuttered windows and shrouded public fountains; sprigs of sa'karian, black and white berries intermixed as symbol of death and rebirth, adorned every door. The capital of Ophir mourned its dead King in fear and uncertainty, yet none in that city knew that what they felt was as a flickering lamp flame to the storm-lashed fire-death of a great forest beside the terror that awaited their wakening.

As he galloped through the archway of the house where his company was quartered, Conan bellowed. "To me! Out with you, and to horse! Move, damn you to Zandru's Hells!" Stillness lay heavily on the blackened building; his words echoed hollowly from the courtyard walls as the others clattered in behind him. "Taurianus!" he called. "Boros!"

A door open with the protest of rusty hinges, showing a tiny light, and four figures moved into the court. Slowly the shadowy shapes resolved into Boros, Julia, and two of his company holding shielded lanterns. The armored men were the two remaining besides those behind him who had come with him from Nemedia.

"Where are the others?" Conan demanded.

"Gone," Boros answered hollowly. "Taurianus—Erlik roast his soul for eternity—convinced most of them you were dead, since you didn't return. Half followed him to join the nobles against Iskandrian. The rest?" His thin shoulders shrugged. "Faded away to hide as best they can. Without you, fear corroded their hearts."

Conan fought the urge to rain curses upon Taurianus' head. There was no time; the torches still burned atop the mountain. What must be done, must be done with the men he had. But he would lead no man blind to face sorcerers, and perhaps a god.

"Boros," he said grimly, "tell of Al'Kiir. But briefly, old man. The time of his coming is near, perhaps before first light, if we do not stop it."

Boros gasped and, tugging at his beard, spoke in a quavering voice, filled with all his years, of days before even ancient Ophir existed and the rites of Al'Kiir, of the Circle of the Right-Hand Path and the imprisonment of the demonic god, of those who would bring the abominable worship again into the world and the god whose horror they celebrated. When he was done there was silence, broken only by the call of an owl. Each man's breath was audible, and they all spoke of fear.

"If we go to Iskandrian with this tale," Conan said finally, "he will think it a ruse of the nobles and slay us, or imprison us for madmen until it is too late. But every word is as true and as dire as a spear thrust to the heart. Boros has told you what comes, what fate may lie in store for your sister, or wife or daughter, because she is comely and spirited. I ride to Tor Al'Kiir to stop it. Who rides with me?"

For a long moment only silence answered him, then Julia stepped forward, her chin held high. "If there is no courage among these who call themselves men, at least I will go with you."

"You will go to your sleeping mat," Machaon growled, "or I'll bind you in such a package as Karela made of you, to keep you safe against my return." The girl moved hurriedly behind Boros, eyeing the grizzled mercenary warily as if unsure how much of his threat he meant. Machaon nodded with satisfaction, then turned in his saddle to Conan. "I've seen more of wizards following you, Cimmerian, than one man has a right to expect in a lifetime. But I cannot see that once more will make any difference."

"An owl calling on a moonless night means death," Narus said glumly, "but I've never seen a god. I, too, ride with you, Cimmerian."

One by one, then, the other seven mercenaries pledged to follow also, voices cold with humiliation at being surpassed in courage by a girl, with anger and determination to protect some particular woman from the bloody rites. And still with fear. Yet they would come.

Conan eyed their scant number in the pale light of the lanterns and sighed. "We will be enough," he said, as much to convince himself as anything else, "because we must. We must. Claran, Memtes, get your horses." The two men named set their lanterns on the ground and ran for the stables. "We ride as soon as they return," he went on. "We must needs scale the mountain afoot, for our horses cannot climb those slopes, but—"

"Wait, Conan," Boros broke in. "Make haste slowly, or you but hasten to your death. You must acquire the Staff of Avanrakash."

"There is no time, old man," Conan said grimly. He twisted impatiently in his saddle to peer through the night toward the deeper blackness of Tor Al'Kiir. The torch lights still were there, beckoning him, taunting him to his core. What befell Karela while he sat his horse like a statue?

"Do you go forth to confront a lion," the bearded man chided, "would you then say there was no time to fetch spear or bow? That you must face it with bare hands? You go to face Al'Kiir. Think your courage and steel will avail you against a god? As well slit your own throat right here."

Conan's massive hands tightened on the reins in frustration until his knuckles cracked. He did not fear death, though he sought it no more than any other man, but his death would be of no use if Karela were still sacrificed, if Al'Kiir was freed again. Decision came swiftly, spurred by necessity. He tossed his reins to Machaon and dismounted.

"Take my horse with you to the mountain," he commanded as he tugged his hauberk off over his head. Such work as he had now to do was not best done in armor. He dropped to the ground to pull off his boots. "I will meet you at the crossroads at the foot of the mountain."

"Do you know where this staff the old man speaks of is to be found?" Machaon asked.

"In the throne room," Boros said. "By ancient law, at the death of a King the scepter and crown must be left on the throne for nine days and nine nights. Valentius has usurped custom by donning the crown so quickly, but he will not dare flout it altogether."

"The royal palace!" Machaon exclaimed. "Cimmerian, you are mad to think you can enter there. Come! We will do the best we can with honest steel."

"I was a thief once," Conan replied. "Twill not be the first palace I've entered by ways other than the door." Stripped now to his breechcloth, he slung his swordbelt across his massive chest so that his sword hung down his back, dagger and pouch beneath his left arm. Claran and Memtes trotted their horses from the stable, hooves ringing on the thick slates of the court. "I will be at the crossroads, with the staff," the Cimmerian said, "without fail. Be you there also."

With ground-eating pantherish strides, Conan loped into the night. Behind him Machaon and the others clattered out of the courtyard and turned their mounts in the other direction, toward the North Gate, but he was already one with the darkness, a deadly ghost racing through unlit streets that were empty of other human forms. Every door was barred, every window shuttered, as the inhabitants of the city cowered in fear of what might come; only occasional scavenging dogs, gaunt-ribbed and half-wild, prowled the moonless streets, and they shied away from the huge shape that shared the way with them. Beneath his leathery-soled feet the paving stones felt like the rocks of his native Cimmeria, and the feel gave wings to his stride as when he raced up mountains as a boy. His great lungs pumped with the effort of his running, for this time he raced not for the pride of winning, but for Karela, and for every woman who would lose life or more if he failed.

Again an owl cried, and Conan's mind went to Narus' words. Perhaps the cry did mean death, his or someone else's. Crom, the fierce god of the harsh and icy land where he was born, gave a man life and will, but the grim Lord of the Mound never promised that life would be long, nor that will would always prevail. A man could but fight and keep fighting so long as breath or life remained.

The Cimmerian did not slow until the massive walls of the royal palace loomed before him, crenelations and towertops only shadows against the ebon sky. The thick, iron-sheathed gates were closed and barred, the portcullis down, but he spared not a glance in that direction. Such was not his means of entry this night.

His fingers felt across the surface of the wall, featureless in the blackness. Long centuries past had the great wall been built, of stones each weighing more than twenty times as much as a big man. Only the largest trebuchet could hurl boulders weighty enough to trouble its solidity, but Conan did not mean to batter a way through. Those years had leeched at the mortar between the great stones, leaving gaps that made an easy path for one mountain-born.

With agile sureness Conan climbed, fingers and toes searching out the grooves where wind and rain and time had worn away the mortar, mighty muscles straining to pull him up where there was but room for fingernails to grip. Below was only the long, bone-shattering drop to pavement now swathed in the night, yet he did not slow in his swift ascent of that sheer wall. Time pressed on him too greatly to allow room for caution.

At the top of the wall he paused between two tall merlons topped with stone leopards, ears straining for the scuff of boots on the rampart, the creak of leather and armor. A combat there with guards would surely doom his quest before it had truly begun. There was no sound. Conan drew himself through the crennel. No guards were atop the wall. The palace was silent as a tomb. It seemed Iskandrian had left only men for the gates; the White Eagle would strike hard, as was his wont.

From the rampart a curving ramp led down toward the outer bailey.

There, however, he would surely be seen, no matter how few guards had been left behind or how many servants hid in fear that too-ardent service to him who now wore the crown might be punished if he lost it. Rooftops must be his path. The nearest, a wing of the palace, lay but an easy jump from the ramp for a vigorous man. Easy if the approaching run could be made on level ground rather than down a steep ramp, and if a three-story drop to the granite paving of the bailey were ignored.

Conan measured distances and angles, then took a deep breath and sprinted down the ramp. At the sixth great stride he flung himself across the chasm. Fingertips caught at the edge of the roof. One tile broke free, spiraling into the dark to shatter on the stones below; for an instant the Cimmerian hung by one hand. Slowly he hauled himself up, swung to hook a leg over the edge. The tile he held to shifted under his hand. Then he was flat on the roof, carefully setting aside the loose tile and quieting his breath as he waited to see if the noise of the first tile's fall drew attention. Still nothing stirred.

Like a jungle beast Conan was up and running, feet sure on the slanting tiles, climbing granite gargoyles to a higher level, leaping from a balcony tiled in black and white marble to clutch at a high peaked gable, edging with chest pressed flat against smooth granite along a ledge wide enough only for the balls of his feet, then climbing again, past mullioned windows and trefoils, until at last he scrambled through a narrow ventilation arch and looked down from great height on the vast throne room of the royal palace.

Great golden lamps hung on thick chains of the same metal from the vaulted ceiling, their bright flames lighting well the floor far below, a floor mosaicked in huge representations of the leopards and eagles that were the royal symbols of Ophir. In the middle of that floor was a black-shrouded bier on which Valdric's body lay in state, clothed in ornate robes of gold embroidered purple set with pearls. No living man was there to keep vigil over the dead King.

Conan's eyes sought the throne. Like unto the great chair in which Antimides had sat it was, covered in leopards and eagles, but larger still and of solid gold. The beasts' eyes were rubies, and claws and talons clutched emeralds as large as the joint of a man's thumb. Of the crown there was no sign. Ancient law or no, the Cimmerian thought, Valentius had not found it in himself to part with the royal diadem for even nine days once he had gained it. Yet what he sought was there. Across the arms of the throne lay the scepter of Ophir, its golden length glittering with an encrustation of all manner of gems.

Carefully Conan let himself down inside the throne room, using the scrolls and arabesques carved in the marble walls to climb down until he reached their end, some twenty feet above the floor. Here great tapestries hung. He ripped loose a corner of one—a scene of a crowned King hunting deer from horseback—and let himself drop, swinging on it as at the end of a rope. His feet brushed the floor, and he released the tapestry to run to the throne.

Almost hesitantly he hefted the long scepter. So much had he risked on the word of a drunk, and so much depended on it. Hastily he produced his dagger and began prying away soft gold and sparkling jewels, letting them fall to the purple velvet cushion of the throne. At the sight of wood beneath he grunted in satisfaction, but continued until he had stripped away all the outer sheath. He was left with a plain wooden staff as long as his outstretched arms and as thick as his two thumbs together.

Yet could it be in truth the Staff of Avanrakash, he wondered. He felt no magical qualities in it, and it showed no signs of its supposed great age. In fact, had it been a walking staff he would have thought it cut no more than a few days previous.

"But it *was* within the scepter," he breathed, "and it is all I have." For luck he scooped a handful of gems from the cushion, not bothering to see what they were, and stuffed them into his pouch.

"A common thief," Taramenon said from the door to the throne room. "Will not Synelle be surprised when she returns to find your head on a spike atop the River Gate?"

Conan reached over his shoulder; his sword slid easily into his grasp. The staff clutched in his left hand, he strode toward the tall noble. He had no words to say, no time for words. Even so in a corner of his mind lust flared at the mention of the woman's name. Synelle. How could he have gone so long without thinking of her? How could he have gone so long without touching her? The frozen rage of battles forced the thoughts down, smothered them.

Taramenon threw aside his fur-trimmed scarlet cape and drew his own blade. "I but stepped in here a moment to spit in Valdric's face. To offer obeisance to a corpse that was half-rotted before even it died turned my stomach. Finding you is a pleasant surprise I did not expect." Abruptly rage contorted his face into an ugly mask. "I will tell her of your death when I see her this night. Your filthy hands will never touch her again, you barbarian swine!" Snarling he rushed forward, swinging his blade in a mighty chop at Conan's head.

The Cimmerian's broadsword met Taramenon's with a tremendous clash. The Ophirean's eyes widened at the force of the blow, but on the instant he struck again. Again Conan's blade met his in a shower of sparks. Taramenon fought with all the deadly finesse of one who was the finest swordsman in Ophir, his longsword as agile and swift and deadly as a

Kothian viper; Conan fought with the cold ferocity of a northland beserker, his steel the lightning of the Cimmerian crags. Conan had no time to waste in defense—he must conquer, and quickly, or the noise of the fight would draw others, and he might well be overwhelmed by sheer numbers—but his constant attack left no room to Taramenon for aught *but* defense.

Sweat rolled down the face of the finest blade in Ophir as he found himself forced back, ever back, by an implacable demon with a face of stone and icy blue eyes, eyes in which depths he could read his own death. Panic clouded Taramenon's face, and for the first time in his life he knew fear. "Guards!" he screamed. "A thief! Guards!"

In that brief instant of divided attention Conan's blade engaged that of the tall Ophirean, brought it down, around, thrust under it. Chain-mail links snapped, razor steel sliced through muscle and bone, and the Cimmerian's sword hilt slammed against Taramenon's chest.

Conan stared into dark incredulous eyes. "Synelle is mine," he grated. "Mine!"

Blood bubbled from Taramenon's mouth, and he fell. Conan stared at the body in wonder before remembering to pull his sword free. Why had he said such a thing? Synelle was of no import in this. Karela was important, Al'Kiir and the staff and getting to the crossroads quickly. Yet images suppressed by events rose unbidden, sleek thighs and satin skin and swelling breasts and . . . Shaking his head woozily he half-staggered to Taramenon's discarded cape to clean his bloody blade and cut strips to bind the staff across his back. Was he going mad, he wondered. Visions of Synelle kept crowding his brain, as if time spent not thinking of her had to be made up. Desperately he forced them back. The crossroads, he thought. The crossroads, and no time.

Running to the half-torn-down tapestry, he began to climb. Synelle. The crossroads, and no time.

XX

Karela grunted as the sack in which she was carried was upended, dumping her, still bound and naked, onto cold stone. After the darkness light blinded her, filling her eyes with tears. The tears infuriated her; she would not have those who had taken her prisoner think they had reduced her to crying. Blinking, she was at last able to make out the roughly cut stone walls of what seemed to be a small cave, lit by rush torches in black iron sconces.

She was not alone, she realized. Synelle was there, and four other women, alabastrine-skinned blondes who seemed to wear variations of one face. The noblewoman was not dressed as when last Karela had seen her. Now she wore bracelets of black iron chain on each wrist, and two narrow strips of ebon silk, before and behind, leaving the outer curves of hips and breasts bare, were all her garb save for a belt of golden links. Karela stared when she saw the buckle. It was the head of the malevolent bronze she had sold—tried to sell, she thought ruefully—but rendered in gold. A chaplet of gold chain encircled Synelle's silvery tresses, severely braided into a coronet, and on that golden band, too, were the four horns of that demonic figure.

The other women were dressed as was Synelle, but the narrow belts cinching their waists were of black iron, and dark metal enclosed their ankles and necks as well. Their hair, neatly coiled about their heads, bore no headdress. With bowed heads their humbly alert eyes watched the exotically beautiful noblewoman.

Karela swallowed hard, and was reminded again how dry was her throat. Had she the use of her mouth she would tell this Synelle she could have Conan. It would be a lie—she would not be driven from her business with the Cimmerian by this pale-haired trull who called herself a lady—but lying seemed much the better part of valor at the moment.

Synelle nodded, and the four women in iron belts produced leather straps. Karela jerked futilely at her bonds despite herself. If only she had a dagger, or but a single hand free, or even her tongue to shout her defiance at them.

"Listen to me, wench," Synelle said. "These women will prepare you. If you fight, they will beat you, but in any event they will carry out my orders. I would have you as little marked as possible, so if you will submit, nod your head."

Karela tried to shout through her gag. Submit! Did this fool woman think she was some milksop maiden to be frightened by threats? Her green eyes hurled all her silent fury at Synelle.

Abruptly Synelle moved, placing a foot on Karela's knees, bound beneath her chin, to roll her onto her back and hold her there. "A taste, then. Cut well in."

The other women darted forward, their leather straps slicing beneath Karela's corded heels, raining blows on her helpless buttocks, drawn taut by her tying.

Her green eyes bulged in her head, and she had an instant to be grateful for the gag that held back her cries, then her head was nodding frantically. Derketo! There was no use in being beaten while lying trussed like a pig for market.

Synelle motioned the women back. "I was sure you would be reasonable."

Karela tried to meet the dark eyes staring down at her, then closed her own in humiliation. It was clear from the look on Synelle's face that she had never doubted that the red-haired woman could be brought to heel. Let them free her, Karela prayed, and she would show them the worth of pledge wrung from whips. She would . . .

Suddenly the cords binding her were severed. Karela caught a flash of a dagger. She moved to grab it . . . and sprawled in boneless agony on the stone floor, muscles stiff from long confinement barely able to do more than twitch. Slowly, painfully, she brought a hand up to drag the gag from her mouth. She wanted to weep. The dagger was gone from sight, and she had neither seen who had held it nor where it was hidden.

Even as she dropped the wadded cloth two of the women pulled her to her feet. She gasped with the pain; had they not supported her she could not have stood. One of the others began drawing an ivory comb through her tangled locks, while the last wiped her sweat away with soft, damp clothes.

Karela worked her mouth for the moisture to speak. "I'll not sell you to a tavern," she managed. "I'll tear your heart out with my bare hands."

"Good," Synelle said. "I feared your spirit might have been broken. Often the journey here, bound, is enough for that. It is well that it was not in your case."

Karela sneered. "You want the pleasure of breaking me yourself, then? You will not have it, because you cannot do it. And if you want Conan back—"

"Conan!" the noblewoman cut her off, dark eyes widening in surprise. "How do you come to know of the barbarian?"

"We were once," Karela began, then spluttered to a halt. She was tired, and spoke of things of which she had no wish to speak. "No matter how I know of him. If you want him, you'll cease your threats and bargain."

Synelle trilled with laughter. "So you think I merely attempt to dispose of a rival. I should be furious that such as you could think of yourself as my rival, but I find it merely amusing. I expect he is a man who has known many women in his time, and if you are one of that number I see he has little discrimination in his choosing. That is at an end, now." She held out a slender palm. "I hold the barbarian there, wench. He will crawl to me on his belly when I call him, dance like a bear for a tin whistle at my command. And you think to be my rival?" She threw back her head and laughed even harder.

"No woman could treat Conan so," Karela snapped. "I know, for I have tried, and by Derketo, I am ten times the woman you are."

"You are suitable for the rites," the silver-haired woman said coolly, "but I am High Priestess of Al'Kiir. Yet were I not, you would still not be woman enough to serve as my bowermaid. My tirewomen were nobly born in Corinthia, and she who draws my bath and rubs me with oils was a princess in far Vendhya, yet to obey my slightest wish is now the whole of their lives. What can a jade of a bandit be beside such as they, who are but my slaves?"

Karela opened her mouth for another retort, and gasped when a black-armored man in a horned helmet appeared in the entrance to the cavern. For an instant she had thought it was the creature the bronze represented. Foolishness, she berated herself. Such a creature could not exist.

"Has Taramenon come yet?" Synelle demanded of the man.

"No, my lady. Nor any message of him."

"He will suffer for this," Synelle said heatedly. "He defies me, and I will see him suffer for it!" Drawing a deep breath, she smoothed the already taut black silk over her rounded breasts. "We will proceed without him. When he comes, he is to be seized and bound. There are rites other than the gift of women."

"Taramenon, my lady?" the man said in shocked tones.

"You heard my command!" Synelle made a brusque gesture, and the armored figure bowed himself from her presence.

Karela had been listening intently, hoping for some fragment of information that might help her escape, but now she became aware of how the four women were dressing her, the tiny white tarla blossoms woven into her hair, the diaphanous layers of blue silk meant to be removed one by one for the titillation of a groom.

"What travesty is there?" she growled. "You *do* think me a rival, but if you mean to rid yourself of me in this way, you are mad! I'll marry no man! Do you hear me, you pasty-faced trull?"

A cruel smile curled Synelle's lips, and the look on her face sent a chill through Karela's blood. "You will marry no *man*," the haughty noblewoman said softly. "Tonight you will wed a god, and I will become ruler of Ophir."

The tall white marker at the crossroads, a square marble pillar inscribed with the distances to the borders of Nemedia and Aquilonia, loomed out of the night ahead of Conan. No sound broke the silence save his labored breath and the steady slap of his running feet on the paving stones. Beyond the marker reared the dark mass of Tor Al'Kiir, a huge granite outcropping dominating the flat country about it.

The big Cimmerian crouched beside the marble plinth, eyes straining at the blackness. There was so sign of his men. Softly he imitated the cry of a Nemedian nighthawk.

The muted jingle of tight-strapped harness announced the sudden appearance of Machaon and the rest, leading their horses. Memtes, bringing up the rear, gripped the reins of Conan's big Aquilonian black as well as those of his own mount. Bows and quivers were slung on their backs.

"I thought it best to keep from sight," the tattooed veteran told Conan quietly. "As we arrived, two score men-at-arms passed, chasing another band as large, and twice parties of light cavalry have gone by at the gallop. Scouts, the last, no doubt."

"Unless I miss my guess," Narus added in a low voice that would not travel far, "Iskandrian seeks action this night, and the nobles seek to avoid him until their strength is gathered. Never did I think that when the final battle for Ophir occurred, I would be scaling a mountain."

"Go to Taurianus, then," Conan growled, "if you seek glory!" Irritably he shook his black-maned head. Such edginess was not his usual manner, but his thoughts scarcely seemed his own. With a desperation foreign to him he fought to cling to his purpose of mind, struggled against images of Synelle and lust that threatened to overwhelm him.

"Is that the famous staff?" Machaon asked. "It has no look of magic to me."

"It is," the Cimmerian replied, "and it has." He hoped he did not lie. Unfastening the strips of cloth that held the length of wood, he clutched it in one hand and drew his sword with the other. "This is the last chance to change your minds. Let any man unsure of what he does step aside." The soft and deadly susuration of steel sliding from scabbards was his answer. Conan nodded grimly. "Then hide the horses in yon copse of trees and follow me."

"Your armor," Machaon said. "'Tis on your saddle."

"There is no time," Conan said, and without waiting for the others he started up the stony slope.

Crom was not a god men prayed to; he gave nothing beyond his first gift. But now Conan offered a prayer to any god that would listen. If he died for it, let him be in time.

A silent file of purposeful men fell in behind him in his climb, on their way to beard a god in his den.

The lash struck across her shoulders again, and Karela gritted her teeth against the howl she wanted to let pass. Bound between posts topped with the obscene head of Al'Kiir, she knelt, all but the last layer of thin blue silk torn away from her sweat-slick body. It was not the pain from the incessant bite of leather that made her want to cry out, or not alone; she would have died before giving her tormentors the satisfaction of acknowledging that. But the burning stripes that made scarlet lattices on her body were as pin-pricks beside the flaming desire the ointment with which Synelle had anointed her brought unbidden. Uncontrollably Karela writhed, and wept for the humiliation of it.

The silvery-haired noblewoman danced before her, spinning and dipping, chanting words that defied hearing in rhythm to haunting flutes and the pounding of scabbarded swords on the stone floor of the vaulting cavern. Between Synelle and Karela stood the bronze she had stolen from Conan, but its evil was overpowered by the waves of horror that radiated from the huge sanguinary image that dominated the chamber. Three ebon eyes that seemed to drink in light held her own. She tried to tear her eyes from that hellborn gaze, she prayed for the strength to pull away, but like a bird hypnotized by a serpent she had no will left.

The lashes struck, again and again. Her hands quivered in her bonds with the effort of not shrieking, for that demonic scarlet figure had begun to vibrate, giving off a hum that blended with the flutes and wrenched at the core of her that made her a woman. Conan, she cried silently, where are you?

Stirring where neither time nor space existed, where endless nihility was all. Awakening, almost full, as pleasure overwhelming lanced through the impenetrable shield. Irritation, vaster than the minds of all men together could encompass, flared.

Would these torments never cease, these returnings of ancient memories near gone and better forgotten? Would not . . . Full awareness for the first time in eons, awareness cold enough to freeze suns and stay worlds in their motion. There was direction. A single pristine strand of crystalline desire and pain stretching into the infinite. Slowly, with a wariness born of long centuries of disappointment, from the midst of nothingness the gleaming thread of worship was followed.

Conan peered around the edge of a huge, moss-covered block of marble which had once been intended for construction. Crickets chirped in the dark, and a nightbird gave a haunting cry. All else was still.

Roofless walls of niveous stone and truncated alabaster columns, never completed and now wreathed by thick vines, covered the leveled top of the mountain. Among the columns were more than a score of men in black armor and horned helms, the torches a third of them carried casting flickering shadows over the weather-beaten ruins. He wanted to sigh with relief at the symbol picked out in scarlet on their chests. It was clearly the head of the image Karela had stolen, the head of Al'Kiir. Not until that moment had he allowed himself to fear he might be coming to the wrong place.

The black-armored man had to be guarding an entrance to chambers below, Conan thought, where the horrible rite was to take place. Boros had said the tomb lay buried in the heart of the mountain. At least, they were supposed to be standing guard. The sinister reputation of Tor Al'Kiir made it unlikely anyone would come there, most especially in the night, and that made them careless. Some leaned against pale fluted marble. Others sat and talked among themselves. No eye was directed outward to watch for intruders.

Conan signaled with his hands; long practiced, the nine men behind him slid soundlessly away. The Cimmerian counted silently, knowing how long it would take each man to reach his place.

"Now!" he shouted, and burst from concealment to hurl himself at the guards. As he had known it would, his shout and the appearance of a lone man charging froze them for an instant, long enough for nine bowstrings to twang, for nine feathered shafts to drink life.

The guards of Al'Kiir had been chosen for their skill, though, and even as their comrades were falling the survivors darted for cover behind the columns. But then Conan was among them. Thrusting the staff like a lance he took a man under the chin; throat cartiledge snapped loudly, and blood spilled from a mouth that could no longer scream.

"For Conan!" he heard behind him. "Conan!"

A blade thrust at him, and his ancient steel severed the arm that held it. He ducked beneath a decapitating cut and, wielding his broadsword like an axe, chopped through his attacker's midsection almost to the spine. Kicking the body away, he straightened to find no black-armored man standing. His mercenaries stood among the bodies, gripping bloody swords and warily watching for more of the enemy.

"Are they all dead?" Conan demanded.

Machaon shook his head. "Two managed to run down there." He pointed to a dark opening where steps had led down into the mountain.

"Crom!" the Cimmerian muttered. With quick strides he moved to the opening and started down. Wordlessly the others followed.

Sweat trickling down her sleek form, Synelle moved in the ancient forms and patterns, her body swaying and bending in an exaltation of lust and pain. Time-forgotten words spilled from her mouth, echoed against the walls, supplicating and glorifying her dire god. The monstrous horned malevolence before which she danced pulsated like the string of a harp. The drone that came from it now drowned out the flutes and the pounding scabbards and even the slap of leather on flesh, yet seemed to merge with and amplify her voice.

A part of her mind noted that the auburn-haired woman, naked now to the lash, sagged in her bonds, but struggled still against surrender. Not once had a cry passed her lips. That was well, Synelle thought, not pausing an instant in either movements or incantation. She was certain that the success she seemed to be having was as much due to the stubborn pride of this Karela as to the bronze image. Much better than any of the haughty noblewomen, who in the end always wept and begged and offered their bodies to the men whipping them in exchange for even a moment's surcease.

One of her guards, his chain-mail rent and bloodied, burst into the chamber. "We are attacked, my lady!" he gasped. "Hundreds of them! They cry, for Conan!"

Synelle faltered, then desperately continued with dance and invocation. To stop now would mean disaster, doom better undreamed of. Yet her mind spun. Conan? It was impossible. But then it was impossible that any should dare brave the night slopes of Tor Al'Kiir. Then who . . .

Thoughts and words and movement died as one. All sound stopped as the great horned head turned toward her and three lidless eyes, black as death, regarded her like dark flames of unholy life.

Men in black chain-mail, their horned helmets making them seem more demons than men in the dim light of fires burned low in iron cressets, appeared as if from the walls to defend the roughcut stone passage. Demons they might appear, yet they died like men. Into the midst of them Conan waded, his ancient broadsword tirelessly rising and falling in furious butchery, till its length was stained crimson and blood fell from it as if the steel itself had wounds. A charnel house he made, and those who dared confront him died. Many could not face that gory blade nor the deathly cold eyes of he who wielded it, and darted past the one man to face instead the nine behind.

The Cimmerian spared no thought for those who refused him combat. What they guarded and what he sought lay ahead, and he did not cease his slaying until he had hacked his way into a huge cavern. The blood chilled in his veins at what he saw.

Twenty more of the black-armored men stood there, but they were as frozen as he, and seemed as insignificant as ants beside what else the chamber contained. Karela, her lush nakedness welted, hanging by her wrists from two wooden pillars. Synelle, oddly garbed in black silk that clung damply to her, a horned chaplet on her brow. And beyond her a shape out of madmen's nightmares, its skin the color of dead men's blood. Al'Kiir awakened threw back his head, and from a broad fanged gash of a mouth came laughter to curdle the heart of heroes.

Even as the evil god's laughter stunned Conan's mind, Synelle's presence filled it. The staff fell from his fingers, and he took a step toward her.

The dark-eyed noblewoman pointed a slender finger at the young giant. As if commanding more wine she said, "Kill him."

The strange lethargy that had affected him of late when he was about her slowed Conan's hand, but his sword took the head of the first man to turn toward him before that man had his blade half-drawn. Nobles could prate while they lounged at their ease of chivalry in battle, though they rarely practiced it; a son of the bleak northland knew only how to fight to win.

The others came at him then, but he retreated to the entrance, wide enough for only three at a time to get near. With a frenzy approaching madness he fought, and his steel did murderous work among them. Synelle filled his brain. He would get to Synelle if he must wade to his waist in blood.

A scream drew his eye beyond the men struggling to slay him. Al'Kiir had seized Synelle in a clawed hand that almost encircled her narrow waist, lifting her before that triad of ebon eyes for inspection.

Conan redoubled his efforts, and the fury of his attack, seeming reckless of death, forced the mail-clad men to fall back before him.

"Not me!" Synelle screamed, her face contorted in terror. "I am thy faithful slave, o mighty Al'Kiir! Thy priestess! She is the one brought for thy delight!"

Al'Kiir turned his horned head to Karela, and his lipless mouth curled in a fanged smile. He took a step toward her, reaching out.

"No!" Conan roared, desperation clawing at him. "Not Karela!" His foot struck something that rolled with the sound of wood on stone. The Staff of Avanrakash.

Ignoring the men who still faced him, Conan seized the staff from the floor and hurled it like a javelin. Straight to the chest of the monstrous figure the plain wooden staff flew, struck, and pierced. Al'Kiir's free hand tugged at the length of wood, but it could as well have been anchored with barbs. Black ichor poured out around it, and the horned god shrieked, a piercing cry that went on without end, shattering thought and turning muscles to water.

Steel clattered to the stone floor as black-mailed men dropped their swords and fled, pushing past Conan as if he held no weapon at all. And he, in turn, paid them no heed, for the scream that would not stop allowed room for awareness of nothing else.

Around the staff drops of ichor hardened like beads of obsidian, and the hardening widened, spreading steadily through the malevolent shape.

Synelle plucked frantically at the claw-tipped fingers that held her; her long legs kicked wildly. "Release me," she pleaded. "Release thy faithful priestess, o mighty Al'Kiir." Now she struggled with fingers of stone. Slowly, as if it moved with difficulty, the horned head turned to look at her. "Release me!" she screamed. "Release me! No! Mitra, save me!" Her kicking slowed, then her legs were frozen, her cries stilled. Her pale skin gleamed like polished marble in the light from the torches. There was silence.

Flight. Flight from pain great enough to slay a thousand worlds. Flight back to the hated prison of nothingness. Yet something had been brought along. It was clothed in the flesh it had once worn, and a beautiful, naked woman, dark of eye and silvery of hair, floated in the void, mouth working with screams that were not worth hearing. Evil joy, black as the depths of the pit. Long centuries of delight would come from this one before the pitiful spark that was human essence faded and was gone. But the pain did not end. It grew instead. The crystalline thread that linked this place of nonexistence with that other world was still intact, unseverable. Yet it must be ended, least endless eons of agony follow. It must be ended.

Conan shook his head as if waking from a fever dream, and ran to Karela. Quickly he severed her bonds, caught her as she would have fallen.

The beautiful red-haired bandit turned her sweat-streaked face up to him. "I knew you would come," she whispered hoarsely. "I prayed for you to rescue me, and I hate you for it."

The Cimmerian could not help smiling. Whatever had happened to her, Karela was unchanged. Sheathing his sword, he picked her up in his arms. Sighing weakly, she put her arms around his neck and pressed her face to his chest. He thought he felt the wetness of tears.

His gaze went to the stone shape pierced by the wooden staff, the sanguinary horned monstrosity clutching the alabaster figure of a struggling woman, her face frozen in horror for eternity. All the raging feelings and confusions that had filled him were gone as if they had never been. Bewitched, he thought angrily. Synelle had ensorceled him. He hoped that wherever she was she had time for regret.

Machaon and Narus ran into the chamber, bloody swords in hand, and skidded to a halt, staring in awe. "I'll not task what happened here," the gaunt-faced man said, "for I misdoubt I'd believe it."

"They flee from us, Cimmerian," Machaon said. "Ten of them together, and they ran down a side passage at the sight of us. Whatever you did took all the heart right out of them."

"The others?" Conan asked, and the tattooed mercenary shook his head grimly.

"Dead. But they collected their ferryman's fees and more."

Suddenly Narus pointed at the huge stone figure. "It's—it's—" He stammered, unable to get any more words out.

Conan spun. The petrified body of the god was quivering. A hum came from it, a hum that quickly rose in pitch until it pierced the ears like driven nails.

"Run!" the Cimmerian shouted, but could not hear his own words through the burning pain that clawed at his skull.

The other two men needed no urging, though. The three of them sped through the rough-hewn stone passages, Conan keeping up easily despite carrying Karela. In their headlong flight they leaped over the bodies of the dead, but saw no one living. And the mind-killing vibration followed them up sloping tunnels, level after level, up the stone steps to the ruins.

As the Cimmerian dashed out among the over-grown columns, the skull-piercing sound ceased. Birds and crickets had fled; the loudest noise to be heard was their own blood thrumming in their ears. Before a breath could be drawn in the silence, the mountain shook. Half-built columns toppled and mossy walls collapsed, blocks of marble large enough to crush a man splashing dirt like water, but the sound of their fall was swallowed by the rumbling that rose from the granite bowels of Tor Al'Kiir.

Dodging through clouds of dust and flying chips of shattered rock, Conan hurtled down the slope, Karela's naked form clutched to his chest. The side of a mountain in the night was no place to be during an earthquake, but neither was the midst of crumbling marble walls. He had

a feeling the only safe place to be in *this* earthquake was as far from Tor
Al'Kiir as it was possible to run. And run he did, over ground that danced
like the deck of a ship in a storm, fighting to keep his balance for rocks
bouncing beneath his feet and stones flying through the air like hail. He
no longer knew if Machaon and Narus ran with him, nor could he spare a
thought for them. They were men, and must take their risks. Conan had to
get Karela to safety, for some primal instinct warned him that worse was
to come.

With a sound like the splitting of the earth, the peak of Tor Al'Kiir
erupted in fire, mountaintop and alabaster columns and marble walls alike
flung high into a sky now lit by a fiery glow. The blast threw Conan into
the air; he twisted so that his own huge frame took the bone-jarring
impact of landing. It was no longer possible to gain his feet. He put his
body over that of Karela, sheltering her from the stones that filled the air.
As he did one image remained burned into his brain, a single flame
towering a thousand paces from the destroyed top of Tor Al'Kiir, a single
flame that took the form of the Staff of Avanrakash.

Epilogue

I n the paleness before full dawn Conan peered toward Ianthe, towers thrusting into the early morning mist, glazed red roof tiles beginning to gleam with the light of a sun not yet risen. An army approached the city, men-at-arms with gaily colored pennons streaming, long columns of infantry with shields slung on their backs, tall plumes of dust rising beneath thousands of pacing hooves and tramping feet. A victorious army, he thought. But whose?

Avoiding looking at the steaming, cratered top of Tor Al'Kiir, he picked his way through the huge, misshapen boulders that now littered the mountain slope. A quarter of its height had the great granite mound lost in the night, and what lay at its new peak the Cimmerian neither knew nor wanted to know.

Narus' voice came to him, tinged with a bitter note. "Women should not be allowed to gamble. Almost I think you changed dice on me. At least let my buy back—"

"No," Karela cut him off as Conan rejoined his three companions. She wore Narus' breeches, tight across the curves of her hips and voluminous in the legs, with his scarlet cloak wrapped about her shoulders and his sword across her knees. The inner slopes of her full breasts showed at the gap in the cloak. "I have more need of something to wear than of gold. And I did not switch the dice. You were too busy filling your filthy eyes and leering at the sight of me uncovered to pay mind of what you were doing."

Machaon laughed, and the gaunt man grunted, attempting to pull his hauberk down far enough to cover his bony knees.

"We must be moving," Conan announced. "There has been a battle, it seems, and whoever won there will be mercenaries without patrons or leaders, men to re-form the company. Crom, there may be enough for you each to have your own Free-Company."

Machaon, sitting with his back against one of the building stones that had once stood atop the mountain, shook his head. "I have been longer in this trade, Cimmerian, than you have lived, and this night past has at last given me my full. I own some land in Koth. I shall put up my sword, and become a farmer."

"You?" Conan said incredulously. "A month of grubbing in the dirt, and you'll tear apart the nearest village with your bare hands, just for the need of a fight."

" 'Tis not quite as you imagine," the grizzled veteran chuckled. "There are ten men working the land now. I will be a man of substance, as such as counted among farmers. I shall fetch Julia from the city, and marry her if she will have me. A farmer needs a wife to give him strong sons."

Conan frowned at Narus. "And do you, too, intend to become a farmer?"

"I've no love of dirt," the hollow-faced man replied, snatching the dice from Karela, who had been examining them idly, "but . . . Conan, wizards I did not mind so much, and those men who looked like a snake had been at their mothers were no worse than a horde of blood-drunk Picts, but this god you found us has had my heart in my mouth more than I can remember since the Battle of Black River, when I was a fresh youth without need of shaving. For a time I seek a quiet city, with buxom wenches to bounce on a bed and," he rattled the dice in cupped hands, rolled them on the ground, "young lads with more coin than sense."

"They had best be *very* young," Karela laughed. "Do you intend to gain any of their coin. Eh, Cimmerian?" Narus glared at her and grumbled under his breath.

As Conan opened his mouth, a flash of white caught his eye, cloth fluttering in the breeze down slope. "Crom!" he muttered. It was Boros and Julia. "I'll wring his scrawny neck for bringing her here," he growled. The others scrambled to their feet to follow him down the mountainside.

When Conan reached the girl and the old man, he saw they were not alone. Julia knelt beside Taurianus, tearing strips from her white robes to try to staunch the blood oozing from a dozen rents in the Ophirean's hauberk. The man's hair was matted with dirt and blood, and a bubble of scarlet appeared at his lips with each labored breath.

Boros flung up his hands as soon as he saw Conan. "Do not blame me. I tried to stop her, but I have not your strength. I thought it best to come along and protect her as best I could. She said she was worried about Machaon."

"About all of them," Julia said, her face reddening. "Conan, we found him lying here. Can you not help him?"

The Cimmerian needed no close examination of Taurianus' wounds to see the man would not survive them. The ground about him was already blackened with his blood. "So the nobles lost," he said quietly. A mercenary fighting on the victorious side would not have crawled away to die.

The Ophirean's eyes fluttered open. "We caught the Eagle," he rasped, and continued with frequent pauses to struggle for breath. "We left our camp—with fires lit—and Iskandrian—fell on it—in the night. Then we took him—in the rear. We would have—destroyed him—but a giant flame—cleft the sky—and the white-haired devil—shouted the gods— were with them. Some cried—it was the Staff—of Avanrakash. Panic seized us—by the throat. We fled—and his warriors cut us down. Enjoy your time—Cimmerian. Iskandrian—is impaling—every mercenary— he catches." Suddenly he lurched up onto one elbow and stretched out a clawed hand toward Conan. "I am a better man—than you!" Blood welled in his mouth, and he fell back. Once he jerked, then was still, dull eyes staring at the sky.

"A giant flame," Narus said softly. "You are a man of destiny, Cimmerian. You make kings even you do not mean to."

Conan shrugged off the words irritably. He cared not who wore the crown of Ophir, except insofar as it affected his prospects. With Iskandrian at Valentius' side—perhaps, he thought, it was time to start thinking of the fopling as Moranthes II—there would be no chance to gather more men, and possibly no men left alive to gather. " 'Twill be Argos for me," he said.

"You!" Machaon snapped abruptly, and Julia jumped. "Did I not tell you to remain in Ianthe? Must I fetch a switch for you here and now? The life of a poor farmer's wife is hard, and she must learn to obey. Would you have our only pig die because you did not feed it when I told you?"

"You have no right to threaten me," the auburn-haired girl burst out. "You cannot . . ." Her words trailed off, and she sat back on her heels. "Wife? Did you say wife?" Taking a deep breath, she said earnestly, "Machaon, I will care for your pig as if it were my beloved sister."

"There's no need to go so far as that," Machaon laughed. His face sobered as he turned to Conan. "A long road we've traveled together, Cimmerian, but it has come to its ending. And as I've no desire to let Iskandrian rummage in my guts with a stake, I'll take my leave now. I wish to be far from Ianthe before this day is done."

"And I," Narus added. " 'Tis Tarantia for me, for they do say the nobles of Aquilonia are free with their coin and love to gamble."

"Fare you well," Conan told them. "And take a pull at the hellhorn for me, if you get there before me."

Julia ran to clasp Machaon's arm, and, with Narus, they started down the mountain.

"After that fool wench's display," Karela muttered, "I need a drink, or I'll be sick to my stomach."

Conan eyed her thoughtfully. "Events hie me to Argos, for 'tis said Free-Companies are being hired there. Come with me, Karela. Together, in a year, we'll rule the country."

The red-haired beauty stared at him, stricken. "Do you not understand why I cannot, Cimmerian? By the Teats of Derketo, man, you wake in me longings to be like that simpering wench, Julia! You make me embrace weakness, make me want to let you protect me. Think you I'm a woman to fold your blankets and cook your meals?"

"I've never asked such of you," he protested, but she ignored him.

"One day I would find myself walking a pace behind you, silent lest I should miss your words, and I'd plant a dagger in your back for it. Then I would likely weep myself to madness for the doing of what you brought on yourself. I will not have it, Conan. I will not!"

A sense of loss filled him, but pride would not allow it to touch his face. "At least you have gained one thing. This time I flee, and you remain in Ophir."

"No, Conan. The vermin that formed my band are not worth the effort of gathering them again. I go to the east." Her head came up, and her eyes glowed like emeralds. "The plains of Zamora shall know the Red Hawk again."

He fumbled in his pouch and drew out half the gems he had taken from the scepter of Ophir. "Here," he said gruffly. Karela did not move. "Can you not take a parting gift from a friend?" Hesitantly a slender hand came to his; he let the gems pour into it.

"You are a better man than you know, Cimmerian," she whispered, "and I am a fool." Her lips brushed his, and she was gone, running with the cloak a scarlet banner behind her.

Conan watched until she passed out of sight below.

"Even the gods cannot understand the brain of a woman," Boros crackled. "Men, on the other hand, rarely think with their brains at all."

Conan glared at the bearded man. He had forgotten Boros was still there. "Now you can return to the taverns and your drinking," he said sourly.

"Not in Ophir," Boros said. He tugged at his beard and glanced nervously toward the ruined mountaintop. "A god cannot be killed as if it were an ordinary demon. Al'Kiir still lives—somewhere. Suppose his body is buried yet up there? Suppose another of those images exists? I will not be in this country if someone else attempts to raise him. Argos, I think. The sea air will be good for my lungs, and I can take ship for distant lands if I hear evil word from Ophir."

"Not in my company," Conan growled. "I travel alone."

"I can work magicks to make the journey easier," Boros protested, but the Cimmerian was already making his way down the mountain. Chattering continuously the gray-bearded man scrambled after Conan, who refused to respond to his importunings.

Once more he was on his own, Conan thought, with only his sword and his wits, but he had been so often before. There were the gems in his pouch, of course. They would fetch something. And Argos lay ahead, Argos and thoughts he had never entertained before. If chance could bring a fool like Valentius to a throne, why could he not find a path? Why indeed? Smiling, he quickened his pace.

Conan
the
Indestructible

By L. Sprague de Camp

The greatest hero of the magic-rife Hyborian Age was a northern barbarian, Conan the Cimmerian, about whose deeds a cycle of legend revolves. While these legends are largely based on the attested facts of Conan's life, some tales are inconsistent with others. So we must reconcile the contradictions in the saga as best we can.

In Conan's veins flowed the blood of the people of Atlantis, the brilliant city-state swallowed by the sea 8,000 years before his time. He was born into a clan that claimed a homeland in the northwest corner of Cimmeria, along the shadowy borders of Vanaheim and the Pictish wilderness. His grandfather had fled his own people because of a blood feud and sought refuge with the people of the North. Conan himself first saw daylight on a battlefield during a raid by the Vanir.

Before he had weathered fifteen snows, the young Cimmerian's fighting skills were acclaimed around the council fires. In that year the Cimmerians, usually at one another's throats, joined forces to repel the war-like Gundermen who, intent on colonizing southern Cimmeria, had pushed across the Aquilonian border and established the frontier post of Venarium. Conan joined the howling, blood-mad horde that swept out of the northern hills, stormed over the stockade walls, and drove the Aquilonians back across their frontier.

At the sack of Venarium, Conan, still short of his full growth, stood six feet tall and weighed 180 pounds. He had the vigilance and stealth of the born woodsman, the iron-hardness of the mountain man, and the Herculean physique of his blacksmith father. After the plunder of the Aquilonian outpost, Conan returned for a time to his tribe.

Restless under the conflicting passions of his adolescence, Conan spent several months with a band of Æsir as they raided the Vanir and the Hyperboreans. He soon learned that some Hyperborean citadels were ruled by a caste of widely-feared magicians, called Witchmen. Undaunted, he took part in a foray against Haloga Castle, when he found that Hyperborean slavers had captured Rann, the daughter of Njal, chief of the Æsir band.

Conan gained entrance to the castle and spirited out Rann Njalsdatter; but on the flight out of Hyperborea, Njal's band was overtaken by an army of living dead. Conan and the other Æsir survivors were led away to slavery ("Legions of the Dead").

Conan did not long remain a captive. Working at night, he ground away at one link of his chain until it was weak enough to break. Then one stormy night, whirling a four-foot length of heavy chain, he fought his way out of the slave pen and vanished into the downpour.

Another account of Conan's early years tells a different tale. This narrative, on a badly broken clay prism from Nippur, states that Conan was enslaved as a boy of ten or twelve by Vanir raiders and set to work turning a grist mill. When he reached his full growth, he was bought by a Hyrkanian pitmaster who traveled with a band of professional fighters staging contests for the amusement of the Vanir and Æsir. At this time Conan received his training with weapons. Later he escaped and made his way south to Zamora (*Conan the Barbarian*).

Of the two versions, the records of Conan's enslavement by the Hyrkanians at sixteen, found in a papyrus in the British Museum, appear much more legible and self-consistent. But this question may never be settled.

Although free, the youth found himself half a hostile kingdom away from home. Instinctively he fled into the mountains at the southern extremity of Hyperborea. Pursued by a pack of wolves, he took refuge in a cave. Here he discovered the seated mummy of a gigantic chieftain of ancient times, with a heavy bronze sword across its knees. When Conan seized the sword, the corpse arose and attacked him ("The Thing in the Crypt")

Continuing southward into Zamora, Conan came to Arenjun, the notorious "City of Thieves." Green to civilization and, save for some rudimentary barbaric ideas of honor and chivalry, wholly lawless by nature, he carved a niche for himself as a professional thief.

Being young and more daring than adroit, Conan's progress in his new profession was slow until he joined forces with Taurus of Nemedia in a quest for the fabulous jewel called the "Heart of the Elephant." The gem lay in the almost impregnable tower of the infamous mage Yara, captor of the extraterrestrial being Yag-Kosha ("The Tower of the Elephant").

Seeking greater opportunities to ply his trade, Conan wandered westward to the capital of Zamora, Shadizar the Wicked. For a time his thievery prospered, although the whores of Shadizar soon relieved him of his gains. During one larceny, he was captured by the men of

Queen Taramis of Shadizar, who sent him on a mission to recover a magical horn wherewith to rescurrect an ancient, evil god. Taramis' plot led to her own destruction (*Conan the Destroyer*).

The barbarian's next exploit involved a fellow thief, a girl named Tamira. The Lady Jondra, an arrogant aristocrat of Shadizar, owned a pair of priceless rubies. Baskaran Imalla, a religious fanatic raising a cult among the Kezankian hillmen, coveted the jewels to gain control over a fire-breathing dragon he had raised from an egg. Conan and Tamira both yearned for the rubies; Tamira took a post as lady's maid to Jondra for a chance to steal them.

An ardent huntress, Jondra set forth with her maid and her men-at-arms to slay Baskaran's dragon. Baskaran captured the two women and was about to offer them to his pet as a snack when Conan intervened (*Conan the Magnificent*).

Soon Conan was embroiled in another adventure. A stranger hired the youth to steal a casket of gems sent by the King of Zamora to the King of Turan. The stranger, a priest of the serpent-god Set, wanted the jewels for magic against his enemy, the renegade priest Amanar.

Amanar's emissaries, who were hominoid reptiles, had stolen the gems. Although wary of magic, Conan set out to recover the loot. He became involved with a bandette, Karela, called the Red Hawk, who proved the ultimate bitch; when Conan saved her from rape, she tried to kill him. Amanar's party had also carried off to the renegade's stronghold a dancing girl whom Conan had promised to help (*Conan the Invincible*).

Soon rumors of treasure sent Conan to the nearby ruins of ancient Larsha, just ahead of the soldiers dispatched to arrest him. After all but their leader, Captain Nestor, had perished in an accident arranged by Conan, Nestor and Conan joined forces to plunder the treasure; but ill luck deprived them of their gains ("The Hall of the Dead").

Conan's recent adventures had left him with an aversion to warlocks and Eastern sorceries. He fled northwestward through Corinthia into Nemedia, the second most powerful Hyborian kingdom. In Nemedia he resumed his profession successfully enough to bring his larcenies to the notice of Aztrias Petanius, ne'er-do-well nephew of the governor. Oppressed by gambling debts, this young gentleman hired the outlander to purloin a Zamorian goblet, carved from a single diamond, that stood in the temple-museum of a wealthy collector.

Conan's appearance in the temple-museum coincided with its master's sudden demise and brought the young thief to the unwelcome attention of Demetrio, of the city's Inquisitorial Council. This caper also gave Conan his second experience with the dark magic of the serpent-brood of

Set, conjured up by the Stygian sorcerer Thoth-Amon ("The God in the Bowl").

Having made Nemedia too hot to hold him, Conan drifted south into Corinthia, where he continued to occupy himself with the acquisition of other persons' property. By diligent application, the Cimmerian earned the repute of one of the boldest thieves in Corinthia. Poor judgment of women, however, cast him into chains until a turn in local politics brought freedom and a new career. An ambitious nobleman, Murilo, turned him loose to slit the throat of the Red Priest, Nabonidus, the scheming power behind the local throne. This venture gathered a prize collection of rogues in Nabodinus's mansion and ended in a mire of blood and treachery ("Rogues in the House").

Conan wandered back to Arenjun and began to earn a semi-honest living by stealing back for their owners valuable objects that others had filched from them. He undertook to recover a magical gem, the Eye of Erlik, from the wizard Hissar Zul and return it to its owner, the Khan of Zamboula.

There is some question about the chronology of Conan's life at this point. A recently-translated tablet from Asshurbanipal's library states that Conan was about seventeen at the time. This would place the episode right after that of "The Tower of the Elephant," which indeed is mentioned in the cuneiform. But from internal evidence, this event seems to have taken place several years later. For one thing, Conan appears too clever, mature, and sophisticated; for another, the fragmentary medieval Arabic manuscript *Kitab al-Qunn* implies that Conan was well into his twenties by then.

The first translator of the Asshurbanipal tablet, Prof. Dr. Andreas von Fuss of the Münchner Staatsmuseum, read Conan's age as "17." In Babylonian cuneiform, "17" is expressed by two circles followed by three vertical wedges, with a horizontal wedge above the three for "minus"—hence "twenty minus three." But Academician Leonid Skram of the Moscow Archaeological Institute asserts that the depression over the vertical wedges is merely a dent made by the pick of a careless excavator, and the numeral properly reads "23."

Anyhow, Conan learned of the Eye of Erlik when he heard a discussion between an adventuress, Isparana, and her confederate. He invaded the wizard's mansion, but the wizard caught Conan and deprived him of his soul. Conan's soul was imprisoned in a mirror, there to remain until a crowned ruler broke the glass. Hissar Zul thus compelled Conan to follow Isparana and recover the talisman; but when the Cimmerian returned the Eye to Hissar Zul, the ungrateful mage tried to slay him (*Conan and the Sorcerer*).

Conan, his soul still englassed, accepted legitimate employment as bodyguard to a Khaurani noblewoman, Khashtris. This lady set out for Khauran with Conan, another guard, Shubal, and several retainers. When the other servants plotted to rob and murder their employer, Conan and Shubal saved her and escorted her to Khauran. There Conan found the widowed Queen Ialamis being courted by a young nobleman who was not at all what he seemed (*Conan the Mercenary*).

With his soul restored, Conan learned from an Iranistani, Khassek, that the Khan of Zamboula still wanted the Eye of Erlik. In Zamboula, the Turanian governor, Akter Khan, had hired the wizard Zafra, who ensorcelled swords so that they would slay on command. En route, Conan encountered Isparana, with whom he developed a lust-hate relationship. Unaware of the magical swords, Conan continued to Zamboula and delivered the amulet. But the nefarious Zafra convinced the Khan that Conan was dangerous and should be killed on general principles (*Conan: The Sword of Skelos*).

Conan had enjoyed his taste of Hyborian-Age intrigue. It became clear that there was no basic difference between the opportunities in the palace and those in the Rats' Den, whereas the pickings were far better in high places. Besides, he wearied of the furtive, squalid life of a thief.

He was not, however, yet committed to a strictly law-abiding life. When unemployed, he took time out for a venture in smuggling. An attempt to poison him sent him to Vendhya, a land of wealth and squalor, philosophy and fanatacism, idealism and treachery (*Conan the Victorious*).

Soon after, Conan turned up in the Turanian seaport of Aghrapur. A new cult had established headquarters there under the warlock Jhandar, who needed victims to be drained of blood and reanimated as servants. Conan refused the offer of a former fellow thief, Emilio, to take part in a raid on Jhandar's stronghold to steal a fabulous ruby necklace. A Turanian sergeant, Akeba, did however persuade Conan to go with him to rescue Akeba's daughter, who had vanished into the cult (*Conan the Unconquered*).

After Jhandar's fall, Akeba urged Conan to take service in the Turanian army. The Cimmerian did not at first find military life congenial, being too self-willed and hot-tempered to easily submit to discipline. Moreover, as he was at this time an indifferent horseman and archer, Conan was relegated to a low-paid irregular unit.

Still, a chance soon arose to show his mettle. King Yildiz launched an expedition against a rebellious satrap. By sorcery, the satrap wiped out the force sent against him. Young Conan alone survived to enter the magic-maddened satrap's city of Yaralet ("The Hand of Nergal").

Returning in triumph to the glittering capital of Aghrapur, Conan gained a place in King Yildiz's guard of honor. At first he endured the gibes of fellow troopers at his clumsy horsemanship and inaccurate archery. But the gibes died away as the other guardsmen discovered Conan's sledge-hammer fists and as his skills improved.

Conan was chosen, along with a Kushite mercenary named Juma, to escort King Yildiz's daughter Zosara to her wedding with Khan Kujula, chief of the Kuigar nomads. In the foothills of the Talakma Mountains, the party was attacked by a strange force of squat, brown, lacquer-armored horsemen. Only Conan, Juma, and the princess survived. They were taken to the subtropical valley of Meru and to the capital, Shamballah, where Conan and Juma were chained to an oar of the Meruvian state galley, about to set forth on a cruise.

On the galley's return to Shamballah, Conan and Juma escaped and made their way into the city. They reached the temple of Yama as the deformed little god-king of Meru was celebrating his marriage to Zosara ("The City of Skulls").

Back at Aghrapur, Conan was promoted to captain. His growing repute as a good man in a tight spot, however, led King Yildiz's generals to pick the barbarian for especially hazardous missions. Once they sent Conan to escort an emissary to the predatory tribesmen of the Khozgari Hills, hoping to dissuade them by bribes and threats from plundering the Turanians of the lowlands. The Khozgarians, respecting only immediate, overwhelming force, attacked the detachment, killing the emissary and all but two of the soldiers, Conan and Jamal.

To assure their safe passage back to civilization, Conan and Jamal captured Shanya, the daughter of the Khozgari chief. Their route led them to a misty highland. Jamal and the horses were slain, and Conan had to battle a horde of hairless apes and invade the stronghold of an ancient, dying race ("The People of the Summit").

Another time, Conan was dispatched thousands of miles eastward, to fabled Khitai, to convey to King Shu of Kusan a letter from King Yildiz proposing a treaty of friendship and trade. The wise old Khitan king sent his visitors back with a letter of acceptance. As a guide, however, the king appointed a foppish little nobleman, Duke Feng, who had entirely different objectives ("The Curse of the Monolith," first published as "Conan and the Cenotaph").

Conan continued in his service in Turan for about two years, traveling widely and learning the elements of organized, civilized warfare. As usual, trouble was his bedfellow. After one of his more unruly adventures, involving the mistress of his superior officer, Conan deserted and headed for Zamora. In Shadizar he heard that the Temple of Zath, the spider god, in the Zamorian city of Yezud, was recruiting soldiers. Hastening to Yezud, Conan found that a Brythunian free company had taken all the available mercenary posts. He became the town's blacksmith because as a boy he had been apprenticed in this trade.

Conan learned from an emissary of King Yildiz, Lord Parvez, that High Priest Feridun was holding Yildiz's favorite wife, Jamilah, in captivity. Parvez hired Conan to abduct Jamilah. Meanwhile Conan had set his heart on the eight huge gems that formed the eyes of an enormous statue of the spider god. As he was loosening the jewels, the approach of priests forced him to flee to a crypt below the naos. The temple dancing girl Rudabeh, with whom Conan was truly in love for the first time in his life, descended into the crypt to warn him of the doom awaiting him there (*Conan and the Spider God*).

Conan next rode off to Shadizar to track down a rumor of treasure. He obtained a map showing the location of a ruby-studded golden idol in the Kezankian Mountains; but thieves stole his map. Conan, pursuing them, had a brush with Kezankian hillmen and had to join forces with the very rogues he was tracking. He found the treasure, only to lose it under strange circumstances ("The Bloodstained God").

Fed up with magic, Conan headed for the Cimmerian hills. After a time in the simple, routine life of his native village, however, he grew restless enough to join his old friends, the Æsir, in a raid into Vanaheim. In a bitter struggle on the snow-covered plain, both forces were wiped out— all but Conan, who wandered off to a strange encounter with the legendary Atali, daughter of the frost giant Ymir ("The Frost Giant's Daughter").

Haunted by Atali's icy beauty, Conan headed back toward the South, where, despite his often-voiced scorn of civilization, the golden spires of teeming cities beckoned. In the Eiglophian Mountains, Conan rescued a young woman from cannibals, but through overconfidence lost her to the dreaded monster that haunted glaciers ("The Lair of the Ice Worm").

Conan then returned to the Hyborian lands, which include Aquilonia, Argos, Brythunia, Corinthia, Koth, Nemedia, Ophir, and Zingara. These countries were named for the Hyborian peoples who, as barbarians, had 3,000 years earlier conquered the empire of Acheron and built civilized realms on its ruins.

In Belverus, the capital of Nemedia, the ambitious Lord Albanus dabbled in sorcery to usurp the throne of King Garian. To Belverus came Conan, seeking a patron with money to enable him to hire his own free company. Albanus gave a magical sword to a confederate, Lord Melius, who went mad and attacked people in the street until killed. As he picked up the ensorcelled sword, Conan was accosted by Hordo, a one-eyed thief and smuggler whom he had known as Karela's lieutenant.

Conan sold the magical sword, hired his own free company, and taught his men mounted archery. Then he persuaded King Garian to hire him. But Albanus had made a man of clay and by his sorcery given it the exact appearance of the king. Then he imprisoned the king, substituted his golem, and framed Conan for murder (*Conan the Defender*).

Conan next brought his free company to Ianthe, capital of Ophir. There the Lady Synelle, a platinum-blonde sorceress, wished to bring to life the demon-god Al'Kirr. Conan bought a statuette of this demon-god and soon found that various parties were trying to steal it from him. He and his company took service under Synelle, not knowing her plans.

Then the bandette Karela reappeared and, as usual, tried to murder Conan. Synelle hired her to steal the statuette, which the witch needed for her sorcery. She also planned to sacrifice Karela (*Conan the Triumphant*).

Conan went on to Argos; but since that kingdom was at peace, there were no jobs for mercenaries. A misunderstanding with the law compelled Conan to leap to the deck of a ship as it left the pier. This was the merchant galley *Argus*, bound for the coasts of Kush.

A major epoch in Conan's life was about to begin. The *Argus* was taken by Bêlit, the Shemite captain of the pirate ship *Tigress*, whose ruthless black corsairs had made her mistress of the Kushite littoral. Conan won both Bêlit and a partnership in her bloody trade ("Queen of the Black Coast," Chapter 1).

Years before, Bêlit, daughter of a Shemite trader, had been abducted with her brother Jehanan by Stygian slavers. Now she asked her lover Conan to try to rescue the youth. The barbarian slipped into Khemi, the Stygian seaport, was captured, but escaped to the eastern end of Stygia, the province of Taia, where a revolt against Stygian oppression was brewing (*Conan the Rebel*).

Conan and Bêlit resumed their piratical careers, preying mainly on Stygian vessels. Then an ill fate took them up the black Zarkheba River to the lost city of an ancient winged race ("Queen of the Black Coast," Chapters 2–5).

As Bêlit's burning funeral ship wafted out to sea, a downhearted Conan turned his back on the sea, which he would not follow again for years. He plunged inland and joined the warlike Bamulas, a black tribe whose power swiftly grew under his leadership.

The chief of a neighboring tribe, the Bakalahs, planned a treacherous attack on another neighbor and invited Conan and his Bamulas to take part in the sack and massacre. Conan accepted but, learning that an

Ophirean girl, Livia, was held captive in Bakalah, he out-betrayed the Bakalahs. Livia ran off during the slaughter and wandered into a mysterious valley, where only Conan's timely arrival saved her from being sacrificed to an extraterrestrial being ("The Vale of Lost Women").

Before Conan could build his own black empire, he was thwarted by a succession of natural catastrophes as well as by the intrigues of hostile Bamulas. Forced to flee, he headed north. After a narrow escape from pursuing lions on the veldt, Conan took shelter in a mysterious ruined castle of prehuman origin. He had a brush with Stygian slavers and a malign supernatural entity ("The Castle of Terror").

Continuing on, Conan reached the semicivilized kingdom of Kush. This was the land to which the name "Kush" properly applied; although Conan, like other Northerners, tended to use the term loosely to mean any of the black countries south of Stygia. In Meroê, the capital, Conan rescued from a hostile mob the young Queen of Kush, the arrogant, impulsive, fierce, cruel, and voluptuous Tananda.

Conan became embroiled in a labyrinthine intrigue between Tananda and an ambitious nobleman who commanded a piglike demon. The problem was aggravated by the presence of Diana, a Nemedian slave girl to whom Conan, despite the jealous fury of Tananda, took a fancy. Events culminated in a night of insurrection and slaughter ("The Snout in the Dark").

Dissatisfied with his achievements in the black countries, Conan wandered to the meadowlands of Shem and became a soldier of Akkharia, a Shemite city-state. He joined a band of volunteers to liberate a neighboring city-state; but through the teachery of Othbaal, cousin of the mad King Akhîrom of Pelishtia, the volunteers were destroyed—all but Conan, who survived to track the plotter to Asgalun, the Pelishti capital. There Conan became involved in a polygonal power war among the mad Akhîrom, the treacherous Othbaal, a Stygian witch, and a company of black mercenaries. In the final hurly-burly of sorcery, steel, and blood, Conan grabbed Othbaal's red-haired mistress, Rufia, and galloped north ("Hawks Over Shem").

Conan's movements at this time are uncertain. One tale, sometimes assigned to this period, tells of Conan's service as a mercenary in Zingara. A Ptolemaic papyrus in the British Museum alleges that in Kordava, the capital, a captain in the regular army forced a quarrel on Conan. When Conan killed his assailant, he was condemned to hang. A fellow condemnee, Santiddio, belonged to an underground conspiracy, the White Rose, that hoped to topple King Rimanendo. As other conspirators created a disturbance in the crowd that gathered for the hanging, Conan and Santiddio escaped.

Mordermi, head of an outlaw band allied with the White Rose, enlisted Conan in his movement. The conspiracy was carried on in the Pit, a warren of tunnels beneath the city. When the King sent an army to clean out the Pit, the insurrectionists were saved by Callidos, a Stygian sorcerer. King Rimanendo was slain and Mordermi became king. When he proved as tyrannical as his predecessor, Conan raised another revolt; then, refusing the crown for himself, he departed (*Conan: The Road of Kings*).

This tale involves many questions. If authentic, it may belong in Conan's earlier mercenary period, around the time of *Conan the Defender*. But there is no corroboration in other narratives of the idea that Conan ever visited Zingara before his late thirties, the time of *Conan the Buccaneer*. Moreover, none of the rulers of Zingara mentioned in the papyrus appear on the list of kings of Zingara in the Byzantine manuscript *Hoi Anaktes tês Tzingêras*. Hence some students deem the papyrus either spurious or a case of confusion between Conan and some other hero. Everything else known about Conan indicates that, if he had indeed been offered the Zingaran crown, he would have grabbed it with both hands.

We next hear of Conan after he took service under Amalric of Nemedia, the general of Queen-Regent Yasmela of the little border kingdom of Khoraja. While Yasmela's brother, King Khossus, was a prisoner in Ophir, Yasmela's borders were assailed by the forces of the veiled sorcerer Natohk—actually the 3,000-years-dead Thugra Khotan of the ruined city of Kuthchemes.

Obeying an oracle of Mitra, the supreme Hyborian god, Yasmela made Conan captain-general of Khoraja's army. In this rôle he gave battle to Natohk's hosts and rescued the Queen-Regent from the malignant magic of the undead warlock. Conan won the day—and the Queen ("Black Colossus").

Conan, now in his late twenties, settled down as Khorajan commander-in-chief. But the Queen, whose lover he had expected to be, was too preoccupied with affairs of state to have time for frolics. He even proposed marriage, but she explained that such a union would not be sanctioned by Khorajan law and custom. Yet, if Conan could somehow rescue her brother from imprisonment, she might persuade Khossus to change the law.

Conan set forth with Rhazes, an astrologer, and Fronto, a thief who knew a secret passage into the dungeon where Khossus languished. They rescued the King but found themselves trapped by Kothian troops, since Strabonus of Koth had his own reasons for wanting Khossus.

Having surmounted these perils, Conan found that Khossus, a pompous young ass, would not hear of a foreign barbarian's marrying his sister. Instead, he would marry Yasmela off to a nobleman and find a middle-class bride for Conan. Conan said nothing; but in Argos, as their ship cast off, Conan sprang ashore with most of the gold that Khossus had raised and waved the King an ironic farewell ("Shadows in the Dark").

Now nearly thirty, Conan slipped away to revisit his Cimmerian homeland and avenge himself on the Hyperboreans. His blood brothers among the Cimmerians and the Æsir had won wives and sired sons, some as old and almost as big as Conan had been at the sack of Venarium. But his years of blood and battle had stirred his predatory spirit too strongly for him to follow their example. When traders brought word of new wars, Conan galloped off to the Hyborian lands.

A rebel prince of Koth was fighting to overthrow Strabonus, the penurious ruler of that farstretched nation; and Conan found himself among old companions in the princeling's array, until the rebel made peace with his king. Unemployed again, Conan formed an outlaw band, the Free Companions. This troop gravitated to the steppes west of the Sea of Vilayet, where they joined the ruffianly horde known as the *kozaki.*

Conan soon became the leader of this lawless crew and ravaged the western borders of the Turanian Empire until his old employer, King Yildiz, sent a force under Shah Amurath, who lured the *kozaki* deep into Turan and cut them down.

Slaying Amurath and acquiring the Turanian's captive, Princess Olivia of Ophir, Conan rowed out into the Vilayet Sea in a small boat. He and Olivia took refuge on an island, where they found a ruined greenstone city, in which stood strange iron statues. The shadows cast by the moonlight proved as dangerous as the giant carnivorous ape that ranged the isle, or the pirate crew that landed for rest and recreation ("Shadows in the Moonlight").

Conan seized command of the pirates that ravaged the Sea of Vilayet. As chieftain of this mongrel Red Brotherhood, Conan was more than ever a thorn in King Yildiz's flesh. That mild monarch, instead of strangling his brother Teyaspa in the normal Turanian manner, had cooped him up in a castle in the Colchian Mountains. Yildiz now sent his General Artaban to destroy the pirate stronghold at the mouth of the Zaporoska River; but the general became the harried instead of the harrier. Retreating inland, Artaban stumbled upon Teyaspa's whereabouts; and the final conflict involved Conan's outlaws, Artaban's Turanians, and a brood of vampires ("The Road of the Eagles").

Deserted by his sea rovers, Conan appropriated a stallion and headed back to the steppes. Yezdigerd, now on the throne of Turan, proved a far more astute and energetic ruler than his sire. He embarked on a program of imperial conquest.

Conan went to the small border kingdom of Khauran, where he won command of the royal guard of Queen Taramis. This queen had a twin sister, Salome, born a witch and reared by the yellow sorcerers of Khitai. She allied herself with the adventurer Constantius of Koth and planned by imprisoning the Queen to rule in her stead. Conan, who perceived the deception, was trapped and crucified. Cut down by the chieftain Olgerd Vladislav, the Cimmerian was carried off to a Zuagir camp in the desert. Conan waited for his wounds to heal, then applied his daring and ruthlessness to win his place as Olgerd's lieutenant.

When Salome and Constantius began a reign of terror in Khauran, Conan led his Zuagirs against the Khauranian capital. Soon Constantius hung from the cross to which he had nailed Conan, and Conan rode off smiling, to lead his Zuagirs on raids against the Turanians ("A Witch Shall Be Born").

Conan, about thirty and at the height of his physical powers, spent nearly two years with the desert Shemites, first as Olgerd's lieutenant and then, having ousted Olgerd, as sole chief. The circumstances of his leaving the Zuagirs were recently disclosed by a silken scroll in Old Tibetan, spirited out of Tibet by a refugee. This document is now with the Oriental Institute in Chicago.

The energetic King Yezdigerd sent soldiers to trap Conan and his troop. Because of a Zamorian traitor in Conan's ranks, the ambush nearly succeeded. To avenge the betrayal, Conan led his band in pursuit of the Zamorian. When his men deserted, Conan pressed on alone until, near death, he was rescued by Enosh, a chieftain of the isolated desert town of Akhlat.

Akhlat suffered under the rule of a demon in the form of a woman, who fed on the life force of living things. Conan, Enosh informed him, was their prophesied liberator. After it was over, Conan was invited to settle in Akhlat; but, knowing himself ill-suited to a life of humdrum respectability, he instead headed southwest to Zamboula with the horse and money of Vardanes the Zamorian ("Black Tears").

In one colossal debauch, Conan dissipated the fortune he had brought to Zamboula, a Turanian outpost. There lurked the sinister priest of Hanuman, Totrasmek, who sought a famous jewel, the Star of Khorala, for which the Queen of Ophir was said to have offered a roomful of gold. In the ensuing imbroglio, Conan acquired the Star of Khorala and rode westward ("Shadows of Zamboula").

The medieval monkish manuscript *De sidere choralae*, rescued from the bombed ruins of Monte Cassino, continues the tale. Conan reached the capital of Ophir to find that the effeminate Moranthes II, himself under the thumb of the sinister Count Rigello, kept his queen, Marala, under lock and key. Conan scaled the wall of Moranthes's castle and fetched Marala out. Rigello pursued the fugitives nearly to the Aquilonian border, where the Star of Khorala showed its power in an unexpected way ("The Star of Khorala").

Hearing that the *kozaki* had regained their vigor, Conan returned with horse and sword to the harrying of Turan. Although the now-famous northlander arrived all but empty-handed, contingents of the *kozaki* and the Vilayet pirates soon began operating under his command.

Yezdigerd sent Jehungir Agha to entrap the barbarian on the island of Xapur. Coming early to the ambush, Conan found the island's ancient fortress-palace of Dagon restored by magic, and in it the city's malevolent god, in the form of a giant of living iron ("The Devil in Iron").

After escaping from Xapur, Conan built his *kozaki* and pirate raiders into such a formidable threat that King Yezdigerd devoted all his forces to their destruction. After a devastating defeat, the *kozaki* scattered, and Conan retreated southward to take service in the light cavalry of Kobad Shah, King of Iranistan.

Conan got himself into Kobad Shah's bad graces and had to ride for the hills. He found a conspiracy brewing in Yanaidar, the fortress-city of the Hidden Ones. The Sons of Yezm were trying to revive an ancient cult and unite the surviving devotees of the old gods in order to rule the world. The adventure ended with the rout of the contending forces by the gray ghouls of Yanaidar, and Conan rode eastward ("The Flame Knife").

Conan reappeared in the Himelian Mountains, on the northwest frontier of Vendhya, as a war chief of the savage Afghuli tribesmen. Now in his early thirties, the warlike barbarian was known and feared throughout the world of the Hyborian Age.

No man to be bothered with niceties, Yezdigerd employed the magic of the wizard Khemsa, an adept of the dreaded Black Circle, to remove the Vendhyan king from his path. The dead king's sister, the Devi Yasmina, set out to avenge him but was captured by Conan. Conan and his captive pursued the sorcerous Khemsa, only to see him slain by the magic of the Seers of Yimsha, who also abducted Yasmina ("The People of the Black Circle").

When Conan's plans for welding the hill tribes into a single power failed, Conan, hearing of wars in the West, rode thither. Almuric, a prince of Koth, had rebelled against the hated Strabonus. While Conan joined Almuric's bristling host, Strabonus's fellow kings came to that monarch's aid. Almuric's motley horde was driven south, to be annihilated at last by combined Stygian and Kushite forces.

Escaping into the desert, Conan and the camp follower Natala came to age-old Xuthal, a phantom city of living dead men and their creeping shadow-god, Thog. The Stygian woman Thalis, the effective ruler of Xuthal, double-crossed Conan once too often ("The Slithering Shadow").

Conan beat his way back to the Hyborian lands. Seeking further employment, he joined the mercenary army that a Zingaran, Prince Zapayo da Kova, was raising for Argos. It was planned that Koth should invade Stygia from the north, while the Argosseans approached the realm from the south by sea. Koth, however, made a separate peace with Stygia, leaving Conan's army of mercenaries trapped in the Stygian deserts.

Conan fled with Amalric, a young Aquilonian soldier. Soon Conan was captured by nomads, while Amalric escaped. When Amalric caught up again with Conan, Amalric had with him the girl Lissa, whom he had saved from the cannibal god of her native city. Conan had meanwhile become commander of the cavalry of the city of Tombalku. Two kings ruled Tombalku: the Negro Sakumbe and the mixed-blood Zehbeh. When Zehbeh and his faction were driven out, Sakumbe made Conan his co-king. But then the wizard Askia slew Sakumbe by magic. Conan, having avenged his black friend, escaped with Amalric and Lissa ("Drums of Tombalku").

Conan beat his way to the coast, where he joined the Barachan pirates. He was now about thirty-five. As second mate of the *Hawk*, he landed on the island of the Stygian sorcerer Siptah, said to have a magical jewel of fabulous properties.

Siptah dwelt in a cylindrical tower without doors or windows, attended by a winged demon. Conan smoked the unearthly being out but was carried off in its talons to the top of the tower. Inside the tower Conan found the wizard long dead; but the magical gem proved of unexpected help in coping with the demon ("The Gem in the Tower").

Conan remained about two years with the Barachans, according to a set of clay tablets in pre-Sumerian cuneiform. Used to the tightly organized armies of the Hyborian kingdoms, Conan found the organization of the Barachan bands too loose and anarchic to afford an opportunity to rise to leadership. Slipping out of a tight spot at the pirate rendezvous at Tortage, he found that the only alternative to a cut throat was braving the Western Ocean in a leaky skiff. When the *Wastrel*, the ship of the buccaneer Zaporavo, came in sight, Conan climbed aboard.

The Cimmerian soon won the respect of the crew and the enmity of its captain, whose Kordavan mistress, the sleek Sancha, cast too friendly an eye on the black-maned giant. Zaporavo drove his ship westward to an uncharted island, where Conan forced a duel on the captain and killed him, while Sancha was carried off by strange black beings to a living pool worshiped by these entities ("The Pool of the Black Ones").

Conan persuaded the officials at Kordava to transfer Zaporavo's privateering license to him, whereupon he spent about two years in this authorized piracy. As usual, plots were brewing against the Zingaran monarchy. King Ferdrugo was old and apparently failing, with no successor but his nubile daughter Chabela. Duke Villagro enlisted the Stygian super-sorcerer Thoth-Amon, the High Priest of Set, in a plot to obtain Chabela as his bride. Suspicious, the princess took the royal yacht down the coast to consult her uncle. A privateer in league with Villagro captured the yacht and abducted the girl. Chabela escaped and met Conan, who obtained the magical Cobra Crown, also sought by Thoth-Amon.

A storm drove Conan's ship to the coast of Kush, where Conan was confronted by black warriors headed by his old comrade-in-arms, Juma. While the chief welcomed the privateers, a tribesman stole the Cobra Crown. Conan set off in pursuit, with Princess Chabela following him. Both were captured by slavers and sold to the black Queen of the Amazons. The Queen made Chabela her slave and Conan her fancy man. Then, jealous of Chabela, she flogged the girl, imprisoned Conan, and condemned both to be devoured by a man-eating tree (*Conan the Buccaneer*).

Having rescued the Zingaran princess, Conan shrugged off hints of marriage and returned to privateering. But other Zingarans, jealous, brought him down off the coast of Shem. Escaping inland, Conan joined the Free Companions, a mercenary company. Instead of rich plunder, however, he found himself in dull guard duty on the black frontier of Stygia, where the wine was sour and the pickings poor.

Conan's boredom ended with the appearance of the pirette, Valeria of the Red Brotherhood. When she left the camp, he followed her south. The pair took refuge in a city occupied by the feuding clans of Xotalanc and Tecuhltli. Siding with the latter, the two northerners soon found themselves in trouble with that clan's leader, the ageless witch Tascela ("Red Nails").

Conan's amour with Valeria, however hot at the start, did not last long. Valeria returned to the sea; Conan tried his luck once more in the black kingdoms. Hearing of the "Teeth of Gwahlur," a cache of priceless jewels hidden in Keshan, he sold his services to its irascible king to train the Keshani army.

Thutmekri, the Stygian emissary of the twin kings of Zembabwei, also had designs on the jewels. The Cimmerian, outmatched in intrigue, made tracks for the valley where the ruins of Alkmeenon and its treasure lay hidden. In a wild adventure with the undead goddess Yelaya, the Corinthian girl Muriela, the black priests headed by Gorulga, and the grim gray servants of the long-dead Bît-Yakin, Conan kept his head but lost his loot. ("Jewels of Gwahlur").

Heading for Punt with Muriela, Conan embarked on a scheme to relieve the worshipers of an ivory goddess of their abundant gold. Learning that Thutmekri had preceded him and had already poisoned King Lalibeha's mind against him, Conan and his companion took refuge in the temple of the goddess Nebethet.

When the King, Thutmekri, and High Priest Zaramba arrived at the temple, Conan staged a charade wherein Muriela spoke with the voice of the goddess. The results surprised all, including Conan ("The Ivory Goddess").

In Zembabwei, the city of the twin kings, Conan joined a trading caravan that he squired northward along the desert borders, bringing it safely into Shem. Now in his late thirties, the restless adventurer heard that the Aquilonians were spreading westward into the Pictish wilderness. So thither, seeking work for his sword, went Conan. He enrolled as a scout at Fort Tuscelan, where a fierce war raged with the Picts.

In the forests across the river, the wizard Zogar Sag was gathering his swamp demons to aid the Picts. While Conan failed to prevent the destruction of Fort Tuscelan, he managed to warn settlers around Velitrium and to cause the death of Zogar Sag ("Beyond the Black River").

Conan rose rapidly in the Aquilonian service. As captain, his company was once defeated by the machinations of a traitorous superior. Learning that this officer, Viscount Lucian, was about to betray the province to the Picts, Conan exposed the traitor and routed the Picts ("Moon of Blood").

Promoted to general, Conan defeated the Picts in a great battle at Velitrium and was called back to the capital, Tarantia, to receive the nation's accolades. Then, having roused the suspicions of the depraved and foolish King Numedides, he was drugged and chained in the Ivory Tower under sentence of death.

The barbarian, however, had friends as well as foes. Soon he was spirited out of prison and turned loose with horse and sword. He struck out across the dank forests of Pictland toward the distant sea. In the forest, the Cimmerian came upon a cavern in which lay the corpse and the demon-guarded treasure of the pirate Tranicos. From the west, others—a Zingaran count and two bands of pirates—were hunting the same fortune: a Zingaran refugee count and two bands of pirates, while the Stygian sorcerer Thoth-Amon took a hand in the game ("The Treasure of Tranicos").

Rescued by an Aquilonian galley, Conan was chosen to lead a revolt against Numedides. While the revolution stormed along, civil war raged on the Pictish frontier. Lord Valerian, a partisan of Numedides, schemed to bring the Picts down on the town of Schohira. A scout, Gault Hager's son, undertook to upset this scheme by killing the Pictish wizard ("Wolves Beyond the Border").

Storming the capital city and slaying Numedides on the steps of his throne—which he promptly took for his own—Conan, now in his early forties, found himself ruler of the greatest Hyborian nation (*Conan the Liberator*).

A king's life, however, proved no bed of houris. Within a year, an exiled count had gathered a group of plotters to oust the barbarian from the throne. Conan might have lost crown and head but for the timely intervention of the long-dead sage Epimitreus ("The Phoenix of the Sword").

No sooner had the mutterings of revolt died down than Conan was treacherously captured by the kings of Ophir and Koth. He was imprisoned in the tower of the wizard Tsotha-lanti in the Kothian capital. Conan escaped with the help of a fellow prisoner, who was Tsotha-lanti's wizardly rival Pelias. By Pelias's magic, Conan was whisked to Tarantia in time to slay a pretender and to lead an army against his treacherous fellow kings ("The Scarlet Citadel").

For nearly two years, Aquilonia thrived under Conan's firm but tolerant rule. The lawless, hard-bitten adventurer of former years had, through force of circumstance, matured into an able and responsible statesman. But a plot was brewing in neighboring Nemedia to destroy the King of Aquilonia by sorcery from an elder day.

Conan, about forty-five, showed few signs of age save a network of scars on his mighty frame and a more cautious approach to wine, women and bloodshed. Although he kept a harem of luscious concubines, he had never taken an official queen; hence he had no legitimate son to inherit the throne, a fact whereof his ememies sought to take advantage.

The plotters resurrected Xaltotun, the greatest sorcerer of the ancient empire of Acheron, which fell before the Hyborian savages 3,000 years earlier. By Xaltotun's magic, the King of Nemedia was slain and replaced by his brother Tarascus. Black sorcery defeated Conan's army; Conan was imprisoned, and the exile Valerius took his throne.

Escaping from a dungeon with the aid of the harem girl Zenobia, Conan returned to Aquilonia to rally his loyal forces against Valerius. From the priests of Asura, he learned that Xaltotun's power could be broken only by means of a strange jewel, the "Heart of Ahriman." The trail of the jewel led to a pyramid in the Stygian desert outside black-walled Khemi. Winning the Heart of Ahriman, Conan returned to face his foes (*Conan the Conqueror*, originally published as *The Hour of the Dragon*).

After regaining his kingdom, Conan made Zenobia his queen. But, at the ball celebrating her elevation, the Queen was borne off by a demon sent by the Khitan sorcerer Yah Chieng. Conan's quest for his bride carried him across the known world, meeting old friends and foes. In purple-towered Paikang, with the help of a magical ring, he freed Zenobia and slew the wizard (*Conan the Avenger*, originally published as *The Return of Conan*).

Home again, the way grew smoother. Zenobia gave him heirs: a son named Conan but commonly called Conn, another son called Taurus, and a daughter. When Conn was twelve, his father took him on a hunting trip to Gunderland. Conan was now in his late fifties. His sword arm was a little slower than in his youth, and his black mane and the fierce mustache of his later years were traced with gray; but his strength still surpassed that of two ordinary men.

When Conn was lured away by the Witchmen of Hyperborea, who demanded that Conan come to their stronghold alone, Conan went. He found Louhi, the High Priestess of the Witchmen, in conference with three others of the world's leading sorcerers: Troth-Amon of Stygia; the god-king of Kambuja; and the black lord of Zembabwei. In the ensuing holocaust, Louhi and the Kambujan perished, while Thoth-Amon and the other sorcerer vanished by magic ("The Witch of the Mists").

Old King Ferdrugo of Zingara had died, and his throne remained vacant as the nobles intrigued over the succession. Duke Pantho of Guarralid invaded Poitain, in southern Aquilonia. Conan, suspecting sorcery, crushed the invaders. Learning that Thoth-Amon was behind Pantho's madness, Conan set out with his army to settle matters with the Stygian. He pursued his foe to Thoth-Amon's stronghold in Stygia ("Black Sphinx of Nebthu"), to Zembabwei ("Red Moon of Zembabwei"), and to the last realm of the serpent folk in the far south ("Shadows in the Skull").

For several years, Conan's rule was peaceful. But time did that which no combination of foes had been able to do. The Cimmerian's skin became wrinkled and his hair gray; old wounds ached in damp weather. Conan's beloved consort Zenobia died giving birth to their second daughter.

Then catastrophe shattered King Conan's mood of half-resigned discontent. Supernatural entities, the Red Shadows, began seizing and carrying off his subjects. Conan was baffled until in a dream he again visited the sage Epimitreus. He was told to abdicate in favor of Prince Conn and set out across the Western Ocean.

Conan discovered that the Red Shadows had been sent by the priest-wizards of Antillia, a chain of islands in the western part of the ocean, whither the survivors of Atlantis had fled 8,000 years before. These priests offered human sacrifices to their devil-god Xotli on such a scale that their own population faced extermination.

In Antillia, Conan's ship was taken, but he escaped into the city of Ptahuacan. After conflicts with giant rats and dragons, he emerged atop the sacrificial pyramid just as his crewmen were about to be sacrificed. Supernatural conflict, revolution, and seismic catastrophe ensued. In the end, Conan sailed off to explore the continents to the west (*Conan of the Isles*).

Whether he died there, or whether there is truth in the tale that he strode out of the West to stand at his son's side in a final battle against Aquilonia's foes, will be revealed only to him who looks, as Kull of Valusia once did, into the mystic mirrors of Tuzun Thune.

L. Sprague de Camp
Villanova, Pennsylvania
May 1984

Conan
the
Destroyer

1

The bloody sun baked the Zamoran plain, and baked, too, the procession that made its way across those rocky flats and rolling hills. The riders were armored in ebon breastplates and nasaled helms. Sable was the chain-mail that covered their arms, and sable the greaves that rose from booted feet to dark-breeched knees. No accoutrement of theirs but was the hue of deepest night. Their horses, too, were sheathed in black iron, chanfons and crinets covering heads and necks, peytrals protecting their chests. A long, curved sword hung at each warriors' hip, and spike-headed maces swung at every high-pommeled saddle, but the hands that should have grasped lances held instead wooden clubs and long staves. Nets did they carry, as well, thick woven and weighted, stout enough to hold tigers.

Last in the procession was a high-wheeled cart, drawn by two horses, and on it was bound a large cage of iron bars as thick as a man's wrist. The cart's driver worked his long whip ceaselessly across the backs of his team, for despite the heat of the sun and the weight of their armor the column kept a rapid pace, and it would be more than his life was worth did he delay it a moment in reaching its goal.

He who led the column was a head taller than any other man there, and broader of shoulder by more than a handspan. He was marked as a warrior of note, a man of position, by the intricate gold chasing of his gleaming sable breastplate, elaborate arabesques surrounding a leaping lion. It was a symbol he had chosen many years before, and many said he fought with the ferocity of that beast. Thin, age-whitened scars, one across the bridge of his broad nose and another running from the corner of his left eye to the point of his chin, proclaimed him no newcomer to the profession of arms. Now those scars were all but hidden under dust that clung to the sweat pouring from his face.

"Useless," he muttered beneath his breath. "No Erlik-accursed use at all."

"There is always a use in what I do, Bombatta."

The big man stiffened as one of the riders, masked in soft black leather as well as helmeted, galloped up beside him. He had not thought his voice would carry further than his own ears.

"I see no need," he began, but the other cut him off with a voice distorted by the mask, yet carrying the note of command.

"What must be done, must be done as it is written in the Scrolls of Skelos. Exactly as it is written, Bombatta."

"As you command," he replied grudgingly, "so do I obey."

"Of course, Bombatta. But I hear a question unspoken. Speak it." The tall warrior hesitated. "Speak it, Bombatta. I command you."

"What we now seek," Bombatta said slowly, "or rather where to seek . . . surely *that* cannot be in the scrolls."

The black-masked rider's laugh was muffled behind the dark leather. Bombatta colored at the mocking tone.

"Ah, Bombatta. Think you my powers are limited to knowledge of the Scrolls? Do you think I know only what is written there?"

"No." His reply was as curt as he dared make it.

"Then obey me, Bombatta. Obey, and trust that we will find what we seek."

"As you command, so do I obey."

The huge warrior dug his heels into the flanks of his mount, careless of the men behind who must keep up. More speed, he knew, would be taken as a show of obedience, a sign of trust in the commands he had been given. Let the others mutter angrily in their sweat. He kicked his horse again, ignoring the lather that was beginning to fleck the animal's neck. His doubts were unshaken, but he had been too long in climbing to his present post to lose it now, not if he had to gallop men and horses alike to their deaths.

The plains of Zamora oft saw unusual sights, so often that few were any longer truly considered unusual by those who witnessed them. Madness, bandits and holy vows had at different times produced a man in the robes of a noble who scattered gold coins to the sands, a column of naked men mounted backwards on their horses, and a procession of maidens, wearing naught but blue paint from forehead to toes, who danced and chanted their way through blistering heat. And any who sought to link event with cause would find surprises.

There had been many others, some stranger still, yet few had seemed odder than the two men laboring far from any city or village, beneath the blazing sun in a hollow at the foot of a rock-strewn hill. Their hobbled horses cropped sparse, tough grass nearby.

The first man was a tall, heavily-muscled youth. Massive arms straining, he lifted a thick, flat slab of rock, as long as a man was tall, atop four gray boulders he had rolled together. To level the slab he pushed fist-sized stones beneath it. About his neck, on a rawhide thong, hung an amulet of gold in the shape of a dragon.

The sapphire-eyed young man seemed more a warrior than a builder. A broadsword of ancient pattern hung at his belt, and both its hilt and that of his dagger showed the wear of frequent use. His face, a square-cut black mane held back from it by a leather cord, showed only a lack of years to the casual observer. Those who looked deeply, however, could see several ordinary lifetimes' experience written there, lifetimes of blood and steel.

The sky-eyed youth's companion was his antithesis both physically and in occupation. Short, wiry and black-eyed, with greasy black hair tied behind his neck to fall below his shoulders, the second man stood to his thighs in a narrow pit, laboring to deepen it with a broken-handled shovel. Two bulging leather sacks sat on the ground beside the hole. Continually the wiry fellow dashed sweat from his eyes and cursed work of a sort he was unused to, but whenever his gaze fell on those sacks he set to again with a will.

Finally, though, he tossed the broken shovel aside. "It's deep enough, eh, Conan?"

The muscular youth did not hear. He frowned at the thing he had built. It was an altar, something with which he had little experience. But in the harsh mountain wastes of his native Cimmeria he had learned that debts must be repaid, whatever the cost, whatever the difficulty.

"Conan, is it deep enough?"

The Cimmerian eyed his companion grimly. "If you hadn't opened your mouth at the wrong time, Malak, we'd not have to bury the gems. Amphrates wouldn't know who stole his jewels, the City Guard wouldn't know who stole the jewels, and we could be sitting in Abuletes' tavern drinking wine, with dancing girls on our knees, instead of sweating out on the plains. Dig it deeper."

"I did not mean to shout your name," Malak grumbled. He fumbled open one of the leather bags and scooped out a handful of sapphires and rubies, emeralds and opals. Green glittered in his eyes as he poured the polished stones back again, a sparkling stream of blue and crimson and green and gold. With a regretful sigh he tugged the drawstring tight. "I just didn't think he would have so much. I was surprised. I did not do it apurpose."

"Dig, Malak," Conan said, looking now at the altar rather than the other man.

The Cimmerian closed his big hand around the golden amulet. Valeria had given it to him, and it seemed to him he felt her near him when he touched it. Valeria, lover, warrior and thief all in one bundle of lithe golden-haired beauty. Then she died, ripping the joy from his life. He had seen her die. But as well he had seen her return, come again to fight at his side, to save his life. Debts must be repaid.

Malak had taken up the broken-handled shovel again, but instead of digging he eyed the altar. "I did not think you believed in the gods, Cimmerian. I've never seen you pray."

"The god of my land is Crom," Conan replied, "the Dark Lord of the Mound. At birth he gives a man life and will, and never another gift. He will not pay heed to votive offerings, nor listen to prayers or pleadings. What a man does with the gifts Crom has given him are his own affair."

"But the altar?" Malak prompted when he fell silent.

"This is a different land, with different gods. They are not my gods, but Valeria believed." Frowning, Conan released the dragon amulet. "Mayhap her gods listen, as the priests claim they do. Perhaps I can do something to help her fate with them."

"Who knows what will sway gods," Malak said, shrugging. The wiry thief lifted himself from the hole and sat crosslegged beside the leather sacks. "Even the priests do not agree, so how can you—" The clatter of galloping hooves from beyond the hill cut off his words.

With a yelp Malak snatched for the leather sacks. In an instant he had thrust several of the gems into his mouth—his face contorted painfully as he swallowed—and tossed the sacks into the hole. Desperately he began shoveling dirt back in, kicking in stones, anything to fill it before the riders arrived.

Conan put a hand to the leather-wrapped hilt of his broadsword and waited calmly, cool blue eyes watching the hill for the first of the newcomers. They could be anyone, he told himself. They could be concerned with matters other than Malak and himself. But he did not believe it.

11

As a lone horseman in black nasaled helm and gold-chased ebon breastplate crested the hill, Malak laughed shakily. "One man. He may be big, but we can handle one man, if he tries—"

"I heard more than a single horse," Conan said.

"Erlik take them," Malak groaned. Jamming the broken-handled shovel under the edge of a small boulder, he levered the stone toward the hole. "Our horses," he panted. "We can outrun them." The boulder toppled into the narrow pit, plugging it.

Conan snorted, but gave no other answer. The watcher's horse was weighed down with as much armor as its rider, it was true. The two of them would gain a lead, but a short-lived one, he knew. Their mounts were the sort available on short notice to men who had obvious need of leaving Shadizar quickly, though each had cost as much in gems as a king's charger. At a gallop the animals would founder inside half a league, leaving them afoot to be run down at their pursuer's leisure.

The watcher had stopped on the crest of the hill.

"What does he wait for?" Malak demanded, tugging two daggers from his belt. "If we are to die, I see no reason—"

Abruptly the black-armored warrior raised his arm, moved it from side to side. Over the hilltop burst more than fourscore yelling armored riders, an ebon wave that split to either side of the man who still sat with upraised arm. At a dead gallop the warriors roared to the right and left, sweeping out to encircle Conan and Malak at a distance of three hundred paces.

"You would think we were an army," Conan said. "Someone thinks we are dangerous, Malak."

"So many," Malak moaned, and cast a regretful glance at their horses, now whinnying fretfully and dancing as if they wished to run. He seemed ready to run with them. "The gold for hiring these would keep a man in

339

luxury for months. Who would have thought Amphrates would become so angry?"

"Perhaps he did not like having his gems stolen," Conan said drily.

"We did not take *all* that he had," the wiry thief muttered. "He could be grateful that something was left. He could spend a coin or two for incense in the temples, to thank the gods for what remained. He did not have to . . ."

The Cimmerian was barely aware of his companion's tirade. He had learned long since to listen selectively to the small man, simply no longer hearing Malak's moans of what could have been or should have been, but obviously was not.

At the moment the steely-eyed northlander was intent on four of the encircling warriors, four men who had ridden together and now fumbled with a long bundle one of them bore before his saddle. He glanced back at the hilltop. Another rider, masked, now sat beside the first, watching what occurred below.

Abruptly the tall watcher raised a curled brass horn, like the hunting horns used by nobles. A loud note rang from the hilltop, and the four who had worked at the bundle suddenly unfurled it between them and broke into a gallop, straight for the two men afoot. Four others galloped out to join them.

The big Cimmerian's frown deepened. It was a net they held, and the outriders bore long clubs, as if they would cut off a quarry that sought to evade capture.

Malak took two nervous steps toward the horses.

"Wait." Despite Conan's youth there was a note of command in his voice that stopped the smaller man. "Wait for them, or we are meat for the taking." Malak nodded grimly and tightened his grip on his daggers.

Closer the horsemen thundered. A hundred paces. Fifty. Ten. Shouts of triumph broke from the charging warriors.

"Now," Conan said, and leaped . . . toward the net. Groaning, Malak followed.

As he leaped, the Cimmerian's broadsword finally left its worn sha-green scabbard. Driven by massive shoulders the blade sheared through a corner of the net. The rider who had held that corner galloped on with a startled yell, holding only a fragment of thick rope. The warrior following behind dropped his reins and drew the curved tulwar at his belt. Conan ducked under the slash, then thrust up, his steel sliding under the black breast-plate. The impaled warrior seem to leap backwards from the saddle of his charging horse.

Even as the man fell, Conan tugged free his bloodied steel and spun, warned by a primitive instinct for danger. The face looming above him was twisted with rage beneath the dark helmet's rim, contorted as if the man wished he swung a sword rather than a club. Yet that thick billet, longer than a man's arm, could crack a skull if landed hard enough, and the club-wielder swung with a will. The Cimmerian's blade flashed upward, through flesh and bone. Club and still-clutching hand sailed through the air. As the shrieking man grabbed his scarlet-fountaining wrist with his remaining hand, his horse bolted, carrying him away. Hastily Conan sought for a new enemy.

Malak was grappling with one of the net-carriers, attempting to pull him from the saddle. One of the small thief's daggers darted into the gap between helmet and breastplate. With a gurgling scream the horseman toppled, carrying Malak to the ground with him. The dark-eyed thief bounded quickly to his feet, daggers at the ready. The other man did not move.

For a frozen instant Conan and his companion faced the five remaining of their attackers. The net lay abandoned on the ground, now. The two who had helped bear the net rested their hands on their sword hilts. Those with clubs seemed more hesitant. Suddenly one man threw down his club; before his sword was half drawn another blast of the horn rang out. The sword was resheathed with an oath, and all five galloped back toward the encircling line.

Malak licked his lips. "Why are they trying to capture us? I don't understand."

"Perhaps Amphrates is even madder than we thought," Conan replied grimly. "Perhaps he wants to see how much the Torturers' Guild can make us scream before we die."

"Mitra!" Malak breathed. "Why did you have to tell me something like that?"

Conan shrugged. "You asked." Again the horn sounded. "Get ready. They're coming again."

Again four riders bore the net spread between them, but this time the outriders brought their number up to a full score. As the horsemen pounded toward them, Conan motioned unobtrusively; Malak shrugged and nodded. The two men stood, waiting, as they had before. Closer the net came, and closer. Only three strides from the men on the ground, half the outriders swung in close to the net. This time there would be no unimpeded cutting of the net or killing of its bearers.

As the outriders closed with the net, Conan leaped to the left and Malak to the right. Netbearers and outriders galloped between them, cursing and trying to turn their horses. A club swung at Conan's head. Its wielder grunted in surprise when his wrist slapped into the Cimmerian's palm, yelled in disbelief as the massive youth jerked him from the saddle.

Conan's fisted hilt struck once, spraying blood and teeth, and his opponent slumped.

Drumming hooves alerted him to an attacker coming from behind. His hand closed on the long club as it fell from nerveless fingers, and he rose, spinning into a backhand blow with the staff. The thick length of wood cracked as it slammed across the midsection of a charging horseman. Eyes bulging and air rushing from him in one long strangled gasp, the rider bent as if seeking to fold himself around the club, and his horse galloped out from under him.

"Conan!"

Before his last opponent had struck the ground Conan was seeking the reason for Malak's cry. Two of the black-armored warriors were leaning from their saddles to club at a bloody, writhing shape on the ground.

With a wild yell the Cimmerian was on them, ensanguined steel slashing. Two corpses fell away from him as he dragged the small thief to his feet, dazed of eye and with scarlet rivulets streaming down his face. The net-bearers were coming once more, he saw, and Malak was barely able to stand, certainly in no shape to fight.

Muscles bulging in a massive shoulder and arm, Conan hurled his companion aside and leaped for the net. His hand closed on it, and he heaved. A surprised warrior was catapulted from his saddle to land atop the grid of thick ropes, tangling in it as he rolled. A club smashed into the Cimmerian's back, staggering him, but he whirled, roaring, and drove his blade under iron breastplate.

There was no hope of escape. He knew that. Too many men crowded around him, striking with staves and clubs. Dust pounded up by dancing hooves coated his sweated body. The coppery stench of blood was in his nostrils, and his ears were filled with the din of men shouting their rage that he would not fall. Soon he must go down, but he would not surrender. His blade was a whirlwind of razor steel, encarnadining whatever it touched. By fury alone he hacked a way through the press of mounted men, but the mass swirled and enclosed him again.

Loudly the horn sounded, the brazen note slicing through the tumult. And the men who had crowded so about him drew back. With obvious reluctance they abandoned their silent dead and groaning wounded, galloping back to form once more their circle at three hundred paces' distance.

In wonder Conan watched them go. Blood trickled in the dust on his face, and stained the back and chest of his tunic. Malak was gone, he saw. No, not gone. Captured. Netted, an arm and a leg sticking through the thick mesh, like a pig on its way to market. Regret coursed through the Cimmerian, and a determination not to end so.

Slowly he turned, attempting to keep an eye on all of those about him. Horses wandered riderless between the circle and him. He might seize one of those and fight his way clear, if he was willing to abandon Malak. He made no move toward a horse. Close to him there were bodies, some still, some twitching. A few cried out for succor, or stretched a hand toward the black-armored watchers.

"Come, then!" Conan shouted at the iron circle. "Let us finish it, an you have the stomach!" Here and there a horse moved as if its rider had shifted angrily, but only silence answered him.

The rattle of rocks sliding down the hill announced the arrival of the two who had remained on the hilltop. The big man in the gold-chased armor stopped at ten paces distance from the Cimmerian, but the leather-masked rider halved that before drawing rein. Conan set himself. He could make out little of the one who approached, for the mask covered all but eyes, and a cloak of black wool swathed all else, but if single combat was sought, Conan was ready.

The lone figure's hands rose to remove the nasaled helmet. Then the mask came off, and the Cimmerian gasped despite himself. A woman faced him, dark eyes smouldering above high cheekbones, raven hair pinned in tight coils about her head. Beautiful she was, with the beauty that can only come to the woman who has left girlhood behind, but there was a fierceness to that beauty, in the firm set to her lovely jaw and the penetrating quality of her gaze. Her cloak was thrown back to reveal riding breeches and tunic of sable silk, clinging to every curve of full breast and rounded thigh. Conan drew a deep breath. Of all women, he had never expected to be confronted by this one.

"You are the one called Conan." Her voice was sensuous, yet imperious.

Conan did not answer. That she had left her perfumed palace and bright gardens for the heat of the plains was surprise enough, but that she had come seeking him—and such he did not now doubt—was more than merely worrisome. Yet he had lived long enough among those who called themselves civilized and him barbarian to know some rules of survival among them. He would give no information until he knew more.

The mounted woman's delicate brows drew down at his silence. "You know who I am, do you not?"

"You are Taramis," Conan replied simply, and her frown deepened.

"Princess Taramis." She emphasized the first word. His face lost none of its grimness, nor did his sword lower from its ready position. She was tall for a woman, and she drew herself up to the last hairsbreadth of her height. "I am the Princess Royal of Zamora. Tiridates, your king, is my brother."

"Tiridates is not *my* king," Conan said.

Taramis smiled as if she found herself back on a familiar path. "Yes," she breathed. "You are a northlander, a barbarian, are you not? And a thief?"

Conan stiffened. It was all he could do not to check the encircling horsemen to see if some were drifting closer with their nets, yet he knew the true danger lay with the woman before him. "What do you want of me?" he demanded.

"Serve me, Conan the thief."

He had had patrons of the moment before, those who gave him gold for a particular theft, and at that moment it seemed his alternative was to battle the remaining black-armored warriors. Yet perversity touched him. "No."

"You refuse me?" Taramis said incredulously.

"I do not like being hunted like an animal. I am no wild boar to be netted."

"I can give you wealth beyond your imaginings, titles and position. You could be a lord in a marble palace instead of a thief in squalid alleys."

Conan shook his head slowly. "You have but one thing in your gift that I want, and I will not ask it of you."

"Only one? What is that, barbar?"

"My freedom," the Cimmerian smiled. It was the smile of a wolf at bay. "And that I will take myself."

The dark-eyed Zamoran princess looked at him wonderingly. "Do you truly believe you can defeat all of my warriors?"

"Mayhap they can kill me, but that is freedom of another sort, to die rather than yield."

Still staring, she spoke as if unaware that she did so. "The scrolls spoke truly." Abruptly she shook herself. "I *will* have you in my service, Conan, and you will ask to enter it."

The tall warrior in gold-chased armor spoke. "It is not seemly for you to bargain with his sort. Let me face him, and we will carry him back to Shadizar in a net like his accomplice."

Without taking her eyes from Conan, Taramis gestured as if waving away a gnat. "Be silent, Bombatta."

One hand she stretched toward the Cimmerian, palm out, fingers moving as if she palped something. The air seemed to stir across Conan's broad chest, and he felt the hairs on his arms lift. He found he had taken a step back. Planting his feet, he firmed his grip on his sword hilt.

Taramis' hand dropped, and her eyes went to the crude structure of stones he had built. "All men have a heart's desire, something they would kill for, or die for." From the neck of her tunic she drew a chain of delicate golden links from which depended a teardrop of clear crystal. The crystal she clasped tightly in her left hand, and her right pointed to the rough altar. "See now what is your seeking, Conan."

From between her fingers closed about the crystal came a pulse of crimson light. Among the encircling warriors horses snorted nervously. Only Taramis' mount was still, although with eyes rolling and flanks trembling. Once more came the flash, and again, and again, until an unceasing glow of purest vermilion shone from her fist.

Suddenly there were flames on the bare stone of the altar, and the warriors' mounts danced and reared in terror. Had Conan sought to flee then, he would have found none opposing, for every rider's whole energy was given to controlling his fear-struck animal, but the big Cimmerian did not even notice them. Among the flames lay a figure, a woman, long blonde hair arranged over her shoulders, firm-muscled body sleekly curved and unblemished.

He clamped his teeth on a name, and muttered instead, "Sorcery!"

"Aye, sorcery." Taramis' voice was soft, but it cut unnaturally through the terrified screaming of the horses. "Sorcery that can give you what you seek, Conan. Valeria."

"She is dead," Conan said roughly. "Dead, and there's an end to it."

"Is it an end, barbar?" Within the fires, the form's head turned. Clear blue eyes gazed into Conan's. The womanly shape sat up, held out a hand to the Cimmerian. "I can give her back to you," Taramis said. "I can return her to this world."

Conan snarled. "As a living corpse? I have encountered such. Better to remain dead."

"No corpse, barbar. Warm flesh. Supple flesh. I can give her to you, and make her as you wish. Would you be certain of her devotion for all time? I can assure it. Would you have her crawl to your feet, worship you as a god? I—"

"No!" The Cimmerian's breath was ragged in this throat. "She was a warrior. I will not have . . ." He let his hoarse words die.

"So you believe, now?" The dark-eyed woman gestured; the flames and Valeria's image alike vanished, leaving bare, unscorched stone. About her neck the teardrop crystal hung clear once again. "I can do as I say."

Slowly Conan's sword lowered. He had no liking for sorcery, not even when practiced by those mages he knew to have no malign intent, and such were few indeed. But . . . a debt to be repaid. A life freely given in place of his. "Free Malak," he said wearily.

Bombatta sneered. "Having cleaned the streets of Shadizar of a thief, you think we would loose the little scum? He is no use to anyone in this world."

"One thief more or less will make no difference in Shadizar," Conan said, "and he is a friend. Either he goes free, or our further talking will be done with steel."

The huge warrior opened his mouth again, but Taramis silenced him with a look. "Free the little thief," she said quietly.

Bombatta's face was a tight mask of anger and frustration. Viciously he pulled his horse around and galloped to those who guarded the net-wrapped Malak. In moments the ropes had been cut and the wiry man was rolled out on the stony ground.

"They nearly broke my bones," Malak called as he trotted toward Conan. "What was that with the fire? Why are we still ali—?" His eyes fell on Taramis and widened. "Aiiee!" He began to jerk fawning bows, all the while casting frantically questioning looks at the Cimmerian. "We are honest men, O most honored princess, no matter what you may have heard from lying tongues in Shadizar. We . . . hire ourselves out as . . . as caravan guards. Why, never have we taken so much as a pomegranate without payment. You must believe—"

"Begone, little man," Taramis said, "before I tell you how much truth I know of you."

Eying Conan doubtfully, Malak took a hesitant step toward their horses.

"We must part for a time," Conan told him, "even as we did after the fight in the Inn of the Three Crowns. Go, and fare you well."

With a last, helpless look at the surrounding guards, the small man darted for his mount.

When Malak had galloped out of sight over the hill—laying his quirt to his horse and staring back over his shoulder as if he still did not believe he was actually free to go—Conan turned back to Taramis. "What is it you wish me to do?" he asked.

"In good time, you will be told," the beauteous woman replied. The smile that played on her lips was tinged with triumph. "For now, there are words I would hear from you."

Conan did not hesitate. "I would enter your service, Taramis." A debt must be repaid, whatever the cost.

III

S hadizar was a city of golden domes and alabaster spires thrusting toward the cerulean sky from the dust and stones of the Zamoran plain. Crystal pure fountains splashed among fig trees in shaded courtyards, and a glaring sun was reflected from gleaming white walls that sheltered dark cool within. Shadizar the Wicked was the city called, and a score more of names, each less complimentary than the last and all well-earned.

Within the great granite city walls pleasure was sought as avidly as gold, and one was oft exchanged for the other. Sleek lords licked their lips over quivering maidens as over pastries. Hot-eyed ladies stalked their prey like sinuous, sensuous cats. One nobly-born husband and wife, each committed to a life of fleshy delights not encompassing the other, were currently the butt of many jokes, for after intrigues and machinations too involved for recounting they discovered too late that each had managed to arrange an assignation with the other.

Yet if perversion and debauchery were the soul of Shadizar, it was trade that provided the gold to purchase them. From the far reaches of the world they knew came the caravans, from Turan and Corinthia, from Iranistan and Khoraja, from Koth and Shem. Pearls, silks and gold, ivory, perfumes and spices, all provided the music for the licentious pavane of the City of Ten Thousand Sins.

The streets of the city were crowded with commerce as Conan rode into the city with Taramis' party of black-armored warriors. Rough-tunicked men carrying baskets of fruit dodged the whips of muleteers who drove their trains of braying beasts down streets lined with brightly striped shop awnings and tables displaying samples of the goods to be found within. Haughty, silk-clad nobles and fat merchants in somber velvets, leather-aproned apprentices and harlots wearing little but jingling girdles of coin, all dodged between the long-striding camels of caravans driven by dusty men of foreign mien and greedy eyes. From building to building the air was solid with the bleats and squawks of sheep and chickens bound for sale, the cries of peddlers and strumpets hawking their wares, beggars pleading and merchants bargaining. Over all hung a stench compounded of equal parts of spices, offal, perfume and sweat.

Taramis did not allow herself to be slowed by the congestion of the narrow streets. Half of her warriors drove a wedge before her, using the long clubs they still carried to beat aside those who were too slow to clear the way. The rest of the ebon-armored guards brought up the rear, with Conan and Taramis in the middle. And guards they were, the big Cimmerian thought, for all the talk that he had entered the noblewoman's service. He bent from the saddle to scoop a fat pear from a fruitmonger's cart and forced himself to sink into a lazy slouch as he rode, seemingly with no thought but eating the succulent fruit and staring at the crowds.

The teeming throngs of people were driven to the sides of the street, merchants and trulls, nobles and beggars crowded together, trampling blankets of trinkets displayed there, overturning tables before shops. Sullen faces stared at the procession. Bloody faces marked those who had been slow of foot. Most were silent, but the guards just ahead of Taramis shook their clubs at the onlookers and scattered shouts rose of "All hail to the Princess Taramis!" or "The gods' blessings on Princess Taramis!"

Conan's eye fell on a caravan forced into a side-street ahead. The lead camel, people jammed about its feet, jerked continually at the halter-rope held by a slim, dark-skinned man in a dirty turban. The camels behind, catching its feelings, grunted and shifted nervously.

As Conan rode past the caravan, he tossed aside the core of the pear. Right into the lead camel's nose. With a wild bray the dusty gray beast reared, pulling its halter-rope from the turbaned man's hand. For an instant it seemed not to realize that it was free. Then it bolted, with half a score more camels on its heels, straight through the column of black-armored warriors. The Cimmerian gave his horse its head, and it joined the stampede.

Shouts rose behind him, but Conan bent low over his saddle and let his horse gallop. Scattering peddlers and marketers, the knot of camels, with Conan in its center, rounded a slight bend in the street. The pursuit—there would certainly be pursuit—could not see him, but that shelter could last only moments. He threw himself from the saddle. A heavy blow caught him in the ribs as he rolled beneath the feet of the galloping camels. Then he was springing to his feet, leaping past a staring, open-mouthed tradesman to crouch behind a pile of tight-woven baskets. Hooves pounding the paving stones cleared the street again, and a score of grim-faced warriors in ebon armor thundered by, Bombatta at their head.

Slowly Conan straightened, hitching his swordbelt back into place as the horsemen disappeared down the street. He rubbed at the spot where the camel had kicked him. Camels were malicious beasts, he thought. Not like horses. He had never been able to get along with camels. Abruptly he realized the basket weaver yet stared at him.

"Good baskets," Conan told the man, "but not what I want." The open-mouthed tradesman was still staring when he hurriedly crossed the street and ducked into a narrow alley that stank of urine and rotting garbage.

Down the pinched, twisting alleys the Cimmerian sped, cursing when his feet slid in the slick filth. Whenever he came to a street he paused only long enough to look for men in black nasaled helmets before darting across and into another alley. In a zig-zag pattern he made his way the breadth of Shadizar until, in the shadow of the southern wall of the city, he slipped through the back door of the tavern of Manetes.

The hall inside was dark and cool, though heavy with the smells of bad cooking. Serving girls gave the big Cimmerian startled glances as they hurried to and from the kitchens, for patrons did not ordinarily enter the tavern from the crooked alley behind. Nor did the tall young man with sword and dagger at his belt and blue ice in his eyes look like the usual patron.

In the common room muleteers and camel drivers and carters, out-landers for the most part, filled the tables, the odor of sweat and animals dueling with the smell of sour wine. Supple-hipped doxies in narrow strips of thin, brightly colored silk or less paraded their offerings between the tables scattered across the sand-covered floor. More than one jade eyed the broad-shouldered Cimmerian warmly; some, on the laps of men who had already crossed their palms with silver, earned growls and even cuffs, but the men saved their anger for the wenches. Even those who thought themselves fierce as mastiffs recognized the wolf in the massively muscled youth and directed their thoughts, and their anger, to others than him.

Conan was unaware of the stir he left behind him. Once he was sure the common room held no black-armored warriors he had no interest in who else was there. Swiftly he approached the bar where Manetes held sway.

Tall and thin to the point of boniness, the tavernkeeper's dark eyes were set deep in a cadaverous face. The man's starveling looks did not seem to hurt his custom, however, though Conan had never been able discern why.

"Is Malak here?" Conan asked the innkeeper quietly.

"Top of the stairs," Manetes replied. "Third door on the right." He wiped thin hands on a dirty apron and cast his eyes suspiciously behind the Cimmerian as if looking for pursuit. "Is there trouble in this?"

"Not for you," Conan told him, and headed for the stairs. He had no worries concerning the gaunt-faced man's discretion. There was the matter of saving Manetes' daughter from the clutches of two Iranistanis who had intended her for sale in Aghrapur. Manetes would keep silent if there were hot irons at his feet.

On the second floor Conan slapped open the indicated door, and jerked back as a slashing dagger barely missed his throat. " 'Tis me, you fool!" he growled.

Grinning nervously, Malak sheathed his blade and backed into the room. Conan slammed the door behind him as he entered.

"Sorry," the wiry thief laughed shakily. "It's just . . . well . . . Mitra's Mercies, Conan, Taramis herself out there hunting us, and that fire—that was sorcery, was it not?—and I did not know what had happened to you, and . . . How did you get free? I'd almost forgotten the fight at the Inn of the Three Crowns, and meeting here after. Do we leave the city now? Did they dig up the gems? We'll go there first thing and dig them up ourselves. Those stones will keep us—"

"Calm yourself," Conan said. "We are not leaving Shadizar. At least, not yet. I have a commission from Taramis."

"What kind of commission?" Malak asked warily. "And how much gold is she offering?"

"What she wants, I don't know yet. As for price . . . Taramis claims she can bring Valeria back."

The smaller man's breath hissed in through clenched teeth. His dark eyes darted as if looking for a way out. "Sorcery," he managed at last. "I *knew* that fire was sorcery. But do you think she has *that* much power? And even if she does, can you trust her?"

"I must take the chance, for Valeria. I owe . . ." He shook his head. Malak was a friend, but he would not understand. "You have no such reason, so I will give you my half of Abulates' gems if you will help me."

Malak brightened immediately. "You did not not have to make this offer, Cimmerian. We are companions, eh? Still, I will accept it, just so everything is fair. That is, so long as I don't have to enter Taramis' palace. She put three of my cousins in her dungeon a few years gone, and two of them died there."

"She doesn't know you from Hannuman's goose-girl, Malak. Still, I will not ask it of you, and you can be sure Taramis won't. On the plain all she wanted of you was that you leave."

"That just shows how little she knows of talent," the small thief huffed. "If she wants a thief, who is better than me? What am I saying? I'll burn incense in Mitra's temple to give thanks that she chose you rather than me. What do you want me to do?"

"I will go to Taramis' palace. You watch it carefully. I do not know where I may have to go, and I may not have time to seek you out first if I must leave the city. Also, find out where Akiro is."

"Another sorcerer?" Malak exclaimed.

A sorcerer, indeed, was Akiro. A short, plump man with yellow skin like the men of far Khitai, though he had never named any land as his place of birth, he had aided Conan once before with his powers. The Cimmerian did not trust him, entirely—he did not truly trust any wizard—but Akiro had liked Valeria. Perhaps that would weigh in the balance.

"I may have need of him in this, Malak, to watch Taramis' sorceries, to make sure Valeria is not returned with some bond-spell on her."

"I will find him, Cimmerian. Do you have time for a drink to luck, or must you return to Taramis' palace immediately?"

"I must go there for the first time," Conan laughed. "I left her company without farewells, and her guards scour the streets for me. But I hope to reach the palace without killing any of them."

Malak shook his head. "You will be lucky if she is not angry enough to have a pike decorated with your head."

"She may be angry enough, but she will not do it. She sought not just any thief, Malak, but me. She knew my name, and she rode onto the plain to find me. Whatever she intends, Conan of Cimmeria is necessary to it."

IV

To the city that surrounded it, the palace of Taramis presented the look of a fortress, though not, of course, so much a one as the Royal Palace. That would have been a good way to be shortened a head, drunkard though Tiridates might be. Taramis' crenellated granite walls stood four times the height of a tall man, being thus two paces shorter than those of the King. Square towers stood at the four corners of the walls, and two more flanked the tall, iron-bound gates.

Those gates stood open as Conan approached, guarded by two warriors in nasaled helms and black breastplates, with long-bladed spears slanted smartly. Other pairs stood, as rigid as the stone they guarded, atop the towers, and more along the walls. The big Cimmerian's lip curled in contempt for such guards. Like statues, they were, and as much use. On a moonlit night a blind thief could find his way between them without being seen.

The sun now dropped toward the western horizon, and the guards at the massive gates were near the end of their watch, bored and with their minds filled with the food and wine and serving girls that awaited them in their barracks. Conan was within three paces before they realized that he truly meant to enter rather than merely pass by. In their experience, men such as he did not enter the palace of the Princess Royal unless on their way to her dungeons. Their spears dropped as one, long points presented to his chest.

"Be off with you," one of them growled.

"I am here to see Taramis," Conan announced.

Their eyes ran over the sweat-caked dust that covered him, and sneers painted their faces. He who had spoken before opened his mouth. "You were told to—"

Suddenly Bombatta was there, flinging a guard to either side as if he barely noticed they had been in his way. The guards slammed against the thick, iron-bound planks of the open gates and collapsed groggily.

Bombatta stood where they had been, glaring at Conan, his hand opening and closing on his sword hilt.

"You dare come here after——?" The massive scar-faced warrior drew a shuddering breath. His black eyes were on a level with Conan's. "Where in Zandru's Nine Hells did you get to?"

"The camels frightened my horse," Conan said carelessly. "Besides, I needed a tankard or two of wine to clear the dust from my throat after the ride back to Shadizar."

Bombatta ground his teeth. "Come with me," he snapped, spinning to reenter the palace. The guards, just now rising to their feet, stayed carefully out of his way, but he shouted, "Togra! Replace those buffoons at the gate!" as soon as he was inside the walls.

Conan followed, but he was no lackey to hurry after the other, as he must were he to catch up. Instead he took his own pace, ignoring Bombatta's darkening face as he had to slow his own steps or leave the Cimmerian behind.

A broad, flagstoned way led from the gate to the palace proper through an elaborate garden where marble fountains splashed and shimmered with watery mists and alabaster spires rose to treble the height of the outer wall. Here tall trees cast a pool of gentle shade. There open spaces were filled with flowering shrubs and plants brought from as far as Vendhya and Zingara. Formal walks laced through it all, and merely within Conan's sight half a score gardeners, their short tunics and bare legs marking them slave, labored to increase its beauty.

A portico of tall fluted columns surrounded the palace itself, and within was a profusion of courtyards floored with polished marble and over-looked by balconies piercing niveous walls that gleamed even in the fading light. Tapestries of wondrous workmanship draped the corridors, and fine carpets from Vendhya were strewn in profusion. Slaves scurried to light golden lamps against the coming night.

Ever inward Bombatta led, until Conan wondered if he were being taken through the entire palace. Then he entered a courtyard and stopped, neither noticing nor caring that the other man had stopped as well. Pedestals stood about the court, on each a symbol carved in alabaster or porphyry or obsidian. Some he recognized from the charts of astrologers. Others he was glad he did not know; his gaze did not linger on those. Among the pedestals stood knots of men in robes of saffron and black, embroidered with arcane signs in varying degrees of complexity. Others, in robes of gold, held to themselves apart. All their eyes swung to him as he stepped into the court, eager eyes, eyes that weighed and measured and evaluated.

"The man Conan," Bombatta said, and the Cimmerian realized he addressed not the watching men, but Taramis, on a balcony overlooking them all.

The voluptuous noblewoman still wore her travel-stained garments, and her face was filled with arrogant fury. Her eyes locked with Conan's. She seemed to be waiting for him to look away, and when he did not, her head jerked irritably. "Have him washed," she commanded, "and brought to me." Without another word she left the balcony, even her back eloquent of rage.

Her anger was no greater than Conan's own, however. "*Have* me washed!" he growled. "I am no horse!" To his surprise, Bombatta's scarred face reflected his ire.

"The baths are this way, thief!" The ebon-armored man all but snarled the words, and strode off, not looking to see if Conan followed.

The Cimmerian hesitated only a moment, though. He would welcome the chance to sluice away the dust; it was only the means of its offering— if it could be called an offer—that rankled.

The room to which Conan was led had walls mosaicked in images of blue skies and river rushes, and in its center was a large, white-tiled pool. Beyond the pool was a low couch and a small table bearing vials of oils. It was the bath-attendants who brought a smile to his face, though. Four girls flashed dark-eyed glances at him and hid giggles behind their hands. Their hair was uniformly black and pinned in identical coils tight about their heads, but short tunics of white linen fit snugly over curves that ranged from slender to generous.

"You will be sent for, thief," Bombatta said.

Conan's smile faded. "Your tone begins to grate at me," he said coolly.

"If you were not needed . . ."

"Do not let that stay your hand. I shall still be here . . . after."

Bombatta's hand twitched toward his sword; then, the scars on his face livid, he stalked from the chamber.

The four girls had fallen silent during the exchange. Now they huddled together, staring at Conan with frightened eyes.

"I will not bite you," Conan told them gently.

Hesitantly they moved to him, simultaneously beginning to tug at his garments and chatter.

"I thought you were going to fight him, my lord."

"Bombatta is a fierce warrior, my lord. A dangerous man."

"Of course, my lord, you are as tall as he. I thought no man could be as tall as Bombatta."

"But Bombatta is bigger. Not that I doubt your strength, my lord."

"Hold," Conan laughed, fending them off. "One at a time. Firstly, I am no lord. Secondly, I can wash myself. And thirdly, how are you called?"

"I am Aniya, my lord," the slenderest of them answered. "These are Taphis, Anouk and Lyella. And to wash you is what we are for, my lord."

Conan ran an appreciative eye over her lithe curves. "I can think of better things," he murmured. To his surprise Aniya blushed deeply.

"It—it is forbidden, my lord," she stammered. "We are sealed to the Sleeping God." Gasps came from the other three, and Aniya's face paled as quickly as it had colored.

"The Sleeping God?" Conan said. "What god is that?"

"Please, my lord," Aniya moaned, "it must not be spoken of. Please. If you reveal what I have said, I . . . I will be punished."

"I will hold my silence," Conan promised. But for all he said, they would speak no further word that did not concern his bathing.

He held still for being soaped and rinsed, then soaped and rinsed again. They dried him with soft toweling, then massaged fragrant oils into his skin. Not the most fragrant, to be sure. He managed to avoid those, though he still thought he smelled as perfumed as a noble fop by the time they were done. They were dressing him in robes of white silk when a bald and wizened man entered.

"I am Jarvaneus," the old man said, bowing slightly, "Chief Steward to the Princess Taramis." His tone indicated he considered that position infinitely higher than that of a thief. "If you are finished, I will take you to—" He coughed as Conan took up his sword belt. "There is no need for that here."

Conan fastened the belt and settled the broadsword and dagger into place. He had little liking of being unarmed in any circumstances, and the more he learned the less he wanted to be so in Taramis' palace. "Take me to Taramis," he said.

Jarvaneus choked. "I will take you to the *Princess* Taramis."

The Cimmerian waved him to lead on.

Surprise upon surprise, Conan thought when the old man left him. It was no audience chamber he had been taken to. Golden lamps gave light against the deepening night. A huge, round bed veiled with sheer, white silk took up one end of the great room. The marble-tiled floor was strewn with rugs from Vendhya and Iranistan, and in its center stood a low table of polished brass on which rested a crystal flagon of wine and two goblets of beaten gold. Taramis, swathed in black silk robes from neck to toe, reclined on cushions piled beside the table.

They were not alone in the room. In each corner stood a black-armored warrior, unhelmeted and with his sword slung across his back so that the hilt stuck above his right shoulder. Straight ahead these men stared, not moving a muscle, not seeming to breathe or to blink.

"My bodyguards," Taramis said, gesturing to the four. "The best of

Bombatta's warriors, almost as good as he himself. But do not let them worry you. They attack only at my command. Wine?"

She rose smoothly and bent to fill the goblets. Conan's breath caught in his throat. The black silk had tightened across her rounded buttocks as she bent. In its multitude of folds, the garment was opaque, but in a single layer it was as mist. And Taramis wore naught beneath it but sleek skin. As she came toward him with the wine, he found he could not take his eyes from the slight sway of her heavy breasts.

"I said, if you wish food, I will have something brought for you." The noblewoman's voice was thick with amusement.

Conan started, colored, then colored deeper when he realized what he had done. "No. No, I want nothing to eat." Furious with himself, he took a goblet. What was he about, he wondered, staring like a boy who had never seen a woman before. If he could not keep his wits better than that, he had as well give it over. He cleared his throat. "There is a commission you want me to carry out. I cannot do it until I know what it is."

"You want this Valeria returned to you?" She moved closer, till her breasts brushed against his chest. Even through his tunic they seemed to burn like two hot coals.

"I want her alive again." He stepped to the cushions—casually, he hoped—and lay back. Taramis came to stand over him; he looked up, and had to pull his eyes away from the tantalizing line of thigh and belly and breast. He did not see the small smile that flashed across her lips.

"Hold hard in your mind to what you want, thief, and do as I command."

"You still have not told me what I must do." He had to suppress a sigh of relief when she moved away from him and began to pace.

"I have a niece, the Lady Jehnna," Taramis said slowly. "She has lived her life in seclusion. Her parents, my brother and his wife, died when she was little more than an infant. The shock was too much for her. The child is . . . delicate, her mind fragile. But now she must go on a journey, and you must accompany her."

Conan choked on a mouthful of wine. "*I* must accompany her?" he said when he had his breath back. "I am not accustomed to being a companion to noblewomen. I mean, it is not the sort of thing I do."

"You mean you are a thief," Taramis said, and smiled when he shifted uncomfortably. "I have not turned you over to the City Guard yet, Conan. Why should I now? It is a thief I need, for Jehnna must steal a key, a key only she can touch, and also the treasure that key will open the way to for her. Who better to aid her in that than the best thief in Zamora?"

The big youth felt as though his head was spinning. Carefully he set the goblet on the table. The last thing he needed then was wine. "I am to take this child, this Lady Jehnna, on a journey, and help her steal an ensorceled key and a treasure," he said wonderingly. "If you say this is the service you require in return for Valeria, I will do it, though I cannot see why she does not travel with a retinue of servants and a hundred of your guards instead of with one thief."

"Because the Scrolls of Skelos say she must journey without such." Taramis stopped, biting at her lower lip.

"These scrolls," he began, but the silk-draped woman waved a quick hand in dismissal.

"Prophecies," she said hastily. "They tell what must be done, and how. Put them from your mind. They are in an ancient tongue known only to . . . scholars." She eyed him consideringly, then went on. "There is some vagueness about numbers, but only two companions are mentioned specifically. I have decided to risk sending no more than that. The two will be yourself and Bombatta."

Conan grunted, abandoning the scrolls for more immediate concerns. Bombatta to ride with him? Well, he would deal with the man when and if he had to. "Where is this key to be found?"

"The Lady Jehnna will show you."

"It will be best if I have a map," he told her, "and a plan of the place where the key is kept. The treasure, too. And what manner of treasure is it? Will we need pack animals to carry it?"

"The Lady Jehnna will know it when she sees it, my fine thief. And she can hold it in her hands, which no one else can do. That is all you need to know. As for a map, there is none, can be none, outside of Jehnna's head. At her birth spells were cast to attune her to this key. She will sense the key as you journey, and know how to reach it. When the key is her hand, she will become attuned to the treasure in the same way."

Conan sighed. That she wished to keep some things secret from him was no surprise. Many patrons found it hard to completely trust a thief, even when he was in their hire. Still, it did not make matters easier. "Is there aught else I should know, or prepare for? Remember that too many surprises may mean not only my death, but that of your niece."

"Jehnna must not be harmed!" Taramis snapped.

"I will keep her safe, but I cannot do it in complete ignorance. If you know something more . . ."

"Very well. I . . . am reliably informed that the key is now in the possession of a man called Amon-Rama, a Stygian."

"A sorcerer." He could not believe otherwise, after all else he had heard.

"Aye, a sorcerer. You see, I tell you everything that I know. I wish success for this journey as much or more than you. Are you frightened, or can you face what comes? Remember your Valeria."

His face hardened at her words. "I have said I will do it, and I will."

"Very well," Taramis said. "Now, one final thing, as important as all the rest, at least to you. On the seventh night from now will there be a configuration of the stars that occurs but once in a thousand years. It is during that configuration that I can bring Valeria back to you. *If* you have returned to me with the treasure and the Lady Jehnna." Her raised hand forestalled the protest he was forming. "My astrologers can locate neither the key nor the treasure, but they assure me both can be found and returned here within the time."

"They assure you," he laughed grimly.

He peered into his goblet, and drained the rest of the wine in one gulp. An hour before, he thought, he had waded to his knees in sorcery, and cautiously. Now he knew he waded to his neck, and in the fog.

Suddenly a scream ripped through the palace, a girl's scream. Again it came, and again. Conan leaped to his feet, a hand going to his sword. He saw the guards tense, and realized it was in response to him. The screams had brought no stir from them.

"It is my niece," Taramis said hastily. "Jehnna suffers nightmares. Sit, Conan. Sit. I will return when I have seen to her comfort." And to the Cimmerian's surprise the Princess Royal of Zamora ran from the room.

Taramis did not not have far to run, and anger lent her speed. She had thought the nightmares dealt with, gone to plague their nights no more. Her niece was curled into a ball in the middle of her bed, sobbing convulsively in the dim light of the moon shining through arched windows. Taramis was not surprised to find no servant in attendance. They knew only she could deal with the dark visions that tormented Jehnna's night. The noblewoman knelt beside the bed and put her hands on Jehnna's shoulders.

The girl started, then saw Taramis and clutched at her. "It was a dream!" she wept. "A horrible dream!" Not yet eighteen, Jehnna was slender and pretty, but now her large, dark eyes swam with tears and her full lips trembled beyond control.

"Only a dream," Taramis soothed, stroking the girl's long, black hair. "No more than a dream."

"But I saw—I saw—"

"Ssssh. Rest, Jehnna. Tomorrow you begin your grand adventure. You cannot let dreams frighten you now."

"But it frightened me so," Jehnna faltered.

"Hush, child."

Lightly Taramis rested her fingertips on Jehnna's temples, and chanted beneath her breath. Slowly the girl's sobs quieted, her tremblings stilled. When her breathing took on the slow, deep rhythm of sleep, Taramis straightened. A hundred times she had thought the dream and the memories of the dream were banished, but each time the accursed dream returned to haunt her. She rubbed at her own temples. The same power that gave the girl her destiny made it harder each time to push away the nightmare. But without that power and destiny there would have been no nightmares. Jehnna was the One spoken of in the scrolls, and that was what was important. This time the banishment would last long enough. It had to.

All of her life had Taramis been on this path, truly since infancy. As soon as she was old enough to be aware of herself, her own aunt, the Princess Elfaine, began to teach her of the only two ways a woman could truly have power, seduction and sorcery. When Elfaine died, the child Taramis, but ten years of age, did not attend the funereal rites. Older heads thought her absence was an indication of her grief. In actuality she had been ransacking her aunt's private chambers, stealing the sorcerous tomes and magical artifacts that Elfaine had spent a lifetime collecting. And there she found the Scrolls of Skelos. Within a phasing of the moon she began the twenty years of labor that now approached culmination.

She became aware of Bombatta standing in the doorway, staring at the girl on the bed. Swiftly she crossed the room and took him by the arms. For a moment he resisted; then he allowed himself to be drawn into the darkened corridor.

"You no longer even hide it, do you?" she said with deceptive quiet. "You desire my niece. Do not attempt to deny it."

He towered over her, but he shifted from foot to foot like a boy awaiting chastisement. "I cannot help myself," he muttered finally. "You are fire and passion. She is innocence and purity. I cannot help myself."

"And she must remain innocent. It is written in the Scrolls of Skelos."

In truth, the scrolls did not require Jehnna to be virgin, merely innocent of the slightest seed of evil, a pure soul incapable of thinking wrong or harm toward anyone or of believing that anyone might mean such toward her. Her carefully cloistered life had assured that. But Taramis had seen what was happening in Bombatta long before he had become aware of it himself, and nurtured his belief.

"Even were it not," she told him, "you are mine, and I will not share what is mine."

"I like it not that you are alone with the thief," he growled.

"Alone?" Taramis laughed. "The four best of your guards stand ready to seize him or cut him down should he threaten me." The huge warrior spoke under his breath, and she frowned. "Speak loudly enough for me to hear, Bombatta. I do not like things hidden from me."

For a long moment he stared at her, black eyes burning, then said, "I cannot bear the thought of the thief looking at you, wanting you, touching you . . ."

"You forget yourself." Each word slashed like an icy razor. Bombatta took a step back, then slowly sank to his knees, head bent.

"Forgive me," he muttered. "But this Conan cannot be trusted. He is an outlander, a thief."

"Fool! The scrolls say that Jehnna must be accompanied by a thief with eyes the color of the sky. There is not another such in Shadizar, perhaps not in all of Zamora. You will do as I have commanded you. You will follow the instruction of the scrolls exactly. Exactly, Bombatta."

"As you command," he murmured, "so do I obey."

Taramis touched his head, much as she might fondle the head of one of her wolfhounds. "Of course, Bombatta." She felt flushed with victory, for it certainly would come now. The Horn of Dagoth would be hers. Immortality and power would be hers. The knowledge sent sparks through her, and flashes of heat that coiled in her belly. Her hand trembled on Bombatta's black hair. She took a deep breath. "Rest assured that all will occur as I have planned, Bombatta. Now return to your chambers and sleep. Sleep, and dream of our triumph."

Unmoving on his knees, Bombatta watched her go, his obsidian eyes glittering in the dark.

Conan got to his feet as Taramis entered the bedchamber. "Your niece?" he asked.

"She is better. She sleeps." The voluptuous noblewoman raised a hand, and the ebon-clad guards marched from the room without a word. "Do *you* sleep, thief, or are you awake? It is late, and you would talk of my niece." Folds of diaphanous silk moved as she walked, showing flashes of bare skin beneath.

The Cimmerian eyed her doubtfully. With a serving girl or even a rich merchant's daughter, he would have been certain what she meant. With a princess he was unsure.

"Are you still a man?" she laughed. "Has mourning for your beloved Valeria unmanned you?"

Conan growled. He knew he could not explain to Taramis what had stood and did stand between Valeria and himself. He was not sure he had it entirely clear in his own mind. But of one thing he was sure. "I am a man," he said.

Taramis' hands went to her neck. Black silk cascaded to pool about her feet. There was challenge in her dark eyes, and her rounded nudity. "Prove it," she taunted.

Disdaining the bed, Conan bore her to the floor and gave the proofs she asked.

V

Conan stared into the fire of dried dung—small, so as to attract no unwanted attention from others who might be spending the night on the Zamoran plain—and thought briefly of other, sorcerous flames on a crude stone altar. A full day's ride from Shadizar, and still Malak had not appeared. The Cimmerian did not like admitting to a need for anyone's aid, but he was more certain than ever that he would need Akiro before this journey was done. And after, if Taramis delivered what she promised. Where in Zandru's Nine Hells was Malak?

Scowling, he pulled himself from the useless reverie and found himself studying his companions. Or rather, one of them.

Bombatta solicitously filled a silver cup from one of their goatskin waterbags and offered it to Jehnna. With a thankful smile she reached one hand from under her cloak of the palest white wool, pulled tight about her against the chill of the night. The girl was not at all what Conan expected and he still had not accustomed himself to the difference. Taramis had spoken of her niece as a child, and he had formed an image of a girl of nine or ten years, not one of his own age, with a slender body that moved beneath her concealing robes with the unconscious grace of a gazelle.

"Our direction," the Cimmerian said abruptly. "Do we continue the same way on the morn, Jehnna?"

"The Lady Jehnna, thief," Bombatta corrected in a growl.

Jehnna blinked, as if startled at being addressed. Her brown eyes, as large and tremulous as those of a newborn fawn, stared at him for a moment, then turned to Bombatta. She addressed her answer to the black-armored warrior. "I will know more later, but for now, I know only that we must ride to the west."

Toward the Karpash Mountains, Conan thought. They were a rugged, towering range where a man could easily become lost if he had neither a familiarity with the region nor a guide with the same. Maps showed only the major passes, used as trade routes. And the people, if not so fierce as Kezankian hillmen, were yet far from friendly toward strangers. They had a way of smiling in welcome until they put the knife into your ribs.

The Cimmerian was not surprised that she had not answered him directly. Since leaving Taramis' palace before dawn she had spoken no word to him, only to Bombatta. But he was skilled in his chosen profession, and knowledge was as life's blood to a thief. "How do you know the way?" he asked. "Does the key draw you to it?"

"She is not to be questioned, thief," Bombatta growled.

A wolf howled in the night, the long, mournful sound seeming to blend with the crescent-mooned darkness.

"What was that, Bombatta?" Jehnna asked curiously.

The scar-faced man gave a last glare to Conan before replying. "Only an animal, child. Like a dog."

Her brown eyes turned eager. "Will we see one?"

"Perhaps, child."

Conan shook his head. The girl seemed to delight in everything, and to know of nothing. The empty streets of Shadizar as they rode from the city, the tents and sleeping camels of a caravan outside the city gates, the pack of hyenas that had followed them at a distance for half the day without ever quite gathering the nerve to attack, all fascinated her equally, bringing bright-eyed stares and questions to Bombatta.

"What I do not know can kill us," Conan said.

"Do not frighten her, thief!" Bombatta snapped.

Jehnna laid a hand on the tall warrior's chain-mailed arm. "I am not frightened, Bombatta. My good Bombatta."

"Then tell me how you know where to find the key," Conan insisted. "Or tell Bombatta, if you still will not speak to me."

Her eyes flickered to Conan, then settled on a space halfway between the Cimmerian and the black-armored warrior. "I do not *know* exactly how I know the way, only that I do. It is as if I remember having been this way before." She shook her head and gave a small laugh. "Of course, it cannot be that. I do not in truth remember ever having left the palace of my aunt until this day."

"If you can tell me where we are to go," Conan said, "even if only vaguely, I may be able to take us by a shorter route than the one you know." Thinking of the configuration of stars Taramis had said was necessary for restoring Valeria to life, he touched the golden amulet hanging at his neck and added, "Time is short."

Once more Jehnna gave a slight shake of her head. "If what I see before me is the proper way to go, then I . . . remember it. But I must see it first." Abruptly she laughed and let herself fall back to stare up at the sky.

"Besides, I do not want this journey to end quickly. I wish it could last forever and ever."

"It cannot, child," Bombatta said. "We must be back in Shadizar in six more nights."

It was all Conan could do to keep his face expressionless. The configuration would occur in six nights, but Bombatta had no care for Valeria's return. What else was to occur on that night?

"Now it is time for you to sleep, girl," the scarred man went on. "We must travel onward early." He began preparing her bed, clearing rocks away from a space of ground, then digging at the earth with his dagger.

"Please, Bombatta," Jehnna said, "can I not remain awake a little longer? The stars look so different here than from the palace gardens. It seems I could almost touch them." Bombatta wordlessly spread blankets over the softened ground. "Oh, very well," she sighed, then covered a yawn with her hand. "It's just that I want to experience everything, and there is so much."

As she lay down, Bombatta put another blanket over her with surprising gentleness. "I will let you experience as much as I can," he said softly. "As much as I can, child, but we must be back in Shadizar in six nights more."

Pillowing her head on her arms, Jehnna mumbled sleepily.

A lover, Conan thought, watching the way Bombatta remained bent over the girl. Were Jehnna not so obviously a virgin he would have been sure the other man was her lover.

Rising to his feet, Bombatta walked to the fire and began to kick dirt over it. "I will take the first watch, thief," he said. Without another word he returned to Jehnna's side, drew his sword, and sat crosslegged with the naked blade across his knees.

Conan's mouth tightened. The man had placed himself between Jehnna and the Cimmerian, as if it were he who must be guarded against. Not taking his eyes from Bombatta, Conan stretched out on the ground, one hand gripping his own swordhilt. He drew no blanket over himself. He was inured to more cold than the Zamoran plain had to offer, and a blanket would slow him an instant should he need to bring his sword into play. Such could be fatal against a man with steel already in his fist. Yet even through his distrust of Bombatta, he wondered about the new mystery that had been added to the rest. What was to occur in Shadizar in six nights? His mind was still on that when he allowed sleep to overtake him.

The rufescent sun beat down fiercely on the mounted trio making their way westward across the Zamoran plains, and Jehnna tugged the hood of her snowy cloak lower in a vain attempt to find coolness in its shadow on her face. She knew Bombatta was right when he said the cloak protected her from the sun—she had held a hand out from under the cloak long enough to feel the strength of the sun's direct rays, and been convinced— but that did not lessen the heat. This was one experience she felt she could do without. Ahead loomed the gray bulk of snow-capped mountains, the Karpash Mountains, promising both cool and wetness. She licked her lips, but they were dry almost as she was done.

"The mountains, Bombatta," she said. "We shall reach them soon?"

He turned toward her, and a thrill of fear shot through her at his scarred, sweaty visage in the ebon helmet. Foolishness, she told herself. To be afraid of Bombatta, whom she had known all of her life? Foolishness indeed.

"Not soon, child," he replied. "Tomorrow. In the morning, perhaps."

"But they seem so near," she protested.

"It is the air of the plains, child. Distances seem nothing to the eye. The mountains are many leagues distant yet."

Jehnna thought of asking for another drink of water, but she had seen Bombatta eyeing the waterskins after her last drink, weighing what remained. He had taken only two drinks since waking. Her eyes went to Conan, leading them, with the packhorse's rope tied to his saddle. The northlander had taken one swallow of water on waking and had not looked at the waterbags since. Now he rode easily, one hand resting lightly on his sword hilt, eyes always searching ahead, apparently not even noticing that the sun had broiled them since dawn and was still not halfway to its zenith.

What a strange young man he was, she thought, though she had little with which to make comparison. He was no older than her, she was sure, but his eyes—such a peculiar color for eyes, blue—seemed unimaginably older. Thirst did not bother him, nor the heat. Could anything slow him? Rain, or wind, or snow? She had heard stories about snow in the mountains, piled as high as a palace. No, she was certain he would go on, deterred by nothing. Perhaps that was why her aunt had sent him. Perhaps he was a hero, a prince in disguise, as in the stories some of the serving girls told her when her aunt was not there.

She shot a glance at Bombatta from the corner of her eye. "Is he handsome, Bombatta?"

"Is who handsome?" he asked gruffly.

"Conan."

His head swiveled toward her; for an instant she was afraid again. "You should not think of such things." His voice was hard, with no trace of the gentleness he usually had with her. "Especially not about him."

"Do not be mad at me, Bombatta," she pleaded. "I love you, and I do not want you to ever be angry with me."

A pained look flashed across his face. "I . . . love you, too, Jehnna. I am not angry with you. It is just that . . . Do not think about the thief. Put him from your mind entirely. That is best."

"I do not see how I can do that, when he rides with us. Besides, Bombatta, I think perhaps he *is* handsome, as in the stories about princes."

"He is no prince," Bombatta snorted.

Jehnna felt a flash of disappointment, but went on. "Even so, I think he is. Handsome, I mean. But I have no one to compare him with, save you and the male slaves and servants in Taramis' palace, and I cannot see any of them as handsome. They are always kneeling and bowing and groveling." Bombatta's face had been growing harder as she spoke; she hunted among her words for something that might have offended him. "Oh, of course you are handsome, Bombatta. I did not mean to imply that you are not."

The big man's teeth ground audibly. "I told you not to think of such things."

"He is bigger than any of the slaves. He's almost as big as you, Bombatta. Do you think he is as strong as you? Perhaps that is why Taramis sent him with us, because he is as strong as you, and as brave as you, and as great a warrior."

"Jehnna!"

She jumped in her saddle, and stared. He had never shouted at her before. Never.

Breathing hard, he rode with one fist on his hip, staring straight ahead. Finally he said, "This Conan is a thief, child. Only a thief, and no more. The Princess Taramis had her own reasons for sending him with us. It is not for me to question them, nor for you."

Jehnna chewed at her lip as she mulled over what she had just learned. When Taramis told her the day for her journey had come, she had been overjoyed. It meant the fulfilling of her destiny. She would find the Horn of Dagoth and return it to her aunt, and great honor would be bestowed on her. But if Conan was a thief, and Taramis had sent him with them . . .

"Bombatta, are we going to *steal* the Horn of Dagoth?"

He made a chopping motion with his hand, and looked quickly toward Conan. The blue-eyed young giant still rode before them, too far ahead to hear words that were not shouted. From the stiffness of his back Jehnna thought he was deliberately ignoring Bombatta and her. For some reason she did not quite understand, it annoyed her that he might ignore her. And on purpose.

"Child," Bombatta said quietly, "Taramis told you not to mention that name in the hearing of anyone but her or me. You know that. It is our secret."

"He cannot hear us," she protested. "And *are* we going to—"

"No!" His tone became overly patient, the way it did when she had pushed him to a limit. "No, Jehnna, we do not steal. No one save you can touch the key. No one save you can touch the Horn. No one in the entire world. Is that not proof that your destiny is true? You cannot doubt your aunt, or me."

"Of course not, Bombatta. It is just . . . oh, I'm sorry. I did not mean to make a bother." The scar-faced warrior muttered something angrily under his breath; she stared at him. "What, Bombatta?"

Instead of answering, he galloped ahead of her, toward Conan.

She stared after him, and abruptly realized someone had ridden over a hill to the north of them and was fast approaching, leading another horse behind him on a rope. He was an ugly little man, she saw as he came closer, short and wiry, in a leather jerkin and dirty breeches. Suddenly her mind puzzled out what it was that Bombatta had muttered. Malak, he had said.

Conan permitted himself a grin when Malak appeared, riding across the hilltop, a saddled horse behind him on a lead rope. He shifted the smooth pebble he was using to bring moisture to his mouth from under his tongue to his cheek. "Ho, Malak!" he called.

"Ho, Conan!" A broad grin split the wiry thief's face. "I had a hard time finding you, Cimmerian. I am no tracker, you know. I am a man of the cities, a civilized—"

Bombatta cut between the two of them, reining in with a spray of dust and rocks. He ignored Conan to glare at the small man, whose smile faded slowly under that murderous gaze.

"The Princess Taramis gave you your life," Bombatta snarled. "You should have lost yourself in a pigsty while you had the chance."

"I asked him to come," Conan said.

Bombatta pulled his horse around, his scars livid lines across his face. "*You* asked him! What made you think you could decide who came on this journey, thief? The Princess Taramis—"

"Taramis wants me to accompany Jehnna," Conan cut him off, "and I want Malak."

"And I say no!"

Conan took a deep breath. He would remain calm. He would not kill this fool. "Then continue the quest without me," he said with more coolness than he felt.

It was Bombatta's turn to take a deep breath. His teeth grated, though, as he failed in showing the same outward equilibrium as the Cimmerian. "There are reasons, thief, that you cannot know. You and I and the Lady Jehnna must go on alone."

"Taramis said the numbers were vague," Conan said, and was pleased to see the other's face go slack with surprise.

"She told you that?"

Conan nodded. "Taramis does not want us to fail. She told me everything."

"Of course," Bombatta said slowly, but there was that about his tone that suddenly made Conan doubt his own words. Yet surely she would not have kept anything back if that would hinder their chances for success.

"Well?" Conan said. "Does Malak ride with us, or do he and I go our own way?"

Bombatta's hand tightened on his sword hilt until his knuckles paled. "Keep the little wretch, then," he breathed hoarsely. "But make no mistake, thief. If we fail because of him, I'll slice both of you for dog meat. And keep a proper respect about you for the Princess Taramis and the Lady Jehnna!" Sawing at his reins, he galloped back to Jehnna, who sat her horse watching worriedly.

"I do not think that man likes me," Malak laughed weakly.

"You have survived other men who did not like you," Conan replied. "You will survive Bombatta. A sorry beast," he added, then gestured to Malak's spare horse when the small man raised a questioning eyebrow.

Malak chuckled. "It was all I could steal. It's for Akiro."

"Is he close? I have no time to seek him very far."

"Not far. The way you're traveling, and to the south."

"Then we must ride," Conan said. "Time is lacking."

Malak fell in beside him as he started forward again. The Cimmerian twisted in his high-pommeled saddle to make sure Bombatta and the girl were following. They were, but still at the distance they had maintained all morning. Conan was not sure if Bombatta simply wanted to avoid his dust, or if the other warrior simply did not want to ride with him. He suspected the latter, and did not care save for missing the opportunities to look at Jehnna.

As they rode, Malak continually glanced at him and muttered to himself. After a time he said, "Uh, Conan? What was all that about reasons why I shouldn't be here, and Taramis telling you everything?"

"I wondered when you would ask," Conan grinned, and detailed all that Taramis had said to him. At least, all that related to the seeking of the key and the treasure. Some things, said in his arms, the big youth would definitely not relate.

When he was done Malak shook his head dazedly. "And I thought all I had to worry about was this bringing Valeria back to life. Aiiee! Listen to me! All, I say, as if it was done by every street corner fakir in Shadizar. That's what comes of being too close to too much sorcery, Cimmerian. You're beginning to take it for granted. That is when it will kill you, or worse. Mark my words." He mumbled something quickly, and Conan recognized a prayer to Bel, the Shemitish god of thieves.

"It is not so bad as it could be," the Cimmerian said.

"Not so bad!" Malak all but squealed. "A girl with a map in her head. There is sorcery there, grant me? A magical key guarded by a wizard, and a sorcerous treasure no doubt under the protection of another mage, if not two or three. This is more than a prudent man should expose himself to. Listen. I know three sisters in Arenjun. Triplets, with bodies to make a man weep and a father who's deaf. I'll even let you have two of them. We put Shadizar from our minds, as if we have never been there, or even heard of it. Taramis would never find us in Arenjun, even if she thought to look. Nor would Amphrates. What do you think? We ride for Arenjun, right?"

"And Valeria?" Conan said quietly. "Do I put her from my mind also? Go to Arenjun, if you wish, Malak. I have been there, and have no reason to return."

"You mean to go on, then?" Malak said. "No matter what I do?" Conan nodded grimly. The smaller man closed his eyes and murmured another prayer, this time to Kyala, the Iranistani goddess of luck. "Very well," he said at last. "I will go with you, Cimmerian. But only because you're giving me your half of Amphrates' gems. This is business."

"Of course it is," Conan said lightly. "I would never accuse you of doing anything out of friendship."

"Of course not," Malak said, then frowned suspiciously at the Cimmerian as if he suspected he had not gotten the straight of the exchange. "At least there is one good thing about all of this."

"What is that?" Conan asked.

"Why, as we are the best thieves in Shadizar," Malak laughed, "which is to say the best in the world, this Amon-Rama will not know we have entered his domain until long after we are gone."

VI

O nce the mountain had brought forth molten rock from the bowels of the earth. A millennium ago had come its final eruption, shaking the ground like the sea in storm for a thousand leagues in all directions, toppling cities and thrones and dynasties. It had blackened the skies with its ash, and in a final, deadly joke, the mountain of fire brought snows where the green of spring should have been and ice in place of the heat of summer for three years. The villagers of the Karpash Mountains no longer remembered why, but they knew it for a mountain of death, and knew their souls were forfeit should they set foot on it.

Half of the mountain had gone in that last, titanic explosion, leaving a long oblong crater with a deep lake, nearly half a league across, at its bottom. Two sides of the great pit were sheer walls, towering a hundred times the height of a man. The other two were gentler slopes, and at the foot of one, abutting the lake, sat a palace such as only one pair of human eyes had ever seen.

Like a gigantic, infinitely faceted gem, the palace was, with towers and turrets and domes of adamantine crystal. No join of stonework showed at any place in it. It seemed a monstrous carving from a single mountainous diamond, glittering in the sun.

In the center of that jewel palace was a huge domed chamber, its mirrored walls hidden behind long golden draperies. In the center of the room stood a narrow, pellucid plinth supporting a gem redder than red, a stone glowing as if fire and heart's blood had been compressed and solidified to form it.

Amon-Rama, once a thaumaturge of the Black Ring of Stygia, moved closer to the thin spire, his scarlet hooded robes flowing liquidly about his tall, lean form. His swarthy, narrow face was that of a predator; his nose had the raptor's hook. Ten thousand soulless sorceries had extinguished the last light in his black eyes. Like claws his hands curled about the gem, but he was careful not to touch it. The Heart of Ahriman. Every time his eyes fell on it he exulted.

It was when his former compatriots discovered his possession of the Heart that they expelled him from the Black Circle. Some things even those dark mages feared to know. Some hidden powers they dared not risk unveiling. His thin lip curled contemptuously. He feared nothing, dared anything. Merely by gaining the gem he had gone beyond the fools. They would have slain him, had they managed to find the courage, but each one of them knew his powers, now that the Heart was his, and feared the counter-stroke should their attempt fail.

On either side of the Heart his long fingers set themselves in a precise fashion, and he began to chant in a language dead for a thousand years. "A'bath taa'bak, udamai mor'aas. A'bath taa'bak, endal cafa'ar. A'bath taa'bak, A'bath mor'aas, A'bath cafa'ar."

The crystal walls of the palace chimed faintly with the words, and with each word the glow of the Heart of Ahriman deepened, deepened and clarified. Still more crimson than rubies and blood, it yet became clear as water, and within its depths figures moved across stony hills.

Amon-Rama's eyes narrowed as he studied the shapes. Riders. One girl and three men, with two extra horses. The pattern formed by his fingers changed slightly, and the girl seemed suddenly to fill the gem.

The girl, he thought, and smiled cruelly. She was the One, the One he had sought these many years. She was attuned to the Heart of Ahriman, and the Heart to her. The woman in Shadizar thought to use her. This Taramis had courage, that she dared think of using the Heart for its ultimate purpose, and she possessed no small ability in the use of powers, yet she reckoned without Amon-Rama. There were many powers of the stone, many uses other than that one she intended. Once the girl, the One, was in his grasp, he would have access to all of those powers. And he would know which to use, and which not to. He would let this foolish Taramis live, he thought, as a naked bondmaid cowering at his feet. But that was for later.

"Come to me, girl," he whispered. "Bring her to me, my brave warriors. Bring the One to me."

Yet again his fingers formed a new shape about the stone, and he chanted, this time in words never meant to be uttered by a human throat, never meant to be heard by a human ear. They burned in the air like purest pain, and the crystal walls groaned with the agony of them. The Heart of Ahriman glowed redder, brighter, ever brighter. The fierce sanguine light split and coalesced and split again, casting his bloody shadow on every surface of the room till it seemed as if a score of men were there, fifty men, a hundred. And still he chanted, and brighter still grew the piercing light.

A sense of urgency built in Conan, intensifying with his horse's every stride toward the towering Karpash range, so near, now. So near. He must turn aside to find Akiro, he told himself, but the rejoinder came that time was desperately short. Every hour spent seeking the rotund wizard was an hour less available to search out the key, somewhere in the mountains ahead, an hour less to find the treasure and return to Shadizar. Each hour's delay was the risk of being an hour late, the risk that Valeria would not be reborn. The necessity of finding Akiro faded gradually to insignificance; the need to reach the mountains became paramount. Above all else, he must take Jehnna to the mountains.

"Here, Conan."

The Cimmerian turned his head at Malak's words, but he did not slow his mount.

"Akiro," Malak said. He gestured with the hand holding the lead rope of the spare horse. "We must turn south here. That is, we were going to . . . I thought we . . ." With a shaky laugh, he shook his head. "Maybe it isn't important after all."

Doubtfully Conan reined in. Frowning, he gazed toward the mountains, then to the south, then once more to the mountains. Akiro *was* important; speed was of the essence, delay intolerable.

Bombatta and Jehnna drew their horses up beside the two mis-matched thieves. Strands of the girl's raven hair stuck to her flushed face, and her gaze was fixed on the gray heights filling the horizon.

The black-armored warrior scowled through his sweat. "Why have you stopped, barbar?"

Conan's jaw tightened, but he made no answer. Irritably he twitched the halter rope of the pack mule. Time, he thought. Time. He knew that he wasted time sitting his horse there, neither seeking out the old mage nor riding for the mountains. But which was the correct decision?

"Erlik curse you, barbar, we must keep moving. We are almost to the mountains. We must reach the Heart—the key, we must reach the key quickly!"

Malak broke in on Bombatta's tirade. "What about Akiro, Cimmerian? Do we find him, or not? By Ogun's Toenails, I no longer know *what* to do."

A strangled curse erupted from the scarred man's throat. "Another, barbar? You would add still another to our number? Taramis may say you are essential, but I say you endanger us all! One more in our party may be enough to rupture the prophecy! Or do you care for that at all? Do you just seek delay, fearing to face what lies before us? Do you, you stinking, northland coward?" He ended on a shout, with a handbreadth of sword bared and bloodlust eager on his face.

Conan stared back with glacial eyes. Rage, beyond his strength to control, burst into white heat. His words were flat and hard. "Draw your sword, Zamoran. Draw it and die. I can take Jehnna to the key just as easily without you."

Abruptly Jehnna rode her horse between the two glaring men. To the surprise of both, her large brown eyes snapped with fire. "Cease this, both of you!" she commanded sharply. "You are to escort me to the key. How can you do that if you squabble like two dogs in an alley?"

Conan blinked in disbelief. Had a mouse attacked a cat he could not have been more taken aback.

Bombatta's jaw had dropped open as she spoke. Now he snapped it shut, but he sheathed his steel as well. "We go to the mountains," he told her gruffly.

Ruthlessly Conan quenched the anger that threatened to flare again, controlled his emotions as tightly as the leather wrappings of his swordhilt. Outwardly calm, he turned his horse south.

"You cannot!" Jehnna protested. A small fist pounded on the pommel of her saddle in frustration. The imperious air was gone like gossamer on the wind. "Conan! You are supposed to go the way I show you. You are *supposed* to!"

With a sigh the big Cimmerian stopped and looked back over his shoulder. "Jehnna, this is no game played in the gardens of your aunt's palace. I do what I must, not what anyone thinks I am supposed to do."

"I think it's very much like a game," Jehnna said sulkily. "Like a giant maze, only now you refuse to play."

"In this maze," Conan told her, "death may lie around any turning."

"Of course not!" The slender girl's face was a portrait of shock. "My aunt has raised me for this. It is my destiny. She would not have sent me if I might be harmed."

Conan stared. "Of course not," he said slowly. "Jehnna, I will take you to the key, and the treasure, and back to Shadizar, and I promise I will allow no harm to come to you. But you must come with me, now, for we may well need the abilities of the man I seek."

Hesitantly, Jehnna nodded. "Very well. I will come with you."

Once more Conan started south, and Malak and Jehnna rode close behind. Scarred face as dark as a thunderhead, Bombatta followed at a distance.

There were no shadows in the chamber of mirrors within the crystal palace. The vermilion blaze was gone, and the Heart of Ahriman gave off only its normal sanguine glow.

Amon-Rama staggered slightly as he walked away from the crystalline plinth that supported the gem. His narrow face seemed narrower still, and pale beneath its swarthiness. There was effort involved in working sorceries at a distance. He needed rest and sustenance before he could try again.

For the moment, however, he thought less of food or sleep than of the failure of his enchantment. He had been unable to see what occurred on the plain; the Heart could not be used to scry and as a nexus of power at one and the same time. He rejected out of hand the possibility that the girl had had anything to do with it. She was the One, true, but no wielder of thaumaturgies. Her life had but one purpose, and sorcery was forbidden to her by the very nature of what was required of her.

That left only the men with her. They were not mages either. He would have detected vibrations of their power when first he viewed them in the Heart, had that been so. Any talisman capable of shielding them from the energies he had unleashed would have showed as clearly as a wizard. That left only a single answer, however impossible it seemed. One of them—one of the two warriors, surely—possessed a force of will so strong as to pass belief.

The Stygian necromancer's smile was cruel. An adamantine will. Beyond acquisition of the girl, there might be sport to be had from such a one.

But first, food and wine and sleep. Wearily Amon-Rama left the chamber of mirrors. On its thin, transparent column the Heart of Ahriman smouldered malevolently.

VII

The sanguinary sun sat on the mountain tops, a burning ball that baked the four riders even as daylight dwindled. Bombatta had cursed steadily since they turned south, but he did it under his breath, and Conan did not try to hear what was said. Had he heard, he might have had to take action, and he had decided that Jehnna should not have to see the other man slain, pleasant though the idea might seem were she not there.

"Over this next hill, Conan," Malak said suddenly. "Selket stab me if Akiro's camp does not lie there. If I was not lied to in Shadizar."

"Three times have you said that," Jehnna said irritably.

The wiry man shrugged and grinned. "Even I make mistakes now and again, my lady. But this time, I assure you, I am right."

Stones turned beneath the hooves of Conan's mount as it made its way up the slope. The Cimmerian was beginning to wonder if Malak even had an idea in which country Akiro was to be found. Then he topped the hill, and growled, "Hannuman's Stones!"

"Watch your tongue before Jehnna!" Bombatta snarled, but as he reached Conan's side he muttered, "Black Erlik's Bowels and Bladder!"

Below them was indeed Akiro's camp, a crude hut of clay and stone built into the side of a hill. The plump, yellow-skinned wizard, however, was bound hand and foot to a thick, upright post set in the ground before the hut, and about his feet piled branches were just leaping into flame. Three men, their backs to those on the hill, stood in front of the growing fire with heads thrown back to chant at the sky and arms outstretched so that their long, white robes hung beneath them like wings. More than a score of others, their filthy, tattered rags contrasting sharply with the triad's pristine garments, watched, howling and shaking their spears in approbation.

"I never liked Akiro all that much," Malak said weakly.

"We need him," Conan replied. He looked at Bombatta, not asking the question, but the Zamoran saw it in his eyes.

"No, barbar. If this is the man you've brought us all this way to find, then he is your affair."

"Why are you all talking," Jehnna demanded angrily, "instead of helping that poor man down there? Bombatta?"

"My duty is to guard you, child. Would you have me take you among those savages below, or leave you here alone when there might be others about?"

"There is still time to ride for Arenjun," Malak suggested.

"Go straight for Akiro, Malak." Conan's broadsword came easily into his hand, the setting sun lighting its length with premonitory crimson. "He cannot stand those flames much longer." With that he kicked his horse into a gallop down the hill.

"Donar help me," Malak hissed at the Cimmerian's back, "think you of the kind of men who can tie up a wizard!" Muttering quick prayers to half a score of gods, the small thief loosed the horse he had brought for Akiro and followed.

Silently Conan charged, the clash of shod hooves on stone drowned beneath the yells and chants of the spearmen before him. His horse burst into a knot of them, throwing suddenly screaming men to either side like a ship breasting a wave. Others scrambled toward him, spears dropping to the ready, but he ignored them for the moment. The white-clad trio had not ceased their chanting, nor looked away from Akiro. Wizardry of some kind it surely was, and the Cimmerian was just as sure it must be halted if Akiro was to be saved.

The center of the three went down beneath the hooves of Conan's horse with a startled scream and the crunch of bone. The big youth had no compunction about riding him down from behind. This was no sport, but rather war in miniature. These men meant to kill a friend of his, and he would stop them how he could.

The long-robed man to his right snarled at him, produced a dagger from his voluminous sleeve. The Cimmerian could not help staring in horror even as his sword went up. That snarling mouth held teeth filed to points, and below it hung a necklace of shriveled human hands. Small hands. Children's hands.

Conan made his first sound then since leaving the hilltop, a roar of rage as his steel slashed into that foul, sharp-toothed gap. With a gurgling scream the man jerked himself off the blade. Clawed hands rose to clutch at a ruined face; blood poured between quivering fingers, and spreading scarlet stained the pale robe.

Then Conan had no more time to think of the wizard, if such he was, or of the last of the three, who seemed to have disappeared. Shock had frozen the trio's followers at first. Now they came at a rush.

The first spear to thrust at him Conan grabbed just behind the head, ripping it from the grasp of a man whose throat was torn out by the Cimmerian's broadsword an instant later. With the haft of that spear he beat aside another thrust while his blade was slicing yet another shaft in two. Desperately he shifted his hold on the spear and sank its long point into the face of one of his attackers. His steel clove a skull to the eyes.

Three were dead in as many heartbeats, and the rest fell back. They were enough to sweep over him by sheer weight of numbers, but some would surely die. They had proof of that, now, and none wanted to be in the forefront. They shuffled nervously, edging forward, darks eyes burning with a mixture of fear and shame at that fear.

Carefully, not taking his eyes from the slowly approaching spearmen, Conan stepped down from his horse. They would have the advantage, with their long spears, should he remain mounted. Not, he told himself wryly, that there was not some advantage for them merely in out-numbering him twenty to one. Best to take the initiative. He eyed their straggly line, chose the weakest point, and set himself to attack.

Suddenly a ball of fire shot past his shoulder to strike a ragged spearman in the face and explode in lumps of charred flesh.

Conan jumped in spite of himself, and looked over his shoulder. Beside the fire Malak capered wildly, grinning like a fool. In front of the wiry little thief stood Akiro, his rough brown tunic and cross-gaitered leggings still smouldering in patches. The old wizard's lips moved as if he were chanting, but no sound emerged that Conan could hear. Parchment-skinned hands moved in elaborate patterns, ending in a clap at chest height. And when Akiro's hands parted another fireball hurtled from between his palms. Immediately he began gesturing again, but two corpses with blackened stumps where their heads had been were more than enough. Howling with terror the rag-clad spearmen threw down their weapons and ran into the deepening twilight. Their cries faded quickly to the south.

"Misbegotten, half-breed spawn of diseased camels!" Akiro muttered. He peered at his hands, blew on his palms, dusted them together. His wispy gray hair and long mustaches stood out in disarrayed spikes. He smoothed them angrily. "I will teach them a lesson to make their grandchildren's grandchildren shake at the mention of my name. I will make their blood freeze and their bones quiver like jelly."

"Akiro," Conan said. Malak squatted to listen, an interested expression on his face.

"I will visit them with a plague of boils to the tenth generation. I will make their herds fail, and their manhoods whither, and their teeth fall out!"

"Akiro," Conan said.

The saffron-skinned mage shook a fist in the direction of the fleeing men. "They claimed I maligned their gods. Gods!" He grimaced and spat. "Fool shamans do not know a fire elemental when they see one. I told them if they sacrificed one more child I would bring lightning down on their heads, and by the Nine-Fold Path of Power, I will do it!"

"Maybe you can't," Malak said. "I mean, they managed to tie you up and half cook you. Maybe you had better leave them alone."

Akiro's faced smoothed to an utter lack of expression. "Do not fear, Malak," he said mildly. "I will not make your stones fall off." Malak toppled over backwards, staring with bulging eyes at the wizard. "Is that proper respect that I see on your face?" Akiro asked gently. "Then I shall recount what happened. The three shamans, who call themselves priests, managed to put a spell on me while I slept. A minor spell, but it enabled their followers to fall on me and bind me." His tone hardened as he spoke, and his voice rose higher word by word. "They tied my hands, so I could make no gesture of significance. They stuffed rags into my mouth," he paused to spit, "so I could utter no words of power. Then they proposed to sacrifice me to their gods. Gods! I will show them gods! I shall be a demon in their pantheon, at least, before I am done! I—That girl."

Conan blinked. He had decided to let Akiro run out of wind—it was the only thing to do when the old mage got the bit firmly between his teeth like this—but the sudden softening of voice and change of subject caught him by surprise. Bombatta, he realized, was finally bringing Jehnna down from the hill. The pair of them were barely visible shapes in the dusk, and Conan, for all his mountain-bred vision, would not have wagered that either was a woman had he not known it already.

"She is an innocent," Akiro said, and Malak laughed shrilly.

"You mean that you can tell from here that she's never—"

"Hold your tongue, Malak!" the old man snapped. "This has naught to do with the flesh. It is of the spirit, and it is a terrible thing."

"Terrible!" Conan exclaimed. "It is not what I would chose for myself, but terrible?"

Akiro nodded. "Such must be protected like children till they gain some knowledge of the world, else they are fated to be prey. It is rare that an innocent occurs naturally. Most have been raised so for some sorcerous purpose."

"Raised so," Conan murmured, frowning. Well away from the hut, and the bodies before it, Bombatta was helping Jehnna down from her mount.

The black-armored warrior stood between her and the charnel scene, not allowing her to look.

"Valeria," Akiro said, and the Cimmerian started.

"She is part of why I came to you, Akiro."

"Wait." Akiro bustled into the rude hut. Oaths and the clatter of rummaging drifted out. When he returned he handed Conan a small, polished stone vial sealed with beeswax. "This is for Valeria," he said.

"I do not understand," Conan said.

Akiro pursed his lips and tugged at his mustaches, one with either hand. "Long did I study this question, Cimmerian. I tossed the Bones of Fate, read the stars, told the K'far cards, all to find an answer for what troubles you."

"I am troubled no longer, Akiro. At least—"

"Do not dissemble with me," the wizard cut him off. "How can I help if you do not speak truth to me? Valeria's life and yours were most strongly intertwined. She was at once lover and companion warrior. She died in your place, and so strong was the bond between you that even death could not stop her returning to save you. Cimmerian, that great a bond between life and death is dangerous. Valeria would sever it herself if she knew, but some knowledge is hidden to those beyond the dark."

"Akiro, I do not want the bond severed, and it is not necessary."

"Listen to me, you stubborn northlander. You cannot cut your way out of this with a sword. I know your fate if you will not listen. The cards, the bones, the stars, all agree. Eventually the bond will pull you into a living death. You will find yourself trapped halfway between the world of the living and the world of the dead, but in neither, able to touch neither, for the rest of time. Only forgetfulness can save you. I went to great pains to concoct the potion in that vial. It will wipe from your mind all memory of Valeria. Naught connected to her will remain. Believe me, Cimmerian, could she know the choice you face, Valeria would tell you to drink from that vial without delay. She was not one to shirk a hard decision."

"And if Valeria could return once more?" Conan asked quietly. "Not for moments, as she did before, but to live the rest of the life she should have had. What then, Akiro?"

The rotund mage was silent for a long moment. His eyes traveled to Jehnna, and he licked his lips slowly. "I think we must clear away these bodies so we can eat," he said finally. "I shall need food in me to hear this."

VIII

T he old wizard would not take back his vial, and finally Conan stuffed it into his belt pouch. In the end it was he and Malak who dragged the corpses away. Akiro muttered vaguely about his back and his aged bones, though there was considerable muscle under those layers of fat. Bombatta again refused to leave Jehnna, or to let her come close enough to see what the big Cimmerian and his diminutive friend carried to the far side of the hill.

Akiro had said he required food before listening, and now he insisted on it. Rabbits taken that morning by the wizard—by the normal means of a sling and stone—were spitted and roasted, and a half-filled basket of small Corinthian oranges was produced from the hut. Finally the last bones were gnawed, and orange peels were tossed into the fire that cast a golden pool before the small hut. Bombatta took a wetstone from his pouch and bent himself to tending his tulwar's edge. Malak began juggling three of the oranges to the delight of Jehnna, though he dropped one at every second pass.

"'Tis a part of the trick," the wiry thief said as he picked an orange from the ground for the fourth time. "To make the later things I do seem even greater by comparison."

Akiro touched Conan on the arm and motioned with his head to the darkness. The two men withdrew from the fire; none of the others seemed to notice their going.

When they had gone far enough that their voices would not carry back to the hut, Akiro said, "Now tell me how Valeria is to be brought back to life."

Conan eyed the plump mage speculatively, though he could see nothing of his visage but shadows in the moonlight. Wizards did things in their own way and for their own reasons, even the most benign of them. Not that many could be called benign. Even Akiro, with whom he had traveled before, was largely a mystery to him. But then, was there *anyone* in all of this whom he could afford to trust totally?

"Taramis," Conan began, "the Princess Royal, has promised to return Valeria to me. Not as a shade, nor as an animated corpse, but living, as once she lived."

The wizard was silent for a time, tugging at the long mustaches that framed his mouth. "I would not have thought to find one of such power alive in the world today," he said finally. "Most especially not as a princess of the Zamoran Royal house."

"You think she lies?" Conan sighed, but Akiro shook his head.

"Perhaps not. It is written that Malthaneus of Ophir did this thing a thousand years gone, and possibly Ahmad Al-Rashid, in Samara, twice so far in the past. It could be that it is time for the world to once more see such wonders."

"Then you believe Taramis can do as she promised."

"Of course," Akiro continued musingly, "Malthaneus was the greatest white wizard since the Circle of the Right-Hand Path was broken in the days before Acheron, and Ahmad Al-Rashid, it is said, was thrice-blessed by Mitra himself."

"You jump about like a monkey," Conan growled. "Can you not say one thing or another and stick to it?"

"I can say that this thing has been done in the past. I can say that Taramis *may* be able to do it." He paused, and Conan thought his bushy gray brows had drawn down into a frown. "But why should she do it for you?"

In as few words as possible the Cimmerian told of the quest on which he accompanied Jehnna, of the key and the treasure and the short time that remained.

"A Stygian," Akiro muttered when he had finished. "It is said that there is no people without some spark of good in them, but never have I found a Stygian I would trust long enough to turn around twice."

"He must be a powerful sorcerer," Conan said. "No doubt too powerful for you."

Akiro wheezed a short laugh. "Do not try that game on me, youngling. I am too old to be snared so easily. I have those accursed hedge-wizards to deal with."

"I would not find your company amiss, Akiro."

"I am too old to go riding off into the mountains, Cimmerian. Come, let us go back to the fire. The nights are cold here, and the fire is warm." Rubbing his hands together, the gray-haired mage did not wait for Conan to follow.

"At least Bombatta will be quieted," Conan muttered. "He has been afraid Malak or you would upset some part of the prophecy of Skelos."

Akiro froze with one foot lifted for his next step. Slowly he turned back to face the big youth. "Skelos?"

"Aye, the Scrolls of Skelos. They tell what is to be found on this quest, and what must be done for it to succeed, or so says Taramis. You know of this Skelos?"

"A thaumaturge centuries dead," Akiro replied absently, "who wrote many volumes of sorcerous lore. All now as rare as virgins in Shadizar." He thrust his head forward, staring intently at Conan through the darkness. "Taramis has these in her possession? The Scrolls of Skelos?"

"She quoted from them as if she does. She must. Where are you going?"

Akiro was disappearing toward the hut with a quickness that belied his complaints of feebleness. "Time is short, you say," he called over his shoulder. "We must leave for the mountains before first light, and I need my sleep."

Smiling, Conan strolled after him. Betimes, he thought, the best snare was one you did not know you had laid.

When the Cimmerian reached the fire Jehnna sat staring into the flames with daydreaming eyes. Bombatta, still drawing the wetstone along his blade, shot irritable glances at Malak, who sprawled beneath a blanket with snores like ripping sailcloth coming from his open mouth. The scar-faced warrior was not the only one bothered by the all-intrusive sound. From within the hut came angry mutters, of which only the words ". . . need my sleep," ". . . old bones," and ". . . like an ox with a bad belly," were recognizable.

Abruptly Akiro's frowning face appeared in the doorway of the hut, eyes fixed intently on Malak and lips moving. Malak's snore ended as if sliced by a razor. With a gasp the wiry thief bolted upright, staring about him fearfully. Akiro was no longer to be seen. Hesitantly, one hand feeling at his throat, Malak stretched himself out again. His breathing deepened quickly, but barely enough to be heard above the crackle of the fire. Moments later snorting rumbles began to erupt from the hut.

Jehnna giggled. "Is he going with us?"

"Yes." Conan sat crosslegged beside her. "We will leave before the sun rises."

"In the direction I say, this time?"

"In the direction you say."

He could feel her eyes on him; they made him unaccustomedly awkward. He had no small experience with women. He could deal with impudent serving girls and old merchants' too-young wives, with brazen doxies and nobles' hot-eyed daughters. This girl was a virgin and more. An innocent, Akiro termed her, and Conan thought the word fit. Still, there was one thing that did *not* fit with that description.

"Before," Conan said, "when Bombatta and I all but came to blows, you changed, for a space of moments at least. You sounded much like Taramis."

"For a few moments I *was* Taramis." His eyes widened, and she giggled. "Oh, not in truth. I did not want the two of you to fight, so I pretended that I was my aunt, and that two of the servants were squabbling."

"I am no servant," Conan said sharply.

Jehnna seemed taken aback. "Why do you sound offended? You serve my aunt, and me. Bombatta is not offended that he is my aunt's servant."

The sussuration of wetstone on steel stopped, unnoticed by the two at the fire.

"He can bend his knee if he wishes," Conan said. "I hire my sword and my skill for a day, or for ten, but I am servant to no man, woman or god."

"All the same," she replied, "I am glad that you accompany me. I cannot remember ever speaking more than two words together to anyone other than my aunt, or Bombatta, or my dressing maids. You are very different, and interesting. It is all different and interesting. The sky and the stars and so many leagues and leagues of open space."

He stared into her big brown eyes and felt a hundred years older than she. As lovely a maiden as he had ever seen, he thought, and so very truly the innocent indeed, unknowing of the feelings she could raise in a man. "It is a dangerous land," he muttered, "and the mountains are more so, even without a Stygian sorcerer. This is no place for you."

"It is my destiny," she said simply, and he grunted.

"Why? Because it is written in the Scrolls of Skelos?"

"Because I was marked at birth. Look."

Before his astonished eyes Jehnna tugged down the neck of her robes, shrugging, until her satiny olive-skinned breasts were bared almost to the nipples. Sweet mounds made to nestle in a man's palms, the Cimmerian thought, his throat suddenly tight.

"See?" Jehnna said. "Here. This mark I bore at birth, naming my destiny. It is described in the scrolls, but it was the gods who chose me."

There was a birthmark, he saw, in the valley between her breasts. A red eight-pointed star, no bigger than a man's thumbnail and as precisely formed as if drawn by a craftsman.

Abruptly curved steel slashed down to shine in the firelight between them.

"Do not touch her, thief," Bombatta grated. "Not ever!"

Conan opened his mouth for an angry reply, then realized that he had indeed been stretching a hand toward the girl. The gleaming blade hung before his fingertips as if it was the tulwar he had meant to stroke.

Furious with himself, Cimmerian straightened, returning Bombatta's glare.

Jehnna's eyes traveled from one man to the other, a strange expression crossing her face as if thoughts new and disturbing had come to her.

"It is late," Conan said harshly. "Best we all sleep, for we must travel early."

Bombatta held out his free hand to help Jehnna rise, still holding his blade before her as if it were a shield. Conan's eyes did not leave those of the scarred warrior while the huge Zamoran backed away, leading Jehnna. The girl glanced once at the tall Cimmerian youth, her eyes troubled, but she allowed herself to be bundled into her blankets without speaking. As on the previous night Bombatta set himself before her as a guard.

Muttering curses under his breath, Conan wrapped himself in his own blankets. This was foolishness, he told himself. There were women enough in the world that he did not let himself be entangled by a girl who likely did not even know what she did. She was a child, no matter her age. He slept, and his sleep was filled with dreams of lush-bodied Taramis and the night of lust they had shared. Yet often, in those dreams, he would look, and it would be not Taramis he held, but Jehnna. His sleep was not a restful one.

Blackness hung thickly over Shadizar, and the tapestried halls of Taramis' palace were empty as she made her way from her sleeping chamber. The only sound was the brushing of her long silken robe on the polished marble tiles of the corridors. Her astrologers and the priests of the ancient worship she revived came often to the great hall she entered, but the nocturnal visits that she made with increasing frequency, she made alone.

About the edges of the room cunningly hooded golden lamps gave off a soft glow that could have been moonlight, so pale was it. The floor was black marble, polished to a mirror sheen, and fluted alabaster columns supported the high, arched ceiling, tiled with onyx and set with sapphires and diamonds to represent the night sky, the sky as it would be on one night in each thousand years.

Centered beneath that false sky was a couch carved of crimson marble, polished with the hair of virgins, and on it lay what seemed to be the alabaster statue of a man with his eyes closed, nude and half again as large as any living man, more handsome than any mortal man could ever be. But a single thing marred the perfection. Sunk to the depth of half a finger joint in the broad forehead was a black depression, a circle as wide as man's hand. There was about the figure a sense of timeless waiting.

Slowly Taramis approached the marble couch, stopping at its foot. Her gaze roamed the alabaster form, and her breath quickened. Many men had she had in her life, choosing the first most carefully at sixteen, choosing each since with as great a care. Men she knew as well as she knew the rooms of her own palace. But what would it be like to be the lover of . . . a god?

She slipped her robe from her shoulders and sank naked to her knees at the feet of the figure. No word in the Scrolls of Skelos required this of her, but she wanted more than even they promised.

Pressing her face to those cold, alabaster soles she whispered, "I am thine, O great Dagoth."

A compulsion to go further than ever before seized her, and she rained moaning kisses on those feet. Slowly she worked her way upwards, leaving no portion of that pale surface undampened by her ardent lips, caressing it with her lush roundness, until she writhed atop the great form as she would atop a man. Trembling fingers reached up to softly stroke the face.

"I am thine, O great Dagoth," she whispered again, "and forever will I be thine. When thou wakeneth I will build temples to thee, overturning the temples of other gods, but I will be more than thy priestess. Thy godly flesh will merge with mine, and I will hold myself chaste hereafter, save for thee. I will sit on thy right hand, and by thy grace will I receive the ultimate powers over life and death. Once more will the sacrifices be made to thee, and once more to thee will the nations bow. All this I vow, O great Dagoth, and seal it with my flesh and my soul."

Suddenly her breath caught in her throat. That on which she lay had still the hardness of stone, but now it held the warmth of life. Not daring to believe, fearing that perhaps it was but the heat of her own body, absorbed, she brought her hands down over the broad, perfect shoulders to the deep chest. Everywhere was the warmth.

Almost at once it was gone again, and her last doubts were shattered by the unnatural quickness of its going. Her god had given her a sign. Her offering would be accepted; the rewards would be hers. Smiling, she let her own sleep claim her there, lying atop the form of the Sleeping God.

IX

Conan's eyes narrowed as he studied what lay ahead. Shadows stretched before him, and behind the sun had not yet risen two handbreadths above the horizon. There were shadows in plenty on the sheer rock wall that faced them half a league on, the narrow lines of folds and creases in the stone, but no sign of any pass.

"Jehnna?" he called, looking over his shoulder.

He did not have to say more. All had fallen silent as they saw what they approached, and even the slender girl wore a worried frown.

"We must go this way," she said insistently. "I know this is the right way. Straight ahead now. I know it."

Conan booted his horse into a trot. Whatever lay ahead—and there had better be *something*, by all the gods—he was impatient to find out what it was.

He scanned the cliffs, running a league to the north and south of the point they rode toward. The lowest was at least fifty paces in height and topped with a jutting overhang, the highest was ten times that. Occasional vertical crevices and shadowed chimneys split the continuous front, but in those two leagues was nothing that even hinted at a passage through.

He could climb it, he knew. He had climbed higher cliffs and sheerer in the wind-swept mountain fastnesses of his native Cimmeria. Malak likely could, as well, and perhaps even Bombatta, but Akiro was no scaler of cliffs, and the Cimmerian could see no way at all to get Jehnna over them unless she grew wings. Wings. He hummed thoughtfully. Actual wings were out of the question, of course, but perhaps Akiro could provide an answer. Mayhap the old man could use his powers to lift himself and the girl to the top of the cliff while the rest of them climbed in more ordinary fashion.

Abruptly he realized what lay directly ahead of him. Straight ahead, she had said, and straight ahead was a narrow crevice, but a crevice that stretched deep into the cliff, losing his eyes with a sharp bend in fifty paces. He could not be so lucky, he was sure, that this would not be their path. Wings, he thought, would have been much better.

Conan looked around at the others. It was clear by their faces that they all saw what he had seen. Even Bombatta wore a doubtful grimace, and Malak was muttering prayers under his breath. Only Jehnna appeared sure, and even so the Cimmerian could not help asking.

"This?" She nodded firmly, and he sighed. "I will go first," he said, loosening his broadsword in its worn leather scabbard. "Malak behind me, then Akiro and the packhorse, then Jehnna. Bombatta, you bring up the rear." The scar-faced warrior nodded, easing his own curved blade. "And keep a watch above," he finished. Though, he thought, what they could do if someone began dropping boulders or worse on them he could not imagine.

"Shakuru's Burning Teeth," Malak said sourly. "We could have been in Arenjun by now."

Not answering, Conan rode into the narrow opening, and the rest followed. The sky became a thin strip directly overhead, and light faded till it almost seemed twilight was upon them once more. The high walls were barely separated enough to allow horse and rider to pass. Gray stone slid past, often no more than a fingerwidth from knees on either side.

On they rode, twisting, turning, doubling back on themselves, till only Conan's instincts told him that they still moved westward. The sun stood directly overhead, now, throwing a cascade of fading shadows into the snaking gap.

Suddenly Conan drew rein, his nostrils flaring.

"What is it?" Bombatta called hoarsely.

"Have you no nose?" the Cimmerian demanded.

"Woodsmoke," Akiro said.

"Aye," Conan agreed. "And more than a campfire."

"What do we do?" Malak wanted to know, and Conan snorted with brief laughter.

"What can we do, my friend? We ride on and see what's burned."

Three more bends the strait passage took, and then they were out of it. Out of the narrow crack through the mountain, and into a large village that butted against the steep side of the valley. Crude huts lined dusty paths that could not properly be called streets. On the far side of the village Conan noted half-a-score wispy columns of smoke, remnants of whatever had burned. A few naked children yelled and tumbled in the dirt with bony dogs, while their ragged elders, as filthy as the small ones if not more so, stared in dark-eyed surprise and wariness at the newcomers.

"Pull up the hood of your cloak, Jehnna," the Cimmerian said quietly.

"It is hot," she protested, but Bombatta jerked the white hood forward, hiding her face in its shade.

Conan nodded. As outlanders they might well have trouble just riding through this village, and most assuredly there was no way around it. There was no need to increase the chance by letting it be known they included a beautiful young girl in their number.

"Do not stop for anything," he told the others, "until we are well beyond this place. Not for anything." Resting a hand on his swordhilt, he twitched his reins and started forward. They rode in the same order in which they had traveled the narrow passage.

"Malak," Akiro said, "if you see something you desire in this place, try not to steal it."

"Eh?" Malak jerked his hand back from a basket of figs. "Fidesa's Teats, old man, I am not a fool."

Suspicious eyes followed them, covetous eyes that caressed their horses and weapons, speculative eyes that tried to pierce Jehnna's cloak. Yet they were not many for such a place, and as they came on the source of the smoke, ten patches of ash that had once been huts, Conan saw why there were not more. The villagers had gathered to watch a brutal entertainment.

Six soldiers in boiled leather breastplates and red-crested helms stood leaning on their spears and laughing in a wide circle around a woman who clutched a wooden staff taller than she and as thick as a man's two thumbs. Her skin, as black as polished ebony, proclaimed her origin far to the south. A tightly bound strip of cloth about her small breasts and a slightly wider bit about her loins were all of the garb on her hard-muscled body, and a thick rope bound about one ankle kept her within a pace of a stake driven into the ground.

"Those men are not Zamorans," Jehnna said. "This is Zamoran land, is it not?"

Conan did not think that it was the proper moment to explain the border situation to her. The men wore the armor of one of the Corinthian city-states. The mountains, on the border between Zamora and Corinthia, were claimed by both, and the villages paid such taxes as they could not avoid to whomever sent soldiers, denying the sovereignty of either when there were no soldiers.

The black woman stooped slowly, not taking her eyes from the encircling soldiers, to feel the knot at her ankle. As her fingers touched the rope, one of the Corinthians dashed forward, jabbing with his spear. The woman leaped back as far as the rope would allow, the staff spinning in her hands like a thing alive. The spearman stopped his rush, laughing, and another, behind her, jumped forward. Again she darted away from the spearpoint, then had to dodge yet another.

"What did this woman do to deserve this?" Jehnna demanded. Conan stifled an oath, and gripped his sword hilt more firmly.

A dirty-faced man on the edge of the crowd looked up at Jehnna, frowning. "She's a bandit." He twisted his neck, trying to see her face under the edge of her hood. "We took another, and killed him slow, but the soldiers came before we could get to her."

"They'll do for her," another man said, joining the attempt to make out Jehnna's features. A swollen bruise stood out blue beneath the grime on his forehead. "They shouldn't have given that stick back, though. She killed a man with it, and near got away." His gaze slid from Jehnna to each of the others in turn, and his mouth pursed thoughtfully.

"Bombatta," Jehnna said, "you must stop them. Whatever she has done, these men have no right to treat her so. They are Corinthians, and this is Zamoran land."

"Bandits and thieves deserve to die," the scar-faced Zamoran said harshly. "And it is time we were going on." He snatched for her bridle, missing as she pulled her horse around to face Conan.

"And will you do nothing either?" she demanded.

Conan drew a deep breath, but the situation had gone beyond cursing. More villagers were turning to look at them, weighing the value of their possessions with intent eyes, trying to see if Jehnna were pretty enough for the auction block. Such were not usually dangerous in the open and the daylight, but their blood was heated by the bandits' raid, and by the soldiers' cruel sport. The desire was there, writ plain on their faces in licked lips and shifting glances. In moments, soldiers or no, daylight or no, these men would try for fresh prey, and an attempt to leave now would only set off the eruption on the instant.

"Stand ready," the Cimmerian commanded quietly.

"Bel watch over us," Malak breathed as Conan moved his horse into the crowd.

Wondering villagers parted slowly before him as he rode slowly toward the soldiers. Casually, nodding to the Corinthians, he rode into their circle. They frowned at each other, at him, obviously unsure what he was about. He drew his broadsword.

"Do not kill her and spoil the fun!" one of the Corinthians shouted. The sable-skinned woman stepped smoothly to the limits of the rope, her staff at the ready and untrusting eyes on his face.

Conan gave her a smile he hoped was reassuring. His blade flashed in the sun, slashing through the rope close to her ankle. Their eyes met; she had not moved a muscle. There was no fear in her, he thought admiringly.

"What did he do?" a soldier called. "I could not see. Did he strike her?"

As casually as he had entered the circle, Conan rode out of it, heedless of the doubtful glances the Corinthians cast at him. Before the Cimmerian reached his companions the black woman took advantage of her chance. Staff moaning with the speed of its whirling, she attacked.

"Ride!" Conan roared.

The thick butt of the woman's weapon crushed a soldier's throat before her captors had time to realize she was truly free of the rope. The wooden shaft crashed against a crested helmet, buckling the Corinthian's knees, then spun to shiver a spear from another's grasp and rebound into his face with the crunch of bone and a spray of blood.

Shouting villagers scattered before Conan's waving sword and prancing horse. Bombatta struggled to reach Jehnna's reins, while she protested, yelling words the Cimmerian could not hear and pointing at the woman who fought.

Three soldiers had gone down in almost the space of as many breaths, and the three remaining hesitated at closing with the woman responsible. She whirled the long staff about her head, giving a high, ululating cry. The three exchanged glances and reached their decision. As one man, they ran. Again the woman gave voice to her battle cry, this time in triumph. Then she disappeared after the soldiers.

Angrily Conan snatched Jehnna's reins from her hands. She tried to speak, but he booted his horse to a gallop, pulling hers behind, and all she could do was cling to the high pommel of her saddle. Villagers shook fists at them, and here or there a spear or rusty sword, but they made no effort to hinder the speeding riders.

Only when the village was out of sight around a bend in the valley did Conan slow, and return the girl's reins to her.

She snatched them from his hand and glared. "Why did we leave that woman in the village? She—"

"She has more chance now than she did an hour gone," Conan barked. "Did we come here to rescue bandits, or to find a key?" He made an effort to control his anger. She had no idea of the danger in which she had placed them, not even now.

A clatter of hooves in the distance brought a growl from Bombatta. "The Corinthians. There's little chance they will leave us out of their report."

"They will leave out the dark-skinned woman," Akiro observed drily, "and make us many more than we are. To be driven off by a large party of armed men is one thing, to be defeated by a single woman another."

Jehnna looked from one to another of them. "We had to do it," she maintained stubbornly. "That woman could not have deserved to be tormented."

"Which way?" Conan asked, breathing heavily.

Jehnna pointed silently down the valley. At least, the Cimmerian thought, it was not back toward the village. There was no talk among them as they resumed their journey.

X

The valley down which they fled from the village led into another valley, that into yet another, and the third into a twisting, steep-walled canyon scattered with huge boulders, some half-buried in the stony soil. The Karpash Mountains loomed about them, gray peaks often capped with snow, their dark lower slopes sparsely spotted with stunted trees.

Conan eyed the sun, halfway to its setting now, and thought of the time left. Only three more days, and they had not even found the key yet, much less the treasure. And if they did not return to Shadizar with both by the night of the third day . . . Face grim, he touched the golden dragon amulet hanging at his neck.

Malak brought his horse up beside the Cimmerian. "We are being followed, Conan."

Conan nodded. "I know."

"There is only one, but he's getting closer."

"Then we had best dissuade him," Conan said. "You and Akiro keep on with the girl. I will catch up to you." He dropped back until he rode with Bombatta at the rear. "We are being followed," he told the scarred man.

"I know," Bombatta replied.

"Let us convince him not to, you and I."

Bombatta frowned doubtfully at Jehnna before giving a reluctant nod.

As the others continued on their way, the two men swung their horses from the line of march, one to either side. Two of the great boulders that dotted the valley shielded them from whomever came up the trail after them. Jehnna twisted in her saddle to look back, but Conan motioned quickly for her to turn back. The follower must be given no warning that he was discovered. The girl and her two companions disappeared behind another bend of the canyon. Conan drew his sword and rested it across the saddle before him. He did not have long to wait.

Stones rattling beneath shod hooves heralded the approach of their pursuer, and Conan frowned at the noise. The man did not seem to care if he was detected. The Cimmerian exchanged glances with Bombatta, and the two set themselves.

The first glimpse of a horse appeared between the boulders that hid them, and Conan charged out. "Hold!" he shouted, and then his jaw dropped in surprise. Beside him, Bombatta began to curse.

The ebon-skinned woman from the village started and stared, then drew herself up. Her horse, two hands shorter than theirs, bore a Corinthian military saddle, and behind it hung a leather waterbag. "I am Zula," she announced proudly, "a warrior of the People of the Mountain, who live to the south of the land called Keshan. I would know the name of he who gave me my life again."

"I am called Conan," the Cimmerian said, "of Cimmeria."

Zula peered at his face intently. "I did not truly believe your eyes before. Do many people in this Cimmeria have eyes like sapphire?"

"Erlik take his eyes," Bombatta snapped, "and you as well, woman! You have heard his name. Now be on your way, and bother us no more!"

The woman did not look at him, or seem even to have heard him. "I will ride with you, Conan of Cimmeria. Perhaps I can repay the life you gave me."

Conan shook his head slowly. This talk of a life to be repaid was so strong a reminder of Valeria that it must be an omen, but of what kind? "What I did was not done to save your life, but rather to allow us to escape that village without having to fight our way out. You owe me nothing."

"Reasons do not matter," she said. "Only actions. And for your actions I live and am free, where else I would be dead or captive."

Before Conan could frame an answer they were joined by Jehnna and the others.

He gave the two men with her a withering look. "Did I not say I would catch up to you? What if there had been a score of villagers on our trail? Is this how you look after Jehnna?"

Malak grinned weakly and became engrossed in study of the pack horse's lead rope. Akiro shrugged, saying, "I am too old to make a woman do what she does not wish to do."

"Do not be silly, Conan," Jehnna said. "Malak said there was only one, and you agreed. My ears are not failing." She shifted her attention to Zula. "The villagers called you a bandit."

"They lied," the dark woman replied scornfully. "There is a smaller village four leagues to the south, from which these people stole several young women. With other warriors I took payment for the recovery of these women. In the night we came, firing storage huts to draw the attention of these dogs who call themselves men. The women we found, but T'car, who was my battle companion, took a spear thrust and could not escape, and I could not leave him."

"And so you both were captured," Jehnna said breathlessly. "It was a brave thing you did, a thing such as romances are made of."

"He was my battle companion," Zula said simply.

Jehnna jerked a nod, as if reaching a decision. "You will come with us."

"No!" Bombatta shouted. "Mitra's mercies, Jehnna, will you endanger everything? Remember the prophecy."

"I remember nothing that says I cannot have a woman with me." Jehnna's tone was firm, but still she turned to Conan. "Say that she may accompany me. You have Malak and Akiro. I have only Bombatta, and he shouts at me of late. He never shouted at me before."

"She could not even keep up with us on that Corinthian sheep," Malak laughed.

Zula eyed him calmly. "I will ride you into the ground, little man, even after you attain full growth."

Conan touched the amulet on his chest. Bombatta could be right; perhaps they *did* endanger the fulfilling of the prophecy, and thus the rebirth of Valeria. But there was the matter of the omen. A life to be repaid. "I will not say no," he said finally.

Bombatta cursed, but Jehnna overrode him with her enthusiasm. "Then you will ride with me, and be my companion."

"I will ride with Conan," Zula said. "And so with you." Jehnna smiled as if she had not caught the distinction the ebon woman made.

"Let us *all* ride, then," Conan said, and turned his horse once more down the canyon.

In the sanguine glow of the gem Amon-Rama studied the moving figures. Two more, he thought, and concentrated his study on the rotund, yellow-skinned man with the wispy gray hair and mustaches. There was power there. A wizard. His thin mouth twisted in a malevolent smile. Not enough power. Merely more sport.

"Come to me," he whispered. "Bring the One to me."

". . . And when you have carried this key and this treasure to Shadizar," Zula said, "what then?"

Jehnna looked at the other woman in surprise. She had never thought of such a question. "Why, I will live in the palace, as I always have." That brought a vaguely dissatisfied frown to her face. But what else was she to do? "This is my destiny," she said firmly.

Zula only grunted.

Feeling ill at ease without knowing why, Jehnna let her eyes travel ahead, to wiry, laughing Malak and round-bellied, wise-eyed Akiro, to broad-shouldered Conan, riding in the lead as they wended their way around a snow-tipped mountain. Bombatta still brought up the rear, his gaze always on the heights, searching for danger in the fading, reddish-gold light that announced the imminence of dusk.

It was the Cimmerian who held her thoughts, however. He was so different from what she had expected. Akiro, and even Malak, had their places in the stories her dressing maids told, but the tall northlander fit nowhere in those tales of handsome princes and lovely princesses. And it was not just him. He made *her* feel very peculiar, indeed, in ways she did not recognize. None of her feelings seemed to correspond to what she imagined she would feel like if he were to recite long poems to her eyes. It was difficult to imagine him doing that, in any case. Or to see him giving her a single, golden rose for her to weep crystal tears over while he went far away. Conan might rather sweep her fiercely to his saddle before him and . . . and what? She was not sure, but she was certain that whatever he would do would be something not in the stories.

Zula, she thought, might have useful advice, but something made her feel awkward about simply asking. But perhaps if she made her way to it in slow steps . . .

"Women warriors," she said abruptly, "are strange to me. Are all women of your land warriors?"

The dark woman nodded. "Our mountains are surrounded by enemies, and we are few. Too few to allow us your ways, where only men are warriors, and some few women who want to be. All of us must fight, if we would live."

"I did not know there were women in my land who are warriors," Jehnna said, diverted for the moment. "Could I be a warrior?" It would certainly be a different thing than living the rest of her life in Taramis' gardens, she thought.

"Perhaps," Zula replied, "if you were willing to accept hard training, and if you have the heart. It is a harsh life, though, and you must ever be ready for death. Your own, or that of someone close to you."

The sadness in the other woman's voice reminded Jehnna of her purpose. "T'car," she said softly. "You called him your battle companion. Was he your . . . your true love?"

"My lover, you mean? Aye, he was my lover, and in all ways as good a man as I have ever known."

"How . . . how did it begin? Between you and T'car, that is."

Zula laughed, as if at a fond memory. "Many women wanted him, for he was a proud and handsome man, but I told them they must fight me if they would lie with him. None of them could stand against me, and when T'car saw, he took me into his hut."

Jehnna blinked. It certainly did not sound like any of the stories. "So you simply decided he would be yours, chose him. Do men like that?"

"Some men, child, if they know themselves men. Others have not the stomach for it."

"And which of the men riding with us would you chose? Malak, perhaps?"

The black woman snorted. "That has no humor even if it is meant to be a joke. I would choose Conan."

"Because he saved your life?" Jehnna felt a flash of anger, and could not understand it. "Why not Bombatta?"

"That one would be brutal, thinking it made him seem strong, yet I could bend him to my will like bending a reed. Conan can be strong and gentle at the same time, and he would not bend easily if at all. As well lie with a rabbit as with a man you can bend too easily." Zula gave her a sidelong glance; Jehnna knew her face was flushed, and the other woman's obvious amusement made her color deepen. "Do not worry, child. I will not try to take him from you."

Jehnna found herself stammering. "Take him . . . but he is not . . . I mean . . ." She drew a deep breath and tried to sit very straight in her saddle, as Taramis did at her most imperious. "Do not call me child," she said frostily. "I am a woman."

"Of course. Forgive me, Jehnna." Zula was silent for a time before continuing. "Among my people there is a custom at the death of a lover. I will lie with no man for one year from the day of T'car's dying. He would have done the same had I died."

It was Jehnna's turn to ride in silence, mulling over what had been said. Little of it seemed to be of any use to her. There were no women to challenge over Conan, even if she knew how to fight them, and even if she was sure that was what she wanted. As for the rest . . .

"Zula, thrice now you have spoken of lying with a man. What does that mean?"

The black woman's face went slack with amazement. "By all the gods," she breathed, "You *are* a child."

Jehnna opened her mouth for an angry retort, and froze with it open. Before them lay another mountain, or rather half of a mountain, for its top had long since disappeared. Even from below it was plain that a vast crater holed that truncated peak.

"Conan," she whispered, then shouted it, "Conan! The key! I can feel it pulling me! The key is in that crater!" Eagerly she urged her horse to a gallop.

XI

"Wait, Jehnna," Conan called for the tenth time, but he knew it was already too late. She had outdistanced all of them, and even as he spoke she topped the crater's rim and disappeared.

Cursing, he sped after her as fast as his horse would take the mountain slope. The others were strung out behind him in a long line, but he could not wait for them. Over the rim he galloped, and gasped as he started down the other side.

At the bottom of the mammoth pit lay a lake unruffled by any breeze, its dark blue speaking of great depth. On either side of the glassy waters rose sheer walls. Below him was a small beach of black sand, rushes growing on its edges. Jehnna's mount was already halfway to the water in its headlong plunge. And on the far side of the lake stood a palace of crystal, an impossible structure of glittering facets that made the hair stand up on the back of his neck.

By the time he caught up to her, Jehnna's panting horse had its muzzle in the lake, and the girl stared with eager eyes at the distant crystalline towers. The crater's deepness created an early dusk on the sands.

"The key is in that palace?" Conan said.

She nodded excitedly. "Yes. I can feel it, pulling me."

"We must leave the crater, then," he told her, "and go around the side of the mountain. There is no way from here except to swim."

The others began to arrive, first Bombatta and Zula almost together, then Akiro, and lastly Malak, with the packhorse.

"Are you all right, child?" Bombatta shouted at the same instant that Zula cried, "Jehnna, are you unharmed?" The scar-faced man and the ebon woman glared at one another.

"This is the way," Jehnna said insistently. "This is the proper way."

"How?" Conan demanded.

Even Bombatta looked doubtful. "We could go around, child. It can make no difference."

"This is the way," Jehnna repeated.

Suddenly Malak leaped down from his horse and waded into the rushes. When he came out again he was dragging a long, narrow boat of hides stretched over a wooden frame. He held up a handful of cords and bone fish-hooks. "Villagers provide the way, eh?" he grinned. "The fisherman will not care if we borrow his boat. There are paddles in it, too."

"Convenient," Akiro murmured, "to find it here. Mayhap too convenient."

"What do you mean?" Conan asked.

The wizard tugged at a dangling gray mustache and peered toward the palace, sparkling still even now that direct sunlight was gone. "I do not think the Karpash Mountain folk are fishermen. And even if they were, would you fish in a place where *that* was?"

"But . . . here it is," Malak protested. "You cannot deny your eyes."

"I can deny any of my senses," Akiro replied mildly, "except those of the mind. As for the boat, perhaps someone knew we were coming."

With a gasp the small thief dropped the boat and fishing lines as if they were serpents. He stepped back from them quickly, wiping his palms on his leather jerkin. "The Stygian knows we are coming? Banba's Buttocks!"

"We make a cold camp just the same," Conan said, stepping down from his saddle. "If he does *not* know we are here, there is no point to telling him with a fire."

"We must cross now," Jehnna said. "Now. The key is there, I tell you."

"It will still be there in the morning," the Cimmerian replied. With clear reluctance she took her eyes from the palace for the first time since reaching the beach, her jaw firming determinedly, but he went on before she could speak. "I have as much reason not to delay as have you, Jehnna. We will cross with the dawn."

"The thief is right, child," Bombatta said. He gestured to the lake, its waters blackening as sunlight failed. "Did the boat tip over in that, you could drown before I found you. I cannot risk that."

Jehnna lapsed into sulky silence, and Conan turned his attentions to Malak. "You can go, if you wish. Neither of us reckoned with this Amon-Rama knowing about us. Consider the jewels yours."

"Jewels?" Bombatta echoed, but the two friends ignored him.

Malak took a step toward his horse, then stopped. "Conan, I . . . If we had a chance, Cimmerian, but he knows we're coming. Balor's Glaring Eye! You heard Akiro."

"I heard," Conan said.

"You are staying?" Malak asked, and Conan nodded. The wiry man sighed. "I cannot travel in these mountains in the night," he muttered. "I will leave in the morning."

"Now that that is settled," Akiro said, climbing from his horse with a groan, "I am hungry." He dug his fists into the small of his back and stretched. "There is dried lamb in the packs. And figs."

A heavy, solemn air hung over everyone as they set about making camp. The crater had the effect of making each of them grow silent and introspective, all save Jehnna, and she was rapt with the approach to a part of her destiny.

Soon the horses were hobbled, the dried meat and fruit had been consumed, and full night was on them. Jehnna wrapped herself in her blankets, and Zula, to everyone's surprise, sat crosslegged beside the slender girl, crooning soothingly while she fell asleep. Bombatta glowered jealously, but the black woman's fierce glare whenever one of the men came close to Jehnna was enough to make even him keep his distance.

As the full moon rose higher the darkness lessened, for it seemed as if the crater in some fashion trapped and held that canescent glow. The air took on a thick pearlescence of unearthly paleness, where faces could be dimly yet distinctly seen. Conan and Akiro sat alone amid the blanket-swathed mounds that marked where the others slept. They sat, and stared across the dark waters at the palace, shining yet illumining nothing, as a diamond on black velvet shone by holding every glimmer of light.

"This place presses in on me," the Cimmerian said finally. "I cannot like it."

"It is not a place to be liked, except by sorcerers," Akiro replied. He moved his hands before him as if caressing the pale light. "I can sense the flow of power from the very rocks. This is a place where bonds are loosed, and the ties that hold the ordinary whole are undone. Here barriers are weak, and names may summon the dead."

Conan shivered, and told himself there was a chill in the air. "I will be glad to be gone from it, back to Shadizar with the things Taramis seeks."

Suddenly a shriek tore the night, and Jehnna twisted in her blankets, staring with unseeing eyes as she screamed. "No! No! Stop!"

Bombatta leaped from his sleep with tulwar in hand, while Malak cursed and struggled with his blankets, a dagger in each fist. Zula hugged the slender girl to her breast and murmured softly.

Suddenly Jehnna threw her arms about the black woman. Sobs convulsed her. "It was horrible," she wept hoarsely. "Horrible!"

"A dream," Bombatta said, sheathing his blade hastily. He knelt beside the girl and tried to take her from Zula, but she clung even more tightly. "Only a dream, child," he said softly. "Nothing more. Go back to sleep."

Zula glared at him over the girl she held. "Dreams are important. Dreams can tell the future. She must speak of it."

"I agree," Akiro said. "There are often portents in dreams. Speak, Jehnna."

"It was only a dream," Bombatta growled. "Who can say what she might dream in this evil place."

"Speak," Akiro said again to the girl.

Saying the words softly within Zula's comforting arms, Jehnna began. Her dark eyes were still wide with terror. "I was an infant, barely able to walk by myself. I woke and saw my nurse asleep, and I slipped from the nursery. I wanted my mother. Down many corridors I ran, until I came to the room where I knew my mother slept, and my father. Their bed lay in the middle of the floor, and sheer hangings from the ceiling surrounded it. I could see them there, sleeping. And another figure, as well, like a boy. It crouched at the head of the bed, looking down at my mother and my father. The dim light of the lamps gleamed strangely on the figure's hands. One hand raised, and I saw . . . . I saw it held a dagger. The dagger fell, and my father made a strange sound, groaning as if he were hurt. My mother woke, then. She screamed a name, and another dagger slashed. There was blood everywhere. I ran. I wanted to scream, but it was as if I had no tongue. All I could do was run and run and run and—"

Zula gave her a fierce shake, then hugged her even closer. "It is all right, Jehnna. You are safe, now. Safe."

"The name," Akiro prompted. "What was the name?"

Jehnna peeked hesitantly out of the circle of Zula's arms. "Taramis," she whispered. "It was Taramis. Oh, why would I dream this? Why?"

No one made a sound until Bombatta said, "A dream of madness. A foul dream brought on by this foul place. Even my sleep is troubled by things that never were."

"So it seems," Akiro said at last. "You will see to her?" he asked Zula.

The ebon woman nodded, and stroked Jehnna's hair as she began again the soft crooning that had brought sleep before. Bombatta sat on the other side of the girl, as if he, too, would guard her sleep this time. The two warriors, man and woman, stared at each other unblinkingly.

In company with Akiro Conan walked slowly to the water's edge, its black sheen undisturbed by the smallest ripple. "When Jehnna was barely old enough to walk," the Cimmerian said slowly, "Taramis was perhaps sixteen. Just barely the age to be invested with her brother's titles and estates."

"Perhaps it was just a dream."

"Perhaps," Conan said. "Perhaps."

* * *

Amon-Rama peered into the crimson depths of the Heart of Ahriman, frowning at the sleeping figures. None remained awake on the far side of the night-shrouded lake. Last to slumber had been the yellow-skinned wizard, peering into the sky and attempting—this brought a momentary sneer to the Stygian's hawk-nosed face—attempting to touch the powers cupped in the crater. The wizard had retired long after the others breathed deep and slow beneath their blankets. But now even he slept. On the morn they would come, and . . .

His frown deepened to a scowl. On the morn. Long had he waited, and now there were but hours more to wait, yet he itched with impatience. Naught could go wrong at so late a moment. So why did he feel as if ants crawled on his skin?

He released his concentration from the Heart, and the glow faded, leaving only a gem more scarlet than rubies. He would not spend a night so. There would be an end to it.

Swiftly he strode from the mirrored chamber, through crystal halls whose smallest golden ornament would have been a delight to kings, up to the top of the tallest glittering spire of the palace. From that towering height he looked once toward the far shore, as if his unaided eyes could pierce the unnaturally pale night, then produced from beneath his hooded vermilion robes a black chalk compounded from the burned bones of murdered men and the life's breath of virgins.

In quick strokes he scribed a pentagram, leaving one break so it would be safe for him to enter. In each point of the star he drew two symbols, one the same and one different in each of the five. The like symbols would add their warding to the protective power of the pentagram. The other five would summon. Holding his robes carefully so as to smudge no part of the pattern—there could be disaster in that!—he stepped within, and completed the last segment of the unholy diagram.

Slowly at first, then with greater force, he began to chant, until he howled the words at the night. Yet he heard no word he spoke. Such words were not meant for men. His ear could not hear them. Only with long years of painful practice could he speak them. In that place where bonds were broken, Amon-Rama invoked spirits of change and dissolution.

Bit by bit the paleness of the night seem to gather around him, thickening, swirling, enfolding, hiding him as in a pillar of smoke. And that smoke grew and shaped, changed. Wings stretched forth in a span four times the height of a man. Massive talons scraped at the adamantine crystal of the towertop. Within the scribed lines of power stood a gigantic bird, a fierce-beaked eagle, but all of smoke that swirled and roiled within.

The great wings beat—there was no sound, as if they did not beat at the air of this world—and the monstrous form rose into the night. Swiftly the vaporous creature flew, until it circled far above the black sand beach. Ethereal pinions folded, and the bird-shape swooped.

Unerring it struck, straight at the slender form of the girl. Huge wings smote doward to brake; no flutter of air disturbed the blankets of the black woman or the scar-faced man sleeping on either side. Talons closed firmly about her slender body, but she did not wake, nor give any sign that she felt any other than deep, normal sleep.

Upward the smoky creature flew, then, wings seeming to sweep the breadth of the sky as they hurtled it back across the raven lake to the coruscant spire. As it lowered toward that vitric tower, the bird-form dissolved once more to a pillar of smoke, a pillar that touched down within the pentagram, swirled, and dissipated to reveal Amon-Rama bearing Jehnna in his red-robed arms.

Carefully he scrubbed out a section of the diagram with his foot, then stepped out. The rest he could dispose of later. Now there was a matter more important. The lifeless-eyed necromancer smiled thinly—it touched no more than his lips—down at the lovely face she turned up to him in her unbroken sleep. A matter infinitely more important.

Crystalline stairs that chimed beneath his hurried tread carried him down into the palace. To the chamber of mirrors, he hastened, and beyond, to a room like no other in that sparkling-faceted structure, nor like any other to be found on the face of the earth.

Elsewhere in that crystal palace was there always light and brightness, without need of lamp or sun. Here was darkness. The walls seemed tapestried with blackest shadow, if walls there were, or ceiling or floor, for the chamber appeared to extend in all direction infinitely, and no spark of light in it save two. Brightness framed the doorway that gave entrance from the chamber of mirrors, but that brightness failed abruptly at the very door. No pool of light stretched from it. The second light was indeed a pool, a soft glow without apparent source that surrounded a huge bed piled high with silken cushions. On that bed Amon-Rama laid his slight burden.

He looked down at her, no expression in his flat black eyes, then slowly traced one hand along the line from slim ankle to rounded thigh to tiny waist to swelling breast. Normal vices had been burned out of him by his thaumaturgies long years ago, but others remained, others that gave him dark pleasures. And, he thought, as he had not the same use for the girl as that foolish woman, Taramis, there was no reason for him not to indulge himself in them. But when his sport with the others was done. Now that the girl, the One, was finally in his grasp, his impatience was gone. Now was a time for preparations.

"Hear me now!" he called, his voice rolling into vast distances. "No door, no window, no crack nor opening to air. So do I say it, so must it be!"

The crystal palace tolled brazenly like a great bell, and it was so. The palace was sealed.

"Let us see first how they deal with that," he murmured.

With a final glance at Jehnna's unmoving form, he made his way from the place. When he had shut the door behind him, only the one pool of light remained, and Jehnna floated in the midst of infinite dark.

XII

erily pearlescent darkness still filled the crater when Conan woke, but he did not need a paling of the sky to the east to tell him that dawn approached. To cross the lake at dawn they must be awake before dawn, therefore he had awakened in good time. It was a useful trick he had, though he would admit that too much wine could befuddle it.

Tossing aside his blankets, he sheathed the bared broadsword that had lain by him through the night and rose, stretching. He frowned as his eye fell on Jehnna's empty blankets. Swiftly he scanned the slope of the crater above their camp. The horses stood with heads down, sleeping. Nothing moved.

He bent to prod Akiro and Malak. "Wake," he said quietly. "Jehnna is gone. Up with you."

Leaving then—Malak spluttering and cursing, Akiro muttering direly about his age and need for sleep—Conan strode to where Bombatta and Zula slept, one to either side of the empty blankets where Jehnna had been. He glared at the scar-faced warrior, snoring in a low buzz, and planted his booted foot in the man's ribs.

With a startled yelp Bombatta came awake. A heartbeat later he was snarling to his feet, hand darting to his tulwar. "I will kill you, thief! I—"

"Jehnna is gone," Conan said with grim coldness. "You all but tie her to you, then let her disappear. She could be dead!"

Bombatta's fury vanished with the first words. He stared at her blankets as if struck in the head.

"The horses are all here," Malak called.

The ebon-armored man shook himself. "Of course they are!" he roared. "Jehnna would not ride away from her destiny."

"Destiny!" Zula sneered. "You call it her destiny. Why can she not choose her own destiny?"

"If you have done something with her," Bombatta grated, and the black woman bristled back.

"I? I would never harm her! It is you who think she is a plaything, to be used as you see fit!"

The scars stood out as white lines across the big warrior's face. "You diseased she-jackal! I will carve you—"

"Fight later!" Conan snapped. "Now we must find Jehnna!"

Tension between the two lessened, but did not disappear. Bombatta sheathed his half-bared tulwar with a growl deep in his throat, and Zula's lip curled angrily as she lowered the staff she held in both hands.

Akiro had knelt by Jehnna's blankets and begun running his hands over them. Now his lips moved silently, and his eyes closed. When he opened them again only dead-white spheres showed. Malak gagged loudly and turned away.

"The girl was taken by a bird," the old man announced.

"Old fool," Bombatta muttered, but Akiro continued as if he had not spoken.

"A great bird, a bird of smoke that moved without sound. It carried her in its talons." His eyelids dropped, and opened on normal black eyes.

"A fool?" Conan said to Bombatta. "You are the fool. And me. We should have expected the Stygian to do something."

"Where did this bird take her?" Zula asked.

Akiro pointed across the lake to the crystal palace. "There, of course."

"Then we must follow," she said.

Conan nodded wordless agreement. As one he and Bombatta ran to the hide boat, wrestled it to the water.

"But it may be ensorceled," Malak protested. "Akiro said so."

"We must take the chance," Conan replied. He stood knee deep in the water beside the narrow vessel. "In! Quickly!"

In a quick scramble they filled the boat, Zula in the middle between Akiro and Malak, Conan and Bombatta on the ends. Paddles in the big men's hands dug furiously at the water, and the slim boat knifed away from the shore.

"Sigyn's Bowl!" Malak howled abruptly. "I forgot! I am leaving this morning! Turn back!"

Conan did not slow the steady work of his powerful arms and shoulders. "Swim," he said curtly.

The small thief looked at the liquid beneath them and shuddered. "Water is for drinking," he muttered, "when there is no wine."

With neither wind nor wave to hinder and two strong men working the paddles, the hide boat all but flew over the lake. Ripples from its passage spread incredibly far, for no other thing disturbed that glassy surface. The crystal palace loomed before them. Along its border with the water there was a landing, perfectly ordinary except that it, too, seemed carved from a single huge gem. The sun topped the crater's rim as they reached the palace, and the vast structure became a riot of scintillation.

Conan held the boat close to the strange landing while the others clambered out. When he was on the glittering stone as well, he lifted the hide boat from the water. A thief did not last long in Shadizar who failed to plan for his exits and escapes. For now the lake was still, but he would not risk something sweeping the craft away, not until he knew of some other means of leaving that unnatural palace.

The boat secured, he turned his attention to the palace. Smooth, sparkling walls met his eyes. Far to the right and left were the ends of crystal colonnades with tall, fluted columns of pellucid stone. Above rose featureless, vitreous expanses of sheer wall topped by faceted domes and glittering spires stretching toward the sky.

"Fascinating," Akiro murmured, stroking his fingertips over the crystal wall. "There are no joins. It is truly one single gem. All of it. Fascinating."

"Better it were ordinary marble," Conan said roughly. "I could contrive a means to scale that. Come. We must find a doorway of some sort."

"There is none," Akiro said without breaking his abstract reverie.

"How," Conan began, then thought better of asking how the wizard knew there were no doors. "Then how in Zandru's Nine Hells do we get in?" he asked instead.

Akiro blinked in surprise. "Oh, that part is easy." He walked to the edge of the landing and pointed to the water. "Down there is an opening. I could sense it the very first time I tried, perhaps because it is the *only* opening I found. It is big enough for our uses."

"A means of getting water from the lake?" Zula said doubtfully.

"I do not like water," Malak grumbled, but it was the palace he eyed nervously.

Conan knelt beside the round-bellied mage and peered at the water's surface. It was unruffled once more, and he could see nothing but his own image. It could not be possible, he told himself, that this Amon-Rama would build a palace with no way in, then leave such a simple entrance as this. A trap, he thought, with Jehnna for bait. Then let the trapper discover what manner of creature it was he meant to snare. He breathed deeply to flush his lungs with air, and dove into the lake. Only a small splashed marked his entrance.

There was a grayish clarity to the water below the surface. The Cimmerian took himself deeper with powerful strokes, searching along the face of the landing. The crystal surface was unmarked by the slimes and green things that grew on normal stonework immersed so.

Quickly he found the opening, a great pipe nearly as wide as his outstretched arms, with a cross-hatch of thick iron bars across it. Seizing the bars, he braced his feet against the wall beside the pipe and heaved. Nothing gave, not even the slightest. Harder he pulled, till his sinews creaked, and still to no avail. Abruptly he was startled to see other hands beside his own. He looked up and stared into the straining face of Bombatta, stripped of his black armor. Conan threw himself into redoubled effort. Bone and thew quivered, and lungs burned.

Suddenly, with a sharp crack, one bar tore loose in a shower of jewel-like shards. The grating shifted in Conan's hands, and he found he had more leverage. Crystal splintered and broke, and one by one the other bars came free.

Letting the grate fall, the Cimmerian sped back to the surface. As his head broke water he gulped air. He did not look around when Bombatta surfaced beside him. From the landing's edge three anxious faces peered down.

"The way is open," Conan said between pants. "Come."

"Wait but a moment," Akiro said. "Regain your breath. We must make a plan."

"No time," Conan replied. One last breath he drew, then rolled over and swam downward again.

With a quick twist he turned into the pipe, powerful strokes carrying him deeper. The light faded behind him, and he swam in darkness. Thirty paces, now. Forty, and his lungs demanded air. Fifty. And suddenly there was a glow ahead. Swiftly he swam toward it, then turned upward toward the light's source, moving arms and legs to slow his ascent. He broke the surface with only the sound of a droplet falling.

He was in a well, he saw, walled with the same smooth crystal as made up the palace. A wooden bucket was sunk in the water next to him, its rope pulled taut. Carefully he tugged the rope. It did not give.

A deadly smile came onto his face. Amon-Rama no doubt thought himself secure, and his trap subtle. In the northlands, though, there was an ancient saying. To trap a Cimmerian is to trap your own death.

Someone surfaced beside him with a splash that echoed from the well's walls, but he did not look to see who it was. He would allow only one thought, now. Grasping the rope, he climbed hand over hand with a grim face. The Cimmerian had entered the trap, and he hunted.

In the chamber of mirrors Amon-Rama thoughtfully tapped his pointed chin with a long, thin finger. They were inside the palace. He had forgotten the pipe that brought water to his well, and they had found his oversight quickly. Good sport was indicated.

With a malevolent smile he lightly touched a mirrored wall. It was not, of course, as if these interlopers had some chance of escape or—all the powers of darkness forfend!—victory. This palace was his in ways no king could dream of. The shriek of the crystal as the bars were torn free. That had come to him. The tread of their feet in the corridors, the disturbing of the air by their breath, all came to him. But then, he found sport in other ways than offering true hope to his prey. Their false belief in false hope sufficed, and even greater sport came when all hope was stripped away.

Now was time for preparations. He spoke a word, raised his hands, and the golden draperies shrouding the walls rolled neatly upwards revealing the five score great mirrors that surrounded the chamber. Each mirror reflected the clear plinth that held the glowing Heart of Ahriman, but none showed Amon-Rama. A lifetime drenched in darkest thaumaturgies had many peculiar effects on the earthly body of the practitioner. He *had* no reflection to be shown in any surface.

Only two breaks were there in the phalanx of mirrors. One was the door to the corridor. Through the other he could see endless dark and the bed on which Jehnna's still sleeping form lay. It was through this last that Amon-Rama moved. A sound rolled round the chamber, like the splash of a rock in a pool of water, and there was but a single gap unmirrored in the wall. Five score and one reflections of the Heart of Ahriman waited with the original.

Akiro pulled himself from the well with a grunt and, ignoring the water that dripped from him, stood staring at gem-like walls and ornaments of gold and silver so finely wrought that it seemed the mind of man could not have conceived them. Everywhere were tapestries of other-worldly scenes and carpets that changed in infinite variety of color and pattern as he watched.

"Akiro?" Malak said.

The rotund wizard shook his head admiringly. All done with sorcery; no one of these things had ever been crafted by a human hand. It was magnificent.

"Akiro?"

Irritably the mage turned to regard the small thief. Malak's hair hung in his face, and a pool of water about his feet splashed with a rain of drops from his garments. He looked like a drowned rat, Akiro thought, then quickly scrubbed his own dripping hair from his face. "Yes?" he snapped.

"They are going," Malak said.

Akiro looked in the direction the other pointed, and bit back an oath that would have curdled the air. Bombata and Zula were disappearing around a bend in the corridor, and Conan was no longer to be seen. "Fools," he muttered. "Wait!" As swiftly as he could make his old bones move, he ran after them, with Malak dogging his heels. "Half-wits!" the old mage growled. "You do not wander about a wizard's lair as if it were a merchant's garden! Here, anything can happen!"

As he rounded the corner, Akiro saw the others ahead, with Conan far in the lead. Sword in hand, the Cimmerian darted through a doorway at the end of the corridor, and in the same instant a door slid down with a clang, sealing the passage behind him. Bombatta and Zula rushed forward to pound on the door, he with his sword hilt, she with her staff.

Cursing under his breath Akiro ran to help, but for moments after reaching them he could only stare. The door was as transparent as glass—clearly they could see Conan, looking warily about a mirrored chamber, his broadsword at the ready—yet the blows of Bombatta and Zula rebounded as if from an iron-bound castle gate. As if to add to the hollow booming, all began to shout at once.

"Can he not hear us?" Malak cried. "Conan! Ogun's Toenails! Conan!"

Zula dropped to her knees, feeling along the bottom of the door. "If we can lift . . . there is no crack! None!"

"Stand back," Bombatta roared, taking a two-handed grip on his sword. "I'll break it if it can be broken."

"*All* of you stand back," Akiro shouted over them. "And be quiet," he added. He rummaged in his pouch, sighing as he tossed aside powders ruined by the wet, yet continued to speak hastily the while. "This is no tavern brawl, to be settled with brute might. This Stygian is a sorcerer of puissance. Treat him as such, or we will all . . . ah, here it is." Smiling in satisfaction, he brought out a small vial covered entirely with purest beeswax and marked with a seal of power.

"I do not see Jehnna," Bombatta said suddenly. "The thief must be left to his fate. Jehnna must be found."

"She is here," Akiro said, not looking up from the task of peeling away the wax. The peeling must be done properly, or the contents would be useless. "Can you not sense . . . of course you cannot. The nexus is here, the center of all the powers of this palace."

The last of the wax fell away, revealing a darkly shimmering compound that seemed at once grease and smoke. To this he touched the tip of the smallest finger of his left hand, and scribed a rune on the right-hand side of the transparent door. With the smallest finger of his right hand he drew the same symbol on the left-hand side of the door.

Akiro frowned as the runes began to hiss, as if boiling, but there was nothing to be done for it. Quickly he began to chant in silence. There were powers invoked with words spoken aloud, but he had found those dangerous, unreliable or foul, and often all three. Pressure built; he could feel it inside his head. They were spirits he summoned, spirits concerned with opening things that could not be opened, spirits concerned with lifting what could not be lifted. The pressure grew, and he knew they obeyed the calling. The pressure grew, and sweat beaded on his forehead. The pressure grew, and grew, and . . .

With a gasp, he slumped and would have fallen had he not caught himself against the door.

"Well?" Bombatta demanded.

Shaking, Akiro stared at the door in wonder. The pressure was still there, enough to burst the gate of a castle, and to no effect. "A wizard most puissant," he whispered, then added as he peered into the mirrored chamber, "If you believe in gods, then pray."

XIII

Slowly Conan moved around the mirrored chamber, broadsword held ready for any attack. The huge mirrors cast back his stalking form, multiplied ten thousand times as reflections of reflections were in turn reflected, and that of the glowing crimson gem that stood on a slim crystalline spire in the center of the room. Without break was the wall of grim images, and he realized that he was no longer certain which had fallen to hide the door through which he had entered.

He had avoided the gem before. The glow and its color told him all he needed of its nature. Never had he seen anything so scarlet; the hue alone made him want to squint. Such items of sorcerous power were dangerous when not understood—as he had learned in hard lessons—and scarcely less so when comprehension was complete. Still it was the only thing in the chamber other than himself. Slowly he approached the narrow plinth, and stretched forth a hand.

"You provide little sport, barbarian."

Spinning, the big Cimmerian searched for the source of the words, and when he found it he was hardly less surprised than at hearing them in the first place.

One tall mirror no longer depicted him, but rather a man in hooded, blood-red robes. At least, he assumed it was a man from the voice and the size. The deep hood hid the face in shadow, while the robe hung in vermilion folds to the floor and even the hands were covered by long sleeves that depended to points.

"I will provide no sport at all for you, Stygian," Conan said. "Release the girl, or—"

"You become tiresome." A score of voices behind him spoke the words, and all were the Stygian's voice. Suspecting some form of trick to divert him, Conan risked a glance back. And stared, Twenty mirrors now held the hooded form.

"I will keep the girl, and you can do nothing."

411

"She is the One, and the One is mine."

"Muscles and steel avail you naught against *my* power."

Conan felt as if his head were whirling. Each time there were more scarlet-robed images in the mirrors, chorusing the words, until he was surrounded by the mage, multiplied more than a hundred times. Hairs on his arms and the back of his neck stirred, and his teeth bared in a snarl. Yet many times had he met fear, and that stealer of will and strength was as familiar to him as the dark form of death. If the latter would one day surely conquer him, the former had no power he had not defeated a thousand times before.

"You think to frighten me, sorcerer? I spit on your power, for you hide behind it like a cowering dog. You have not the courage to face me like a man."

"Brave words," the multitudinous reflections murmured in oily tones. "Perhaps I shall face you." Abruptly two of the images split in twain. From each of those mirrors one shape streaked in a blur of scarlet; the two blurs struck, merged, and the shape of the mage stood at one end of the chamber as well as in the mirrors. "Perhaps you will give some small sport, after all. You will not like it, barbar. I will kill you slowly, and you will scream for death long before it comes. Your strength will be as that of a child against me."

With every word more of the mirrored forms divided, more flashes of crimson blazed across the chamber to sink into the hooded figure, and with each the figure grew slightly larger.

Twice, as blood-red streaks passed close to him, Conan struck at them with his sword. The steel whistled through them as through the air, with only a tingling along his arms to tell him the blade had met anything. The Cimmerian stood then, waiting rather than waste his effort in futility, until at last each mirror had given up its portion of the red-robed form that faced him. Taller than he by a head, it was, and twice as broad.

"This you call facing me?" Conan sneered. "Well, come then."

The huge shape stripped back its hood, and as Conan started in spite of himself, hundred-fold laughter rolled from the mirrors. An ape's head glared at him from atop the scarlet robes, as black as pitch and with gleaming white fangs made for the ripping of flesh. Its eyes held malevolent ebon fire. A tiger's claws tipped its thick, hairy fingers. Slowly it shredded the robes, revealing a massive, ebon-haired body and heavy, bowed legs. No sound came from it, not even that of breathing.

A creation of sorcery it most certainly was, Conan thought, but perhaps it still could bleed. With a roar he bounded the length of the chamber, his broadsword a razor-edged windmill. Like a leopard the creature danced away from him, moving faster than he would have believed anything of that bulk could possibly move. And even in its dodging it struck—almost casually, it seemed—opening four crimson-welling slashes across his chest.

Grimly Conan followed. Three more times he struck at the great beast. Three more times, with silent snarls, it avoided his steel like quicksilver, and blood now dripped from his thigh, his shoulder, and his forehead. Full-throated laughter flowed from the mirrors in counterpoint to the frustrated curses the Cimmerian muttered under his breath. The creature's every move was lightning, exhibiting none of the clumsiness of its shape. He had not so much as touched it yet.

Abruptly the monstrous sable ape charged, seized him in an instant, lifted him toward that slathering fanged mouth. He was too close to hack or stab with his sword, yet he slashed his blade sideways across the snarling face, slicing a gash through eye and nose and mouth. Claws dug into his ribs as green ichor rose in the wound, and the one remaining bulged in agony. With a heave of its massive arms Conan was sent hurtling across the chamber.

It could be hurt, flashed through the Cimmerian's mind, and then he slammed into the wall, all the air leaving his lungs, and slid to the floor. Desperately he struggled to breathe, fought to regain his feet before the beast could reach him. He staggered to his feet ... and stared in amazement.

The huge ape had sunk to all fours, and its mouth hung open as if it would moan if it were not mute. Yet that agonized sound was supplied a hundred times over by the images of the mage. In every mirror the form of the necromancer sagged and groaned in pain.

Not in every mirror, Conan realized suddenly. The mirror he had struck in his flight was crossed by a web of cracks and showed only shattered reflections, including, now, his own once more. He swung his blade against the next mirror. As the silvery surface fragmented beneath the blow, the figure of Amon-Rama within vanished, and the groans of the others became cries.

"I have you, sorcerer!" Conan shouted above the shrill ululations.

Along the wall he ran as fast as he could, pausing only to smash at each mirror as he passed. Image after image of the thaumaturge disappeared to the splintering of glass, to cries becoming howls, then shrieks.

The skittering of claws on the crystal floor warned the Cimmerian, and he threw himself into a roll just as the ape-creature lunged at him. His broadsword flashed as he came to his feet. A gash ran down the beast's ribs, while he had gained another along his own ribs. It was slower, he thought; no faster, now, than a fast man. Still, he ran across the chamber, ignoring the monstrous form. Defeating the creature was no part of defeating Amon-Rama.

At the far wall Conan stabbed his sword viciously at the image of the necromancer in mirror after mirror. The screams now spoke of pain beyond knowing, and of desperation, as well. From the corner of his eye, Conan saw the huge ape scrambling toward him again, its lone black eye burning with a frantic light. Yet even in its haste, he noted, it circled wide around the glowing red gem.

Abruptly, with a splashing sound as if he had stabbed into water, Conan's sword pierced the surface of a mirror. He could only stare. His blade went *into* the mirror, and into, as well, the image of Amon-Rama within. Silence was thick in the chamber, broken only by an occasional tinkling as a bit of broken mirror fell to the crystal floor. All of the unbroken mirrors save the one his sword transfixed now showed only normal reflections. The ape-beast was gone as if it had never been, though the burning of his gashes told him it most assuredly had been real.

Beneath the scarlet hood in the mirror a hawk-nosed face was painted with disbelief, and raven eyes shone hatred at the big youth. A ball of light suddenly oozed from the place where the blade entered the mage's robes, flowed down the sword and exploded, hurling Conan away like a flung stone. Shaking his head, the Cimmerian got dazedly to his feet just as Amon-Rama stepped out of the mirror, its surface first bulging around him, then suddenly vanishing into vapor.

The necromancer did not look at Conan. Once he touched the sword that thrust from his chest as if to convince himself of its actuality. With staggering steps he moved toward the crimson gem atop its slim pelucid column.

"Cannot be," the Stygian muttered. "All power would have been mine. All power . . ."

His hand closed about the glowing stone, and the wail that ripped from him then, going on as if it would never end, made all the other sounds he had uttered pale to whispers. Scarlet light glared from between his fingers, brighter and brighter, until it seemed that his hand itself had taken on the color.

"Crom!" Conan whispered as he realized the hand *had* become crimson.

And the redness spread, up the sorcerer's arm and through him, till he was as a statue of congealed blood, yet keening still. Abruptly the form collapsed into a sanguinary pool that boiled and bubbled, vermilion steam rising till naught was left save his broadsword lying on the crystal floor. And the gem, hanging unsupported in the air.

Carefully, with more than one hesitant glance at the crimson stone floating above his blade, Conan retrieved his weapon. The leather-wrapped hilt was hot in his hand, but the sword seemed unharmed. Swiftly he backed away from the sorcerous stone, and his skin crawled. Almost had he touched the accursed thing, before Amon-Rama began his fatal game.

With a deafening crash another of the mirrors burst, and Conan's companions poured into the chamber.

". . . and I told you it would work," Akiro was saying. "It took only the death of the sorcerer, releasing his hold on his majicks."

"Ravana's Weeping Eyes," Malak said scornfully. "You said he was lucky. There was no luck. This Stygian should have known better than to oppose Malak and Conan."

Akiro turned his attention to the Cimmerian. "You *were* lucky. One day your luck will run out like the sands from a glass, and what then?"

"You saw?" Conan asked, now that he could get a word in edgewise.

Akiro nodded, and Zula shivered. "That ape," she murmured, looking about as if she suspected it might only be hiding.

"It is gone," Conan said. "Let us find Jehnna and this Mitra-accursed key, and be gone as well."

As though her name had summoned her Jehnna appeared, stepping through the gap left by the mirror from which Amon-Rama had come. Behind her was blackness made darker by the glittering crystal and mirrors in the chamber. She did not look at any of them, but walked slowly, surely, to the radiant red gem, hanging still where the Stygian sorcerer had left it.

"No!" Conan and Bombatta shouted together, but before either man could move she plucked the stone from the air.

"The Heart of Ahriman," she said softly, smiling at the blood-red jewel in her hand. "This is the key, Conan."

"That?" Conan began, then cut off as a tremor shook the floor. The walls shivered, and ominous crackings sounded.

"I should have known," Akiro mused. "It was Amon-Rama's will that held it, and with him dead——" Abruptly he stopped to glare at the others. "Well? Did you not hear me? Run, or we are all as dead as the Stygian!" As if for punctuation another quaver ran through the palace.

"The well!" Conan commanded, though the thought of that swim with the possibility that the palace might collapse atop them all was not one he enjoyed.

Akiro shook his head. "Allow me to show what I can do without the interference of Amon-Rama." He gave Malak a significant look. "Watch." Chanting silently, he moved his arms in strange patterns—it looked to Conan much like what he had seen at the wizard's camp, yet in some fashion different—clapped his hands, and a fiery sphere shot from between his palms to strike a mirrored wall. There was no eruption, this time. Rather the ball of the fire spread and hollowed, like the flames of a hot coal touched to parchment. In only a moment it extinguished, leaving behind a roughly circular doorway melted in the crystal wall. "There," Akiro said. "Now, Malak, have you seen anything to surpass—"

This time the palace danced and swayed, and a portion of another crystalline wall fell with a shattering crash.

"We'll talk of our triumphs later," Conan said, grabbing Jehnna's arm. The others hesitated not a moment in following him through the way Akiro had provided.

Down glittering corridors of ethereal beauty they ran, and when the corridor bent away from the direction they wished to go Akiro melted yet another hole in the sparkling crystal walls. Faster and faster the shocks came, until they blended into one continuous gyration of the entire palace. Ornaments of unearthly exquisiteness burst apart, walls toppled in bounding chunks of pellucid stone, and twice entire stretches of the ceiling fell in solid blocks behind them.

Then Akiro's magic burned its way through yet again, and they rushed out onto the landing. The lake was in turmoil, choppy waves radiating out from the palace. Conan heaved the hide boat, heavier for Bombatta's armor already lashed in its bottom, to the water, handed Jehnna into it, then had to hold the craft against the scar-faced warrior's attempt to push off before the others could scramble aboard.

When all were in, Conan leaped into the boat and snatched up a paddle. "Now," he growled at Bombatta. The other man dug his paddle in without speaking.

Behind them the crystal palace scintillated with all the hues of the rainbow gone mad. Lightnings leaped from tall spires, *up* into cloudless skies.

"Faster," Akiro urged, staring anxiously over his shoulder. "Faster!" He glared at Conan and Bombatta, wielding their paddles with all their might, and grunted. Trailing his hands in the water, the wizard began to chant, and slowly the water mounded beneath the boat. Swelling, the wave rushed forward, carrying the frail vessel faster than all their stroking could have. Malak loudly tried to pray his way through all known pantheons.

"Too much magic," Conan grumbled.

"Perhaps," Akiro replied, "you would rather wait until that palace—"

With a roar like the rending of the earth the crystal palace burst asunder. A hammering wind smote their backs, and then the wave they rode was caught and overwhelmed by a greater wave. Bow down at a precipitous angle, the hide craft hurtled across the lake. All Conan could do was dig in his paddle and hope to hold them straight. Did they turn sideways to that wall of water, all was lost.

The beach of black sand approached at incredible velocity, then disappeared beneath the wave. Abruptly the bow of the boat struck against the crater's slope, and the vessel cartwheeled, catapulting them all into frothing water.

Conan struggled to his feet, fighting the water's attempt to pull his legs from under him. Jehnna, floundering, swept by him, and he seized a handful of her robes and pulled her to him. She flung one arm around his neck and clung to him, panting, as the water rushed away, leaving them standing a quarter of the way up the slope of the crater.

"Are you all right?" he asked her.

She nodded, then held up the hand not clutching him. "And I did not lose the key." A crimson glow seeped between her fingers.

The Cimmerian shivered, and did not try to stop her when she moved away from him. From beneath her dripping robes she produced a black velvet bag into which she slipped the gem.

Conan shook his head. The longer this journey went on, the less he wanted to do with it. And yet—his hand closed around the golden amulet at his neck, the amulet Valeria had given him—and yet there were reasons.

He was surprised to realize that all of the party were not only alive but on their feet, if soaked and bedraggled, and staring at one another in disbelief that they still lived. Fear had apparently driven the horses despite their hobbles, for they stood, whickering nervously, higher still on the slope. The boat lay below them, and from there to the water were scattered the remains of their camp, such as was left. The cooking pot was gone, and half the water bags, and a single blanket remained tangled in the rushes.

On the far side of the lake the only sign that the palace had ever been was a vast hole which the waters of the lake were quickly filling. Akiro stared toward it with something approaching sadness on his face. "All a creation of his will," he said quietly. "It was magnificent."

"Magnificent?" Zula's voice squeaked with incredulity. "Magnificent?"

"I would as soon be far away from it," Jehnna said. "And I can sense the treasure, now that I hold the key." At that Bombatta hurried to her, hovering protectively and glaring at Zula and Conan as if the greatest danger came from them.

Malak rubbed his hands together, and lowered his voice for the Cimmerian's ear alone. "Treasure. I like the sound of that better than wizards. We will help ourselves to whatever the girl does not want, eh? Soon we'll be in Shadizar, living like kings."

"Soon," Conan agreed. His eyes on Jehnna were troubled, and his hand tightened on the amulet until the golden dragon dug into his palm. "Soon."

XIV

I t was possible, Conan reflected as he rode southward, that Akiro's cures were worse than the wounds they were meant to heal. Gray-flanked mountains reared about him, cut with a hundred narrow valleys that could serve as roads for attack and an endless string of pinched passes where ambush could blossom in blood, but he found it hard to keep his mind on anything but the bandages, smeared with foul-smelling ointment, that covered the gashes the ape-creature had opened. Worse than the stench, they itched with a fury. Surreptitiously he scratched at the linen folds wrapped around his chest.

"Do not do that," Jehnna said briskly. "Akiro says they must not be disturbed."

"They are foolishness," Conan grumbled. "I have had scratches such as these before. Wash the blood off, then let the air to them. That's all I ever needed before."

"They are *not* scratches," she said firmly.

"And this grease stinks."

" 'Tis a pleasant herbal smell. I begin to wonder if you have sense enough to take care of yourself." She went on, oblivious to his dumb-founded stare. "You will leave your bandages alone. Akiro says that his ointment will heal your wounds completely in only two days. He said I must keep an eye on you, but truly I did not believe it."

Conan twisted in his high-pommeled saddle to glare back at the wispy-haired wizard. Akiro met his stare calmly, and the others were watching him as well. Malak and Zula wore looks of smug amusement. Bombatta seemed lost in thought, but his eyes rested on Conan in a fashion that made it clear he would not have wept had the ape-inflicted gashes proved fatal.

"I must say you do not seem grateful," Jehnna continued. "Akiro labors to make you well, and you—"

"Mitra's Mercies, girl," Conan said abruptly "do you have to go on so?"

Hurt clouded her face, and the look in her big eyes made him feel it was his fault. "Forgive me," she said shortly, and let her mount fall back. Malak replaced her.

"Sometimes," Conan told the small thief, "I think I liked that girl more when she was affrighted of her own shadow."

"I like them with more to fill the arm," Malak said, and flinched at the Cimmerian's cold gaze. "Ah, look you, it's not the girl I want to talk of. Do you know where we are?"

Conan nodded. "I know."

"Then why are you not turning another way? Inti put his hand over us! Another league at most, and we'll be getting close to the village where we found Zula." The wiry man made a sound half sigh and half groan. "They'll not be glad to see us again, Cimmerian. It will be luck if we get no more than a fistful of arrows from ambush."

"I know," Conan said again. He looked back at Jehnna. She rode with her head down and the hood of her pale cloak pulled far forward to hide her face. Every line of her spoke of a deep sulk. "Must we ride all the way back to the village?" he called.

Jehnna jerked erect, blinking. "What? The village?" She looked around, then pointed to the east, to a strait pass rising between two dark, snow-capped peaks. "We must go that way."

"Praise all the gods," Malak breathed, and at that moment two-score mounted Corinthian soldiers burst upon them with longswords gleaming in their fists.

Conan wasted no wind on curses; he had not a moment for it in any case. His broadsword came into his hand barely in time to block an overhand strike that would have split his skull. He kicked a foot free of its stirrup to boot another Corinthian in red-crested helm from his saddle, and as if it were all one motion slashed open his first attacker's throat. He saw Malak bend beneath a flashing blade to sink his dagger under the bottom of a polished breastplate, then another cavalryman was upon him.

"Conan!" The shrill scream reached him even as he engaged. "Conan!"

The one glance the Cimmerian could spare was enough to freeze the breath in his throat. A laughing soldier had his hand tangled in Jehnna's dark hair, and their two horses danced in a circle, only her frantic grip on the tall pommel of her saddle keeping her from being unseated.

One glance Conan could spare, and when his eyes turned back to his opponent the Corinthian gasped at what he saw in those icy sapphires, for it was his own death. The man was no mean hand with his long cavalry sword, but he had no chance against the grim northland fury he faced now. Thrice their blades met, then Conan was turning away from a bloody corpse that toppled to the rocky ground behind him.

Desperately Conan raced his horse for Jehnna. The slender girl had loosed one hand from her saddle to clutch at the first in her hair; her other hand had only a precarious, clawed hold on the pommel. The horses pranced and circled, and the Corinthian threw back his head in gales of laughter.

"Erlik take you, dog!" Conan snarled, and stood in his stirrups so that his backhand blow had all the strength of his massive body driving the whipping blade.

So great was his rage that he barely felt the shock as his razor steel sheared through the laughing soldier's neck. Mouth frozen forever in mirth the Corinthian's head flew from his shoulders; blood fountained from a torso that remained erect for moments longer, then rolled over the rump of the prancing horse. Fingers twisted in Jehnna's hair almost pulled her from her saddle before they slackened in death. She slumped across the pommel, sobbing wildly and staring with bulging eyes at the headless body beneath her horse's hooves.

It took Conan no more than an instant to take in the situation on the small battlefield. Malak now rode one of the smaller, Corinthian horses, and even as the Cimmerian looked he leaped from that to another, pulling back the rider's head by the red crest on his helmet and slitting his throat. Flashes and roars accompanied Akiro on his mad dashes about the narrow valley. Every time the rotund wizard found time to breathe he began the arm motions that heralded his major displays of power, but each time horsemen in polished breastplates would close about him and, with a shouted curse, Akiro would startle them with a burst of light and a clap of thunder. the deflagrations and deafening bangs hurt no one, though, and the old man was finding less time after each to try his greater wizardries. Zula and Bombatta each attempted to fight to Jehnna's side, but flashing tulwar and whirling staff were hard pressed simply to keep back the soldiers who strove to cut them down.

In the first fury of battle the very numbers of the Corinthians made it inevitable that the balance of dead would favor the Zamorans, but there were simply too many riders in red-crested helms. And dying bravely and stupidly when there were alternatives was one custom of the cities that had never found favor with Conan.

"Scatter!" he roared. Two cavalrymen closed with the big Cimmerian; his blade swept in a circle, severing a swordarm at the elbow, axing deep into the second man's shoulder. He wrenched his steel free without slackening his bellow. "Scatter! They are too many! Scatter!" Seizing Jehnna's reins, Conan booted his horse toward the narrow pass she had indicated as the way they must go.

Three Corinthians spurred to put themselves in the fugitives' way.

Surprised grins of anticipation blossomed on their faces when Conan did not wheel in another direction; the grins turned to consternation when the Cimmerian galloped straight into them, his tall Zamoran mount bowling over a smaller animal. The Corinthian screamed as his thrashing horse rolled atop him, grinding him into the stony ground.

Stunned, the pair remaining fell back on defending themselves rather than attacking. Burdened with pulling Jehnna's mount behind him, Conan knew he would have been hardpressed at best to fight a way past. Cold and methodically deadly, he taught them of their fatal mistake. He rode on from two fresh corpses—and one Corinthian screaming and coughing frothy blood—with eyes locked on the narrow pass, eyes as grim as death.

He could not afford to look back, and the knowledge gnawed at him. What if he did look back, and saw one of the others in need? He could not ride back to help. Jehnna must be gotten to the treasure, then to Shadizar with treasure and key, for Valeria. And even without Valeria, he knew he could not abandon the girl. She would get her throat cut, or be dragged behind a boulder by a cavalryman who thought it safe to ignore the unequal fight for a time. Teeth clenching till his jaw ached, he rode, and tried not to hear the sounds of battle fading behind.

XV

The valleys were purple with the shadows of mountains when finally Conan drew rein. He had not galloped all that time—the horses could not have stood such a pace for so long on flat ground, let alone in a maze of twisting valleys—but the animals could not travel forever even at a sensible speed. Besides, he was of a mind to find a place for the night before it was too dark to see.

He glanced back at Jehnna, to see how she was bearing up. The slender girl's cheeks were stained with dust and tear-tracks, and she was sunk in the wide-eyed silence with which she had first greeted him. She held to her saddle with both hands, and showed no more desire to take her own reins now than she had at any time during their flight. She had replied to his few comments only with shakes or nods of her head, though he reluctantly admitted his gruffness of the past few hours might have had something to do with that. All she appeared to want to do was stare at him, and it was beginning to make him nervous. If being in the middle of a battle had driven her mad . . .

"Are you all right?" he demanded roughly. "Well? Speak to me, girl!"

"You were . . . terrible," she said softly. "They might as well have held switches instead of swords."

"It was not a sport," he muttered, "not the game you still seem to think it." Wondering why he suddenly felt so angry, he resumed looking for a place for camp.

"It is just that I have never seen such a thing before," she continued. "What Zula did, in the village, what happened at Akiro's hut, they were different. I . . . I was apart from them. They were like entertainments, like jugglers or a dancing bear."

He could not help growling his reply. "Men died in those . . . entertainments. Better that they should die than we should, but that does not change the fact of it. No man should die for entertainment." He saw a likely spot, half a score boulders, taller than a man on horseback, set

423

close together and near to a steep slope. Twitching his reins, he turned toward them.

"I did not mean to offend you, Conan."

"I am not offended," he replied sharply.

He led her horse between two of the boulders, just far apart enough to admit him, and found a space between the great stones and the precipitous slope that was more than large enough for them and the animals. The boulders would keep off the worst of the mountain winds and, more importantly, shield them from searchers. Dismounting, he helped Jehnna down and set about unsaddling the horses.

"Build a fire," she said, hugging her cloak about her. "I am cold."

"No fire." Even had there been anything to burn he would not have risked giving away their hiding place. "Here," he said, and tossed the saddle blankets at her.

"They smell," she sniffed, but as he squatted to check their meager supplies he saw that she had draped them about her shoulders over the cloak of white wool, albeit with much wrinkling of her nose.

He had had a waterskin and a pouch of dried meat tied behind his saddle, and there was enough of the meat for several days. Water, however, could be a problem. The skin was only half full.

"Do you think they got away, too?" she asked suddenly. "Bombatta, I mean, and Zula, and the others?"

"Perhaps." Abruptly he tore the bandage from his head, and began unwinding the one about his chest.

"No!" Jehnna cried. "You must leave them. Akiro says—"

"Akiro and the others could be dead because of these," he growled. "Because of me." He used the bandages to wipe off the wizard's greasy ointment. To his surprise the gashes were only slightly swollen pink lines, as if they had had days of healing already. "I was worrying about these, about the itching and the stink. If I had had my mind about me those Corinthians would never have been able to take us by surprise so easily." With an oath he tossed the wadded cloth aside.

"It was not your fault," she protested. "It was me. I was sulking like a child when I should have been telling you the way to go. Had I not been, we would have turned aside before they attacked us."

Conan shook his head. " 'Tis foolishness, Jehnna. In this twisted maze you could have seen the true way but moments sooner, at best, and the Corinthians would have attacked as soon as we turned away from them." He chewed on a strip of dried mutton, as tough as ill-tanned leather and of equal taste, while she frowned pensively.

"Perhaps I could not have done anything more," she said at last, "but I see your point concerning yourself. You, of course, can see around corners and through stone, and so should have warned us. It is quite wonderful to know we had two wizards in our party. But why did you not give us wings, so we could fly away?"

Conan choked on a bit of mutton. Regaining his breath, he glared at her, but she looked back as a wide-eyed vision of innocence. It was possible, he thought, that she was innocent enough to mean exactly what she said, to actually believe that he . . . No! He was not fool enough to believe that of anyone. He opened his mouth for a retort, and closed it again with the certainty that anything he said would only end in making him feel truly the fool.

"Eat," he said sourly, throwing the pouch of dried meat at her feet.

She chose a piece delicately. He could not be sure, but he thought, as she nibbled at it with small white teeth, that he detected the edges of a smile. It did little for his disposition.

Light faded from the sky, and amethyst twilight descended on the mountains. Finishing the meager meal, Jehnna began to shift about as if seeking for a more comfortable spot on the stony ground. She hitched the blankets this way and that, finally complaining, "I am cold, Conan. Do something."

"No fire," he said curtly. "You have the blankets."

"Well, get beneath them with me, then. If you'll not allow me a fire, at least you can share the warmth of your body."

Conan stared. More innocent than any child, he thought. "I cannot. That is, I will not."

"Why not?" she demanded. "I am freezing. Did not my aunt send you along to protect me?"

Conan laughed and groaned at the same time. Ask the wolf to protect the sheepfold. He shook his head to rid it of unwanted thoughts. "You must have a care of Taramis, Jehnna, when you are back in Shadizar."

"Of my aunt? But why?"

"I have no true reason," he said slowly. "But kings and queens, princes and princesses, do not think as do ordinary folk. They do not see right or wrong the same way."

"Are you troubled by the dream I had? Bombatta was right. It was just a dream, Conan. Anyone could have bad dreams in a place like that crater. Taramis loves me. She has cared for me since I was a child."

"Be that as it may, Jehnna, should you ever have need for help, send word to the tavern of Abuletes, in Shadizar, and I will come. I know many places where you would be safe."

"I will," she said, but he knew she did not believe in even the possibility of it. "I am still cold," she went on, smiling and lifting a corner of one blanket.

A moment longer the big Cimmerian hesitated. Then, telling himself that it was indeed becoming colder, that a sharing of warmth could harm nothing, he removed his sword belt and seated himself next to her. She pulled not only a saddle blanket, smelling strongly of horse, over his shoulders, but part of her cloak as well. The blankets began to slide from them, and as they shifted to secure them he realized that she was leaning against him. Instinctively he put an arm around her. His hand landed on the warm curve of her hip, jumped away as if burned, brushed the soft roundness of a breast, then settled on the indentation of her waist.

" 'Tis warmer than I thought," he muttered. There was sweat on his forehead. "Perhaps I should move." How much forbearance, he wondered, could even the gods ask of a man?

Jehnna snuggled herself more firmly against him, touching the golden dragon at his chest with a single finger. "Tell me of Valeria." He stiffened, and she glanced up at him. "I overheard you and Malak. And Akiro. I am not deaf, Conan. What kind of woman was she?"

"A woman," he replied. But the off-handedness of that would not let him leave it. "She was a woman in thousands upon thousands, perhaps the only one of her kind in the world. She was a warrior, friend, companion . . ."

". . . And lover?" she supplied when he let his words trail off. He drew breath, but she hurried on before he could speak. "Can there be room in your life for another woman?"

How to explain about Valeria and him, he thought. Valeria, a woman who would neither own nor be owned, a woman who could come to his bed with the passion of a tigress and two hours later nudge him so he did not miss eyeing a particularly toothsome serving wench. "There are things about men and women," he found himself saying, "that you simply would not understand, girl."

"Much you know," she retorted hotly. "Zula and I had long talks about the proper methods of . . . of handling a man."

Abruptly she seized his free hand and thrust it beneath her robes. Involuntarily he cupped a warm, hard-tipped mound. The thought returned to him, made to nestle in the palms of a man's hands.

"You know not what you are doing," he said hoarsely.

Before the words were out of his mouth she threw herself on him. So great was his surprise that he toppled over backwards, so that she lay atop him.

"Then show me," she murmured, and honey lips drove rational thoughts from his head.

The cold night wind swept hard out of the plain across Shadizar, as if seeking to scour the city of its corruption.

It was an omen that the wind blew so, Taramis thought. A symbol of the sweeping away of old ways, and the coming of a new dawn. Her robes of sky blue slashed with gold had been chosen as well to speak of that new sunrise, that inexorable new coming.

Her dark eyes surveyed the courtyard, the largest in her palace. Tiled with huge blocks of pale, polished marble, it was surrounded by an alabaster colonnade. The balconies overlooking the court were empty, and no light showed at any window. Guards within the palace made sure no slave's curious eye fell on what occurred there this night.

Before her rested the great form of Dagoth on its couch of crimson marble. More perfect than any mere mortal male born of woman, she thought. In a circle about her and the massive shape of the Sleeping God stood the priests of the new religion, of the ancient religion reborn. Shimmering golden robes covered the priests to their sandled feet, and on each head was a golden crown with a single point above the brow graven with an open eye, symbol that though the god slept, never did they sleep in his service.

The crown with the tallest point was on the head of he who stood by her right hand, his snowy beard fanning over his chest, his parchment-skinned face the very picture of kindly mildness. His tall staff of gold was topped with a blue diamond carved into an eye of twice human size. He was Xanteres, the high priest. And highest indeed he was, Taramis thought, after herself.

"'Tis the third night," she said suddenly, and a sigh as of exultation rose from the circle of priests. "The third night from the Night of Awakening."

"Blessed be the Night of Awakening," intoned the priests.

"The Sleeping God will never die," she called, and their reply came back to her.

"Where there is faith, there is no death!"

Taramis held her arms straight out to either side. "Let us anoint our god with the first of his anointings."

"All glory to she who anoints the Sleeping God," they chanted.

Flutes began to play, softly and slowly at first, then quickening, rising higher. Two more crowned priests appeared from the colonnade. Between them was a girl, her raven hair pinned in tight coils about her small head, her body swathed in robes of pristine white. At the circle the two priests slipped the robes from her, and she entered, unashamed in her slender nakedness. Her eyes, on the form of Dagoth, bore a look of purest rapture as she stopped at the god's head. Taramis and Xanteres moved together, one to either side of the girl.

"Aniya," Taramis said. The naked girl reluctantly tore her gaze from the Sleeping God. "You," Taramis said, "are the first chosen, above your sisters, for your purity."

"This poor one is honored greatly," the girl whispered.

"At your birth were you sealed to the Sleeping God. Do you now willingly serve him?" Taramis knew the answer even before the light of ecstacy appeared in the girl's eyes. The cruel-eyed noblewoman had prepared both long and well.

"This poor one begs to serve," the girl replied, her voice soft yet eager. The flutes now shrieked in frenzy.

"O great Dagoth," Taramis cried, "accept this, our offering and pledge to thee. Accept thy first anointing, against the Night of thy Return."

His face still a portrait of gentleness, Xanteres' clawed fingers gripped Aniya's hair, bent her forward over the head of the alabaster form, then bent back her head so that her neck was a tight curve of smooth skin. From within his robes he produced a dagger with a gilded blade, and the gilded steel bit smoothly into the smooth curve. A crimson fountain splashed over the god's face.

"O great Dagoth," Taramis shouted, "thy servants anoint thee!"

"O great Dagoth," the priests echoed, "thy servants anoint thee!"

Taramis sank to her knees, bowed her head to the marble. Wrapped in her own intentness, she was unaware of the rustle as the priests knelt and bowed as well. "O great Dagoth," she prayed, "thy servants await the Night of thy Coming! *I* await the Night of thy Coming."

The massed voices of the priests followed fervently on hers. "O great Dagoth, thy servants await the Night of thy Coming."

Aniya's body jerked one last time and was still where it had fallen, forgotten, her glazing eyes staring at the no longer spreading pool of her blood on the pale tiles.

XVI

Conan's horse picked its way along the stony valley floor, its rider wearing a stony expression. He kept his mind focused on the way before him, not allowing thoughts to stray.

"We must go on," Jehnna told him, and his face hardened more. "I know the way, and we must go on."

He waited until they topped a notch, its far slope leading into another valley, before speaking. "I can have you safe in Shadizar in two days. One, if we near kill the horses." From that rise he could see out of the mountains toward the rising sun, out onto the Zamoran plain. Two days, he thought, without pushing the animals too hard. No thoughts but how far the horses could travel, and how fast.

"It is my destiny!" she protested.

"Your destiny is not to die in these mountains. I will return you to your aunt's palace."

"You cannot interfere with my destiny!"

"Erlik take your destiny," he growled.

She drew alongside of him. "What of Valeria?" she demanded. "Yes, I heard that, too. I know what reward my aunt promised you."

It was a titanic effort to keep his face free of emotion, but Conan did it. A debt to be repaid, no matter the cost. But cost to himself, not to Jehnna. "I can protect you as we travel, but not if we hunt danger. Or do you think this treasure will simply be lying about unguarded?"

"Valeria—"

"She'd not ask me to trade your life for hers," he snapped. "Now be quiet, and follow me."

For a time she was indeed silent, though sulking and muttering angrily under her breath. Occupied with his own troubles, Conan refused to acknowledge her anger.

Abruptly she said, "It is there. I know it is, Conan. We must go there. Please!"

Despite a resolve not to, he looked where she was pointing. The gray-sloped mountain was not high, but near the base its stone flanks split unnaturally into hundreds of granite fingers and spires. A maze, he remembered Jehnna calling this journey. That was a maze in truth, where an army could lie in wait unseen until you were in their midst. It was no place to take a young girl, not in the Karpash Mountains, not even if the treasure Taramis wanted was in there. They would circle to the south, he decided, giving that particular mountain a wide berth. He rode on in silence.

"Conan!"

He closed his ears, refused to hear.

"Conan!"

Suddenly it impinged on the Cimmerian's mind that it was not Jehnna's voice he heard. His hand went to the worn hilt of his broadsword. That the caller knew his name could mean much or little. Then, from where a fold of land had momentarily hidden it, a horse appeared, with a Corinthian military saddle and a wiry, dark-eyed rider.

A broad grin split Conan's face. "Malak!" he shouted "I feared you were dead."

"Not I!" the small thief roared back. "I am too handsome to die!"

On Malak's heels the others came, Bombatta and Zula, Akiro easing his seat in his saddle and complaining about his old bones. The black woman rode straight to Jehnna, and the two of them put their heads together for talk pitched not to travel to any ears but their own.

"What happened with the Corinthians?" Conan demanded. "And how did you find us?"

Akiro opened his mouth, but Malak rushed in. "When they saw you two topping the pass, about half the fools rode off shouting about being first to ride the girl. Don't you all glare at me! Mitra, they said it, not me! In any case, cutting the numbers down gave Akiro a chance to work. Tell them what you did, Akiro."

Akiro opened his mouth again.

"He made a tiger appear," Malak laughed. "It was as big as an elephant! Fidesa witness my words! The horses went mad." He caught the old wizard's gaze on him, and subsided with a weak, "You tell the rest, Akiro."

"It was a small illusion," Akiro said. He did not take his eyes off Malak as he spoke, as if afraid that did he look away the wiry man would cut him off again. "Even with fewer of the Corinthians, I had no time for more. It was of sight and smell only, and could not even move, but the horses, to our great luck, did not know that. They did indeed go mad. Ours as well. But it enabled us to escape. Without the packhorse, as you see, but with our skins in one piece."

There was a deal too much of sorcery on this journey to suit Conan, but he could not complain when it saved his friends' lives. Instead he said, "It was fortuitous you found us. We entered these accursed mountains together, and it is well that we leave together."

Malak started to speak, then snapped his mouth firmly shut at Akiro's glare.

"Fortune had naught to do with it," the yellow-skinned mage said. "It was this." He held a leather cord with a small, carved stone dangling at its end. With a deft motion he set the stone to spinning in a circle, yet almost immediately the circle lengthened and narrowed until the stone swung back and forth in a line that pointed directly at Conan.

The Cimmerian drew a deep breath. Yet more sorcery! "I do not like such things associated with me," he said, and was pleased that he had not yelled it.

"Not with you," Akiro assured him. "With the amulet. Such a thing is much less complex than a living person, and thus easier to fix on. Had I had some of your hair, or some garments you had worn, I could have found you much more quickly."

"Crom!" Conan breathed. His hair! He would never allow a sorcerer to have such, no matter how much a friend he seemed at the moment.

Akiro went on as if the Cimmerian had not spoken. "With only an inanimate object as a focus, the circle barely changed at first. It was very difficult to read a direction. Much like finding your way through a building in the dark, by feel."

"And Bombatta did not want to follow it," Malak burst out. "He said he didn't trust Akiro." His last words trailed off to a murmur, and he gave a worried look at Akiro.

"It is all right," Akiro said. "I was finished."

All the while they talked Bombatta had sat his horse, glaring from Conan to Jehnna and back again. Now he growled, "Did he harm you, child?"

Jehnna looked up, startled, from her conversation with Zula. "What? Why, what do you mean, Bombatta? Conan protects me, even as you do."

Her answer did not seem to satisfy the black-armored man. His face darkened, and the scars on it became livid. He looked at Akiro, hesitated visibly, then spoke. "I must know, wizard. Is she still an innocent?"

"Bombatta!" Jehnna protested, and Zula spoke close behind her.

"That is no question to be asked, or answered," the black woman growled.

"Tell me true, wizard," Bombatta said insistently, "for our lives and more, much more than you can know, depend on it."

Akiro pursed his lips, then nodded slowly. "She is an innocent. I sense it so strongly, I wonder that the rest of you cannot." As Bombatta sagged with a relieved sigh, the round-bellied mage moved his horse closer to Conan's and lowered his voice. "It is a thing of the spirit and not of the flesh, as I said once before," he murmured.

Conan colored, and colored more when he realized that he had. "You pry," he muttered. "Do not use your wizardry on me."

"Use the vial I gave you," Akiro said. "Use it, and ride away from here. Take the girl, if you wish. I do not doubt you could persuade her to go with you. In another night or two." A faint leer touched his lips, and was gone. "There can be nothing in this for you, Cimmerian, save more wounds of the kind that neither show nor heal."

Conan scowled silently, denying the temptation to put his hand to his belt-pouch to see if the small stone vial was still there. Valeria, and a debt still unpaid. He became aware of Jehnna's voice.

"He says he will not take me, but I know it is there. I know!"

Bombatta turned a scowling visage to the Cimmerian. "Well, thief, do you abandon your precious Valeria? Did those Corinthians frighten your manhood from you? Or did you ever have—?"

Conan's eyes were so cold that the scar-faced warrior cut off his words. Bombatta's emotions were writ plain on his features, realization of what he had done, anger at having been afrighted even for a moment, rage that the others had seen it. He gripped his tulwar so hard that the hilt creaked, but the big Cimmerian made no move toward his own weapon.

Patience, Conan told himself. In the rugged mountain ranges of Cimmeria a man without patience was a man who was soon dead. There would be time for killing later. When he spoke his voice was icy calm.

"I would not take her where she wants to go without other eyes to watch, and more blades to guard her. We have them, now." He pulled his horse up beside Bombatta's. "Let us not delay, Zamoran. We must be back in Shadizar by tomorrow night, and we have matters to settle, you and I, when this is done."

"I will look forward to it," Bombatta snarled.

"And I," Conan said, starting forward again, "will look back upon it."

XVII

Half a day's riding it took to reach those broken fingers of stone, and they looked no better to Conan once he was in them than they had from a distance. Quickly the rough gray walls rose around them, and the way narrowed until they were forced to ride in single file. Hundreds of confined passages crossed and re-crossed like miniature canyons, with thick stone separating them. Sometimes half a score choices of direction were presented at once, and each was more cramped and crooked than the one before.

"To the right," Jehnna said from directly behind him. "The right, I said. No, not that one. That one over there! It's close, now. Oh, we could move twice as fast if you'd only let me lead."

"No!" Bombatta shouted.

Conan said nothing, reining in to study the possibilities ahead, three narrow corridors through the stone leading off in different directions. Very narrow corridors. It was not the first time Jehnna had asked to lead the way, and he had long since tired of explaining the dangers to her. Bombatta now refused to leave her side because, he claimed, he did not trust the Cimmerian not to allow her to go ahead of him. After Bombatta's display at the rejoining, Conan was sure the Zamoran simply did not want to leave her alone with him, but the problem before him left no time to worry about that.

"Why have we stopped?" Jehnna demanded. "That is the way. Right there." She pointed to the center gap.

"It is too narrow for the horses," Conan said. With some difficulty, for the gray walls were already close, he swung down from his saddle and moved ahead of his horse. "We will have to leave them."

He did not like doing it. Hobbled, they would not wander far, but even a short distance could make a difference in this. And without horses there was no hope in Zandru's Nine Hells of reaching Shadizar in time. The others had dismounted and were fastening hobbles between their mounts' forelegs, or pushing past the animals to join him.

"Malak," he said, "best you stay with the horses."

The small thief started and stared at the stone around them with a sickly look. "Here? Sigyn's Bowl, Conan, I don't think we should divide ourselves. Keep our forces together, eh? A man can't even breath in here."

About to make a sharp retort, Conan stopped. He himself had been thinking much about how close the stone was, how it seemed almost to cut off the air. But he was not one to be affected by tight passages or close spaces. He studied the others' faces, trying to see if any of them felt what he did. Jehnna was all impatience, while Zula had the set face of one who expected combat at any moment. Bombatta glowered, as usual, and Akiro appeared thoughtful, also as usual. Perhaps it was all in his imagination. And perhaps not.

"Yes, we'll stay together," he said. He drew his sword in one hand, his dagger in the other. "Thus will I mark our way," with the dagger he scratched an arrow on the stone, pointing toward the horses, "that we can find the horses again. Stay close."

To Jehnna's eager urging Conan moved down the rough-walled passage, though not so quickly as she would have liked, and every ten paces he scratched another arrow on the stone. If the worst came, he thought, even Jehnna could find the animals with these. Even alone she might have a chance of escape.

At times they had to turn sideways, stone scraping their chests and backs, for some stretches were so strait not even Zula or Jehnna could walk through them normally. However Conan walked, he kept his sword advanced and his dagger ready for anything that managed to get past the longer blade. As he moved deeper into the maze, his sense of something ill grew. Almost could he put a name now to what seemed to permeate the stone through which they made their way. It was like the remembrance of a memory of the stench of death, so faint the nose could not smell it, so tenuous the mind could not grasp it, yet there to be touched by the most primitive instincts.

He looked back at the others, and this time found his unease mirrored on their faces, all save Jehnna's.

"Why do we move so slowly?" the slender girl demanded. Vainly, she tried to push past the big Cimmerian, but there was barely width enough for him to pass alone. "We are almost there."

"Akiro?" Conan said.

The gray-haired wizard's face was twisted as if he had a bad taste in his mouth. "I have sensed it since we entered these passages, but it grows stronger as we go. It is . . . a foulness." He stopped to spit. "But it is old, ancient, and I do not think it threatens us. We are more than a few centuries too late for that."

Conan nodded, and continued on, but he was not convinced. His own senses might not be magical, but they had kept him alive in many places where he could well have died, and they told him there was danger here. He kept a firm grip on his weapons.

With startling suddenness the passage spilled out into a large open area. Here the rock had been cut away, and the stone remaining carved in intricate patterns to floor a great courtyard that fronted a temple hewn from the very side of the mountain. Massive fluted columns ran across the face of the temple, and once a score of obsidian statues, four times the height of a man, had stood between them. Now only one remained, an ebon warrior holding a tall spear, with the features of his face worn away by wind and rain. Of the others only shattered chunks of black stone and the stumps of their legs remained.

Conan sheathed his dagger and grabbed Jehnna's arm as she tried to run to the temple. "Take care, girl," he told her. "I'll risk much here, but you I risk as little as possible."

Bombatta seized her other arm, and the two men stared coldly at one another above her head. The promise of death was strong between them. It was another reason to wish the journey done, Conan thought. Such promises as that could not remain unfulfilled forever.

"Let me go," Jehnna said, twisting in their grasp. "I must find the Horn. It is inside there. Let me go!"

Zula, sneering at both men, put her hands on Jehnna's shoulders. "Will you tear her apart, then? Or perhaps crush her between you?"

Conan let his hand fall away, and Bombatta was only an instant behind. Zula drew the girl away, speaking softly in her ear. Conan met Bombatta's glare unblinkingly.

"This will be settled, thief," the scar-faced man said.

"In Shadizar," Conan said, and the other jerked a nod of agreement.

When Conan reached the temple, Akiro was attempting to trace with his finger weather-worn carving in the pedestal on which the obsidian statue stood. Little was left.

"What are you trying to do?" Malak laughed at the old wizard. "Read decorative carving? And to speak of it, I've seen better scrollwork done by a one-eyed drunkard."

Sighing, Akiro straightened and dusted his hands. "I could read it, in part at least, were it not so badly eroded. It is script, not scrollwork. This place is much older even than I believed. The last writings in this language were done more than three thousand years ago, and even then it was a dead tongue. Only scattered fragments remain. Perhaps I can find more inside."

"We are not here to decipher old languages," Bombatta growled.

Privately Conan agreed, but all he said was, "Let us get on with it, then."

Rock doves burst from their nests high behind the massive columns, their wingbeats like an explosion in the stillness, as Conan strode to the tall bronze doors, covered with the verdigris of centuries. Through the thick green could be seen a huge open eye worked deeply into the metal of each door. A large bronze ring hung below each eye.

"We'll never get that open," Malak said, eyeing the corrosion.

Conan grasped one thick ring for an experimental heave. To his surprise the door swung out with a squeal of hinges long ungreased. It was but chance that it opened so, he told himself. If men used those doors, they would grease the hinges. He did not like the relief he felt at that. Still, he told himself, he was there to see to Jehnna's safety, not to flaunt his own bravery.

"Keep a sharp eye," he commanded, "and your guard up." Then he led the way inside.

Beyond the great doors the dust of centuries lay thick on the floor. Torches stood along the intricately carved walls in golden brackets, untarnished by the years but festooned in cobwebs. Above them the ceiling was lost in shadows, and the vast hall stretched before them into darkness.

Suddenly Zula screamed as a spider, its outstretched legs wide enough to cover a man's hand, ran across her bare foot.

"Only a spider," Malak said, crushing it beneath his foot. He kicked the pulped remains away. "No need to be afraid of a—" The wiry thief cut off with a yelp as Zula's staff whistled toward his face and halted, quivering, no more than a finger-width from his nose. His eyes crossed staring at it.

"I am not afraid," Zula hissed. "I simply do not like spiders." Rustlings sounded deeper in the hall, and she peered in that direction nervously. "And rats. I especially do not like rats."

Conan lifted a torch down from the wall and sheathed his sword to dig into his pouch for flint and steel. "If these still burn," he began.

Akiro's lips moved, and fire suddenly danced atop his bunched fingers. He touched it to the torch, which burst aflame with a crackle that was loud in the still hall. "It will burn," he said.

"Can you not wait until you are asked?" Conan said drily as he stuffed the lighting implements back. Akiro shrugged apologetically.

Bombatta and Malak lit torches from Conan's, and they started warily down the great hall. Their feet disturbed dust unmarked save for the small tracks of rats. The bones of small animals and birds lay scattered about, some buried in the dust, some atop it. Long had it been since anything had moved there save the rodents and their prey. The chattering of rats, held back by fire and the strange smell of humans, followed them, and the torches' flames were reflected in hundreds of tiny, hungry eyes. Zula muttered and swiveled her head as if trying to watch all ways at once. Malak no longer made fun of her discomfort; he rigidly avoided looking at those glittering eyes, and mixed curses and prayers to a score of gods in a low monotone.

At the far end of the hall were broad stone steps leading up to a dais atop which sat a high-back throne of marble. Before that throne lay a small pile of age-dried bones, and on its seat another pile with a human skull in its midst, empty, shadowed eye-sockets staring at Conan and his companions. Armor, garments, a crown, whatever that man had once worn, were all long gone to dust.

Jehnna pointed to their right, to a wide, arched doorway half-hidden in the darkness. "There," she said. "That is the way."

Conan found himself relieved that the treasure—the horn, had not Jehnna called it?—was not on that throne. Many years before he had taken the sword he carried from a throne not too different from this one, and it had not been an experience he would care to repeat.

Bombatta had moved to the archway as soon as the girl spoke, and thrust his torch through it. "Stairs!" he muttered. "How much deeper into the bowels of this place must we go?"

"As deep as we must," Conan said. And pushing Bombatta aside, he started down.

XVIII

The wide stairs spiraled down into the depths of the mountain, and here Conan could see signs of the earthquake that had toppled the statues in front of the temple. Cracks spider-webbed the walls, and once there was a jog in the stairs, as if someone had cut neatly through them then pushed one part a handspan to the side. True spiders had been there once, as well. Thick cobwebs clogged the passage, but at the touch of the Cimmerian's torch they hissed and flared and melted away.

"I do not like this, Conan," Malak whispered loudly. "Ogon strike me, but I don't."

"Then wait above," Conan replied.

"With the rats!" The small man's voice was a squeak, and Zula chuckled, though not strongly.

A final turn and the stairs led into a long chamber with a high vaulted ceiling supported by what seemed at first glance to be golden columns, a row of them along each wall. Nearly half the columns were toppled, though, their broken pieces littering the dusty, mosaicked floor, and the pieces showed thin hammered gold-leaf atop ordinary gray stone. The ceiling was worked in a profusion of strange symbols, only one of which Conan could even recognize. An open eye, as on the bronze doors, repeated over and over among the other designs. What it meant he could not begin to guess.

"Conan," Akiro called, "this seems the only way out other than the stairs."

The wizard stood at the far end of the chamber by a broad door that seemed of iron, yet had no spot of rust on it. It had no hinges either, Conan saw, as if it were merely a huge metal plate set in the stone.

"This is the way," Jehnna whispered eagerly. She stared intently at the door, or at something beyond. "We must go on."

The door's dark gray surface was smooth except for the inevitable open eye in its center and two snarling demons' heads near the bottom. Tusks, like those of a wild boar, curved out from the open mouths of those grotesque heads. If the door could not be pushed open, Conan thought, then possibly ... He rapped his sword sharply against each of the grimacing demon heads. From one gaping mouth wriggled a scarlet centipede; its bite was sure, slow and agonized death. Malak leaped from its way as it scurried for a hiding place among the fallen columns.

Sheathing his sword, Conan handed his torch to Zula and squatted before the door. One hand he placed in each demon mouth. As he had thought, his hands fit easily. He heaved upward.

"Handles," Malak exclaimed.

With every muscle straining, Conan began to wonder if he had been right in reaching the same conclusion as the smaller man. The metal slab moved no more than if it were a part of the mountain. Suddenly Bombatta was there beside him, grasping one of the demon heads. Conan shifted both hands to the other, and redoubled his effort. Tendons stood out along his neck and thighs, and every sinew of him cried out. Silver flecks danced before his eyes. And the iron slab lurched up a handsbreadth. Slowly then, with a metallic racheting noise, the door rose, until Conan and Bombatta between them held it above their heads.

"In," Conan rasped. "Quickly."

The others of the party squeezed hurriedly by the two big men, then Bombatta released his hold and followed. Conan's thews quivered with the strain of holding the weighty door alone, yet he hesitated. When he released it, it would come down, and look as he might, he could see no demons' open mouths nor other means of lifting it from the other side. They would be trapped. But if he could not find a way to prop it open, he would *have* to let it fall.

Murmuring to himself thoughtfully, Akiro stepped to the wall beside the door, where a bronze rod ending in a large knob, embossed with the ever-present open eye, projected from the stone. The mage put a hand on the knob, pushed, and the rod sank into the wall.

Conan blinked. There seemed to be a lessening of the weight on him. He eased his upward pressure slightly. The door did not move. With a sour grunt he stepped from under it.

"I thank you," he told Akiro, "but now that I think of it, could you not have opened this yourself?"

"I could have," Akiro replied mildly, "but you said I should wait to be asked. As I was not—"

"Where are the others?" Conan cut him off.

The light of Akiro's torch lit one end of a narrow corridor, and there was no sign of anyone other than the two of them, nor any light from the other torches. Cursing, the Cimmerian set out down that hall at a run, with Akiro panting in his footsteps. The corridor opened into a large, circular chamber, and both men skidded to a halt in amazement. The others were already there, holding their torches high while they stared about them.

Directly opposite the door through which they entered a monstrous head of carved black stone, fanged and glaring, as tall as a big man, projected from the wall. Two other doorways, set equidistant around the circle from the first, led from the chamber. Or rather, one did, for the other was broken and choked with rubble that spilled in a fan into the room. The rest of the walls were carved in bas-relief, images of fabled beasts, gilded, with gems set for their eyes while others formed hooves and claws and horns. At intervals around the walls great plaques of gold were set, covered with strange script. The low domed ceiling was tied with onyx and set with diamonds and sapphires, twinkling in the light of the torches, as if to represent a night sky.

Akiro rushed to one of the golden plaques and ran his fingers over the deep-carved script as if he did not believe his eyes. "This is the same language as outside, and more of it than exists in one place anywhere else in the world. I can . . . yes, I can make it out. Listen." He spoke on slowly, pausing to trace letters. "And on the thirteenth day of the Last Battle, the gods did come to war, and the mountains did tremble at their footsteps."

The rotund wizard went on, but Conan was more interested in what Jehnna was doing under Bombatta's watchful eye. She alone had not goggled at the riches of the chamber. Her eyes were only for the massive, terrible head of black stone. Now she stood before it, looking nowhere else. Beneath her feet was a circle of runes carved in the marble of the floor, and woven among them was a five-pointed star with straight lines joining its points.

Conan's breath caught in his throat. He knew the symbol of the star of old, knew it to his regret. A pentagram, a focus of sorcerous powers. He half-raised a hand to stop her. But there was Valeria. And Jehnna said this was her destiny, that she had been born to do this thing. The hand he had raised clenched into a fist until his knuckles cracked. He could do nothing else but see it through to the end.

From beneath her robes Jehnna produced the black velvet bag in which she carried the Heart of Ahriman. As the blood-red gem slipped into her palm its sanguine glow filled the chamber, and the jewels set in the ceiling seemed to glitter more fiercely. Carefully she set the Heart down before her in the pentagram; there was a small niche carved into which it fit exactly. As she straightened awareness faded from her eyes. In a trance, she chanted, and her words rang round the walls.

As she intoned the words, the radiance of the Heart increased, yet now it was focused, shining only on the great stone head, bathing it in crimson light. The black stone eyes especially seemed to reflect its glow, and crimson shadows danced in their depths, depths that had not been there moments before.

"It lives," Zula hissed, and Malak began muttering prayers.

"You must stop her," Akiro said suddenly, urgency riddling his voice. "Quickly, Conan, you must—" He broke off with a moan of denial that seemed wrung from his bones.

Soundlessly the stone jaws of the monstrous head opened, spreading wide enough to swallow three men whole, and in that mouth burned fire such as no eye there had ever before seen. Blood turned to flame, it was, and Conan found himself stepping back, a hand before to his face to shield him from heat that seemed to sear the very air. Though it pained his eyes to look, the Cimmerian saw a crystal spire in the midst of those flames. It was a pellucid column such as the one on which the Heart of Ahriman had rested in Amon-Rama's place, but atop this one was a horn of gold, like the horn of a bull. Neither spire nor horn seemed touched by the fiery tempest that roared about them.

Jehnna still stared as if not at this world, but worlds beyond. Her large eyes were blank, and her face lacked all expression. Slowly her hands rose to her shoulders, and her robes fell to her feet. Naked, she stood, slender curves bathed with the light of the flames before her, the birthmark between her small breasts glowing like those fires. With quick, unhesitating steps, she moved forward. Not a muscle moving, Bombatta watched her, and the light in his dark eyes could have been a reflection of the fiery furnace.

"No!" Conan shouted, yet even as he did it was too late.

Into the roaring flames Jehnna stepped. About her the fire flared as if in fury at her invasion, licking at her slim nudity, yet she moved deeper, unaware and unharmed. In both hands she lifted the golden horn, and with it walked from the blazing furnace, back to the pentagram.

For a moment she stood there, and all in the room seemed frozen where they stood. Then she sighed, sagged, and would have fallen had not Zula rushed to support her. Quickly the black woman pulled the girl's robes up about her.

"It is done," Bombatta said softly. "The Horn is in the hands of the One."

"Conan," Akiro said shakily, "there is something you must know."

Abruptly there was a wind in the chamber, an icy gale of eerie howls that they felt to their bones, yet which did not so much as bend the flames of the torches. Then it was gone as suddenly as it had come, and the fires in that huge mouth were gone, as well, but the chill of the wind remained.

"Conan," Akiro said again.

"Later," Conan snapped. One too many pieces of sorcery had he seen for a single day, and this last had come at no one's bidding that he could tell. "We leave *now!*" And barely waiting for Jehnna to gather the Heart of Ahriman, he hurried them from the chamber.

XIX

I t was a procession that Conan led back along the narrow corridor, and he did not care for the feeling of it. Jehnna carried the golden horn hugged tightly to her bosom, and Bombatta and Zula hovered protectively on either side of her, interspersing solicitous looks for the slender girl with cold stares at each other. Though glad beyond measure that she was unharmed, the Cimmerian was troubled by what Jehnna had experienced, and troubled as well by the artifact she carried so carefully.

Akiro tugged at Conan's elbow. "I must talk with you," he said quietly, glancing back at Bombatta. "In private. It is urgent."

"Yes," Conan agreed distractedly. He had come in contact with sorcery many times before in his young life, many more than he wished to remember. Betimes he found he could sense it, and what he sensed from the golden object the girl clutched to her breast was the odor of evil. Very much he wanted to be gone from that place, to be back in Shadizar with the thing done. "In private, Akiro," he murmured. "Later."

Malak ran before them, dancing in his eagerness to leave. "Hurry!" he called over his shoulder. "This place is ill! Mitra's Bones! Hurry!" He darted from view ahead, and his words faded away.

"Fool," Conan muttered. "This is no time to be separated." Then he was into the chamber of gilded columns, and he fell silent as well.

Malak was there, rolling his eyes nervously. Also there were more than a score of warriors in black leather armor of archaic design, leaning on long spears. The smallest of the men was head and shoulders taller than Conan or Bombatta. They were as black as the obsidian statue before the temple, and Conan was relieved to see their chests rise and fall with breathing. They were men, not statues come to life. That had been his first thought.

Two of the warriors stepped forward. One had a crest of long white hair spilling down the back of his bronze helmet; the other wore no helmet, but rather a black leather skull-cap from which hung long fringes of red hair. He with the white crest spoke. To Jehnna.

"Long have we waited for you, for the One. We have slept, as our god sleeps, and we have awaited the day of your coming. The Night of Awakening approaches."

Bombatta shifted uneasily, and Akiro's breath whistled between his teeth.

"This girl has no part in your ways," Conan said. "We crave pardon if we have disturbed your temple, but we have far to travel, and we must go."

All the while he noted the disposition of the ebon warriors. He had no wish to fight if it could be avoided, but these men seemed to be saying that this was their temple, for all it looked not to have known a human tread in centuries. And men often grew violent when they thought strangers interfered with their religion.

"You may go," the towering black warrior replied. "For bringing us the girl, the One, your lives are given to you. But she remains with us."

Making every attempt to seem casual, Conan stepped between the tall warrior and Jehnna. "She is not the One you seek," he said, but the ebon man ignored him and spoke again to Jehnna.

"For all the years we have slept, guarding the Horn of Dagoth, waiting for you, for the One who could touch the Horn. Now will the Sleeping God be awakened, and his vengeance will spread against those who betrayed—"

Conan caught a flicker of motion out of the corner of his eye as Bombatta's arm whipped forward, and a dagger blossomed in the tall man's throat. Blood poured from the black giant's mouth as he fell, and pandemonium broke loose in the chamber.

"Back!" Conan shouted. There was no way forward except through huge men who were raising their spears and snarling with fury. "Back! Quickly!" The Cimmerian thrust his torch into one tall warrior's face, beat aside another's spear thrust, and ran a third through the middle.

A metallic racheting caught his ear. Sword dancing desperately to hold off an ever-increasing number of spears, he risked a quick glance over his shoulder. The great iron door was descending in jerks, and it did not have far to fall. With a roar he attacked, his blade a grim blur of razor steel before him, the sheer fury of him forcing his opponents back despite their greater numbers. With a suddenness that caught them all off-guard, he whirled and threw himself into a rolling dive toward the rapidly closing doorway. The bottom of the iron door scraped his shoulder, then he was through, and the slab settled against the floor with a heavy, grating thud.

Akiro, Malak and Zula stared down at him worriedly, but there was no time for their worry. "We must hurry," he said as he scrambled to his feet. "'Tis likely they got a spear point or two under the edge of that trying to stab me, and if so they'll lever it up soon enough."

"I will see what I can do about that," Akiro said. Delving in his pouch, he drew out materials and began drawing symbols on the metal of the door.

"You could have given me a little warning," Conan muttered to Malak. "A shout that you were letting the door fall."

"Bombatta caught us all by surprise," Malak replied. "He grabbed Jehnna and darted in here before any of the rest of us could move. I guess he pulled that rod out as soon as he was past the door."

"There," Akiro said, stepping back from his labors. A string of faintly glowing symbols, each of which resisted efforts to focus the eye on it, stretched across the door from side to side. "That should hold them for a time."

Conan found he was no longer interested in whether the door held or not. "Where *is* Jehnna?" he demanded. "And Bombatta?"

Zula spun to stare down the dark hall. "I was so worried about you," she whispered, "that I did not . . . If he has hurt her . . ."

Conan did not wait to hear the rest. He sped toward the chamber of the great stone head as fast as his legs would carry him. It was empty. Without hesitation he took the one way out other than the way he had come, the unblocked, third corridor.

Grim thoughts filled the Cimmerian's head. Perhaps Bombatta meant to try spiriting Jehnna back to Shadizar without him, to cheat him of his reward. It would be like the Zamoran, he thought, to rob Valeria of a chance at rebirth just to strike at him. There would be no waiting until Shadizar now. The time for accounting had come.

The corridor ran straight as an arrow, without bend or fork, without a doorway leading to another chamber. Like a tunnel, the corridor had been carved from the living rock of the mountain, its walls, ceiling and floor polished as smooth as marble. Dust dulled and covered all, now, and it was in that dust that the light of his torch showed the traces of those he followed, signs as plain to his keen eyes as ruts in a wagon road. The spaces between the tracks told him they, too, were running.

Suddenly the hallway spilled into a large, square chamber filled with thick, fluted columns set close together and supporting a ceiling lined with cracks and fissures. Many of the columns were filled with cracks as well, some seeming to need only a breath to topple. Dust-covered implements lay among them, fallen braziers with high, tripod legs, things that might have been tall stands to hold torches, others the purposes of which he could not guess.

Conan's torch was enough for him to make another door ahead, a deeper black rectangle in the shadows. The tracks in the dust led toward that door as well, but he stopped his headlong dash. Bombatta could be hidden anywhere among those myriad columns, and tracks so plain could lead to an ambush. In a cautious crouch, poised to spring in any direction, broadsword at the ready, the big Cimmerian advanced. His eyes probed the dark about him for the slightest hint of movement.

"Jehnna," he called softly, then louder, "Jehnna!" The name echoed, and he shouted over it, louder still, "Jehnna!"

Then he saw Bombatta, standing beside the far doorway with a thick rod of rusted iron, a good three paces long, in his hands. The Zamoran moved quickly for such a big man. He thrust the rod crossways between two cracked pillars like a lever and heaved.

Time seemed to slow for Conan as the columns bowed outwards in opposite directions, began to fall in chunks. The ceiling above him groaned; bits of stone and dirt pelted him.

In one smooth motion the Cimmerian turned and threw himself back the way he had come, away from collapsing stone. The roar of falling rock reverberated through the chamber. Something struck Conan's head, and darkness swallowed him.

Jehnna crouched where Bombatta had left her, peering down the corridor down which they had fled. He had fled, she thought angrily. She had been dragged behind him like a bundle. Until reaching this spot he had refused to listen to her pleas that he help the others, then he told her to wait and dashed back. It was all very well that he put her safety first, but he should have listened to her sooner. Golden-red sunlight shone through a crack at the top of a huge stone slab behind her, but she did not look at it. Daylight and the way back to Shadizar lay on the other side of that thick slab, but Conan was still behind her, in the depths of the mountain. What if he were injured, and needed her? What if . . .

Running footsteps announced Bombatta's return. He scrambled up the slope of the corridor in haste.

"Is he unharmed?" she demanded.

Dust and dirt covered the scar-faced man, and blood trickled from a scratch on his cheek. He started past her, then stopped suddenly, his face paling. "Where's the horn, child?" he demanded. "Zandru's Nine Hells, if you've lost it . . ."

"It is here." She showed him the bundle she had made, wrapped in strips torn from her cloak. It was her destiny, she knew, this quest for the Horn of Dagoth, but there was something about the golden object that made her want not to touch it. The Heart of Ahriman and the Horn of

Dagoth were together, swathed in layers of white wool, and she truly wished there were more layers. Many more. "Where is . . . where are the others?"

"Dead," Bombatta replied curtly. Huge muscles straining, he threw his weight against the massive slab of stone.

Jehnna sat as if poleaxed. Dead? Conan could not be dead. She could not imagine him as dead. Or the others, she told herself quickly. Zula, Akiro, even Malak, had taken on special meaning to her. She did not want to think of any of them being harmed. But the tall youth with the strange sapphire eyes and the hands that were so gentle when they did not hold a sword, he was more than special. "I cannot believe it," she whispered. The great slab fell outwards with a crash, raising a cloud of dust and letting in a flood of fading sunlight. "I heard him call my name. I know that I did."

"Come, Jehnna. We have little time, child."

Bombatta seized her wrist in his huge hand, pulling her after him through the opening. They were on the very edge of the large courtyard before the temple. The sun sat crimson on the mountaintops to the west. With a wary eye on the tall bronze temple doors and cursing under his breath, Bombatta hurried her into the maze of high stone fingers and spires.

"I will not believe Conan is dead," she told him.

"One of the marks," the black-armored man said, pointing to an arrow scratched in the rock. "Now to find the horses. We can cover leagues before full dark."

"Bombatta, I will not believe it. Did you see him fall?"

"I saw," Bombatta said harshly. He did not slow his pace, and his iron grip on her wrist made certain she kept up. "He was running, like the thief and dog that he was, and the black warriors cut him down. Him, and the others, as well. I had to pull down the ceiling to block them off from us. Ah, the horses."

The hobbled animals were still bunched together. Jehnna could not have told whether they had wandered from where they were left even had she thought of it, and her mind was on other matters.

"Perhaps he was only wounded," she began, then cut off at the strange look Bombatta was giving her. His eyes burned with intensity.

"We could go anywhere," he said softly. "We could go to Aghrapur. A Turanian wizard, or even King Yildiz himself, would give enough for those things you carry to keep us in luxury for the rest of our lives." Abruptly he lifted her onto a saddle. "Guard them well, Jehnna," he said, and began loosing the horses' hobbles. He tied the reins of each horse he freed to those of the next, and when he mounted he had the other four animals on a long lead.

"What are you doing?" she demanded. "We cannot take those."

"We will need them," Bombatta said. "It is a long way to Aghrapur."

"We go to Shadizar, not Aghrapur. And I will not leave the others without horses so long as there is any chance one of them remains alive. If you wish to take the horses, then you must take me back into the temple and show me their bodies."

Bombatta shook his head. "It is too dangerous for you."

"Dangerous or not," she insisted, "I will not leave him so."

The fury that clouded the massive warrior's face made her want to cower. It took all of her will to keep her back straight, to look him in the eye with outward calm.

Dropping the reins of the other horses, he moved his own closer to hers. "Him! Him, and again him! We could have gone anywhere." Every word came from him like a piece of iron. "Anywhere, child." Abruptly his scarred visage twisted in pain. Jehnna stared; she had never before seen Bombatta show pain. The agonized grimace lasted but a moment, then his face was normal again, save that in going from his eyes the burning seemed to have left them dull and flat. "We go to Shadizar," he said hoarsely and, taking the reins from her hands, began to lead her through the maze.

Jehnna clutched the bundle, containing all she had come so far to find, tightly against her breast, and would not allow herself to look back. Conan or her destiny. One at the cost of the other. She wondered how there could be such pain. How could the gods allow it? Slumping, no longer able to find the strength to sit straight, she wept softly and let herself be led.

XX

Through thick clouds of smothering darkness Conan clawed his way back to consciousness and scrambled to his feet with sword in hand. Akiro and Zula stared at him in amazement. Malak tossed a fist-sized rock into the shadows between the columns and dusted his hands.

"About time you were awake," the small thief said. "By Mehen's Scales, I was beginning to think you were going to sleep until we were all dead."

"How long?" Conan said. He felt the side of his head. It was tender, and a fan of dried blood descended from his hair.

Malak shrugged, but Akiro said, "Perhaps two turns of the glass, perhaps a little longer. It is difficult to tell exactly. We found you lying like a stunned ox. I did what I could, but it is best with head injuries to let wakefulness come naturally."

"I have a few herbs that help blows to the head," Zula said, "but there is no water to steep them in."

The Cimmerian nodded, and immediately wished he had not as the chamber seemed to spin around. Desperately he fought off the dizziness. He could allow no weakness now.

The far end of the dim chamber was now a mass of stone, fragments of fluted columns mixed with chunks of the mountain above in sizes from that Malak had held to boulders larger than a man. Three of the rusted metal stands Conan had thought made to hold torches had been set upright. Their torches burned atop them, casting a pale yellow pool about the four, a pool that quickly faded into shadows among the columns. Not all the light came from the torches, however. From down the unblocked passage came a flickering azure glow that was painful to the eye.

"What is that blue light?" Conan asked.

"A ward," Akiro told him. "I managed to lay nine sets before those tall fellows got the door open. Then I had to trigger the first and could lay no more. It is dangerous to place one of those while another burns close by."

449

"How long," Conan began, and got his answer before he could complete the question.

The azure flickering increased in speed, and Akiro bent to draw symbols in the dust with a finger and mouth his silent incantations. With a last flash of brilliant blue the light was gone. In an instant it began again, and a shriek echoed down the corridor as it did.

Akiro tilted his head as if listening, then sighed. "One was very fast, but not their wizard, worse luck. If Bombatta had to slay one of them, he could as well have killed the one with the red crest. He is their mage, and without him they would never even have gotten that door open, much less reached my wards. And I must fight him with little more than my bare hands."

"I do not see why he had to kill any of them," Zula said angrily. "They offered no violence toward us, only speaking to . . ." Her words trailed off with a sympathetic look at Conan, but he ignored it.

"I doubt they would have let us go without a fight," he said. "Not with Jehnna. In any case, I'll not let them spear me like a wild pig just because Bombatta started it."

"That's it," Malak said. "Ogon's Toenails, if a man attacks you, you carve him, and if it's all a mistake you can burn a little incense in the temples for his spirit."

"Not always the best way," Akiro said drily. "But those men are foul."

"I saw no foulness in them," Zula protested, and the wizard snorted.

"That is because you are not a mage, nor did you read the plaques, as I did. The unease we felt as we entered was put there by those men, and by those who came before them, over centuries. Human sacrifice was the least of it. They make the shamans you res—ah, assisted me with, seem as babes at play."

"I care not if they're cannibals," Conan said. "It is past time for us to be getting out of here. Bombatta and Jehnna get closer to Shadizar with every moment, and I do not doubt he'll do his best to leave us out of what has happened when he tells Taramis of it. I do not intend to be cheated of my promised reward."

Akiro looked at him pityingly, and Zula gaped. "But I thought . . . we thought . . . Jehnna . . ." She gestured helplessly at the jumbled stone filling the other end of the chamber.

"Bombatta pulled that down," Conan said. "He could not wait to face me in Shadizar. But I cannot think he pulled it down on his own head, nor on Jehnna's. We will dig our way out, and follow. There is but a night and a day left before we must be back in Shadizar."

"You intend to dig through the mountain?" Malak said incredulously. The other two looked at the Cimmerian as if he had gone mad.

"I saw this chamber when it was whole," Conan told them as he strode to the mass of rock. "I know how much of it is gone." He seized a torso-sized piece of a column and heaved it loose; smaller stones slid free and bounced around his feet. "The passage Bombatta followed is no more than three or four paces from us. And we have only to clear a way wide enough to squeeze through." He carried the stone well into the columns before dropping it. There was room there for all they had to move and more. When he returned, the others remained where they had been, still staring at him. "Well?" he demanded. "Would you rather die here?" Without a word Zula came to dig at the stone.

Malak came more slowly, and not without a look over his shoulder at the old wizard. "Aren't you going to help, Akiro? You could wave your arms, and make all this disappear."

"You display your ignorance openly," Akiro snorted. "In any case, I must watch to trigger the next ward when this one fails. Unless you want your first warning of those spearmen to be when one spits you like a lamb."

"You trigger all of them now, old man. Then you could help."

The gray-haired wizard laughed derisively. "Do I teach you how to steal, my small thief? Be about something you know how to do."

Conan labored like an automaton, fixing his mind on the goal of freedom, refusing to allow the immensity of the task to daunt him. Two stones he moved for every one moved by Zula and Malak together. Sweat oiled him till he glistened in the torchlight, and there was always more sweat to wash away the dust. When, with a loud rumble, rock cascaded from above to replace all they had done, he chivied the others back to work without ceasing himself. He must reach Jehnna. He must repay his debt to Valeria. Jehnna. Valeria. The two swirled in his mind till he could not tell which drove him most.

When another ward failed and Akiro chanted to replace it, Malak stopped to watch, knuckling the small of his back. "You really read those plaques, Akiro?" he asked.

"Work," Conan said, and after one glance at the Cimmerian's grim face Malak bent back to the stones.

Akiro, however, seemed to want to talk. He settled himself against a column and began. "Yes, I read them. Enough of them, at least. The golden horn that . . ." He frowned at Conan, then went on. "It is the Horn of Dagoth."

"The black warrior called it that," Malak panted.

"Do not interrupt," the wizard replied acerbically. "Millennia ago there was a war between the gods, which was not a rare thing in those times. In a great battle Dagoth was defeated by having the Horn ripped from his head and carried far away. The Horn carried what might be called his life-force, and without it he slowly turned to stone. According to the plaques, he sleeps, and when the Horn is placed again on his head he will wake."

"So that is why Taramis wants it," Conan said, still laboring. "To wake a god. Surely a god could bring Valeria back to life."

"Yes," Akiro sighed, "I suppose Dagoth could restore her to the living."

"So Taramis did not lie," Conan said with satisfaction.

As if he had received rest and cool water the Cimmerian increased his efforts. As the others slowed, he carried stones with greater speed. Zula fell trying to keep up with him, and could not stand. Conan paused to carry her back to Akiro, then rushed back to his labor. Later, when Malak dropped, the Cimmerian merely dragged him clear of the path he must follow from the stony blockage to where he threw the rocks.

He knew vaguely that they had dug past the end of the chamber, into the corridor, and still rock was piled before him. He knew it in a dim recess of his mind, but to acknowledge it might be the beginning of defeat, and he suppressed it ruthlessly without even being aware that he did so. Time lost all meaning to him. Effort lost all meaning. As if he were himself made of stone, incapable of tiring, he attacked the barrier relentlessly. Twin images drew him on. Valeria. Jehnna. He would not stop while life remained.

He tugged at a stone jammed into the tangle, tugged harder. It came free, and as it did the wall of rocks fell toward him. He stumbled back, cursing, barely avoiding being buried to the waist. Starting to turn away with the stone, he stopped abruptly with the realization that he had been looking over piled stone at a pale spot of light in the distance. He looked again, just to be sure he was not imagining it. The glow was still there. Letting the stone he had fall, he moved back to the chamber of columns.

Akiro sat crosslegged, staring gravely at the azure light from the corridor. Zula barely looked up, but Malak said tiredly from where he lay, "So you're finished, too, eh, Cimmerian? Well, we gave it a good try. Erlik take us, if we didn't."

"I am through," Conan said. "There is light. Sunlight, maybe." Malak made a strange sound, and quivered. It took Conan a moment to realize the small thief was laughing.

"We made it," Malak wheezed. "By Zandru's Darkest Hell and Mitra's Bones, they cannot stop us, Cimmerian."

"You are certain, Conan?" Akiro said worriedly.

"It could be torches in another chamber," Conan replied, "but there would have to be scores of them. The passage slopes upward. It must break ground." Or it could rise into the mountain, he thought, but would not say it. The light could be from sorcery or Zandru's Seventh Hell, but he needed to reach the surface above, and he would not admit it could be anything else.

"We must hope for sunlight," Akiro said finally. "The seventh ward yet holds, though not for much longer, and two more wait. You must get Zula and Malak out of here as quickly as possible. I will follow as soon as I can." He scurried back to his post at the mouth of the corridor. "Go man, or you may yet kill us all."

Conan helped Zula to her feet, and turned to find Malak already wavering erect. The black woman tried to walk on her own, too, but the big Cimmerian found himself helping the pair to scramble over the last mound of stones and stagger upward toward the light. That glow seemed to have a restorative quality, for by the time Akiro caught up to them, both Zula and Malak were climbing without support and making good speed.

Even so, the old wizard called out, "Hurry! Hurry!" And there was that in his voice that made them move even faster.

The corridor ended in a rectangular opening, and the four stumbled out into the temple courtyard and the light of a sun not-yet fully risen in the east. Malak and Zula stared at it as if they had not believed they would ever see a sunrise again.

Conan had eyes only for the temple, with its huge columns and fallen statues. Unless the tall warriors were fools, he thought, there would be sentries. Yet as he hastened them all across the carven stones of the courtyard nothing moved from the temple save rock doves, flapping out from their nests high behind the columns. Then he realized there was no need to put sentries above when all of your enemies were trapped like rats beneath the mountain.

In the maze the thirsty whickering of the horses drew them quickly to the animals. Conan noted the missing hobbles and the tied reins, then the four of them were hurrying for the waterskins. Despite a throat that felt like gravel Conan first poured water into his horse's mouth. When it was his turn he tipped back his head and drank until forced to breath, let the water splash over his face while he gulped air, then drank more. He finished by giving his horse another drink. The animal would have more need to be refreshed than he, for he intended to ride it hard.

Suddenly the ground quivered beneath their feet. Conan grabbed the reins, but before he could soothe his mount another tremor shook the earth, followed by a rumbling boom from the direction of the temple.

Malak, clinging to a trembling horse, muttered, "What in the Nine-Fold Names of Khepra was that?"

Akiro coughed smugly. "I changed the incantation slightly. When they broke through the seventh ward, the last two were triggered together.

Those spearman will not wake from this sleep, nor rise from this tomb to slaughter innocents for Dagoth." He smiled suddenly at Malak. "Do you see now why I could not invoke all the wards at once?"

" 'Tis good they will not trouble us further," Conan said, climbing into his saddle, "but we must ride if we are to reach Shadizar by the ceremony tonight. I will not let Bombatta cheat me of Valeria's life."

The smile disappeared from Akiro's face. "I did not tell you, Conan, when I thought we would die, for a man should not be burdened at his death with matters he cannot change. In truth, even now I fear it is too late. I tried to stop it when it could have been stopped, before she entered the furnace, but I was too slow."

"You babble, Akiro," Conan growled. "Speak what is on your mind, or let me ride for Shadizar."

"It was all on the plaques," Akiro said. "The Rite of Awakening takes three nights, and on each night a girl is sacrificed. On the Third Night, the sacrifice is the One who Bears the Horn, the innocent. It will be Jehnna."

"Perhaps it is not her," Zula said pleadingly. "Not even Bombatta would take her back to that."

"Bombatta called her the One," the old wizard sighed. "He knows she is to die."

Conan touched the dragon amulet on his chest. Pain filled him, and he wanted to howl it aloud as he had never given voice to pain before. Valeria. "Jehnna will not die," he said through clenched teeth.

"I like the girl, too," Malak protested, ignoring Zula's glare, "but, Badb's Holy Buttocks, we're all exhausted, and we could not reach Shadizar before nightfall if we killed the horses trying."

"Then when my horse dies," Conan replied grimly, "I will run, then crawl. But before all the gods I vow, Jehnna will survive this night if I must die for it." Without waiting to see if the others followed, he kicked his horse into motion, into a race with the rising sun.

XXI

From a balcony Taramis looked down on the marble-tiled courtyard where rested the Sleeping God, a canopy of fringed golden silk raised to shield him from the blazing sun. In a circle about the canopy, unprotected and perspiring, knelt half a score of priests in their robes and crowns of gold, chanting their prayers. Since the First Anointing there had continually been a circle of priests offering their devotions to Dagoth, with only a pause the night before for the Second Anointing.

Taramis ran her eyes over the other balconies overlooking this court, yet she knew there would be no one there to observe who should not see. For three days this part of her palace had been all but sealed from the rest. No slave or servant would come near to it without her express command, even if guards had not been posted with orders to slay any who tried. It was not that that cut at her like a whip's lash. She knew very well what it was that truly preyed on her mind, what it was she did not want to think about.

Hesitantly she looked at the sun, then jerked her gaze away. Already that distended yellow ball was past the zenith. *Well* past the zenith. And tonight came a configuration of the stars that would not come again for a thousand years. If Bombatta did not bring the girl in the next few hours, if the girl did not have what she had been sent for. . . . Taramis bit at her lip, heedless of the blood that came. It could not be so. It would not be so. She refused to die knowing that power and immortality would come to someone else a thousand years hence.

A deferential cough made her whirl, ready to flay whomever had dared to disturb her.

Xanteres stood in the doorway, his face as deceptively gentle as ever, but a gleam of exultation in his dark eyes. "She is come," he said grandly. "Bombatta has brought her."

Taramis abandoned dignity. She pushed past the white-bearded high priest and ran, speeding down corridors and stairs till she came to the great alabaster-columned entry hall of the palace, with its high, vaulted ceiling. And there, dusty, bedraggled and travel-stained, stood Bombatta, with his helmet under his arm, and Jehnna, clutching a dusty bundle, barely recognizable as once-white wool, to her bosom. Taramis hardly even noticed the massive black-armored warrior. Her eyes were all for the girl.

"Do you have it?" she whispered, approaching slowly. "By all that is sacred and holy, child, do you have it?"

Hesitantly, Jehnna held out the bundle she had clasped to her breasts. She swayed, and Taramis saw that she was exhausted. But the time for rest was not yet. Other, more important matters came first.

The tall Zamoran noblewoman looked around frantically for the high priest, ready to shout for him, but he was there. Reverently Xanteres held forward an elaborate golden casket within which were crystal supports wrought with all of Taramis' sorcerous skill and cunning.

"Place them there, child," Taramis said.

From the bundle Jehnna produced the Heart of Ahriman, sanguinely glowing, and placed it in the casket. Taramis held her breath. The dirty white wool dropped to the marble floor, and Jehnna was cradling the golden Horn of Dagoth in her hands.

As that, too, was laid on crystal supports within the casket, Taramis' hand twitched with the desire to touch it. Not yet, she reminded herself. Now it was death for any hand but Jehnna's. Later it would be hers alone to know.

With great reluctance Taramis closed the golden casket. "Take it," she commanded the high priest. "Guard it with your life." Xanteres bowed himself from her presence, and she turned her attention back to Jehnna and Bombatta. The girl swayed again. "Where are the bath girls?" Taramis demanded. "Must I have the fool wenches flayed?"

Two white-robed young women, black hair pinned in curls close to their heads, sped into the hall and fell to their knees before Taramis.

"The Lady Jehnna is travel weary," the beauteous princess told them. "She must be bathed and massaged. She must be properly garbed."

Jehnna smiled warmly, if tiredly, at the woman as they hurried to her. "It is so good to see you again," she said. "It seems years since I have had a proper bath. But where are Aniya and Lyella?"

The white-robed women's faces went blank, and Taramis hastened to fill the silence. "They are ill, child. You will see them later. Take her away! Can you not see she is near collapse?" She watched them lead Jehnna from the hall, then turned smiling to Bombatta. "It is done, then," she sighed.

"It is done," he said, but something in his eyes made her frown.

Her mind raced, searching for what could possibly be left yet undone. "The thief?" she said. "He is dead?"

"He is dead," Bombatta replied.

"You put your sword through him."

"No, but—"

Her hand flashed out, cracked against his face. "When the One holds the Horn," she quoted, "the sky-eyed thief must die. An he lives, danger comes on his shoulder and death rides his right hand." She drew a deep breath. "You *know* what is written in the scrolls."

"He lies entombed with half a mountain atop him," Bombatta growled sullenly.

"Fool! If you did not handle his corpse . . . I will not take a chance, Bombatta, not even a small chance, not now. It is all too close to fruition. Treble the guard."

"For one thief who is certainly dead?" he barked.

"Do it!" she commanded coldly. "Let not so much as a mouse pass the palace walls without a spear in it." Not waiting for his reply she turned away. The Horn was at last in her possession, and if she could not touch it, she could at least gaze upon it. She had to gaze upon it.

The city of Shadizar was called "the Wicked," and what the eyes of its citizens had not seen had never happened under the heavens, yet the crowds in the streets gave wide passage to the four who rode into the city as dusk drew near. Weary and lathered were their horses, and the four— one a woman—seemed no less travel-worn, yet there was a grimness in their eyes, most especially in the strange blue eyes of the young giant who led them, that made even City Guardsmen decide to look elsewhere for evildoers and bribes.

Conan knew where a stable stood not far from Taramis' palace, and the horses were no sooner turned over to a hostler than he hurried into the streets.

Akiro caught up to him with an effort. "Slow down, my young friend. You must have a plan." Malak and Zula joined them, and the look of the four was enough to gain them as clear a path as when they had ridden.

"There is no time for slowing," Conan growled. "Or have you not looked at the sun?"

Ahead of them Taramis' palace came in view. The tall, iron-bound gates were closed, and six guards stood before them with slanted spears. On the walls more guards were appearing every moment, until they stood two paces apart all the way around the palace.

The wizard pushed Conan to the mouth of an alley. "Now will you agree to a plan?"

Malak snatched an orange from a fruit-monger's cart that stood beside the alley. The peddler opened his mouth, looked at the small man's companions, and closed it again.

"Now I see there is no use to a plan," Conan replied slowly. "I must try to rescue her, for I have vowed it, but I fear that I and any who go with me will die in the attempt. It is best the rest of you leave."

"I will go with you," Zula said fiercely. "I owe you a life, and I will follow you until it is repaid."

"You are fools," Akiro said despairingly. "Do you mean to attack the palace as if you were an army?"

The fruit-monger's mouth fell open.

"What about you, wizard?" Malak asked around a mouthful of orange. "Can you not help with some incantation or spell?"

"No doubt," Akiro said drily, "I could hurl a fireball that would destroy those gates as if they were made of parchment. But I must stand in the open to do it, with the result that someone will probably put a spear in me, leaving the three of you to battle tenscore guards, if not twice so many."

Eyes wide, the fruit-monger threw his weight behind his cart and pushed it away as fast as his legs would carry him.

"That does not sound like such a good idea to me," Malak laughed weakly. "Mitra, who would believe anyone would go to all this trouble to get into that place, considering what my cousin went through to get out."

"I thought your cousin died in those dungeons," Conan said absently. His eyes and his mind were still on the palace and the fast-approaching night.

Malak shook his head, trying to avoid Zula's glaring frown. "Two of them died. One escaped . . ." He trailed off as Conan swiveled his head to look at him. Akiro raised a quizzical eyebrow. "That is, he did die. All of them died. I know nothing about tunnels or anything of that sort. I don't remember. I swear it!"

"I could break his head," Zula said thoughtfully.

"Then he could not talk," Akiro said. "But he does not need his manhood for speech. I could shrivel that."

Conan merely fingered the hilt of his dagger.

The small thief looked from one pair of eyes to another, then sighed. "Oh, very well. I'll show you."

Conan gestured him to lead on, then followed quickly on his heels as Malak started down the alley.

It was a snaking path the little man took, along alleys slick with offal and stinking of urine and excrement, and it led away from the palace. At last, behind a stone building many streets away, he ducked into a shadowed doorway. The Cimmerian trod on his heels down rough steps in deeper dark and musty air.

"We need light," Conan sighed reluctantly. "Akiro?"

Abruptly there was light, a ball of it resting on the wizard's fingertips. They were in a cellar, filled with sagging crates and splintered barrels. Dust and cobwebs lay thickly on everything. Akiro found a torch among the rubble and transfered the fire from his fingers to that.

"There is a way from this place to a palace?" Zula said disbelievingly.

On hand and knees Malak counted the large, square stones of the floor along one wall. "Here," he said, pointing to one that seemed no different from any other. "This is the one. If I remember it right."

"You had better," Zula said darkly.

Conan knelt by the stone. At one side there was just enough gap for him to get a grip with his fingertips. He pulled the block up, worked his fingers under it, and heaved it over. Below it was a dark hole, slightly smaller than the stone slab. He seized the torch from Akiro and thrust it into the opening. It was walled in stone, and along one side there were holes spaced properly for hands and feet.

"Ah!" said Akiro. "Whoever built that palace was a wise man. However strong a fortress, it is always wisdom to have a bolt-hole or two. I do not doubt there are others."

Conan swung his legs into the hole. "Then it will take us inside the palace walls."

"Are you not forgetting tenscore guards?" Malak demanded. "Sigyn's Bowl, Cimmerian, they will not be one fewer because you are inside."

"You are right," Conan said. "This improves our chances but little. You have done your part, my friend. You need not come further."

Zula spat loudly, and Malak twisted his mouth. "Amphrates' jewels," he breathed heavily, "had best be worth more gold than I think they are."

With a grin Conan began his descent.

XXII

D usk rolled across Shadizar as Taramis looked down once more upon the courtyard where the Sleeping God lay. The canopy was gone now, and a different circle of golden-robed priests prayed around the god. Her four bodyguards, and six more black-armored warriors hand-picked by Bombatta, stood watch about the courtyard. She did not like that. They knew what they served, but they had never seen any part of the ceremonies, and there should be no outsiders to witness what would happen this night. But Bombatta's stupidity had made it necessary.

True, it was unlikely in the extreme that the thief still lived. Even did he live, surely one man, and he a thief out of the streets, could do nothing to hinder her plans in the slightest. But the Scrolls of Skelos spoke of the possibility . . . no, they spoke of the certainty of danger if the thief lived. And that fool Bombatta had the temerity to sulk somewhere in the palace because she had upbraided him. Something would have to be done about Bombatta when this night was over.

With a last look at the darkening sky, she returned to her chambers. There was much yet to be done.

From the chest of ebony inlaid with silver she took a twist of parchment. Wine she poured from a crystal flagon into a goblet of chased gold. The parchment gave up a white powder which dissolved quickly in the wine. A second goblet stood beside the first on the lacquered tray. It was not sorcery, this potion, but it had no taste and would do its work well, and all spells were forbidden this night save those required by the Rite of Awakening.

She clapped her hands, and, when a slave woman in short white tunic appeared, commanded, "Bid the Lady Jehnna attend me." Soon now, she thought. Soon.

Thrusting the torch ahead of him, Conan ran in a half-crouch down the low-ceilinged tunnel, its stone walls gray with mold.

"Not so fast," Malak complained. "Mitra's Bones, could not whoever built this have given it enough height for a man to stand up?"

"You can almost stand as it is," Zula said, prodding the small thief to greater speed with her staff in his ribs.

Malak glared at her, but only said, "I hope at least they have stairs at the other end. I don't fancy another climb of fifty paces in the dark."

Conan cursed as the torchlight showed him a blank wall ahead, then he became aware that the ceiling was higher here. He straightened, and found himself in another shaft like the one they had descended, complete with holes along one wall for hands and for feet. Without hesitation he climbed.

"A plan," Akiro called after him hoarsely. "You know not what is up there."

Conan climbed on. It was not easy with the torch in one hand. The method required keeping both feet in place and balancing while the one free hand darted to a higher handhold. A single miss in that quick grab, and the long fall back down the shaft was inevitable. Too, it was a way of climbing that should have been done slowly and carefully, but Conan had no time for being careful. He pushed on as if it were stairsteps he climbed.

At the top of the shaft there was a black iron bracket on one stone wall for the torch, and a foothole on the opposite side of the shaft from those he had climbed, so that a man could straddle it if he did not mind getting close to the torch's flame. The stone above had a ring in its center, no doubt to aid closing the bolt-hole behind refugees should the palace's lords and ladies ever find the need to use the route. There had been none on the stone at the other end, as no one had ever been expected to enter from that direction.

The torch seared Conan's back as he heaved against the stone above him. With a mighty shove he toppled it away from the shaft, and raised his head into a dungeon lit only by the obstructed glow of his torch. The walls were a rough-cut stone, and the floor was covered with pale straw dried to dusty brittleness. A small creature chittered and rustled away as the Cimmerian climbed out.

Pausing only to secure the torch, Conan moved to the thick, iron-bound door. An iron plate on the outside of the door covered a slot for checking on prisoners. A careful push showed the huge lock was not fastened. Slowly he cracked the door, grimacing at the squeal of the crudely-wrought iron hinges. The stone-walled hallway outside was empty and dark.

"You should have waited," Akiro panted, scrambling from the shaft. "You had no way to know what lay on this side of that stone."

"It had to be a dungeon," Conan said. "Malak's cousin could hardly have made his escape from the great hall, or from Taramis' bedchamber."

The old wizard stared at him, astounded. "Logical. I did not expect such thinking from you. You always seem to go at problems with a sword, rather than logical thought."

Malak, who was allowing Zula to help him into the cell, muttered, offended, "How do you know my cousin did not escape from Taramis' bedchamber? All the men of my family have a great attraction for women."

Zula snorted, and Malak opened his mouth again, but Conan cut short any argument with a sharp gesture. "Do that later," he said, and slipped into the hall.

A choice of direction was easy. One way lay more darkness, the other a glow of light. Dropping his torch on the bare stone floor of the corridor, Conan drew his sword and moved toward the light. Short of the dim glow that spilled into the hall he stopped in consternation.

This was the jailer's chamber, a large cube with a rough cot in one corner, well lit by torches in iron sconces. On the far side stairs led upward, and at a table of crude-hewn planks by those stairs sat the jailer, a big balding man with as much hair on his arms and legs as he had once had on his head. He chewed at a joint of beef held in one thick-fingered hand, while the other scratched casually beneath his leather jerkin. He faced the hall where Conan stood hidden only by darkness, and from where he sat he could be halfway up the stairs shouting an alarm before the Cimmerian could reach the table.

As Conan tensed to take the chance, Zula touched him on the arm and shook her head. Swiftly she doffed the strip of cloth that covered her small breasts. Malak licked his lips ostentatiously, but she ignored him, tucking the cloth into the other piece she wore about her loins. Then, with a welcoming smile on her face, she padded into the jailer's chamber, using her staff as if it were a walking stick.

The balding man froze with the joint half-raised to his mouth. "Where in Zandru's Nine Hells did you come from?" he growled. "You're no prisoner of mine."

Zula did not speak, but the roll of her slim hips increased as she continued toward him.

The jailor tossed the joint onto the table, missing a cracked pottery plate, and scrubbed the back of a broad hand across his greasy mouth as he stood and moved around the table. "If you're not a prisoner, you're not supposed to be here," he said thickly. "And being where you're not supposed to be can get you put to the question. Painful, that. Why don't you talk? You got a tongue? No matter. If you want to avoid the hot irons and the strapado, wench, you're going to treat me like a walking god and the love of your life, all rolled into one."

He reached for her, then. Zula's face did not change as her staff, suddenly gripped with two hands, whipped up into the big man's crotch. A strangled squawk burst from his throat, and his eyes bulged almost out of his fat face. He doubled over, and her staff whirled around to crack the side of his balding head. With a sigh, he crumpled to the floor stones. Calmly Zula donned her halter once more.

"Most effective," Akiro said with a smile, as the others joined her. Malak studiously avoided looking at her bosom even after she was covered.

Conan did not wait for talk. The coming of night weighed him like massive stones on his shoulders. Sword in hand, he raced up the stairs, barely hearing the clatter as the rest followed behind.

"You sent for me, my aunt?" Jehnna said from the door.

Taramis put on a smile, pleasant and, she believed, familial. One more role the girl had to fill, she thought, and for that Jehnna had been prepared well. Thin black silk covered her to the floor, hugging her slender curves. Her black hair, dressed simply, flowed about her shoulders, and her face was bare of any trace of kohl or rouge. A scrubbed face for innocence, and black silk for the Night. And the girl's black contrasted well with her own scarlet silk, slashed to show her voluptuous curves to best advantage before the god.

"Yes, child," Taramis answered. "This is your natal day, and tonight you fulfill your destiny. Come, drink a celebration cup with me." She filled the second goblet, then held out the first to the girl. "You are a woman, now, and old enough for wine."

Jehnna took the goblet hesitantly, peering at the dark ruby liquid within. "I have often wondered about wine," she said.

"Drink," Taramis told her. "Drink deeply. It is best so." She held her breath while Jehnna hesitated further, then let it out when the slender girl raised the goblet, drinking as commanded, deeply.

Jehnna gave a little laugh as she lowered the almost empty goblet. "It warms so, swirling all through me it seems."

"Do you feel lightheaded? That happens, sometimes."

"I feel . . . I feel . . ." Jehnna trailed off with a slight giggle.

Tarmis took the golden cup from unresisting fingers and studied the girl's large eyes. Wine would not act so fast, even on one so unfamiliar with it as Jehnna, but the powder should. It *had* to have taken effect. "Kneel, child," she said.

Smiling as if it were the most ordinary thing to be told to do, Jehnna knelt.

The powder worked quite as well as a spell, Taramis thought. There would be no hesitation at a fatal moment. Aloud, she said, "Stand up, child." Even as Jehnna rose she went on. "Xanteres! She is ready."

The mild-faced high priest hurried into the room with the golden casket in his hands. He reached to open it himself, but Taramis brushed his thin hand aside. It was her place to do this. When the casket lid was lifted, she barely saw the glowing Heart of Ahriman. On the morrow, when it was safe for her to touch the stone, many wonders of great power could she do with the Heart. Tonight, only the Horn of Dagoth had importance.

"Take up the Horn, child," Taramis said, then watched jealously as Jehnna's fingers curled around its curving golden length.

In the courtyard four brazen gongs sounded their rolling tones. Full night drew nigh.

"Come, child," Taramis said. And, bearing the Horn of Dagoth before her, Jehnna followed toward her destiny.

Treading carefully, silently, Conan made his way down a palace corridor, unheeding of rare Vendhyan carpets on the marble floor or ancient Iranistani tapestries lining the walls where golden lamps flickered. Warily his companions followed him. Taramis' guards were everywhere. Twice already they had been forced to hide in a crossing hall, Conan gritting his teeth in frustration, while half a score of the black-armored men marched past. As much as urgency spurred him, it would be impossible to engage such a squad without an alarm being given. And Jehnna *must* be found before any alarm, if there was to be a hope of getting her out alive.

The Cimmerian stepped into the intersection of two corridors, and the creak of leather gave him a chance to live. On either side of him, leaning against the wall where he could not see them before, was a guard in ebon breastplate and nasaled helm. Their hands streaked for their swords as he appeared. There was no time to think of what to do; he must act.

With a two-handed grip on his hilt Conan pivoted to the left, driving his blade through the guard's breastplate while the other's sword was yet half-drawn. In one motion he pulled his steel free and continued his spin. The other man had his tulwar drawn, and was making the mistake of raising it to slash rather than thrusting. The tip of Conan's streaking blade slashed across the undersides of the man's upraised arms. As the guard jerked his arms down in reflex at the agony, Conan completed his turn, taking a step closer as his sword twisted in a narrow loop and bit deeply into the black helmet. The second corpse struck the marble floor within a heartbeat of the first.

Malak whistled in admiration, and Zula stared in awe. "You are fast," she breathed. "Never have I seen—"

"These men," Conan cut her off, "will be found soon, or missed, whether we hide them or not."

"You mean the tenscore guards are going to know we're here?" Malak's voice was shrill. "Danh's Bony Rump!"

"Go back to the dungeon," Zula said scornfully. "The way out is yet open."

Malak grimaced, then drew his daggers. "I always wanted to be a hero," he said weakly.

Conan growled them all to silence. "I mean there is no more time for caution. We must find Jehnna. *Quickly.*" Like a hunting leopard he sped on, driven by the darkness that thickened the sky outside.

A gasp of awe rose from the assembled priests—all of them were there, now—when the small procession entered the courtyard, and Taramis basked in it. She knew it was for the girl behind her, for the One and the golden Horn of Dagoth that she bore, but she, Taramis, had brought it to be.

The voluptuous noblewoman stepped aside, revealing Jehnna and her burden clearly, and the golden-robed priests fell to their knees. Xanteres, who had exchanged the casket for his tall staff of gold tipped with its azure diamond eye, moved to the other side of the girl, stroking his full white beard in self-satisfaction, to gain his share of the adulation.

"The Sleeping God will never die," Taramis intoned.

"Where there is faith," came the response from the kneeling priests, "there is no death."

She flung wide her arms. "This is the Night of Awakening," she cried, "for the One has come!" The reply echoed from the walls.

"All glory to the One, who serves the Sleeping God!"

The half score black-armored guards, their spears precisely slanted, but standing well back so as to be out of the way, shifted uneasily. From the colonnade came the piping of flutes, beginning their litany of coming sacrifice and anointment. The velvet black sky arched above, glittering stars set in a pattern they would not attain again for another thousand years. The moment had come.

Power, Taramis thought while the echos still shivered the air. Power and immortality were hers.

Conan slid to a halt as a man stepped into the corridor ahead of him, a man black-armored and even more massive than he, with a naked tulwar in his hand.

"I knew you must come this way, thief," Bombatta said softly. His scarred face was grimmer than ever before behind the nasal of his sable helm. "When I found the bodies, I knew then that you lived. And I knew you would run to the great court to save her. But if I cannot have Jehnna, no mortal man will have her." His blade came up, gleaming in the lamplight. "She goes to the god, thief."

Motioning the others to hang back, Conan moved closer. In the confines of the tapestried hall they could only hinder, not help. The Cimmerian gripped his sword with both hands, holding it erect before him.

"Have you lost your tongue?" Bombatta demanded. "In moments the girl dies in the very center of this palace, I tell you. Rage at your loss, thief. Let me know your despair and lose my own in the slaying of you."

"This is no time for talking," Conan replied. "It is a time for dying."

The two blades moved, then, as one. The clanging of steel on steel filled the hall as they wove a deadly lace between the two big men. Attack and counterattack, thrust and riposte, followed so closely one on the other that it seemed as though lightning flashed and danced.

Abruptly Conan's broadsword was torn from his grasp. Triumph flared in Bombatta's face, but even as the blow struck Conan's foot lashed out, sending the giant Zamoran's blade spinning. The two men crashed together, grappling. For an instant each strove to reach his dagger, then Bombatta's huge hands closed on Conan's head and twisted, and the Cimmerian gripped the black helm, one hand on its bottom edge, the other above the dark nasal. Feet shifted and scuffled for balance, and hard-drawn breath was the sound of battle, now. Massive thews bulged, and joints popped with the strain.

A grinding crack sounded, not loud, yet seeming to drown all else, and Conan found that he supported a boneless mass. For an instant he stared into those black eyes, as death filmed them, then let Bombatta fall.

"Time is running out," Zula said, "and we still do not know where to find her."

Working his neck, Conan retrieved his sword. "But we do. He told us. The great court in the center of the palace."

"He also said she was to die in moments," Malak reminded him.

"Then there is no time to stand here talking," Conan said. "Come."

"O great Dagoth," Taramis intoned, "on the Night of Awakening we, thy servants, come to thee."

The flutes shrilled madly as she took Jehnna's arm. Xanteres took the other, and between them they led the girl to the head of the great reclining form of the god, its noble forehead marred by the dark, circular depression. Holding the Horn before her, Jehnna moved unresistingly.

"O great Dagoth," the tall princess chanted, "on the Night of Awakening, they servants call to thee." In a whisper she spoke to Jehnna. "The Horn, child. Place the Horn as you were told."

Jehnna blinked, hesitated, and Taramis' breath caught at the fear that the potion's effect might have worn off. Then slowly the slender girl set the base of the golden Horn into the depression in Dagoth's forehead.

A tremor passed through the huge, alabastrine form. Marble hardness softened, and took on the hue of human skin. The eyelids fluttered.

Relief flooded through Taramis. Nothing could halt it, now. The Sleeping God was awaking. And the Horn was no longer sacrosanct to Dagoth and the One, alone. But it all had to be finished, and quickly now.

"O great Dagoth," she called, "accept this, our offering and pledge to thee. Accept thy third anointing, the Anointing of the One."

Jehnna did not even start as Xanteres tangled his left hand in her hair and bent her forward over the recumbent god's head. A gilded dagger flashed in his hand as he raised it.

Bursting into the great courtyard, Conan took in the scene before him, the black-armored guards, the kneeling priests in gold, the huge, horned form that seemed to be just beginning to stir. And Jehnna, throat arched for the knife in the hands of the white-bearded man.

An instant it took him to see, and in that same instant he was moving. His sword was tossed from right hand to left, the fisted pommel smashed into the ebon helmet of a guard, his right hand tore the spear from the guard's grasp. As the dagger moved toward Jehnna he threw. The spear lanced a dark streak across the courtyard, and the dagger dropped to the marble tiles as the white-bearded man, a wavering shriek rising from his throat, clutched at the thick black shaft that pierced him.

An instant, and in that instant the courtyard swirled into chaos. Black-armored guards turned to battle Conan, who suddenly found Malak fighting at his side. Zula dashed across the court, beating golden-robed priests from her path with her staff, to seize Jehnna's arm and drag her away from the huge, now-quivering form.

"There is yet time," Taramis screamed. "It must be done! It must be!" On hand and knees she scrambled for the fallen dagger.

And the huge form of Dagoth sat up, the shape of a gigantic man, too handsome for humankind, with a golden horn standing out from his forehead. The air in the court turned chill as it moved, and no man or woman there but froze. The noble head turned, great golden eyes surveying the courtyard. Then suddenly the head was thrown back, and Dagoth howled. Staggering to his feet, he howled such agony as had never been known on the face of the earth.

As if the terrible sound had freed him from paralysis, Conan found he could move again. He gripped his sword and set himself, but the guards before him threw down their spears and fled, brushing past him as if what else was in that courtyard made the steel in his hands no longer worth fearing.

Dagoth's form rippled, now, as though knots grew beneath the skin. Bulging, writhing, it grew and changed. In the twinkling of an eye its skin became coarse. The brow sloped back, and the jaw grew forward, fangs thrusting past lips. Arms and legs thickened, and claws sprouted on the ends of fingers. The skin of the back split, and leathery wings as of a monstrous bat came forth. Grotesquely male, hunched and twisted, yet three times the height of a man, Dagoth stood, and only the huge golden eyes were unchanged.

Those eyes came to rest on Taramis, kneeling with the dagger clutched to her breasts and her face slack with horror. "You!" It was as if thunder had spoken, and with the tongue of thunder. "Out of your own mouth, Taramis, are you promised to me!"

Hope dawned on Taramis' face. "Yes," she breathed. Leaping to her feet she ran toward the god. "I am promised to thee," she cried. "And thou wilt gift me with power and immortality. Thou wilt—"

Clawed hands pulled the noblewoman to Dagoth, and the huge wings folded around them, hiding her. From beneath those wings came a crystalline wail of purest pain and disbelief. The wings opened, and Dagoth tossed aside a robe of scarlet silk.

"Thus it is," the thunder roared, "to know a god, and be known by a god!"

Zula had stopped to stare in horror at the garment that was all that remained of Taramis, and Jehnna stood beside her, seemingly unaware of what occurred about her.

Dashing forward, Conan grabbed each woman in turn, pushing them toward the shelter of the palace. "Run!" he commanded, and they ran.

"No, mortal!" came the thunder. "She is the One, and the One is mine!"

Conan felt the ground tremble as Dagoth took a step. The women could never outdistance that monstrous form. Time would have to be bought for them. Certain for the first time in his life that he faced something he could not defeat, Conan turned to confront the god.

Suddenly a fireball streaked over his head to strike Dagoth's chest. It bounced away like a pebble from a mountain, yet even as it did another struck, and another. "Run, Cimmerian!" Akiro shouted. "Erlik take you, run! I cannot hold such as this forever!"

Dagoth's wings stiffened, then snapped together behind his back like a thunderclap. And as if that sound had called invisible lightning Akiro was flung into the air and hurled backwards.

"And you, mortal!" Dagoth thundered at Conan. "Would you oppose a god? Know the fear of what you do."

Then did Conan feel fear rolling over him, fear primordial, fear so strong that it felt as though his very bones would split asunder. Overpowering waves of it crashed on him, pushing that which called itself Conan of Cimmeria back, back beyond knowledge of civilization or fire or speech, back to the ancient creature that knew no gods, the creature that survived its lack of claws and fangs because it was more deadly than leopard or bear. That creature knew but one response to fear. With a roar the cave sloth knew and feared, Conan attacked.

His broadsword slashed deep, and Dagoth laughed like a storm at sea as bloodless wounds healed even as they were made. Claw-tipped hands seized the Cimmerian, lifted him toward gaping fangs, and still Conan hacked with a mad fury that would not quit till death overtook him.

Yet as he fought, dim words penetrated Conan's brain. "The horn!" Part of him struggled to listen, while the greater part raged to kill. Akiro, that small part thought. "He is only vulnerable through the horn!" the wizard shouted.

Conan was raised before the golden eyes, and he returned their gaze unafraid. Fear had been purged from him by the blood-red madness that screamed to slay or die.

The Cimmerian laughed as he let his sword fall and seized the horn; it was like seizing lightning, yet he voiced his deathly grim laughter. Massive shoulders knotted, he tore the golden horn from that monstrous head. Pain flared in the god's xanthic eyes, and the fanged mouth opened wider to rip at the human who had wounded him. But the insane rage of the attacker had not left Conan. As he ripped the horn free, he reversed it, thrust it point first into one of the golden globes that stared at him, shoved it deep with all his might.

The howl that Dagoth had loosed before was a whisper to the scream that came from him now. Conan was flung through the air, spinning end over end, to crash to the marble tiles. Higher and higher the shriek rose. Suddenly it could not be heard at all, but now the Cimmerian's skull vibrated, and white-hot daggers bored at his ears. Clawing at his head, he struggled to rise. He must fight. He must kill. He must . . .

A measure of sanity returned to him amid the pain as he realized that he was seeing stars. *Through* Dagoth. The gigantic shape still loomed in the center of the courtyard, clawed hands clutching its face, blood like rubies welling between the taloned fingers, the blood of a god dropping to shatter like crystal on the marble beneath his feet, but even as the Cimmerian watched the form grew dimmer, less distinct. In gossamer outline Dagoth hung against the night sky. Abruptly he was gone, and with him the pain from Conan's head.

Unsteadily the Cimmerian surveyed the courtyard. The priests were fled, and of the black-armored guards none remained save those he and Malak had slain. Zula crouched beside Jehnna, cradling the slender girl in her arms. "She collapsed," the black woman told Conan, "when you tore out that horn. But it is only a sleep, I think. She will be well."

"Hey, Conan," Malak called. The small thief was propped against the marble pillar of the colonnade. Akiro, who moved as if he were one bruise from head to foot, was binding a cloth about Malak's bloody thigh. "I took a spear, but we won. Hannuman's Stones, man, we won!"

"Perhaps," Conan said tiredly. He grasped the dragon amulet on his chest as if he would crush it.

"Perhaps."

Epilogue

From an alabaster balcony of the vast marble palace that had once been Taramis', Conan watched the sun rise from the far horizon. It was the second time he had watched a sunrise from that same spot. A day and a night to rest and think, to reach decisions. He had made his decisions, then given a few commands, and showed a handbreadth of steel when those commands were questioned.

"My Lord Conan," said a servant behind him, "the Princess Jehnna b-begs your presence." The woman blushed, flustered at stammering, flustered because a Zamoran noblewoman never begged. Most especially not a princess.

"I am not a lord," Conan said, then quickly added, "Take me to the Princess Jehnna," before she could become flustered further.

The tapestry-hung chamber to which he was led was meant for informal audiences, with a dais only one step high and an unadorned, high-backed chair of polished ebony for a throne. Jehnna looked well on it, he thought, in her robes of white silk. The others were much recovered from their ordeals as well, Malak surreptitiously fingering a golden bowl, Akiro looking impatient with a bundle of tightly rolled scrolls under his arm, Zula leaning on her staff near Jehnna's throne as if she were a bodyguard.

"Conan," Jehnna said brightly as he entered, "it has come. King Tiridates has invested me as Princess Royal of Zamora and confirmed me in Taramis' estates."

"I congratulate you," he said, and she frowned at him doubtfully.

The frown cleared quickly though, and she said, "I have asked you all to come to me this morning because I have a favor to ask of each of you. You, first, Malak." The small man jerked his hand from the bowl as if burned. "I ask you to remain here with me, Malak," she went on, "living in my palace. Thus I will always be reminded that a man can be a fool, yet be brave and good."

"Even my mother never called me good," Malak said slowly. His eyes drifted to the bowl. "But I will stay in your palace. For a time."

"Best to put a guard on him, then," Akiro said drily, and grinned at the offended glare he got from Malak.

"You, also, Akiro," Jehnna said, "must stay with me. You are a man of great wisdom, and I will need wise counsel in the days, the years, to come."

"Impossible," the wizard replied. "You have given me the Scrolls of Skelos, and some bush-shamans on the Kothian border are carrying on vile practices that I have vowed to end."

"I can put soldiers at your disposal to deal with the shamans," Jehnna told him, then added slyly, "And Taramis gathered several rooms full of magical volumes and instruments which you would be free to study for as long as you remained here."

"Soldiers," Akiro mused. "I suppose soldiers could deal with such hedge-shamans as those. Ah, how many rooms full, exactly?"

"Many," Jehnna laughed. "Zula, you must stay, as well. You have showed me that a woman need not be confined by others' boundaries, but there is much yet to teach. The staff, for instance."

The black woman sighed regretfully. "I cannot. I owe a life to Conan, and I must follow him until I can re—"

"No!" Conan said sharply. "The debt cannot be repaid in that way."

"But—"

"It cannot, Zula. It has come to me that some debts cannot be repaid directly the one owed. Find another life to save, and I will be repaid by that."

Zula nodded slowly before turning back to Jehnna. "I will stay, Jehnna, and gladly."

"Conan," Jehnna said, and hurried on when he opened his mouth. "Listen to me, Conan. Stay with me. Sit beside me."

"I cannot," Conan said gently.

"But why not? By all the gods, I want you, and I need you."

"I live by my wits and my sword. Would you have me become a lapdog? 'Tis all I could be, here. I am not made for palaces and silks."

"Then I will go with you," she said, and stiffened when he laughed.

"The Turanians have a saying, Jehnna. The eagle does not run in the hills, the leopard does not fly in the sky. You would take to my life as ill as I would take to yours. Never a day but I must fight for my life or ride for it. That is the road I travel, and you cannot come with me."

"But, Conan—"

"Fare you well, Jehnna, and all the gods grant you happiness."

He turned his back on her then, and walked from the room. He thought he heard her call after him, but he would not look back or listen. As he had commanded, his horse waited, saddled, before the palace.

The sun was almost to its zenith by the time he reached the rough stone altar on the plains. The wind had swept dirt and sand against it, and he thought Malak might have some difficulty finding exactly where Amphrates' jewels were buried, but otherwise nothing had changed.

Slipping the dragon amulet from about his neck, he laid it on the altar. From his pouch he took the vial Akiro had given him. So long ago, it seemed. Some debts could not be repaid to the one to whom they were owed.

"Fare you well, Valeria," he said softly. And, scraping the seal from the vial, he drank.

Heat rushed along his limbs, and he squeezed his eyes shut, his horse dancing from an involuntary jerk on the reins. When he opened them again, the heat was gone. He found shards of a vial crushed in his fist, and wondered how they had come there. A glint of gold in the sun caught his eye. A pendant, he saw, in the shape of a dragon, resting atop a strange pile of stones. He bent from the saddle, but before his fingers touched the gold, he stopped. There was something, something he did not understand, that told him he should not take it. Sorcery, he decided.

Well, there was gold aplenty in Shadizar that was not sorcerous, and willing wenches to sit on his knee and help spend all he stole. With a laugh, he kicked his horse into a gallop for the city. Never once was he tempted to look back.

THE CONAN CHRONICLES 1

Robert Jordan

Before Robert Jordan conquered the bestseller lists with his phenomenally successful Wheel of Time series, he revived the legendary fantasy hero Conan the Cimmerian. These widely acclaimed adventures introduced the world-famous barbarian to a new generation of readers.

This volume contains three tales, *Conan the Invincible*, *Conan the Defender* and *Conan the Unconquered*, all of which feature the storytelling magic and epic splendour that have made Robert Jordan one of the best-loved fantasy authors of all time.

THE WHEEL OF TIME®

Robert Jordan

The Wheel of Time® turns and Ages come and go, leaving memories that become legend. Legend fades to myth, and even myth is long forgotten when the Age that gave it birth returns again. In the Third Age, an Age of Prophecy, the World and Time themselves hang in the balance. What was, what will be, and what is, may yet fall under the shadow.

All available from Orbit

"Solid as a steel blade, and glowing with true magic"
Fred Saberhagen

The World of Robert Jordan's
THE WHEEL OF TIME®

Robert Jordan and Teresa Patterson

Since the publication in 1990 of *The Eye of the World*, Book One
of The Wheel of Time ®, these magnificent volumes have
transported readers to a world so strikingly real, so rich in detail
and complexity, it seems to rise from memory rather than the
printed page. This indispensable companion to The Wheel of
Time® is for everyone interested in the history and
background of this incredible series.

Including:

More than seventy full-colour paintings of maps, landscapes,
characters and objects of Power

A comprehensive guide to the history, geography and nations

Never-before-told legends

Previously unknown peoples and lands

Potents of what may come to pass

With this magnificent illustrated guide, the reader can enjoy the
world and history of The Wheel of Time® in all its splendour.

THE DRAGONBONE CHAIR

CHAIR

MEMORY, SORROW AND THORN
Book One

Tad Williams

A thrilling, heartstopping quest that blends the machinations of a
king gone mad with the politics of empire, breathtaking suspense
with the pity of war, a brilliantly conceived world of ancient
days with the joys—and terrors—of magic . . .

"Reminiscent of Tolkien's *Lord of the Rings* . . .
an epic fantasy you can get lost in for days,
not just hours" *LOCUS*

Also available from Orbit in the
Memory, Sorrow and Thorn series

STONE OF FAREWELL
TO GREEN ANGEL TOWER: SIEGE
TO GREEN ANGEL TOWER: STORM

RUNNING WITH THE DEMON

Terry Brooks

Terry Brooks turned fantasy fiction on its head with
The Sword of Shannara. Now, in *Running with the Demon*,
he's done it again.

On the hottest Fourth of July weekend in decades, two men have
come to Hopewell, site of a long and bitter steel strike. One is a
demon, a dark servant of the Void, who will use the anger and
frustration of the community to achieve a terrible secret goal.
The other is John Ross, a Knight of the Word, a man who, while
he sleeps, lives in the hell the world will become if he fails to
change its course on waking. Ross has been given the ability to
see the future. But does he have the power to change it?

At stake is the soul of a fourteen-year-old girl mysteriously linked
to both men. And the lives of the people of Hopewell. This
Fourth of July, while friends and families picnic in Sinnissippi
Park and fireworks explode in celebration of freedom and
independence, the fate of Humanity will be decided . . .

Running with the Demon is an exquisite tale that weaves together
family drama, fading innocence, cataclysm and enlightenment.
It will change for ever the way you think about fantasy.

Also available from Orbit:

A KNIGHT OF THE WORD
ANGEL FIRE EAST

A CAVERN OF BLACK ICE

Book One of Sword of Shadows

J. V. Jones

The majestic first book in a major new fantasy series by the
bestselling author of The Book of Words trilogy.

When Raif and Drey Sevrance return home to their clan as the
only survivors of a vicious attack in which both their father and
the clan chief were killed, everything changes for Raif. Uneasy
with the new chief's reign of brutality and his brother's
acceptance of it, Raif welcomes his Uncle Angus Lok's invitation
to accompany him to Spire Vanis.

Asarhia March—Ash for short—is the beautiful ward of
Penthero Iss, Overlord of Spire Vanis. Suspicious of Penthero's
increasing interest in her developing body, when Ash overhears
him planning to imprison her she flees, only to be cornered at the
city gate by a band of the Overlord's elite guards. But as they
close in on her, Angus Lok—observed by a bemused Raif—
plunges into the midst of the guards and snatches her to safety.

For Angus knows that as this girl grows to womanhood she will
develop powers which could destroy herself and the world if she
doesn't learn to control them. And only Raif can protect her on
her journey to understanding.

"A triumph ... J. V. Jones writes with a kind of hellish possession
and a concept so clear it crackles from each page"
SFX on *The Barbed Coil*

VISIT THE ORBIT BLOG AT

www.orbitbooks.net

FEATURING

**BREAKING NEWS
FORTHCOMING RELEASES
LINKS TO AUTHOR SITES
EXCLUSIVE INTERVIEWS
EARLY EXTRACTS**

AND COMMENTARY FROM
OUR EDITORS

**With regular updates from our team,
orbitbooks.net is your source
for all things orbital**

•

**While you're there, join our e-mail list
to receive information on special offers,
giveaways, and more**

•

**Find us on Facebook at www.facebook.com/orbitbooks
Follow us on Twitter @orbitbooks**

imagine. explore. engage.

orbit

www.orbitbooks.net